I0652980

Swill of Pearls

A Novel by
Babs Kobaly

Copyright © 2014 by Babs Kobaly

All rights reserved

ISBN-13: 978-0615926353

Swill of Pearls
Dedication

*For everyone who aches for the hidden, unique, unappreciated splendor
within the least, the lost, the homeless*

For those who thrill to simpler, wilder ways of Gypsies and Indians

For he who heeds the artist within each and every one of us

For everyone who seeks goodness and beauty wherever they happen to be

For my own librarians: Maxine, Ruth, and Marjorie

For proof–readers, Robin, Wendy, Sallie, Carol, Gay, Ruth, and many others

For Tony and Penny, Mike and Virginia for first drafts

For Eddie Barker who loved Bowie and Fawna

*For Johnnie who pulled, tore and punched his weary way through 29 revisions,
becoming, as well as breadwinner, the homemaker in my place*

For Andy–helping everywhere and always standing by

For all of my family who helped by being themselves, and waiting

*For Myron, sis – Laurie, Michael, Doug, Robin, Dave, Bonnie, Meta, Tammy,
Kathy, Kim, and others whose support helped so much
in making this book finally happen*

For mother–igniting the love of plants, and father–leaving the author's urge in me

*And for a friend–someone who leaves you with all of your freedom intact,
but obliges you to be fully what you are*

CONTENTS

1. Waterfront Wake

"Damn! The biggest story to ever hit this stagnant slum-hole. And where was I? Vacationing! Reading all about it in the New York Times." The editor stormed through the door of the Waterfront Wake and slid a suitcase across the room.

He jerked his coat open and loosened his tie. "But who ever hears of the Waterfront Wake?" He shrugged his shoulders. "Every copy is sold before it even hits the streets. Jeez, Dom, do you sleep in those clothes?"

"When you're not here, boss, I've gotta run this show alone, you know," the lone reporter squirmed in his chair.

"Why are cops stationed at the morgue and that crummy run-down trailer park? How did that dismal art gallery across the street become an overnight shrine? Why is old Main Street just a muted mob of people?" The editor looked out the window and threw up his hands, "Has everyone gone crazy? This is 1950, man! Any kid could tell we're all bein' duped! Those pictures they're blubberin' over aren't any classy collages, ya know. They're only glorified garbage pieced together by some over-shocked powderpuff Picasso."

Dom looked into space. "You'd never understand."

"Why is this whole damned country 'on hold'? Why are they calling it 'the' funeral?" He ran the back of his hand up Dom's cheek. "Jeez! Have they quit sellin' razor blades?"

Sounds like my ex-wife, thought Dom, breathing a tired sigh. He snuffed a cigarette and finished cold coffee while the editor ranted on.

"Tell me, Dom, how could a drunken peeper and a sleazy fortuneteller deserve all that space in national news? Jeez, Waterfront is only a two-bit town in California!" He picked up the marked newspaper on Dom's desk.

"How in hell has the manager of Last Resort, shabbiest trailer park in creation, earned 'first-name' privileges in every metropolis, in every whistlestop throughout America?" He paced back and forth. "Who is this so-called trailer park manager that everyone just calls, 'Robbie'?"

Dom wiped at his white hair streaking it with black. He yawned, dropped his head on one arm and held up a stack of dog-eared notepads in the other hand. "It's almost all here, boss. You know, I've been practically living at that burned-out trailer, that old art gallery and the morgue, since..."

The editor ignored him, sat on Dom's cluttered desk and read from the Wake. "What a phony lineup of tenant names: Gussy, Fay Rose, Enoch, Lolli, Juju, Pug, Doll, Bowie and Quila, pronounced 'Keela'. Where's their background?"

Dom waved his notes again without raising his head. "It's almost all here, boss."

"Almost? Then why in hell are you glued to that chair?"

Despite his exhaustion, the question pumped adrenaline into Dom's weary body.

Grabbing camera, pencils, and pad, he headed for the door.

"Snappy answers now!" the editor demanded. "Then non-stop human interest. Deadlines twice daily. Milk it! Ooze it! String it out! Even the New York Times is stealin' our stuff. What a break!" He grabbed the phone to enlist more help.

Dom was almost out the door when the editor shouted again, "And trail that drunken Indian peeper! What-ziz-name? Bowie. I want writin' that bleeds and weeps and vomits. Go!"

Dom started to press to his lips the crucifix hiding beneath his shirt. Instead, he yanked it off its chain and dumped it next to the change in his pocket. He needn't plead or thank any mysterious "someone" out there ever again. Earsplitting orders to write as he had always, always wanted to were still echoing in his head.

He stepped off the curb joining solemn throngs of people massed in the street, waiting to enter the spacious old art gallery.

Somewhere inside of those once-gloomy rooms perhaps the peeper was lost in the crowd again, weary, dirty, still in shock, gently touching or lightly dusting off a picture with loving breath, just to be part of that strange scene again. Dom would already be geared up with his camera while Bowie was tenderly tucking into a collage fresh hollyhock petals, a snag of tangled hair, a sliver of used soap or some other disgusting, pitiful or precious discard, just to restore things to life for yet another day.

Slowly inching across the crowded blacktop, toward the people-jammed stairway, Dom sighed with relief. Without the pressure of ads, obituaries, police calls, school and club news to cover and compose all alone, he was finally free to allow warm ink to flow from his heart instead of being coldly measured by the clock. Soon he might even have enough background to write the book of his dreams–If only he could find a starting place.

If only he could enliven this tale just as each trailer tenant had lived it, exactly as Bowie, the drunken peeping Tom had watched it with his own compassionate eyes. If only he could capture artistically like Ginny/Gussy had on humble collages that now walled this entire gallery. If only he could write truthfully just as she had scribbled inside her weird little blood-soaked diary. Dom held his camera high and squeezed in tighter among sad, yet eager, jam-packed bodies oozing up the gallery steps.

Suddenly he glimpsed drunk, pitiful Bowie, up there ahead of him, pushing into the funnel of people one-stepping through clogged doorways. Reporters scribbled and flashed as Bowie eluded them.

Tightly stuck now in this mass of warm humanity, Dom hung the camera around his neck, allowing himself to drift, to become a basic part of this wondrous, loving, hurting agony of which Bowie was the real heart–Of which Bowie was the real heart! At last it finally happened, the inspiration he had been hoping for, a magic moment when he wasn't just the reporter but a living part of it all, knowing for sure now exactly how desperate Bowie felt.

He had found a starting place.

2. Quila's Wagon

Wild-eyed, Bowie pulled the moth-eaten fur coat much tighter around his trembling drunken body as very slowly the door of the trailer park's dark storeroom was creaking open. Out of deafening silence came a faint clicking noise and the crackle of paper. The weathered door scraped shut again and footsteps faded into the night. He relaxed in his makeshift bedroom, the little hollow that existed beneath old clothes hanging above his body.

Distant sounds of a restless sea joined the ringing in his ears. His sensitive nose was accustomed to nightly smoldering of the incinerator, but he squeezed his eyes tighter against the friendless April night.

Frantic to return to the familiarity of his Other World, he tried to conjure up the round ghostly web that always waited somewhere in his mind. Soon it should hang there shimmering between dazed eyes and misty past. There he could drift his tired, confused spirit between tines of the feather always entangled there. He waited. Though peopled with faceless beings, his dreams (unlike this filthy monotonous place) would soon spread out, full of mountains, streams and deserts. He waited... But nothing appeared in the blackness.

He groped for the always-within-reach bottle of wine beside him. Hysterically, he felt all around his body, but it just wasn't there. While deep in his usual drunken stupor, the bottle must have been stolen. Now there was nothing to soothe the starving wolf in his stomach, nothing to shield him from the terror of reality.

Wide awake now, he was cat-curious as he felt between studs along the bottom of the wall. All of his cigarettes were gone, his little pile of butts and the last book of matches. Someone must be overly sure of Bowie's habits, a master at waiting. Someone was aware that his very last dregs of wine had been watered down, that his gut was gnawing upon itself, that his eyes had had their fill of others' lives, loves and food. Someone must have been waiting, waiting until Bowie felt totally hopeless in every single way.

He sat up in the darkness, dismayed, then felt above him in a certain pocket of an old jacket. Could there be a forgotten butt or a loose match in that familiar space? No! Even his worn toothbrush, gappy-toothed comb and dirty spare shoestring for tying long hair were gone. He sat there against the wall, dumbfounded, with clothes hanging in his face. What was there left now of Bowie for anyone to even notice? Long ago, even his wallet and identification had been lost.

He struggled out of his furry shelter, groped his way to an outer wall and felt for the wad of paper that usually blocked fresh air, new sights and sounds beyond that peephole. But a folded half-pack of cigarettes and a book of matches had been substituted for crumpled paper. Ha, the thief had some plan, for the matches had all been lighted. He put the cigarettes in his pocket, then nudged the fur coat until it was hidden. He rearranged the hangers, then slowly let himself out the door.

Though well past midnight, the controlled hiss of a teakettle and the aroma of fresh baking taunted his ears and nose. Standing motionless at the corner of the washhouse, he watched the strange Gypsy wagon. On the ragged door-curtain of this only still-lighted trailer there flickered a teasing hook-nosed silhouette, tasting something from a large spoon. Quickly he pressed back as a darting figure moved silently from trailer to trailer, seeking deep shadows until it reached Quila's dimly lighted wagon. Tiny porch steps groaned as someone ascended, leaned over, then hurried back down the steps.

Bowie crept from his sheltering shadow and Quila's dog, Mange, whined a soft greeting from the latticed space that they often shared beneath the wagon. Weathered boards only whispered as moccasins felt their way upward and he reached for the fascinating milk bottle that waited in the moonlight. The empty bottle was put outside every night, then taken inside again, one or more times before dawn. Sometimes it jingled with coins, or was fragrant with tea leaves or coffee. Often there was nothing in the bottle. Sometimes there was only a sack of vegetables or a dog bone wrapped in paper beside the bottle. Maybe tonight (by some miracle.) there might be a stray match in the bottom.

He shook the bottle, peered inside, returned it, disappointed. Only a few coins were inside and, like Quila, her bottle smelled of musty herbs and old saliva. Placing his foot in just the right silent place, he started backward down the steps. Quila's windowed door flew open anyway, flapping against the wagon's wall, flushing startled birds that always drowsed in faded scrollings of the eaves. That same witchlike silhouette that had flickered on the curtain now peered from escaping candlelight. Knotty fingers picked up the bottle.

"Got a match?" he whispered feebly.

"Come in," commanded Quila as she turned to go inside. "Been expectin' ye!'

Bowie hesitated at the threshold; the small doorway was black from smoke. Perhaps he should feel pride instead of terror at her invitation. Unless his peeking counted, never before had anyone been inside this eerie little trailer that Quila called her "wagon." Late at night— the tenants whispered–Quila mumbled strange words over bubbling brews, which sometimes seemed to whisk away a tenant in the middle of the night. He wiped blackness off on his jeans.

It was impossible to stand upright in the low-ceilinged interior. This space was fashioned for small dark people like Quila, who had shuffled over to the candlelit table. She huddled into flowing folds of her long black dress as she settled onto a stool. Leaning over, she warmed her hands above the kerosene stove. Bowie closed the door and hunched to the other stool.

Smoked-up walls were paneled in carved squares that framed hanging cooking spoons, a washbasin, wooden bowls and a black fry pan. A rack of slots held rusty carving tools. Twosomes of metal plates and bowls, a couple of pottery cups and two jars instead of glasses were snugly waiting on a narrow box-like shelf above the table. Cloth pouches of labeled spices hung from bent nails on the underside of the shelf.

There was very little room on the small tabletop, so Quila tossed the milk bottle into a gloomy sleeping recess, where a dusty tambourine and a web-covered guitar hung on either side of the opening.

Bowie hid his astonishment. The entire niche was charred and appeared to have crumbled at one time, onto a ragged burnt-edged quilt. Only blackened shreds remained of the curtain that used to cover the recess. So that was why there was always a streak of soot somewhere on Quila's hand or cheek. Above the alcove were scorched remnants of two carved names intricately entwined, upheld by smoke-blackened wooden babies.

A metal teapot steeping at the back of the stove was sending up steam to mingle with musty-smelling plants hanging upside-down from the ceiling. Dusty spider webs that seemed to be holding things together were at least absent from an old trunk standing beneath a cupboard on the opposite wall. On the clasp of the trunk was a lock, and Bowie knew that the key to it hung low around Quila's neck, inside her dress. She never removed the key chain, not even when she kneeled on the floor to unlock the trunk, not even when she stripped to her bodice and knee-length bloomers for sleeping or washing, not even when she wanted to keep cool or save wear on the threadbare black dress.

Quila scrutinized him while she took one cigarette from a metal box at the back of her table.

Bowie's whole body tensed. He squeezed his eyes shut.

I wonder, thought Quila, if designs on this lid match fragments still lost in his memory? She shrugged, leaned over the candle, lit the skinny hand-rolled cigarette, then studied Bowie's discomfort while she smoked all alone.

In time she turned to the stove and ladled stew from a heavy-looking black pot. Eagerly Bowie spooned up meat, kraut and beans that she had served in a metal bowl. She opened the oven, sniffed, then used the hem of her dress to remove a pan of bread. She loosened the fragrant loaf with her evidently numb fingers and overturned it on the bare table. While she twisted off a piece of steamy sourdough and put it down before him, his eyes were glued to one finger of her scarred, cramped-looking hand. She was wearing a big ring with a real beetle encased in it.

He grabbed the bread, then quickly looked away. Quila's fingers were gruesome and always sooty, and he could see that these same frightening fingers had gathered toadstools for flavoring and common weeds to flesh out the stew. He had watched through an obscure knothole while she scrubbed this same dirty bowl with fresh sand, or merely wiped clean her black pot with a chunk of bread, which she popped into her hideous mouth. Tonight he just didn't care. He was famished. He held out his empty bowl and she refilled it.

Quila looked at him closely now with one eye shut while the other peered through a gap between closed fingers. "Been watchin' ye, Redman," she cackled. "Blendin' with scen'ry, movin' with shade." Bowie lowered his eyes and spooned more stew into his eager mouth.

Quila flashed her jagged smile. "A man like ye hears skeletons rattlin' in the tightest trailer 'closets,' sees invisible smoke curlin' from the deadest sinful 'embers,' smells taint on the sweetest 'rose' of 'em all." Quila rested her cigarette in an overflowing ashtray and nudged it closer toward him. Herb-filled smoke spiraled toward him, quieting Bowie's mind, making his eyes weak and staring. Golden loops that always dangled from Quila's ears glimmered in the candlelight, creating a tired hypnotic feeling inside his head. He tugged at the brim of his hat, for her evil little eyes were sliding all over him, measuring as though for a graveyard plot.

Bowie looked nothing like he had when Quila had first seen him that long-ago evening at the manager's doorstep. Aye, things were somewhat the same: medium build, but skinny now instead of firm and muscular, and high gaunt cheekbones with strong features. He had walked into the park sadly, yet proud and colorful as a Gypsy king leading his shy quiet queen. His deep blue embroidered velvet shirt, denim jeans and leather moccasins were brand new then, but now she knew those were his only clothes. She could tell from the very first that his pride was deeply suffering.

And, of course, he had had "that something," insisting to Robbie, the manager, that Bowie and his beautiful pregnant wife just belonged here at Last Resort.

His shirt had been worn outside his jeans then, held snugly with a fancy belt of silver dollars twinkling around his firm waist. Knotted leather thongs with beads and feathers at their tips had tasseled down between each coin. She smirked: now that same belt lay hidden in Quila's trunk, awaiting some necessity when she could snip off the needed coins—one at a time. (There had been so many shocked people in the little gray trailer that horrible night. Nobody had even noticed that Quila had quickly transferred that fascinating belt and the elaborate box beside it to the secret "pocket" of her sleeve.)

On that evening when Bowie first arrived the tenants had stared in disbelief. Here was no cigar-store Indian, no circus freak that had entered their park. That very day he must have bedded his bow and said goodbye to a trusted horse. Yet Quila could tell by the way he walked and the sharpness of his haircut that he also used to wear a uniform.

She took a long draw on the stub of her cigarette and slowly blew a line of numbing smoke beneath his eyes. Within months Bowie had lost his beautiful wife, his newborn baby, and all the rest of his pride. He couldn't even remember the gruesome reasons why. Now, with Robbie's silent permission, Bowie merely floated through life in a drunken fog, homeless, numbly waiting, hoping for some token of the past, some fleeting desire or any reason at all to even keep on living. His military haircut had disappeared and strands hung limp and dirty on his shoulders. He totally forgot to jerk out long hairs that soon were scattered over his chin.

Now after years at Last Resort, tenants scarcely noticed him anymore for he and the shadows were one.

Gone was the eager, healthy way of walking. Hunching, creeping and slithering had molded his body. The peculiar red dirt that blanketed the park had permanently stained his worn-thin velvet shirt and tattered jeans. Even by candlelight, she could see that a layer of that same redness now powdered his once strong face and dulled the forgotten sheen of his hair.

Bowie's eating finally slowed a bit and Quila began to drum her fingers on the tabletop.

Patiently she had waited until every wall in the washhouse, all of the toilet and shower stalls, the storeroom, the tool room and all of the trailers were somehow fixed for Bowie's better peeping. Occasionally he even climbed up and hid among dark rafters of the toilet rooms. The earth beneath every trailer belly knew well the shape of his prone listening body. The curved prints of his holey moccasins had tamped hard the dirt behind and around every trailer. His middle and index fingers were scorched from forgotten cigarettes.

Against him now, in all of the trailer park, there was no secret place.

Quila chuckled. Bowie had been created to order for her unique purposes.

She put an elbow on the table and looked out at Bowie through another slot of her bony fingers in order to focus more clearly. The rock of which his face was chiseled had already started to crumble, and the arrow he seemed to have for a backbone was ready for bending. Quila took down the pottery cups, stirred the teapot with a stick, and poured some wild-smelling tea. She scraped out the last of the stew and jerked off another hunk of bread for him.

Often, Quila had eavesdropped on Bowie's growling stomach. From the uncovered sweeping slot on the floor she could hear and decipher several things about him as he slept, drank or mumbled below her, using the dog space under her wagon as a hidden lookout.

Once as she walked in the foothills with Mange, she came across Bowie's simple camp. There was less and less at that time of year to fill the cans that he cooked with. She could see that wild tea was made from only yellowed leaves and old dried fruits still clinging to dormant bushes. She smelled his larger stewing can; it must have been simmering tough jackrabbits, skinny birds and wild sage.

Daily now as Bowie watched and listened to others, Quila spied him ever tightening the frayed rope that he used for a belt as he nibbled desperately on wild grasses, pigweeds and mustards barely sprouting around the park.

She had waited long enough. From now on, she smirked, it's just you and me against these non-Gypsies, these lily-white Gorgios.

"Eat up," she urged. Taking a long drag on the last inch of her cigarette, she ground it into the ashtray. "Ye've been sleepin' 'neath me wagon long enuf. Yer rent be overdue!"

"Rent?" he smirked. "I live nowhere." He wiped his bowl spotless with his last bit of bread and stuffed it into his mouth.

"Ye've been crowdin' Mange's kennel fer many a moon cycle, ye have!"

"You don't expect money for that, do you?"

She grinned. "No, not money. "She lit another cigarette from the candle, then leaned toward him slightly, letting narcotic smoke curl into his breath again. She aimed her worn eyes at Bowie, for he had unconsciously pushed his hat up and back on his head.

The whole park thought Bowie was trying to hide his long bunched-up hair with that filthy shapeless hat, but Quila knew differently. It was not his hair but his eye that he was hiding. Intently she had watched the progress of Bowie's strange right eye, the one that missed all the evil of Last Resort. From so much squinting as he peeked with his left eye, the right one was beginning to draw permanently together. To a few of the tenants who had unexpectedly seen the eye it was pitifully love and life-starved and the lack was almost a concrete thing. Ugh! Close-up, it was just as they whispered and she lowered her eyes: repulsive as a soiled sphincter muscle. But those were not the words they used.

Bowie squirmed.

Aha, his well feeling is beginning to warn him, she thought. Whenever the glaze of wine wore off, or whenever he had had enough food, he quit the continual tugging at his hat. But this was merely a short intermission before the quiet Indian became frantic for more anesthetic against his agony of remembering. If he could only get enough wine at one time Quila, was quite sure that he would drown his aimless boring life. Quickly he jerked down his hat. He must have caught her staring.

Bowie stood and edged toward the door, for Quila (whose chilly bones chattered at hot breezes) had given herself away. Not because she was hot, but in nervous anticipation she had pushed up her black sleeves. Like dingy clay, her mask of a face cracked into its crook-nosed smile. As if by magic, from one flowing sleeve she took out a familiar brand of cheap wine, then divided this – his own watery mix – into the empty cups. She lined them close in front of herself.

Suspiciously Bowie reached for the door latch, but Quila was sitting closer and her hand had beaten him there. With her other hand, she slyly took something from her dress top, tossed it on the table and settled back to study his reaction.

It was only a bloodied bundle of animal hide closed with a leather thong. But Bowie's fluttering heart knew well that it contained something very precious, some clue to his dim past. He could have grabbed it in an instant but instinctively guessed that only Quila in her own good time could decipher it for him. Otherwise, she wouldn't have risked blackmailing him with it, now at the very beginning, right under his anxious hands. Quila would never lay out her "big card" first unless it was something that would be good for a long, long time.

Bowie could feel his face harden as he turned it into stone. It allowed no glimmer of understanding to betray him as he sat back down on his stool. He forced his eyes to widen with awe and fright. Slowly, trying to look entranced, he reached for the leather bundle, while an unexpected sob seemed suddenly caught in his throat.

Quila smiled complacently, her scarred facial muscles causing her nose to curve left as she swooped out with her claw of a hand and plunged the leather pawn back into the flat bosom of her dress. "Me eyes be burnin' out! I need me a 'stalkin' horse'," she propositioned.

Bowie shook his head. This can't be true. Nothing is real anymore. Quila is just some witch from an old storybook. Her shapeless dress, clear to her ankles, is lifted from the Middle Ages. Her speech is shoveled from moldy crypts. Her hands grasp at things like withered five-hook burrs. What she's asking is unbelievable.

Quila took the lid from a candy box that stood on edge at the back of her table. She put her finger on several of the chocolates, pushed down on each one to test its softness. Finally one caved in at the pressure and Quila popped it into her mouth. Now she hunched down lower, grabbed his eyes in hers and rambled on in her crackly voice.

"A stalkin' horse I be a-needin'," she repeated, licking chocolate from her fingers. "One who knows that a fly be sure ta wait in certain ointments, a snake in certain grasses, a worm in certain apples. One who knows that if ye want ta snatch a bee ye merely wait beside a flower.

"I need someone who stalks like you, Bowie, 'gainst the wind. Someone who tracks like you, 'gainst the light." Pausing, she patted her bosom where a tip of the leather thong was peeking out. "One who knows that daily hunger and a savage thirst fer wine could create a very effective alliance," she cackled. She squinted at him through the widest jagged opening between her fingers.

The teakettle had quit its low hissing, the stove was cooling off. In the strained silence Bowie suddenly realized that Quila had set a trap for him, and wide-eyed he had raced smack into its waiting jaws. Bowie often fought off the hideous unwanted pity that slithered into his being when Quila sometimes wheezed with almost every breath. But now, out of the silence, there came a new sound. Beneath the table she was nervously flicking two thumb nails together, and it was that same little clicking that had awakened him in the storeroom.

His face obeyed him. He felt his lip corners branching out like rock veins on his granite cheeks, forming a wicked smile that was merely expedient. Two can play your game, you old dung beetle. Especially if food and wine are included in the bargain. Knowing well that he'd have to really sweat to keep Quila supplied with enough of the tenants' small secrets–so that their big ones could remain forever safe and undisturbed in his vague memory–Bowie grabbed his cup and quickly clinked it against Quila's before draining it.

The stew and most of the bread were gone, the mugs empty, and the gruesome bargain sealed. Bowie started for the door but Quila's hand was there again, restraining him. She turned around on her stool and looked out, far past the shreds that barely covered the window of her door. Her frail body seemed to rattle as she breathed.

"I'd hoped it would yet be awhile, even though we've long been in Aries. But I could hear in a heartbeat the stranger's telltale steps." She shuddered as though some ghost had grabbed her body, "It's all about ta begin."

"Aye," she whispered, "with less than a drop o' printer's ink, this dreary town will be reborn. This wonderful, stagnant trailer park will renew its image–almost overnight". She shuddered. "Non-Gypsies are constantly wishin' fer snow in summer and sunshine in the wintertime. But this artsy little white girl, in her very own innocent way, will be the inspiration fer somethin' bigger than anythin' we've ever seen! Her name–fer now at least–be Ginny."

Quila spread another line of smoke beneath his drowsy eyes.

"I'd like ye ta start yer spyin' on this new little stranger. The one in the gray trailer beside the trash yard," she ordered. "The trailer ye like so well," she smirked. "Just bring me Ginny's symbols, Bowie. Habits! Fetishes! I'll do the figurin' out!"

One at a time, she took from her pocketed sleeve and put before him a half-used book of matches, one fresh shoestring, a new toothbrush, and a comb with all of its teeth intact. Then she reached beneath the table and took out half a bottle of wine from a narrow shelf. Suddenly angry, Bowie totally understood now that Quila would ration out every daily need to him.

As the candle lowered, her eyes became beetles trapped in a maze of wrinkles. Her hair in the sputtering light was a tangle of wispy threads and her earloops quivered like giant dewdrops caught in this spider's lair. Bowie sat back on his stool and tried not to tremble.

Quila leaned over and whispered, "Spy me somethin' quickly, me once-proud eagle. Perhaps, with a wee drop o' luck we can whisk this Ginny right back where she came from!" She patted her bosom, "And then the leather packet would be all yers!"

Pushing the bottle toward him she added quizzically, "Why now would such a pansy seek this gutter ta hide in?

3. Ginny Arrives

Bowie eased down Quila's rickety stairs and crept back to the dark, safe little storeroom. He stashed fresh supplies in the jacket pocket above him, snuggled deep into comforting fur, sipped the new wine and closed his eyes, remembering. Had he really wanted to, Bowie could already have told the fortuneteller much about the new little tenant. She had arrived that very morning in the "Month when Growth Begins," as Quila called it.

Awakening with a jerk, Bowie had hit his head on the axle of Quila's wagon above him. Like a hawk's shadow profound silence was sweeping ominously through the quail-like chatter of trailer women doing their Monday morning work. Noise was normal. Morning was always a jumble of clattering garbage can lids, cranky cars, rebellious children and undertones of women cursing flies, clogged drains and the stubborn wash machine. It was the sudden lack of noise that switched the women's attention to footsteps that had turned into this barren, neglected, hostile trailer park.

For many months Quila had been preparing these women, forecasting this simple event: "Watch for her in the Month when Growth Begins!" But surely, this particular stranger could never be a threat, thought Bowie. She seemed just a little bird blown off her course, glad to find any place to alight.

Eyes closed, he breathed deeply of clean elusive scent while the stranger flitted past the wagon. She moved with an inborn purpose long forgotten in this rut of dried-up ambition, like she was beginning some grand journey, instead of just descending into a lower world. Inches above him he felt a weight shifting as Quila, sensing something different about the dull predictable morning, pulled aside her shabby curtain.

Daylight woven by latticework at the bottom of Quila's wagon created a checkered carpet around him. He yawned, rubbed dust from his eyes, stretched cramped limbs, and in his usual drunken daze waited while the park awoke to its dreary life again. His movements awakened old Mange who wearily thumped his tail while Bowie scratched behind his ears. Uncorking the frighteningly low bottle between his knees, he took a few swallows—barely enough to keep steady his level of vagueness.

Overnight, new cobwebs veiled the view from his right. Forking them down with his fingers, he glanced beneath Kasha's trailer and into her shady yard. Something subtle as waving grass on a quiet dune moved in the single sunny spot. There, slyly studying the new female's clothing, and her simple way of walking, was Lolli. Twisting her shapely tan body on its sun towel, she squinted her eyes to better see this little stranger that Quila had predicted.

Angling his hips, Bowie glanced into the washhouse to sum up the hush that had fallen. "There she is! New posy for the Pigpen!" someone whispered loudly.

Sitting on the long bench opposite utility basins, Fay Rose stared after the stranger, delaying the small board she was aiming at Juju's bared bottom. Mala's foot, suspended by the walk-by, was ready to resume kicking the stubborn coin-operated wash machine. Leaving an unfilled water jug, one woman left abruptly and Bowie watched as a clean eyespot appeared on her grease-fogged window.

A single noise split the silence and grew louder. Like one brave chirping in a field of hushed crickets, Robbie appeared, jangling rhythmically the keys that hung from a belt loop. Water sloshed as the big coffeepot was rinsed and filled, then Robbie jangled back to her usually overcrowded trailer. Nothing startles, shocks nor insults Robbie, thought Bowie. Emotions are never wasted. They're all deposited, saved for some inevitable crisis, it seems. He tucked the profound tidbit into the shadowy file of his mind. Like a master switch Robbie's nonchalance reactivated the park. Fay Rose coughed, gagged, lit another cigarette, pushed impatiently at her waist-length unnaturally red hair and wiped at a wisp that was caught in a dab of pink calamine on her cheek. She gathered her flimsy negligee tighter about her thin body, then resumed her task of teaching Juju not to lick butter wrappers she kept finding in the trash yard. Bowie flinched: in the world of his sleep, children were never struck. Especially not to release frustration.

"I'll yank ya tongueless the next time ya dig one up, I'll yank ya tongueless!" Fay's stabbing voice droned on as she beat the silent child until the flimsy board broke in half. Jerking up on the soiled, polka-dotted cloth the child was diapered in, Fay Rose shoved her away, then sashayed back to her own trailer, swishing her hair like a red mop behind her.

"God-damn you, you money-slurpin' monster, WORK!" Mala screeched, kicking the machine again. She was furious now, not only at the weary wash machine but at Fay Rose, the prissy-looking stranger and the whole wide world as well. Bowie smirked at such mild language coming from Mala, who could out swear the whole Navy and shouted only four-lettered blasphemies at everything from her six different-fathered children to her inadequate aid checks. Again she kicked the machine, and with a pathetic sputter it finally resumed its weary "swish-swash" as Mala began overloading it again from filthy scattered mounds.

Having rinsed a strainer of string beans, the woman Pug headed her large shapeless body toward Robbie's trailer for the next process of snapping. Other women finished their work and followed after her, while females from outside the park straggled up the driveway to join them. The door creaked above Bowie, and Quila carefully descended the weathered stairs to follow after the memory of Robbie's jangle. She shuffled a deck of cards in the air as she walked. "Sic after them, vicious tick!" Bowie whispered.

Mala's clothes were filling up the lines that stretched beside the washhouse. She could seldom afford any bleach and her dingy wash declared it. Underneath blowing bedclothes, Bowie's eyes followed the new girl's feet as they kicked a path among cans and debris scattered from the trash yard to the front door of the little gray trailer.

Some of the park's children were there as usual amongst the trash, looking for something to play with. Some were jumping endlessly on the rusty bedspring, their eyes vacant and bored. It was almost as if this mindless jumping were the only activity in dull unchallenged days that kept the spirit of childhood still throbbing within them. Bowie took a small mouthful of wine, rinsed it around in his mouth, then swallowed. Children paused to titter at the futility of the stranger's path-making, then resumed their lifeless playing. As the newcomer reached into her purse for the doorknob, the black cat Spade managed an angry hiss as she ran between the stranger's legs dragging a mass of intestines.

Through a gap in the hanging clothes, Bowie watched the new girl insert the door handle and twist it. (Why did this simple act always seem so strangely familiar?) She seemed to be hurrying as though the vile smolder of the incinerator and the feel of laughing eyes were overpowering. At last the door opened and she stepped up high, for there was no doorstep. Inside, she slammed the door once, twice.

Tensely Bowie waited. On the third slam the door caught—just as he knew it would. The new glass pane fell out of the back window, tinkled to the ground and Bowie relaxed. He knew somehow without seeing that a crude magazine rack had also fallen from the curved front wall. How maddening to know only these insignificant details.

Why must he keep returning to this tiny nondescript trailer, the only thing that kept him at Last Resort? Watching and guarding it, hating any change in its sad neglect. How often he had held his hands, his heart or his ear against its peeling paint, hoping to pull from its shabby walls some answers. Why were weird butterflies always threatening his sanity? Why those nightmares of a fleeing horse with an arrow in its bloody chest? And why did a ghostly round web keep hanging behind his eyelids, always helping him to forget? Forget what? Meanwhile, why did he have to hate anyone who lived there? He had uncorked the wine, closed his eyes, then corked it up again—merely smelling of its last precious mouthfuls.

At once he loved, yet feared that trailer. Often he leaned nose-close to it, for even from the outside, the inside walls smelled faintly of familiar animal fat and cornmeal simmering with wild herbs. The very framework of its feeble structure seemed to be smothering secrets.

From between his thighs he grabbed the bottle and uncorked it again. Blood-warm, one single mouthful of fluid caressed his throat and soothed his mind. Like often, when he was overtired, the shimmering web appeared before his closed eyes and there was the same feather caught in its woven strands. His spirit tried to leave his body to float between the downy veins and drift toward sleep and dreams.

But that stifling cloud of butterflies appeared again from nowhere. Double black spots on the wings were like big sad eyes watching, condemning him. Then suddenly, as always, the eyespots turned into clots of ravenous flies eagerly leaving their hosts, determined to feed on his sanity. Swatting the empty air around him and struggling for consciousness, he again hit his forehead on the wagon's axle as he tried to sit up. Too little wine! Oblivion was what he desperately needed, not just a brief blackout!

But it wasn't a dream that had nudged into his sleep nor a fly exploring sweat beads on his dusty upper lip. His skin had bristled at "some nearness." Through lowered lashes he saw a child staring in at his checkered cell. Her eyes were sad blue pools, their edges muddied with tear stains. She clutched a crumpled butter wrapper and trailed a piece of dirty black silk behind her filthy bare feet. Relieved, Bowie lifted and twisted his hips, removed a flattened pack from his back pocket and lit a mashed cigarette with one of his last matches. He held the flickering match out through a square hole and, without smiling, the child blew it out. Smoking, as always in his practiced way, he exhaled slowly so nothing could possibly be seen or smelled. Outside the lattice wall the child licked her wrapper slowly.

Looking beneath the next-door trailer, Bowie saw a few women gathering under the only tree in the park. Here at times – in the yard of the Jewish woman, Kasha–Lolli ruled a lesser kingdom than Robbie's. In lacy shade of the cottonwood, women sat like living smoke stacks, each perched upon her own wooden doorstep, warding off the morning's work with cigarettes, idle talk and pots of strong black coffee. As usual Lolli was stretched out on her brown towel, fanning flies with her wide hat and petting her dainty white poodle. Regularly she smoothed herself with lotion, then sunned her body in the one bright patch of the shady yard, while keeping an eye and ear on the rest of things going on around her.

He closed his eyes, started to drift. But a freakish sea breeze suddenly swept into his lookout and he woke with a shudder. Always suspended around him were everyday odors of foul rags and half-burned garbage smoldering in the incinerator. But now these usual odors were mingled with a new blend of moldy seaweed, briny driftwood and the fishy smell of barnacled columns that held up the old pier way down on the beach. The smell was startling, as though, along with the strange footsteps, the outside world had suddenly found a tiny crack in this solid rut.

But it was time to move. The ground began hinting of the iceman's coming. Bowie humped toward the two-way hanging door that Robbie had made for Quila's dog. Yet, it was strangely wide enough for Bowie, too. As the truck turned into the park Bowie scrambled through the little door. He sucked out the last drops of wine, ran his tongue along the inside lip, and quietly slid the empty bottle into Quila's trash barrel.

He molded his body to the back of the Gypsy wagon and peeked around the edge. Children were appearing from all over the park and Bowie loved to watch and listen as they gathered for the one regular happy time in their dull days. As always they surrounded the truck making it immovable until the iceman laughingly chipped enough ice to satisfy their eager hands, their pockets or out-stretched dress fronts. When finished with his rounds he would entertain them with a fist puppet, whose features were made of lipstick, whose bonnet was made of a bandanna kerchief.

A new zest trickled through the monotonous conversation beneath the cottonwood, stirring ripples of laughter. With gentle ways and trusting face the iceman was a regular spark for sexy conversation. Shyly he always evaded their various invitations as he worked.

A sudden whirlwind coincided with children's laughter and Bowie could wait no longer. Whirlwinds always filled him with a wild and bittersweet longing for which he could name no fulfillment and tears welled up in his eyes. Twirling debris in a cone of red dirt spun past Quila's wagon as Bowie darted across the driveway to the familiar storeroom.

Before entering, he spared one knowing backward glance and, as he almost smiled, a twitching black rag disappeared into the refuge he had just vacated. Bowie knew that the child would now snuggle up to the patient Mange. Sucking her thumb through her black rag, here the child enjoyed the only warmth and security that she had ever found.

Inside the dark storeroom Bowie slapped red dust from his clothes. From knotholes in all four walls he removed wads of paper to permit air and sound to enter the windowless room. Stretching out on the furry coat he groped in shadows until his hand closed around the comforting shape of his very last, now watered-down bottle of wine. His hungry body was shaking too hard for planning beyond that final moment. He took a small swig, held it in his mouth, pulled off his worn shirt and balled it up to pillow his head. He took off his hat and untied the shoestring that held his long hair in a bunch that could be hidden in the hat. He swallowed very slowly, then put the bottle close beside him and settled with his thoughts into the long, lonely, hungry, desperate hours that stretched ahead. If anything of importance happened, he would know of it by hushed tones or shrill excitement that passed through thin walls of the storeroom.

It will be hard, he had thought, nestling deeper into fuzzy warmth, to hate this little cream puff who would live in "his" trailer. She was so out of place. A piece of fragile pastry in a gutter. The kind that makes a man ache to protect her. Warm and soft as the underside of a bird's wing, as vulnerable and naked as a nestling under Bowie's penetrating hawk's eye.

Surely the tenants realized that the yellow of the stranger's hair came from a bottle. Such drugstore phoniness just didn't suit the fine-boned body, the ladylike walk. Did anyone notice that the flowered skirt was not her own? It was way too long for her small height. It must be too wide as well, for it hung where it should not. And those sockless, sun-lacking feet belonged in sedate shoes with hosiery, not in sandals too big for her. Only the prim purse that peeked from under an armpit looked like it really belonged to the girl.

Bowie doubted that even Lolli, as she itemized the stranger's clothes, had noticed the real clue: the girl's right fist had been clenched as she walked, but not in anger or rebellion. That fist had carried something far more important to her than the baggage she lacked. Whatever her treasure was, the tender little stranger had pressed it to her heart with the same devotion that Juju clutched her dirty rag.

In the darkness, he lit a cigarette with the new matches that Quila had just given him; he took a long gulp from the new bottle of wine and tried to drag his mind up to Now.

Oh well, perhaps this really wasn't "the" girl that Quila had predicted. This one was far too plain and gentle to revolutionize the rut that Last Resort preferred to stay in. Yet, there must be something about her that was like all of the rest whom Robbie permitted to live here. Was she without skills or talents? Was she "lost"? Was she broke and without a job? Or was she merely just ashamed of something? Another long, appreciative swallow of the brand new red forgetfulness. As usual, Today and Yesterday had mingled into and out of each other. The cigarette fell from his fingers and he floated into nothingness.

4. Playing House

Before even opening her eyes the next morning, Ginny could hear dawn arriving in a burst of slamming doors and banging trashcan lids. The air was overpowering with a stench of smoldering cloth and half-burned garbage. But from the open door of the big trailer next door, she could hear and smell perking coffee and the splat of pancakes pouring onto a griddle. Smiling, she opened her eyes.

Having slept in her clothes, she merely re-pinned her skirt tighter. Of first importance was not food but coverings for the curtainless windows of the bare trailer. The only window even partially covered was a front one where an ice sign hid the broken section of glass.

But what to use for curtain material? The drawers and cupboards revealed nothing but linings of newspapers. Ginny sat at the table for awhile with clasped hands beneath her chin and eyes closed, remembering how much her mother hated for her to do this. Suddenly she jumped up. Thank goodness, Eloise–in her motherly way–always insisted that Ginny carry a manicure kit in her purse. First she folded and tore nine paper shades to scroll around the curtain rods. With the tiny scissors it took longer to create the double-triangular "curtains" with scallops along their edges to hang across the tops of the shades.

"Why, this is like playing house!" Crouching outside her window, Bowie heard her laughing as she admired the make-believe curtains.

The water tank beneath the breakfast nook seat must be filled, as the manager explained. She rushed out for the hose, remembering too late that there was no step there. She ran to one of the toilet stalls where her stomach retched without results.

Sunlight was warming the trailer when Ginny finished the only other tasks possible with meager tools. The water tank was filled. The floor, icebox and stove were scrubbed with wet crumpled newspapers and the mirror on the closet door was shined. Cracked windows were polished and opened. A cockroach and three lazy flies had been coaxed outside. Slowly she had waited until each one of a small line of ants crawled onto a piece of newspaper and were also transferred. She stuffed a wet wad of newspaper into their entryway.

There was nothing to do now but see what the neighborhood offered. She stood outside where a step should be and slammed the door until it caught – three times. She knew that inside, the closet door had popped open and one magazine rack had fallen again from the curved front wall. Sighing, she stuffed the doorknob into her purse. As she passed the washhouse a woman cursed and kicked a wash machine. In adjoining basins, a toast-brown girl soaped a poodle with its paws on the rim of a sink and a faded shell of a young woman wrinkled her nose while she rinsed a diaper. No one spoke or looked up as Ginny passed.

She stepped outside the park, off the strange red dirt that covered the place, and onto the encroaching sand. She could see that downhill, one block and past a sea wall, waves were scalloping the beach. In the distant curve of the shore was a pier, filled with little shops and amusement stalls, stretching out into rolling waters. Trailing unseen behind her was Bowie, just a shadow among old houses, second-rate motels, faded cars, ragged fences, scraggly trees and shrubs. Ginny passed by shabby boys playing in the street with a baseball made of rags. Little girls sat at the curbing using stones to play with instead of a ball and jacks.

Although she walked for an hour, zigzagging among the block-long streets beside the little hillside, every neighborhood seemed like the rest, lined with drab rickety dwellings in the midst of yards that were merely sand piles spilling over, erasing sidewalks. Lines of washing often filled the narrow spaces between flimsy bungalows that seemed to lean in the breeze. Ginny waved at an old lady rocking her body as she sat in a straight chair on her crumbling porch. She nodded at a crippled black man who sat on splintering steps, just staring. Ginny was shocked. She had no idea that poverty existed so close to home. This area of Waterfront was so different from shady well-manicured lawns, highly polished late-model cars, rambling stone walls and spacious two-story homes in her own serene neighborhood. Several times, Ginny was almost lost but the giant cottonwood towering over everything else in the neighborhood kept pinpointing the exact location of the trailer park.

It was still early when she started back. Passing the pier, Eloise's voice still echoed throughout the years, " Now, Ginny, don't go near the old part of town, all alone!" The pier seemed to funnel out from the edge of town, drawing to it what little bit of life and laughter were still lingering among the fading shops of main street. How different this was from the new part of town. She wandered into the big depressing art gallery across the street from a dingy newspaper office. Only one drab room was open, displaying canvases of more colorful places. Even the dark mortuary next door to the gallery looked like it was seldom needed.

Once she thought she glimpsed Luanna, the young new housekeeper and cook that now worked for Ginny's mother. Yes, Luanna in a peasant blouse, bright skirt and brown sandals (all just like Ginny's) was entering a shop in the Plaza. Ginny longed to run after her, to seek out her sweet simplicity and understanding, to apologize for borrowing some of her clothes. What an industrious worker she was for daddy Dom's big parsonage. But Luanna had been born Indian and too late. Civilization confused and repulsed her. Still, Luanna would understand Ginny's leaving and her reasons, but Eloise—never. It would only prove that Eloise was right as usual and Dom, dear daddy, was wrong again.

Instead of hurrying past the business section, Ginny pulled Luanna's peasant blouse down low on her snow-white shoulders. Bowie peeked as she added a swing to her hips, a toss to her goldened hair. Evidently, someone was looking for a natural-moving, subtle kind of girl.

For the first time in her life she was really noticed, Ginny thought, as men turned their heads for a better view. Why, it would be so easy, she summed up their greedy glances. In the next town over, near the Metropolitan Art School (her home for the past two years), there had been three girls who walked like this. Older men paid for their apartments and picked them up in fancy cars. But Ginny was well past the stores now, and Bowie watched as she pulled her sleeves back up and resumed her natural little birdlike walk.

The highlight of Ginny's excursion was the discovery of a big house being used as a secondhand store and pawnshop. It stood on the street directly behind her own trailer but separated from it by the many-leveled, add-on fence surrounding the park. At the entrance to the store she picked a familiar leaf and smelled it. Yes, it was a bay leaf. From behind the bush where he was spying, Bowie could see that someone else was peeking out from behind a curtain in the store as Ginny tucked some tree leaves into her blouse. Geraniums with leaves that smelled like cloves were lining the walkway to the building. Slyly Ginny also picked some of these fragrant leaves and pushed them down into her blouse.

When Ginny had finished exploring the interesting store, the owner Flo, a kindly but curt spinster-of-a-woman asked Ginny to join her for tea, "from the bay tree that shades my yard and the rose geraniums that lined the pathway as you entered." Ginny felt herself blushing, hoping that warm odors from inside her blouse could not be detected from the outside. Flo served little piecrust cookies that smelled delicious, and it was hard to not take more than two.

Ginny left the gold pendant Flo had admired and picked up the apple box that held her barter. She walked around the block again and started up the short street that would dwindle to a dead end just past the trailer park's entrance. Even from a block away she could see that a narrow path led beyond the park and into some wooded hills.

What a long way around, she sighed as she walked, wishing for a gate in the back fence that could lead directly from the second-hand store to her own trailer.

The day was hot and the box got heavier as she passed tattered signs intended to sway the tourists, weekenders and Navy wives: Seabreeze Resort, Restful Resort, Resort of the West Wind. And finally there it was at the very end of the street with the cottonwood, like a giant exclamation point. Carved disrespectfully on the post of the big mailbox was merely, "last resort!"

Even as she stepped from the sandy sidewalk and onto the red dirt again, she could smell smoldering rags and rotten garbage. The trailers, about fifteen of them, sat like drab bread loaves discarded in three uneven rows. Into the aisles between, possessions slopped over like gritty unwanted dough.

Beside the west fence the cottonwood spread dappled shade over one trailer and its yard. Yet the pretty brownette still sat on a towel toasting herself in the one sunny patch of the yard. She looked like she had been "waffled" into her skin-colored quilted sunsuit. With a large-brimmed hat, she fanned flies and chewed gum loudly, as if it were a chore instead of a pleasure. Through curly hair of the poodle in her lap, she ran slim fingers, seeming to enjoy its whiteness. What a waste, Ginny thought, of the only shady spot in the whole park.

Now the girl's drumming palms on her bare thighs seemed to catch the beat of Ginny's walk, turning it into a laughable tempo, making it uncomfortable to pass by the space.

Aside from the shade of the unappreciated tree, there was nothing else green to relieve the utter neglect of peeling paint, disrepair and junk-littered yards. It seemed so odd for the whole place to lie so fallow in the midst of red earth that spread like an unrecognized fertile blanket over the entire park. Outside the strange red square, the entire neighborhood was covered with sand.

As Ginny passed the washhouse, a woman cursed and kicked the silent wash machine and two other women worked at adjoining tubs. Ginny cringed as one woman scrubbed a frying pan where the dog had been bathed this morning, and another woman washed lettuce where dirty diapers had been rinsed. Even though she smiled, nobody spoke as Ginny passed and the silence was almost hostile.

She hurried now, for the smells of lunchtime puckered her mouth, widened her nostrils and her stomach wrenched in agony. She waved flies away from the door, and as she inserted the handle noisy bantering in the washhouse resumed. Bowie had darted in and out, following the stranger until he reached the hidden safety beneath Quila's wagon.

Entering her trailer, Ginny could hear the clatter of pie tins being dealt around a bare table in the trailer next door. At home in the parsonage Luanna would be doing the same chore with Eloise's gilt-edged china—but soundlessly, for Eloise insisted upon a silence cloth beneath her immaculate linen. Ginny put down her box and carefully urged a fly out of the door.

From her apple box Ginny proudly rinsed or put away the odd assortment she had chosen in trade. Aside from newspaper curtains, these were her first household possessions: two worn washcloths but no towel, a rusty skillet, dented saucepan, a sack of partly-burned candles, stubby whiskbroom, a chipped plate and a cup that didn't match, a spoon, a dull knife, some tacks and a flashlight that worked only when it was thumped. Underneath everything Flo had hidden something Ginny had forgotten about—matches.

The evening stretched long and lonely before Ginny. Bowie poked a wire through a hole in one screen and pushed aside a paper curtain. He watched from the back of her trailer as Ginny pulled wax drippings off a lighted candle and chewed them to ease her growling stomach. For nothing else to do she wiped at tears, closed the windows, curled up on the bare mattress and fell asleep shivering.

The next morning Ginny left her trailer early to search in the trash for a board of some kind. Finding one, she had soon scraped a "yard" in front of the trailer and beside the encroaching debris of the trash yard. Bowie watched from under Quila's wagon as the girl proudly sat in the doorway admiring her simple work. She was fanning herself and her feet were propped on her new apple box step. She didn't notice the iceman making his rounds until he stood before her, the big cube of ice dripping from his shoulder.

"Your sign's out!"

"Sign? Oh!" She remembered the broken window covered by the ice sign, then scrambled inside and opened the door of the icebox.

Despite his efforts not to, Syd stared in disbelief at scalloped newspapers like dainty drawn-back curtains at every window.

Here was something else new, he thought. A female all aglow from work instead of the pale scraggly ones he'd just delivered to, some still in their morning robes, smelling like stale coffee and soggy ashtrays. But this girl smelled faintly of bay or cloves, and clean yellow hair was damp against her face. There was something proudly pitiful about her and about the fan that she had been using. It was made of pleated newspaper and its top edge had been daintily scalloped with scissors.

And he hadn't had to thread his way through bones, broken glass, jagged cans, blowing papers and scattered garbage, as he had always done with other tenants who lived so close to the trash yard. He had walked over a clean, freshly scraped area around the sad little trailer. Pleasantly missing were inevitable boxes of overflow that walled in so many of the other trailers. He smiled, for the floor wasn't sticky or gritty beneath his feet. Though fresh and sparkly clean after the dirty cluttered ones he'd just delivered to, this trailer and its icebox were totally bare. There weren't even flies in this trailer.

"May I pay you next—next week?" she stammered.

"First one's always free," Syd lied, reddened, and stepped hurriedly down from the trailer.

What was she doing here, so sheltered and coddled that he had an almost uncontrollable urge to pick her up and cuddle her like a pet lamb?

That afternoon seemed endless to Ginny. She decided to rinse her under things in the tiny trailer sink, then wrung them out tightly. She spread them over one of the clotheslines and went to shower leisurely while the damp clothes soaked up warm sunshine. The shower stall was so narrow that her elbows were scraped and bleeding when she finished. She dried herself with the wrung-out washcloth, dressed, and left the shower. Beneath Quila's wagon Bowie was watching Ginny squeeze her skirt between her knees while she removed the still-damp undergarments from the line.

Two grubby boys, twins evidently, began pelting each other with debris from the trash yard. First a moldy tomato, then an eggshell full of mud whizzed past Ginny's head. Then a large shriveled yam landed at her feet.

Quickly she grabbed it, buried it between damp clothes hanging on her arm and tried to walk nonchalantly back to her trailer. Bowie left his wagon lookout and soon was standing against the back fence where he could peek, unseen, from a gap beside a paper curtain.

Water would soon be boiling on the stove and Ginny stood over the sink poised and ready to peel with her dull knife, when she saw a tiny green leaf on the yam. Quickly, before she could change her mind, she cut the yam in half and dropped one piece into the new chipped cup, pumped water over it and put it on the breakfast nook table. The other half she pared, washed, diced, and dropped into the boiling water.

"Bread and beauty both beneath my very eyes," she breathed aloud, "and me almost too proud and blind to see it!" It was one of Dom's favorite Sunday sermons. Something about, "Sell half your loaf and with the dole buy hyacinths to feed the soul!" She could almost hear his soft Irish voice and smell the hyacinths that he had passed out to all of the ladies seated in church.

"Well," Ginny patted the piece of yam in the cup, "you'll never be a hyacinth but in this greenless place you'll certainly be food for my soul!"

Ginny pumped water to rinse dirt from her washcloth and underclothes, wrung them tightly and hung them on hangers in the bare closet. With an odd sort of pride that she had never known before, she finally sat down to her meager dinner of yam mashed with a little hot water. Bowie enjoyed watching her linger over every small bite. She could hardly wait for night. Maybe there was another yam somewhere in the trashcans.

The park was dark and quiet when finally Ginny took her flashlight and slipped out the trailer door. The skinny cat snarled menacingly, its yellow eyes smoldering, its twitching tail like a warning finger as Ginny waited flat against her trailer until her eyes adjusted to faint moonlight. She gasped as a rat skittered over her foot and a cockroach grazed her arm as it fell from the trailer wall.

Shaking with hunger and revulsion, she thumped the flashlight and stood over the first garbage can, wincing at its topping of coffee grounds, potato peels, and moldy cereal. She moved to the next can, which was overflowing with bones, thick gravy, and a bowl-shaped "something" that sprouted green "hair." The next can was smelly from some ugly mess that looked and smelled like vomit.

As she turned in disgust, back toward the trailer a familiar voice seemed to taunt at her: "She's not tough enough, Dominic. She'll never be a gardener. I wonder what would happen if she were ever really hungry. She'd rather accept a puny 'store' potato than dig for a giant one in rich damp earth. She could never squash a ravenous worm or enjoy the feel of rich manure with those flawless hands. You just can't pretty everything up for her, Dom! Tell her the facts and punishments. The child is already too much yours! You'd both be lost without my shoulders. When will you two learn that life is neither free nor beautiful?"

"Ginny's hands are beautiful," Ginny could almost hear Dom whisper again as she wiped a tear from her cheek.

"And why wouldn't they be beautiful?" Eloise had shouted as she looked at her own worn hands. "All she wants to do is draw and read and think!"

"But her hands make everything she does say and do seem so special. Here, let me set those plants for you, Ginny. You can't burn the log before the kindling, Eloise," Dom said softly as he held Ginny's hands in his. "A child must crawl and wander, enjoy and feel of its path before it can walk a straight line."

"And, pray tell, who's going to disinfect, deodorize, and perfume that path? No, Dom, she'll always take the easy way. If any path is hard or offensive, our gentle little Ginny will always find a convenient detour."

Quickly Ginny turned back to another trashcan and sunk her fingers into bones, gravy, and mold. She overturned the first layer and exposed a bed of squirming maggots. But for Eloise's mocking laughter in her head, she would have screamed. Instead she lifted the squirmy layer and settled it into another can. She shook the worms from her hands, then frantically stooped to rub away with dirt their wiggly memory from her fingers.

Now she moved things around with a stick she had found. But what was this? She thumped the failing flashlight, and there, smiling up at her through broken glass and more squirming maggots was a sad little cloth mouth. Blowing maggots aside, she exposed a rag doll with a cigarette burn on its soggy cheek. She shook away worms and glass, wrung stale beer from the smelly little body, then put it on her new porch step.

In the next can she unearthed a seed catalogue, some flour left in a sack, dried-out food coloring, and an unused nail polish brush. At the foot of the incinerator she was starting to sift out a thin piece of charcoal when she got that bristly feeling of being watched.

She froze, remembering Flo's parting words. "Renters in your trailer, Ginny, never last a month. They all complain of an eerie presence, a strange smell or goose-shivery feelings of invisible eyes always watching. I'm sure that if you're aware of this you can accept these conditions. I'd like to see you stick around. You'd be a real change for Last Resort!"

Reluctantly, Ginny slipped back into the trailer with no more yams, but arms full of other discoveries. Yes, the trailer did have a strange odor, and her skin did prickle up as soon as she closed the door. But so what, this really was her own "last resort."

She pumped water in the sink and rinsed the doll until it didn't smell. The flour had a weevil and the catalogue was damp. She had cut herself and was bleeding, so she ripped out the hem of her skirt and tore it into bandage widths. The skirt was too long, anyway.

"Besides," she explained to the empty trailer, "who else has ever had a cut finger tied up in cloth flowers? A bright little bandage that will always remind me of a good friend!"

For no real reason, maybe because she felt so possessionless, Ginny cleaned the nail polish brush with wet newspapers and added a bit of water to the dried jar of food coloring. She caught the weevil with a spoon, gently lifted it outside, then put the flour sack and the seed catalogue on the top shelf of the kitchen cupboard. In the breezeless night she suddenly felt a slight movement and even though the paper shades were unrolled now and some of their tips secured with tacks, she felt like a nude artists' model posing in front of a class. Quickly she squeezed the last bit of water from the rag doll and sat it upright on the table. As the doll leaned against the curved wall, the burn on its face wasn't as black as it used to be. In fact, it seemed to be beaming, just for her eyes, alone.

She blew out the candle and undressed. Sitting against the fence, Bowie could hear and feel her getting down on her knees. But in moonlight from the transom, he could see that she wasn't praying. Instead, she sat back up on the bed and dramatically wiped her hands three times.

"No! No! No! Not just on knees with hands together. Not just in church. Not just with somebody else's tiresome songs and prayers. Here and now, I can indulge in my own un-traditions. My every breath and thought, my every desire, discouragement and sigh, my every laugh, blunder and creation are already prayer. And the designation changes with every heartbeat. It is not only God. It is Love, Grace, Beauty, Serendipity, Compassion, Darkness, Dawn, Moonlight, Silence, and Friend. Now I can just talk to, share with, and marvel at the awesome mystery and miracle that is all of life!" Puzzled, Bowie smoked the last of his cigarette.

Now she was just lying down in bed, softly talking to the empty trailer. "I'm so thankful! My primary thought in life is being proven: 'Less is more.' I already know that I will learn here what my mother says I lack the most: humility and gratitude."

She can't last long, mused Bowie, snuffing his cigarette in a crack of the back fence. She's too different.

Another day passed and Ginny was at the bitter end of hunger. She sat at the table by candlelight with her eyes closed, her elbows on the table, and her chin propped up in her hands. Eloise called this Ginny's "escape position," but Ginny called it "wistful waiting."

Suddenly Dom's voice was in her ears: "Even the lowliest person has some jewel to offer. But mostly, these tiny gems are never recognized until and if we really need them."

That very morning Ginny had watched a horribly birth-marked little waif as she licked on a butter wrapper. Suddenly Ginny opened her eyes. Yes! Then there must always be a trace of butter left on each wrapper. And grains of salt and sugar, flakes and drops of this and that in almost all containers.

And thus, Ginny began her study of the tenants and of what they threw away.

5. The Tenants

What an odd bunch lives in this lackluster place, Ginny had thought. Yet, within a week of observation, she found the people highly interesting, completely different from the bland sort she was used to as a pastor's daughter. Here, some of the tenants seemed to be coming and going all of the time, in a constant turnover. But there were also those who chose to stay, regardless of possible vacancies elsewhere. In time each permanent resident contributed something for Ginny to use. Intently, Bowie observed her progress.

The manager, Robbie, a rugged-looking woman, sometimes sat (like Ginny had first seen her) in an old chair tilted against the washhouse wall as she folded and wove cellophane wrappers from cigarette packs into a zigzagging chain that always hung around her neck. She drank black coffee, smoked incessantly, or chewed tobacco and spit out its vulgar juice while she listened and talked to a motley crowd of girls that usually surrounded her. Sometimes she laughed, in a way that magically touched Ginny, like the sound of rippling water suddenly appearing in a dark forest. Girls from the park, the neighborhood, the pier, the beach, and the beer parlor down the street sat around Robbie on the bench or the floor, smoking, drinking coffee, sharing jokes, laughing, making Ginny feel like such an outsider.

"No watering, loud parties, or outside plants," Robbie had said as she pocketed the six twenties Ginny handed her. Robbie masked her surprise in a cloud of exhaled smoke. "And," she added defiantly, "we have a welcome peeping Tom. Actually, he's listening more than he's peeking. Harmless, homeless, naive, amnesiac. Until he can find his way back to 'Now,' he has to be tolerated, ignored, expected, and understood. Yours is that little gray trailer over there by the trash yard that we call the 'Pigpen.' Rent starts tomorrow. Here's the only 'key' that works." Robbie took a doorknob from her back pocket and handed it to Ginny.

"Six months in advance," Ginny had repeated, trying not to squirm as lazy flies tickled her nose and explored her legs. It was hard not to stare at the oddly handsome woman with the dark curly hair, in ragged jeans, rumpled shirt, and grubby work shoes. In a constant cloud of seeming hive smoke, Robbie was a queen bee surrounded by adoring sister bees.

Robbie gave a sort of reign and routine to otherwise dull days at the park. Twice or more daily, with a big bunch of keys hanging from her belt, she jangled out to the washhouse to draw water for her big coffee pot that never seemed to be out of use. It was a strange sort of coffee klatch that went on in the washhouse or in Robbie's trailer, Flo had told her. Often, after wild laughter, someone might even bolt out of the washhouse or Robbie's trailer, never to return, or, if a resident of the court, to be gone that night, trailer and all.

Once, when Robbie walked by, Ginny caught her staring up at the newspaper curtains as though wondering when Ginny herself might join her crowded "Den," as she called her trailer kitchen. But here in this uncivilized place where all the women smoked, drank, and cursed as frequently as churchgoers praised the Lord, how could anyone relate to a nineteen-year-old, who had never even smelled of cigarettes or liquor except on the breaths of derelicts that her father smuggled into the kitchen of the parsonage. What could anyone here have in common with someone who couldn't cuss and didn't even care to remember a "funny" story?

Most of Robbie's trash sacks contained only empty wine and beer bottles, cigarette butts, ashes, empty cans, and cigarette packs (without their cellophane wrappers). There were also one or more strange soggy "trays," made from cut-off, folded-down paper sacks. Without even knowing it, Robbie had something else, more interesting, to offer Ginny. Strangely, this event happened whenever Robbie played that same sad record all day long, that everyone called "Doll's Song." Nobody seemed to visit Robbie's trailer on those days. On those nights there always appeared on Robbie's doorstep a snack or dinner in a paper sack whose folded-down top was secured with clothespins. By bedtime, if the sack were still on the doorstep, as quietly as she had put it there, Pug, the large lady in the trailer next door, sighed, removed the clothespins, dumped the food from the plate right back into the clean sack, carried it out with her own trash, and took the plate inside to wash. Eagerly, Ginny began to look forward to the sudden hearing of that record, and those clean samples of Pug's wonderful, homey cooking.

The opposite side of the trailer park was kingdomed into another domain. There the sulky, dusky Lolli waited, watching for opportunities to impose a lesser reign at her own trailer, when Robbie and Doll were both gone. Meanwhile, fanning away flies, petting her poodle, oiling her beautiful limbs, Lolli lazed beside the shade of the big cottonwood. This only tree in the trailer park spread leafy arms across the space where Kasha, the Jewish woman lived. "Queen" Lolli lounged there in patches of sunshine, as though her brown towel were a throne. Instead of merely talking, she drawled her drawn-out words, loudly cracking her gum, lifting her eyebrows, and making cruel insinuations. Constantly she drummed on things, in a way that Ginny could almost read her thoughts. When Robbie was home, usually only Kasha and Lolli had coffee in Kasha's yard. But when Robbie and, or Doll were gone, many of the girls had coffee at Lolli's, but they never stayed very long. When Robbie was home, they usually stayed at her trailer all day long and sometimes far into the night.

Lolli was lazy, thank goodness. She never mended things, or used leftovers. But in small ways, which were big to Ginny, Lolli was tidy as a cat. She wrapped leftovers in packets of newspaper before throwing them away. Iced tea was too troublesome; Lolli drank pop continually, and with these empty bottles, which Lolli never returned, Ginny had money for ice every week as well as a pack of gum to be cut in little pieces for easing frequent hunger pangs. Lolli couldn't stand bananas with spots, potatoes or onions with sprouts, or shriveled grapefruit with seeds starting to leaf. Ginny squeezed the now sweeter, older grapefruit for juice and saved the seeds for dessert: they tasted so much like flowers. She mashed the overripe bananas and pretended they were puddings. Adding hot water to Lolli's old catsup bottles, she poured the bland liquid over cooked potato skins, which she decorated with onion tops. She finely diced the mushy onion bodies and simmered them to broth.

Ginny always checked Lolli's discarded pop bottles before returning them for deposit money. Lolli sometimes filled them with bacon fat, which she seemed to abhor. Ginny melted the bottled fat in hot water, stirred it into some of the flour she had sifted through a piece of screen, added a little water, and stirred again. Lolli also threw out heels of bread, and over them Ginny poured her tolerable sort of gravy.

All that Pug threw out were sacks of peelings, bean snips, and pits. After careful separation and washing, peels and snips made a fair broth, while fruit skins and pits boiled down to a drink that was tolerable over chipped ice. But after Pug got done with a bone, it had already given up all of its color and flavor to an all-night-simmering soup. Though none of the other women bothered, Pug was always scrubbing on a board, and Bowie enjoyed watching Ginny walk through instead of around Pug's sweet-smelling laundry as it blew on the lines. "That's a gift in itself. Food for my soul," she confided to the empty trailer.

Eagerly, Ginny watched for Quila's discarded candy boxes. Quila was obliged to leave the chewy and nutty candies untouched, her old teeth merely stumps, the gums shrinking away as if in horror of touching them.

But Quila was so colorful. According to Flo, the little old dried-up woman in the fascinating but faded trailer was a real Gypsy fortuneteller.

"But Gypsies eat poisonous nightshade berries," Flo whispered. "They put scratchy nettles and thorny cactus pads into soups. They pluck eerie forecasts right out of the very air, mystifying and terrorizing not only the tenants, but the whole neighborhood as well. Just by walking past someone, Quila can feel the chill of disaster."

Flo confided that Gypsies put squashed toads on boils, and washed themselves with goat urine. "Wary neighbors," she said, "whisk clothes off lines, lock windows, cross themselves, or rush children inside when Quila goes to the store." Ginny steered clear of her.

Yet, in the evenings, when Quila sat on her tiny porch, birds really trusted her and flitted happily all around as she cooed and fed them breadcrumbs. And her old dog Mange trustingly rested his head on her knee and looked up adoringly into her dry, wrinkled face.

In one of the sidewalk trailers the thin flashy girl, Fay Rose, conducted an unlovely trade. Fay had a chronic cough, flushed cheeks and big green eyes that constantly searched for understanding, warmth, or friendship in all the wrong places. In French, she whispered endearments to her twin boys, "the Chips." But in English, she shouted curses to her badly birth-marked, black-curled daughter, Juju. Fay wore toothpicks in her pierced ears, curlers all over her head, and pink calamine blotches always dotting her daytime face.

Yet in the evenings, she swished her beautiful long hair like a brush dipped in Titian red as she strutted away from Last Resort in a different outfit every night. Then she moved her bony body in ways that actually made her seem to acquire some instant curves.

Fay never seemed to have much but cans to throw away, but old bouquets that sailors brought her made very useful materials. Gently gathering the best parts from trashcans, Ginny snipped the blossoms into potpourris to lift up her sometimes-flagging spirits.

But Fay's dead roses still smelled so good that Ginny coaxed them into fragrant brews, and began to gather her own odd tea mix, adding bay and rose geranium leaves to the crumbled roses, and dregs from spice cans found in the trash yard.

Ginny seldom saw the Indian, Bowie; he had nothing anyway to add to her life. But someday, when she had the right materials, she wanted to sketch the patience, anticipation, and appreciation that she had spied in him one evening. Standing on a stack of newspapers, she had looked across the trash yard fence and into Flo's yard, pondering how to make the journey shorter to her favorite store. And there was Bowie below her, hunched down on his knees, entranced, waiting for a twisted moonflower bud to open. When finally it unfolded, she saw him smile for the very first time, as he closed his eyes. He smelled of the flower's snowy whiteness as though it were priceless perfume instead of only a common weed.

Ginny wasn't sure how other tenants disposed of trash or garbage, so mostly she ate from sacks that belonged to Pug and newspaper packets Lolli dumped in the Pigpen.

Each night now, Ginny waited patiently for the last two lights, Quila's and Pug's, to flick out. This was the moment in every day that she looked forward to the most, as eagerly as old Lambeth (in the tiny trailer next to Robbie's) watched for overdue buses filled with new faces to arrive at the Plaza bus stop that he haunted. Ginny waited as eagerly as Enoch in his faded maroon trailer listened for the thud of his evening Wake. She waited almost as longingly as Robbie did for each return of Doll. Then Ginny took her sacks and cleaned jars to the trashcans or to the overflowing incinerator that often hadn't even been lighted that day.

Thumping her flashlight, she quietly sorted through refuse. Spade was always there already, snarling and hissing at Ginny's intrusion. Ginny already had one small jar half filled with drops of bleach, another almost full of soapbox rinsings. Soon she would have enough soapy liquid to wash her outer clothes and enough bleach to whiten dingy underwear.

Now she ran her fingers through trash and garbage laughingly, almost wishing that Eloise could see her fingers now, so bruised and cut from sifting and sorting, as though digging for priceless treasure. But usually, when there was something really clean or usable in the Pigpen like meaty ham bones that Lolli wrapped in newspaper to throw out, instead of using in a bean pot, Spade had an uncanny way of discovering them first, seeming to sense and enjoy Ginny's disappointment.

Though nights were somewhat rewarding, the days dragged by in loneliness. Ginny was obsessed by thoughts of food, the unappreciated beauty of the tree, laughter from the Den, and the coming again of a promising dark night. After sweeping with the blunt whiskbroom, mopping with a rag, and coaxing or lifting outside various insects that still found their way inside, there was nothing to do for the day. She found herself idly dusting whenever a car passed by, poking a bit of rag or paper into another possible ant or cockroach entry, and counting the number of times that children jumped on the old bedspring. There was nothing even to read but old newspapers, torn magazines, soggy catalogues, and filthy words on restroom walls.

Yet now, Ginny found that she really appreciated the small amount of work there was to do. It was actually fun now to wash, sweep, dust, and mop with no one around to prod, hurry, instruct, or shame her.

She often spent afternoons sitting on the red dirt as she leaned against the mailbox, waiting for letters that never came for her. Tenants looked at her contemptuously as she squinted one eye and studied them, the trailer court, the tree, the Pigpen, nearby mountains, or children playing through her cupped finger "frames." Often she sketched in the dirt with her fingers, or pretended to draw things in the air.

Ginny blamed her loneliness on her mother's upbringing. Eloise had taught her to be selective with friends, food, and books. Eloise had insisted that a closed door was to be knocked upon, that one must be invited to tea, that adolescents were to be seen and not heard, and that those older than one's self were to be called by their last names. These unrefined people never knocked, nor did they await invitations to tea or coffee. Nor, as far as she knew, did they have any last names to be called by. And the mail that Ginny sorted through every day never gave her any clues.

Now that she could scavenge at least one bland "meal" a day, Ginny thought of other things. Though she longed to sweep with a real broom, sit in a proper chair, soak in a hot bath, sleep between crisp sheets, snuggle beneath warm blankets, and fill her stomach to the bursting point, most of all she longed to draw again, not to capture the stark unloveliness around her, but to dress it up, if only for her own imagination. For nothing else to do, she began to scrub the wooden trailer walls with an old toothbrush and remnants of a cleanser can. She removed not only the last of the varnish on the walls, but a strange mutton-like odor that rushed out at her whenever she entered the trailer.

One night she found a stubby pencil in the incinerator. Laboriously she sharpened it with her dull knife, then realized she had no paper. Disgusted, she fell onto the bed and held the sharpened useless prize at arm's length, scaling imaginary trees, mountains, and figures against the ceiling, as she had often done in art school. She giggled. One of the knotholes in the pine wall looked like a cartoon of the tenant, Enoch, balancing a weenie on his nose.

Sitting on her knees, she darkened the outline of Enoch with a pencil. Why, there were puppies and pigs there too, and clouds, strange faces with funny features, flowers and little children, all waiting to be taken from the anonymity of knotty-pine and given life. Remembering the dried-out bottle of food coloring, the nail polish brush, and slivers of charcoal sifted from the incinerator, Ginny knew that her own voiceless inner self had had good reasons for saving them.

Outlining, then brushing diluted food coloring into clean, thirsty wood, Ginny worked long into the night on her strange "mural." Then slowly, she seemed to feel, rather than hear, faint rustles of clothing outside in the stillness. She blew out the candle and curled up into a ball that her skirt could almost cover. But in a few minutes, Bowie could hear her talking to the night again. "Thank goodness it's true that slowness really is beautiful, and that work really is wonderful when you do it at your own pace, in your own simple way. And thank goodness that art really is always waiting—wherever one might be. But mostly, I'm so thankful for discovering that having nothing conventional to eat or to work with, can really be such a strange asset—at least for me!"

6. Eating with Enoch

Next evening at the washhouse while pretending to scrub her fingernails, Ginny watched Enoch flooding his lettuce, minutely examining each leaf. From under Quila's wagon, Bowie also watched with interest. Usually Ginny avoided Enoch, for the smallest occurrence could remind him of a morbid fact that he just could not resist sharing.

But Ginny was out of butane. Her scanty meals had to be raw for now. Even making "tea" was disappointing. Water brought from the washhouse was never hot enough to release the flavor of various plant parts that she continued to gather. Maybe Enoch would discard one of those large outer lettuce leaves and forget it there in the sink.

"You'd be amazed at the 'monsters' that tenant these green walls!" Enoch suddenly exclaimed, looking over at Ginny. He retrieved one outer leaf. "Come, let me show you." Eagerly Ginny followed him to his trailer.

Although Ginny hated to be cornered by Enoch, she realized there was much to learn from him. Slyly, Ginny had watched as he dipped toothpowder from a jar labeled "Soda+Salt." He scooped hand soap from a jar of white gel to which he was always adding soap slivers. He had no need for an iron, for he hung washed pants on stretchers, and damp white tee shirts on hangers. He was a kind, big-eared, overly clean man with an energetic walk. A weak smile framed his large overhanging teeth with lips too pink to be manly. The hair, which easily could have covered a bald head, instead grew only at the back, in one thick, rust-colored clump that he combed forward. His tennis shoes were spotlessly white and mended with vari-colored thread. He was wifeless, childless, and friendless, from head-to-toe a natural target for ridicule.

Enoch's worst habit was obsession with death. He could find any excuse for a sordid conversation. Like the time when Ginny fished out a gob of hair from a clogged sink.

"Did you know," he quickly began, "that some scientists tell a dead person's sex, age, and race by examining a single hair? Some dead people have hair growing out of huge moles. Some bodies are covered with warts, scales, or the wrong kind or number of sex glands." He talked faster now, to be sure of finishing. "Some 'deads' have horns on their noses, heads, or personal parts! Some have hair roots that ooze a gooey liquid!" Ginny had swallowed hard and hurried to the Pigpen carrying the gob of dripping hair–instead of merely dropping it into the trash can beside the sinks.

Ginny stepped inside of Enoch's trailer and saw that it was an orderly maze of labeled jars, sacks, old cookbooks, and stacked newspapers with narrow passages between. Dusting a cracked hand lens, he tried in vain to find an aphid for Ginny to look at.

"Never mind. What are you having for dinner? Let's sup together." Ginny was frowning. "Come now! It takes more muscles to frown than it does to smile. 'Cheerful looks make every meal a feast,' my Marnie" (he said the name caressingly) "always said." He motioned to a stack of newspapers, lower than the rest. "Sit down. We're having mulligatawny." From the open window, Bowie closed his eyes and feasted on steamy aroma.

The curry was thin and peppery, but a warm and welcome change for Ginny. Enoch himself teetered upon a low three-legged stool, as though four legs were just too superfluous. After the meal, Enoch shared how he prolonged leather shoes by constant cleaning and polishing with petroleum jelly. He showed her how he mended tennis shoes, then made decorative stitches over a patch. Then proudly he pointed out ships he would sail on some day and countries he planned to visit; his walls were papered with maps and travelogues.

Rescuing a tasty morsel with his tongue, Enoch took it out, identified it, and returned it to his front teeth to munch. "Even when I was a tiny apron-hanger," he looked around the walls, "Marnie always said that when you wanted something badly enough, you must keep your goals always pictured before you." He wiped away a tear.

When Ginny returned to her trailer, Bowie watched from a gap in a rolled-down shade as she took out a seed catalogue, a little jar of flour paste and manicure scissors. From a newspaper shade on the window at the head of her bed, she snipped out a paper face "with eyes like Tad's," she said out loud. From the catalogue she cut a dozen blooming hollyhocks "As pretty as daddy-Dom used to plant," and, "A picture that looks like the tree." She pasted the hollyhocks and tree on a piece of cardboard. "Thanks, Enoch. I will keep my goals always pictured before me!" Then she sketched her own ugly, shadeless trailer nestled beneath the tree. The paper face she had cut out was now smiling out of her own penciled trailer window. "Someday, maybe," she sighed. She tacked the collage to the closet door, stood back and admired it.

Sitting at the table now, she began to snip out cloth flowers and tear more bandage strips from the hem she had ripped from her faded skirt.

Enoch showed Ginny how to make tea without fuel. In the morning he put tea leaves in a jar of water and placed it in sunshine on the screen of his ceiling transom. When he arrived home in the evening his "transom tea" was just right for sugar, ice, and drinking.

Ginny tried it in her own trailer with her own private mix and it wasn't bad at all. The words of her father, Dom, were clear in her head: "Folks learn eagerly, Eloise, when there's a real need for it. You're so efficient, there's no need in Ginny's trying hard around this house. What is there to do that you haven't already conquered? Why can't you just accept that Ginny was born to discover and create her own little rules?"

Most of the recipes that Enoch created were made in one pot. "Bring whatever you have. We'll make it do. It's not what you make, but what you call it that really counts."

"I hear you're a butcher," said Ginny one night.

"A butcher," mused Enoch, "Some might call me that." He seemed to shiver.

Returning next evening with wine she had found in a hump behind her trailer, with a teaspoonful of sugar grains she had painstakingly collected, with the last of the flour she had sifted from any weevils, two crusts of Lolli's bread, and her last sliver of ice, she handed them to Enoch, ashamedly. "There! It would take a wizard to transform these into a meal!"

Enoch closed his eyes and thought, then poured and beat things into the imagined bowl in his lap. With movements neat as stitches at the back of his mended seat bottoms, Enoch rubbed his hands in eagerness. Daintily, he gathered things from his cupboard, lined them evenly, then leaned over like a sorcerer and began concocting. His stock bone was already bubbling as he added sliced carrots, onions, potatoes, and seasonings. He turned down the flame with a flourish, lidded the pot, and smacked his lips. After more fussing, he handed Ginny an iced drink. "Have a pick-me-up," he offered, clinking his glass to hers.

"Here's to those greedy 'hussies' who keep us from getting rich – our own palates!"

Ginny sniffed, a taboo that until Last Resort she had only smelled. "Sangaree," Enoch explained as Ginny hungrily sipped diluted wine, sweetened, iced, and spiced deliciously.

Enoch now mixed Ginny's flour with oil, baking powder, and canned milk. He dropped teaspoonfuls of the batter, like tiny dumplings into the bubbling seasoned pot of vegetables. From stacks of newspapers he fashioned a table and bench for Ginny.

"Wait," she urged, fumbling in her purse for the manicure scissors. With a few swift cuts on a many-folded newspaper she created a lace-like scalloped "tablecloth."

Proudly Enoch sat the feast before them. "Humble Pie," he announced, presenting a stew dotted with dumplings. "Cambric Tea," he labeled hot water, milk, and sugar she had brought. "Rusk," he declared of crusts, broken into pieces and sprinkled with cinnamon-sugar. They savored each mouthful as Enoch again pictured places he would visit someday.

He picked up one oval-shaped piece of spice-reddened crust. "Did you know that flamingo tongues – they're shaped like this – were once a common delicacy of Roman feasts?

Ginny sank back against a partition of cardboard that separated Enoch's bedroom from the rest of the crudely made trailer, and pinned her skirt looser. "Never have I more enjoyed a meal," she sighed, trying to change the subject.

"Hunger is the best sauce of all," said Enoch, as her delicate hands ceased shaking.

Ginny wasn't like other wasteful women in the park, he noted. She looked longingly, not laughingly, at his cigar box full of razor-pointed pencil stubs, at his bits of thread wrapped neatly on old ice cream bar sticks. Her eyes were more alert after she had seen these treasures. Like Enoch himself, she now walked with her head down, eyes to the ground. Pins, buttons, bobby pins, and needles were like shimmering nuggets and ground anywhere was a potential gold field. Everywhere she went, Enoch noticed, she now was ready for discovering beauty or bounty to take home and use. Some nights Ginny found things in the Pigpen that were useable for their evening meal and sometimes she did not. Then she shared bouquets from vacant lots, or seashells for serving bowls or sauces.

Ginny was tender and ladylike, hard qualities to hang onto when one lived a hand-to-mouth existence. Suspended by wires from the roof of the washhouse were rows of long-unused water pipes, and into one of them a small bird fashioned a nest that included a wad of pink thread.

Enoch watched as Ginny stood on a bench to check if the eggs had hatched.

She waited so patiently for those little birds to hatch, thought Enoch as he picked his teeth and enjoyed the pictures on his walls. Finally the babies flew away, and she took down the nest. As she sat on the long bench in the washhouse, unraveling pinkness and winding it around a stick as he had taught her to, Enoch as always could not resist sharing again.

"Did you know that if you unraveled the alimentary canal of a dead human, it would reach to the top of a three-story building?" Ginny did not seem to appreciate that treasured fact.

Enoch sucked his teeth now, and he noted that Ginny seemed a sickly girl, for in the mornings when vile incinerator smoke engulfed her trailer, she would often rush to the restroom and vomit. Since coming to Last Resort, Ginny's legs had grown skinny and her cheeks were hollowing. Yet she ate with a slow, calm elegance her usual fare of Enoch's concoctions and clean siftings from the trash yard. It was as though she was always thinking: the more I chew a bite, the less I will need, and the more nutrition can be extracted.

Enoch had glimpsed her in the past, walking until footsore and weary, filling up on vapors of neighborhood dinners. It would have been far easier for her to procure a meal than for Fay Rose to do so. Ginny's complexion was speckles, and hair that hung like coils of gold was meant for tossing in a man's face. But since her first week here, every time she left the park, she wore a ragged head square that covered the beauty of her hair.

Enoch sighed. Perhaps he should consider squelching his favorite topic for a while. It always scared females away or made them sick. And it was nice at last to have some decent company. Maybe, if he tried harder when Ginny was around, he could even forget how much, and how fast, the long hot flame of Fay Rose's hair could warm him. Maybe, he could even forget the taunting, lying promise of her jade eyes, and the fever of hot desire that Fay Rose ignited whenever she merely sauntered by.

Ginny wasn't a bit like Fay. She had none of the conniving look, the female wile that his Marnie had always warned him against. Ginny spoke with few, chosen words—not that vulgar mishmash of English and phony French like Fay. Though Ginny's one outfit was growing threadbare, and her thin body often shook with hunger, still she stood straight, without that round-shouldered resignation of other trailer women. She seemed just a babe turned loose in wilderness, with no mother to guide or father to protect her.

For the first time in his life, a female needed the only thing that Enoch could ever share: the knowledge behind his petty, thrifty, unappreciated daily habits. As well, though she often seemed to tremble, Ginny was the only one who had ever seemed even slightly interested in facts that made others disgusted. Never before could he honey tea with anyone, while sharing the exciting tidbit that dead ancients were often preserved in a crock of that same sweetness. Nor could he have admired anyone's bloody floral bandages, and share with them the fascinating fact that bandaging mummies often took six months to complete.

They ate together often, Enoch calling old things by creative new names and Ginny declaring them "Delicious!" He would not think of using questionable, scavenged fare except from Ginny's discriminating hands. It became the highlight of the evening for Ginny to bring the few useable items that she had discovered to add to their supper.

Underneath Enoch's trailer, Bowie had pulled closer to the always-open door a thin mattress that Enoch stored beneath his trailer. Here Bowie could listen, smell and pretend that he was a part of happy occasions. Above him now, he could hear Enoch swatting a fly.

"Ginny, did you know that the progeny of a single fly is in the millions?"

"My, my," gasped Ginny, "can you just imagine what the progeny of a married fly might be?" Bowie could scarcely contain his laughter. "Humph," muttered Enoch.

A few sprouting potatoes Enoch transformed into Fried Murphies. When Ginny saved a jarful of cornmeal leavings, they had tiny skillet muffins, that Enoch called Crumpets. Together they lingered over Chrysanthemum Beets, Blushing Cauliflower, and other quaint, picturesque dishes that usually one only reads about.

Long after a meal was finished, Enoch prolonged the time it took to loudly suck his palate and pick his teeth with a sharpened matchstick. So from the second evening, Ginny brought torn cardboard and the backs of can labels, so she could sketch her host and his unusual trailer, while Enoch talked and sucked and picked.

Actually, Enoch seemed to enjoy the aftertaste as much or even more than the meal itself, as though it were an added bonus, thought Ginny, who had never seen even one toothpick inside the parsonage. Yet, daintily she followed suit with matchsticks Enoch sharpened just for her. Oh well, it won't hurt me to clean my teeth in front of somebody, and to allow Enoch a little earbending. It's worth the food and fun, she thought.

One evening Ginny brought only hardened molasses and a smashed can of ginger, saying, "There, that'll stump you!" Enoch thought for a minute, then mixed things into an imaginary bowl, as Ginny sketched. His eyes kindled up, and after awhile they both sat laughing on their newspaper benches, holding foaming mugs of molasses, ginger, and yeast that he had borrowed from Pug. Enoch labeled that night their "Ginger Beer Bust!"

And then it was all over.

One day Ginny surprised Enoch by scrubbing his linoleum and dusting his bottles and books. She peeked beyond the cardboard wall and into Enoch's tiny bedroom. Wondering at their strangeness, she smoothed the floor pallet, the flat silk pillow, and narrow satin sheets that he slept with. She had never seen this kind of bedding except inside a coffin.

Enoch came home earlier than usual that afternoon, and for a moment just stood there in the open doorway watching Ginny work, remembering Marnie's words: "Son, you are a very plain and practical man. Women will only want you for money. Do for them if you must. But when they 'do' for you, they've got some hidden reason. Pay them back and be done with them." Hurriedly Enoch thanked Ginny and helped her out of the door. When Ginny arrived back at his trailer that night with wizened apples and stale cake in her sack, Enoch's trailer was locked and he was gone. The next night there was a note pinned to his door. "I've made you a present. Try your butane stove tonight."

That night Ginny found her scalloped paper tablecloth wrapped carefully around her jar of strained bacon grease, the same bacon grease that Enoch kept putting off using. He had finally hidden the unwanted grease deep in Pigpen debris. Enoch, with a shudder, had probably been substituting with olive oil. Thinking back, she realized his meals were always bland and weak, that only his collection of spices had made high-flavored soups and stews even palatable. Why, his very zest alone had created a meaty illusion. Just for her benefit.

"Poor Enoch," she said aloud one night as she touched up a sketch of him. "You must have been embarrassed that I found it," and she laughed at the memory of what Enoch had fooled her with, the bone-shaped rock that always sat at the bottom of his boiling kettle. Enoch had a morbid distaste for meat.

Outside Ginny's trailer, Bowie rubbed his aching neck, shook his head, snuffed his cigarette butt into a nail hole and pussyfooted over to Quila's. It had never once occurred to the little stranger, that evening after she straightened Enoch's trailer, that he couldn't wait until he had thanked and shooed her out of the door, that he was extremely excited – not about the cleaning nor the secrets of his "bone" and bedding, but about the way she had shoved all the newspapers into different, neater piles.

Bowie told Quila the seemingly useless information, and that night after supper she rewarded him with a whole bottle of wine.

For a while now, Ginny tried her hand at job-hunting.

"What can you do?" they asked.

"Well, I can draw and paint a little. I have a great vocabulary. I can correct Sunday sermons. I'm good at Latin. I can turn ugliness into beauty. And, and, I'm a good listener!"

It didn't take long for Ginny to discover that these were not marketable skills.

7. Holly

Weeks later Ginny woke abruptly from fitful sleep, aware of deep silence and a feeling of eyes upon her. Outside, the new hollyhock rustled, was quiet, and the new jar of crickets resumed chirping. Ginny smiled sleepily; she had only been dreaming she could smell wine at the open rear window. She drifted back to sleep. Through a gap in the rear curtain, Bowie enjoyed watching moonlight melt her fright into contentment.

The only company the little stranger had had since her aborted friendship with Enoch was the ragged doll at the foot of her bed, and on her dresser, crickets she had found one evening as they sang in Flo's lush greenery. She had housed them in a glass jar, and offered them fruit peels, wildflowers, and drops of water. They performed only at night. Bowie disliked them; they were as alert and ready with warning silence as watchdogs with loud barking. She had no radio, so sounds of the little insects were the stranger's favorite nighttime music and her only living confidants.

Until one night when a full-grown hollyhock plant had scratched with green "fingers" against her kitchen window. At this new sound, the stranger rolled up the paper shade and practically devoured with her disbelieving eyes the spire of heart-shaped leaves and pink flowers that were tapping there. Hazily, Bowie sipped wine as he settled against the fence to remember the long story of how the miraculous hollyhock had gotten there. And, as usual, the tenses of his remembering seemed to wander into and out of the past.

The original hollyhock seeds were small discs drifting one by one to the floor from the little stranger's hand that very first night. She was breathing with a sobbing sound, as Bowie spied her through the curtainless windows sleeping fully clothed on the bare mattress. The last tenant had taken all of the light bulbs, leaving only a candle stub and a few matches.

All that Bowie saw before the flame guttered out was the girl's determined fist, relaxed at last and losing its precious cargo.

No matter how hard she tried, tenants seemed determined to keep the seeds from sprouting in the stranger's front yard. "Here's some special soil for your seeds," laughed Mala as she dumped her night jar on the tiny leaves. All the stranger could do was dilute the spot and hope. The next day Mala picked a new spot that was leafing and dashed again. When the stranger made a string fence, Mala respected it; she dashed the slop outside the little enclosure, but harder now, so that it rolled under the string fence and covered the green tips, which quickly withered away. By the time other seedlings were cracking ground, Fay's twins found that sunken seed basins were unique places to quickly relieve their bladders.

One especially muggy day, Bowie took up the day's watch in the tool room at the north end of the women's side of the washhouse. Leaving the door ajar, he peeked from the hinged crack and watched Juju sifting through trash in the Pigpen.

The child looked so small, trying to piece together a broken cream pitcher to play with. Then there it was again, frightening, engulfing, that old familiar ringing in his ears, so loud it was impossible to hear that little voice whispering to him of something similar in the buried past. He jerked out the wine cork and drank. Like a river of time it bore him farther and farther back to somewhere else, and he slid down flat and slept. There was never any end to his dreaming. It was all one idyllic day.

But a slight spray awakened him, and he peeked again from the door crack. Ignoring Robbie's rules, the stranger was sprinkling around her trailer where more seeds were sprouting. Watching her was Lolli, smoothing her clothes as she hung them, seeming eager with anticipation. Finally, Robbie casually appeared from the washhouse, walked over to the little stranger, grabbed the hose and began spraying the peasant skirt, limping the white blouse, shredding the toilet paper flower at her throat and straggling the yellow hair.

"Around here, water's for bodies, dishes, and clothes – like I already told you," stated Robbie. "A pond lily grows not in the rapids, nor an orchid in a pigpen," she quoted emotionlessly. "Weeds are the only things that grow here without the expense of water. Hardy, ugly, but perfectly contented." And, as Bowie scrambled to hide behind the water heater, Robbie drug the hose back inside the tool room, selected a key from the ring at her waist and locked the door.

"Damn," Lolli grumbled between gum chews. She was doubly disappointed. The stranger hadn't retaliated one little bit, and Lolli's basket of clean clothes was spattered with mud. "Damn! Everyone ALWAYS jumps for Robbie. Even when she opens her mouth to yawn! She'll be measuring our sweat if Doll don't hurry home!" Picking up the basket, she stomped to the washhouse, shaking her muddy bare feet.

The door to Robbie's trailer slammed shut and the tiresome record began again. As always, Bowie could not only hear but he could feel the deep vibrant chords of Robbie's bass with which she often accompanied Doll's Song.

"That tune could haunt a deaf man," Bowie muttered as he waited in the tool room, pondering on the imprisonment that Robbie had unknowingly imposed upon him. Hoisting himself up, he peeked over the man-high partition dividing the tool room from the women's toilets, only to find the adjacent stall now occupied.

But the confinement was not without a strange atonement, for that was the day when Bowie discovered he could climb way up onto the tool room wall, wiggle past a loose board and into the low, peaked attic over the washhouse. Even though there was only room to travel on his belly, here was a way he could move unseen from one side of the washhouse to the other if ever he might need to.

While slithering along in shadows, cold perspiration began to mingle with his already sweaty clothes as he noticed there beside him a familiar-seeming suitcase, covered with dust and cobwebs. He opened the clasp and dumped the contents. A beautiful woven blanket smelling like horse-sweat was wrapped around a roll of skins. The inner one was a bloodied sheepskin that reeked of meat and smoke. Inside of its smallest fold was a black stone knife and a piece of turquoise on a leather neck string. Without any folding or rolling, he hurriedly stuffed things back into the suitcase, then squeezed his eyes shut, covered his ears with his arms and tried to stop his silent sobbing.

Loosening a board at the side of the attic, he lowered his body into the secret bedroom. He shook the hidden liquid forgetfulness, and deeply smelled of it before he drank. He splashed it into his nose, trying to overpower the faint smells of buckskin, a sweaty horse, simmering lamb, and campfire smoke. He splashed wine over his eyes, trying to erase the sight of the long black knife and the bloody sheepskin.

One morning Bowie sat propped against a clothesline pole. He could smell Pug's clean-smelling wash while pretending to doze in sunshine. Past the blowing clothes he sleepily watched the little stranger. She had spotted one tiny plant that continued to green in spite of the daily dousing of greasy dishwater that Mala blindly aimed at that edge of the Pigpen, instead of walking a few more steps to the washhouse. With a spoon, quickly the stranger scraped a trench and rounded up a few wine bottles from the trashcans. Hurriedly she began poking them into the narrow ditch to form the beginnings of a solid glass "fence" before other tenants trekked out to the Pigpen with more of their daily dumpings.

Twining herself around an awning pole, Juju wistfully eyed the stranger as she worked. Impulsively the stranger handed the child a bottle. Juju gasped delightedly and soon she was "planting" bottles as fast as the stranger could sift them from the trashcans.

When no more bottles could be found, the stranger disappeared into her trailer to return with two jelly glasses filled with water and strips of orange rind. The child grabbed one glass, but drank its contents slowly, then removed the peelings and chewed them up. The stranger poured the rest of her own drink into the child's glass, then she bent down, spread the ice around the last greening hollyhock shoot, and stroked its tips with pride.

From nowhere it seemed a big splat of tobacco fell squarely upon the seedling.

It was evident that the stranger knew before she looked up, just whom it was that could aim their spit with such remarkable accuracy. Calmly and quickly, with her spoon she scooped up the tobacco, sprout, mud, and all, and aimed them right back where the tobacco had come from – Robbie's insolent, open mouth. "I was only 'watering' with used ice, Robbie. That I pay for myself!" she shouted. Robbie coughed and sputtered to the washhouse, while Bowie slunk into one of the women's stalls, flushing the toilet to hide his laughter.

Much later that night, the same night that Bowie realized her desperate need for the right someone to talk to, the little stranger almost caught Bowie peeping.

"The night be still, Bowie," Quila had hinted, as he drank the wine she poured. He had waited and waited, but Quila didn't offer to share her evening meal. As he tightened his belt, Bowie slammed out of the wagon door. He was tired of chewing tough jackrabbits and tasteless wild potherbs, but he had no barter for Quila and it was useless to ask her for credit.

For the sake of his stomach he knew it was pointless, but watching the stranger that night seemed irresistible, almost as delightful as watching Pug. Maybe tonight he could find some harmless flaw in her simple, unnatural existence that Quila could tuck away for the future. He dug into an odd new hump beside the back fence and uncovered a half-full bottle of wine. Oh God, he was even losing his short-term memory for he had no recollection of ever burying it. He took several sips as he edged closer to the little trailer.

The stranger was still rummaging in the Pigpen and her trailer was dark as he peeked inside except for star-shine winking down from the ceiling transom. Watching that square of light, he felt the ache of longing, and in one tiny blink, the walls of the trailer changed to sandstone covered with animal skins. The square transom was now a rocky ceiling hole with moonlight shining through, and a soft old voice was filling up his ears. He was in such a hurry to drown the scene that wine went up his nose and slopped down his shirt. He made a mistake and looked inside again. Eyes black as nightshade berries stared out at him, and they were juicing up with tears. "Come back, boy child. Please come back some day." He finished half the liquid in long gulps. If only he could drink enough, he knew that he could leave this miserable life and step into the starlit cave where "some child" was always waiting. But the stranger entered the blackness, lit a candle, and destroyed the somehow familiar cave.

In spite of the trailer's cheerful, clean simplicity inside, on the outside of it Bowie often felt uneasy and confused. Especially near the bedroom end of the trailer, where there was a splintered hole the size of Bowie's fist. There his body often broke into sweat and shudders crept over his skin. An invisible presence seemed to hover between the trailer and the back fence, engulfing him in a wave of nausea. Long swallows of wine and his eyes alone always drug him back to reality inside of the trailer.

Yet now it seemed that baskets and cobs of drying corn should be hanging on those walls. Wild skins should be spreading across those windows instead of scalloped newspapers. And cardboard sketches of the tenants and their trailers were fanned together and propped up against the walls. Yams sprawled leafy green arms across the curtain rods. Wild grasses prickled out of old bottles and chipped jelly glasses. He shook his head in dismay.

Inside, the stranger went brightly about her work, and Bowie's eerie feeling soon passed away, as it always did.

The stranger worked best late in the owl-light. As usual she continued on with her crusade to prettify the surface of something while the thing itself remained the same – old, faded, and worn. Often before, she had attached a bow at the neck or a toilet paper flower to the shoulder, in order to make her blouse seem new. Once she pulled thread from an old dress seam to use for fancy stitching around the neckline and armholes of her blouse. Tonight she was circling the puffed sleeve edges with pink tape ripped from an old dress of Pug's. On Doll, Bowie thought, simplicity was elegance. On Pug simplicity was practical, but on the little stranger simplicity was pitiful, yet bright and endearing. He took several swigs from his bottle and resumed remembering.

Nothing about the stranger was natural to Last Resort. "Alley cat" was the accepted breed here, and regardless of what she did, Ginny was too much of a pedigree for the everyday comfort of tenants.

Most things, to the amusement of Bowie and Quila, the stranger did in private, not in the washhouse. Like brushing her teeth with salt, soda, and a long, thin percolator-hole brush, instead of her finger wiped across some soap, as she first had done. And washing her clothes at night in her tiny trailer sink, instead of in the wash machine. She scented clean clothes with rinsings of old perfume bottles. She wrung things out tightly, then hung the worn underwear, floral bandage strips, peasant skirt, and various sizes of material torn from her Pigpen gleanings, on pieces of string that she tied, wove together, and crisscrossed below her ceiling. The fragrant washing always gave the little trailer a fresh odor like wildflowers on the downside of a breeze. (Where did he get that comparison?) She often stuffed her clean blouse with crunched newspapers, and when it was dry the next day, it was wrinkle-free.

Bowie swiveled tight shoulders and lit another cigarette. Then he continued to study the stranger (as she in turn had been studying everyone else in the park), hoping to find something of value within the reasons for her simplicity, something that could be bartered to Quila for a bite of nourishment or a sweet red "bottle of oblivion," here and there.

The sewing finished, the stranger stuck her pins and needle back into a used bar of soap like Enoch did. She put her renewed blouse back on and admired it in the mirror. Then she sat at the table to shade a sketch with a piece of charred wood. Now and then, she paused to sip of wine. Bowie churned inside, as he suddenly realized that she was drinking from one of his own once-buried bottles. It hadn't taken her long to discover what lay hidden under mysterious humps behind many of the trailers.

On a narrow shelf at the foot of the bed, the stranger's jarred crickets began to chirp as Bowie moved ever so slowly, from one tiny curtain gap to another, all around the trailer, in order to survey the inside more closely. At first the trailer had been empty as an ant-gutted barrel cactus. (Another odd comparison.) Now, in its own way it was becoming exquisite. Like a hummer's nest fashioned with lichen, spider webbing, and tiny blossoms. (Oh God, another example from nowhere. He took a long, long swig.) Since last he spied, the back of the water-stained sink and the space above her pillow were covered with paper flowers cut from a seed catalogue. A short ruffle hung below the mattress now, extending from the bed frame to the spotless floor. Though of much duller colors, the ruffle was vaguely similar to a wildly printed negligee Fay Rose used to wear.

She spoke aloud as she sipped and shaded. "And here is Eloise's tidy, sedate garden – Mama's useful garden," she sighed. And here are daddy's – dear Dom's – own gangling, <u>useless</u> hollyhocks," she whispered, as she angrily pretended to slash long stems and scribble tiers of flowers all over the paper. She turned to other cardboard. "And here are the windows of Daddy's marvelous, cluttered study where he can gaze out at impudent hollyhocks and write beautiful thoughts – write <u>anything</u> but preachy sermons!" She took another long swig and turned to a small cardboard. "And here is my own (thanks to Eloise) sterile, over-clean, uninteresting room."

She picked up a drawing of a prim woman and began to retouch it. "The hair is too casual! Things are never casual with you, Eloise. No room at all for beautiful impulse or impromptu events. For you, seeds hang alphabetically in tidy spaces on the back porch to dry. Only certain 'bouquet flowers' should be allowed to grow, and then be commanded to march along, only in their allotted geometrical spaces!" She picked up the first picture again, looked at the bare areas, and burst into laughter. "But commoners," – she made bold, long strokes now – "hollyhocks just casually overtook things didn't they? 'Take all of the elegant tea roses to the sniffly alderman, Dom. And send a hunk of hollyhocks to the dying darky!'"

Abruptly, the stranger stood up from the breakfast nook bench and teetered over to a narrow drawer beneath the sink. Why, she was tipsy. Probably drank all of that wine on an empty stomach, thought Bowie. She took out an ice pick and an envelope. Bowie froze against the trailer as she pushed up the scrolled paper shade in back of the breakfast nook, began enlarging a hole in the screen, then poked tiny disks through the opening.

"That's the very last of them, daddy-Dom," she said to the empty room. "Maybe they'll have a chance there under the drain, where Robbie can't see them getting free water. If they die, I won't know of it and grieve." She blew out the candle, staggered to the bed, and passed out, without undressing, without even snuggling beneath her handy skirt-of-a-blanket.

Cupping his hands, Bowie lit a match and moved a circle of light over dampness from the icebox drain. With the heel of his hand he pressed the somehow special seeds into the ground. The little stranger deserved a hollyhock. It was the only link to home, it seemed.

Bowie dragged his thoughts back to Now. It was so hard to figure out anything chronologically anymore. Time was only a stream of disconnected flashes meandering through his mind without his bidding. He could not understand Quila's fear of this girl. She had no big or little secret, no devious plan to change things. Only a desperate longing for someone besides the darkness to talk to, and a bit of beauty to brighten up her barren life.

Bowie admired the new hollyhock beside him, then began his roundabout journey back to Quila's to share his memories, before they scattered into nothingness.

As Quila heated his dinner, Bowie sat on the floor picking with his fingernails until he removed a splinter from his ankle. "The posy makes a pleasin' pastime fer those greedy eyes of yers! Did ye pluck me a 'tell-petal'?" urged Quila, noting damp upturned moccasin bottoms as he stretched on her floor trying to straighten out and relax his cramped body.

8. At Lolli's

"She talks to herself! She shares with the darkness!" He scowled at Quila. How could she always know where he'd been, whom he'd been watching? Quila smirked.

On the pretense of walking Mange, she noted much about the park and Bowie's presence here. She peeked behind Ginny's trailer and there was barely room for a stationary body in the narrow space there, much less an ever-moving, listening, peeking body. The fence was bone-dry and jagged behind the trailer and the ground was always muddy from frequent icebox cleanings. Bowie was often digging at fence splinters, and his soft moccasin soles often stayed dark and wet a long time. She smiled as he untied the laces and propped his damp shoes against the edge of the warm stove.

"What does she say?" wheedled Quila, taking a cigarette from the tin box and lighting it from the candle. She poured two jars half-full of wine, then sat back listening. Her earloops teased him with reflections, and sweet narcotic smoke engulfed his being.

As they drank together, he told her about the many sketches, informative monologues, the ever-changing blouse, little jars of watery soap rinsings and bleach, strange edibles rescued from the Pigpen, and the diary of envelope backs tied together with old knotted string.

While fresh in his mind, he wove the tale of hollyhock seeds and the "miraculous" plant now growing in back of the little trailer. Quila laughed at the stranger's naiveté and began to make a dinner for him. Flashing her evil crook-nosed smile as he left, she held up a silver dollar, and slid a new bottle of wine into his hand.

Taking an overlong swig from the bottle, he hurried to bury it behind the stranger's trailer. Then he headed for The Joint, feeling a strange kinship with the new coin. Was that a tiny remnant of oddly familiar solder on one side? He was barely able to part with the dollar. In the week that followed he "earned," devoured, or buried new wine behind several of the trailers. Quila chuckled and said she didn't need to use the facts that he gave her "today." Mostly she stored them up for "someday."

Tonight, the narrow margin between the back fence and the gray trailer was barricaded even higher with more empty boxes prohibiting entry. He crawled on his stomach beneath the trailer, knowing the night's "work" would result in nothing more than a stiff neck. But he was unable to resist the pleasure of pretending for some weird reason that the stranger was dark-skinned and raven-haired. He took a guzzle of sweetness that was buried there. He sat beside the tall new hollyhock, touched its leaves, smiled, and continued his remembering.

Aside from a growing stack of boxes at the entrance to the back of her trailer, the stranger seemed to purposely forget about the hollyhock seeds that she had poked through the screen. She resigned herself to the naked patch of front yard dirt, which, except for its lack of clutter and growing wine bottle fence, matched every other yard in the park.

Bowie hadn't forgotten. He scouted around town, located a blooming hollyhock in back of a church's parsonage, then sunk it, pot and all, into wet dirt beneath the icebox drain.

Within a week, hollyhock leaves had begun to scratch at her window, and blooming "faces" were happily peeking into the little stranger's kitchen. Evidently she knew nothing about plants, for she seemed to accept somehow, the unbelievable growth, as though it were just her own private miracle. And nobody else seemed to discover that the hollyhock grew there. The stranger only rolled up the paper shade at night when she could freely enjoy the brazen beauty.

It became a regular thing to share silent burdens and private thoughts – as though the plant had ears. She looked forward to getting dinner dishes done, then talking to "Holly" while she perfected sketches of the tree and Lolli beneath it, the washhouse and workers in it, the Pigpen, Quila's wagon, Ginny herself, her trailer, and the shabby mailbox. She especially loved to draw while Pug was making meals and the air was full of homey odors.

"Thank you, Holly, for just being," she had said one evening as Bowie sat against the back fence. "You always seem to be listening so intently – like Daddy, Dom. Nodding, then silently encouraging me to find my very own answers. Someday, Daddy, maybe you, at least, will be proud of me for just that one little trait: trying to find and believe in my own answers."

Now, even at night when the paper shades were unscrolled, Bowie could listen outside while Ginny talked to the hidden plant. But Bowie preferred to watch.

Usually the stranger took her bedtime bath in darkness, washing with a rectangular bag made from a folded, sewn-together washrag filled with soap chips rescued from the shower. But on bright moonlit nights, if the shadows fell just right, Bowie could poke with a wire and beyond a paper curtain to watch the beautiful ritual. Moonbeams filtered down through the transom screen and transformed pale hair into translucent "wings" resting on bare shoulders. She never sang, but always hummed while she washed, as though words would disturb the purity of the moment. Sometimes, unconsciously, she hummed Doll's Song, for it had often hung in the air all day, soaking up any space for new ideas.

Before the girl finally slipped clean and bare onto her bed, with her skirt blanketed above her for warmth, she always rolled up the paper scroll-of-a-shade on the curved wall above her, as though to invite the beauty of the night to become a part of herself.

Night was all that the stranger asked inside, though Bowie doubted if women would have accepted had she offered; the stranger had a knack of rubbing people the wrong way.

Living with strangers was unfamiliar, and unconsciously, she added something daily to the list of tenants' grievances. Like deciding to scrub away smutty words on the women's restroom and shower walls. She had worked all night with her stubby whiskbroom rubbed on soap chips. This was all right in itself, but she got bolder and the next night washed the walls of the washhouse. Next morning, though all of the walls were spotless and clean smelling, the wrath of the park descended upon her, for the stranger had scrubbed away all of the phone numbers jotted along the telephone wall. For just a little while, the displeasure of the park put a pall on her bright face, and her mouth seemed to droop instead of turning up.

Then there was the first time she brought laundry to the washhouse, appearing like a fine-boned deer among a crowded corral of workhorses. Innocently she took over Pug's undisputed Monday morning wash time. Why, she actually enjoyed each process, delighted in pouring plops of bleach and watery soap from two little jars, dropping one dime into the coin box like it were pure gold, and joyously feeding her few items into the old wringer, whose worn rollers met like Quila's snaggly teeth.

But the stranger did not hang up that particular wash. Bowie spied the familiar clothing that night in her trailer, hanging on string lines. She must have future plans for Doll's holey blue jeans, Robbie's cigarette-burned denim shirt, and old flowered items of Pug and Fay's. Her own few clothes she always washed inside her trailer, for she was grounded there until they dried enough to wear. Darting in and out among damp clothes, the stranger hummed softly as she worked, while all the rest of the park was sleeping.

She spent a lot of time just sitting at the table with her eyes closed, elbows up, her chin in her palms, and fingers closing her eyes. After these long sessions, she always started something new – like adding untried items to her transom tea. She left it up there every day now, as sunshine soaked the mixture of Fay's discarded flowers, old spices from the Pigpen, and now the honeysuckle and violets blooming in front of the library.

Miraculously, the new hollyhock grew until it was almost taller than the little trailer. One night the stranger crept back behind the boxes, bent the plant down, and cut off the tops, so the flowers could not be seen from the driveway.

It was then that Ginny found the stake that Holly clung to, and the rim of the pot sunken along with the stolen plant. She must have been grateful to Bowie, until she also saw that fence boards nearest her bedroom window were tightly chinked together with old cigarette butts and the ground was littered with spent matches. Bowie finished the last of a bottle, slumped against the fence, and fell asleep.

"Coffee's on!" Lolli hollered over to a surprised Ginny one morning when both Robbie and Doll were gone. "Bring your porch over to Kasha's to sit on."

When Ginny arrived with her apple box seat, the subkingdom was already armed with a cache of smutty jokes. Lolli was lounging on her brown towel as she brushed Whiffet's clean woolly curls. She dabbed her with perfume and tied a fresh bow on her collar.

Each morning now Lolli's bunch of girls droned on, rehashing their love life, gossiping or talking of The Joint, the pier, or Robbie's Den and its happenings. Swearing as they did, and pointedly talking down for her, Ginny always left ashamed of the wasted time. Worst of all, it was warming up. No matter how she tried, no colorful stitching, knot of ribbon, bit of rickrack, or toilet paper flower could any longer disguise the truth–she had but one outfit, the fading skirt, threadbare peasant blouse, and worn brown sandals that she had arrived in.

Soon Robbie and Doll came home and then there were only Ginny, Lolli, and Kasha beneath the tree. Often now, while drinking Kasha's coffee, Ginny enviously watched Quila, Fay, and the neighborhood girls going home from the Den, licking lips or fingers, rubbing tired backs, yet happily invigorated after most of Robbie's klatches. But things were not really so bad. Kasha whose husband worked nights and slept days served Jewish pastries with a big smile, and cream and sugar for the coffee. Fat little Kasha, for some reason, felt unwelcome at Robbie's Den and seemed grateful for anybody's company at her own yard.

But Ginny made a mistake. One evening she asked Lolli's husband, Louie, if he would put a new glass in her window. Louie made an even greater mistake—he did so. The next morning Ginny could hear Lolli having coffee inside Kasha's locked trailer. Lolli was loudly laughing, imitating Ginny's voice and Ginny's words.

9. Doll's Song

Lonely again, Ginny sat at the table with eyes closed and chin on her palms. Finally, she opened her eyes and grinned; she had thought of a plan enabling her to visit Pug every week. Especially when she smelled cookies in the oven or donuts in the deep frying pan.

Bowie was often watching when the stranger knocked on Pug's door asking to borrow a cup of sugar, flour, or oatmeal. Pug always asked the girl inside to share whatever treat she was making. While the stranger sat at the kitchen table drinking coffee, she longingly listened while Guy read to his family of little girls as they waited patiently for Pug's treats to be ready.

"Come and sit with us, my little 'cobblestone'. Dishes can wait," Guy always pleaded as Pug put hot delicious smelling plates of goodies on the table and children gathered around.

The next night, Bowie watched Ginny return the same cup of borrowed food – unused.

The stranger "borrowed" things often now, just to be part of Pug's homey atmosphere. (Pug must have understood, thought Bowie, especially one night when Ginny tripped up. Pug smiled knowingly as the stranger asked, "Could I please borrow a cup of, of, of salt?") At last the lonely stranger got nerve enough to sit on the floor with the children while Guy read to his sleepy little girls, and Pug went about her endless work.

Pug always held the little stranger in her soft plump arms when she reluctantly left the big comfortable trailer, and Pug was always the one who finally terminated the hug. Ginny could have lingered forever, engulfed in the giant warmth and security, as though she had never felt a mother's arms before, thought Bowie.

Ginny now began a serious effort to find free "paint." At night Bowie watched through steaminess as she boiled and cooled, stirred and mixed vegetable peels, old socks, hair ribbons and ties, while keeping notes on her experiments. She also began to collect from the Pigpen all kinds of paper and cardboard to draw and paint upon, storing them in the now safely secured magazine racks that Guy had fixed for her.

Often she merely chewed on candle drips and sipped bland unsweetened transom-tea while she sketched, worked on the ceiling mural, wrote in her diary, talked to Holly and the rag doll, listened to the crickets, or sat in her thinking position.

While sitting this way at the table, the stranger discovered odd things. One was a way for wine to last longer on hot days. She put chipped ice onto a washcloth and tied its edges to make a pouch. Then she rested the strange ice bag into a shell that contained a spoonful of Bowie's wine. Now, as the stranger sketched, she dabbed her neck, forehead, wrists and nose with her "medicine bag," as she called it.

While sitting this way she decided (out loud) to forget the cracked windows, to let them be. The broken one could last until wintertime, and she cut a piece of cardboard to fit the vacant part. The cracked windows she mended with masking tape that someone had tossed because it got stuck on the roll. With charcoal she "painted" chosen lines on the tape, until those windows looked like webs snugly holding the black paper spiders that she had cut out to live there.

In the daytime Ginny paid no attention to the Pigpen, but one afternoon was different. "Ah, dining al fresco!" sneered Quila, coming upon Ginny as she blew off the perfectly good piece of melting chocolate and popped it into her mouth. Most of the day the half-open candy box had perched on the crest of one heaped-up garbage can, strangely undisturbed by morning dumpings. Ginny should have known it was only bait.

In the short time she had been here, every move she made seemed to irritate or amuse the tenants. Now this humiliation. Well, maybe they would all quit expecting blue blood to spout from her cuts and scrapes, or a red carpet to descend from heaven for her to hurry away upon. Maybe now someone would even engage her in a real, everyday conversation, or call her more than merely: Hey, Stranger, Greeny, or worst of all, Posy. Maybe, someday she would seem just another common person they could easily relate to.

Wiping her mouth on the threadbare washcloth that she also used for a towel, Ginny continued on to the shower, chewing thoughtfully on her now chocolate-flavored candle wax.

Like an old pro now, she showered in the tiny, poorly drained shower. It was the mark of a newcomer to have scraped elbows from the narrow cubicle, but Ginny had mastered the hang of it, the awkward knack of standing and moving sideways, and scabs on her elbows were ready to slough off without bleeding. She rescued and rinsed a soap sliver from the floor to take home and add to her soap bag. (In the daytime, she just rinsed off. Soaping was only for nights, when she bathed at her little sink.) Now Ginny scrubbed every angle and plane of the shower stall with her whiskbroom before she rinsed her body and the walls.

The real reason the stranger showered in the daytime was for something to do, to cool off, and listen to the park in general, Bowie reasoned. Just as he also listened and watched the park from various strategic places.

Bowie had gouged four peepholes in the tool room: one toward Robbie's Den and Pug's trailer, one toward Ginny's trailer and the Pigpen, one poked through to the washhouse area, and the other connected the adjoining toilet stall. At night, if he wanted to check on the other toilet stall or the women's shower, Bowie had to climb up on the tool room partition and try to seem like part of dark rafters which supported him. Or he could climb over to an empty stall, lock the door and look through peepholes in the walls—except that that kind of watching wasn't any fun, unless the occupant was talking to herself. Somehow, these females were just not interesting; they did not have dark skin and long black hair.

Basically, peeking from the storeroom (diagonally opposite the tool room) was set up the same, except that one peephole was aimed at Enoch's trailer, and through another one Bowie could check on Lolli, Quila, Kasha, and Mala. Fay Rose was the only "permanent" whose trailer could not be seen from his peeking spots in the washhouse.

With the wrung-out washcloth Ginny dried herself in the shower. While putting on the same clothes she had taken off, her eye was caught by a new hole, waist-high, tiny, but bigger than it was yesterday. Removing wax from her mouth, she formed a cylinder that filled the hole joining the shower room with the next-door toilet stall. As usual, parting with the hunger appeaser was difficult, but her jaws were weary. She paused while smoothing her hair, for outside there was a commotion.

Suddenly the door in the next toilet stall was flung open, shut quietly, and hooked. Brakes screeched, a car door slammed, and there was loud pounding on Pug's screen door.

"Okay, where is she? I know she ran into this filthy park. Oh boy, were they right! I've heard of her: leads a man on, drives him crazy, takes all his money, then never 'pays up'! You know damn well who I mean. They call her 'the Doll!'"

"Never heard of her!" declared Pug.

Cursing, the man slammed the car door and began to slowly prowl around the washhouse. He shouted out the car window, back at Pug. "I'd bet my last dollar, she's past thirty and still has her 'cherry'. Never heard of her. Everybody's heard of her!"

Ginny stooped down and quietly removed wax from the hole.

"You frigid little vamp," a beautiful girl was softly sobbing as she sat and stroked the hideous cat, Spade – that same little demon that Ginny vied with every night in the Pigpen. "Tomcats think they can have you for free," the girl crooned. "Why, the only 'eyeing' you've got in you is for their feeding bowls." Both of the girl's tearful eyes were blackened, her cameo face was a blotch of bruises. Her white dress was bloody and ripped at the neck.

The girl snuggled short blond hair that cupped toward her face into the cat's black fur and whispered, "You're the only one in this whole world that understands me, Spade. We're so alike. Toms don't know any different, 'cause we're soft and cuddly-seeming – while they're so rough and demanding!" She wiped at her tears. "Know why you and me get along, puss? We don't ask nothin'! Who we are? Where we're from? Where we're goin'?" Slowly the girl unhooked the door. Cautiously, she looked out, put the cat outside, and latched the door. She opened her suitcase and changed from her dress and sandals to jeans, a white man's shirt, and tennis shoes. Quietly she lifted the lid of the toilet, dipped her dress into clean water, and rinsed it. With the damp dress she washed her face in painful dabs, then rinsed, and wrung the dress again. She flushed the unused toilet, listened, slowly opened the door, eased it shut and hung the dress on the clothesline.

Once more Ginny caulked the hole with wax. "So this is Doll and she's home again."

To Bowie it was obvious. With the timing of a thunderclap, it was spring.

When Doll was gone, dripping faucets infuriated Robbie. Now water dripped merrily, unnoticed. The women hosed hot trailers and settled dusty yards with fine spray. Children had water fights and Robbie walked through puddles like they were pink clouds. Extra fans ran incessantly and the few men of the park had poker parties in the washhouse every night.

And Bowie loved to watch as Doll merely walked to and from the washhouse to refill the coffeepot. It was poetry, set to music of tender footsteps. She walked so beautifully, like the ground itself was pregnant or was birthing fragile flowers.

But, there were no supper sacks on Robbie's doorstep, and worst of all, now Ginny had to wait later and later for her despicable, enchanting, rewarding treasure hunts in the Pigpen. One good thing, Doll's Song didn't grind away all day in Robbie's Den, scraping away any time for planning or creating new ideas. Instead, women of the park waited anxiously for the smell of Robbie's coffeepot, announcing that Doll was still home and the Den was open to all.

Bowie knocked softly at Quila's door one night and sat down at the table. But Quila was wearing a chunk of turquoise on a chain, and it looked like a piece of captured sky. In the span of a heartbeat, Quila's face became a soft smooth brown and her hair fell down into shiny braids. "She" removed the turquoise that hung from a leather thong and put it around Bowie's neck. "To keep you safe and lucky," said Her gentle voice.

Bowie stood up, knocked over his stool, and bolted out the door. He sobbed in the black storeroom while draining an entire bottle of wine. Trembling in his fur blanket, at last the giant web appeared and he relaxed. Easing his exhausted spirit through feathery tines, he drifted into merciful sleep.

10. The Den

After freshening up one afternoon, Ginny dressed slowly in the shower as she listened through thin walls to gossip beneath the tree and chatter of women loitering in the washhouse.

From snatches of conversation, Ginny had gleaned a lot. She knew that the smallest blue trailer had only a tiny window, one bed, and was dubbed "the cradle." "You can almost count the months before the couple needs larger quarters. What else is there to do?" shrugged Lolli, smiling slyly, snapping her fingers and her gum.

Once after Doll walked by, Ginny heard Lolli comment, "I hear that when her dad, old Lambeth's, rent is due and there's no more credit at the mama-papa store or doctor's office, Doll just rolls a guy at some beer joint."

Lolli was an endless source of information and Ginny often took mental notes through the little cement hole as Lolli chewed gum, drank soda pop, fanned flies, fondled Whiffet, or lovingly oiled her shapely body. Often Ginny stood wet and shivering as she peeked, fascinated with Lolli's fulsome beauty and quick, biased opinions.

"Don't lend things, Kasha. They'll borrow everything – from hairbrush to husband – once you let them begin." "Don't start going to the Den, Kasha. Unless you've time for tea and trivia, unless you love sitting nose-to-armpit with sweaty girls and dirty babies, or you just adore secondhand news. Unless you have no secrets or can afford to pay Quila's bottle its hush-money." "Keep your door locked, Kasha. The Indian drunkie wanders late at night: 'I'm coming, Fawna, wait!' he cries when he's really drunk. I feel sorry for the Posy. Bowie has a 'thing' about her trailer. But Robbie's too mush-hearted to make the crazy wino leave."

Then, as she often did during conversational lulls, Lolli would beat her towel or her bare thighs with the palms of her hands in a rhythm involving, subtly, her whole body.

Ginny heard someone burst from the Den, sobbing. Laughter inside the Den quickly resumed and women under the tree had no need to mute their voices. "Mala's gonna miss good eating," drawled Lolli. "And she could sure use it. Next one's 'in the oven.' But Robbie's playing dumb to Mala, because Quila needs supplies." What did that mean, Ginny pondered?

Ginny watched toast-brown Lolli move her towel from encroaching shade. If only she had her pencil and cardboard. Again, Lolli applied sun lotion. To the artist within Ginny, Lolli was proudly pulling up on fragile net hose and the sheerest of opera gloves.

"Is it true," Kasha spoke in lowered tones, "that Robbie's cupboard has niches filled with jars and cans and things like cheese, popcorn, nuts and pigs' knuckles?"

"Yep! Robbie keeps her harem fed," yawned Lolli, as she shooed a bee with her hat, "as long as they can play poker, look interested, and amuse her once in awhile."

Ginny's heart raced: "as long as they can play poker, look interested, and amuse her once in awhile." Hurriedly she dressed, slammed out the door, scurried to her trailer, propped up her elbows, closed her eyes, and began to plan. Food, utensils, and supplies the Pigpen often offered, but no human companionship, and Ginny was starved as much for that as she was for real food. Now she had finally learned of a place where both could be "bought" with the only thing she had to pay with: insatiable curiosity.

"I've got to try, Holly," she confided, as she opened her eyes and looked through the kitchen window. "Even though it's the hardest, hardest thing I've ever planned to do." Ginny grabbed a pencil stub and some envelope backs, rushed out her trailer, and headed for Flo's.

Late that night, poking a paper shade with his wire threaded through a screen hole, Bowie saw a flower-patched denim shirt of Robbie's being buttoned over Doll's mended blue jeans. Posing in front of the closet mirror, her hair curled in colorful rags, Ginny surveyed her unfamiliar figure. She rolled up the pant legs, cocked her head and turned the cuffs higher. With deliberate sloppiness she twisted shirt sleeves up to her elbow. She lit a cigarette, puffed and coughed, miraculously blew a smoke ring, then rested the butt in a seashell. From now on Bowie sighed, she'd learn fast that smoking relieves a rumbling stomach, shortens lonely hours, and comforts a body's longing need for another's nearness.

The stranger did a weird thing now. From an old mustard jar, she scraped the last moist remnant, rubbed it between the middle and index finger of her right hand, waved it in air, smelled the yellow spot, then waved it some more.

She lifted a bottle of Bowie's wine, looked dismally at the dregs. She opened the icebox, took out her jar of fruit peel punch and added a bit to the wine. She drank slowly, and when the drink was gone slouched her shoulders and stared defiantly into the mirror. "Shit, shit, shit! There Holly, I've finally said it. Durn it! Maybe I can last now in the Den!" Startled, Bowie jumped back, giving the trailer a slight jar.

Disillusioned, he climbed Quila's little steps to share his findings and sample stew.

The next morning, walking toward Robbie's Den for the first time, Ginny chewed on candle drips to quiet anxious rumblings of her empty stomach. At Robbie's doorstep, she spit out the wax, took a deep breath, and bravely opened the door. Bowie was watching through a peephole in the adjacent add-on shed.

What dark, smoke-filled hotness. Ginny cringed. How could such excitement come from this cheerless place? Though bright and sunny outside, here heavy curtains were drawn tight. Doll, Quila, and Robbie sat around a table while Doll dealt cards beneath a spotlight. Other females, sullen and dirty looking, sat on a bare wooden floor, smoking and sipping coffee. Quila was holding a bird and Robbie was splinting its leg with toothpicks and tape. The only noise was a rhythmic thud coming from Pug, sitting in a dark corner pitting fruit.

Stalling until her eyes adjusted, Ginny stood lighting a cigarette.

"Spit!" came a sputter as the match burned her fingers. The painfully practiced word had exploded liked a lisped shibboleth and the women snickered as Ginny entered.

She sat beside Doll, sized up the situation, and over-anted: five of the new cigarettes that she had bought for today. "Deal me in," she said too casually, and, without hands she shifted her cigarette inexpertly to the other side of her mouth.

In Robbie's tarpaper storeroom, Bowie wiped his forehead. These females will chew her up. He shifted his cramped position beneath a window slit. What was the stranger going to talk about? She who swept with a whiskbroom, who knew nothing, and cared less about baseball, gossip, or last night at The Joint. A girl who talked to flowers, drew crazy pictures on her ceiling, rummaged at midnight in the Pigpen, went into ecstasy over a sunset, and talked out loud to darkness as though it were

God. She even marveled at the planes and stitches of a growing web for hours, watching spiders by flashlight. Bowie tensed himself for the worst.

But the stranger said nothing.

Instead, her eyes strayed to the record player and the bass viol propped against a wall. Hungrily her eyes slid among wooden cubbyholes, which honeycombed the opposite kitchen wall. In shadows she could see a motley assortment there: sugar, coffee, soap, potatoes, cheese in cloths. Smaller niches were stuffed with mail, apples, nuts, an onion or two. And, according to Lolli, cans and cans of odd things that the average person has never even heard of.

"We don't tolerate speleologists here," snarled Robbie, adding another toothpick to the fragile bird's leg and reeling off more tape to secure it.

"Study'n caves ain't one of ma hobbies," Ginny drawled. Other women had no idea about what they were talking. "I prefer to study artists' lives, words, interesting facts, and people," Ginny added, forgetting her original crude way of talking.

Robbie raised an appreciative eyebrow. Ginny picked up her cards, feeling, but not daring to scrutinize the carved tabletop of an artistic knife doodler. She dropped a card and leaning down to get it, felt the floor strewn with whittlings, peanut shells, and butts. As she rescued the card, her elbow grazed Robbie's knee and Robbie seemed to recoil, unduly.

Ginny arranged her cards, waiting uneasily. Hopelessness was almost tangible all around her. Homelessness, prostitution, and worthlessness haunted many eyes. One girl with tattoos at the swell of her breast nursed a baby while she smoked. Two girls held hands in the shadows. And Eloise's voice was echoing, "No company is better than bad company, Dom. Why do you insist on bringing derelicts into our kitchen?" What was it that Dom always replied as he loosened his parson's collar? "Eloise, Jesus traveled in the worst company!"

Outside, Bowie eased. Flo had taught the stranger rudiments of poker, and today she needn't talk much for Robbie was in rare form. Usually Robbie's remarks just bounced off of Fay, Doll, and the others. Now, despite attempts at commonness, Robbie seemed to relax, to become more like her own discriminating self. She sensed that the stranger was going to be a great change from light-minded females. Here at last was someone with a neat vocabulary, who might start topics, color comments, and add fresh air to flat conversations.

Even though Spade pushed through her cat-door, Robbie kept in good temper. Quila smoothed the startled bird, kissed its head, opened the door, and threw it into the air.

As they played cards, Robbie and the little stranger kept the group astir, slowing to press a point, hurrying to skip the boring. Doll kept coffee cups filled, and Quila spiced the air with peppery comments and salty conclusions. At last, Bowie totally relaxed.

The more Ginny's eyes became accustomed to heat, darkness, and smoke, the more her fingers ached for pencils or charcoal. Behind a thick smoke screen sat the fascinating Robbie, like a sorcerer pulling moods from the air. Every motion she made with slow precision. Carefully she opened a pack of cigarettes, removed cellophane, unfolded it, smoothed it, refolded it, then wove the ends into the chain of shiny rickrack hanging around her neck. She crossed the ends and threw them back over her shoulders.

Deepened by meager light beyond the spotlight, compared to webbing of Quila's face, and the seamless complexion of beautiful Doll, Robbie's face seemed bold and sharp. Steam from her coffee spiraled up, transforming gloomy, solemn Robbie into a totally new being.

Morning grew into noon and Doll left to refill the coffeepot. A tearful child knocked at the door, smiled, held up a jelly glass with a flower in it, then burst into tears as he held up his bleeding finger. Robbie smiled, smelled the weedy bloom, and then placed it at the back of the table with other droopy bouquets. As Robbie tended the nasty cut, some of the females left, while others crowded into the Den. Here and there, Pug chose certain girls to hug, or pat on the head as they sat beside her. Robbie lifted the mended child to her other knee, put milk, sugar, and a dash of cinnamon into her fresh cup of coffee and stirred. She dipped out a spoonful, blew on it and offered it to the child, who beamed up at Robbie through his tears. Heavens, thought Ginny, like moths enchanted by Robbie's warmth.

Robbie opened a fresh pack of cigarettes, then folded and wove the cellophane wrapper into the pointy rope at her neck. With a narrow knife that she took from her pocket, she absent-mindedly poked the paper part of the old wrapper into a windowsill slit. Outside, Bowie tried in vain to burn the paper wadding with his cigarette, then moved to another window slit.

Robbie put the smiling child outside the door with a piece of licorice. She lit a cigarette and passed the pack around. Standing thoughtfully in front of her odd cupboard, she carefully chose a can. She took a paper sack from a drawer, creased it, ripped it off at the top, folded a heavy rim around it, then molded the cutoff top into the bottom of her instant tray.

Again she took the unbending knife from her pocket, cut bread and cheese into little squares, then added them to the tray. She opened the tin of meat, divided it minutely while Doll made beautiful curves as she speared the pieces with toothpicks and neatly arranged them. Robbie opened bottles of cold beer and divided them – an inch or so into every empty coffee mug. She joked, gestured and laughed as she worked, making Ginny feel happy, bubbly and welcome. While everyone ate, Robbie gave a brief rundown and short comment on today's worldly news. A few girls listened intently, others seemed oblivious.

Bowie turned his back. Holding the tarpaper door closed with moccasined toes, instead of a tired finger, he lit another cigarette, then settled against the trailer. Somehow, what the rest of the world was doing never made sense to Bowie.

Fascinated, Ginny watched Robbie's hands as she talked. They did not flutter in the way of women. Even without voice, they talked with a flowing tomboy kind of motion. Robbie was a craftsman with spoken words; Ginny watched them forming flawlessly from Robbie's strangely strong and beautiful mouth. And, whenever Robbie laughed, the sound for Ginny and all of the women seemed to ripple through their hearts like liquid sunshine.

The room got hotter, filling with smoke, the stench of diapers, and sweaty clothes. Pushing aside one curtain, Doll slightly opened a window and turned on a fan. Girls sat all over the floor, against the wall, or on their haunches. How uncomfortable, thought Ginny. Robbie called each girl by name, then subtly drew each one into conversation. But Ginny soon became aware that the show was all for Doll, who sat in complete repose, behind the "footlights," listening half-heartedly, fondling Spade like she were made of priceless fur.

Perhaps, thought Bowie as he fanned himself with his hat, the stranger's plan was going to work. But the thought was short-lived, for Quila, whose every word was carefully calculated anyway, was becoming too quiet and withdrawn. Bowie turned around to the window, snuffed his butt in a crack, and settled himself down again to see as well as hear.

Quila's eyes, like span worms, were inching over the stranger. Even from his peephole, Bowie could sense the stranger's growing discomfort. After her beer was gone, she forced herself to pour coffee around the room without being asked. It was nearing the dregs and vile, but she downed hers without the sputter he knew they all expected.

Still, Quila sat silent. As the food squares disappeared, deep silence developed. The girls coughed and cleared their throats, but nobody could break the hush. Pug got up, took a fussy baby from one girl, and quickly left the Den. The girls looked relieved for the dirty diaper was overpowering even the smokiness of the room. Faintly, Quila's wheeze could be heard as she breathed the heavy air. Nervously, underneath the table she flicked her thumbnails together. It was so quiet that from one corner of the kitchen, Bowie's keen ears could catch the sizzle from a punched hole in the cap of the cider jug that Robbie called the "gurglet."

"Uh, could I have another light?" Robbie lighted the girl's cigarette, then slowly blew out the match. Silence still continued while Ginny searched her mind for trivia which she and her father used to bandy back and forth. Yet all she could apply here was one of Enoch's morbid stories. Ginny picked up Robbie's spent match from the ashtray.

"Did you know, Robbie, that thousands of young girls died to create this match? One step in the manufacturing was to lick each match point to stiffen it after being dipped into a radioactive chemical. That chemical attacked the teeth, jaws, and finally the entire body. Most died before reaching their thirties."

"Jeez!" cried one girl. Bowie could see that Robbie was surprised and appreciative.

Suddenly Quila quit her nail clicking, pushed up her sleeves, and took the stranger's hand. A gnarled finger – the pointer with a dead beetle ring on it–rudely traced across a bloody floral-bandaged finger, then moved to the stranger's palm.

"Lily-fingers!" Quila sneered. "Strangers ta scrub boards!" Silence. She spit on a rag from her sleeve and wiped it between two of the girl's right fingertips. "Yer 'nicotine' comes off, m' dearie," she croaked. "It still smells," she sniffed, "lak stale mustard!" Bowie cringed, remembering details he'd shared. Quila reached up and parted the stranger's hair.

Rudely Quila leaned over, poured beer on the floorboards and nobody seemed surprised. "May me very brains flow out, jest the way this ale does, if I ain't dead right! Yer nay the lightskirt ye'd like us ta believe. Yer bleached roots be still in darkness, sweetie, but yer forced tongue betrays a cloistered mind. And," she snickered, "underneath that planned dirt, ye smell squeaky clean and spicy as Flo's scented geranium leaves!" Quila shook her head in disgust, "Transparent as a toady eggstring, ye be!" Bowie almost stopped breathing.

"Why _did_ you finally come?" demanded Robbie.

"I was starved," blurted the little stranger, and Bowie gasped aloud before she continued, "– starved for some intelligent conversation!"

Robbie looked pleased. Bowie could tell the stranger's practice to seem like others – to make her cigarette droop, to drink coffee vilely black, to look Robbie square without blinking, to seem like she were cussing while kicking the washing machine – had not been wasted.

"I like a girl with guts," said Robbie.

"Aye," conceded Quila with reluctance. "Her tongue be speedy, and sharp as well!"

But Robbie stood abruptly for the stranger's eyes were glued, sticky and soft upon Robbie. "Come on, you old hens; time to scatter. I've dirt to move and paper to hang. Besides, I'm out of coffee." Robbie grabbed a broom whose handle was already filled with skewered toilet paper rolls and pretended to sweep women into the twilight.

Bowie's early for dinner, mused Quila, sensing stealthy footsteps. But Bowie paused on the porch outside of Quila's door. He was famished but with nothing to barter.

Quila settled herself at the table to wait and wonder when Bowie was going to knock. She drummed her fingers impatiently. Daytimes, she mused, Bowie divided his time. Under her own trailer he waited and listened to Lolli's group when Doll was gone, or he hid and slept in one of the two dark storerooms at each diagonal end of the washhouse. Subconsciously he filed away odd habits and comments of each tenant and routines of the park in general, sleuthing for significant variations. When Doll was home, although Bowie spent most of his time in the tarpaper shed beside the Den, it was never all day.

Today Bowie was trapped in the hot dark shed. The bus-watcher, old Lambeth, hadn't gone to town at all today, but preferred to sit across from Robbie's shed, rubbing his aching finger joints, or dozing on his doorstep awaiting the few words that his daughter, Doll, might speak to him on passing. He had dressed meticulously, as usual, slicking down with saliva his stubby white mustache and sideburns, wearing his hat brim much higher, for he needn't be hiding from the view of passengers who entered and alighted from buses at the Plaza.

"I felt ye peekin' there today," Quila said when Bowie, swinging at startled porch birds, decided to knock and enter. He stretched as high and as wide as he could in the confining wagon, cracked tired knuckles and rubbed the toes inside his right moccasin before he sat down. Waiting until evening for just the right moment to slink from the sweaty shed into the coolness outside must have been merciless. But patience was his highest virtue.

Robbie had slit a "door" – an upside-down ell – in the tarpaper that formed a roof over, and an envelope around the many boxes that pressed against the back of her trailer. Once inside the door, Bowie scooted the boxes apart until a space was hollowed, just outside of Robbie's kitchen windows. There he sat on stacked boxes, his eye to slits beneath or around the curtained windows. He kept one finger joint, or one moccasin, curled around the door edge of tarpaper in back of him, to keep it totally shut.

"Ye ought ta paint yer finger black, else bring it in when someone's walkin' by," Quila chided. "Robbie must know ye be there. She almost chinked ye out fer good with that last wrapper. One more thing. There be smoke under the sill today. Ye'll burn this park down someday, ye firebrand, if ye don't quit snuffin' butts in these dry trailers! Especially Robbie's. She stuffs cracks with rags and paper, y' know, ta keep heat and cold outside."

"Was it you that finally pulled the wrapper out?"

As usual Quila ignored any question aimed at her. Instead she took out a brand new kind of wine, shined the bottle with the hem of her dress, and lavishly poured his mug almost to overflowing. She said nothing until he drank, smacked, and put out his mug for more.

She looked deeply into Bowie's eye, the one that peeked and didn't squint. She patted her sunken bosom where it bulged unnaturally over the bundle always waiting there to remind him. Her voice lowered mysteriously, "I want ye ta listen well and remember this above all else," she waited dramatically, then glanced up briefly at the rag-curtained window. "Robbie and Doll are primey-aged. What do they do about it? Where do they go when they take off in Robbie's car? Where do they go when they hop a freight train? Who do they meet?"

Too slowly, Bowie pulled the grimy hat down lower over his eyes.

"All right! Save yer crown jewel," she bargained. "Someday you'll be needin' that kind o' trade. Fer now," she poured his mug full again, "think hard! Dig deep! Me cupboard and pots be bare. Just dazzle me with some lesser gem. I'll be content ta wait."

11.   Donuts and Poppycock

On the second day that Ginny came to the crowded Den, she brought along cardboard from old food packages and the stubby pencil she had rescued.

Bowie watched the stranger sketch as Doll poured coffee for the crowd of females gathered there. Robbie was folding, creasing, and tucking another cellophane strip into the slow-growing zigzag that waited around her neck for the constant additions every day. She crossed and tossed behind her the shiny ends, then started to make her well-known "Robbie-tray" as the girls called it, folding the sack's cut-off top part in half and fitting it into the bottom of the finished tray to soak up grease or moisture and create a steadiness.

Robbie counted heads, then into the tray she divided four homemade donuts that Pug had brought, while Quila toothpicked the tiny pieces.

Pug took off her apron and stepped over to a girl called Stray, who was patting a baby as it slept across her lap. An almost buttonless shirt was barely covering Stray's bra-less chest. Pug wrapped the startled girl in her apron, pulled off the girl's shirt, then sat down in her chair to move the cuff buttons to where they were more needed.

Robbie pounded the table with a giant metal serving spoon. "Did you know," she asked, as Doll passed the portions as though they were made of gold, "that a donut's hole grows smaller in bad times when bakers offer more cake to customers and less air? During good times people don't care how big the hole gets!"

"Did you also know," Ginny looked up from sketching, "what dough from the donut hole is often used for? It's fried for little kids, so there'll be big, regular donuts for adults."

Robbie looked up in surprise. Other girls seldom added to Robbie's comments.

"Is that true, honey?" Robbie asked of the little girl on her knee. The child nodded and Robbie pushed her own dole of donut closer to the child and poured more coffee.

For lunch Robbie took sardines and crackers from niches of her unusual cupboard. With an ice-cream stick she added mayonnaise, and mashed fish inside the can so she could use it for a disposable serving dish, smirked Bowie, watching. Robbie banged the spoon, and with a lemon wedge in her hand, waited for silence. Ginny turned to a fresh cardboard.

The new buttons were secure now so Pug decided to mend a hole in Stray's shirt. She felt around the edges of the cushion on her chair and brought up a wooden darning egg. Bowie turned his eyes to Fay Rose; it always made Fay uncomfortable for Pug to feel for things at the edges of her seat. She did not seem to like it either whenever Pug began to knit. For no apparent reason, Fay got up from her place on the floor, ground out the last of her cigarette in an ashtray, tossed her hair as though it were full of hidden taint, and left the Den.

"In Middle Ages," Robbie began as the door slammed behind Fay, "it was believed that if a person swallowed a fish bone, lemon juice would dissolve it away and crackers would move it on down." Robbie squeezed juice into the fish and stirred, then handed ice-cream sticks to Quila and Doll. While Robbie prepared a paper tray, Quila and Doll spread mix on the crackers and lined them up in the tray. Outside, the smell was hard to bear, though Bowie knew that Quila's sleeve would be hiding at least some crackers to add to his evening meal.

Ginny passed the tray around, remembering as she did, long and lovely days out on the pier fishing alone with Dom. "Is this a sardine fish?" little Ginny had asked.

"Do you know there's no such thing as a sardine fish?" asked Ginny. "They're any of several small fishes only suitable for canning. A sardine is also an insignificant person." Robbie looked up again in surprise. Once again the little stranger had added interest and value to something Robbie had said or prepared.

"Like you!" Robbie pretended to shout to the little girl who still sat on her knee. "You insignificant little sardine. You just ate both of your own crackers and mine as well!" Laughing, Robbie hugged and comforted the frightened child, put her and her mended doll down on the bench, and poured another round of coffee. Ginny noticed that Robbie had lifted and released the child as if she were made of fragile glass.

Within the week, Ginny began to understand what Lolli meant by "tea and trivia." To others less sensitive and inquisitive than Ginny, Robbie could seem to be frittering her time away with snacks and trivial small talk. But Ginny was soon happily aware that Robbie was usually hard at work all by herself, not only at filling the empty stomachs of all kinds and nationalities of lost, lonely, jobless girls, but creating a homey, entertaining, enlightening atmosphere. She was teaching the art of "making do" with whatever little there might be to eat. As well, she was restoring shattered egos, extending shallow minds, unearthing hidden potentials, encouraging uniqueness, and doing everything possible to avoid doing dishes.

Ginny began bringing larger cardboards. For smaller details, she practiced on the backs of can labels painstakingly removed each night after raiding the Pigpen. Cardboards and labels she held together with safety pins. She was constantly sketching various tenants, a steady stream of hungry neighborhood girls, and children with little problems for Robbie to solve. And Pug was also always at work there in her dark little corner – either for Robbie's girls or for her own big family. Pug seemed so happy to just be a part of the atmosphere.

Robbie often told the group what would be served the next day, hoping that somebody else would make some effort to add newness to the sessions. Sometimes she did not tell them anything, because at the end of the month she had little to share with anybody.

Today it was nearing the end of the month and coffee, too. As the girls filed into the Den, Bowie was watching from a new slit he had made in the windowsill. Robbie counted ten heads then held up a single peeled orange. She pulled apart the ten sections, sighed, then put the sections together again, made two cuts and handed Quila the toothpick box.

Robbie made a paper tray, Quila did toothpicks, and Robbie began the day's topic.

"Okay," said Robbie, "each must tell three things that can be done with an orange before you get any of your own three allotted pieces. To begin with, you can see that an orange can be peeled, sectioned, and cut." Robbie chose three pieces and passed the tray.

"What's to say after juice, sherbet, and icing?" complained Dago, choosing three bites.

"My grandfather," said black little Opal, "pinched orange peels over a candle to watch orange-oil making sparks. He dried orange peels on fences for smell-good fires. And I hope to wear orange blossoms at my own wedding, someday." Opal picked three pieces.

"What about fruit salad, marmalade, and mixing the juice into whiskey or gin." Ginny put her sketch boards against the back of her bench, and left hurriedly.

"Add to Jell-O. Float slices in punch. And," a long silence with no Ginny to fill it up, "poke a hole, add a straw, squeeze it, and suck out the juice." The girl sighed and took three.

"An orange can be thrown, rolled, or juggled," said one of the Oriental girls from the pier as she removed her own three bits.

"An orange can be used to get someone's attention, as a weapon, or extra vitamin C."

"Half the rind could be an emergency cup, glass, or bowl."

"The other half to heat water in the sun, wash a few dishes in, serve food or drinks."

It looked like all but Ginny's pieces were gone.

"But Robbie, there's so much more!" cried the girl who had first complained. "An orange cup for an ashtray, a game to guess how many seeds it holds, and —"

But Robbie was pumping water into a pitcher, cracking ice with her metal spoon, and scissoring thin curls from the orange skin. She dropped both ice and peelings into empty coffee mugs, while Doll filled them with water and passed them around.

"Now," announced Robbie, "everybody squeeze your eyes shut tight, while magically I turn this water into cocktails." Bowie snickered quietly while Robbie walked around and dramatically stirred everyone's water with a long feather.

Amidst all the laughter there was a knock. A tear-stained little face looked in. A whimpering little dog was in the boy's arms, and he held up a drooping rose. Robbie smelled the pathetic rose with her eyes closed then put it with other sad blooms and sagging greenery envased at the back of her table. Robbie sat the neighbor boy beside her, pushed her own "cocktail" towards him, and started work on the fox tail grass embedded in the puppy's paw.

Ginny hurried through the screen door, glad to see her place was still vacant. She unscrewed a jar and doled out glistening pieces of sugary orange peel into every hand. "Dried peelings are great for tea, potpourri, and candied orange peels." Robbie smiled in disbelief, then handed her the last bits of orange that had been saved for her. The rest of the afternoon was spent listening to Quila's tales of carnival life, while everyone chewed slowly on Ginny's glistening orange peels and sipped blandly flavored water as though it were ambrosia.

The next day was Sunday but Robbie had saved things back for the Sunday bunch. There were only four in Robbie's Den at lunchtime – Robbie, Doll, Quila, and Ginny. On the table were a paper tray of steamed and plucked artichoke leaves and a shallow can of thinned mayonnaise that Robbie was sprinkling with herbs. Robbie dipped a leaf into the mix, pulled the base of it through her teeth, and threw the spent part into another sack.

"The grocery man told me that freshest artichokes squeak when rubbed against each other. This was the squeakiest one in the bin."

"Did he also tell you," Ginny asked, "that unharvested artichoke plants develop into flowers six inches wide? In my mother's garden they made spectacular dried arrangements."

Too soon the leaves were gone. Robbie removed spiky leaflets from the heart, cut it into fourths, dropped them into the remainder of the mayonnaise-mix, and stirred

"Artichokes remind me of some people," commented Robbie as she smiled at Quila, then at Doll. "They're tough and spiky, but if you take the time and trouble to get to their centers, their softened hearts can be well worth the effort."

"Humph!" said Quila. Doll just smiled into space.

It took longer to eat those four delicious pieces of heart, thought Bowie outside his window slit, than it took to devour the whole tray of leaves. Ginny finished first and worked on her sketches. With the evening still young, Robbie turned up the gas and opened the oven door to lessen the chill. The foursome played a few hands of poker, dividing spent artichoke leaves instead of money or toothpicks. There must have been some hidden lesson there, but Bowie was drunk by then, and too woozy to decipher anything.

Later, that cold, cloudy, windy evening, while Bowie was curled beside Mange to keep warm, he realized the air smelled like popcorn, as it did now, every Sunday night. When he arrived back at the window slit, the stranger was sketching again.

The corn was already popped. Robbie minced onions, garlic, wieners, cooked vegetables, and then added chili powder and herbs. With her right hand Robbie cracked some eggs one at a time into her left hand, squeezed the egg until the yolk broke, then spread it over the mixture. Sprinkling popped corn back into the pan, she gave the mess a stir, grated cheese on top, and popped the skillet into a warm oven. She pumped water over her hands and wiped them on a clean rag pulled from the bunch nailed to the wall beside the sink. She threw the rag into the trash then settled on a bench, warming her hands around her coffee mug.

The stranger stopped drawing and looked eagerly at the skillet as Quila opened the oven and hearty fragrance filled the air. She upturned a fresh cardboard as a new assortment of girls trekked into the Den, pouring coffee, lighting cigarettes, and settling on the bare floor.

Outside, Bowie remembered that very first Sunday night when Robbie made this strange concoction. She had scored it into squares, sprinkled it with paprika, then held up a jar of unpopped corn. "We have Indians to thank for popcorn," she had explained. "At the first Thanksgiving this gift to the Pilgrims was an Indian chief's contribution to the feast."

Every Sunday now, Robbie unearthed something new about popcorn. Today she continued the ongoing story as Doll passed warm squares around to the girls' uplifted hands. "Popcorn was probably discovered by accident. I can see it in my mind." She took a long draw on her cigarette, slowly blew out the smoke, and closed her eyes. "One of the ancients must have held an ear of corn over the fire to warm it, heard it make a strange noise, then saw a little white 'flower' mysteriously growing from one side of the ear. What an enchanting surprise that must have been!" There was a long silence. Bowie watched as the girls, especially Doll, closed their eyes and smiled.

"And," added Ginny, "Columbus found natives making corsages of popcorn. And today people make popcorn scallops for Christmas trees, or hang out strings of it for hungry birds in wintertime." Bowie smiled; the little stranger's being here made Robbie's efforts for the Den crowd much more significant. Now Robbie's planning, trips to the library and the store, as well as her satisfaction were much more frequent.

But Ginny had quit sketching. Bowie smiled knowingly – was she too restless?

This particular dish was Robbie's Sunday night favorite. At week's end Robbie always used her funny knife to cut up and mix the week's leftovers. She added popped corn, grated cheese, and eggs, fried it, scored it, and before it had cooled in its paper tray, she had "ragged" the skillet, spoon, spatula, and was done with dishes. Robbie's hatred of dishes, especially greasy ones, was an obvious joke.

Before serving the color-dotted mix, Robbie looked at it with surprise. "This is nonsense, poppycock. How can it taste so good? Popcorn must be the only thing that can increase a cup of nothing into twenty times its size – enough for as many girls as need it. To the Den girls, Sunday evenings were synonymous with Robbie's crunchy, stomach-filling, delicious-smelling "Poppycock."

Outside, the wind turned suddenly fierce and colder. Doll closed the windows, yet Bowie could barely see that Robbie was putting a strip of lemon peel into each mug, filling it with hot water, then putting out an assortment of spices, cayenne, and honey. Unable to hear or smell the fragrant Den, Bowie left the tarpaper shed and spent time hidden on the shadowy rafters, waiting for Ginny to visit the toilets, as she eventually did.

Smiling smugly, he climbed down into the tool room, walked to Quila's empty wagon and snuggled against Mange, awaiting supper that soon might be simmering on Quila's stove.

Fondling Mange's ears, Bowie's thoughts returned to Robbie. Though every day when Doll was home was a milestone, Robbie tried to make Sunday nights predictably overlong and special for all girls that showed up at the Den. Robbie was aware that Sunday nights were especially hard on girls that were away from, or totally without any real home. She seemed to know that this would be all of the Sunday dinner, all of the entertainment, all of the warmth and stimulation that any of the girls would get.

It was not surprising the day after that big wind and all-night rain that followed to smell what Robbie was cooking for brunch. Onions, garlic, and herbs were sautéing in one skillet and in another skillet, bread was toasting. Doll margarined half the slices and heaped on the onion mix, while Quila added toasted tops. Robbie cut sandwiches into fours, Quila toothpicked, and Robbie made the tray, while Doll wiped skillets clean and threw rags away – just the way that Robbie did. Coughing and sniffling, girls kept filing in.

Shivering in makeshift rainwear, girls helped themselves to coffee and huddled on the floor. Doll passed sandwiches, the stranger sketched, and Robbie banged her spoon.

She held up an onion. "This is the plant that's painted all over Egyptian tombs. Alexander the Great lavished it on his troops to give them strength for battle. The most famous of all the lily family – the humble little onion!" Ginny looked at the eager faces and smiled. If this session of Robbie's had appeared anywhere as a school course in "Becoming Enchanted with Everyday Life," not one of them would have showed the slightest interest.

Robbie cut an onion. "No matter what color – white, yellow or red – it has nine perfect rings. Now, what else do we know about onions?" Ginny smiled again. Robbie has a knack for getting people to realize that they really know more than they think they do.

"Onions have a strong taste, awful odor, and make you cry."

"Helps cure coughs and colds."

A long pause and everybody looked at Ginny for a last comment.

"Uh, you can scissor the greening tops for a week of salad garnish." Another pause.

"One of my father, Dom's, favorite sermons," remembered Ginny, "was how one strong person can change an entire crowd. He dramatically lifted an onion from a bowl, saying: 'Let onion atoms lurk within the bowl and, half-suspected, animate the whole!'"

"They sho nuff gonna animate my whole 'bowl,'" declared little Opal as she took the last piece of sandwich. "At choir practice tonight, everyone will pass out from jes smellin' ma strength." While everyone was laughing, Ginny took something from her pocket.

"Here is my contribution." She put a tangerine on the table and carefully removed the skin. "Some people call this the 'kid glove orange' because the skin comes off so easily like a kidskin glove. Peeling it never soils your fingers. And, Opal, it might make that strong bulb we've all been eating, smell more like the lily family that it's supposed to belong to!" Robbie smiled with appreciation, opened another pack of cigarettes, and began to weave another cellophane into the chain around her neck.

12. Fortunes

The next morning, Bowie smelled tea brewing instead of coffee perking in the Den. Except for Quila's crooked smile, eager hand-rubbing, and nervous fingernail-clicking, the atmosphere was gloomy: Doll was not there. But Quila had waited patiently for times like this – perfect for fortunes – and this was one of those times. Robbie sat silent as her ashtray overflowed.

There was fighting, shouting, and banging at the door. "I'm fust! I got the mostest in my foot!" Robbie put out her cigarette and went to the cupboard for tweezers, peroxide, a bandage roll, and licorice. The Chips wrestled their way inside and poked blooming weeds into Robbie's hand. They sat on the floor while Robbie stuffed the plants into jars of water. Robbie put one foot of each boy on her lap. They sucked on licorice as Robbie took turns back and forth on each foot removing pieces of glass. The boys seemed immune to pain and barely winced as the stranger recorded the odd scene.

Bowie watched Quila as she sat among the females gloating over her own teacup like a house spider weaving a silken cage around a hapless moth. The trouble was, nobody ever knew for which "moth" the "cage" was intended until it was too late. To all the girls of the Den, uneasiness was just a necessary part of the "admission price." Quila put her elbows up on the table and one eye peered out from a gnarly space between her fingers.

Sometimes Quila merely "told" her own tea leaves, "read" her own cards, or revealed her own zodiacal horoscope, picking random symbols and objects and dibbling them on the surface of a conversation with a mysterious lowering of her eyes or voice. In different groups and conversations, different chords were formed, different girls felt entrapped.

Having woven her invisible net, Quila would then sit back to watch a victim ensnare herself.

Often, Bowie realized that Quila had no idea which girl she had snared, even when she found payment in the bottle. But it mattered not, for Quila had little faith in her talents even when she was serious. She figured it was all just a matter of Bowie's spying, her own homework, odds, and good luck. Quila's old eyes would not permit real study or accuracy. So she threw in a little salt of common sense, along with a keen awareness of human frailties, and stirred them all with uncanny intuition in which she alone did not believe. The girls seemed intrigued by Quila's fortunes. Even when they were caught themselves, it seemed small payment for the regular food, fun, warmth, and security of the Den.

With Bowie's daily "equipment," Quila dug pitfalls and somebody was always sure to fall in. It also helped her aim to know when Mala received a support check, when the stranger bought her first box of real tea, when new tenants seemed elated over mail, and when it was payday at the nearby paper factory where most of the neighborhood people worked. Bowie also hung in shadows of The Joint, listening to and watching the same girls there, while he nursed wine that Quila paid for, and stored up facts to trade for meals.

Quite by accident, Quila discovered a habit that blended quite well with her method of making a living – she habitually carried in her big sleeves odd objects or newly "acquired" possessions. One reason was merely for the pleasure in feeling of them and seeing them with her mind instead of her failing eyes. Secondly, when nothing she said produced results, she could pull out some object and fondle it, looking very mysterious. Then casually she would glance from one person to another, slowly, all around the crowded room.

This way she found that Fay reacted to a knitting needle that Quila found peeking from Pug's cushion. Pug reacted to a wedding band. Bowie had been startled one evening after supper when Quila caressed a lock of black hair that she usually kept locked in her trunk.

And, with fortunes, Quila, Bowie, and Robbie kept a tight reign on those who were permitted to stay at Last Resort. If Robbie or Bowie saw or felt that someone was a thief, an irritant, or a troublemaker, Quila merely whisked them away with a threatening fortune.

Quila twirled her teacup, recalling. Sunday night Bowie's pant bottoms still had a dusty telltale stripe of matted dust on them that he brushed off as he sat at Quila's table. But his mouth was set against spilling whatever his eyes had seen from the toilet rafters.

Quila talked circles around him until Bowie felt caught like a dog trapped by his own rope. Her tongue distracted him while her constant curiosity searched for hidden clues.

"What saw ye from the rafters?" she whispered.

"The stranger stands astraddle," he parried. "Afraid of our bugs," he shrugged.

"Since when?" She held the wine bottle suspended over his empty mug, and the smell of stew from the cocked lid on her bubbling pot was overpowering. It was a little thing really. Everyone new eventually got the problem and paid the bottle because of it. It did not matter to others, but Quila and Bowie knew that it would matter a lot to the little stranger.

"Two days."

"Hah!" Quila poured generously of the wine and dipped into her black kettle to serve him. "Like I thought. Fay's 'sailor-bugs.' Always dependable fer a few staples."

Such an innocent happening. Like the percolator brush, which the stranger dug from the trash, washed, sterilized, and used in private for brushing her teeth. Or beanbags she found on the fence ledge, robbed of beans, refilled with tiny stones, and sewed up again before their owner returned to find them. Each event had produced payment for Quila's bottle.

Yesterday the stranger squirmed all through the afternoon coffee klatch until she felt herself wilting under Quila's peevish eyes. "Yer wiggly as a sheep with a botfly," Quila complained. And the stranger had left the Den abruptly, for the itch had become unbearable.

"Durn that Fay Rose," the stranger swore in her own fashion. Between two thumbnails she squeezed the bug hard before she realized that in her hurry she had forgotten to plug the knotholes. Bowie took a long swig, then dragged his mind back to the present and the scene inside the Den.

When Ginny returned to the Den, Robbie had removed glass, disinfected the dirty wounds, and was bandaging two little feet while the Chips chewed on the last of their licorice.

"Can't ja bandage our other feet too, so's we can play like kids with shoes?"

Robbie laughed a ripple of understanding. "Okay, one more time!" She quickly bandaged the other two feet and the Chips limped happily out the door.

Next morning, Doll was still gone so Robbie would just be in and out for a cup of tea or a cigarette. Largely she would be repairing the wash machine, plumbing, or light fixtures.

"Drink up m'dears," Quila urged as Robbie slammed out the door. From his peeking spot outside, Bowie could tell that the sensitive stranger felt danger lurking whenever Robbie left the Den. Quickly, Quila stirred a whirlpool in her own cup. "I feel so full o' fortunes this morn!" She drank her tea, then swirled the dregs to coat the cup. Turning it upside down, she twirled it three times while other women uncomfortably followed suit. Bowie could hear Quila's wheeze and her nails clicking beneath the table.

Girls sat patiently watching like always, as though Quila's hands were divining rods that could tell where fascinating waters waited. Quila adjusted the spotlight and picked up Ginny's cup. She ignored the wing at the cup's bottom – good messages were coming to the lonely stranger. Quila would have to make "arrangements" with the postman. Now, instead of revealing the real fortune, she "saw" what she had to see and couched it in cryptic words.

"Behold! A 'Rose aphid' I see! That's all." Quila looked at the girls who sat on the floor, then all around the table. As always, her eyes lingered slyly on every one. Then she looked across at Ginny and flashed her jagged smile. "Squashed 'tween two 'sore thumbs' it be!" She had delivered the fortune opaquely to the major audience, but it was crystal clear to the stranger. Outside, Bowie wanted to hide from himself.

"Pass the sugar, will ye, Ginny? Quila's eyes fastened on the stranger. "I jest can't seem to get enuf sweetness lately. It turns me tongue sa sour and vengeful."

That night Ginny paid Quila's bottle the sugar that it had taken so long to save. She felt a strange delight in sewing up a narrow flowered bag with a string closure, one that would easily fit into the milk bottle, that Quila might use for other things as well. Ginny was becoming a part of the park now and expected pain to be mixed with the pleasure. But she had not expected the bottle to already contain a wax paper bundle of brown sugar.

Ginny found little in the Pigpen lately, so next morning she flooded with milk the tea that Robbie offered, and took a teaspoon of sugar. Doll had not returned, and the gloom of the Den attracted only Ginny, Pug, and Quila, who waited with cards and an evil twisted grin.

"Deal out," said Robbie. "I'll be right back."

Quila dealt, and then waited with her head cocked until she heard the storeroom door open. Immediately she put out a feeler, "Ye haven't lost yer milk teeth m'lass!" She pointed to Ginny's cup of white tea. "Yer mother must be missin' ye," she said innocently enough.

Please don't, Ginny pleaded with her eyes. Not until I have proved myself. She drank her tea swiftly and prepared to leave. But Quila reached for her empty cup, turned it upside down on the bare table, twirled, and began to read its contents. "Not too many churches in town. But here's a large, windowed parsonage, m'dearie, right in yer cup. Hollyhocks all over the backyard." Quila sat back, waiting for a reaction. But Robbie walked in, and even from outside the window slit, Bowie could tell that the timing was terrible.

"The women's shower sure stays clean lately," said Robbie as she picked up her cards.

Until the stranger came, thought Quila, the women's shower was poorly drained and rimmed with stale water and scum. Now, Bowie told her, when the stranger showered, she scrubbed the walls, floor, and corners with her whiskbroom. This way soap slivers were fairly clean before she added them to the rag-of-a-bag that she bathed with at night.

Outside Bowie waited, not breathing, for Quila could maximize the merest detail into something sordid. Quila shuddered, making her golden earloops seem to tremble. "People scrape together the craziest collections, don't they, Ginny?" Quila whispered. So, she has decided to let the former threat alone, smiled Bowie. This was more immediate, more colorful, and she soon let the stranger guess what the harmless tidbit was worth. That night, Bowie flipped a fifty-cent piece as he headed for The Joint. Small payment, he sighed, for feeling so sick and sorry that the stranger had to pay for her love of cleanliness.

Just last week, he remembered as he neared The Joint, the incident of the nails in the women's toilets. "How filthy, all over the floor," said the stranger as she waded into a toilet stall. "Why can't they sit on tubs in their own trailers?" Above, in the tool room rafters, Bowie had watched, dismayed as Ginny wiggled and twisted until she had pulled out every nail in both of the women's toilet stalls.

With a hammer in her hand and a mouthful of nails, Robbie stormed from the crowded Den that afternoon. "Wish I knew who the hell rips out goddamn nails on the women's side. I've better things to do than replace douche bag hooks. Cool a cup of coffee, Quila!"

As the screen slammed, Quila had looked from face to face and finally rested her gaze where she expected to – on the down turned eyes of Ginny. Bowie shook his head sadly – the stranger just kept on "asking for it," and Quila was always there to keep on "giving it" to her.

"Stir me coffee, will ye dearie?" Quila settled back and slowly rubbed her knotty fingers. She looked up at the little stranger, grabbed, and held her attention. "Me auld fingers sure be beggin' fer that special 'goosegrease' the druggist always saves fer me."

Poor girl, Bowie sighed outside of Robbie's window, so sensitive, just made for Quila's every whim. Anyone else would just say yes, they did pull out the goddamn nails. So what? Would the stranger give up ice or candles to pay for Quila's ointment this week?

Ginny had left abruptly, furious that she blushed so easily. In hurrying home, she noticed Doll disappearing into a toilet stall. She seemed to be sobbing. By the time Ginny was settled in her own trailer, Robbie's white convertible, St. Vitus, was warming up, and soon Robbie and Doll took off in a cloud of red dust.

13.   Doll and Robbie

As the thumping, coughing, rattling car turned out of Last Resort, Bowie watched from inside the latticework shadows.

Nobody knew where Doll really lived. Perhaps, he thought, wherever her suitcase happened to be at bedtime. Mostly she found a lodgment of sorts with her frail old father, Lambeth, in the trailer next to Robbie's. When there, Doll tidied her father's bare little home, washed, and cooked sometimes for the two of them.

Often, after Doll contrived a good setup at The Joint or out at the bar on the pier, she would hurry home in a flashy car. She and Robbie would take off for a drive while the drunk slept it off. More often, Doll returned bruised, scratched, or bloody. Ignoring the latchstring Lambeth left hanging out for her, she tapped instead on Pug's door, or slept the night in a vacant trailer.

If her hair was a different color, Doll stayed with a barmaid at The Joint until her wounds healed and policemen stopped questioning. But it seemed to Bowie that Robbie would much prefer for Doll to come home for healing, hiding, and rest, for Robbie took morbid delight in Doll's wounds and strange satisfaction in tending them. "Put up a good fight, didn't you?" Bowie overheard Robbie whisper as – gash and bruise alike – she tended more carefully than a surgeon stitching spider nerves.

Doll always wore the same clothes: white tennis shoes with no socks, blue jeans, and a man's white, untucked shirt that detoured from straight lines, betraying interesting hillsides and nooks of her beautiful body. In their mind's eye, men who saw her explored them all. Pretty to the pith, thought Bowie whenever he saw her, and oh, so ripe. Enshrined she was in those immaculate, nondescript clothes. When she moved it was in her own way, slow and soft – like a ballerina under water. Bowie swept dirt from a mound beside the wagon's wheel, uncorked the bottle there, and took a long swallow.

Nobody knew the real color of Doll's hair. When first Bowie saw her hair, it was long, straight, and light brown – smooth and sleek as a young fawn frightened by two children. Bowie erased the sudden picture from his mind by splashing wine into his face, then went back to remembering. Soon Doll's hair had a copperish sheen. Once when he followed Robbie and Doll to the seashore, he saw it dove-colored and pearly with seafoam. Again, it was black, sparkling with rain as she and Robbie came laughing out of a storm. Once Doll was gone for a long, long time and Robbie was sullen and silent. The voice of the dripping faucet screamed like a giant clock ticking unused time, and Doll's Song gouged an endless, throbbing rut in everyone's days. Finally Doll returned with bruises, a black eye, and lemony hair. Then at times from so much change, her hair was too short, unhealthy almost, and had a pink cast or a bluish tinge by candlelight. Sometimes it was even sort of greenish and soft like a clump of rabbit's foot grass beside a quiet pool. No, not rabbit's foot grass beside a quiet pool. Vague remembrance of certain scenes made his body tremble. Another swig from the warm bottle stashed between his knees.

As Robbie's car now struggled out of the park, Doll's hair was close and short upon her head, looking from that distance like water rippling across a gray rock – a rock perfect for grinding corn. Bowie drained the bottle in his hand, inched out of the dog's door, and quietly lowered the bottle into Quila's waste barrel. He slipped over to Robbie's trailer where a full bottle was stashed in the tarpaper shed.

Drinking slowly, he resumed thinking beneath Robbie's empty, hollow-seeming trailer above him, where it was cooler than in the tarpaper room. There was about Doll an unstudied spiritual grace. Especially in spring when she seemed to be floating in silent lullabies, as though her feet revered the pregnant earth. Her usually dull, hazily eyes sparkled around children with their same innocence, and around expectant women with their same anticipation.

Yet all of her affection, maternal and otherwise, she lavished only upon that she-cat, Spade. Though a demon with other tenants, Spade was Doll's ever-willing companion. When Doll was gone, Spade waited on the fence, under a streetside trailer, or beside the mailbox with an uncanny sense that always knew exactly when it was time for Doll's first step onto the red dirt and back into Spade's loveless life again.

Doll never used makeup, yet her complexion seemed to glow and her lips and cheeks were always flushed with childlike radiance. Yes, Doll was beautiful, but what for? Men interested her like wads of gum on a heel after being used; they were merely sticky and hard to get rid of.

Too often, like today, the law had come looking for Doll. When strangers quit poking around and Doll reappeared, Robbie had scrambled from under the white coupe that forever needed tinkering. "It's time!" Robbie cried eagerly as she grabbed Doll and easily lifted her into the car. If they had not gas enough for the car, like two kids they would have streaked off on foot through nearby hills to hop a freight train as it chugged up a nearby incline. While running, Robbie insisted on carrying Doll's suitcase, her own few things always gathered into a bandanna and hurriedly tied through a belt loop of her jeans.

Sometimes on leaving, Robbie dropped keys at Quila's feet. "Behave, you long-tongued old fossil!" she would loudly whisper. And sometimes, like today with no explanation, keys had been thrown to Lolli as they passed her lazing on the towel.

Before the clatter of Robbie's car died down, before dust that had been raised had time to resettle, Lolli had grabbed Robbie's limelight and "installed" it in her own trailer. Though it usually took her all week to get around to cleaning, in ten minutes now she blew dust around, swept dirt out the door, made the bed, put coffee to perk, and whipped up something to bake. She tried hard to have something better than Robbie had to offer the girls, and the smell of baking was always enough to entice them. Yet strangely, nobody stayed long. From beneath Lolli's trailer, the fragrance would have been intolerable without anticipation of the extra goody that Quila often hid in her sleeve for Bowie's supper.

Lolli went around jangling the keys Robbie had entrusted to her, slinging orders, changing washdays, and playing the tyrant.

When they would finally return, Doll would be brown as turned earth and Robbie, ruddy-cheeked, her fair hands sunburned and splashed with new freckles. As usual, their seemingly pathless journey would have led back to the sea and the pier at Waterfront. St. Vitus as she loudly sputtered home alerted girls as far away as the town; otherwise, how could the Den become so crowded, so soon?

A lonely boring week finally passed. Hoping for this moment, Bowie was napping under the coolness of Robbie's trailer when the familiar car sputtered into the park again.

Bowie took a deep breath. Like a wrapper of freshly opened soap, Doll's clothes seemed to always remember the fragrance of exquisite cleanness. Now Bowie enjoyed her wake as, cuddling Spade, she gracefully stepped up into Robbie's trailer. Close on her heels came the coffee crowd, smelly as wet horse blankets, yet chattering like a flock of birds.

It was great to have them back, to hear familiar voices drifting from the floorboards, to smell coffee perking, to hear happy laughter. He scooted out into the tarpaper room where he watched from one of the slits that he had enlarged while everyone was gone.

Doll was complaining as she opened a window, "Robbie delights in talking to the artist while sailors are getting tattooed out on the pier. Finds some kind of sadistic pleasure in it, I guess. Every time a good-looking prospect began eyeing us on the beach, Robbie left for the pier. Whenever she started to get drunk that's also where I'd find her. Passed out in Blackie's back room or happily asleep, both arms and curly head on his worktable."

The trailer shook as Doll tousled Robbie's hair. "Do you think I could ever get her to swim? To wash off the sweat? Never! We did the town every night, fell on the sand, exhausted, until daybreak. I got ashamed of her!" Playfully she tweaked Robbie's nose. "We showered at a friend's, then back to the sty where we're like the rest of the little pigs."

She rumpled Robbie's curls again, stretched one out to its farthest possibility, then let it bounce right back again. "Loves the sea yet won't even put one foot in it! Afraid I'd see naked toes!" Doll unbuttoned her shirt, "God, it's hot!" Robbie got up, and the screen slammed behind her.

Bowie noted from a tarpaper crack that Robbie was almost swaggering away, the nearest thing to content probably sparkling in those now pansy-soft blue, blue eyes.

Doll's words as the screen slammed were clear. "I never saw such a modest one. You'd think she had three breasts. She's a funny duck, but I love her exactly as she is!"

14. Vegetable Sauté

It must be the beginning of a month, thought Bowie, watching as Robbie overstocked her bare icebox. Most of the vegetables had been begged from neighborhood gardeners. But Quila had gathered mushrooms from under a certain tree on the morning after a rain.

As girls crowded in and helped themselves to fresh coffee, Bowie realized for the first time that some girls arranged themselves in a particular order. Orientals sat together and Mexican girls too. White girls were scattered, but the black girl, Opal, always seemed alone in the crowd. The stranger sat quietly sketching, yet her body seemed tense with anticipation.

Robbie had finished steaming a variety of vegetables: bunches of broccoli and cauliflower, rings of green peppers, cubes of squash, okra, and eggplant, slices of parsnips and carrots, and cleaned wild mushrooms that a grumbling Quila had unloaded from her sleeve. The room was homey with the odor of cooking and coffee and the sound of laughing conversation.

Doll was there and Robbie's laughter bubbled over, flowed through the girls, danced off the walls, filling them with warmth and energy. Heavy clouds hung low and girls shivered as they stepped inside, breathing deeply of warm air as they left chilly gloom as though to fill themselves with everything they lacked, everything that being in the Den represented.

Pug stepped over to a thin, sniffling girl. "Here, Bones!" Pug handed her a "handkerchief" pulled from Robbie's wall nail. The girl seems happier to smell the freshness than to use it on her nose, thought Ginny as she sketched the girl's lonely, unloved expression.

With her metal spoon, Robbie transferred steaming vegetables into a skillet for sautéing, salting, and peppering, then she overturned them onto clean rags inside a paper tray. Pulling another rag from the nail, she wiped the skillet, tossed the rag, and slid the skillet back onto the stove.

Now she sorted cauliflower into another rag-bottomed tray and slid toothpicks toward Doll. With the same spoon, Robbie pounded the table, paused dramatically, and looked around the room, including every girl in a caring gaze. She spoke slowly. "Most people have prejudices: the color of one's cheek, the tilt of another's nose, one's politics, job or religion. But all people seem to be prejudiced against cooked vegetables." Everybody groaned.

"In most cases prejudice continues because nobody takes time to carefully introduce us to the unique personalities behind pre-judgments." Uh oh, thought Bowie, a personalized lecture is coming up and no one will even recognize it.

After Robbie salted and peppered, Quila passed the tray while everybody speared one piece of cauliflower with a toothpick. But nobody ate, Bowie noticed. By now everyone knew that Robbie must first finish her introduction.

"Poor cauliflower," Robbie spoke slowly again, "an overprotected cabbage, whose flowers have been forced to become crowded, misshapen, and white." Each girl looked closely at her own steamy whiteness with new appreciation. "As blossoms begin to form, at least in private gardens, big leaves below are tied up over its head like arms, to protect it from sun and rain. This causes everything to crowd together and turn white, instead of green and flowery. When ready for market, leaves are cut level with heads. Now that's a lot of trouble."

Robbie held up her own buttery, steaming cauliflower, nibbling on it as if it were the last piece left in the whole wide world. "Do you realize that I am totally enjoying a deformed, wrong-colored, very intentional freak?"

"Not too bad," one girl remarked.

"Very interesting," said Stray.

"Can I have some more?"

"Now broccoli," said Robbie while Doll and Quila hurriedly sorted hot pieces into one of the rag-bottomed trays that Robbie continued to create, "is called 'Queen of the Cabbage Clan.' Weather has not been kept from her developing buds, and she has been picked at the peak of tasty perfection."

"Strange," she observed, tasting of the broccoli as though it had cost a fortune, "if it wasn't explained, or my eyes were closed, I couldn't tell albino freaks from classy queens." Ginny could not sketch and turn her pages fast enough. On the next pass-around, Doll put two pieces of broccoli into every girl's hand, while Robbie filled the coffee cups.

Robbie pounded the table with her spoon again. "I really enjoy squashes," she smiled, as several girls made faces. The same women scrambled to sort again and Robbie cut squashes into even smaller pieces as more girls entered, and everyone scooted around to make room. "Squash names are so colorful, but they taste a lot alike. These tender summer ones are long-necks, crook-necks and scallops." Robbie held up a piece of each different squash and ate it like food of the Gods. "My mother used squash blossoms to dress up a salad."

Robbie nodded appreciatively to Ginny, picked up a slice of bell pepper and pounded again with her spoon. "Bell peppers add 'rings of music' to other foods, with notes of color and flavor. But these green bells are just big berries that aren't even ripe until they're red." Quila looked tired, so Ginny put down her sketches, secured her pencil above one ear, then took a few turns herself at passing the tray.

"Parsnips," some girls shuddered, "have a peculiar, sweetish taste that turns most people off. And that's too bad! Cooks should take advantage of that sweetness and add a little nutmeg." Robbie slid a can of nutmeg across the table to Doll. "Parsnips are fed to cows to increase milk production. That means an extra portion for you, Mala." It seemed to Bowie that the girls could hardly wait for their share, anymore.

The tallest, skinniest female that Ginny had ever seen stepped into the Den, scraping her head on the doorway as she entered. Pug took an overall look at her and stood up.

"What's your name, sweetheart?"

"Just call me 'Too-Tall,' everyone else does." Pug took off her apron. "Give me your jeans, honey. There's at least four inches waiting at the bottoms of those pants. Let's see if there's enough to cover up those shivering ankles." The surprised girl removed her pants and happily huddled into Pug's apron, while Pug searched around her seat pillow for a spool of dark thread with a big-eyed needle in its strands. Pug just held her tongue out and Ginny popped a piece of parsnip on it.

"Carrots!" Robbie banged her spoon again, as Doll and Ginny sorted. "In the past, carrots were only used for medicine." Quila clenched her lips against revealing that Gypsies grated the orange magic for poultices. "Nowadays, carrots are used for coloring butter. They're also great for eyes, so give Quila doubles."

Robbie looked intently now at Ginny, until she definitely had her particular attention. "Poor people save thick ends of carrots and all root vegetables, except potatoes, to grow in little watered dishes for windowsill gardens of salad leaves. Sprinkle these with ginger, Doll." Bowie noticed that Ginny was hastily making notes at the bottoms of her sketches.

Outside, Bowie could not tell if it was the sautéing and seasoning, Robbie's dramatic introductions, the warm crowded company, or the fact that the girls were always famished, but everybody was enjoying herself eating vegetables for breakfast.

Robbie sorted okra. "Little okras," explained Robbie, "can grow to foot-long adults. Connoisseurs prefer these tender infants." Quila was squirming. Okra's slimy qualities were a perfect Gypsy remedy for constipation. But why share this wisdom?

Robbie sorted eggplant, then popped a square into her mouth. She loudly licked her lips, and, smiled Bowie, nobody groaned this time. "This is a cube from a small eggplant body. Allowed to grow it would become a football and be just as tough and tasteless."

Now Robbie held a potato wedge, smelling it with delight. "Peelings remain on these 'earth-apples,' as Frenchmen call them. Vitamins and minerals hide just beneath the skin. Sprinkle with basil." Robbie slid a spice can toward Doll. Who would believe this, thought Bowie. Robbie was teaching a whole curriculum of subjects, disguised as entertainment. "Few people know that potato 'eyes' are just the buds of new leaves. Or that the real fruit of a potato is just a worthless green berry." Quila pursed her lips tightly lest she add that, to Gypsies, raw potatoes have more power to draw poison than any other vegetable.

Ginny took her portion before Doll passed the tray, and added, "Does anyone know what the expression 'small potatoes' means?" The girls looked blank. "It's a slangy way of saying that something is small, inferior, insignificant. Like, Last Resort is probably small potatoes compared to city trailer parks." Robbie gave Ginny a subtle bow of respect.

Someone knocked and entered. Poor, fat, miserable girl thought Ginny, turning up fresh cardboard. Does she hack her hair with pruning shears? Like children that came to Robbie's door, the girl held up a single flowering weed. Robbie admired its bland beauty, then stuck it into a jar already filled with droopy moonflowers and wild dandelions that had not yet opened. "My name's Shag," she timidly announced. "I heard that everyone is welcome here."

"Sit over here, sweetheart, in my already warmed-up chair. I have to leave for awhile," explained Pug, as she wove her way to the doorway through scattered girls.

Robbie held up a steamy mushroom and whispered, "These are 'fairy umbrellas,' that hide in wild places that only Gypsies know of, and in tame cellars, dark caves, and rock quarries where growers keep water and temperature steady." She slowed down even more, determined to get her next point across. "They don't look strong at all, but if humans had the strength of a mushroom, they too could always struggle upward and win their day in the sun." Doll salted and peppered, gave Shag a toothpick, and passed the mushrooms around.

Ginny took her share, then added, "And, 'to mushroom' means to elevate quickly overnight, like mushrooms, to a higher position or rank. Like, 'a mushroom artist' is an upstart, who rises rapidly, from nowhere, it often seems." Robbie gave Ginny a subtle salute. Bowie smiled, for sometimes he sensed that these little gems of wordy wisdom were wasted on everyone save Robbie. But, Bowie could see that Ginny did not even care.

"Are there more fairy umbrellas? They're great!"

"I'd like more earth-apples and green music bells," said Bones.

"I'd like more green and white bouquets." Girls crowded around the trays and kept on spearing until every morsel was gone.

Again, Robbie pounded her spoon. "I'm so proud of you all!" she declared. "Even the last pieces of okra and eggplant were fought over. Today, we've made friends with what used to be vegetable foes. So, tomorrow we're going to have a champagne and caviar celebration. But, it's going to cost you. You each have to bring one disposable item to both eat and drink from. I hate doing dishes!" Bowie saw that Robbie was assessing Doll's reaction. Yes, Robbie seemed to decide – Doll will be here. I've aroused her curiosity.

Ginny helped to empty ashtrays and rinse cups. Leaving Robbie's doorstep, she saw Pug giving Shag a haircut. Ginny sat on Robbie's step and sketched the little happening.

That night after Ginny's Pigpen search, Bowie watched as she cut a few inches off the fat ends of limp carrots and put them in a saucer of water. Since Robbie's revelation that salad greens could be grown in a saucer, the stranger became an indoor gardener. Soon edible leaves in dish gardens were not only growing from vegetables that Robbie had used, but also from stumps of turnips, rutabagas, radishes, and celery that she found in the Pigpen. Soon she was daily scissoring the biggest, yet still very tiny, leaves onto her dinner plate, until the very last ounce of the little stump's lacy green energy had been forced outside of itself. Yet, every time Ginny ate the tiny leaves, she held them up for appreciation. Bowie always wiped his eyes as she thankfully nibbled tiny green miracles that seemed to have come from nowhere, nowhere but Robbie's imagination.

15. Champagne and Caviar

The next morning as Bowie settled himself in front of a slit, Robbie stood at her table amidst the roomful of girls. Before her was a bottle of wine, a pitcher of ice, and seltzer water. All of the girls seemed filled with eagerness. At last, silence was so total Bowie could hear bubbles again, coming from the hole punched in the lid of the gurglet which always seemed to be waiting in its dark corner of the Den, waiting for something unnamed. Robbie hit the table softly with her big spoon.

"Champagne," said Robbie in a loud whisper, as she gazed around the room giving each girl her undivided warmth, "is only a fancy name for expensive fizzy wine. Who cares whether it's made in the fields of France, or here on this table in Waterfront?" She uncorked the wine and smelled its cheap fragrance with her eyes closed and nose pointed heavenward. She pried off the lid of the seltzer and dramatically poured the bottles together over the pitcher of ice. Then she walked among the group, pouring about a jiggerful of the mix into the strange assortment of containers that, laughingly, they each held up to be filled – an avocado skin, a small cabbage leaf, half a crackerjack box, flat tin cans, orange rinds, part of a broken bowl, a scooped out bell pepper half, an egg shell. And then there was Ginny, who merely held up one cupped hand, while the other kept on sketching.

Robbie looked pleased. "This really is an odd, disposable assortment to drink from."

"But," said Ginny, shading hair with her thumb, "the strangest cup of all belonged to Napoleon, because, according to Enoch, he drank from the skull of an adventurer."

Robbie raised her mug toward Ginny and her reliable, fascinating memory.

A dark, greasy-looking girl entered and sat down, trying to be inconspicuous. Girls immediately changed seating positions, until the newcomer was obviously sitting apart. Pug got up from her chair and took the girl's hand. "Sweetheart, I need your special help." They left the Den together, and the girls resumed their original places with apparent relief.

"Whew, I smell why they call her 'Skunk' behind her back," whispered Dago, as the girls drank from weird cups and Ginny captured them on cardboard.

Even from outside, Bowie could feel Robbie's growing respect for Ginny. Robbie often told the girls the day before, just what the next day's fare was going to be, hoping in vain that someday, someone else would contribute a new fact, use, or idea. But Ginny was the only one who had ever made any effort to look up a word, think a bit, recall a little, or even make hurried trips to the library, as Bowie told Quila, and she often related to Robbie. Robbie raised her mug again, "Here's to the washing away of prejudices!" Bowie looked around the room at everyone laughing and tapping together their strange little "glasses" before they drank, and he felt as happy as though he were part of the scene, himself. Doll walked around refilling the containers, while Robbie tried not to show admiration with her eyes.

Robbie held her mug higher, "Prejudice is just a 'vegetable' that nobody has introduced." Everyone touched their own container to Robbie's before they drank.

"Now, close your eyes," demanded Robbie. "I want you to feel, taste, and understand caviar, before you look at it." Bowie had watched last night as Robbie made tapioca. Instead of using sugar and vanilla in the whole batch, she had reserved some of the clear grains. Later she salted and put them in her icebox, beside the real tapioca. Now, she was serving salty tapioca into the odd containers that girls had just emptied of "champagne."

"Caviar is so expensive!" Robbie rapped the table loudly with the metal spoon. Then she doled out meager portions with an ice cream bar stick. Now her voice was hushed as she slowly looked around. "There is only one precious spoonful for each girl. So really relish this. Roll it around on your tongue before you chew, and savor the feel and taste.

"Has everybody swallowed theirs?" The girls nodded.

"Now, if I should say that you had just eaten real caviar, a teaspoonful of unripe, salted eggs that had been stolen from a smelly, dead fish's belly, I'll bet you'd never pay a penny to get another taste!" The girls all groaned, made faces, or stuck out their tongues while Ginny sketched as fast as she could. "But," Robbie added, "if instead, I told you that these milky-white balls were really little 'pearls' from the tropical cassava plant, you just might be interested." Now Robbie dished up the real recipe of tapioca, but still handed out nothing to eat it with. Everybody shrugged, then merely tongued it up with delight, and then licked their "bowl." "You see, it is how we are first introduced to a food, a thing, a race, or a person that makes all the difference. You can see now how important a real, unbiased mother and father should be." Robbie looked into the almost empty pitcher.

"Now, before I'll make any more champagne" she pointed to the shy Oriental girls, "I want you delicate scallop-eyed 'squashes' to stop hiding by yourselves, and mix in with those" – she pointed to Dago and her friend –"olive-skinned 'potatoes'. And then, I want you to crowd that beautiful black 'eggplant'" – she pointed to Opal – "into the center of you all."

Pug knocked on the open screen door and Skunk entered, wearing Guy's trousers and a shirt that came down past her knees. Two more shirts were hanging from her arm. Even her hair looked squeaky clean, and now she smelled like Pug's laundry mixed with baby powder.

"Let me introduce you to Rosy. We just burned her only-one-outfit-twin out there in the incinerator!" Eagerly, girls made room for the smiling girl. Robbie dished tapioca into jar lids, and poured the rest of the champagne into two mugs for Rosy and Pug.

Sweet "caviar" was continually teaspooned around and tongued out of all the weird containers. Nobody seemed to mind that the room had become one big combination "salad" seasoned with love and understanding, mixed together with Robbie's careful planning, and Pug's gentle touch. And the little stranger with her too-short pencils, chips of charcoal, and scraps of old cardboard was still trying to put her woozy impressions into picture form.

On the day after the champagne celebration, Bowie settled himself to watch as Robbie peeled, cut, and arranged a paper tray full of raw vegetables. Then Robbie mixed mayonnaise, avocado, and spices into a dip. She was spooning the dip into jar lids as girls began to arrive.

Although Robbie had worked hard on the beautiful arrangement, she found no joy in the serving, for Doll was not there. Robbie had not had time to set a new stage the day before, had not made time to insure that Doll's imagination had been teased into staying home, instead of pursuing her livelihood. When finally she did arrive, with Spade in her arms, the food and girls were gone.

Robbie turned the mournful, scratchy record off and poured coffee that was overstrong from waiting.

16. Spices

The morning was foggy and cold but Robbie's Den, which already smelled of fresh coffee, seemed warm and cozy to Bowie as he settled himself outside the best viewing slit. Of course it seems warm, he thought, Doll is here today, and Bowie could see that Robbie had had a readiness, a simple plan for such an unexpected occasion.

The plan took little preparation. As girls continued to trudge through the doorway, Robbie added cream and sugar to the fragrant coffee, stirred it with her big spoon, then put it back on the lowered burner. She lined up spice cans on the table, and settled one of Pug's little girls on her lap. There were no cups in sight, so everyone waited patiently for Robbie's plan to unfold.

"Spices!" She thumped the table with her dripping spoon, and dramatically pointed to little cans in front of her. Bowie could almost feel Quila squirming. "Dammit," she had complained to Bowie one night, "why do spices always, always stir up in me body so many old facts, old memories, old needs to still be helpin' instead o' usin' people?"

Robbie continued, "Spices are fragrant plants used to flavor food and beverages. Spices have little food value, but they do increase appetite and stimulate digestion. Before iceboxes, canning, or refrigeration, spices made old or tainted food taste better. Spices have played an important part in history. In man's early searching for them, spices helped to prove the world was round. Their possession created powerful cities. Spices have influenced wars and made men rich. This is <u>my</u> collection, my own set of <u>sweet</u> spicery. What does your collection have in it, Tex?"

"Well," drawled Tex, "does salt, pepper, and chili powder make up a 'spicery'?" Everybody laughed.

"What about you, Ginny?"

She looked up from her sketching. "Well, uh, I like to mix mine together for simplicity. I just have two shakers, labeled 'Sweet Spice' and 'Herbal Spice'." Quila stifled a snicker, and outside Bowie felt guilty again for sharing the stranger's humble secrets.

Doll stood before the stove and poured a dozen cups half full of coffee, while Quila served them around the room.

"Well, Ginny, most cooks use spices alone or a chosen few at a time," continued Robbie, "because most foods and most people have their own unique preferences. A good way to start learning your own sweet spicy preferences is to try them in your coffee." The girls all murmured in surprise.

"Like ginger," said Robbie sprinkling into her own cup and stirring with an ice cream stick. She handed the can and stick to Ginny, who walked around the room tapping a generous shake into the rest of the mugs, and then stirring. "Ginger is perfect for a day like today. It creates heat that stays inside the body. Gets rid of the 'blahs' as it speeds up circulation. Soothes headaches, cramps, colds, flu, and even arthritis!"

"So sprinkle me twice, dearie," laughed Quila, as she rubbed her bony fingers.

"Ginger's not only great in pumpkin pie or gingerbread. It's great for stomach aches, nausea, and vomiting."

"So sprinkle Mala three times!" cried Quila in a fit of laughter.

"Tastes great!" said Bones.

"Scads better than coffee alone," added Too-Tall. Everyone drank quickly, and Doll poured the measured rounds again, while Ginny stood poised for tapping and stirring a new spice. Nobody seemed to resent, thought Bowie, the measured half-cups of coffee. Nobody seemed to realize that Robbie was getting low on coffee.

"Cardamom tastes like ginger, touched with pine. Stimulating, stomach-soothing, and masking bad breath." Robbie held up the can.

"The Chinese sprinkle cardamom on cereal. Americans use it to enhance curries, squash, and sweet potatoes. Today, let's enjoy it because it smells like holidays." Robbie tapped into her own coffee, tasted, and tapped again. So Ginny sprinkled twice in each cup and gave a longer stir. Girls sniffed, closed their eyes as Robbie had, and sipped.

"Ah, cinnamon," Robbie smelled of a spicy stick and rolled it like an expensive cigar. "Once more valuable than gold. A treasure that spurred world exploration." Each girl stirred with Robbie's cinnamon stick, shook it over her cup, then passed it along. "Light and delicate, but waiting inside is a warrior, eager to fight colds, flu, bacteria, and fungus." Quila was visibly stirred, for it was happening again, those old times of helping and herbing for other people were racing through her memory. If Jofranka were alive she would see nothing in Quila now but an evil, blackmailing con artist. Hiddenly, Quila crossed herself.

Stray held up a bare foot. "Here, Robbie? Nothing works on athlete's foot."

"Cinnamon," Robbie continued through laughter while holding her cup up high, "your valuable trees are kept dwarfed to better harvest your treasure. Fragrant bark is carefully peeled, and as it dries it curls into rolls called quills." Bowie noted that the girls looked carefully now at the wet stick when it was passed around again, after Doll refilled the empty cups.

"Cinnamon is the color of a small grizzly bear, a fern, a precious stone, and a duck."

"And," Ginny softly interrupted, "Pug's beautiful curly hair is the color of cinnamon."

"So is my skin," declared Opal, sniffing her arm. "But it shore don't smell like cinnamon!" She took the stick from her cup, shook it, and dropped it into Mala's cup.

"Hold it! Skip Mala," cried Quila. "To Gypsies, cinnamon is a female stimulant. And Mala wouldn't want twins!" Everybody laughed except Quila. She was holding her traitorous, impetuous mouth. But behind her hand she was smiling. It felt wonderful for people to enjoy her knowledge, instead of cringing at blackmailing secrets.

Although it was way past lunchtime and there was no food in sight, girls seemed to be sipping slowly, not wanting the session to end. But Robbie is slowing down, thought Bowie. Evidently, she had only planned to use one or two spices at a time. Yet Doll was unexpectedly fascinated by the topic and showing no indication of boredom or leaving.

"Now, cloves." Robbie cleared her tired throat. "Fragrance like carnations." She smelled the open can. "Most cooks team it with squash, pea soup, or tea. Few know that in the seventeenth century Dutchmen destroyed clove trees, except in certain places, in order to..." all of the girls waited breathlessly, "create a scarcity and keep the prices high."

Ginny looked up from her sketch. "Whole cloves are just the unopened buds of those tropical trees. When dried, cloves look like nails. In French the word for nails is cloves."

Robbie's eyes widened in appreciation, before she continued. "Although insects run from the smell of cloves, inhaling cloves can beckon human sleep and banish the blues."

Quila could not help herself, "Or stir up yer hubby's lust," she whispered to herself.

Robbie sprinkled clove powder into her own cup, stirred it, then handed the can to Ginny. Robbie put the child from her lap, then actually danced around the room jabbing her steamy cup among the girls, blowing its warmth into dark corners, filling the room with fragrance. Why, thought Quila, Robbie was showering a happiness that she had never released before. "Ah, how the steam can freshen smoky rooms, ward off disease, make mountainous problems dissolve into molehills." She took a deep breath and let it out slowly. As she watched the fascinated Doll, Robbie closed her eyes. "Can't you feel that subtle power?"

Dago looked into her own cup and sighed, "I theenk it would take an awful lot of powder, Robbie, to even make a leetle molehill." All the girls were laughing, and only Bowie could feel the foggy cold and sudden wind outside as it shook the tarpaper all around him.

"And then there is nutmeg, the kernel of a fruit that hangs like a golden pear." Robbie caught the eyes of Doll, then looked up past the ceiling, then caught another girl's eyes – up, down, up, down – personally willing each girl to stay interested, to brave heights and mentally capture her own golden treasure: to get involved. "Sixty to seventy feet up, nutmeg fruits stretch into tropical air. Few people know that this spice helps you cope with reality, to rise above it without being addictive. Next time, instead of drowning in booze," Robbie's voice was slowing, "just pour a cup of coffee, put on your favorite record, and generously sprinkle nutmeg in your coffee. Then just wait for anger or guilt to fade, for love and self-forgiveness to take over," she was almost whispering, "for peace to enter your world."

"Hurry, I've been waitin' for something simple as that," urged a barmaid.

"Wow! I thought that nutmeg was only for dressing up eggnog and custard," said a girl from the pier as Doll poured the last round of coffee and Quila sprinkled the cups.

As the girls continued drinking, Robbie left the Den, returned with a pot of water, and soon the odor of fresh coffee filled the air again.

"I remember a certain Gypsy bridegroom," whispered Quila, loudly, "who drank nutmeg fer three days straight to keep him ready and eager. It all started when this not-so-handsome Gypsy met this very beautiful Gorgio."

True or not, it seemed to Bowie, as he shivered, that as they drank more of the nutmeg-coffee, girls really were becoming contented and dreamy, just as Robbie said they would. While Quila sat back with a warm cup in her gnarled hands and wove for them a story of Gypsy days, Robbie lit a candle and turned off the spotlight. In darkness, Bowie smiled; Robbie's eyes could secretly caress Doll as much as they wanted. Girls helped themselves to coffee and kept sowing spicy promises into their coffee cups. The next afternoon when Ginny asked the grocery man for nutmeg, he was all out. "Never saw anything like it! A run on nutmeg and it's not even close to Christmas time!"

17. Thanksgiving in Summer

After the spicy coffee klatch Robbie ran out of ideas and Doll disappeared for a while. Now there was only strong black coffee, cigarette smoke, Quila's fortunes or cards and long uncomfortable silences. The only smile was Quila's crook-nosed grin as she dealt cards or scanned the girls' hands. Girls began to pick on each other, complain and argue over sitting spaces. The stranger found nothing worth sketching. Robbie sat silent, her ashtray overflowing, making notes, hatching, it seemed to Bowie, some future idea. Bowie turned around in the hot blackness, held the tarpaper door with moccasined toes, lit a new cigarette and settled back to remember, to fill his mind with something positive.

For a week of nights Bowie had pushed the little stranger's newspaper curtains with a thin wire to get a better view of the new project she was working on.

Shortly after she'd discovered hidden treasure in the Pigpen and became a regular at the Den, Ginny had started to save discarded clothes. She even begged some of the prettiest ones from Pug who always kept her family's old or outgrown clothes for rags and mops. The stranger washed, de-buttoned and ripped the discarded clothes into squares or rectangles. She folded and stored them under her breakfast nook cushions to "iron" them for some future project. Now she was sewing them up like pillowcases.

It wasn't time for bed one night, yet Ginny paused in her nightly sewing to close her eyes and talk out loud to the empty trailer. "Oh, if only these 'impossible pillows' could turn out to be something very special." She spread out her arms and touched the materials folded on her bed. "Wouldn't it be wonderful if they could radiate that same kind of mothering and fathering that Robbie's Den girls have always longed for. If only they could enclose the same aura of caring as Pug and Gus create for their little girls and that Robbie's big heart and careful planning try so hard to accomplish! If only they could be an extension of 'home' and all of the unconditional love that home should be–but usually isn't."

She lifted certain pieces of material and held them to her cheek. "Perhaps some of the hurting and neglect that might still linger in these clothes that Fay, Juju and Mala have worn will be diluted. I want so much to help in mending that shattered look in the eyes of every girl who finds her way to Robbie's Den. But most of all, may I just have the courage to even take these stupid things, someday, to Robbie's Den!"

She sat on the bed and poked crumpled newspapers into a flowery pillowcase made from one of Pug's old dresses, and into another one created from an outgrown shirt of Guy's.

Stuffing about a dozen cases, she stood some of their various shapes down on the floor, and some of them up on the table and benches. She took down dried curls of orange rind hanging from curtain tops and broke some into each "pillow." She sprinkled from an assortment of new spices bought with Lolli's empty pop bottles. She spoke out loud.

"Cloves, Robbie, to soothe problems, freshen stale air in the Den and ward off diseases. Cinnamon to fight colds and flu. Ginger for inner warmth, to shoo the 'blahs' away and soothe headaches. Cardamom turns dull days into holidays. And nutmeg for that dreamy sense of well-being." At the last she crumbled dried bay leaves from Flo's front yard into all of the openings. "Flo says bay leaves make every spice smell stronger."

It had taken over an hour for Ginny to sew the tops together. Bowie had laughed as she crunched, beat and threw each pillow into the air to stir around the odors. She coughed and sneezed in the dusty air, and even Bowie could smell the spicy mixture from outside. Ginny strung one tip of each pillow onto the point of a giant blanket pin, then propped the lot up on the table and benches. "Now I can carry them all at once, Holly," she explained.

Inside the Den Bowie could hear the silent girls rinsing and plunking their cups upside-down on the counter top, disappointed that Robbie had no intention, whatever, of making any more coffee. Sadly they drifted back out into the hungry, gloomy, boring, hopeless day. Bowie snuffed his cigarette into a trailer seam and left the shed.

Things seemed even worse in the Den as Bowie watched the next morning. Robbie just listened while the girls drank black coffee, filled the air with smoke and complained about their problems and shortcomings. The stranger wasn't inspired to sketch.

"Look at us!" Mala stood and shouted. "We're all just great big losers! Sitting here all day long, day after day, after day. Satisfied with crumbs from Robbie's cupboard and tidbits from her mind. Nobody wants to hire us or marry us!"

"Sit yourself down!" commanded Robbie and everyone jumped at her loud voice. "This tortuous time could just be a necessary interval! We're strong enough to go ahead. There can even be strength in a bunch of losers! During the American Revolution there were eight whole companies of soldiers made up entirely of cripples, invalids, blind men and men missing arms and legs. Even so-called losers have much to offer, much to be thankful for!" Did Bowie detect a sob in Robbie's voice? Was she trying to convince herself?

Robbie banged her metal spoon on the coffeepot, hard and loud, while everybody jumped. "I declare tomorrow evening to be our very own thanksgiving in summer! Everyone's invited, so go home and let me plan!"

The Den was indeed fragrant with the odors of Thanksgiving as girls filed eagerly through the door the next evening. Even Lolli and Fay were there. Finally, when Robbie stood up, everyone was silent.

Robbie read from a scrap of paper: "'Said gentleman Gay on Thanksgiving Day, if you want a good time give something away, give anything away!'" Feeling in her pockets Robbie found a dollar bill that was almost torn in half. Looking around she presented it to Mala with a deep bow. Bowie smiled for Mala had just lost another housekeeping job.

Dago had nothing but two scissored butts that she was saving for intolerable hunger pangs. Opal was shaking, so Dago handed her the hunger appeasers, then bowed herself.

Amiko put a quarter on the table beside Pug. Soon there were three dimes, five nickels, six pennies, half a candy bar, sticks of gum, a small comb, three black cough drops, a rolled-up comic book and a little mound of carrots that Pug had just prepared.

While girls were still filling the tabletop with "gifts," Ginny left and soon returned. There she stood now in the doorway completely hidden by pillows that she was carrying on two big safety pins. As she handed the pillows around to the girls nobody seemed to recognize that the strange assortment had been made from Robbie's torn jeans, a threadbare blanket of Orry's, Juju's velvet, taffeta and denim diapers, one of Fay's old negligees, Pug's cotton dresses and a flannel shirt of Guy's.

"I call these 'Impossible Pillows,' Robbie. My contribution to Thanksgiving."

The girls giggled as they settled themselves on or against the fresh smelling, crackling new pillows. Robbie shook her head in disbelief. At last Ginny took a pencil from behind her ear and started to draw the mound of gifts and all of the girls smelling, arranging and punching the colorful pillows.

"At this Thanksgiving," Robbie banged her spoon on the table, "there will be no formal tablecloths or napkins." She unfolded a sheet and spread it over the table. "Tablecloths, themselves, were the very first napkins," she explained. She picked up one corner of the cloth, pretending to blow her nose and clean her ears. "Tablecloths were originally meant to serve as towels with which guests could wipe their hands, their faces and their etceteras." She took bottles of chilled wine from the icebox and put them at the back of the table.

"We will also have no spoons, forks or knives – only fingers and toothpicks. Table knives were not invented until the 1600s. Before that, diners brought their own knives which between meals served them well as daggers. The same knives that people ate and killed with became in time the first scalpels to save lives."

"Daggers were also," interrupted the little stranger, "the first palette knives that artists used to paint broad splashes of color and rugged lines." Robbie smiled and nodded.

"Forks," continued Robbie, "were invented by an Italian lady, too refined to pick up meat with fingers. First forks were two-pronged affairs. First spoons were crude ladles made by cavemen from gouged-out stones. Egyptians and Romans later had spoons made of gold."

"Here utensils are made of wood or skin!" Girls snickered.

Suddenly the door opened and Doll walked in with Spade in her arms. Bowie watched as Robbie hid her radiance. Sniffing meat in the air, Doll patted Spade, kissed her, scooted her out the door and latched the little entrance.

"First we're having tea." Like always, as though Robbie gave silent orders, Doll began to carry through. She filled several cups from the teapot on the stove and placed them in front of Robbie. Robbie stood, dramatically poised with a box of salt and a teaspoon.

"In western China they use salt, not sugar, in tea." From a saltbox Robbie poured a spoonful into every cup and stirred. Everybody groaned as Doll passed the cups around.

"Robbie!" cried the first girl who gingerly tasted her tea. "That's sugar not salt!"

"Next!" Robbie interrupted their relieved laughter while she finished a paper tray. She took a wedge of cheese from her icebox and cut little squares with her pocketknife. Quila speared the cubes while Robbie waited for everyone's attention.

"For the very first time let's really appreciate and savor this common food."

Doll passed around the tidbits and since Robbie was eating her square, the rest did so as well. She swallowed the last bite, wiped her hands in the air, and then dramatically held up one finger for silence. "Why," she whispered loudly, "would anyone gag at a mere mention of the candied bees, the chocolated ants or pickled bull scrotums that are sold out on the pier? All of you are now happily devouring rennet, which is the inner lining of the fourth stomach of a dead calf. Without it milk would never curdle right and cheese could never form." They all made wry faces yet continued to nibble their cheese.

"Now the main course!" Robbie rubbed her hands with enthusiasm, took a paper tray of sliced turkey from the oven and passed seasoned pieces around with only her fingers. The rest of the slices Robbie covered with a patterned cloth from the nail beside the sink.

Robbie held her own slice high above her head. "Here's to the bird that nobody really loves, except when he's in their mouth." Robbie took a bite, chewed and swallowed. "Poor Mr. Turkey, so firm and fat he can barely fly from the ground anymore. Brainless as a rock, he can starve in the midst of food, yet can also strangle to death on his own over-gorged crop. Personality? None at all! Just a huge eating machine that tastes good!"

"He does taste good, doesn't he?" They nodded suspiciously. "Sure glad he tastes all right. Couldn't find anything to boil him in except this." Robbie held up her chamber pot and everybody threw something – pillows, shoes, socks, a wad of gum and a mashed cigarette package. Robbie laughed and ducked and Ginny furiously sketched. Doll passed out more turkey slices, and girls wiped their fingers and mouths on Robbie's giant "napkin."

"Time for dessert!" declared Robbie. "Now what do you think makes pumpkin pie?" Robbie opened the oven and brought out a tray of still-warm orange squash cut into bite-sized squares. She drizzled warm butter overall and Doll sprinkled cinnamon-sugar. Ginny paused from sketching long enough to pass the paper tray.

"For poor folks 'pumpkin pie' is any orange squash – if butter, sugar and spices are in their kitchen!" (Robbie looked at Ginny until she was sure that the useful fact had been recorded at the bottom of her current sketch.) Doll doled out the mock pumpkin pie. The tea was gone so Doll did refills with wine from the back of the table.

"Okay, you freeloaders," teased Robbie, "it's time to pay the cook! Think real hard. We're going to pull the breastbone to see who wins their wish. What personal trait or quality would you like to whisk away?" Robbie wiped her hands on the tablecloth.

"I feel like a dwarf," said one Japanese girl in a voice that could barely be heard.

"But there's a special place for even little dwarfs, Amiko!" Robbie leaned over to pat her head. "A famous spy was only a dwarf. Disguised as a baby, he could hide secrets in his cradle cloths. He did what no one else could do." Robbie drank some wine and began walking among the girls like a comedian, waving her hands, gesturing.

"Attila, the Hun was a dwarf. The father of our constitution, our fourth President, James Madison was only 56" high," she gestured. "He weighed only a hundred pounds, and didn't have big brown eyes and shiny hair like Amiko does. He was very plain and unimpressive. And you?" Robbie pointed.

"My nose is hooked."

"In ancient Rome that was a sign of leadership." Robbie stooped and gently held the girl's chin in her hand while the stranger hurriedly turned up a new cardboard. "Nora, I like your nose. It goes so perfectly with elegant eyes." Outside, Bowie grinned: Robbie never said directly, "You're beautiful." Too hard to accept with humility. Besides, these girls would never believe her. Instead, Robbie admired sparkle in someone's eyes, the way straight hair still made tiny curls on a temple, character in bony hands or the unique little heart that freckles had made on a cheek.

Doll poured another round of wine into the teacups. Impossible pillows crackled coldly with every move, but warm bodies were releasing spicy scents.

"I never finished grade school," Fay Rose confessed.

"You're in very good company. Neither did Mark Twain or Thomas Edison!"

"I hate being an orphan," lamented Opal. "Nobody really understands." Opal couldn't handle wine and her voice had begun to waver.

"President Andrew Jackson would understand. His father died before he was born. His mother and brother died from smallpox, which he had too. His wife died just before his inauguration. But Andrew, himself, carried on in spite of his own tuberculosis."

"They weren't black," whispered Opal.

The Den seemed overly quiet.

"Regardless," insisted Robbie, "you are unique in all of the world, Opal. Your special skin enfolds a space that nobody else can ever live within. Your special eyes can see with a fire that no one else can even feel." Robbie hunched down and held Opal's hands. "Your fingers can accomplish tasks that nobody else might even know exist. Even now, your inner being aches for a particular love, out there somewhere, that it cannot be whole without. Maybe it's a sister's or even the love of a substitute mother."

"Yes," objected Opal, "but I'll always be unfortunate! My Gypsy gramma named me after that unlucky stone, the Opal. My black papa committed suicide when I was a-comin'. Then Mama, herself, up and died when I was born. Gramma hated me!" Opal burst into tears. "She screamed that I was blacker than prison toilets that always needed scrubbing; blacker even than the loss of my mama, her favorite snow-white child!" Opal was sobbing.

"Once I scrubbed my face until it bled. I held a match to my arm until it sizzled! But black don't wash off, burn off or wear off!" Pug held her arms out to the shaking girl, then nestled Opal into her big comforting lap. She smoothed Opal's short kinky hair. Within the long silence Lolli got up from the floor and left. Bowie could swear that angry tears were gathering in her eyes.

"I have horrible acne. Nobody ever touches me. I hate to apply for jobs."

Robbie held the girl's scarred cheeks in her hands. "George Washington had the highest job in the country and his face was horribly scarred from smallpox."

"I can't do anything right!" Mala objected. "Men always leave me. My kids are getting bratty. Regardless of all the people in it, my house is cold and lonesome."

"Lincoln couldn't do anything right. He failed at everything, except for being a wonderful President. Too big, too homely. The only thing he was good at was telling fabulous stories. One thing you've always done right, Mala: you always have beautiful, handsome children!" Mala had never stopped to consider this, but now she fairly beamed.

Doll timidly raised her hand. "Something about me too, Mala, always attracts the wrong men. Why can't I attract a good man, a kind man, a sort of rich man in his own unique way? Isn't there even one man out there who puts people, animals and children above instant sex?" Pug reached over and patted Doll, then pulled her hand away and wiped her eyes. Robbie picked up a corner of the tablecloth and wiped her entire face.

Robbie's sheet-of-a-tablecloth must be smelling like turkey, wine and pumpkin pie, thought Bowie. The hem must be filling up with smudges of lipstick and sticky fingerprints. The rest of the food on the table was disappearing. Five of the wine bottles were empty, and as the sixth began to work, the girls didn't seem to mind anymore that another's head was in her lap, that they were leaning all over each other. Nobody seemed to notice that a blue-jeaned leg or a bare foot was in somebody else's space. Nobody seemed to notice that the stranger was running out of cardboard, labels, and ambition.

Doll was tired of pouring wine and merely passed the bottle around.

"What about you, Robbie?"

"My hearing's going bad."

"That never stopped Edison or Beethoven," reminded Ginny. "Besides, ears are only a single way of hearing. Deaf people hear with fingers and eyes. Insects hear with body hairs. Robbie and Pug, now, they hear with great big hearts!" Robbie looked embarrassed.

"Okay, Pug, you didn't think we'd forget about you!"

Pug spread her hands out in front of Opal's body. "All of my finger and toenails turn up instead of down!"

"That's not bad. A British lady had six toes on one foot, six fingers on one hand, and three breasts! Worst of all, she wasn't married to wonderful Gus, but to Henry VIII!" The only one that laughed was Ginny. Robbie lit a cigarette. "What about you, Ginny?"

"I'm just afraid to be my real self."

Slowly, Robbie blew out a long breath of smoke, then smiled. "But, you seem to be getting a lot of practice."

Dago raised her hand, "I have one eye that's crossed."

Robbie was stumped for an example. Ginny held up her pencil and volunteered. "The artist El Greco became famous in spite of faulty eyes. Because of his strange seeing, many of his paintings seemed to be sliding off a corner of his canvasses. Yet he was a great success. That little fault was a trademark to admirers who were aware of its possible existence."

Ginny looked around in dazed amazement. "Hey, that's what Robbie's been trying to teach us and herself as well." She began to weave. "We're all just lounging around like losers, waiting for some kind of spark to ignite us into our own kind of activity."

Ginny quit sketching; pictures were looking vague and wavery. She stood and steadied herself against the table, then pointed her cup around the room as her other hand held up her elbow. "Listen, all you females who wish you were somebody else!" (The bashful stranger let out a long burp. It made Bowie chuckle, because it didn't ruffle her composure.)

"Enoch told me a story that should make us all ashamed to be complaining. A Roman Emperor once collected all of the dwarfs, cripples and freaks that he could find and brought them to the Coliseum. There they were ordered to fight each other to death with meat cleavers. At least we're none of us freaks, we live in America, it's the twentieth century, and nobody has that kind of cruel control over people!" The little stranger raised her cup above her head in an angle that almost spilled its contents, then she drained it.

Robbie blew off the wishbone. "Hate to disappoint you, girls, but there's only one wishbone to every turkey. So the cook gets the privilege of pulling. Here Quila, you haven't wished yet. Whoops, you got the short end. Anyway, what was the trait that you hoped to wish away?"

"Me arthritis, it's killin' me!"

"Well," Robbie giggled, sounding unlike her usual self. "You'll just have to go out and get yourself pregnant. They say that it works every time." The girls started to snicker but their laughter sounded tired. They all began to stretch and weave.

"Before you leave, choose a trade-gift from the table." Robbie steadied herself with one hand on the table and held out her empty mug. "And always remember: we're never so boor or proke that we can't shind fomthing to sare! Well, anyway."

Robbie lit a candle and Doll switched off the lights. Robbie tried to bang on the coffeepot but dropped the big spoon on the floor. "It's time for the final toast!" she slurred the words.

Robbie raised her cup high and squeezed her eyes together as though trying to clear them. "It's okay that I got the long end, because I already had my wish – that everyone would know how important it was to share your shortness, your funny nose, your lack of parents and education, your lack of confidence, your turned-up toenails, your pimples – everything!"

Bowie watched intently, for Robbie was looking into Doll's eyes. She raised her mug, and Bowie could barely hear. "I'm thankful I'm me," said Robbie softly, "that I live at Last Resort, that it's today instead of yesterday – or tomorrow!" She looked around the room.

"Be glad we're different. People 'out there' are trying so hard to be copies. But we <u>know</u> we don't fit. We are the lucky ones, though we still don't believe it. 'They' have money, education, power. But with all their acquiring, most have never been able to buy the really important thing: friendship with their own uniqueness. 'Out there' people are trapped in a rigid, materialistic sameness that would be deadly to the rest of us!" Silence. Nobody had ever seen herself in this light, or given herself any credit for feeling this way.

"I'm thankful Americans use sugar and not salt in tea." Arkie raised her cup.

"We don't eat bees, ants or pickled scrotums."

"I'm thankful for Ginny's spicy, loud new pillows." Another raised a cup.

Trash gathered coins on the end table. "Been out of soap for weeks."

"I'm thankful for this comic book," said Mala. "It's my kid's birthday."

"Who cares if 'they' use silverware! Today at least, I'm thankful for my own black fingers, Robbie's full toothpicks, and a warm loving lap when I really needed one."

Bowie shifted position. There were no noises or lights in the rest of the park, so Bowie let the tarpaper door hang open. For five hours, with a sheet, toothpicks, paper sacks and facts from the library, Robbie had turned tea and turkey, cheese, wine and squash into a memorable Thanksgiving.

"Now," drawled Robbie, standing up, wobbling, trying to pour more wine, "we have proved that in every lack there awaits some advantage. From now on, let's all be glad we're not smart, gorgeous or rich. We don't yet have that wasteful need to 'be somebody.' We can live in the beautiful 'now,' floating, savoring and spending each wonderful second. We needn't cling to nightmares about past history or dreads about the future."

With both hands Robbie pointed her cup to Pug, while swaying in every direction. "Some people have their beautiful cinnamon hair so tangled up in an old history book, they can't even purn the tage." She drained the cup and almost dropped it on the table.

Robbie floundered to her bedroom. Pug kissed Opal and helped her to stand. She transferred soggy trays to the trashcan and folded the "napkin" to take home for washing.

Holding, dropping and retrieving sketches, Ginny staggered home. Not a bad trade, she grinned, remembering the fragrant, crackly pillows. She had traded only time, old clothes, wadded newspapers, dried peelings, bay leaves and spices for a fabulous turkey dinner and five hours of entertainment that could never, never be forgotten.

18.   Picturesque Names

Back in her trailer now Ginny lit a candle and sat before the big dictionary. She began to leaf through it, then fell asleep on its open pages. Bowie settled himself beside Ginny's new hollyhock and took a long swallow of wine. He lit a cigarette and set himself to remembering the story of the big dictionary Ginny had found almost as soon as she had discovered the Pigpen's varied potential. Pug and her family had had a lot to do with how Ginny began to use the book. Bowie closed his eyes as Ginny began to lightly snore.

Every morning so she could clean her trailer, Pug shucked her seven daughters out of the door, kissing or hugging each one, fussing with their hair or clothes as they went off to school or play. "Like little peas from a big green pod," Ginny often mused out loud as she sketched the girls from her doorstep. "All in skirts and tops from the same bolt of material, well-fed, well-loved, scrubbed, curled and eager to undo Pug's handiwork. What a wonderful mother," Ginny sighed. "How easy to locate them in a hurry!"

On weekends the first one out was usually Cassy, a sad lovely creature of thirteen. Like a rosebud tucked under Cassy's arm was two-year-old Pal who seemed too wise for her age but was late in walking. Then, carrying Orry the baby, out walked Missy, a tall and quiet girl of nine with an intense disliking of men. Peg, the seven-year-old popped out like a cork; she never walked where there was room to run. Then out nudged the small mischievous one, called Elfin. Lastly came the little oftimes nudist, Pat.

Somehow, this seemed to Ginny an odd assortment of names. In most big families back at the parsonage, many of the names seemed to start with the same letter or to have some kind of similarity. But these names: Cassy, Pal, Orry, Missy, Peg, Elfin and Pat?

Bowie had been watching one afternoon when Ginny first started to visit the Den. Little Pat was sitting on Robbie's lap drinking spoons of coffee while Robbie re-glued the child's storybook. Ginny, Pug, Doll, Quila and a few neighborhood girls were having iced coffee in cups. Two seemingly nameless, vagrant girls were juggling nursing babies, cups and cigarettes. Doll was wondering if her latest conquest really had money or was shamming her with flowery proposals. For the hundredth time, it seemed to Bowie outside, Quila asked the new friend's occupation and told Doll that he was not "the" man for her.

"Well, strew me some patrin, anyway," sighed Quila with a dramatic sweep of her arm. Doll laid out a stolen item or two from the absent man's pocket. At Quila's words little Pat had suddenly looked up at Quila quizzically, as though her name had been called. Robbie glanced at Pug, then at Ginny and seemed to pale. For no apparent reason Robbie picked the child up gently, gave her some licorice and put her out of the door to go play.

"That was nothing unusual for Robbie to pale at," thought Ginny as she sketched. According to Flo, Doll often brought some man's pocket items to be analyzed by Quila. Quila's comment that time – as she closed her eyes and fingered the items – was, as always, about the same: "He's nay the price o' beer, much less a weddin' loop!"

"Someday," sighed Doll, her eyes misty and her voice faraway, "I'll find me a rich man, who's sweet and gentle, one that I can really love."

Ginny might never have found the key to Robbie's pallor – and many other "keys" – had she not acquired the afternoon habit of lingering in the shower while listening to talk beneath the tree, in the washhouse or under the clotheslines.

"Can you imagine, Kasha," Lolli's mouth had been full of clothespins, "what Louie got for our anniversary? A giant dictionary! Of all the gutty digs! Besides, the print's so small a dwarf would dread to read it. I fed it to the 'Pigpen Posy'. Maybe she can digest it. I'm not about to even try. I'll just tell Louie that someone borrowed it, then moved away."

It was like a blow in the stomach but the nickname was not without compensation. That night Ginny found the book deliberately hidden under a mound of soggy coffee grounds. Her very first book.

When it was cleaned and dried somewhat, "What shall I look up?" Ginny pondered with eagerness. Then she remembered: "patrin," the only challenging word she had heard since her arrival. The dictionary was big and heavy and at the back it offered foreign words and phrases, proper and biographical names.

"Patrin," she read aloud, "sticks, grass, leaves, etc. left as marks by Gypsies to indicate the route taken." Then she remembered. Whenever little Pat was missing, her sisters could always find her by toys or droppings scattered behind her. It was like a game and little Pat would be hiding, waiting for the searchers, ready to be scolded and tended to, waving her diaper gleefully in one hand.

"So Pat is really Patrin. Why should Robbie even care if I should find this out?" she suddenly spoke out loud to the empty room. Just a trifle, the trailer had shaken in the breezeless night, like a startled leaner quickly pulling away from it.

Ginny blew out the candle, curled up on the bed and waited in the darkness. Spade's purring had finally drifted down from the open transom and released her to sleep.

Later another incident seemed to contain an element of Patrin's same mystery. Doll was gone and only Robbie, Ginny, Quila, Pug and Orry were in the Den as Bowie watched. "Ah, this baby, she's so good and quiet, I worry about her," lamented Pug. "My mother had six children before she had me and every one of us drove her crazy with our constant motion." Pug settled Orry in the big chair and then sat down on the bench beside Robbie to have a cup of coffee. "Orry's the same age as Juju, yet she never tries to walk," sighed Pug. "Just sits there contentedly, watching, smiling and laughing all through the day."

Quila, in one of her rare sympathetic moments, reached over and put a bony hand on the child's curly head. She looked into her placid baby eyes. "Never fret, Pug, this one'll be a seer," she predicted, "the seventh child of a seventh child."

Abruptly Pug stood up, gathered Orry into her arms, and as Quila stared after her in astonishment, Pug left without a word. She had never touched her coffee. Pug seldom showed any emotion, thought Bowie. As silent and controlled as the eye of a storm, but now that calm eye was about to ooze a tear. Something had disturbed Robbie too, for Bowie had seen restraint marks on Robbie's cheeks, on her tightened jaw and lowered eyelids.

From outside Bowie could barely hear Robbie's words. "Why don't you watch what you say, Quila. Pug lost another child – before it was ever really born."

Robbie grabbed a wine bottle from the icebox and held it high, "Here's to all of the lost Pugs, Bowies, Lollis and Fays with two feet in yesterday and a fence before tomorrow."

Robbie hurried everybody out the door. "Flyaway, all of you and your fetishes." For some reason Robbie locked the door, turned on the record and proceeded to get good and drunk. It was useless for Bowie to stay sweating any longer in Robbie's storage shed.

That night the only late light had been Ginny's. She loved the night, like an owl or a bat. And Bowie enjoyed watching her.

Ginny had looked methodically through the O's in her new dictionary until she found it. "Orra," she read and spelled it aloud, "the runt of a brood, last, odd, leftover." The thrill of discovery made the usual late-night hunger pangs seem almost bearable.

She took a piece of hard wax from its jar and began to chew. She put her elbows up on the table, leaned her chin on her hands and looked out past the rolled-down shade. "Holly, nobody but Robbie could have named Pug's youngest children. The names are far too picturesque for Pug to think of. Only someone who calls a narrow-necked cider jug a "gurglet" could have named those children." She closed her eyes and rested her head on the open dictionary. "What about the rest of Pug's children; has Robbie named them too? If so, there must be more to Pug and Robbie's silent relationship than meets the eye, for only Pal, Pat and Orry were born at Last Resort, at least according to Flo. What of Cassy, Missy, Elfin and Peg?"

Ginny raised her head and opened her eyes wide. "I'll bet Robbie named them all!" she exclaimed in fascination, as though she had found out something that Bowie, still listening outside, hadn't already guessed. Excited, Ginny had turned to the C-section and began searching for nouns that could be shortened to "Cassy."

Each day now Ginny managed to be first at the mailbox, sitting on the ground against the post and sketching until the mailman arrived. Each time she sifted patiently through letters before the other tenants arrived. How strange that there was never a letter addressed to Fay Rose, Mala, Lolli or Pug. The letters they claimed were addressed to Suzette, Marsha, Chloe or Madonna. Quila, Enoch, Robbie or Bowie never checked the mail, nor did they ever seem to receive any. There was never mail for Ginny.

"Expectin' a billet dieu, dearie?" sneered a voice one day as Ginny looked through the mail. Ginny turned, surprised not at the contempt in Quila's question but by the fact that Quila had spoken to her at all. Quila seldom passed the time of day with anyone outside the Den unless she had some plan behind it.

"Why no, not necessarily a love letter," replied Ginny warily, but Quila had already gathered her daily cup of new sand for dishwashing and was halfway back to her wagon.

Ginny had come to realize that everyone but the postman used Robbie's nicknames. To the park's daytime denizens the pet names seemed to be an invisible badge of acceptance.

"You've got to be pretty wishy-washy around here, to stay unnamed by Robbie!" Lolli taunted within earshot. Ginny alone, of all the regular tenants, remained like a sore thumb with only the labels "Hey," "Greeny," "Stranger," "Posy" or her given name of Ginny.

"Fay Rose – how do you spell that?" asked Ginny one day at the Den, with too much nonchalance.

"Any way you please," retorted Robbie wedging a piece of cheese with the ever-present, unbending knife.

"But how do you spell it?"

"I don't!" said Robbie with finality as she stood and slammed out the screen door. It amused Robbie to have her brain picked, but only with the utmost finesse, Ginny realized.

"Don't irritate Robbie," whispered a neighborhood girl who often had coffee at the Den. "Strange things happen. Your mail disappears. Water runs out in the shower or you get scalded. You never get a regular washday. The door is locked at the Den during coffee time. Phone calls won't get to you. You'll want to move." Suddenly remembering Pug, silent in her usual place, the girl put her hand to her mouth and quickly left.

To forget her curiosity and her frequent nauseous hunger, Ginny had gathered up a long board and two stacks of wooden boxes from the Pigpen. Standing balanced on the board she began sewing with a bent needle, until rag patches nearly covered her holey awning. Bowie watched her painting the awning's framework with an old sponge and green paint leavings found in the Pigpen. While the paint was drying she went to one of the toilet stalls and returned to her trailer with a roll of toilet paper hidden in her blouse. She came outside again in a few hours and began twisting knotted string around the dried poles. Using bunched-up toilet paper "flowers" that she had created, she twisted them into the strange vinelike spirals. As Bowie watched he wondered for the hundredth time, how could Quila ever think that such a weird girl could make any change in Last Resort?

Ginny had rested on her porch box, idly sifting the red earth through her fingers. "What does Robbie have to do with this mysterious red "blanket"? And why is nobody supposed to dig or plant in it?"

From the corner of his eye Enoch had been watching Ginny as he finished smoothing his threesome of pants which hung from stretchers on the line. He missed Ginny and the dinners they used to have together. She was the only one who had ever had the slightest interest in, or maybe it was tolerance of, his hobby. Walking toward her, Enoch dug the toe of his foot into the red dirt at the edge of her porch.

"Did you know that there are over thirty times as many people buried in this earth as there are now living on top of it?" Ginny squirmed on her apple box, smiled vaguely, then decided it was time to get the hose from the tool room and fill up her water tank.

That night Bowie had been listening when Ginny found something new and exciting while thumbing through the Ps in the dictionary. "Surely, Robbie alone has named each one of Pug's little girls. And, the nicknames that Robbie has given to each of the regular tenants might also have secret meanings."

"That's a clever name for somebody to have given Suzette: Fay Rose. 'Pharose' is a lighthouse beacon to attract or guide sailors," she said when she and Robbie were alone one morning. Ginny expected at least a withering glance. But Robbie merely smiled in awed appreciation, passed the fruit bowl and struck up a silent bargain with her eyes, for others were now arriving. Mysterious nicknames were one of Robbie's few rewarding pastimes and Ginny wasn't about to drain the mystery, just enjoy the thrill of each discovery.

Bowie began to shiver in the darkness behind the gray trailer. He took another sip and buried the bottle again, stood, stretched, and poked his wire at the paper curtain. The woozy little stranger was still fast asleep with her head on the dictionary, and the candle was almost spent. He hurried back beneath Quila's wagon where at least the warmth of Mange's body could be shared.

19. Meet Gussy

Glutted with card games, the next afternoon Robbie lit a fat candle and switched off the spotlight. With fresh coffee and a cigarette she settled back into shadows. Bowie was watching and listening from the slightly opened window, as slowly the Den filled up with females. Soon they were sitting wall-to-wall, against and upon Ginny's fragrant crackling pillows, on the arm of Pug's big chair, all over the benches and floor. Ginny sketched, drank coffee and added her own smoke to the over-crowded Den. A tension, an expectation knit them all together into a unit that laughed and joked as one, but without Robbie.

Doll got tired of the empty cups. She refilled the pot herself and put more coffee on to perk. Ginny captured with her pencil spidery shadows that were creeping down the walls as the candle lowered. Still, Robbie said nothing. Pug's ceaseless knitting didn't help. It dug the silence deeper. Despite the fan, the room was like an oven in its dense cloud of smoke. Ginny had rolled the sleeves up high on an old shirt of Robbie's, whose front was now patterned with sewn-on flowers. Others tied their blouses in knots beneath their bosoms, undid buttons and pinned up their hair. Sweat trickled down Robbie's hairline and twisted her curls even tighter, yet she never loosened a single shirt button, rolled up her sleeves or made herself comfortable in any way. Nor did anyone press her, for they all had glimpsed pink tips of ugly scars that sometimes peeked from wristbands of her shirt.

As usual, everyone but Robbie ran hurriedly back and forth to the toilets, afraid that they might miss whatever the tension was foretelling, or lose their sitting space. A child peeked into the doorway and handed Robbie a fistful of weeds. He sat on her lap while Robbie moved the candle closer and straightened the wheels on a toy car. The little stranger captured it all on cardboards as Robbie sugared and creamed her own (usually black) coffee and spooned some out to the child. Finishing the picture, Ginny took a folded newspaper fan from her shirt pocket and tried to freshen the air around her. Robbie gave the child some licorice and opened the door for him to leave.

There was an insurmountable lull at last, so profound that bubbles of ferment escaping from the apple cider jug could plainly be heard. Quila's wheeze as she breathed and her nervous flicking fingernails became obvious. The only visible movements were from Quila's flashing earloops as she nervously looked around, and the swishing of Ginny's scalloped fan. Pug's knitting slowed almost to a standstill, and Spade lifted her head curiously from the bench beside Doll.

Outside the slit his nervous sweat gathered and Bowie was barely breathing.

Without using hands, Robbie shifted her cigarette to the other corner of her mouth and slowly blew out a long curling wisp of smoke.

"Bring the gurglet, Doll." Walking to its dark corner, Doll brought out the sizzling jug, which had evidently been waiting for just such an occasion.

Robbie twisted off the hole-punched lid, then spoke very slowly. "From exactly the same slime," she stared into space, "one of us creates a little castle, while all of the rest are hiding in hovels. One of us finds interest, use or beauty in every single thing that does or doesn't happen around her, while all of the rest see only the swill of life. One alone has discovered that pearls are hiding everywhere." Robbie stood up. "This cider's going to hatch pink elephants if we wait any longer. It's time for a baptism party," she announced with a mischievous smile. "Spit! Durn! Hades! Love child! She can't even cuss without gussying it up in frills!"

Everyone looked at Ginny as her paper fan paused and she looked around the room. She shriveled on her bench for she could see it in their shadowed eyes: she'd never really be one of them. She said restroom instead of "can," cigarette instead of "weed." She winced at "my old man" and "shack-up time." At night she coughed when passing darkened trailers. She often laughed, but seldom cared to understand crude jokes. Refinement was as much a part of her as skin. She could not hide the squeaky-clean sound of her words, the innocence in her voice. Her very walk was too naive for this place.

Dramatically, Robbie paused as she held the heavy jug easily aloft on one shoulder. Ginny quickly turned to a new cardboard and nervously started to sketch the happening. Robbie took a long testing swig before sending the jug on its rounds. Quila looked uneasy, observed Bowie. This method of drinking always stirred up something painful that was stuffed down deep inside of her.

Robbie stared into space. "Methinks, we'll call the little stranger –" It was suddenly so quiet that even Bowie could hear the gurgling as Robbie drank again "–Gussy!"

It was so easy, so smooth, so informal. At first Ginny was not really sure. But yes! She really was finally tagged: she belonged. And everyone was clapping. With her silvery sword of a tongue, Robbie had dubbed her. The gurglet made its rounds on the shoulder of every girl. The words might just as well have been, "I christen thee, friend!" Ginny's – no, Gussy's – heart soared, its joyful wing beats throbbed ecstatically in her wrists and visibly warmed her cheeks. Robbie had finally accepted her. Just as she was.

Switching to another peeking gap, Bowie watched Robbie turn on the lights, blow out the candle and happily take things from nooks and niches in her cupboard and icebox.

Doll made a paper sack tray while Robbie divided cheese and inserted toothpicks. Robbie put dabs of peanut butter on crackers and Quila dotted them with raisins. Robbie rinsed grapes, halved them, then arranged everything on a rag inside the tray. One girl sitting on the floor was inspired to strum the guitar that always hung, unused, from her shoulder.

Bowie smiled with anticipation as Quila slyly transferred some whole grapes and raisins to her sleeves. Robbie was in a rare, happy mood: her nostrils flared like a fine horse in a wild wind. Gussy was out of cardboard, so she just sat back on her bench. So what, said the smile on her face: This is my very own christening party and I am determined to enjoy it.

Spade quivered as Robbie sat down to open a can of sardines. The cat jumped from Doll's lap to the floor and leaped up beside Robbie. Robbie stroked Spade's fur the wrong way, tweaked her ear and put her outside. She rinsed her hands, separated the fish into bite-sized pieces, threw away the ice cream stick, and handed the can to Quila for toothpicks.

"I like any animal but a cat," growled mood dampened Robbie. "Take, take! Never give!" If anything could oust Gussy now, her eyes lowered, it would be Robbie's suspicion of being used.

From then on, Gussy appeared at the Den, not in jeans and a shirt, Bowie noted, but in her old faded skirt, with the peasant blouse worn outside of it. From so many washings and constant borrowings, there was an unplanned fringe on the skirt's now much shorter bottom, and Gussy's pretty knees were beginning to peek. Gussy ate more sparingly now. But slyly she dropped pieces of bread, crackers, grapes or whatever else would not leave a telltale signpost, into several flower-patterned patch pockets which now held stubby pencils, pieces of charcoal in a matchbox, old can labels and sizes of cardboard.

Bowie watched intently as Gussy's days now shortened up and richened greatly. Her trailer was overflowing with stacks and stacks of sketches. She was having a tough time keeping cardboard and can labels ahead of her drawings.

The hub of each day now was Robbie's trailer – newspaper, theater, club, and café. Like a belled clock were those clanking keys as they tolled the time of the morning coffee klatch, thought Bowie, as, eyes closed on his furry bed, he waited for the smell of ready coffee. It was always the same: the trip to the sink to dump used grounds into the trashcan, to swirl the metal basket with its coffee dregs down the drain (along with dog hairs, the smell of foul diapers and rancid grease), then the fast swish of the pot itself, and the refill with fresh water. Last, was the clanking of Robbie's keys going back to the Den. Coffee was on and the Den began to fill with females. In minutes Gussy's stomach could stop grinding, her nausea would settle down, conversation would be rich and stimulating, the world would be tolerable again – and Bowie could lose himself in the lives of other people for yet another day.

Robbie's Den gave a cycle, a daily expectation in the midst of monotony. Outside Robbie's window Bowie waited, tied his hair back in a cooler way, and smoked. He began to halfway listen, for, as often happened while the coffee was perking or being poured, Robbie was first sharing a brief rundown and comment on national and world news.

As usual, noted Gussy as she sketched, Robbie was being too sharing with her meager earnings. The pigeonholes that made up her cupboards had today, as often, produced some dividable everyday item or exotic food, about which Robbie seemed to know the entire natural history. Sometimes she sprinkled a spice into the coffee and gave the enchanted drinkers even more of a peek into that spice's background. Usually Robbie didn't ask how each girl wanted her coffee served. The first cup often had milk and sugar in it, and that was that: the girls needed the extra nutrition and energy, Robbie seemed to be thinking.

Now Robbie was sprinkling ginger into all of the cups before pouring coffee. Each girl smelled her cup with delight, while Gussy captured at the bottoms of her sketches fascinating new tidbits that flowed from Robbie's lips.

Robbie knew every obvious and obscure holiday that had ever been observed, thought Gussy (and many that only existed in her mind). One day she declared it was "Nobody Can Cuss Day!" Everyone roared at her announcement, but no one was allowed to cuss (in ordinary words) without the forfeit of a cigarette, or an order to leave the Den.

Every klatch was an occasion now when Doll was home. Not only tenants and neighbors were attracted, but odd characters from the beach, the pier or The Joint down the street, where Robbie sometimes strummed her bass and Doll often sang for tips.

But there were no men.

Always females observed Gussy. Of any race or color. Sometimes, like today, they would even be sitting on top of each other, glad for the tiniest space in the Den.

Some were beef-witted cows caring for nothing at the time, just drifting mindlessly through life. Some were skinny as shoestrings and just as lifeless. Their hair was too short and mannish or too long and straggly. They were dirty, untidy, seemed homeless, carried "logs" on their shoulders, swore, and smelled like booze. Mostly, the girls wore men's jeans and shirts, and were known only by nicknames. Gussy scribbled at the bottoms of her sketches: Tex, Shag, Trash, Dago, Frisco, Chi, Philly, Stray, Arkie, Too-Tall, Butte, Charlie and such.

Their eyes were furtive, their stomachs bottomless. Like addicted moths around Robbie's intriguing flame, they were constantly drawn, thought Gussy again and again. She constantly sketched and shaded with her fingers, while Robbie maneuvered among them like an entertainer working the crowd, making them laugh, touching them briefly.

The girls often had tattoos somewhere and Gussy had a whole series of their crude homemade pictures hurriedly sketched on the backs of can labels.

Common as weeds, most of them were. But once in a great while, Robbie coaxed a seemingly budless girl into surprising bloom. Robbie would ask the girl what she wanted to do in life. Then Robbie pointed out that the girl already had the basic qualifications for her goal. Her last question was always the same. "Why are you wasting time HERE, when you could be in school?" These few never stuck around very long, but everyone sensed somehow that now they were "headed somewhere." The others – average, mediocre girls – Robbie slyly studied, until somewhere she found a vague little asset with which she could pleasantly surprise the girl, by innocently sharing it aloud with the rest.

"How can you stand such riffraff, Robbie?" Gussy had asked one day, when only she and Robbie were left alone in the Den. "The way they dress, the way they smell."

"You really do have a mania for dressing things up, don't you?" mocked Robbie. "If a person wants 'dressing up,' she'll find her own time, her own style. Besides," slowly Robbie blew out a match, "some people are very ridiculous dressed up as society would have them.

"It took me a long time to learn that, Gussy. No matter how we dress, act or think, there really is room, somewhere, for every one of us." Robbie poured them both more coffee. "The trouble is, we don't realize that it's an extra special room made for each individual with his own set of peculiarities and humble talents."

Robbie had tapped a can of cloves over both of their cups and stirred. "You know, if we could peek into each other's agony, we could never judge."

Truly, thought Gussy tenderly, if one of the girls were dog-eared, pigeon-toed and giraffe-necked, Robbie would still think of her as basically quite an interesting animal and would find room for her somewhere in the cramped Den.

Until she asked questions.

"Why haven't you ever married, Robbie?" (Some asked questions that the regular tenants would never voice, even if they were dying of curiosity.) And the clicking, snapping, peeling or shelling that Pug was always doing would increase in tempo.

"Ha! You _are_ blind!" Robbie would pale or flinch, but never blush.

Or they'd try to catch her, "Roberta?" they'd insinuate, when her curly hair fell endearingly into her eyes.

"Real friends never ask," said Robbie as she pushed her hair aside, cracked her knuckles or took a long draw on her cigarette.

"Whadaya do with those long coils of cellophane that you're always weavin'?"

"Oh, you can do a lot of things with a coil like this." Robbie showed them a purse she was making for Pug. Or suddenly she'd grab the bold questioner with a cellophane coil around her neck. She'd tighten it, until the offender gasped. "You can do a lot of things with a chain like this," she would calmly repeat. Gagging, the girl left hurriedly to seldom return.

Some made the mistake of touching Robbie. But Robbie seemed to actually suffer at bodily contact like an old one with rheumatic arthritis, thought Bowie outside, as he took a deep swallow of wine and patiently waited for something new to see or hear.

Witless, most of the girls spoke spasmodic, ill-timed clichés and generalities, or merely echoed Robbie's viewpoints. Whatever was heavy sank to the depths of most of their shallow minds. Only the watered-down, trite things leaked out at mouth-level.

Some spoke timidly, with no conviction at all.

"Speak up!" Robbie would finally bellow. "We all need practice in sharing. Ideas should not be stillborn," she would add when someone, aside from Gussy or Quila, would make a provocative statement.

Today, Doll had suddenly left. Robbie had soon sampled everything within the small sweep of these careless minds. Like looking for non-existent pearls, Gussy thought as she added faces to penciled oysters on her paper. The talk became too boring, and since Robbie had no incentive to plan, she stopped the conversation with a yawn. "Ad nauseam, ad nauseam," she sighed and retired to her bedroom for a nap. From then on, Quila took over with her insidious cards and carefully plotted fortune telling.

As he seemed to be doing more often lately, Bowie sighed in disappointment, then made his way back to the storeroom. Hoping that Doll wouldn't stay away too long, he drank himself into a stupor in order to sleep away the endless boredom.

20. Holding Her Seat

That night Bowie had nothing to trade, so he watched through peepholes in Quila's trailer as she sat at her candlelit table practicing card skills. Only Bowie and Robbie knew that Quila's flowing outer sleeves were hiding secret inner sleeves with convenient elastic at the wrists. Secretly she could shove a card up into the loose, drooping edge of an outer sleeve and into the gripping inner one. Then, even if she shook her sleeve, the card had vanished.

Tonight she handled certain cards with greasy fingers and carefully spattered drops of strong tea in chosen places. Bowie grimaced, remembering a player who got close enough to study the cards. Quila coughed in the girl's face and began to violently scratch herself. But there was nothing new here, so Bowie decided to sleep beneath the wagon, entwined with the warmth of Mange.

The next morning when Gussy entered the Den, Doll was still not there. A fresh mixture of characters was sitting around for Quila to work upon, and Robbie was outside unstopping sinks again. Word sure got around fast, thought Gussy, that Robbie was a soft touch and always good for free snacks and novel entertainment. But, Gussy paused in her drawing and looked around; of all the trailer tenants only Quila, Pug, Mala, Fay Rose and Doll remained as permanent Den guests.

As she was sketching her, Gussy wondered again why Fay Rose had lasted so long. Fay was always coughing and holding a fist against her chest as though it were ready to fly apart. Instinctively, Gussy knew that Mala had been ousted for a while, because her scratchy voice blasted and damned at everything that touched upon her miserable life, until Robbie's nerves were raw. But to Gussy's ears the shoddy thinking and tuneless voice of Fay were much harder to bear. Fay could never stimulate curiosity. Yet here, as with Bowie, Pug and Quila, there seemed to be some senseless loyalty, sympathy and protectiveness.

Amidst the fast turnover, Gussy began to feel like a modern-day Scheherazade, prolonging her own inevitable fate.

"How can you draw in this darkness?" they would ask.

"Just impressions," Gussy would reply.

But at night Bowie watched her transfer sketches to larger cardboards that she kept cutting from boxes found in the trash yard. Before shading original sketches, Gussy studied them with a chip from a broken magnifying glass, for hidden among the penciled hair strands, in eye wrinkles and clothing folds were tucked Robbie's verbal gems: quips, toasts, new words and ideas to look up – clues to the assurance of Gussy's daily welcome at the Den.

Then, to the backs of old envelopes Gussy transferred her bits of information. She poked holes in the left margins and tied the little scrap of a book together with knotted-together shoelaces. Page-by-page, she began a long plod through the big dictionary, adding footnotes and embellishments to the little diary that largely rolled from Robbie's tongue. As well, she added page numbers from the dictionary concerning any information pertaining to common foods that Robbie might be interested in. And often she thought the same thought: did anyone else ever realize that Robbie was using food to lure females back to her Den again and again until they could soak up enough warmth, encouragement and self-esteem to possibly break out of their own cocoon of lonely, hopeless misery?

Here in this odd diary, Gussy also recorded the day's events, her feelings and things that she had learned, felt or read about that day. As she wrote, Bowie listened, for out loud she shared her little entries with Holly and the darkness.

She's a sly one, Bowie smiled, for never a hint or a reference dropped from Robbie's lips that wasn't captured by Gussy in fine lines of her sketches. Sometimes, in exchange for enough of Lolli's discarded pop bottles, Gussy bought some preferred tidbit that Robbie had mentioned and casually included it in the coffee klatch. She also spent a lot of time now at the library.

And, like Robbie, Gussy made the most of simple occasions. That's where the others fail, Bowie thought. He snuffed a butt in a seam of the little gray trailer, stood up and stretched. Except for Quila and Gussy, other girls seldom added anything, tangible or otherwise, to the gatherings. But Robbie didn't seem to care anymore, as long as Doll was in the Den occasionally, and the girls were fed, happy and mentally stimulated. The day, itself, was all that Robbie lived for; she seemed to have no other goals or ambitions.

Gussy had also observed that Robbie had an appetite for odd facts, interesting in themselves, but of no practical use. Whenever an icebreaker was desperately needed, Robbie soon came to know that Gussy's memoried list could be depended upon.

Instead of going to the toilet, Gussy often hurried to her trailer where the diary and the dictionary were always open on her table. There she looked up a word or stretched out on her bed to hopefully think up something mental or material to add to the daily klatch.

Thus, Gussy not only held her seat at the Den, but also edged past Quila in Robbie's esteem.

21. Doll and Juju

Doll was home again! That afternoon she was the last to leave Robbie's trailer with Spade still nestled in her arms. As Doll opened the screen door, a child in a filthy nightgown seemed to blow away from the stepping box.

"Like a blighted black rose," thought Doll, as Juju scurried away. One hand was full of dust curls, butts and raisins hurriedly scooped from Robbie's doorstep. From the other hand streaked her reddish-black rag. Frowning suspiciously back at Doll, the child ran squarely into Fay Rose who grabbed her by the hair and pulled her to the men's shower.

"She smells like bilge water. Shower her!" Fay shouted into the Chips as she shoved the child inside.

Doll waited until Fay was well out of sight. She put the cat down, then went to open the shower door. Juju was cringing in a corner of the narrow stall, for Doll had interrupted one Chip and the proof of his shame dribbled yellow from Juju's curly bangs. Doll turned off the shower, grabbed a handful of each boy's hair and shook him.

"Promise me," she whispered furiously, "whenever the child's to be bathed, you'll call me! Whenever I'm home," she added. "If ever you don't, you little sons-of-a-bitch, I'll sic that old witch, Quila, on you!" She grabbed their little noses and shook them back and forth. "She'll put a giant hex on you, that'll make your noses longer than baseball bats! And your weenies–!" They jerked away from her, crossed their knees, and held their bare crotches. "–they'll shrivel up into shreds!" She pushed them both hard against the concrete wall, picked up Juju, and slammed out the door.

Bowie watched from under Quila's wagon as Doll, enraged, rinsed out one of the sinks, ran it half-full of warm water, pulled off Juju's soiled nightgown, removed safety pins and threw the muddy, dripping diaper into the trash can. Angered as her fingers caressed boniness, Doll tenderly washed the festered little body with her gentle hands and lather from a soap chip. As the child soaked in clean water, in another basin Doll rinsed and scrubbed the nightgown and the ragged black rag, using Pug's washboard and her bar of brown laundry soap. She wrung the clothes tightly and hung them on the line.

It was pure delight to dry the child, exploring with her own worn towel the tiny finger pads, the soft little ear channels, the dimpled knees and elbows. It was the very first time that Doll had ever bathed or really touched a child.

Dried now, Juju stood on the floor wrapped in Doll's towel, as water drained from the sink. Doll answered the insistent telephone, watching the child while she talked. Juju had leaned her forehead against the row of laundry sinks, and though Juju looked happy, she was watching her own big tears as they plopped into a puddle on the floor.

Why, I've never seen her cry before, thought Doll, no matter how hard Fay has spanked her. I've – everybody – has always thought that she was dumb, unfeeling. "Fay's not home," lied Doll, slamming down the receiver.

Full force, Doll ran new water, bubbling over soap flakes that someone had left on the washhouse bench. She hung the towel out in the sunshine while she bathed the child again. This time she washed her hair, leisurely, carefully, as a continuous tear ran down her own cheek. Doll played with the beautiful soapiness of Juju's curls, making peaks and swirls and twists, before she rinsed it. While the child soaked in clean water, Doll dried her hair, then patiently untangled it with her own brush, delighting in a springiness that had never been there before.

Bowie watched and thought. Each curl is a joy to unwind, as if Doll were the very first explorer on a rain-fresh grassy meadow. Quickly, he needed to erase some happy memory, and almost drowned himself with a long, hasty gulp of forgetfulness.

Now Doll unrolled, brushed, and caressed with her eyes every single curl. She pulled each one out to its farthest, then laughing, she let it bounce right back again, like she often did with Robbie's curl.

When Doll finally decided to halt the brushing, it was only because it was getting dusk. The long bath had soaked and soothed away the rash, but Juju's skin was becoming wrinkled and she was shivering. Doll's towel was old and threadbare, easy to tear in half for a diaper. With the other half she finished drying Juju, then put over her head the slightly damp, but sun-warmed and whitened gown.

As she had always wanted to do, she tied the ragged sleeve edges into little knots, then tied the stretched back hem into a big knot so Juju could walk without tripping.

At last, although reluctantly, Doll handed Juju her clean black rag, and the child crushed it to her cheek. But it smelled like Doll now. Of sunshine, fresh air and soap. There was no hint of Fay within the ragged silk.

Sitting on the bench, Doll cradled the damp little body in her arms, smoothed the fragrant curly head, and hummed a lullaby while the astonished little Juju fell asleep.

22. Fay Rose

"Bowie, there must be somethin' spicy about Fay Rose," urged Quila as she poured one cup of dark tea slowly, as if it were precious. She trailed a spoonful of sugar from a narrow cloth bag to her cup. While the tea cooled, she sat with eyes closed, saving them. Her other hand was rubbing a square blue sapphire, which she often wore around her neck for clear thinking.

"Were Fay more discriminatin' Juju's black-haired sire would be somethin' to really dwell upon, Bowie." She peered out between bony knuckles. Was she wrong, or did his jaw tighten ever so slightly?

"Fay lies in mud, how can she fall farther?" He looked eagerly at the stew pot.

"Aye, but even a scarlet lady has 'er pride. I could take a long time to tear it down."

"How do you blacken a crow?" he snarled.

"That's yer problem!" she stood up, and patting her bosom where she kept the teasing roll of leather, she flung open the door for him to carry out his empty, complaining stomach.

Soon Bowie was behind Fay's trailer hidden from the street by the crumbling front wall of the park. With the piece of wire that he always carried, Bowie had long ago widened the tiny hole in the wall of Fay's bedroom. He had tied a rag on the end of a stick to block the hole when he wasn't using it. Two enlarged window slits helped when Fay was out of sight. He lit a flattened, half-smoked butt that had been stuffed into a trailer seam. He pulled out the chink rag and settled himself to siphon what seemed to be useless fuel for Quila's barter. Fay was rummaging in a bag of clothes at the foot of her bed.

Fay Rose got her clothes by the pound, it seemed. Her closet bulged with them. It was often past dusk as she reached beneath her bed where she kept the newest bag of used clothing that Flo weeded out from her second-hand store every month. Handing Fay the bulging bag, Flo also tucked inside a few feathers, belts, ribbons and gaudy jewelry at the last minute (God-awful things, no doubt, that hurt Flo's prim little eyes, Bowie smirked). In exchange Fay often swept the floors, folded, dusted or rearranged displays.

But Fay was practical. Or was she just lazy and meanly discriminating, Bowie debated. She and the boys wore the chosen items first, until they were soiled or sweaty. Then Fay stuffed them into bags behind her trailer. She never washed them before she brought some inside, to crudely cut up for diapers and shove into a drawer. Sometimes she was in a hurry and used the dirty clothes uncut, just as they were. Later she sacked up the soiled, smelly "diapers," dumped them with the garbage or burned them with her trash.

Rummaging through a new bag now, Fay brought out a pair of boy's pants. If she folded the waist down and used suspenders, they'd fit now. She pulled out a boy's tee shirt and held it up. It would come to their knees, but it would do. She folded the items into the boys' drawer. She held up a blue dress that was about Juju's size. Quickly she ripped the seams and stuffed pieces into the diaper drawer. With a sick feeling, Bowie realized he had never seen Juju in a dress. She only wore strange diapers and a dirty nightgown.

Fingering through the bag again, Fay felt the warmth of velvet, heard the rustle of taffeta, and her eyes lit up as they caught sight of shiny satin. A blouse, a bright skirt and a silk sash Fay took from the bag. First dampening them with water flipped from her fingertips, she barely ironed them all on a crudely padded board that now slanted from her dresser and down to the bed. When finished with an item, she proudly fanned it out on the bedspread to dry.

Bowie shook his head sadly. Fay delighted in the complexity of her costumes. She had the same childlike imagination of a four-year-old playing dress-up. But also, Fay had a grown-up flair, Bowie conceded, for putting things together: adding a belt and blousing a top that was too big, adding a jacket or shawl to cover, when something looked too small.

Fay is a night-bloomer. A dead stick she is in the daytime, thought Bowie as he lit a new cigarette and waited for her to sashay to and from the shower, still in her flimsy negligee, tossing behind her the only thing she really had going for her: a thick mop of red hair. Sleeping, smoking, reading simple novels, dipping into the candy box beneath her bed, Fay squandered daytimes. After dusk she blossomed, always breathtaking as a one-night-blooming cactus. Close-up though, it was easy to tell how hard she was hoping the new costume, brightened hair, delicately curved eyebrows and unnaturally widened lips would be noticed, and not the frequent hacking cough that shook her flat, childlike chest.

Bowie pillowed his head on bumpy clothes bags, swigged a bit, then closed his eyes while he waited. Often, Bowie followed Fay when her cheeks were ablaze without help from her rouge pot, when her eyes were overcast with pain. On those nights she left her children alone and walked beside the sea wall, sometimes as though listening for spirit voices, sometimes like she were taunting some seething, waiting monster beyond the crashing waves. Wildly then, she searched faces of aimless walkers like herself, or sailors and their girls, who giggled or were insulted by her scrutiny. But she trembled strangely when dark-haired men happened to walk past her.

Fay loved the sea. It brought tall blond sailors stepping out of buses, rushing into arms. But always there seemed to be one for whom there were no arms, who accepted the invitation in Fay's eyes, the ritualistic promise she whispered before he followed her.

In half an hour, Fay had showered and refaced herself. Her bosom was filled and inviting. She was ready for the evening's adventure. Daintily she stepped down from her bedroom door. Kicking Spade from her path, she sailed out of the park.

If she weren't first seen, she'd be heard or smelled. Her face was painted chalkstone. Her scant breasts stretched big and taut now under green velvet. As she walked down the street, her slim hips tossed around themselves a flowered skirt tied at her tiny waist with a scarlet sash. Her hair was a red-brown foxy tail flirting along behind her, ready to lure new prey back to her lair. Tinkling bracelets hooped her wrists. She reeked of a kitchen-smelling perfume – so unlike the calm, faceless, phantom girl that dwelt in Bowie's darkened mind.

Quickly, Bowie drained the bottle in his hand, then dug around in dirt humps until he found another one, half gone already. He took a long swallow for he could smell Her materializing from the murk of his mind, as pure and exciting as fresh rain. For makeup she would wear but the flush of a campfire after dark or a summer's dawn on her cheeks. His phantom never craved to adorn herself with lasting conventional jewelry. Her ornaments were short-lived as a day moth: a purple aster tucked into her hair, or a halo of wild daisies that he, himself, had fashioned. But her eyes were becoming visible, dark as mountain berries, and as usual they would be juicing up and ready to overflow. He drank the rest of the bottle in one gasping rush. With his head buried among the lumpy bags, he fell into restless sleep. He'd dump the empty bottles later and bury tonight's expected new one under Fay's bedroom window.

Within the hour Fay returned from the Plaza, and Bowie soon awakened groggily at the sound of clinking shells beckoning Fay's back door to open. For some odd reason, Fay kept a lidless shoebox filled with seashells nailed beneath her back window. The Chips and Juju's bottom sides remembered well by now that children never, never touched Fay's seashells. Her patrons just took a handful out, threw them against the back window, and most of them were caught beneath it in the same box. Hearing the shells, Fay automatically locked the door to the kitchen, dimmed the lights in her bedroom and cranked up the record player.

"Ma'am, yer enuf ta stagger a preacher, within a inch of pearly gates! That ya are," sighed the sailor. So young, eager, awkward and away from home for the first time, groaned Bowie. But Fay had a knack with sailors. Mingled with dregs of a French accent, the soft flattery and dreamy atmosphere that Fay created were cool hands on ship-fevered brows.

Bowie flattened himself against Fay's trailer, so he could see past the curtain to watch as she took a birthday candle from its box. Bowie thought he had finally figured out the daytime use of the candles: perhaps it took the time of a candle's span (about fifteen minutes) for the Chips to get to the corner store and back. But what strange reasoning made the ritual necessary at night, when stores were closed and children asleep, he could not understand.

Daintily Fay settled onto the bedspread like a butterfly on a thistle tuft. Her orange floor-length lounging skirt was split clear up to one bare thigh, but there were false flowers at her high black neckline. Inviting as her bosom might be on parade, in her bedroom Fay never permitted any petting of her upper parts; some kind of bodice wear always clothed her in bed. She lit the candle, snapped off the dim light, and Bowie could see only flickering shadows.

"Ya don't smell lak other gals, ma'am," the sailor boy was entranced. "It's a smell lak ah gits when a sailor shouts 'Land'! Lak upturned earth, 'n' ripe fields, all in one whiff." He paused, "Mostly though, ya smell jes lak ma Mama's cookin'!"

He must have felt of Fay's bony arms or heard her flat hungry stomach complaining. Before he left he said naively, "Ah wish there was money ta leave with ya. There's only mah ticket fer home, this time."

Fay snapped on the light and smiled a resigned smile. She reached up and unfastened a campaign pin from his breast.

"A glad good bargain, Miss Fay," he said in approval, "somethin' ta remember Plunkett by." She handed him his hat, and when he had left, she reached under her bed and dropped the campaign pin along with all the others, inside of an almost full cigar box. Then Fay traipsed, as always with her little satchel, to the shower, as with every trip, pulling out another ravel of her reputation.

Plunkett returned often, bearing bouquets, milk, fresh eggs, bacon, apples, and a tender proposal. "Please wait fer me?" he pleaded, slipping bills beneath her pillow.

But then one night, before Plunkett's candle darkened, seashells sounded again upon the window, and another man's impatient voice was at the door. Crushed, Plunkett tiptoed past the sleeping children, and closed Fay's door for the last time.

Bowie had finally come to realize that Fay was particular about her men. She could have enticed any stray sea dog as he ambled past her on blue land legs, but just any sailor wouldn't do.

The pattern was always the same. Shells beckoning at the rear window, the back door opening silently, a few minutes of music and candlelight. Again the door opened, and a young man walked quickly down the street, looking sheepish and pulling at his clothes as though shoved out before he was ready to leave. As he walked through the darkness, smoothing down his hair, the man would look back, then take the folded cap from his waistband and place it on light hair. Each was about the same size, the same coloring, the same build. The Chips could be two shavings off any one of them.

Why, if a black-headed sailor so much as touched her doorknob, Fay'd scream like a ravished spinster, thought Bowie, snuffing out his cigarette in a windowsill crack. For some reason, Bowie decided to keep this fact for himself.

"Would you mind if I'd call you Woodee'?" he'd hear Fay always whisper when the light snapped out and the record began. "It's my very favorite name."

Stretching his cramped legs out sideways as he sat at her tiny table, almost word for word each night that week, Bowie repeated the scenes, the actions to Quila. She must be happy with him, for now, beside the tasty stew, she always dipped out a teaspoonful of her precious bacon grease that she kept in a can at the very back of her warm stove. And then she spread its tasty flavor out across his hunk of homemade bread. Often now, she even served canned peaches for his dessert.

Bowie decided to give more time to viewing Fay's bedroom at night.

23. Suzette

"Su-ze-ette."

Fay cocked her head but kept on curling bangs. Did she imagine someone calling in the twilight? It couldn't be Woody; he was gone forever. He used to throw new shells against her bedroom window. Afterwards, he'd tell her and the babies about wonderful places he had gathered them. The only way she could live without him was to keep on pretending. She sighed, finished curling the last bangs and began to brush the back of her damp hair.

My name is Suzette, she used to insist, but that was so long ago. "Fay Rose" sounded much more glamorous. There must be hundreds of Suzettes, but who ever heard of Fay Rose? So she clung to Robbie's nickname and repolished it with a French twist of her tongue.

Sailors didn't know Suzette and Fay could forget she ever existed. Except when the candle was lit and "their" record was playing.

"Su-ze-ette?" Nobody else could say it exactly that way. But Fay just shrugged and kept on brushing. The name that inhabited her mind like a mirage, when she really listened was always gone. She had wasted too many nights already-wanting Woody, pretending it was his shells, his candles, his body again and again on her bed. When daylight brought reality, she always vowed to stop. Yet, when darkness came and filled her emptiness with panic, she knew that she would pretend again.

"Su-ze-ette." Sometimes the name seemed to rise from sea mist, a sad, barely audible, three-parted melody, beckoning to Fay irresistibly. It was then that she loved to walk alone by the seawall, allowing faint, distant murmurs to pulse along with her heart. She loved to taste the seaspray, pretending it to be the peanut-salty kiss of Woody on her lips.

Sometimes the name whispered out from sailors mulling around the bus stop. Glimpsing a blond profile, tall, straight as a sugarpine, Fay would run frantically into the wall of blue. Arms from everywhere would block her. Sometimes, as the blond was swallowed up, another sailor sidled up. "You can call ME Woodee, Fay Rose!" If the sailor were dark-haired she'd shiver and run away; if he were blonde, tall and handsome, he seemed to know somehow that he could follow her.

"Suzette! My hands are full!" shouted a live, but groggy voice from the past. Fay froze, ran her fingers through warm bangs and pulled a diaper rag from the bottom drawer.

Bowie's ears perked up as he awoke beneath Quila's wagon: a stranger's voice at Fay's trailer. For days, Doll had been gone and the Den locked. Doll's Song was driving everyone crazy. There was nothing of interest to see or to hear in the whole park. Bowie's head and senses were empty vacuums eager to be filled. Shadowlike, he left Quila's wagon to take up his watch on the streetside of Fay's trailer. He pulled out the chink rag.

Fay grabbed the naked, shivering Juju, patiently waiting, wet from the hurried shower the Chips had grudgingly given. She threaded a soiled tee shirt between the child's legs and pinned it. "Go far away!" Fay whispered furiously. She pinched the child hard, twisted her tender skin, shoved her rudely out the back door.

In a panic Fay smoothed the bed, fluffed the pillows, pushed the box of military ribbons farther under the bed, loosened the biggest blob of candle wax, dropped it into the wastebasket and dumped the saucer into its drawer. Shaking, she grabbed the brush and weakly ran it through her hair. The front screen squeaked open and slammed shut.

She touched the hammering of her heart as a tall, blond, sea-worn-and-freckled sailor stooped through the doorway, dumped packages on the bed and hid the telltale hollow. Lifting her long clean hair, he wove his arms beneath it. "God! Still the same," he breathed.

The screendoor slammed again and the Chips loudly rummaged cupboards. Eating peanuts, Woody stooped back through the doorway. "Freckles big as barnacles!" He reeled against the doorframe. "Eyes, portholes to the sea! Straight as sugarpines! Seaweed hair! Can't deny 'em!" He opened his arms, but the Chips turned away from his heavy breath.

Woody grabbed them both and dizzily twirled around. But the bedroom door was shut and locked. "Give me a minute, Woodee," pleaded Fay. "I want everything to be perfect!"

Bowie scurried to a kitchen peephole. "Ahoy, slivers off me old block!" Sitting the boys on the unmade couch bed, he ruffled their hair. "Jamie and Lindsey," he clucked.

"Nope! Our names is Chip! Quit breathin' all over us! Whadja bring?"

Fay's bolt rattled and Bowie rushed back to the chink hole. The Chips poured into the bedroom, over the bed, began tearing paper and ripping string. Pillow covers from all over the world, a bolt of silk, gaudy jewelry, exotic souvenirs, boxes of those sickening chocolate cherries. (Bowie had onetime watched as Fay gave both the boys a chocolate-covered cherry that she had painted with iodine.) The Chips ransacked through everything twice.

"Peanuts!" they said in disgusted unison, lifting from the pile two small sacks, evidently the only things intended for them. "I liked the last one better," complained one Chip. "Uncle Plunkett always brought–" Woody hadn't heard, he was lifting packages onto the dresser. "Now off with you," he cried, shooing them out the back door, then locking it.

Woody turned around and for the first time in six years got a full view of Suzette.

She always had been a seductive girl, with that long silky "hook" of red hair and that come-hither walk of hers. Woody liked his women slim and striking – but this?

This woman moved with affectedly elegant curves, a mockery of that graceful beauty she had once been. She swished a candy-striped skirt, surrounding him with an odd suffocating odor. Her too-long scarlet nails fingered a ruffle around the neck of a star-blotched blouse. On her skinny arms, like skewer sticks, bracelets were strung, and she jangled with every gesture. Clipped onto each ear with a bobby pin was a satin rosette. She twirled around. "Like me?" she asked in a twangy falsetto, a honeyed, sticky voice for men.

"God, you look like a flag!"

"Thank you, Woody," she said with pathetic pride. "This always was your favorite skirt and blouse. Rosettes," she touched her ears, "are from our pillows. I've saved them in tissue. For when you came back, someday."

But all together? She was gaudy, grotesque, blowzy and cheap. It must be some joke. He had had to get storming drunk to even come here and try to face his past, as the chaplain insisted. Now he wished he had swigged even more.

"Well, I've seen you, how's about unrigging?" He reached for her buttons.

"I'll do it, Cherie." She pulled away. "Undress. Lie down and rest a bit. Turn your head away and close your eye." She turned down the bedspread.

Finally, her cool fingers were fluttering through his blondness, slowly over his eyes, mouth and neck, and down beyond his quivering chest. "It's been so long," she sighed.

Though terribly scratchy now, their favorite record was playing. Lights were dim, like he liked them. He felt a surge of old anticipation as his hands caressed her once-familiar body. But now she felt curveless, fragile as a dragonfly, her negligee like useless gauzy wings.

He trembled. All of her charms were phony now. Without the plumpness of padding the only thing left to feel was horrible pity. "You're still a stunner, Suzette," he lied, then turned his head from her sudden coughing.

"I don't look the same. I haven't felt well."

Trying to forget tawdry bangs reeking of a too-hot curling iron, he closed his bleary eyes and held to his lips the beckoning "finger" of her hair, that fragrant hook that always used to beach him. But it was hard to remember the girl he had left behind. Just the look of her used to rattle his thighs with desire; now they merely quivered to dash away.

"I've tried everything," she sighed.

"Pine tar is an old-fashioned remedy for many things," he said softly. "Remember, you used to call me your sugar pine, said my old 'pine tar' could cure anything. But wait."

From packages heaped on the dresser Woody lifted strings of seashells. "For my mermaid's neck!" He took a box of candles from his pocket. "Here, my little crepe-suzette," he whispered. Pulling her hair aside, he nuzzled her neck then turned from stifling perfume that lingered. "Light up for me, Suzette. Let's see if it still takes but a candlespan – for both of us!" Bowie put the chink rag back into the hole, sat on the ground – bored, and lit a cigarette.

The squeak and sway of the darkened trailer meant the doors were locked again, but this time Juju didn't care. Rubbing her leg where Fay's pinch still smarted, she ran to the streetside of the trailer. Bowie barely had time to slither underneath the trailer as Juju climbed over the bags of old clothes. Then, like she had seen her fascinated brothers do, she stood tiptoe on their box and pulled out the rag on the end of a stick. For the very first time she was finally tall enough to peek through the open hole and into the flickering candlelight.

Frantically, Juju jumped down from the box, stumbled over the clothes bags and ran to the Pigpen where the Chips were playing. She put her black rag to the cheek of one Chip, to the cheek of the other, then back to her own tearful cheek and pointed back to Fay's trailer. She took each Chip by the hand and tugged. "She's tryin' ta tell us somethin' about Mama!" cried one twin, as he carefully added another empty can to the tower they were making.

"Won't go 'til ya say it," jeered the other twin. "Say it, or we'll stuff yer rag clean down yer mouth!" "Say it! Mama! Mama! Mama!"

With one desperate jerk Juju pulled away. She ran for the front door of Fay's trailer to try and force it open. But Fay had forgotten to lock it. Before the lazy screen door slammed, Juju had burst through the dark living room and kitchen and into the candlelit bedroom, where the man was pinning her mother to the bed, hurting her! She flicked on the shadeless bulb that Fay only used for tweezing and squeezing. And the evil candlelight was gone...

Astonished at their nakedness, Juju breathlessly shaped her mouth and blurted it out as the twins had urged her to, as though this giant effort might erase the horror in their eyes.

"Mama! Mama! Mama!"

The man now held a pillow before him, but the same evil candlelight seemed to blaze up in his eyes. "Well, I'll be damned!" Juju fumbled with the back door lock and fled.

Woody stared after the black-headed child, at Fay's auburn hair, then back into the mirror. "I'll be double-damned! In my own woodpile!" he said to his reflection. "How many studs have you stabled, Suzette? Don't tell me. It's stamped into your eyes!"

"Only to remember you," she stammered.

"Hell, Suzette, you can't pull a gutter-waif's black curls over my eyes and call it blond! Or memory!" Her arms, revolting tentacles, surrounded him. He pushed her away and began to dress. He had seen it before, that same hopeless fear, that hardened glint in the eyes of loose women from Fiji to Frisco and back again.

Fay sighed, covered herself with the sheet. Who could believe a prostitute had been raped? The fact that she had always been true to him, in the only fashion left to her, seemed unimportant now. She spoke in a faraway voice: "I'm what the wind and tides – and you – have left of me. I tried the factory, cafes, scrubbing even. 'Too frail,' they always said. We had to eat, Cherie, while we waited."

As he quickly dressed, Woody studied the bedroom, remembering.

Suzette was always a stunner, beguiling, bold and sassy in a bedroom. He had met her in a bedroom, in a filthy house down near the border. But her bedroom, unlike the other girls', had been like a boudoir; and Suzette, clean, fragrant and different from all the rest.

Her hair had been a cool swash of seaweed on his ever-hot cheeks. And he intended to marry her, to get her away from it all. He even quit the sea.

The bedroom was the most sumptuous room in whatever dump they lived in. Usually the only room. Suzette needed no other, they never had company; meals were in bed. His leaves were spent painting the town, sampling nightspots, dancing together while everyone stopped to watch. Only the two of them. Until the twins came – uninvited.

Just skinny, forked twigs, nested in blue blankets, not tugging at his heart, but rooting his feet to the land with greedy mouths and naked limbs. And, instead of to Suzette, he turned back to his old, irresistible mistress, the sea.

24. Woody

"The 'salesroom' is in perfect order, but the hell with the rest of the joint!" he shouted as he jerked up his navy pants.

He pulled open a remembered drawer. "New black lace panties!" He ducked into the messy kitchen, opened and slammed a door. "Maggots and mold in the icebox! Smells worse than bilge water!" He opened the cupboards – every one of them. "Nothing to eat but salt, catsup and cans!" He went back to the bed, running his fingers under the bottom edge of it, feeling for the usual box of chocolate cherries. Instead he brought out the cigar box overflowing with Service ribbons.

Cold facts, like Suzette in bright light, clotted together, a gagging scab in his throat. He felt nauseated and a spasm engulfed his body. With sailor pants still unbuttoned on one side, he staggered out of the bedroom door, down the applebox step and over to a corner of the trailer. Oh God, it was there! The symbol that told the exact trailer: a chalked-on white rose that sailors knew, joked about, and always kept renewed without Fay's knowledge.

Returning to Fay's bedroom, he looked at his fingers, at the whiteness of the chalk upon them. "All I noticed when I first got here was that your letters said it was the first trailer in the farthest row.

"You're 'the fey rose', Suzette," he stammered. "'The dying rose" he whispered to himself. He looked desperately around the room, and pulled aside the heavy curtains. "Oh God, the windows <u>are</u> round!" He buried his head in his hands. "This place is a way mark for sailors. They call it the French Porthole." He was hoarsely whispering now, his eyes blank, staring. "Your reputation is as far-flung as sailor spawn. Your name – I've heard it – on drunken tongues from here to Haiti. I just never put it together. I used to think you were trapped, but this is your natural wallow.

It makes absolutely no difference, does it, that you're a mother now?" Fay tried to reply but his hand was up for silence.

Incredulously, he looked around the bedroom. It was exactly like they said: some nook that Neptune would create for a tawdry goddess, its coverlet of green moss, its low green lighting coming from somewhere whenever she desired it. His eyes slid to the deep cup in the bed's center, the heavy door bolt, the dusty netting with cheap pier prizes caught in its strands. He picked up the familiar saucer with hint of layers and layers of wax. He flung it against the wall, shattering it. "So this is what they mean by the 'fifteen-minute-filly.'

"It's all true!" he sobbed. He fingered the bracelets on both of her wrists. "She does clank with jewelry, like a beggar with a clack-dish!" He sniffed her hair and shuddered. "She does use almond flavoring when she can't afford perfume!"

In a cold sweat of fury, laughing and crying at once, he pulled off his pants again. "You've short-changed me, Fay Rose. I've paid you with gifts from all around the world, yet I got no special gift for myself! What shall I order? Everything's a la carte Fay Rose! That's the way you work it, I hear: a stated price for every 'dish'!"

"But I never needed any special dish, remember?" Ignoring her sputters of protest, lunging at her, he pulled off his shorts, pinned her to the bed, and she sobbed with the sudden weight of him.

"Why are you crying? Squeal like a pig, that's what you are!" She shrieked with pain, and he gave a loud series of rising squeals himself, before collapsing.

He redressed quickly and fastened the double row of buttons on his pants. "You've resold yourself one time too often, Suzette," he said to the panting, coughing, whimpering figure on the bed. He smoothed the big collar of his blouse. "Now you belong to no one and to every one, but never again to me!"

"Please stay," she whispered faintly. "It was always you, every one of them."

But he was gone. Like before, the saltiness of his lips was only seafoam, coating her with memory. She licked her lips lightly, then even that was gone. Bowie replaced the chinkrag and slid down onto the dirt, sobbing soundlessly.

Gathering all of the strength left in her, Fay Rose pulled on her negligee and struggled to the door. Like flushed birds, three children scattered into darkness from listening posts. Fay's eyes burned sap-green and bitter, and they were only on Juju.

"I'll yank ya tongueless for speaking," she breathed. "I'll beat ya brainless for peeking!" she sobbed. She drew the strings of shells from around her neck and twirled them in readiness.

25. The Iceman

Syd's old ice truck rumbled into Last Resort. Summer was in a sultry fever, yet black clouds churned in the west. He'd have to hurry with deliveries or a storm would descend before he could be with the children.

Syd made his rounds more often now, mostly because his garden was prolific and needed daily sharing. Slyly, along with ice, Syd tucked vegetables and fruits into the most bare iceboxes, or left flowers in trailers where cheering was more needed than food.

Along this new route, most of the kids were hot, bored and neglected. Syd's coming was the only high spot in their gloomy lives. For kids at Last Resort, especially, did he grieve. Toyless, they played at jackstraws with used matches, made target towers from stacked cans, played kick the can, explored the Pigpen or jumped tirelessly on the old bedspring that was always there. The only time they seemed cared for was when they were hurt. Syd was enough of a veterinarian already to recognize that someone at the park was taking advantage of the slightest cut to practice professional bandaging.

When deliveries were done, Syd looked forward to driving far enough down the driveway to escape the smoldering incinerator. There he sat on the back of his truck making a fist puppet with lipstick and his handkerchief. The puppet talked to children, while Syd handed out chipped ice, jelly glasses of fresh lemonade, or cut-up fruit.

Like flowers from filth, children popped out from everywhere, their faces smiling just for him. He worried especially about the child with the birthmark, who never smiled or talked. Unless the bit of black twitching rag could be counted, eyes were mostly all he saw of her often bruised and filthy body – eyes of deep blue pools staring sadly from behind or underneath some trailer.

"Come out and talk to me, little one," Syd's puppet coaxed in vain. He always left a piece of fruit somewhere near the little ragamuffin's hiding place.

Today, that same scratchy record that was often playing was filling the air with depressing sadness. Without incidence he left ice and fruit at Lambeth's and Pug's.

As usual, he caught Mala in the midst of her revolting assembly line dishwashing. As a puppy licked seven plates, Mala rinsed them in scalding water, dried them with men's shorts and sorted them out on the table again. Syd left apricots in her fruitless icebox.

Leaving Gussy's trailer, Syd felt the Indian's eyes peering at him from one place or another. Perhaps he had lingered too long in Gussy's clean artistic space. Syd had noticed she was forcing the last bit of life from stumps of vegetables, so he tried to leave things that would not interfere with leafy experiments. He tucked cucumbers and ripe cherries into her almost bare, spotless icebox. As always, he took time to admire her newest drawings.

Then back to the truck to grab more ice. He pounded on Fay's trailer again. She out-slept the latest dozer and kept doors locked against her children, who roamed the park and neighborhood looking for handouts. Shades were pulled as though she feared day-blindness. Sometimes Fay straggled to the door, coughing and yawning, shading her eyes, lips smeary, bangs in sweaty strings dangling in her eyes. The back of her hair would be in curlers or flowing like a lazy red "J" over one skinny shoulder. She always seemed repulsed at something about Syd, about his dark hair, especially. Yet Syd knew that Fay was makeable.

He had seen her one evening at the Plaza, tossing her long red hair. Like beckoning bait, it was catching eyes of hungry sailors. Syd lost himself quickly; he was afraid she might acknowledge him. Hurrying away he could hear the tinkling of her many bracelets.

Fay didn't answer today, and since the door was ajar now, Syd delivered without disturbing her. Trying not to breathe, he opened the door of the icebox and left some fresh tomatoes. He pumped water into a dirty cup and left a fragrant short-stemmed rose inside.

Leaving Fay's trailer, he saw a girl with a suitcase arriving. A black cat had raced to meet her and now wound itself through her legs as she walked. The girl's jeans and white shirt were revealing as a feedsack around an egg timer. She glanced at Syd with contempt. So this was the infamous Doll. Syd realized that the child with the big eyes and dirty rag was missing. This beautiful blond girl was searching and calling for her. She hurried around the park knocking, inquiring, calling. The tiresome record suddenly stopped.

She put down her suitcase and began grilling one of the twins. Syd stood watching with one foot on the running board, ready to swing up into the driver's seat.

"Nobody's seen 'er since last night, honest! Don't know where she's at! Lemme go!"

"Don't lie to me, Chip!" Doll shook him, then headed for Fay's trailer.

"Wha' time zit? Wha' day zis?" blubbered Fay as Doll yanked her outside by her hanging sashes. The rush of light blinded Fay as she staggered down the steps, woozy, coughing, confused, her hand shading the sunglare. Like a scarecrow in ruffles, thought Syd.

"Where is she?" Doll shouted, awakening Bowie who had slept the night through under Quila's wagon. "She always runs to meet me. Like Spade. They just know; they sense when I'm coming!" Doll shrilled, standing off from Fay's stale, winey breath. But Fay only glowered in a sullen sort of suspense. Doll grabbed a handful of Fay's curlers, twisting until Fay screamed. "Give it to me straight out, where is she?"

"In the tool room!" Fay howled with pain. "She can talk, the little bitch! Called me 'Mama' right in front of Woody!" Fay sobbed hysterically.

The catch was high on the door, too high for a child to unlock it from the crack inside. As Doll threw open the door, the stench of Juju's filthy diaper was overwhelming. Scrunched in a corner of darkness, Juju's eyes were puddles of misery dribbling down muddy cheeks. Dropping down beside her, Doll scooped her up and crushed the child to her heart. A soft whimper escaped Juju before Doll realized that bloody welts striped the child's legs and arms, that her bare back had been beaten with some sharply studded strap.

A sticky little blood-caked hand patted Doll's arm. Doll was home at last, anything could be endured. It crystallized in Doll's mind, how much Juju had come to mean to her.

Fay jerked the child from Doll's arms, "I'll care for my own, thank-you!" she said flippantly, trying to hide the child's wounds with her negligee.

Last night, in anger, delirium and pain, it had been hard for Fay (in her high-heeled slippers) to catch up with Juju. Whenever Fay came close enough, she had used the strings of shell from around her neck to reach out farther to do the striking, until finally they had broken and pieces flew around the park. Fay had finally grabbed the child and locked her in the tool room to deal with later. Exhausted, Fay had barely made it back to her trailer without passing out. She had drained a bottle of wine while putting a few curlers in her sweat-soaked hair. Exhaustion and sleep had finally won out over pain in her chest and despair in her heart.

Fidgeting under Fay's tight grasp Juju retched now, and spewed out all of the nourishment she had found in the tool room – wads and wads of chewed toilet paper.

In slow measured words, Doll began to seethe. "This I just can't stomach!" she screamed. "You'd sooner feed your sailor slot-hounds, than your own sweet flesh and blood – you, you wharf rat!" Doll balled up her fist and knocked Fay sprawling against the washhouse.

The backfall left Fay breathless, but forced the last of the sleep and wine from her brain. She scraped up a handful of dirt, flung it in Doll's eyes, then ran. Now everyone got a view of the squall, for Doll chased Fay clear around the park, until one of Fay's slippers twisted and gave her ankle a painful wrench. Stalling for time, Fay kicked her slippers off and flung them at Doll's face, but she dodged them both. Panting, Doll stepped back to gather energy, but her whole body flamed up at the sight of Juju retching again.

Doll plunged at Fay with fists and feet and even her head. Catching Fay on her knees, Doll jumped on her back and rubbed her face in the dirt. "Wallow, you sand-hog, you ship infester!" Jumping up finally, Fay's eyes rested a moment on Doll's forgotten suitcase. She punched Doll hard in the belly to gain a little time.

Watching from under Quila's trailer, Bowie was the only one who didn't strain to see the contents as Fay flung them out, one-by-one from the suitcase, while Doll gasped and held her stomach. There was nothing spectacular or incriminating in the suitcase, as they had all suspected. Bowie had already peeked at the contents.

Laughing shrilly, Fay examined every article before flinging it away. She cringed as she threw a ribboned strand of Juju's curls to the wind, and Doll scrambled after it. Then out flew all of the precious little keepsakes that Juju had given Doll, wrapped separately in tissue paper: a chipped marble, a blue feather, bits of colored glass, a shiny dead bug.

Then Fay began on Doll's clothing. Syd had heard fantastic stories about this Doll. As he sat on the running board, he looked at the white sandals and plain white cotton dress lying in the dirt. Only a perfectly symmetrical shape could get away with that simplicity. Spotless blue-white lingerie, a single strand of white beads, a white towel and washcloth. Now he knew that the stories were contrived. The white dress and accessories were nothing but a uniform in which to perform an unpleasant task. In

152

fact, the clothes seemed to verify simplicity, naturalness, and an unaffected chaste aura about Doll.

Fay grabbed and threw the empty suitcase hard against Quila's steps, trying to smash it. Like two centipedes the scrappers rolled over and over together, scuffling until they reached Gussy's yard, as she sat on her doorstep sketching the battle scenes.

"Somehow, I thought Doll was more ladylike," lamented Gussy, as the two females proceeded to gouge deep white scars in her newly scraped red yard.

"Even the ladybug has its spleen!" replied Robbie arriving on the scene.

The sideshow is as good as the center ring, thought Quila as she watched from her little porch. At a safe distance the Chips were following the scufflers around the driveway. "Split a gut, split a gut," they shouted now beside Syd when Fay was up and strafing with blows and French oaths that only she could understand.

Then Doll was on top of Fay, beating on the weakest spot of her body, her chest.

In desperation, with toenails sharp as knives, Fay raked across Doll's bare ankle, ripping it red with blood. Struggling to their feet now, they both hit out with weary arms and legs, buffeting the dirt into red clouds around them.

Sitting on the back of his truck, from the corner of his eye Syd watched unbelievingly as Juju, with flies clinging to bloody welts, inched on her hands and knees toward him. He unpinned her filthy diaper, helped her out of it, and nudged it to the edge of the driveway. Gently lifting her naked little body into the truck, he laid her on cool burlap, then trickled water from his thermos over her cracked, bleeding lips. Pouring water over his puppet-handkerchief, he wiped the child's filthy face and hands and daubed at her broken skin. She shook with soundless sobs, partly from physical agony, and partly from divided loyalty at the sight of two frenzied women fighting and shrieking over her like dogs.

Until Fay turned and ran toward her own trailer, furiously kicking Spade out of her path, Doll had tried to fight fairly. Now she overtook Fay with vengeance, tripped her, jumped on top of her and began beating again on the spot she had found most vulnerable. Fay began to cough, gag and spit up blood. Frantically weeping, she seemed to reach up with her last volt of energy and ripped Doll's shirt to ragged remnants, then snatched both brassier straps loose. Standing up slowly, Doll weakly held the shreds before her naked beautiful breasts. They both stared at each other, spent and winded.

"I'll tear your guts out, you harlot!" panted Doll when she could get her breath. With a raking of nails she shredded Fay's negligee and then the sheer nightgown beneath it. She tugged until the flimsy garments tore off from around Fay's neck, then tossed them over her head. Grabbing at Fay's brassier until it broke loose, Doll shook the rag stuffings out of it.

Fay was too weak to even whimper in anger or embarrassment at her bare flat chest or her gaunt naked body, and this gave Doll some time to rally. She heaved herself at Fay again, but Fay had the strength at least to dodge. The blow sideswiped her, making her veer across the driveway like a rag-littered tumbleweed. Bowie watched in disbelief as she tried to regain her balance with arms outstretched like a blind, startled child. Without the small upholstery of her thin clothing, Fay seemed overbalanced with just the weight of curlers scraggling from her head. With Doll close behind, Fay's frail little body lurched and reeled toward her own trailer, until by some miracle she fell against the bedroom doorstep with a sickening crunch.

"If it takes my lifetime," Fay murmured before she passed out, "I'll get even."

"If I've awakened you, it will have been well worth it, slut!" panted Doll. Pug appeared, pushed Doll aside, then pulled Fay up the steps and began to slap her cheeks.

Like a bedraggled hen heading toward her injured chick, Doll staggered toward the ice truck and Juju. "Yes, ma'am," Robbie repeated as she passed by Gussy, "even the ladybird has its spleen!" She started toward the Den to ready the gauze and salve.

But, when Doll finally arrived at the Den, she was wearing Syd's jacket, her brassier hung from a pocket, Juju had been rinsed in a sink, and they both were already covered with expert bandaging. Now, all that Doll needed from Robbie was a cup of coffee.

Robbie searched Doll's soft eyes like they were etched with inevitable handwriting.

Syd had turned his head from the shredded shirt that had merely made Doll's bareness more enticing. "Give me your hand," he had offered as Doll tried wearily to ease herself up onto the ice bed where Juju lay. Syd had been amazed at the soapy aroma lingering under the sweat, blood and spit that muddied Doll. Lifting her for that treasured second gave him a strangely secure feeling. Like knowing the roof was tight against storms, the winter barn was stuffed with hay, the cellar rich with golden apples, onions and potatoes.

His arms are different, Doll had thought absently, different from those that clutched at her from behind slopping mugs of beer. He seemed to handle her like she was fragile as a gardenia and just as easily bruised. Those hands were not made for ice tongs. They were molded for swinging an ax, driving a tractor, planting fruit trees, delivering baby animals, and even, she lowered her eyes, for rocking a cradle. Strong, yet gentle enough to set a woman's world right with merely a touch.

Doll had sagged down beside Juju and the child began dabbing at Doll's wounds with her black rag. Syd wrapped icy slush in his wet handkerchief, smoothed Doll's hair from her eyes and gently wiped away the battle dirt. He covered her with an old jacket, jumped down from the truck and began to gather up the items from her suitcase.

Beneath Quila's trailer, Bowie yawned, removed his shirt, pillowed it under his head, then settled back to let the morning's wine begin to work. Fay, and Syd too, had overlooked the only thing of significance in Doll's suitcase, the clue to her whole character. Syd had picked up the yellowing newspaper packet that was fifteen years old. Inside was an oblong article of monthly feminine necessity that had not, and never would be used. But Syd didn't even look inside as he put it back into the suitcase.

Hmm, Doll had thought as she watched Syd take a first aid box from the driver's seat and expertly tend their wounds; he hadn't soothed her with sympathetic words as she expected, or said she was beautiful in spite of the mud and the blood.

26. Fay's Unwelcome Suitor

Syd was dismayed as he steered out of the trailer park. He had misjudged the beautiful Doll. Now he wasn't so sure she was simple, natural and chaste. While tending her wounds, she was judging him like a farmer considering a sire for his favorite mare. She had also kept the wallet in his jacket pocket. Well, she'd be surprised at what lucky "loot" he carried.

Bowie watched that afternoon as Doll emptied Syd's wallet on Robbie's table. Doll was wearing only a shirt of Robbie's while Pug washed and mended her clothes. Gussy was sketching Doll with all of her bruises and bandages. Bowie hadn't known before how smooth and beautiful Doll's legs were, until she had walked to the washhouse to refill the coffeepot.

Quila fingered through the wallet. "Only a dollar, the seed of a peach, a pear, an apple and a grape. Sorry lass," Quila patted Doll's hand and tucked seeds back into the secret wallet space. "Syd has green thumbs, for sure, but very few greenbacks."

What a crazy, fouled-up world, thought Bowie later that evening under Quila's wagon. He pillowed his head on patient Mange while he tossed and turned in drunken restlessness. No one really understands why either Doll or Fay is filled with bitterness and deceit. Bowie felt more sorrow for Fay than Doll. Fay had to support herself and three children with nothing but her exhausted, overused pain-filled little body. Yet Doll supported just herself and her father with only beauty and wits. Doll's resentment and disappointment had had years to dull it; but Fay's wound was still raw and ripped wide open every time she looked into Juju's cold blue eyes or at the child's dirty black curls.

Softly it began to rain, making it easier to recall the night that was seared into Bowie's eyes, that he had tried so hard to erase from his everyday memory.

"Bad weather's abreedin'!" Quila declared of that rosy morning, about four years ago. She stood on her little porch, shook her upturned fist, looked around the sky and sniffed. "Sure as toads have warts, it'll storm afore the next dawn!" She rubbed her rheumatic hands together before shooing away anxious flies seeking shelter in weathered scrolls of her porch.

Bowie knew that she was right. Last night a heavy ring was around the moon; now birds were leaving the thin light air that gathered before a storm. A clean sky had soon sullied itself with dirty clouds. Angry thunder, lightning and wind were soon upon the trailer park.

It seemed that the Devil himself had readied a show of delight for Quila's forecast. That the Devil had a hand in the day, Quila was sure, for Spade kept crossing Fay's path as she went to and from the washhouse while the heavens gathered their forces.

"Ye'd best be mendin' yer ways – fer today at least!" Quila had shouted above the thunder. But Fay just sauntered by as Quila unhooked her broom, scrub board and mop that were nailed on the outside of the wagon. She scurried inside to find room for these lightweights that might blow away.

It was an unseasonable rain, more like a tropical storm. Though the ocean was a block away seaspray could be tasted, churned in with horizontal sheets of rain. The tree was a thrashing wraith flinging away her leaves and branches. Papers, boxes and cans were blowing all over the park. Streamlets gouged through red dirt, and tenants retired early. Underneath Quila's wagon, Bowie finally decided to leave, for a waterway was forming beneath him, meandering under the wagon, pooling in the place that always comforted his hips.

Already drunk, Bowie took up a half-hearted night watch beneath Enoch's trailer, which stood near the center of the park. An old mattress stashed there could keep him dry for awhile. Lightning sizzled and thunder exploded. As he tossed, a familiar-seeming spirit kept running out from his head, throwing pinches of wild tobacco wherever white anger seemed to strike. Bowie had never been so drunk, yet he proceeded to get drunker. Even more than usual he ached with homelessness and hunger. Whenever he awoke he still felt compelled to look and listen. He would try to concentrate, directing heat to the millions of hair pores of his body, forming a protective cocoon that enclosed him from head to foot against wind and cold. How did he know this was possible with only his mind? He should have gone back inside the storeroom but he had been there most of the day and walls were closing in.

Vaguely he felt footsteps. A dark shape had entered the park, paused at the switchbox beside Enoch's trailer, waited for a flash of lightning, then pulled the master switch. The figure turned back into slanting rain and trudged, head down, toward Fay's trailer.

Here was something sightworthy. Bowie took off his water-thirsty moccasins, scooted from under Enoch's trailer and followed discreetly. He ducked behind a trailer as the figure looked around the park. This was no ordinary sailor, pressing tightly against Fay's back door. This one hunched in the upturned collar of a civilian raincoat, hiding his face in a hat pulled lower than necessary.

As the figure knocked, Bowie sloshed through mud in bare feet, pushing into pounding rain until he reached the back of Fay's trailer. Slowly he pulled out the chinkrag he had made and waited for flashing light to soak his eye with vicarious living.

No customer would brave this night, Fay thought, pulling aside a curtain and slightly opening a window in order to smell the rain. She was almost delirious with a new pain in her chest and wine she was drinking to relieve it. There was knocking at the back door.

"Door's open!" she shouted. In weary resignation she prepared herself in darkness.

Without a word the strange suitor entered, and Bowie heard him lock both doors to the bedroom. In constantly flickering light Bowie could see that the man wore a mask. He dropped his raincoat on the floor, shook rain from his hat without removing it, eased his already naked body onto the bed, and now the obliging storm unleashed the worst of its fury.

"Wait!" Fay shouted, feeling for her box of candles. But Bowie could see in flashing lights that the man was already smoothing the hair on her forehead, feeling the softness of her fingertips, sensing the curves of her neck. For the very first time, it seemed to Bowie, Fay would be enjoying instead of merely tolerating this all-too-familiar experience. The man seemed to lightly touch every faint little hill and frightening valley of her love-starved body with tenderness and respect, as though, at last, she were really worthy of being loved. And suddenly (or was it Bowie's imagination, for he had never cared for this part of watching?) the lightning itself became a gentle, throbbing pulse, an ebb and flow, a tender quiver.

When the man had finished, he sobbed, soundlessly. Spent by deep, tender passion, he slept for a moment with his masked face turned away from Fay. For a few seconds vivid nearby lightning filled the room and spotlighted a magnificent body that was covering Fay's.

Was Bowie hallucinating? Was he in the midst of another drunken fantasy?

Sailors had hearts, birds, ships, nudes or "Mother" tattooed upon hairy chests or brawny arms. But this one was tattooed all over with doll-like shapes, holding hands, enclosing his body in a bizarre network of outstretched, connecting arms.

Weakly Fay screamed. She struggled as the man awoke and repositioned his hat. Again he covered the soft bending of her chin, her palms, her brows and ears with tender, yet hungry, kisses. Weakly, she wailed as lightning flashed and little dolls wallowed and writhed all over his skin and hers. Together they rolled and tumbled until, exhausted, Fay gave in.

Again and again the lightning seemed to ebb and flow, pulse and quiver.

Then the man did things that no other sailor had ever done. He held Fay's hair to his lips, threaded it through his fingers, caressed it between his hands. He kissed her eyelids like fragile petals. He felt the childlike bow of her lips with his fingertips. He smoothed the hair from her face, took a kiss from his lips and tucked it into the little groovings of her ears.

There was a lull in the stormy lights and Bowie could see nothing for a while. But the way that Fay was sighing created echoes in Bowie's memory. The man was touching and caressing Fay in sweet, imaginative ways that Bowie himself must have loved some other woman, some other time. But at the very instant of that thought, an odor of weeds and fish surrounded him, and a cloud crossed over a moon that wasn't there. Rain poured down from the brim of his hat and drenched his clothes, as Bowie gulped down half of the bottle stashed under Fay's trailer, and lightening began to flash again.

Bowie could see that Fay was silently screaming now under the man's cupped hand. But not at fantastic tattoos or repetitious lovemaking. As the man was fitfully resting with his masked face turned to the wall, his hat had slipped aside and Bowie could see as well as Fay, that lightning didn't linger in the always blond hair of Fay's sailor boys. The hair this time was a mass of black, rain-tightened curls.

Exhausted, the twosome finally slept, and Fay did not awaken when her customer left. Dawn speckled with clouds soon arrived, and it was way past time to repair "damage" that might have been done. Fay turned over and slept deeply for most of the day.

It had still been black and stormy when the man disappeared. Bowie retrieved his moccasins under Enoch's trailer, then sloshed his way to the dryness of the storeroom. He wrung rain-soaked clothes outside the door, put them on hangers and hung them from unused nails. He wrapped his wet head in an old bathrobe, turned the fur coat inside out, laid his bareness inside its primitive warmth, and pulled the sides up around his clammy skin. His eyes were sore as scorched holes branded into his face, his neck was cramped from twisting. He sucked on the seared finger where his cigarette had burned away, ignored. Still shaking, he finished the bottle beside him. Everything seemed immensely different. He had felt an enormity, an overwhelming secrecy in what he had seen; yet even now, years later, he could not recognize what the mystery was all about. Somehow, he had always known though, that Fay's preference for blond sailors was a thing so deep and tender, he could never consciously use it for barter.

That rainy morning after Doll and Fay's fight, when Bowie arrived cold and soggy at Quila's wagon hoping for an early breakfast, Quila again questioned him of Fay's past. But Bowie surprised himself by bartering something trivial. He'd save the master memories for some real emergency – maybe.

Despite savory odors, a disappointed Quila served only leftover unsweetened tea.

27. Juju's Birth

Returning to the storeroom, Bowie drank a liquid numbing breakfast, and took up his remembering – trying to recall things as Fay Rose would.

"Mama's under the weather," the little Chips explained some time after the visit of Fay's unwanted customer. Fay was headachy each morning now, an ominous nausea gripped her and despair furrowed her face. Bowie had been watching when Fay had secretly borrowed one of Pug's knitting needles tucked in with thread, yarn and a darning egg beside the cushion of Robbie's chair. But the big needle had hurt too much, and Fay thought the bleeding would never, never stop. So she lay in the green trough of her bed, her douche bag full of cracked ice upon her head, and stared most of the days through.

In the fifth month, when the sickness subsided and the last of the five twenties that her strange suitor had stuffed beneath her pillow was gone, Fay heeded seashells on the window only when rent was overdue and the icebox had nothing but a lingering stench within it.

The baby was born in February, the seventh month of Fay's pregnancy, with only a hastily called Pug and old Quila in attendance. No one had guessed that Fay was expecting; she had stayed too skinny. The baby was so frail and tiny and Fay had no desire to name her.

It was Pug who fed the Chips and explained to them somehow. It was Pug who divided her own new baby's clothing, and lined one of her own laundry baskets for a bassinet. It was Pug who opened windows wide, washed curtains and bedding, scrubbed Fay's filthy icebox, stove and cupboards. And it was Pug who plodded back and forth with food to force down the tight lips of Fay's thin feverish face.

On the night that Pug and Quila had first prepared the baby for Fay, Bowie had been listening outside an open window as Enoch knocked and entered with an armful of white cloths, some milk and oranges.

"Twarn't no sailor this time. The Devil hisself sired this one!" Quila was whispering as she wrapped the cleaned baby in a towel. Enoch came over to the bedroom doorway.

"Take the hideous little bastard away!" Fay was sobbing in delirium. She moaned, "Now you'll never understand, Woody!" She tossed and tossed until Pug sat down on the bed, smoothed her hot damp hair and hummed a lullaby. Fay drifted into restless sleep, while Enoch stood entranced, admiring her fragile, childlike beauty, and feeling a sadness and compassion that he had never allowed himself before.

"Marked sure as a skunk." Quila whispered. "Look, where that wicked hand has even slapped this baby's cheek!" A dark red imprint, like the palm of an angry hand curved over one ear and cheek, and vengeful fingernails seemed to have raked down past the baby's chin.

"A common birthmark's not so bad," commented Enoch. "Lambs have been born with seven legs. Goats with two heads!" Pug took the spotless cloths from Enoch, and wrinkled up her nose as she stacked them on the dresser. They smelled like disinfectants; she'd have to wash and air them, before using on a tiny baby and its new mother, she seemed to be thinking. She put the milk and oranges into the clean icebox, thanked and hurried Enoch out of the door, then sat on the bed again, beside the baby's basket.

"I say this mark is a giant star of ultimate good fortune!" murmured Pug with her infinite kindness. She smoothed back the dark curly hair where it insisted on standing up in damp cusps. "Poor misbegotten waif." She picked up the baby as Quila touched a jasper pendant to its little forehead.

"Red as a lick o' flame and just as hot!" lamented Quila. Pug eased herself back against one of Fay's fresh pillows and released her own full breast to feed the listless baby.

When Fay woke up her eyes were green stone. She refused to nurse the child until she was so sore and swollen she begged for release that only a baby could give to her.

For three weeks, though her varicosed legs bulged almost to the bursting point, Pug juggled Fay and her brood as efficiently as just another four bowls of fruit to be peeled.

"Pug, you <u>are</u> round as cobblestone as Gus says and just as content to be walked upon!" laughed Robbie when Pug entered the Den with double rations of peeling and pitting.

One day Fay felt good enough to leave her sweet smelling, whitened sheets and look into her polished mirror. Her straight hair sparkled like copper threads from frequent brushings Pug had given. Her skin was pink from good food and daily scrubbing. She needn't stuff rags into her bra anymore. It was good business; she would continue to nurse the child.

But without Pug's cooking, Bowie noted, Fay's milk soon dried up, and as the child was of no further use to her, Fay brushed her aside as casually as a smudge off her dress. Thank goodness, Pug stopped in a few times each day to change the baby's strange diapers, to let her eagerly nurse from her own full breasts, to cuddle her, and murmur the only words of babytalk that the child might ever hear.

But Fay went back to sailor boys, and Pug couldn't stand to be part of the household any longer.

The child cried constantly at the outermost fringe of Fay's life, pricking her conscience whenever Pug's pointed knitting needles began clicking back and forth from the dark corner of Robbie's Den.

The screaming baby kept falling out of her basket. And though she would never own any shoes, Fay's baby was determined to walk early, because she had to, thought Bowie. She toddled around in her filthy nightgown all day long, like a draggle-tailed puppy. Her back hem was always longer, stretched from Fay's snatching at her as she ran. The sleeves of her nightgown were soon frayed with age. The front was blotched with stains, for the only washing the gown ever got was in the shower, when the Chips used it for her washrag. Before the shower, they always dumped her filthy diaper into the trashcan beside the washing machine. After the shower, they always pulled her naked, shivering, barely dry, to Fay's porch step, where they knocked and waited.

Fay finally came out and sat on the porch step while pinning a colorful diaper on Juju and putting clean pants on the bare Chips; Fay never bothered with underwear. She then handed each of them half a folded mustard sandwich and sent them back to play. She put the Chips dirty pants into the drawer for thicker nighttime diapers. She wrung out the toddler's nightgown and stretched it to dry between two nails on the inside of the door. The third nail was for the children's towel which never seemed to get washed and gave their little bodies a moldy, sour smell. Though she locked the inner screen, Fay often left the outer door open for the breeze to dry things.

To Fay, the child's birthmark was solely a stigma to taunt her, and it was painful for her to even wash the little girl's face. The child's coloring was not at all like Fay's or the Chips'. The toddler's hair was dull and matted for it seldom felt anything but scissors upon it. "I'll snatch ya bald if ya don't quit gettin' so crappy, I'll snatch ya bald!" Fay was always hissing as she crudely hacked another tangle from the child's curly head.

Fay only diapered the child in the Chips' or her own soiled discarded clothes that she had stuffed into a drawer; the overflow was stored in pillowcases behind her trailer. She seldom ripped up the old clothing in order to fit the toddler any better, she was too tired to even care. She just crudely folded the soiled garments and used them in their entirety; they absorbed much more this way, she rationalized. Sometimes the little girl could barely walk with such so much cloth between her twiggy legs. There were big open "vees" on the upper parts of her thighs and deep indentations where safety pins held the edges together at her waist. When soiled, Fay thoughtlessly burned the colorful diapers or threw them out with the rest of her trash. The long smolder was far enough away not to bother her much. Mumurless, the child played in the Pigpen, or, waddling around in her incredible diapers she shadowed Fay, never crying a peep no matter where Fay's hand was slapped across her bare tender skin.

As she grew the child seemed to have no feeling. She wasn't normal. Whereas a child that age was always chirping, humming or babbling, Fay's child never smiled, cried or spoke.

But her red scarred cheek lived a life of its own.

It was the only place on the child where any emotion showed. Yet no one but Bowie seemed to notice. At the sight of a sailor the strange blotch seemed to burn with hatred, for the child was at the mercy of Fay's nightly conquests or failures. To make herself scarce soon became the child's primary aim in life; to get enough to eat ran a close second.

The featureless shadow-girl in Bowie's dreams watched bees and hummers for they led to nectar-filled wildflowers. But this little girl watched for flies and ants that led to crusts of discarded jelly bread and bits of apple still on the core. Rotten oranges she ate rind and all, and she could suck on a prune seed for a whole day. "I'll yank ya toothless," seethed Fay, "if ya don't quit sloppin' garbage, I'll yank ya toothless!"

The child in her bright-colored, strange-textured, bunchy diapers had an unnatural craving for fats and would spend hours looking for butter wrappers in the Pigpen. Yet she never gulped what food that Fay begrudged her. She chewed it painfully slow, lingering over it as long as possible. She got a fourth of the food that was doled out to each Chip, and they too were always famished. Yet they tormented her into sharing her own meager supply.

The height of the Chips' delight came on Sunday mornings when they gathered from the trash cans all of the empty liquor bottles and poured the dregs into the child's bottle. If she didn't get sick, underneath Fay's trailer she would sleep the whole day through. Fay seldom noticed that the child was always late for Sunday dinners, that her plate was almost empty before she even sat down. "I'll shake ya sober, I'll shake ya sober!" Fay shouted when the child arrived at the table reeking and reeling. When Fay had finished shaking her, she was often put to bed without any dinner at all.

The only real pleasure the child got from life came accidentally one evening. Bowie was watching when Fay stepped out of her black silk panties and left them on the floor, for she always traipsed to the shower in only her robe and slippers. Quickly the toddler snatched up the still-warm panties and scuttled outside with them. The panties smelled good like Fay. They were silky like Fay's slim white arms, yet they would never inflict the same punishment. Fay didn't feel like running after her in a negligee, but since the panties might help to keep her happy and out of sight, Fay merely shrugged and continued on to the shower. Bowie began to shiver, and made his way to Mange's warmth beneath the wagon. Mange scooted closer, put his head on Bowie's knee and went back to sleep, while Bowie continued recalling.

The child hid in corners out of Fay's view and kneaded the reddish-black rag the panties soon became. She'd lie on the rag and mash it closer to her body, sucking her thumb through it, smelling its faint almond tinge with shivers of delight. The worst that the Chips could do to her was to throw her rag across the fence, up on a trailer roof or high up in the tree. Then tears rolled silently down her cheeks as she stared at her unreachable treasure. Until someone retrieved it, even food couldn't budge her from the watching spot.

From under Quila's wagon, Bowie had heard Robbie reflecting out loud one day as she sat alone drinking wine in the washhouse and weaving another cellophane into the ever-present chain. "Poor little mite, she drags that rag like a priceless gem through the garbage of her daily life. How strange we humans are, keeping fantasy alive with the warmth of our own minds." Then Robbie had drug an obscure scrap of poetry from the depths of her memory.

> "Hands tied, the wretch she spied
> Her treasure carried yon.
> Then idolized the dusty prize:
> The rag it rested on."

Robbie had held up the wine bottle and pointed it at the nameless little girl, who was sitting on Quila's bottom step, sucking her thumb through her rag. "Yes! I think we'll call you 'Juju' – 'Rag of Magic'!" concluded Robbie, and though nobody else understood why, the name seemed to perfectly fit.

Bowie shifted his position under the wagon, wiped at tears, took another sip of wine and put his arm around Mange. Juju was always running away, after some motherly person who had given her a piece of candy or some fatherly soul who had, unfortunately, patted her on the head in passing. "Maybe," Fay must have thought, "if I just mistreat her long enough, she'll run clear away, or someone will steal her!" But Juju always came back, returning like a black cloudlet to further dim Fay's dull days and changeless nights.

Like most of the park's children Juju was drawn instinctively to Robbie. Robbie could sail a kite higher than any kid in the neighborhood. Little boys respected her because she could spit farther than any of the men in the park. She could fix storybooks, cap guns, little cars and mend a tattered doll so that it seemed to be smiling. She doctored people, birds and dogs but refused to even sympathize with a cat.

"I wish you was my daddy," said one of Mala's middle children one day. Bowie was watching as Robbie dropped a mended toy and walked pathetically back to the Den.

Juju would watch with envy as Robbie threw Cassy into the air or ruffled Missy's curls against her will. The other children would sidle up to Robbie with the faintest of wounds for Robbie could diagnose almost any ailment or bandage any hurt. If they wanted her to, Robbie could make a child look like he'd barely survived a death battle. But Juju could have had her head split wide open and still stand hidden, merely pretending that she was being bandaged. Behind a corner of the washhouse or in the shadow of a trailer the child would hide and watch Robbie as she leaned her chair against the washhouse wall, as she drank ceaseless cups of coffee, laughed and joked with the girls at her feet and wove her endless cellophane chains.

For the first time, Bowie watched the progress, a plan that didn't involve food or flight began to hatch in Juju's curly head. In the pocket of an apron hanging over Bowie's sleeping place, Juju began to save cellophane from cigarette wrappers after she smoothed, straightened and aligned their corners. Bowie began to add his own cellophanes to Juju's little collection for Robbie.

Bowie heard a liquid noise at the front of the wagon and realized that Juju had wet again her fancy diaper. A little pool was forming under Quila's step and Juju's nightgown was hanging down into new red mud. Suddenly Spade dashed past the wagon and Juju was close behind: Doll was home. Soon Bowie was watching Juju's happy, infrequent bathtime.

Until the first day that Doll bathed Juju no one had noticed that a cherub was slumbering inside the dirty little urchin. Had anyone else explored, they'd have been shocked to find, as Doll did, that deep blue pools could be made to sparkle from behind the tangled forest of Juju's lashes, that a little scrubbing would remove bumps that speckled her legs and arms, that her filthy hair when washed was tendriled and clingy as a wild vine.

In order to encourage Juju into soaking longer – until her festered diaper area was watered into wellness and her thin, worn nightgown was almost dry on the line – Doll contrived various games. Leisurely, she played with the curves and points of Juju's soapy hair. She played pouring games with cans and floating games with leaves and flowers. With straws she coaxed more bubbles into the water. Doll rubbed a dab of soap on each of their noses and passed a feather back and forth.

Juju's transformation came slowly, and Fay vaguely attributed it to the Chips. Somehow she never noticed the bathing procedure for Fay seldom went to the washhouse in the daytime. She spent those hours wearily sleeping, listlessly reading magazines and eating chocolates behind locked doors. Vitamins that Doll gave Juju, she drank as eagerly as soda pop, yet Fay ignored the pinkening cheeks. She was only aware that the child was fishy smelling.

From under the wagon now, Bowie could see that Juju was sitting on the bench beside Doll, as she chatted with women doing laundry. But Juju, in her clean towel-of-a-diaper, could not sit still. She was ecstatic with her sudden sense of well-being. Newborn was her hearing for Doll had swabbed her ears. The world was bright and ashimmer for her long matted eyelashes were clean and oiled. Her hair was washed, fluffy and fragrant. It spiraled around her ears where she could watch and touch it. Her nails were buffed pink and rounded; her fingertips tingled to touch things. And, smiled Bowie as he scratched Mange's head, the star-shaped birthmark just didn't seem to show as much against the cleanly scrubbed little face.

Bowie twisted his head more to the right. Mincing fearfully, Juju had taken a few steps out into the driveway (as though Doll would disappear if Juju went too far). Then Juju ran back to the bench to touch Doll's arm. She took a few farther steps and returned. Finally she skipped off ecstatically. Little cloth knots of the now clean, sunwarm nightgown were bobbing on her shoulders, and the big knot in the back was wigwagging like it was attached to a happy screw-tailed little bulldog. Circling the washhouse Juju returned to touch Doll's knee, then galloped joyfully to the mailbox. She returned and Doll ruffled her hair, "Lovely as a black rose," she whispered, burying her nose in fragrant curls.

Juju darted away and returned with a bright stone, then a shiny little bone. Carefully Doll praised each item, then tucked the treasures away in her pocket.

It must be odd for Juju to run to, instead of away from someone, thought Bowie as he watched the little gift-giver from his checkered lookout. Gifts that the giver makes precious. Bits of new turquoise, wild tea in a tiny plant cup, a wad of mint-flavored pinyon gum. Bowie shivered, then drank deeply of the bottle in his hand, and shifted his thoughts back to Juju.

To show her joy Juju began to twirl and lift her hands high into the air – as though to touch a sunbeam or imaginary birds in flight. Watching her, Bowie was lulled into sleep, awakening as usual with the horrible butterflies' spots pursuing him. He struggled to keep his mind on Juju and therefore stay awake.

As long as Doll stayed home it became a daily pleasure to watch Juju after her long bath. Instead of sitting by the hour twirling her rag, twisting it frantically when she was hungry or hiding, Juju began to stalk beetles, frisk with her shadow and play in dirt and water like a normal child. When happily tired, she crawled with her rag into Doll's lap, in the washhouse or Robbie's Den, to be lullabyed to sleep. Still, Juju never spoke nor laughed.

Since their fight Fay never entered the Den when Doll was home, so for hours Doll often sat in the Den brushing Juju's clean damp hair, pausing only to help Robbie serve her wonderful snacks and encourage Juju to eat more.

It was a strange trio that Robbie, Doll and Juju made together, Bowie often thought as he watched from a slit in the shed. Doll making all of the questions and answers, her voice enlovelied by the complement of Juju's silent reactions.

One time Doll tickled and teased Juju, and all of the girls in Robbie's Den instantly hushed in amazement. Everyone stared at Juju as though they had never heard of a laugh before. At first the little noise seemed to originate from a black cave. Then Juju smiled for the very first time and it was like sunlight had entered a deep black hole. Joyful bubbles seemed to escape from her mouth, and everybody clapped.

"I never wanted sons," mused Robbie, caressing Juju's hair that day. Then longingly, almost inaudibly, "But always, for my old age," she sighed, "I have longed for a lovely daughter."

The only fly in Robbie's ointment of content, the only thing marring perfection between the three of them was Spade, and every time the cat jumped to or from Doll's lap, she seemed to look disdainfully at

Robbie and hiss. And whenever Robbie sat on the bench beside Doll, Spade strolled across Robbie's lap, digging her claws into her knees just to remind her of the hatred between them.

28. Den Satire

There came a day when Doll was gone again, as Bowie knew that it would. Juju tired of playing with her shadow, chasing birds, following bees. She often festered in the same foul diaper until nighttime.

All day long Juju searched eyes for understanding. Gussy and Quila had never paid much attention to her, even in the Den. Desperately, Juju hovered around Pug's mammoth dish-towel-of-an-apron; it smelled of splattering meat, drips of sugared coffee and swipes from little jellied mouths. Bowie shook his head. Pug was everything that a grandma should be, yet Juju would never even know one.

Pug looked right past Juju as she hung her endless clean clothes or hurried to Robbie's doorstep with her clothes-pinned sack of cobbler, biscuits or cookies. Late at night she sadly dumped the untouched food back into the sack that she took to the trashcans.

Time stood still and heavy when Doll was gone. It floated formlessly away on endless notes of the sad record, on the throb of Robbie's tired bass, on the wheeze that was growing louder in Quila's fading body while she played solitaire alone in her wagon. Or it ticked away to the impatient drumming of Lolli's palms as she waited for the crowd that didn't come, regardless of Robbie's locked door, regardless of enticing odors coming from Lolli's oven. Most girls didn't come near Last Resort for Doll's Song could be heard before one stepped a foot onto the red dirt. Besides, it was just common knowledge when Doll was gone.

One night Bowie was watching through a windowsill slit of the Den where he had burned away the new paper plug with a lighted cigarette. Robbie was raising her wine bottle inside the locked Den, as she softly toasted Pug's empty chair, the empty benches and pillows. "Here's to trailerites – on wheels going no place. Like on legs that never walk, eyes that never see. Lips that never feel another's warmth."

Doll was still gone the next day, but Robbie was a demon who had turned off the record and unlocked her door to trap company for her lonely misery, but only Pug, Gussy and Quila showed up. Quila was particularly bearish. Bowie watched closely for Gussy seemed like a victim in a lair, fearful of being torn apart by both Quila and Robbie who sat opposite each other glaring across the table. Gussy's only assurance of safety was Pug nervously peeling potatoes in her usual corner of darkness.

"What's the brew today?" inquired Quila, shaking the empty coffeepot.

"I'm land-bored," sulked Robbie, ignoring her while she pulled back a dusty curtain and wistfully looked toward the ocean.

"Better than bein' sea-bored, like someone else we know of," cackled Quila.

"Sea-bored." Robbie's word-loving tongue curved around the sound. "Seaboard: the place where land and sea meet! Aha, that'll tempt our tasters!" Gussy, and Bowie outside the slit, had lost Robbie's drift. "Let's have Rose' on the Rocks!" Robbie half-filled a pitcher with chunks of ice and gurgled over it three bottles of red wine. She squeezed two oranges overall, swirled the pitcher and poured four mugs. She drank her own portion in almost one gulp, refilled it to the top, drank that down as well and refilled it.

Mysteriously, Quila reached over and unhooked Robbie's keys from her belt and, eyes twinkling with mischief, locked the front door, then disappeared into the bedroom.

As though reading her mind, Robbie knocked on the open bedroom door. "Is the sea-maid at home?"

"How do you spell that?" Quila giggled from the other room.

"I don't," replied Robbie. Gussy reddened.

Quila slammed the bedroom door in Robbie's face. "Sorry!" she shouted out, "Sea Maid's in dry dock, bottom needs patchin'. She'll be out directly!" Quila cackled. Robbie had a silly smirk on her face as she poured herself another drink and downed it.

The bedroom door soon opened and Quila slunk out, her dress peeled low over one bony shoulder, the sleeves of a shirt of Robbie's twisted around her waist and Robbie's loop of keys jangling from her skinny wrist.

"Don't you look spiffy!" Robbie laughed sarcastically as she poured, then drank.

Quila lifted her skirt and flaunted the white bloomers beneath. Imitating Fay Rose, she tossed invisible long red hair, then blew on the cupped fingernails of both hands. Gussy had flipped up a new cardboard and was busily sketching.

"Come closer, dearie," Quila beckoned to Robbie and then drained her mug. "I smell jes lak yer mother's cherry pie!"

"Ugh!" said Robbie, covering her nose and pouring more wine.

Outside the peeking slit Bowie cringed for revealing such trivia to Quila. Loathing himself, yet fascinated, he wanted to run to Fay's trailer, take her in his arms and comfort her as one would comfort a fatherless, neglected child. Robbie could never, never have been part of ridiculing Fay if she weren't so full of wine, boredom and longing.

Quila angled a bench, climbed on it, knelt on her knees and giggled. "Board this vessel astern, me hearty, and come in amidships; the sway's not so apt ta make ye seasick!" Pug folded her apron around potatoes, unlocked the door and left.

Laughing, Robbie poured, drank, and then motioned for Gussy to sit in Pug's empty chair. Robbie lined up the other bench with Quila's, longwise, and straddled it. She moved her bench closer and closer to Quila's. Bowie was surprised, along with his disgust. Robbie, of all people was usually so direct in squelching any hint of sex. She was really drunk!

Indignantly, Quila sat upright. "Wait! Ye've no white hat even! The whole world knows this vessel operates only under sea power!" Both became breathless with laughter and almost fell from their benches.

"Wait! Stay, Cherie!" Quila put up her hand, reconsidering. "Yer hair be jest as blond, yer eyes be jest as blue – if I squint real, real hard!" Robbie laughed so hard she was slopping wine on the floor.

"Okay, hit the deck, Matey," shouted Quila. "The candle's lit! Give her the deep six. Sink 'er!" They laughed and laughed and held their stomachs in agony.

Gussy was uneasy, at a loss of how to act, what to say. She wasn't even sketching. Robbie looked her way. "Why bleat so silently, lamb? Don't fight life so hard! So it's ugly! So what? Who cares? Join the herd. Let it be. Stay loose! See?" Robbie held out her arms and teetered on the bench. "It's a lot easier that way," Robbie drawled hazily.

"Pay attention," commanded Quila – the benches were touching. "We're eastin', list west a knot. There! That feels better! A little aport, sailor. Ah! Just right!" Quila was gasping with laughter. "Heave ho! Anchor up! The candle's out, dammit. Yer time is up!"

The joshers both slid off their perches overcome by silent convulsions. They rolled breathlessly on the floor.

"I say, is it still coffee time?" came a voice that Quila had been imitating. It was Fay at the door, ill timed, her scant curves unshaped yet for conquest, enrobed in a soiled negligee, her hair packed in henna. Juju was close on her heels. "I'll grind ya ta grit if ya don't quit follern' me!" Fay seethed as she slammed the screen in Juju's face. Gussy repositioned benches, while Quila took off Robbie's shirt and keys and pulled up the shoulders of her dress.

Robbie had adjourned to her bedroom, and Fay came limping over to the table. Days after her fight with Doll, stiff and bruised, Fay had emerged from her trailer in a way she was to walk forever after. It seemed like her right knee was splinted. Fay only came to the Den now to pay rent, report a problem, or for companionship when Doll was gone. If Doll returned unexpectedly, Fay left the Den, her eyes bitter and revengeful.

Fay had done her nails, waved damp tips and blew on them, as Quila had been doing. Skinny, blooming ocotillos they were to Bowie, who was woozy with wine and heat. Eager to dream himself back into cooler, greener, wilder places, he slid down under the coolness of Robbie's trailer. With Fay's entrance onto the scene there would be nothing interesting to listen for. The only imagination Fay ever had was for combining bizarre colors and textures, and dredging up new ways of condemning Juju. Gussy turned up a new sketch board.

Expectantly, Quila settled onto her bench, shook the empty wine pitcher and studied Fay. To Quila's weak eyes Fay's face was browless and lipless without heavy makeup. Stippled with dabs of calamine, it looked like a giant case of chickenpox. Quila's eyes narrowed as she glanced toward Robbie's quiet bedroom, then she hurried to the corner and picked up the gurglet. As it went the rounds of the threesome, Fay's odd "perfume" became stifling for it was mixed with the odor of Fay's nervous perspiration.

Gussy sensed that Fay felt safe around Quila only when Robbie was nearby to temper her cruel intentions. Though a barb might rest beneath Robbie's witty tongue, stashed under Quila's tongue was a vicious sword, and Gussy quickly sketched comparisons, symbolically. How curious, she thought for the hundredth time, that Fay has lasted so long. She wiped charcoal on her pinkie finger and dabbed calamine blotches onto Fay's paper face.

"Set it back down there for me, will ye dearie?" Quila asked of Fay. As Fay leaned over to put the jug on the floor, a flood of coins rolled out of her bra. "My, yer jangly as Fort Knox," taunted Quila, who always managed to find some sneaky way to tell whether Fay had intrigued a loaded drunk or a broke and homesick boy beneath the last sailor hat.

While Fay retrieved the coins, Quila clucked like a hen eagerly waiting to hatch a nest egg. She fluffed her sleeves as though they were feathers, then huddled into a black ball that sat back concentrating, contriving a fortune from fragments of conversations with Bowie. Bowie awoke in the strained silence and returned to a peeking hole.

Fay reached into the pocket of her negligee and took out a heavy watch that had been one sailor's only asset. "Well, time to regild the lily," she sighed. "I only came to pay some on the rent, and ask if Robbie would stable up my trailer; it's like walkin' on a ship!"

Quila stifled a snicker, but then slapped her hand rudely, twice on the table. Fay sat back apprehensively as Quila dusted off an obscure tidbit from her headful of sordid facts.

"Me dry auld tongue be over-thirsty fer that rare old bourbon the grocer man hides 'neath the cash register, jest fer me!" Quila was whispering loudly. "Its price is $3.00!" She opened her hand in front of Fay. Fay stood abruptly, her eyes blazing. "My, yer ready fire warms me frosty auld heart," said Quila soothingly. "But ye outstretch me patience, Fay. Don't outstretch me tongue as well. I've some real dillies cached beneath it: 'Can I call you Woody?' As though that makes everything all right!"

Fay was sobbing. She emptied her bra cup and threw the coins at Quila. "I knew this park had peepers! Now I can't pay anything on rent!" she cried as she slammed out the door.

"You flap-jowled old dung beetle!" roared Robbie, weaving in the bedroom doorway. "You must be desperate, overturning pebbles in search of shadows! What you label vice, old vulture, may be nothing less than crude virtue! Dirt cheap in your eyes, but priceless if you ever bothered to understand the whole picture!"

Though she swayed now, her voice softened, her eyes looked vacant. "Everyone just takes it for granted that Fay's beautiful hair is a taunting tiger's tail. Nobody bothers to look any deeper. Who would even guess that the tiger is just a little kitten-lost, frightened, always hungry, desperately tired and lonely, with three famished mouths always tugging on her tits!"

Robbie sat down on a bench. Gussy was so entranced, her pencil scarcely moved.

"The wretched must be what they were created, Quila. And thank God, that for many there is some 'black rag of magic', some ritual, some scrap of pretense which makes their daily living tolerable!" Robbie hunched down, looked deep into Quila's eyes. "Who cares what anyone calls their own private 'drug', Quila: 'cigarettes', 'wine', 'Holly', 'black rag', 'scratchy old record', 'Woody'–or 'Mange'?"

"Humph," said Quila.

Robbie lit a cigarette. "Life demands of you a hand-to-mouth existence, but from now on, Quila," she pounded three times on the table, once with every word, "Let! Fay! Alone! She has even <u>more</u> than she can handle." Robbie blew a long breath of smoke.

"My, yer speechful this morn, Robbie!" Quila picked up a butt still smoldering in the ashtray, drew the last bit of life from it, and ground it back into the ashtray. "Yer words be speary ta me tender auld heart. But why the boo-hoo, me bonny? No use acryin' over spilt milksop!" She tucked Fay's change into her sleeve. "There be flaws in every soul!"

"And how like you, Quila, to search for flaws, and be blind to any beauty of a soul!"

"I'll behave now, pet," Quila wheedled. "Sit down. Relax. Yer brow be rutty, Robbie," she reached her hand toward Robbie's forehead.

Robbie slapped her hand away and reeled at the impact. "GET OUT! I'm tired of your molehill mountains and wormhole caverns!" Tread easy, Robbie, thought Bowie, holding his breath. You both really need each other.

"<u>Get</u> <u>out</u>, I said!" Robbie picked up Quila's frail body, opened the screen door and easily dumped the small woman in an angry heap outside the door. Garbling some indignant reply, Quila zigzagged home, and Gussy left the Den as well.

This has happened before, sighed Bowie, snuffing this cigarette. The twosome often sparred with fisted words. And Quila, trying pitifully to seem her normal self, would always come back, nonchalantly cackling to herself, shuffling cards as she stepped through the door, again.

29. Chips

With the Den locked and the tiresome record grinding away again, the afternoon stretched long and hot before Quila, Bowie and Gussy. Gussy had found some dregs of white and brown paint in the Pigpen. She borrowed thinner from Gus to smooth out the thickness and clean her make-do brushes. Creating different shades, she had started to paint Robbie's face on a piece of broken glass. This afternoon she decided to finish it.

Bowie was lying beneath Quila's wagon, sipping wine and keeping an eye on the park. Above him Quila walked back and forth, smoking, drinking wine, shuffling cards and muttering. As though being ousted by Robbie weren't punishment enough, the Chips were spending the afternoon aiming small rocks at Quila's wagon, clacking boards along her area of fence and chanting, "You're-an-old-crabstick! You're-an-old-crabstick!"

Finally Quila pulled aside the ragged door curtain, opened the window, and settled in the stuffy little bed recess to think while she awaited darkness. Evening would lure the twins home, with hopes that the enticing aroma in the air might be coming from Fay's just opened cans. In the meantime, merely ignoring the Chips was the fastest way to discourage them.

Quila chuckled; below, Bowie guessed her thoughts. To the Chips, all the nameless evil they had ever seen, heard or felt was condensed into Quila's body. Bowie had informed her that bigger boys in the neighborhood whispered to the twins that witches like Quila swallowed rats whole and shed their human skins like snakes–among other gruesome things.

Bowie had heard one Chip tell the other that in his dreams Quila's head was a sprouting witch's broom, and her crooked evil smile was hacked from a rotting pumpkin. Just the thought of Quila was frightening as the black hearse housed at the mortuary in the Plaza. Neighbors whispered that if children misbehaved the old Gypsy, Quila, would steal them, cut off their ears and bury them for an evil spell. Sometimes at night, when Bowie was watching Fay's trailer, the Chips woke up screaming from nightmares and pounded on Fay's locked bedroom door. But Fay never responded, and eventually they crawled back under their covers, hugging each other until their sobbing was spent.

"Dragon's blood!" Quila had hissed once as she grabbed the Chips, pinned them against her trailer and painted hexes on them. "They won't come off 'till ye leave me be!" she'd whispered. For a while they quit clacking boards against the fence and aimed rocks at someone else's trailer. But the truce was short-lived. The iodine wore off, and soon they were howling, hooting and shrieking again around her wagon, seeming to sense that because of her weak eyes, her ears were extra sensitive.

Quila tried many things but nothing worked very long. Peppery gum she fooled them with when they raided her milk bottle and sneeze powder when they pestered Mange. "Aw, they're so ornery, they're cute," cooed Fay whenever Quila complained.

There was a small knothole in Quila's wagon that she was forever filling with rags, for the Chips were always squirting water through it. From a store on the pier she finally bought some itching powder, and while the Chips were squirting one day, she crept out to drop some powder on their bare shoulders, mumbling like casting a spell. But that wore off as well and they soon were back again to see what new, enchanting magic Quila might perform this time.

They were always popping up to irritate her, "Little pimples!" She thought she had the answer. Next time they harassed her, with hair awry, mouth askew and eyes asquint, she squeezed and hugged them until they wriggled in angry disgust, squirming away like wet Gypsies. No, thought Quila, not like Gypsies. Young Gypsies would have spent themselves on challenge. Running, wrestling, horseracing. Whew, it was hot! She pulled the bottom of her heavy black dress up over her knees, exposing grimy bloomers.

Hmm, Quila mused. It was only when Doll was sighted that the twins would skid to a stop and leave her area. Then they grabbed at their crotches and scurried away like fleeing goose bumps. Outside her wagon, now, she could hear them whispering and enlarging the knothole in her wall...

At the same time that her body and mind resisted the Chips, her heart too often went out to them. Especially at night when they were tired of playing in the deserted wash house or waiting on Fay's doorstep. They had no toys, nothing whatever to do, and no Gypsy father to teach them how many ways with which a simple stick or stone could be played; no bigger brothers or cousins to teach them to spit at a crack or take a dare. On the verge of tears they would often shake Fay's locked door.

"We're gonna run away if ya lock the door too long!" they shouted in to Fay through gappy-toothed mouths, straining their ears for the reply that never came. They were especially hateful on summer evenings. After returning from some fool's errand that Fay had invented, they sometimes stood watching shadows fuse and giggles move from the lighted front of Fay's trailer to the darkened back of it.

On such nights they were worse than in the daytime, searching for things to defile or wreck, for some sort of deviltry to get attention, and bobbing like a caboose behind them, yet always out of their reach, was Juju. Quila turned her pillow over to the cooler side.

In general, the Chips hated sailors as much as did Juju. Bowie had watched, he told Quila, on nights when sailors were not expected. With Juju fast asleep, Fay awakened the boys and let them gape at her bedroom walls while she shared her wine with them, hummed in a faraway voice, daubed the dim light bulbs with scent, brushed her beautiful hair or tweezed her eyebrows and painted them on anew.

To the Chips, Fay's bedroom was wonderfully unlike any other room in all of the world. Whereas the Chips and Juju's living room beds were hurried makeshift affairs, Fay's bed was soft and bouncy, cool and shiny green. Caught in the fishnet that draped the walls were pier prizes that sailors won for Fay—celluloid dolls and giant feathers, plaster animals, pennants and snap-crickets.

Most fascinating of all was Fay's cigar-box full of striped service ribbons that her sailor friends had won. Quila shook her head sadly. Such tempting objects for little children to play with, yet never once had they dared to touch even one booth prize that hung in the net, even one ribbon that Fay had spread out on the bed for them to admire.

Sometimes, when her breath was already sweet and heavy with wine, Fay invited them to lie down on the bed beside her while she smoothed their hair and called them her "little sugar pines," making them feel deliciously uncomfortable. The Chips finally drifted away from her wagon, and Quila fell asleep.

Doll had been gone for a week, the Den locked, and tenants knew the record by heart. Bowie was watching when lonely Gussy threw a cup full of coffee at the finished painting of Robbie that she had made on glass. Leaving shattered glass, cup and splattered coffee all over her table, walls and floor, she sobbed herself to sleep.

Then suddenly one morning, Doll was in the washhouse running warm water in a sink while gently dabbing muddy tear stains from Juju's cheeks. She worked filthy hair into beautiful lather and soaked the festered little body, trying in vain to make Juju smile again.

Later, an elated Robbie served up coffee and her own brand of news briefs. Bowie listened happily to Robbie's, Gussy's and Quila's conversation. But wordy jewels fell unnoticed before the deaf ears of the inattentive Doll and most of the rest of the audience that sat on Gussy's pillows, drank of Robbie's spiced-up coffee, and filled the smoky Den with laughter. Things seemed almost normal again. But suddenly there was a chilling lull.

Doll heard the ice truck and left hurriedly, smoothing her hair, her hazel eyes sparking with anticipation.

"Hey, Syd!" the Den crowd heard her calling as she ran. Robbie winced.

"Hay-seed!" Robbie mimicked under her breath.

Nobody seemed to breathe.

Gussy fumbled in her mind for some grabline to restore the conversation, but even her memory was limp in the tense silence and heat.

"Uh, have you ever seen an apple, that's cut to reveal its hidden star?" she ventured. "Nature can be so beautiful. It looks like—"

"—And nature can be so blunderous!" roared Robbie as she swept all of the half-full coffee mugs to the floor.

The klatch was over. Everybody quickly fled out the door. Gussy hurried home to try and sketch Robbie's angry actions, her tearful desperate eyes.

30.   Drawing Robbie

Back in her own trailer, Gussy still felt the sting of hot coffee on bare arms and the shocking shatter of cups in her ears. There was also, deep down inside of her, a tinge of hatred for Doll, as soon as the weary record began again. Though Robbie was crushed and smoldering, everybody else had left the Den feeling frostbitten. Worse, Robbie had served nothing but coffee yet, and the afternoon stretched boringly uninterrupted ahead of Gussy, filled with only a growling, nauseous stomach for companionship. She watered the dish gardens and snipped a few leaves to nibble upon.

Bowie watched from the cutout hole in the paper shade as, right in the midst of broken glass, Gussy finished a sketch of angry Robbie and the flying coffee mugs. Then she decided to glue the shattered glass pieces back together again. When most of the pieces had been fitted together, there were still small bits of glass for which she could find no place.

Gussy held the picture to her heart and cried. "Oh, Robbie, I really understand now, like I never could have before: what it must feel like to be continuously shattered, endlessly fitted quickly back together again, merely to seem the same on the surface!"

There was nothing to do now but browse through the thick envelope-scrapbook that had largely grown from Robbie's rich mind. Gussy read and reread much of it again and it was almost like having Robbie in the room.

"It's her voice that's the least feminine thing, Holly," she said, awakening Bowie who catnapped beside the hollyhock. "That voice—beautiful, but sort of masculine. I've got to get that voice into that mouth!" In brazen daylight, some of the sketches were like Robbie when caught outside of the Den: silent and sullen, peeved to even be noticed, it seemed. But, when a heavy bolt of dark material (that Flo couldn't stand) was stretched around the windows, Gussy lit a candle, propped up the best sketch of Robbie and stood back in amazement. Why, she had always thought that only the magic atmosphere in the Den was illusory, but even here, in the right lighting, merely a sketch of Robbie seemed to have changed. She blew out the candle and opened the transom in order to sketch some more.

Outside, Bowie was getting drunk again. Even if it was daylight, he decided to poke the dark material aside and take a peek. Except for the square of daylight from the transom, Gussy's trailer was dark. But suddenly, huge butterflies materialized from the blackness. Some of them floated out through the window screen and fluttered around his face. As usual the black spots left their wings, becoming sad, accusing, glowing eyes that hung by pairs. He slapped them away, shook his head, and closed his eyes on the hovering apparitions. He drained the rest of the bottle, and when he looked inside again the transom was closed and a lighted candle once again flickered in the blackness.

Using pieces of charcoal and her collection of stubby pencils, Gussy smiled before her favorite sketch. In the hot darkness, Robbie's face was slowly growing into a new life, standing out from the background with a weird Rembrandtesque effect. Sweating now, Gussy patted her face and neck with the little bag of ice chips resting in a saucer with a spoonful of wine that she always measured into the bottom. Wine lasted a lot longer this way, smelling instead of drinking its special kind of magic. Gussy sank into a reverie before the picture.

Outside, Bowie decided to only listen and imagine. In daylight it was too risky to peek in the open. He could smell the wine now. He smiled: Gussy needed so little alcohol. She could probably get tipsy on merely the weakened aroma.

"Poor Robbie," sighed Gussy as she shaded here and there. "She really lacks <u>any</u> femininity! Oh well, one never thinks of Robbie as a woman, Robbie is just–Robbie, but never womanly! Her posture is too determined and defiant. There's an intentional droop to her shoulders and her chest is always drawn down, as though ashamed of its flat breasts.

"Robbie doesn't react like a woman–smoke, walk, talk or dress like a woman." Gussy sighed and pressed the cool, wet, euphoric tranquilizer against her nostrils. "Robbie would rather philosophize, inform, tinker with cars, fix toys, patch up kids and animals, walk the beach in silence, talk to people along this dismal street, strum her bass, hop a freight train, drink, smoke and chew tobacco than ever, ever put on some lipstick or wear a dress!"

Gussy added freckles to Robbie's sallow coarse-grained skin. Robbie's hands were sensitive and bony, so Gussy erased the layer of padding that usually softened a woman's hands. She worked and worked, until she could almost feel the same extraordinary courage and character in Robbie's hands and mouth, as she could see in her eyes. For blue, she only had the stub of a pencil, yet when she finished, all of the sketches had Robbie's blue, blue eyes.

It was hard to tell Robbie's age. Gussy darkened lines around the mouth. "Robbie, you have the wonder and curiosity of a child and yet, you also have the wisdom of a prophet." Gussy added a childish sparkle to the eyes, and just a touch of gray at one temple. She held the cold soothing bag against her wrists. "Yet, Robbie you live in a timeless sunset; you've settled back into each Today, into the routine of the Den like there just is no Tomorrow."

Twilight was turning to darkness. Bowie stood up against the fence, stretched, and moved to another window. With his thin wire he again pushed the dark material up, just a trifle. Gussy sat with her back toward Bowie, studying and working on a sketch of Robbie. Other pictures of Robbie were now propped up on the breakfast nook cushions, on the back of the table, on the ledge behind the sink and against the back wall of the bed. Bowie had already watched these other images growing. Robbie's unmistakable blue eyes were staring out of a Sphinx, a cottonwood stump, an oyster, a sorcerer, and a jail with eyelashes for bars.

Gussy sat back thinking as she squeezed and smelled her "medicine bag" as she often called it. At rest, Robbie was a gallant sort of girl when she knew you, thought Gussy. Robbie sat down last if she didn't watch herself, and was often first to retrieve dropped articles. But she was madly embarrassed when these natural manners showed through. Gussy sharpened her pencil on old sandpaper, and dabbed the bag on her neck and shoulders.

"In just the right light, Robbie," Gussy moved the candle, "a sort of down covers your chin." With her thumb she shaded the area a bit. "Your nose is stronger, and your eyebrows are wrong. There! They arch more finely and are too close together. Maybe you should pluck them! They give such a sensitive, fierce look to your face."

Shading the hair mannishly, in the only style that suited Robbie, Gussy now sketched in the way that the hair often tumbled down over one of Robbie's icy blue eyes. In spite of the stuffiness of the trailer, a shiver rushed through her body as the candle lowered, for the sketch was now deceptively virile, fascinating. Gussy shrank from the picture, for instantly she realized that her attraction to Robbie was neither sisterly, nor totally platonic.

Bewildered by her strange self-discovery, for days Gussy ignored Robbie's fragrant coffee and beckoning keys, even though Doll was home again and there was laughter in the Den. Gussy walked instead, smelling with agony the mixings of neighborhood cooking. And when she returned to the park, even Lolli's frizzled eggs smelled divine.

In the end, tired of meager menus and eager to be back in the Den, Gussy rushed to the store for some affordable tidbit to add to Robbie's klatch. That morning in the Den there was only a Robbie–tray of fresh fruit cut into little pieces and speared with toothpicks, to which Gussy added a border of Cracker Jacks. In interesting company it was a feast.

More and more now, Gussy resented Doll. Unexplained absences left Robbie joyless, her natural optimism crumbled, her step was slower, her slouch more pronounced, her voice was drifting and her meaningful gestures were limp. More and more often her door was locked and tenants could hear her plucking aimlessly at her bass. Robbie's vigilance of the trailer park went from casual to blind when Doll was home; when she was not, a dripping faucet infuriated her.

This week the times when the Den was open were few. Strong black coffee was the fare, and most girls avoided the depressing Den. If it had not been for Quila's colorful journeys into Gypsy days and carnival life, Robbie could not have withstood the long intervals. Quila strained valiantly when Doll was away. She was quaint and hard for some women to decipher. But her scrappy way of putting a conversation together with odds and ends of Scotch and Irish, with archaic and poetic loaners, coining new words and thoughts into a fragmentary, disconnected jargon of her own creation was fascinating to word-loving Gussy, and, a partial distraction to Robbie.

All that the tight-lipped Robbie did was smoke, fold, weave, chink little openings in her walls, crack her knuckles, and hack at the wooden table with that unbending pocket knife she always carried. Gone were little news briefs, special snacks and interesting stories. Gone was any concern for the changing assortment of pitiful girls with desperate eyes, often telltale stomachs, scattered lumps and bruises, or here and there a skinny, ragged, nursing baby.

Though Robbie appreciated Quila's efforts, if Doll was gone too long, Robbie's eyes became vacant, and even Quila could not get through to her. To the gloom of her trailer Robbie would retreat like a wounded animal and lock the door for days.

And then, she who could elaborate on every concert or musical artist that Gussy might mention, would play over and over again that one record, a cheap-sounding, simple, haunting melody the whole trailer park knew by heart. It filled the dreary place with unspeakable sadness, unsharable despair. Robbie ate nothing and had only enough energy to light another cigarette, pour more wine and flip the arm of the record player.

"Ex umbra in solem!" (From shadow into sunlight, Gussy translated from school days and the big dictionary she was always studying.) Robbie whispered the phrase joyfully whenever Doll came home. Happily, Bowie watched at each return as the brooding eyes of Robbie ignited with life again, and the lonely room became cozy and overflowing with happy girls, laughter, wonderful aromas and the crackling of Gussy's fragrant pillows.

But, both Gussy and Bowie also noted that Doll talked more to the complacent cat and the answerless Juju than she did to Robbie, anymore. It seemed like she was mad at Robbie for unknowingly luring her back, again and again. She often avoided sitting next to Robbie, and shunned any contact with Robbie's adoring eyes.

"Fine cat! Good girl! Yes, nice little mouse. Want to go out?" Doll brushed Juju's hair, kissed and cuddled her constantly. "Have you really missed me?" Doll seemed completely unaware of the gentle passion confined beneath Robbie's clean shirt and hastily snipped curls. But finally, Robbie speared a tidbit with her knife, another, and then another. She was eating again. Gussy smiled, Quila relaxed, Pug sighed, and happily, Bowie dozed, sipped, smoked, watched and listened beneath Robbie's slightly opened window. And Gussy hastily sharpened her pencils at the bottoms of each fresh piece of cardboard, as endless girls came in the door, depressed, and left again, engulfed in a strange happiness.

Suddenly Bowie came out of his drowse. Robbie had finished relating news, a thing she seldom had the heart to do when Doll was gone, and was whacking the tabletop with her metal spoon. Through the window slit, Bowie could see steaming pots of tea.

"There are usually two types of tea in American markets: black and green. How they are processed or fermented is what makes the difference."

"Oh pshaw!" said Quila impatiently. "I've made tea from every plant that isn't pisonous, and my teas were good fer a body! 'Most every tree in any neighborhood is tree tea: willow, eucalyptus, bay! Grass before it seeds, or dry in the field if ye watch fer pison ergot! And tea flowers like roses, violets. Anything–if it smells good! Why do Gorgios have to have expensive tea from a million miles away? Tea is all around us!" Quila suddenly became aware of her loud words. Angrily she stood, threaded her way between the girls, and slammed the door behind her. Gussy had been recording almost every word she said.

Quila hurried to her wagon, mumbling, shaking, furious that she had allowed this motley bunch of non-Gypsies to peek so deeply into her private knowledge and experience.

After Quila's angry explosion, Robbie seemed to lose interest in the rest of her plan. She merely sugared both teapots, put out the cups and sat down at the table to smoke.

At the peak of the day's heat, Robbie's disciplined hair grew ringleted, the maverick curl separated from the black herd and meandered into her eyes. Bowie noted Gussy sketching in fascination the too-long eyelashes, the mouth that missed by one iota of being masculine. Bitterness in Gussy's eyes started melting, as Doll forgot her resentment, reached up and pulled Robbie's curl like a taut spring, then laughingly let it bounce right back.

Robbie was her old self again, thought Gussy, and it was all right. Robbie poetized the simplest observation. Her tongue was a brush on a full palette of colorful words, and Gussy inescapably fell under the spell of her voice and magic laughter. Drawing less and less, Gussy was smiling more and more, merely enjoying each and every fleeting moment.

Gussy idolized beautiful sounds. At work in her trailer, she usually hummed to shut out swearing, off-color jokes, constant bickering, except when she heard a birdsong, wind in the tree, or a hint of Robbie's voice. And then her face would brighten, just as it did when nighttime descended upon her jar of crickets and freed their wild seeking voices.

That night Gussy removed the labels from several cans, then practiced sketching various features of Robbie on the backs of this constant source of paper. She transferred the improved features to her favorite cardboards of Robbie. Sitting back, she admired the pictures and sipped from a watered-down bottle of wine, to which she had added citrus peels and fragrant neighborhood leaves, before placing it to brew on her transom screen.

It was almost daylight when she finally fell asleep on her sketches. "I don't care if she does love Doll. Robbie is the most wonderful human being that I have ever known!"

31. Penny with a Hole

In the vast abyss of Bowie's mind was a niche overflowing with scraps of strange knowledge. One scrap insisted that Bowie make nightly rounds against the wind, even though he knew tenants had no understanding of scents. Roughly five strides apart were the trailers. If nothing was unusual the entire park could be patrolled in less than half an hour.

Tonight, like a banner, an out-of-place odor lingered outside of Enoch's trailer. Almonds: Fay Rose was inside. Bowie peeked in from the edge of an open window.

Though late, Enoch was cooking a midnight supper when Fay, belled with noisy bracelets, stood at his open door. She hadn't scored, was all dressed up with no place to go.

"Smells good," she said through the screen door, in her usual bored way. In spite of himself, Enoch asked her in, though he had no idea what they would converse about. The one and only thing they had in common was hatred of the cat, Spade.

Enoch detested himself for the excitement he always felt when Fay walked past his open door. Her hair seemed a scarlet finger, twisting to one side, taunting him. Even her recent limp he found endearing. Her makeshift costumes reeked of cedar chests, secondhand stores and a kitchen-sweet perfume. Her profession was boldly obvious. How he could even tolerate her, he who so admired economy and restraint, was beyond him. Why couldn't he be attracted to Gussy, who despite her nearness and dependence on the Pigpen, was always faintly fragrant, walked with grace and even ate her Pigpen fare with elegance? Fay was so extravagant, with ever-flirting hair, phony walk and gestures, restless eyes, lavish makeup, accentuated body, bizarre colors. She was everything that Marney taught him was wrong.

But, as surely as dead meat attracts buzzards, Enoch could not help himself.

She lit a cigarette and perched herself on a pile of newspapers. "How silly to save newspapers! Like saving used rags, potato peels, or one's own sperm."

Enoch grew scarlet, wishing for the first time that he did not eat with the door and windows wide open. However, this was a wonderful opportunity to share. "But indeed, in olden times they did save the sperm of teenage boys for aphrodisiacs! They also saved the paws of bears and tongues of peacocks for the same purpose!" Fay pretended to gag.

As always, Fay was proudly conscious of her clothes, smoothing and admiring them as she smoked. Her restless eyes settled upon labeled jars and neatly rolled paper sacks with rubber bands around them. Rudely she unscrewed the lids of a few jars and smelled them.

"I have my own drugstore," Enoch explained. "If this were ancient Europe, one of those jars would contain powder of Egyptian mummies, to use for gout and sore throat."

"Ugh!" she sniffed and drew back from a strong-smelling finger hole that she had poked in one sack. "A cure is worse than disease!" Fay's twangy voice came floating out to Bowie, vibrating painfully on the nerves of his sensitive ears. "Whatcha makin' in the pot?" Fay lifted the lid and sniffed.

"Sort of an imitation cock-a-leekie: a soup of spices–" Enoch started to explain. But Fay was gasping with laughter. "Cocky leaky? Yuck!" she shrieked, until finally she toppled from the pile of papers and it shuffled down around her. Quickly Enoch went around shutting the door and all of the windows.

"You look so pretty when you laugh," Bowie heard Enoch say softly, as he closed the last window. "I'll bet you're a winsome girl, Fay Rose, beneath those gaudy clothes."

Bowie pressed his ear to a window; everything had quieted. But to Bowie's practiced ears, a tightly closed trailer was like something vaguely crowding into his mind right now-a whispering cave. He took a long swig from his hip bottle and the whisperings dissolved.

"Oh, let me touch it, Enoch," Fay wheedled, "I've never seen so much!" Bowie could see Fay through a scratch that he had recently made in one of the painted-over windowpanes. Her yellow-kerchiefed neck, red blouse, yellow belt and black skirt like the bands of a shiny snake were twining toward Enoch. He was counting hundred dollar bills that had fallen from a big paperclip, a wad of bills that until Fay toppled, had rested secretly between folds of the newspapers.

Later that night, Quila heard eager footfalls padding up her steps.

"Yer befuddled, Bowie, with all that cheap wine ye guzzle. Enoch could never have earned or stored that much money in his trailer!" And Quila refused to feed him. But as she shoved him out the door, he glanced back, long enough to catch wonderment in her eye.

Two mornings later Bowie settled himself inside Robbie's shed. He watched as Quila sat before Enoch's teacup and twirled it, waiting a more dramatic time for reading. Gussy was sketching Enoch's separate features on labels, and Fay was filing her fingernails.

Quila rested her head in her hands. This might prove difficult; Enoch's worst cuss word was "Egads!" and he used it sparingly. His blackest deed? To save on handkerchiefs, he blew his nose in dark corners of the park between his fingers, then shook it off.

"Can ye stand the truth?"

"That's what I'm here for," Enoch trembled.

Ignoring his teacup, Quila took hold of Enoch's hands. He washed them with almost a vengeance, as though trying to shed invisible taint. (I'll have to use everything, thought Quila; I'll probably never again have any chance with Enoch. If one fact doesn't get him, another surely will.) "Aha, I see tables and benches of newspapers, fancy names for entrees from a trash yard, tea brewin' on a roof, and–" she shivered, "sheets stolen from coffins!"

Enoch's eyes were enormous with shock and sweat broke out on his forehead. Stretching one hand out with her right fingers, Quila rested her left ones on the inside of his other wrist. She was quiet, until she could memorize the pattern of his pulse.

The only noise in the Den was from Robbie, carving mindless designs on the table. Aside from Gus, this was the first man who had ever been in Robbie's Den, noted Bowie, for Robbie was uncomfortable around males. Strangely, Robbie had nonchalantly agreed to Fay's request: Enoch was fit, but effeminate. It was virile, rugged men that Robbie shunned, like Syd, the iceman. Robbie took a cigarette, removed cellophane, wove it into her neck chain and threw the pack on the table without passing it around.

"Yer too attached ta moldy, morbid facts, and things about the dead." Quila felt him flinch beneath her grasp. Her fingers turned up his carefully manicured nails.

"As a child ye followed too rigid a health plan. It's time ye chucked pills, deliberately got dirt under yer nails and lived it up a little! Yer still alive, but rigor mortis is start'n' ta set in!"

He looked up suspiciously, "Excessive precaution does no harm!"

Quila ignored him and ran her fingers along the wide, steady heartline. Enoch shuddered, probably remembering those fingers caressing never-washed ears of Mange when she left her trailer porch and those very same fingers being licked when she returned.

"Yer spindly, but yer heart's a hefty giant. Too bad it's knotted up in apron strings. Yer a robot, Enoch. Immaculate! Narrow-minded! But, a mama's boy!"

Spade pushed through her special door, jumped up on one bench and slithered across Enoch's lap to the spot where Doll often sat. Enoch stifled a sneeze as Spade sniffed around for a familiar soapy scent, then curled up in a ball and began to purr with contentment.

"Even yer gestures be too thrifty," Quila snickered. "A real man tears the roof off with a sneeze! Ye ought ta go all out fer <u>somethin'</u>! Be there nothin' or nobody ye ever craved?" Suddenly his pulse quickened beneath her waiting fingers. She noted his avoidance of Fay's mocking green eyes as she stood up. When Fay stepped out the door, she tossed her hair like a scarlet scarf. Bowie had commented to Quila that Enoch unconsciously preened his hair and smoothed his eyebrows, whenever Fay merely sauntered past his trailer.

Furtively, quickly, Enoch whispered in Quila's ear. "Can you brew me a magic potion to make somebody love me?"

Quila tossed one of his hands aside. "Ferget it, Enoch, ye've no sailor hat!"

Tracing the long lifeline on his other hand, Quila summed his future: "Yer ta have a great awakenin', then a healthy, prosperous life!" (IF you can learn to spend yourself and scatter good, instead of SITTING on it, she thought to herself.) "Spend some time collectin' friends, experiences, rather than newspapers and morbid stories that nobody wants ta hear!"

She turned up Enoch's empty teacup. Gazing into it with surprise, her eyes gathered leaf fragments into a mouse at the bottom of the cup with dashes all around it. "Ye'd best be bankin' any cash ye have." She turned the cup a bit. There were ants and bees as well, but Enoch didn't need her to tell him further of his industry and frugality. There was also a ring at the bottom, and, a cross nearby? Quila suddenly trembled, but Enoch was standing up.

Enoch was more than ready to get out of this stuffy room that reeked of cats, sweat, unwashed clothing, overflowing ashtrays and stale coffee. The way Fay had talked he had expected women to be brilliant as a mummy's jewels. But when he had arrived with Fay there were only Quila, Robbie, Gussy and other nondescript females sprawled around the room, sitting on crackling pillows, with cups and ashtrays spread on messy floorboards.

Pug was entering the Den, looking like a fat sausage tied at the joints. A huge dishtowel was stretched around her for an apron. She put some jarlids and paper sacks into kitchen drawers, and pressed some rags against a nail beside the sink, before she sat down in a dark corner of the room to peel potatoes.

"What do I owe you?" Enoch asked hurriedly as he searched for an opening among girls that seemed draped around the room. The trailer already had odd smells, but now, it also smelled of strong soap, bleach and chopped onions. But Quila was still unsatisfied, accustomed to the odors, the mediocrity of the coffee crowd, and Robbie's unkempt trailer.

"Sit down! I'll give me price when I'm through! We play a game with guests. Come now, say the first thing that comes ta yer mouth." Hesitantly, Enoch sat down again.

"Dog!"

"Hairs!" he frowned.

"Cat!" said Quila.

"Sneeze!"

"Mother?"

"Marney."

"Meat!"

"Ugh!"

"Black market!"

"Wrong!"

Quila plainly showed disappointment. She had appraised Enoch's inflections, watched for pauses, understatements, but there were none. Enoch's associations were either innocently true or shrewdly childlike. "Whaddaya do all day?" Quila had overheard Mala's children inquire of Enoch some weeks ago. He had flushed, "Why, er, I suppose you might say that I was a meat man," he cleared his throat, "yes, you might say that." And it soon spread over the park: Enoch was a butcher who dealt in black market meat. Now Quila knew that it could not be true. Yet, whatever his trade, he was reluctant to reveal it.

"What have ye in yer pockets?" Quila asked now. "Strew me some symbols."

Enoch cringed as Quila's gnarled and scarred fingers felt of the many-sized pills, the tiny ball of string, the mound of change whose only distinction was a penny with a hole in it.

Sorry that Fay had enticed him here, Enoch trembled slightly. "Lord, be ye afraid of <u>everythin'</u>?" Quila mocked.

"Nothing to be afraid of; I live a respectable life." Encouraged by Fay's wine one night, he had been suddenly unafraid to seek a fortune from this notorious woman, whose light-fingered tongue picked pockets and pantries of hapless tenants and neighbors. Fay had strutted up with a wine bottle in her hand, wearing a sea blue dress whose scallop of neckline, sleeve and hem even further bewitched her throat, wrists and knees, while making the green of her eyes even more enchanting. She was tinsel and stardust, and Enoch had been blinded.

Innocently, Quila's sleeve brushed across the table and some of Enoch's pocket objects fell. Enoch scrambled to the floor, and Bowie watched Quila closely.

"Where's my penny?" Enoch's voice quivered like a small boy's as he probed dark crevices and threaded overlong among peelings, ashes and wood scrapings beneath the table.

Having palmed one article that might be important, Quila sat back like a simmering saucepan and drank her tea slowly. Bowie watched the twisted smile flash on and off her face. She fingered some object that Bowie knew was soon within one inner sleeve.

Hmm, thought Quila, this coin with a hole is worn with age or rubbing. Enoch is either terribly purse-proud to miss a mere penny, or else the coin is symbolic. Maybe a little blarney could bring out something new, she thought as she poured herself more tea.

Turning as he searched the littered floorboards, Enoch shoved his backside almost up onto the bench beside Quila.

"Hey down there! With all this talk o' places ye've been and are goin' to be, methinks yer jest a longtailed tadpole–all tale and no body!" She thwacked him on the rump that was mended with fancy feminine stitches. But Quila's aim was lower than feeble eyes intended, and her touch seemed to linger overlong. Suddenly Enoch, table and cups, all tilted, then teetered over as Enoch stood straight up from his crouching position, gasping at the hot tea and leaves that had splashed all over him.

His face was flushed and the hair of his red tuft was so like wet, insulted feathers that the roomful of women laughed uncontrollably. Outside, even Bowie could not control himself, but his laughter was lost in the uproar.

"You vulgar old woman! There must be a peek hole in the shower!" he sputtered. Pug gathered her work into her apron, stepped carefully around the girls on the floor and left.

Ha! What have I hit upon, thought Quila, and in complete innocence.

At the door Enoch paused, looking back again at the floor and broken cups.

Quila's mouth widened into her wicked grin. "Ye over prize the penny," she chided. "But I'll be lookin' fer it! Meantime, Mange will be famished fer me payment on yer fortune-tellin': jest a steak er two!" The screen slammed. "See that it's tendered!" she shouted.

Robbie cleaned up, Gussy poured tea into fresh cups, and Quila gently picked up the pieces of Enoch's teacup which had broken on her part of the bench. "Ah, there is the thing I overlooked." A ring, and inside of it a wavy cross, or—it had been jarred, of course—was it more like a ring around a skull in a sea of quiet waves? Trembling, Quila dropped pieces into the sack that Robbie held, then huddled deep into her dress while Gussy filled her new cup.

Enoch hurried to his trailer. Was Quila distorting things? Was he reading words that weren't really there, trapping himself? He had heard of her type of sorcery, how she used ambiguous words, sentences and storyettes to couch or bring out real truths. No, she must possess some master key to pry such intimate secrets from the very walls. Perhaps that redskin, Bowie, had something to do with this, for Enoch sometimes thought he heard scrapings against his trailer at night, as though clothing were sliding from window to window.

That afternoon Enoch purchased the best of steaks and had them tendered by the butcher. At home he rolled them into tight cylinders of paper and tied them. Late that night he slid them into the despicable bottle, and washed his hands overlong. The next day when he took his pants from stretchers on the clothesline, he felt the warm reassuring presence of the holed penny in one pocket, the very first coin that he had ever earned.

32. Peeking at Pug

Someone poked him with a branchlet from the tree. "Come up, Bowie!" Quila urged from outside the latticework. "Ye've harvested enough vile vintage! We'll distill it together."

She waved a new wine bottle in the air when he entered. "Can't sleep: I'm makin' a midnight stew." She sat back on her stool, tenderly fondling a black curl tied in ribbon, wondering why it made Pug edgy for her to do so.

"I'm a wonderin' what Pug keeps hidey under that big garlicky 'front' o' hers!" Quila put the curl on the table and connivingly poured the wine. "She be stayin' overlong in Robbie's Den, fer someone with so little ta add!"

Bowie quivered. The black hair had given him a heart twinge, but it didn't matter: the hair wasn't straight and strong, but soft and coiled. "I haven't been to Pug's for a week!"

"Yer there all week, every night!" Quila whispered as he squirmed. She took down a bowl from the rack, unhooked a serving spoon from the wall and twisted around to the stove.

"You're naggy as a sweat bee." Bowie gulped the bare inch of wine and put out his mug for more.

"Most facts be stretchy, I keep a-tellin' ye! And they's a spice o' wickedness in every one of us," Quila insisted, smoothing again the slight bulge where "his" pouch always waited.

"Pug's clean as air. She is!"

"Well, ye've sniffed deep enough, me bloodhound," Quila hit the cork back into the neck of the bottle. "I know they be a whiff o' taint under all her goody-goody–it lingers in yer eye! A big, complicated thing, fer Lolli has hint of it, too. She's a-teasin' me, savin' it. Methinks she wants me ta help cheat Gussy out o' the tree space!"

Bowie tried not to lower his eyes. "Pug's close-tongued. Gives her man his 'comfort'–regular. Can you make a thing of that?"

"Throw dust in me eyes, will ye?" croaked Quila, as she whisked up the bowl of stew that she had just dished out and dumped it back in the pot. "Ye outstay me patience, Bowie. Food'll still be here, whenever ye blow me hot some embers!"

Now! Bowie urged himself. Why don't you tell her your suspicions? Get it over with. Bowie's hands shook from hunger as Quila gave him a shove. Once out the door, even the stench of the incinerator was welcome after the delicious agony of the unshared stewpot.

Quila was uncanny; her presence stuck like primrose pollen. No! Primrose pollen stuck to unnamed, bare brown feet. Stomach agrowl, he hurried for the storeroom and the half-full bottle that was waiting. He settled back and slowly sipped in darkness. He wondered now if the smell of baking, yeast and spices that permeated the thin walls of Pug's kitchen had somehow rubbed off on him tonight.

Bowie watched Pug more than any of the rest, not to find any evil to barter, but solely for the joy of pretending what contentment life could sometimes hold.

Tonight, the trailer had been shaking slightly against Bowie as he wedged himself into a comfortable place outside of Pug's kitchen window. Gus was reading out loud while Pug scrubbed the last child in one of two large steaming tubs standing on towels in the kitchen. As she groaned and stood up, Bowie could see her stout varicosed legs bulging within the stockings they were always encased in. A little girl stepped from the soapy tub, into the rinsing one and waited contentedly as Pug hung fresh Sunday school clothes on the lowest of seven staggered, different-colored nails inside the doorway of the girls' bedroom.

Pug was always cooking, scrubbing, sewing, serving. On weekdays she was up before dawn in order to finish her work, feed her family, see some off to work or school, settle and satisfy the smaller children with little projects, and be ready for possible morning and afternoon coffee time at Robbie's Den. Pug's kitchen was worn with cleanliness, and most of her dishes were tin, so there would not be any breakage to blame on little children. The kitchen walls were papered with drawings and report cards.

At night, there was one light over the kitchen sink, the stove, the dining table, Pug's huge rocking chair and Gus' big lumpy easy chair. The carpeted floor was usually strewn with seven large pillows, covered with assorted colors of worn velvet slips. Here Pug's little girls sat, played or catnapped. Yet there was always one or more of the girls sprawled over their parents' chairs or tucked into their laps.

On weeknights there was no real bedtime for anyone, just a comfortable sort of pattern. While Pug did supper dishes, Gus supervised the teeth brushing and nightgowns. Then after Gus' horsy rides and mass tickle fights, the children just sat around asking questions until something prompted Gus to tell a nightly story or example. As each child fell asleep, Pug carried her, her special pillow and doll to bed.

On Saturday nights, Gus read bible stories aloud as Pug scrubbed, gowned and tucked each girl into bed. Patterns were exactly the same every day, and no one seemed to want things to ever change. Except that sometimes Robbie dropped in after dinner to bring a new storybook. She sat on the floor with the girls, reading in many voices, dramatically gesturing until even the widest-eyed child was happily asleep on her own pillow or in a cozy lap.

Every meal was also patterned. Breakfast was pancakes, milk and fruit. Lunch was soup that had simmered since last night's meal. Supper was beans or stew, home-baked bread, water, and cobbler. Only for Sunday dinners was there any change: chicken or a roast with vegetables cooked in the same pot; square skillet biscuits scored in the pan, water and Jello. Some nights Pug made donuts or cookies for a special treat.

Pug was the one that women "unbosomed" to and their secrets never went any farther. Pug was as calm, quiet and capable as the simple-hearted mare that pranced about like a mist in Bowie's head–with an arrow sticking out of its bleeding heart. He squeezed his eyes together, trying to shut out a fire exploding with the fuel of a broken bow and buckskin clothes. He unearthed a bottle, uncorked and drank it all, then sucked out the very last drop.

The dying fire faded from his mind but the ghostly horse still pranced around in his head. Pug had the same strong hips and shoulders and wavy chestnut hair sprinkled with gray. Bowie always wanted to reach through the window and pat her head, unfasten big pins from her bun and let the wavy mane blow free. "There, there, tired girl," he'd murmur. "I'm turning you out to pasture, where you'll have nothing to do but eat and rest."

Leaning against the trailer, Bowie pushed himself from the kitchen to the bedroom window. Resting against the fence, he lit a cigarette. Without peeking, he knew that Gus would be on the recessed shelf-of-a-bed in his shorts and stocking feet, reading a magazine, pulling contentedly at thick gray eyebrows, passing by pictures as though they weren't there, 'till he settled down to a western serial. If Pug were the perfect mother, he sighed, Gus was the perfect father. He worked long hours as a truck driver, fixed things around the trailer, spent evenings with the family, and went to bed. There was no time for anything else.

Pug took a mug from the cupboard. He could picture her filling it with coffee, sinking a spoonful of sugar into it and taking it to the icebox for a splat of milk before carrying it in to Guy as she stirred. Bowie blew out a curve of smoke and sighed with longing.

As he turned the pages and read, Gus would be drinking coffee in big appreciative sips. Finally he would yawn, put the empty cup and magazine aside, get up and brush his teeth. He would drop a nightshirt over his head, pull off shorts and drop them in a hamper. Eyes closed and smiling, he would scratch every inch of his tired, sagging flesh, then the scalp beneath his curly gray hair. Gus set the alarm, then unset it with a happy sigh: "Tomorrow's Sunday!" He would slide between crisp sheets and turn down the radio, knowing that Pug's soapy-smelling body would awaken him "when it was time." When the pancake batter was measured, when Pug had had her shower, and the last child was fast asleep. Pug was never variable, as comforting as a worn saddlecloth between Guy and his tiring days.

Sliding back to the kitchen window, Bowie stretched, rolled his head in circles, smoked, and waited while Pug fussed over the untucked smaller girls and closed their door.

Into Pug's stockpot now went the weekly bones and supper leftovers, to simmer with onions, garlic and seasonings throughout the long night's coolness. Pug measured pancake ingredients in the palm of her hand, then set the table. She lowered the burner and turned out the kitchen light.

Bowie scooted back to the bedroom window and pushed the curtain aside with his thin wire. Wearily, Pug entered the bedroom and gathered soap, towel and nightclothes. Gus turned over happily, asleep already. Pug sighed and smiled at the gently snoring figure, and yet, Bowie felt that there was something different about her sigh tonight. Her eye had been caught by the calendar and she paused, instead of letting herself quietly out of the back door.

On ringless fingers she counted to thirty-three, then picked up the only photograph on the dresser, of Pug herself—young, slim and beautiful in a wedding gown. She gazed deeply into the picture. There wasn't a trace of visible romance about Pug, but now her breathing was almost measured. She held the picture closer, then pressed it to her heart.

Slowly she put soap and towel away, hung her clothing on nails in the closet, dropped a shapeless sack of a nightgown over her head and crawled in quietly beside Gus.

Strange, thought Bowie as he snuffed his cigarette in a crack of the trailer, where people hide symbols of something they really cherish, something they can't accept, or something they've lost–Hidden in the "ears" of a hollyhock, in the heart of a mangy dog, in the folds of a yellowed newspaper, in the aroma of a black rag, in the eyes of an old wedding photo–In a bloodied scrap of leather waiting in an old Gypsy's bosom, his heart tried to whisper as he hurried away to careless sounds of laughter at The Joint.

33. Enoch and Fay

One afternoon, as he sometimes did, Bowie took up a watch outside the back window of the Plaza Mortuary. Inside, the mortician took off his black suit and brushed it carefully before hanging it back in the bare closet adjoining the workroom. His dark tie and white shirt he smoothed and also hung on hangers. He removed the black shoes, brushed them carefully and placed them on the empty closet floor. He combed his black toupee, wrapped it in tissue and put it on the dark shelf above the clothes rod. Briefly he combed and arranged his small red topknot of hair. As he slipped out the back door in tee shirt, khakis and carefully mended tennis shoes, nobody could have looked less like a prosperous undertaker, than Enoch.

Nobody admired undertakers, he thought, as he checked the placing of his pocket things while he headed down the Plaza. He, Amos Cunningham, had found that out the hard way. People slyly rubbed handshakes off, and never invited him anywhere. Women thought his hands were clammy, his money tainted. Even in later years, it never occurred to him that his shoptalk was offensive. Death was the only topic at which he excelled.

Nobody appreciated his secrets of preserving color and form that had not been used since Cleopatra's day. Nobody noticed that he spent hours in the library, enchanted by historical facts of death. Nobody realized that he was an expert on that fascinating subject.

Sun was setting as he neared Last Resort, and the wiry undertaker seemed to get taller than five-foot-six; his walk became more erect and he began to whistle through the gap in his front teeth. He was completely unaware of the shadow that flickered in and out behind him.

Enoch could feel a sparkle in his dull eyes this special evening; he had earned another hundred-dollar bill. The feel of it was crisp beside the special penny in his left-hand pocket.

Entering Last Resort, he gingerly skirted Spade, who was curled around the mailbox. Automatically, Enoch squelched a dainty sneeze. He felt a part of this place. Robbie had even given him a pet name. At first Robbie delighted in digging him with all sorts of names, smugly noting his reactions. One day she tagged him permanently with the seemingly meaningless moniker, "Enoch." "I wish you wouldn't call me that," Amos had said in the beginning, (though it was much better than the other names Robbie had first tried out on him.)

"Enoch." Maybe it had some esoteric implication. He looked it up at the library and was pleased to find it meant "teacher" though it puzzled him as Robbie pronounced it. Yes, here he was someone respected though some believed he was only a common butcher.

From the other pocket a bit of red escaped, where he had been fondling the scarf that he had bought while out on the pier. Maybe tonight he could muster enough courage to present the scarf to Fay. His sensitive fingers deciphered silver threads that were woven through it–like the subtle gray that sometimes crept into Fay's shocking red hair.

The park was already gay and loud with a Saturday night air about it. "Saturn's night," Quila mumbled as she hurried past Enoch on her way to the washhouse, "the time of unrestrained revelry and license!" she cackled in anticipation.

Robbie stood at one of the sinks, holding up a dripping wad. "Hair!" she shouted. "Every single week it's hair!" Enoch cleared his throat and stepped into the opportunity.

"Except for vulnerability to fire, human hair is impossible to destroy! Climate, water and most corrosives can't change it. That is why it always clogs the drainpipes."

"You're a real help," said Robbie in disgust.

From under Quila's wagon Bowie watched Enoch's changeless evening routine. Having hung his broken mirror and spread out a protective rag along the rim of the always soiled sink, he washed his hands and dried them overlong. He pulled his mouth apart, checking the overly white teeth, pink gums and tongue. He swiveled his eyes and searched his lids for signs of bloodshot. He poured salt in a glass of water and gargled loudly, filed a nail or two, then tweezed wisps of hair growing irregularly about his cheeks and chin.

"Do you know," Enoch said to the Chips who were watching intently, "that human hair and nails do not grow after the body is dead? Hair is simply the last part to disintegrate!" The boys held hands and ran to sit shivering on the doorstep outside Fay's locked door.

After dinner Enoch took a walk around the neighborhood, prolonging the high spot he planned for this night. By the time he returned, tidied the trailer and readied for the morrow, most of the lights were out in the park. He closed windows tightly, turned off all but one dim light and sampled the wine Fay had left him. The bottle smelled like Fay and had a tinge of red which her lips had left around the opening. After he would put away the money, the liquid magic might enable him to visit Fay and give her the scarf. "I'll leave the rest of this bottle," she teased, "Maybe, someday, it'll do for a little courage!" He took another swallow.

Feeling exhilarated, he crouched and ran his fingers along the edges of one certain stack of newspapers, feeling for the cold curve of the paperclip marker. He took another swallow of wine then again riffled the edges of the papers, turning on more light as he did, to search for at least an indentation where the clip might have slipped from. Frantically he began throwing newspapers all over the trailer. At last he sat on the floor and methodically began searching, opening each newspaper, leafing through it, making an untidy stack on the floor. He grabbed the bottle and poured down wine while it dribbled past his chin. Like a maniac he unfolded and crumpled newspapers until there was hardly room for him to move. A swig or two more, a long gulp and he emptied the bottle.

"Gone–Gone!" he wept loudly. Through a scratch in the window paint that Enoch was always touching up, Bowie watched and shook his head. He pressed flat against the trailer as Enoch veered crazily out the door and headed toward Fay's. Bowie ran to the back of her trailer and removed the chink rag. Somehow, Enoch must have known Fay never locked her bedroom door unless she had a customer, for he knocked, then let himself inside.

"You're not like Woodee'," Fay mumbled drunkenly as she switched on the light.

"Just let me just talk to you, Fay." He sat on the bed. "The money's gone! A million denials, to no avail!" Tears ran down his cheeks, yet he was wildly laughing. Fay put her hand over his mouth. "Don't wake the kids!" she ordered.

"What do I have to show for thirty barren years?" he whispered loudly. "No warmth; no image; no one to care if I suffer or laugh! All of my security," he fisted his hand, "was in that little wad! Help me Fay, help me to forget?" He buried his head in her lap, then looked up hopefully.

Fay laughed disgustedly, her eyes were steely. "My time is valuable!"

"But look what I've brought you." Bowie winced for Enoch's voice was greased with wine and the patience of one coaxing a cat from a tree. He slowly drew the scarf from his pocket and draped it over Fay's hand as though it were woven of priceless threads.

But Fay threw the scarf in his face. "What do you think that is, a ticket to my tent? I get better bargains than that for free, from Flo every week. Scarves don't pay the rent or fill the icebox!" Bowie couldn't believe his ears. Fay must have been hoping that Enoch would spend some real money on her just for friendship.

"Besides," she laughed drunkenly, "I like only sailors; they smell like sweat not hospitals! They boast of the sea and sex! Not stinginess and death! You are short, dull, and boring!"

Enoch looked with disbelief at this hussy. "Women only want your money," Marney had said. Yet here was a little tramp who refused whatever he offered.

"You're getting older, Fay," he tried to be sarcastic. "What if you run out of sailors?"

Her voice was suddenly sad; "I have the whole sea to drink up, if I'd want to. Besides," she was flippant now, "I like only blondes!"

"My, little beggar, you're choosy all of a sudden. What about Juju, your little black-head? What about _her_ father?" Enoch snarled.

"Him!" she shuddered. "If ever I find that bastard, I'll strangle him! With that very black rag that she always drags!" She grabbed the beautiful scarf and violently knotted it, then determined to change the ugly subject. "So, this was to be the payment!" she laughed, quickly ripping down both ends of the scarf and throwing it in his crushed, disbelieving face.

She lit a cigarette, settled against the pillows and smugly studied the astonished Enoch. He had no finesse. His eyes wandered to personal parts of a girl and lingered there.

Posturing in her yellow nightgown with its froth of ruffles at the neck, Fay was for Enoch's eyes, even in drunken despair, a slender goblet of ambrosia, waiting to be enjoyed. He wanted to blow off the foamy ruffles and slowly drain the delectable nectar. No matter how mean she was on the outside, Enoch was sure that sweetness waited within. But she tossed her wine-colored hair and her eyes became haughty.

"Ha, you're so cheap, you'd probably measure your sperm!" she laughed. "I've heard that you always count three squares of toilet paper!"

she whispered teasingly. "And as for lovemaking," she threw a pillow at him, "I'll bet that you couldn't, old maid!" She threw another pillow. "I'll bet you're a lean pig in a padded poke! Like Robbie's name for you, 'harmless, innocuous, Innoc!'"

Though stunned and disappointed at the revelation, wine was dulling everything but anticipation, and scarlet fingers of her hair had teased him for the last time. It was easy to grasp Fay's thin little arms and hold them while he kissed her. Slowly, while she struggled and fought, he ripped away the gaudy neck ruffle and jerked off her flimsy bra. Astonished, he stared at a sunken chest and a body shapeless as a sucked sparerib. In disbelief, he gaped at the bra to see what made her breasts so lifelike.

"Eureka!" he shouted, for though one bra-cup was stuffed with rags, the other was spilling out hundred-dollar bills.

"Monsieur gave them to me, to keep until he asks for them." She had snagged an old French sailor a few days ago, who had put the money in her bosom. "To save from this week's gambling." His eyes—at least—were like Woodee's, she had consoled herself, though blond hair was only a suggestion on the balding head.

Without warning the frozen smile of Enoch's was above Fay. Oh, how he hated and loved her at once—he, who had been so completely self-absorbed, self-generated and self-contented until she had flaunted herself at him. Still pinning her hands behind her, he stuffed the now ragged scarf into her protesting mouth, then unbuttoned his khakis.

"You flagrant little liar and thief," he breathed. "I have slept on morgue pallets and used coffin shrouds to cover me. I have eaten like a pauper, saved like king. And now, I shall not be refused by the likes of you!"

It was the first time he had ever been next to a woman and he was surprised at her odor of snuffed candles and stale almonds. Clumsily he writhed upon her, trying in spite of himself to please her as well. Oh, if only he could make her love him: her voice and her hair could be cooling waves on his stifled heat. But his love and ecstasy were returnless. Her eyes, once green as the sea, now narrowed and changed to the color of bile.

When he had finished he loosened his hold on her wrists and pulled the scarf from her mouth. His hands went soft and clammy around her face, trying to console the fury he had kindled. How could her eyes be so fiery, when her coughing little body felt so cold?

Fay's eyes inched over Enoch's head. Suddenly she tugged hard on one of his long earlobes, and while he was screaming she reached up to his prized possession, the tuft of red hair. In one hard revengeful jerk, she had gouged his scalp and almost snatched him bald.

Enoch staggered down the bedroom steps in a daze, holding his bleeding head, pulling up on his pants...and Robbie was standing there. "That damned Delilah, that damned Delilah," was all that Enoch could manage to whimper.

"What's all the fuss about, Innoc?" asked Robbie calmly. "We could hear all over the park that you got what you obviously came for. All in one big, gagging gulp. And Fay got some payment too. What are you bellyaching about? You've finally proved you're a real man, and Fay has a real scalp for her collection. Oh, is this yours?" Robbie handed him the paperclip with hundred-dollar bills fanning out around it.

Earlier that evening Bowie had awakened beside the hollyhock, for the Chips were excitedly whispering at the edge of the Pigpen. They had discovered Juju's cache within a knothole in a crosspiece of the highest part of the back fence. Usually Juju only had feathers or bugs in there. But she made a mistake and also hid one of Quila's discarded chocolates. Ants had led the Chips to the secret above their heads. But Robbie was collecting all of the garbage cans and newspaper stacks that Juju had used for stepping up on. Now, what could they do?

Well, Enoch must have stacks of newspapers; he was the only one in the park who got a daily paper, and he left his door ajar when he took his evening walk. The Chips decided to borrow some stacks to stand on. Newspapers would never be missed, they thought.

Quila was having evening tea when Robbie knocked on her door. The two of them finally figured out to whom the money belonged that Robbie had found sticking out from a new stack of newspapers when he returned for the last trashcan.

34. Robbie's Fortune

Gussy sketched the weirdness of a candle unexpectedly burning on Robbie's table. Robbie had left hurriedly when Mala rushed to tell her that water wouldn't shut off in one sink. Quila glanced from Gussy to Fay to Pug, then trembled as she watched the candle flicker, gutter and start to form the long "coffin sheet"–that same creepy look that kept appearing in teacups lately.

"Signs are everywhere," muttered Quila. Last night when making scrambled eggs, she cracked an egg with no yolk. Robbie returned and lit a cigarette from the candle.

"Fie, this bake house is drear! Must it always be sa dark?" Quila pushed a heavy curtain aside, coughing at ancient dust, and Robbie promptly pulled the curtain back. "Ye could out frown a gargoyle, Robbie," Quila grumbled.

"See those bottles on that dark shelf, Quila? Good wine, and certain people, spoil when exposed to light." Gussy turned up a new cardboard and began to sketch the bottles.

Outside Robbie's window, Bowie fanned with his hat as he sat in the gloomy shed. For days the spicers, Quila and Gussy, could do nothing to enliven the atmosphere. Doll was gone, and Syd, the iceman was also on vacation. The new man delivered ice as fast as possible. With not a smile, he rushed from the smoldering stench and grubby children who crowded his truck. With nothing to cheer dull days, children were listless and troublesome.

Clocks and dribbling water measured away unused time. Robbie was a scratchy tumbleweed, tossed on an angry wind. Even Spade sensed something, playing wildly on the screen door but refusing to come inside. With Doll gone, Fay was a visitor now whenever the door was unlocked, the record silent, and the smell of fresh coffee or brewing tea was in the air. Today Quila poured black tea for everyone. There was no cream or sugar in sight.

Quila drew much apprehension from Bowie. Even in daytime now, he waited visibly, a vulture hunched in shadows, explaining to her that "something" was beginning.

Robbie slipped the jacket off a new pack, wove it into her cord and passed the pack around. She lit Fay's cigarette, then Gussy's and prepared to light Quila's. Quila drew back. "Last match, you old foreboder," warned Robbie. But Quila crushed the cigarette, shredded it and strewed it beneath the table.

"Superstitions!" muttered Robbie as she lit her own cigarette. From the corner came the sound of accelerated knitting behind Pug's ceaseless fingers.

Fay sat staring as Quila poured herself more tea. Fay drank her own tea without seeming to taste it. Nobody spoke. Then Quila twirled the dregs in Fay's cup and absently turned it upside down on the bare table, while liquid flowed into carvings there.

"Look!" Quila jumped in genuine excitement, while Gussy captured surprise on her face. Quila pointed into Fay's cup, "It's sa clear!" She held the cup to the candle. "A house surrounded by many dots. May I die afore me next meal if it's not so! There be a rich suitor on his way, Fay. Just wait! You'll see!" Fay kept on staring, ignoring her. By now Gussy had finished her tea, twirled her cup and pushed it toward Quila, who turned it over in front of herself. Gussy could feel on one knee warm drops filtering through the table boards.

Quila held the cup close to her eyes. "Scissors!" she declared gloomily. "There's a violent quarrel abrewin'. Ye'd best be careful, dearie, when it hits."

"Let's liven this wake!" Robbie pushed cups to the back of the table. "Get out your cards, Quila, and deal us some good fortunes!"

Robbie walked over, reached down for the gurglet and wiped its mouth on her sleeve. "Ad diaboli," she whispered before she drank.

"Ad vivum!" Gussy toasted when the jug came to her. If only I could let her know that someone understands, she thought, remembering the shattered glass picture of Robbie. If I must fight strange feelings about Robbie, surely I can understand her love and loneliness for Doll. But how to let her know in front of these others, Gussy pondered. If only they shared some secret knowledge. That's it–Latin! Gussy had spent many lonely hours browsing in back of the big dictionary, especially in underlining Latin phrases that she and Dom used to banter back and forth to the disgust of Eloise.

"Corne edito." Eat not your heart–Gussy hoped that Robbie understood.

"Too wise is stupid," replied Robbie under her breath. "In diem vivere!" she toasted, then passed the jug again.

To live for the day, translated Gussy. "No! Ad multos annos!" For many years!

Robbie smiled at Gussy's attempts and looked carefully at faces around her. "Esse quam videri" she said softly and raised the jug again.

To be, rather than just to seem, Gussy's keen ears translated, but her mind was confused. In wine there is truth, she remembered from school days. "In vino veritas," she toasted in the air, then held the jug to her lips.

"Okay, quit the pig Latin!" commanded Quila, dealing cards to Gussy.

But Robbie pulled the cards to herself. "Enough! You've told Gussy every fortune you know of. What's in my future?" Robbie's cheeks rippled with the pressure of gritting teeth. "You've been avoiding it too long."

"'Twould be a misdeal," Quila hedged. "These cards were meant fer another!" Robbie shrugged, took another swig and waited.

"I see a letter," Quila said. "And comin' soon." Gussy lowered her eyes to hide happiness. Fay sighed, pushed on her painful chest with one fist and limped out the door.

Quila shuffled seven times and redealt for Robbie. She picked the cards up one by one, trying to control goose bumps popping out on her arms, a lump leaping into her throat as her eyes confirmed the cards she knew would be in her dealing.

"You're affected by a strange malaise," she said, as Gussy furiously sketched. "And," there was genuine surprise in her voice, "may I die afore this candle, if it's a lie'n I be!" She cocked her head and looked curiously at the cards. "Yer goin' ta be famous almost overnight! What's more, yer gonna take this sleepy town and this crummy trailer park along with ye!"

Robbie exploded with laughter, giving Quila time to quickly gather Robbie's cards.

Easily, Robbie wrenched the pack from her hand. "I know your tricks. Taught you a few myself. Look at me!" Slowly Quila raised her eyes and they verified what Robbie seemed to already know. Robbie looked at the top of the pack and turned up the dreaded black ace.

"Malaise?" Robbie snickered. "Mal-ace is more like it!" she growled. "You've been palming it for weeks." Gussy's pencil was suspended in the waiting moment.

"Well, ye can't live ferever on jest tea and coffee settlin's!" Quila tried flippantly, but Robbie was already slamming out the door.

"Leaves in teacups speak. Palm lines never change. There's no escape. Signs are closin' in. I'm afeared as never yet afore," Quila whispered to herself as she gathered the cards and slipped out the door. Sadly, Bowie watched her fragile, wavering gait from the slit in the tarpaper door. Gussy and Pug looked wordlessly at each other, then drifted out themselves, Pug to gather clothes and Gussy to check the mailbox. Bowie was left alone, tense and hollow. He rearranged his peeking space, then made his way to the haven under Quila's wagon. He drained the last of the bottle there, snuggled up with his head on Mange's chest and absorbed the steady, beating warmth.

Fay sat on her doorstep, rubbing her aching knee, staring vacantly as Gussy checked the mailbox—in vain, as usual. "Don't count on a letter, kid," said Fay. "That lyin' Quila never makes sense. She says Robbie will be an ardent lover to the bitter end. And yet, she also says that Robbie has never, and will never go out with a man in her whole damn life!"

Fay stood and opened her door. "Quila's not only getting old; she's getting blind! She also says that Doll is as chaste as a newborn babe! Shit!" Fay slammed the door.

No matter what she did that afternoon, Gussy was only aware that something was wrong with Robbie's record player, or, perhaps, the record was simply wearing out.

That was the first night Gussy could find absolutely no useable paper or cardboard in the Pigpen. She sat on her doorstep in darkness, elbows on her knees, her head in her hands. Finally, she darted back to the Pigpen and scrounged around with her flashlight until her sack held a ragged book, a shattered balloon and a piece of old linen.

35. Lolli Ousts Kasha

Doll returned the next morning and Gussy could see that her presence refined Robbie's speech and softened her voice. Still, Doll spent little time at the Den. She preferred the company of Syd lately and often went on deliveries with him. By the time Syd arrived in the park, Juju was bathed, Doll's hair was brushed, and a snack for only four was set in Lambeth's trailer. Doll's preference showed in the hollow-eyed look of Robbie who was more withdrawn every day, and cracked her knuckles as though they were Syd's bones. Robbie smoked incessantly now, and sadly folded cellophanes until the coil around her neck was wrapped around there twice.

What worried Quila most was a poised spider near her own cup handle, especially in evening tea: the most imminent of signs! Some person or some thing was ready to undermine the fragile setup of Last Resort.

From beneath Quila's wagon that afternoon Bowie could see into Kasha's yard where she and Lolli were relaxing. Gussy was sitting on her own doorstep while she recorded the little scene.

As Lolli lounged with Whiffet in her lap, she massaged the little dog's neck and clipped long hairs around his mouth. Idly, she looked up at the tree. This tree is greater than all other trees in the neighborhood, Lolli mused. A mistake, in a way, for its masses of cottony seeds fall in messy clouds throughout summer, making Enoch sneeze and sometimes Quila even wears a shawl over her hair. For birds it's a wonderful tree with bugs for food, plenty of nesting places and building material. But why does Gussy gather so much of the cottony stuff?

Everyone wanted the tree space but Lolli knew the unwritten rule. Whenever there was a vacancy under the tree, Gus always moved the Pigpen tenant into that coveted spot. Yes, everybody wanted the tree's protection and shade, except Lolli. She wanted it only because everyone else did. But it belonged to Kasha and she was Lolli's friend—or was she?

"You take better care of that silly lapdog than your own husband, Lolli!" Kasha was saying. "Have you ever rubbed Louie's tired neck at night, clipped his mustache or brushed his hair?" Lolli decided then and there that she had suffered Kasha long enough.

"Say, Kasha," Lolli's voice was casual and she smiled up at the tree. "Let's drop in at Robbie's tomorrow and have Quila read our fortunes!"

"I don't know—" Kasha hesitated. Robbie always added celery to the fare when chubby Kasha walked in. "Here Kasha, it takes more calories to eat celery than it has to begin with!"

"Come on Kasha, you can truly tell Robbie you've lost five pounds this week!"

That night, after Louie had fallen into one of his drunken stupors, Lolli sauntered up to the tree and gave its trunk a smug little pat. She started for Quila's wagon but suddenly Bowie blocked her way. "Nothing about Robbie!" Bowie warned.

"Look who's calling the kettle black!" Lolli taunted.

Bowie could have pushed her aside so easily and told Quila, himself, anything that she wanted to know. But Lolli shoved him away, climbed the wagon steps and softly knocked. Quickly, Bowie slid through Mange's door, and took long gulps from the bottle buried there. Above him they already spoke in whispers, yet Quila was covering her sweeping crack. Bowie put his arm around Mange and tried not to awaken him with trembling.

It didn't take long. Quila's door closed silently behind the informer and Quila sat pondering what Lolli had revealed.

"Stone blind I've been all this time not to see, and stone deaf not to believe," she whispered. She turned her head toward a faint jostle beneath her wagon. It was a dangerous ace that Lolli had traded her, but one too good not to tuck away for the future. She pulled away the floor rug that covered the sweeping crack.

"Yes, yes," she chuckled loudly, "tonight I've found me a gush of information. Too bad Bowie didn't tell me. 'Twas plain he knew all along!" She stomped on the wagon floor. "And we were goin' ta have fresh bread and potato soup, greened with little pigweeds he plucked fer me this mornin'!" She latched the door and loudly began rattling pots and pans.

The Den was alive with gaiety the next morning—Doll was there again. Bowie settled apprehensively beside one of the best peeking slits.

Inside, Lolli drizzled icing over the plate of graham crackers she had brought. But Lolli and Kasha had only come for tea.

When Robbie had seen Kasha enter, she had taken celery from the icebox, washed and cut it into pieces, while Quila was making tea.

"Why do ye make it sa hard, Robbie? Celery's blah and woody! Gypsy girls just press this hollow spot in front of their ear to control appetites." Quila put her hand over her tattletale mouth and shook her head in anger. Quickly Gussy wrote at the bottom of a sketch.

As Gussy shaded with her fingers, she noted that Lolli's eyes were sparkling like brown garnets from the velvet of her eyewhites; but Quila and Bowie only saw that Lolli's hard eyes were cruelly microscopic, taking apart several girls at one time.

Hurriedly, Gussy sketched nervous Kasha, then turned to Lolli. Lolli's eyes prowled the shadows while everyone else talked or joked and Doll sat brushing Juju's hair. Gussy made more quick sketches on several labels, then turned up a big piece of cardboard. Girls sprawled all around the floor and their pillows were scattered everywhere. The air smelled spicy and crackled with every movement they made. Gussy sketched, sipped coffee and smiled.

Quila looked at the disappearing crackers with contempt. Instinct assured her they were only a teasing sample of how superior Lolli's klatches could be, if her trailer were the preferred gathering place. Bowie grinned; whenever the grahams were passed curvaceous Lolli pressed on the Gypsy ear spot, and just passed the plate ahead.

Lolli edged away from Quila for gray hair always matted her shoulders and her clothing smelled musty and stale. Neck ornaments seemed to leave dirty, chalky arcs on her black dress, and there was always a streak of black somewhere on her skin. And, with clawlike fingernails always full of past meals, Quila was often scratching. It was painfully suspicious at the little mama-papa store down the street. There, Lolli had seen Quila scratch herself viciously, squeeze fruit with repulsive hands or smell it with her hooked nose pressed against the peeling. If a customer was nearby, Quila was either chased away or given the soiled article for less, or nothing, depending on the price of the item and who was looking.

Bowie watched with curiosity as Lolli's eyes wandered to Gussy while she drew. He stood on a box to see even more from a higher crack that he discovered. Kasha, Lolli, Gussy and several other girls were pressing on the hollows in front of their ears.

Lolli chuckled to herself. Gussy was so easy to see through. Her fingers were usually cut somewhere from scrounging in the Pigpen after dark. Like now, two fingers were tied with floral strips and blood had been oozing through. Gussy was drawing Robbie now, as she began her tidbits of world news. Why was Robbie always encouraging girls to enjoy crummy lives? What a waste, especially on these dimwits.

Lolli's grahams and Robbie's celery were gone, and Gussy's eyes had begun to settle a bit. Her eyes were always moving, noted Lolli, yet not seductively like a single girl's should. But somewhat like the Chips, Juju and Enoch's, for Gussy was always looking for ideas, scenes to draw or things to somehow reuse. God, she even got ideas from toilet paper!

Lolli watched Gussy pull a sharper pencil from behind one ear and turn up a new cardboard: Pug had entered reeking as usual of garlic, laundry soap and bleach. Pug went directly to Robbie's kitchen and began to empty things gathered into her apron, while Gussy recorded the scene: paper sacks in one drawer, jar lids in another, and small clean cans in the last. Then Pug took squares of cloth and poked them one at a time, onto a nail above the sink. When she finally backed into the big overstuffed chair, she sank into it loudly, as though it was her first rest in years. She pulled socks from beside the chair's cushion and dumped them into her greasy apron. Gussy studied the big woman and smiled while she sketched.

With a pin from the edge of her apron, Pug tacked back a corner of the curtain. She thimbled a fat finger and settled with a wooden darning egg, a needle, thread and a sock.

Lolli seldom wasted time looking at thick-ankled, thick-fingered people like Pug. The slight hunch and careless dressing of those used to hard work made Lolli wince. Huge, useful breasts, low-slung like pot cheese in two cloths, filled her with loathing. Besides, large, broad-bosomed, broad-faced women reminded her of things best forgotten. She wiped moisture from one eye. All that this hipless, waistless woman has to offer a man is sweat. Her hands are forever peeling, mending, pitting, and knitting for others. Why is she so contented?

After Pug's first sock was mended and she had started on another, Lolli watched something strange taking place. Safe in her gloomy nook, Pug's eyes, dull as mud, crept slowly upward. The otherwise clodlike body seemed to come to a tense life as the eyes finally rested upon Robbie and saw that hers seemed to be caressing Doll from behind her thick black lashes.

Lolli's simple intuition puzzled at the silent connection between the older Pug and the younger Robbie. They rarely spoke to each other. If only Lolli could crack the mystery, she might be queen of the park, not Robbie. Everything about Robbie repulsed Lolli, especially her strange, unintentional hold over all of the other women that seemed so drawn to her.

Outside, Bowie watched contemptuous jealousy narrowing Lolli's eyes as she studied Robbie. On Doll and Gussy, Lolli figured, their spotless jeans and shirts were garments. But on Robbie, her ragged jeans and hole-burned shirts were merely cloths that covered her. And Robbie was always spitting and hacking, whittling, cracking her knuckles, smelling of nicotine and alcohol, instead of soap or perfume.

While others talked, played cards or ate, Doll merely sat at the end of one bench, happily brushing Juju's hair, snipping it here and there, or just contentedly cuddling the child. Doll's eyes twinkled more only at the sound of the ice truck's coming. When she left with Juju for awhile, everyone in the Den became tense and quiet until Doll returned.

But now Fay entered (and furiously Gussy began to sketch her) in a tawdry dressing gown, face dotted with pink stuff, hair in curlers and eyes droopy with unfinished sleep. Fay's night self was exactly the opposite, thought Lolli, for then Fay jangled, rustled, or jingled, scattering noise like a southern belle dropping hankies. Today Fay tossed some bills in front of Robbie and glimpsing Doll, she left.

Bowie watched Quila's ugly fingers pouring tea just into Kasha and Lolli's cups, and while they drank, he became aware that Lolli was avoiding Kasha's eyes.

"Fie, it's rent time, agin, and who's ta help these auld eyes discover two spare fives?" Bowie snickered to himself: Quila seldom paid any rent.

Quila made a long agonizing ceremony of getting to the point as she twirled Kasha's empty cup in every direction, squeezed her eyes together tightly, and then began.

"Why, may I be poisoned by me own tea, if I don't see sandwiches high as a Jewish temple. And fie! What is running through their middles? Animals that don't chew cud! Animals with cloven hooves! And look, there on the side–someone scrubbin' walls with bleach, tryin' ta erase that porky smell afore someone comes in the door! Now, why would I see such a strange thing in this teacup?"

That afternoon Gussy had a hankering for shrimp. She had saved enough pop bottles to buy one can, which she drained and was cutting up at one sink in the washhouse. Lolli watched her, then spoke directly to Gussy for the first time since Louie had fixed her window. Lolli's sarcastic voice awakened Bowie beneath Quila's wagon and he could tell that Lolli's plot was continuing just as she had been planning.

"Aren't you gonna clean the crap outa that shrimp?" she sneered as Gussy worked.

"It says cleaned and ready to eat on the label."

"God, you really are green!" Lolli mocked. "Things aren't always what they're labeled, kid!" She looked stealthily around, then picked up a fat shrimp and ran her curved fingernail along its back, gathering up the heretofore-invisible refuse. "Open your eyes, kid! Black scum can be under the purest label. Come here, I want to show you something else."

Dragging Gussy behind her, Lolli cat-footed over to the incinerator. She poked in ashes and lifted charred cloth that was left from men's shorts. As they smoldered she dangled them at the end of her stick.

"Everyone knows why Fay burns what she should be washing. She's lazy! But that's not Robbie's reason. She's ashamed! Yuck! It's bad enough to wear men's outer clothes, but this, ugh! God, it must feel uncomfortable!" She almost whispered now, "I sure would hate to have a queer for one of <u>my</u> best friends!" Having made her point, Lolli hurried away, and Gussy, in a shock of revulsion, reached over and dumped the shrimp into a trashcan.

36. The Tree Space

Later, Bowie was enjoying cool ground beside Holly when he smelled a soapy scent at Gussy's door. "Hi!" said Doll, fondling the black cat. "Lolli gave me an idea. We're both bottle blondes so why not trade bleach jobs? I've got ammonia, soap chips and peroxide, even a bowl and toothbrush. If you do my hair, I'll do yours. We both need touch ups, don't you agree?"

"Well, yes." Gussy hesitated, distrusting anything Lolli would suggest.

"If you don't want to."

"It's just that I haven't supplies."

"I've plenty for two," Doll put Spade on a bench, and began to mix ingredients.

It should have been a pleasure having Doll do her brown-rooted hair, but the mental picture of Doll's fingers linked with Robbie's was discomforting. Finally Gussy picked up a piece of old flannel she had been hemming. While Doll dabbed stinging foam along each new parting, Gussy nervously punched and pulled little stitches around the edge of the cloth.

"Doll," she asked impulsively, "do you ever plan to leave this place?"

"Why leave? Where would I go? There's nothing else I want." Doll wiped her hands, sighed, lifted the cat up to her cheek. "At least, nothing that I can ever have—"

Here it comes, thought Bowie, stone-quiet as his body tensed and waited.

"Eagerly, for fifteen years," Doll explained, "I've waited for what mother told me was God's sign that he wanted me to marry and bear children. It's never come. It would be a crime for me to marry a good young man when I can't have his wonderful children."

Despite Doll's confidence, while Gussy worked on her, there was a strained silence. When Gussy finished and was cleaning up, she could stand it no longer. "Doll, why don't you ever wear dresses, lipstick or perfume? There's talk that you and Robbie are–are–"

"Don't even say it!" With a loud clatter, Doll threw supplies into the bowl. "Guess I was wrong to think that you could be any different." Doll grabbed up the cat, slammed the door and headed for one of the toilets, to get control of herself while the bleach did its work.

From the open toolshed, which Bowie had quietly entered, he could hear Doll whispering to Spade in the next stall. "I have learned to love from Robbie, Spade. I used to know where I was going–nowhere. Now I know that it's somewhere, somehow, and I'm frightened. God, I can't help it! I do love Robbie. I'm afraid of men! Life is so breathless with Robbie around. I need her. I always come back to her! What's the matter with me, Spade? I keep trying and trying to stay away, but I just can't do it for very long!"

That night, Gussy thought it was Spade when the hollyhock trembled in the breezeless night. Later, long after Doll and Robbie had taken off in St. Vitus, Gussy lifted the lid on the first trash can, and there on top of everything was a moonlit "Q", a wreathe made of leaves and hollyhock blossoms, that only Doll could have been responsible for. Gussy hurried into her trailer and rolled up the kitchen shade. Holly stared in accusingly, stripped of flowers, buds and leaves, spindling tall and naked in the sad summer night. Even worse than Holly's fate was the sinking knowledge that never again would Gussy feel welcome at Robbie's Den.

The next morning everyone in the park was buzzing about Quila's strange fortune for Kasha about animals running through sandwiches, for Kasha's trailer had disappeared.

Bowie spent the morning digging in bottle mounds. Disappointed, he headed for the canyon to make a fire and brew plant tea. He drank tea slowly, remembering. He had told Quila such innocent things about the nondescript Jewish woman, whose only delight was food, especially certain food forbidden by religion. He threw the rest of his tea on the fire, then headed back to the park, intending to silently share Gussy's coming disappointment.

All day Gussy waited patiently for the sound of Gus' truck pulling up to the tongue of her trailer and preparing for the transfer to Kasha's vacant spot.

She packed her few dishes. While doing so, she decided to leave Holly, a bit of happiness for the new tenant. She board-scraped around her space, and pushed debris farther back into the Pigpen. She scrubbed the floor, mirror, table, sink, icebox and stove. With nothing more to do, she stuffed bits of paper and rags into possible ant and cockroach entries, helped a fly to freedom outside the door, and gave her dish gardens a good rinsing.

Instead, Gus backed up to Lolli's trailer.

Tearfully, Gussy looked at the tree from her window. Lolli would never appreciate shifting patterns that the tree spread over dirt. She would never bother to tidy branchlets squeaking against tops of her trailer. Never would she dust hot leaves with a cooling spray from the hose, pull off mistletoe or notice perfect holes for nesting sites.

Never ever, like Gussy had done very early one morning, would Lolli climb high enough to see the ocean, distant mountains or Dom's church spire. And never would she discover, then sadly pat deep initials carved high up on the trunk of the tree.

That night Gussy sat with elbows on the table again, chin in her palms, and eyes held shut with her fingers. "It's happy sounds that I'll miss the most–and Robbie," her voice was quivering. There was a long silence. "That's it!" she exclaimed. "Those will be my new and beautiful sounds. I have already found and saved most of the glass, metal and wood."

A few nights later, Bowie was sleeping beneath the wagon, when a sudden breeze created a new combination of sounds. Usually it was quiet in wee hours of night. An occasional dog barked, cats snarled, a coyote howled, waves crashed or a train whistled in the distance. But new sounds were stirring old feelings. He could not return to sleep until he found the source. He crept over to Gussy's from where the sounds were coming.

Something new hung under her awning: a little branch of the tree with knotted strings suspended from it. Tied to the strings were pieces of metal, old wood, little bones and perfume bottles, all making their own kind of music in the breeze. Looking closer at the contraption, his skin got goose-pimply, and his eyes began to deceive him. He rushed to Quila's refuge and drank the rest of the bottle hidden there, for Gussy's wind chimes had suddenly reminded him of rattling seed pods, deer hooves and birds' beaks.

Within a week the hollyhock drooped to a withered stick. Gussy never rolled up the shade where bright little Holly once peeked into her lonely kitchen. Now Gussy seemed almost frantic in her longing for something sweet and living to confide in.

With her trailer beneath the coolness of the tree, and Robbie and Doll gone for a while, Lolli was the first to make friends with any newcomers. Whenever Gussy passed by it was evident that Lolli had told them all about the "Pigpen Posy", as Lolli now called her, and whispered of her gory midnight adventures. Bowie realized that even in her newfound happiness beneath the tree, Lolli had a long memory and would never, it seemed, forget Louie's cheerful fixing of Gussy's window.

It was hard to smell Lolli's perking coffee and fresh baking, yet not be asked to join. Without the food and fun of the Den, Gussy slept odd hours, transferred practice sketches to larger cardboards, marked pages of the dictionary and wrote for hours in her odd diary.

On Lolli's say, so girls kept giving Gussy the cold shoulder. She was never asked to coffee; she was never included in conversations. When she entered the washhouse she got the silent treatment and when she left she could hear backbiters starting in on her.

It should have been easy for Gussy to hate them, but it wasn't in her nature. They closed doors on laughter, cutting it off in the middle, and if Gussy was near they shut windows tighter. When Gussy hurried by, they walked like snooty marchers.

In her loneliness, Gussy began a pitiful ritual, Bowie noted. At dawn, noon and dusk she pretended to have company for meals, setting a place for her guest and calling him, "Tad."

"Oh well, Tad, Christmas is coming." Gussy sighed, "I can't draw all the time. Some of the time I have to 'make'." "Making," Bowie noted, meant new things from the Pigpen: thread from hems to wind on ice cream sticks, buttons snipped from clothing, rectangles cut from colorful dresses, sticks from the tree and sweaters unwound to make balls of yarn.

Bowie knew for sure that the first part of Lolli's plan was to turn Robbie and the park against Gussy, so that she herself could get and keep the tree space. Somehow, he knew this was only step one in Lolli's plan to dethrone Robbie. Yet, Bowie shrugged off the desire to smile at Gussy, to comfort her. It wasn't right, all of those changes in the little trailer. She didn't belong here! And his wine was nowhere safe from Gussy's constant searching.

At last Robbie and Doll returned in a burst of red dust, stopping briefly for the keys. They didn't seem a bit surprised to see Lolli's trailer beneath the shade of the tree.

37. Lolli's Secrets

"Stay Quila, don't go," pleaded Lolli when others left for the Den. "I can help you," she whispered. "Together we can knock down the kingpin and this place can be all ours!"

Quila's face split into a serrated sneer. "Leave kingly backs to cope with kingly cares, m'dear; your back is made of muck!"

"Well, I'll still be around, should you ever fall with Robbie–slavie!"

Quila stared intently in Lolli's direction. "The slave has but one master, sweetie. The ambitious cannot count those he must bend to!" Quila grabbed a homemade cookie for Bowie and tucked it into her sleeve. Then another one for herself before leaving. Lolli plunked her big hat on and headed to the store for some instant approval, without one backward look at dishes in the sink or the last pan of cookies in the oven.

At the sound of Robbie's sputtering, clattering car returning, Bowie had stirred beneath the wagon, but he wasn't finished with a sudden recalling. Mange yawned loudly, snuggled closer and fell asleep again while Bowie resumed his drowsy remembering.

Nighttimes, Bowie briefly watched all of the trailers. Daytimes, the Den had top priority. When Robbie and Doll were gone, Bowie spent his days under the wagon or in the storeroom, half-asleep, listening for statements, exaggerations, flaunts, anything deviating from patterns. Often he listened to children for they had an uncanny, naive perception.

Today, above the din of children, Lolli's voice returned to the park, loud and phony (yet mellow right now). Her voice carried easily to where Bowie napped. "Thank you, dear sweet boy," she cooed, "I'll take the groceries now. He's so jealous–Louie, you know. But I don't dwell on it. To be pacific, he lets no male past the threshold," she lied.

Lolli's treks to the neighborhood store were the highlights of her days. She trailed a large-brimmed hat behind her, seldom wearing it. It was as much a trademark as her cattish sidewise walk and bare brown feet. She always paused before stepping back into the park's driveway for some moon-eyed boy or another often carried her groceries home, insuring her of a grand (though usually unnoticed) entrance. With the boy rewarded, Lolli put groceries away. Then she would return outside with Whiffet, a coke and a fresh stick of gum.

But today there was smoke coming from her open trailer door and it smelled of burned cookies. It took awhile to air and clean her kitchen. At last she shook her brown towel and spread it out near the driveway, away from the shade of the tree, where she could keep an eye on daily happenings and try to not miss Kasha, the only friend that she had ever had.

It seemed to Bowie that Lolli's only business in life was taunting. Daylong was her lazing, and, from where she always stretched out, women had to give her envious looks as they passed to and from work, to the mailbox or store. Lolli stretched her tawny limbs high up into warm sunlight. As she oiled them they glistened and caught the eyes of any appreciative male passerby. The sunsuits she wore were carefully chosen to be the same skin-colored material, seeming to merely add sheen to her body and subtly mark off her limbs.

Through sleepy eyes, she looked to Bowie as uninteresting as a brown gopher snake. Besides, she never walked; she slithered.

It was of no use to closely watch Lolli. She was a deedless girl, doing nothing much of the day but brush her long thick hair, which was the color of bitter acorns, and anoint her beautiful body, which was of the very same tone and sheen. Bowie poured some wine down fast to swamp some gathering memory. Lolli was spreading suntan lotion over her tapered fingers, provocative legs and slim arms, enjoying the silken feel as though caressing a lover's body. Her husband did what work there was to do. "You're too lazy to even curl your hair, Lolli! It's so damned straight!" complained Louie. Lolli's eyes merely sparkled.

Bowie couldn't understand Lolli. She must have been pursued all her life. But going by Louie's shy mannerisms, it was probably Lolli that chased Louie. Why then, did she taunt everyone but Louie? She showed more love for the little panda hiding beneath her pillow. "Pansy-Bear" she called it when all alone. Publicly, all of her passion she unleashed on Whiffet, the creamy-white poodle with no woolly dog smell at all. Whenever she wasn't creaming, brushing or perfuming herself, it was Whiffet. With maternal protectiveness, Lolli hated Spade who spurned the poodle's size, cowardly ways and unnatural smell.

Unlike Fay, Lolli was a daylily. By night her bloom wilted; she was "too tired." When Louie was amorous, she would hedge, "Let's have a drink first, to get in the mood." Then Lolli looked at him with affectionate disdain, patting the table softly, knowing he'd be drunk by bedtime, asleep at the table or off to find drinking cronies. When Louie returned, Whiffet would be happily spread out– on the spot between Louie and Lolli.

But often, as Louie drunkenly slept and snored, Bowie had watched by moonlight as it peeked into a window, while Lolli smoothed Louie's curly dark hair, kissed his eyebrows and whispered in his ear–things she would never, never do when he was awake.

Often Louie returned at night so drunk that he merely slept sitting up in the car, his head drooping farther and farther down, until it hit the horn. Then he awoke with a start, and the procedure began all over again. "Aw, help him in, and let us get some sleep!" someone always shouted, and though Lolli helped him in, she had to "pay" for it too. Finally, she told a grocer boy that her horn often stuck and he told her how to disconnect it.

Bowie's ears pricked up, his eyes opened. Lolli, although sarcastic, was slow to show anger. "You meddling little bastard!" Bowie's subconscious mind reconstructed the scene.

"Whydaya sit in the sun all day when there's shade close by!" one Chip had coaxed.

"It's so beneficiary to my skin," Lolli answered between palm beats on the towel.

"Whydaya use that stuff?" the other Chip pointed to the bottle marked, "Suntan."

"It just helps. Now run along, I'm sleepy." Disgruntled, one Chip kicked a can before him. He turned back to Lolli and shouted: "There's nothin' in that bottle but water!"

"You meddling little bastard!" Lolli hissed again. Bowie didn't breathe.

"I know it's nothin' but water! I tasted it!" the Chip streaked away.

Bowie began stringing facts together. Extremely contented and lulled by more wine, he fell asleep again, contemplating the evening meal and rewarding night. This little happening at Lolli's was something he would not mask in telling Quila. He could always feel Lolli waiting like a coiled rattler to strike at the whole setup of the park. Her brown palms seemed to be always strumming away the minutes, shortening up the hours until it was time.

Women's hands should never be idle like Lolli's, he lamented as he poured the sweet fermented grapes into his twisted memory. Women's hands should be weaving, patting bread, gathering seeds, jerking venison, beating softness into clothes or rocking babies. He frantically drank himself into a stupor. Without seeing Quila, he slept through the night.

Tugging bleary eyes open, the next morning Bowie watched as Lolli, without Kasha or anyone else to coffee with, walked towards the Den.

Quila's fortune that day could have been for any one of them, as, often when she had nothing timely to divulge, she put an extra cup in the middle of the table and read broadly for the whole group. She pulled a generality out of her brain and dibbled bait. "Hmm, I see a pillowcase. Fie, what is on it? Curly dark hairs?" She looked dramatically about the group. "No," she whispered. "Curly light hairs!" She tasted the tea in her own cup and winced. "Sugar ain't nothin' like me favorite honey the grocer saves fer me!"

They all snickered, but the "hush-honey" she loved so well was beside the milk bottle that night. Quila read the grocer's palm and he told her it was Lolli who bought the honey.

Quila listened to Bowie knowingly that night and in a few days she "saw" another pillow. This time it was "covered with curly dog hairs. The dark brown ones be over on the edge o' the cup on the breakfast nook couch. Why now, would anyone prefer a yellow-bellied pooch to a red-blooded man? And why would a body settle fer wild tea, when two pieces o' bacon and two fresh eggs have turned up on their doorstep like magic?"

You can jerk off your loincloth, Lolli, Quila clucked to herself before she fell asleep, before she heard her stair steps creak and felt bare footsteps telling her that she and Bowie would have bacon and eggs for breakfast. You've no secrets left, Lolli, she thought drowsily. Stark as an arctic winter you are, though you're madly in love with Louie! But we'll save that tidbit until the very last. I'll ration out all the little things about you, Lolli. Like Pansy-Bear under your pillow, the strange way you uncurl your hair, fooling around with car wires in the dark. Quila fell asleep, savoring Lolli's "dynamite" for the very, very last blast.

38. Raked Web

It was almost midnight a few nights later when Quila finally heard a hesitant creak on her steps. She took a loaf of sourdough from its muslin cloth and began to slice.

"Yer wet-shod, Bowie!" she complained at muddy spots on her thirsty wooden floor. "Ye've been spyin' on Posy," she prompted as he sat down. "Did ye pluck me a 'tell petal'?"

"Maybe," he stuffed the tasteless bread into his mouth. "Dry as sand," he coughed.

"It's the best we have, m'laddie, and the last!" She brought out a bottle but held it in her lap. "Well?" she bargained.

"The worst she does is root in the Pigpen. And she carries a sack for trash so the park looks much better," he stalled. Quila started to return the bottle.

"Well, I do have three little secrets," he ventured, rapping the table with a mug three times. Eagerly, three times she barely filled it, and as he poured each mug-full down in almost a single gulp, she waited, impatience creeping into the drumming of her fingers.

"Stuffy in here," he pushed the door ajar. "Three secrets? She has moles like beetles on a bun!" he blurted, then bolted out the door. Sticking his head back in, he whispered. "Here!" pointed to his bottom side, slammed the door and ran down the creaky steps.

Quila was tired of his whetting her curiosity with a whiff, a peek and now a humorous hint. Aye, she knew he was struggling against telling her something big, often going hungry and wineless because he had already traded the minor things.

Yes, she knew he worked hard for the little she had to feed him. His muscles ached from long hours of unproductive inactivity, his feet were always falling asleep, his neck was sore and his eyes burned. But it was time to teach Bowie a lesson.

Bowie felt suspicious when the raked "web" first started around Gussy's doorstep, then sprawled into the trash yard. Up to the washhouse it spread fragile fingers and finally clung to tires and leveling blocks of every one of the trailers.

The raking started one evening when Gussy and Quila stood beside the washhouse watching Juju's rag drag frantically back and forth over the driveway, making plaid patterns across the lighted area of dirt. It was way past time for dinner; Juju was shaking with hunger, but mama, Fay, was still entertaining in the darkened back of the trailer. From underneath the wagon Bowie could hear the two women talking.

"Strange how that rag do drag," said Quila to Gussy, who was drawing a pot of hot water. "Look how it makes its own 'footprint.' Everybody has unique footfalls, ye know. Orientals, they kinda shuffle. Indians stalk on the outsides o' their feet, leaving curved 'moons'"—Bowie's heart sank—"where moccasined feet have been. They say that Indians, when they're a-drinkin', sometimes get murderous around white women!" Bowie could see her cross her fingers behind her. "It's funny, how the redskin has such 'a thing' about that little trailer o' yers." Having made her planned point, Quila chuckled and scurried away.

Later, while Bowie was catnapping, Gussy borrowed a hammer from Gus, pulled nails from an old box and straightened them. She drove the nails in two lines through the length of one narrow board. Nailing it to an old broom handle, she used the "rake" like a huge comb, making whorls and stripes in red dirt around her trailer, and as far underneath as she could reach. She removed enough boxes to rake the space between her trailer and the fence. What use was there anymore to stack boxes to hide the place where Holly only used to grow?

But there she found a heart-warming surprise: Holly was in full bloom! But the blooms were not a familiar pink; now they were all a beautiful lavender. Oh well, she had never understood gardening. Carefully she restacked the wall of boxes.

Late at night now, thanks to Quila, Gussy took it for granted that Bowie might be back there. And even though she didn't find the half-moons that she had expected to see zigzagging across any of her rakings, she was careful now to bathe and undress in the dark.

While tenants slept, Gussy's web grew and grew. Like Gussy had watched Juju's rag create frantic unplanned patterns, now she created her own flowing designs.

Bowie wondered if anyone else in the whole world had ever had the privilege of watching an artist at work who had only the moon for lighting, only a makeshift rake for a brush and only dirt for a colored canvas.

Endless days and nights dragged on for Bowie. To avoid Gussy's rakings, he prowled on the other side of the fence line, then climbed back over the splintery barrier, dropping next to a trailer that he wanted to watch that night. He hopped gingerly around the park, for he still had four bottles of wine stashed away, but no food. Now he was sure that Quila was punishing him; she did little cooking lately, and she never answered his frantic knocks. All that he could find in the canyon were tasteless pigweeds, over-dried wild fruits, new grass and leaves from various plants to brew into tea. He watered down the last bottles of wine as he drank them. He tried to sleep the days through and the evenings as well.

Yet always, like tonight, he awoke at silence of the park. Faint pulse of darkness itself, a leaky faucet throbbed from the washhouse. Mange snored peacefully beside him. Movements were only in the Pigpen: scuttles of rats, spirals of smoke and two eerie pupils of Spade twining as she searched. The tortuous odor of Pug's nightly soup soaked the still air and his stomach began to grind on aroma alone. Then, like tiny trumpeters, crickets that Gussy kept in a jar announced the time of day that Bowie and Gussy liked best.

First he vaulted over Quila's side of the fence, following outside of it until he reached Fay's trailer. He scrambled over the rock wall, scooted past clothes bags and pulled out the chinkrag. Immediately, sin bubbled out like marsh gas. But there was nothing new here to trade with Quila. She knew it all. Every detail. Still, he stayed, until evil totally soaked his right eye and it felt like a wad of dirty wet mud. Drawing away, he rubbed the painful eye, but it was the other eye that worried him. He couldn't open it at all!

However unscientific, he knew the eye needed instant beauty to revive it. A tiny breeze was giving voice to Gussy's new wind chimes, and he glanced toward her light.

He became a fly on the fringe of a sticky web, meticulously picking his way toward her trailer. In moonlight he walked now on tiptoe, checking behind him to be sure that curved moons were never following. On fingertips and knees now, with moccasins held up high, he crept beneath Gussy's trailer until he reached the back fence. Gussy was in the Pigpen making little noises that nobody else would be able to decipher. He hunched low, lit a cigarette and sat against the fence to think until she returned to her trailer.

Since falling out with Doll, Gussy never went to the Den. She wouldn't be slipping food into her large blouse pockets anymore, so she had gone back to wearing Doll's threadbare jeans and Robbie's big patched shirts. Now she did most of her work at night. She slept a few hours in daytime, did housework, raked in the evening, or at night when the moon was just right. Patiently she awaited the dying of each day: last swish of the wash machine, last female curse, last garbage lid clatter and the last note of Robbie's record.

While she waited, she sketched by candlelight on every size and kind of cardboard, on every scrap of can label, on any part of paper or other kind of weird "canvas" the Pigpen had to offer. Lately, she also crocheted, mended, cut and hemmed pieces of colorful cloth. She wrapped coat hangers with strips of material, and painted sticks from the tree. She made a cardboard eye with a hole in the middle of it, and an apron with big pockets.

Tonight after scavenging, Gussy enjoyed her session of "painting" dirt by moonlight. Bowie had time to enjoy smoking, listening to Gussy's wind chimes and watching the moon drift among clouds. Reaching across the wine bottle fence, he picked up a windblown toilet paper blossom and refastened it to one of the strings spiraling up an awning pole.

When her weird artistry was finished, Bowie slipped under Gussy's trailer while all around her doorstep and edges of the little trailer she "mended" like a little spider her intricate web of earth, not realizing that the "insect" was already safely waiting inside the net. He waited at the back window, pushing the paper curtain aside with his wire, as slowly Gussy back-stepped up onto her apple box porch, erasing her own footprints as she walked. She left the rake outside, and took inside her sack of gleanings. Then Gussy took plunder from each sack and filed each item into a cupboard, icebox, drawer, magazine rack or the sink to be washed.

With the bag of soap chips she washed herself by candlelight. Watching her was a lovely sight. Moisture on her skin was dew on a primrose. Gussy blew out the candle.

Before, Gussy seemed to enjoy wondering whether Bowie was outside or not, sharing words and thoughts. But she was becoming quiet, and always undressed with the candle out.

Bowie couldn't understand Quila's fears. Gussy was no threat to anything but the gray trailer. She was too innocent, childlike, passive. She couldn't destroy the delicate balance that kept things as they were. She wouldn't want to! "But, it's in the cards, the tea leaves–everywhere!" whispered Quila.

Gussy had pulled off her shirt, Bowie could tell by vague outlines. Over bare shoulders blond hair was fragile wings. She pulled off her jeans as Bowie leaned closer.

Sharply, from behind a cloud, sudden moonlight from the transom filled the trailer and Bowie stared at Gussy. So like his Phantom she looked. In the silence his stomach growled loudly, then he heard footsteps running away. Startled, he ducked beneath the trailer and fled across the giant web of dirt, the trap that was carefully set for him every night.

Earlier, when everyone's light was finally out, Gussy had quietly sprinkled water around her trailer then lightly corrugated the dampness with her strange rake. Now Bowie felt like a crust-hunter, running on snow that was strong enough to support the game, but not the hunter. Entrapped behind him was a jagged line of curved moons.

Quila's light was on. Bowie crept up the steps and knocked, only to hear her bolt. He fell against the door, slid down it, exhausted. "I'm ready, Quila. Starved. It's about Gussy."

"Too late, Bowie! Me and Lolli, we're havin' a midnight snack." Quila chuckled, "And ah, the tidbit that we're sharin'!"

Next morning Gussy found she had captured footprints of a prowler who left crescents fleeing from under her trailer. But there had also been another, who had stood at her front window, and then left hurried barefoot tracks that led to Quila's wagon.

That afternoon Gussy motioned to Bowie, pointed to the prints, like relics preserved in wet patterns. "If I ever see those prints again, I'll swear a warrant for your arrest!"

Bowie was unmoved; he sneered at the fragile child she was. "You wicked peeping Tom," she shouted under her breath, "I'll call the police and have you jailed for prowling. Vagrancy. Drunkenness!" Bowie shrugged. "If that doesn't work, I'll tell them I'm afraid. That sometimes you look at me, living in this particular trailer, and murder is in your eye!" ventured Gussy between clenched teeth. Pleased with herself for taking this wild chance, Gussy watched complacently as Bowie pulled his feet from the patterned dirt like it were quicksand. He reached down and grooved out the telltale curves with his fingernails.

That afternoon, Bowie watched Gussy sketching on her doorstep again. She propped her work beside the trailer while she checked the mailbox. Hurrying over, Bowie saw that Gussy had drawn a bow on a piece of cardboard. It was clear: now she knew that Bowie's business was watching and that he was in partnership with Quila. Gussy had drawn Quila's skinny arm for an arrow shaft and one of her knotty fingers for an arrowhead. The weapon was aimed through a knothole and its gnarly forefinger was wearing Quila's ugly beetle ring.

That evening Bowie waited for Quila to leave the park. Beside the curbing she scooped up sand for scrubbing dishes, as Bowie sneaked into her trailer. He jerked off a chunk of coarse bread, wiped the stew pot, popped it into his mouth and was barely gone before she returned.

39.   Gussy Discovers the Chips and Juju

Vapors of lunch were taking their teasing time that next afternoon, when Quila paused at Gussy's doorstep where she was sketching the washhouse. "Come over ta Robbie's, pet. We'll have ice coffee with our poker. Could use another hand."

"Just waitin' for guts to hang out," said Lolli, walking by with a sly grin on her face. "Take my word. Don't let it happen!"

Gussy felt uneasy and maneuvered, but couldn't resist memories of the Den.

Bowie, sensing a rising crisis in the apparent thaw, got up from beside the coolness of Holly and took the long way, outside of the fence, to Robbie's shed. Bowie spent a lot of time in back of Gussy's trailer now. Without Gussy to keep sessions interesting and lively, Robbie seldom gave a newscast or served anything with an interesting explanation. Even when Doll was there, Robbie's Den just hadn't seemed the same anymore. He peeked inside.

Already deep in a smoke-fog, the Den reeked of intrigue. Gussy's pillows were still scattered, yet strangely, there was nobody there today but Pug, Robbie and Quila. Gussy was surprised they weren't playing for butts or pennies, but a game that she had never heard of called "Strip Poker". Quila must have known the cards. Instead of mixing them up several times, she only made one sloppy shuffle.

Drinking three bottles of red wine, with crackers, cheese and grapes in a Robbie-tray, they practiced for a time, while Quila and Robbie exchanged witticisms. Card-dumb Gussy seemed to easily be ahead. It was wonderful for Bowie to watch Gussy basking again in Robbie's presence. Bee-like, Robbie touched a sterile topic with wordy pollen and it sprung to exciting fertility. The glacial air that Gussy had expected seemed to have melted, as once again Robbie shared her infectious laughter.

But then, Bowie heard nervous clicking of fingernails and shortly, Quila threw out the bait.

"Yer in the seedtime of life, me lass. 'Tis sad ye ain't shoppin' male catalogues." Quila snickered at her pun while Gussy paled. Robbie drained her mug and poured again.

It was past ducking time when Quila handed condolences. "Ye've a greeny look, little church mouse!" Quila offered a stick of gum. "Caulkin' compound, dearie?"

Robbie opened more wine. With helpless despair, Bowie watched Gussy bet everything in her pockets—change, scissored butts, matches; reluctantly, her sandals. Quila fanned her cards and flourished her sleeves in a way that Bowie knew exactly what was happening. Tension was so fierce Pug gathered corn she was shucking, unlocked the door and left. Robbie filled mugs again and Quila locked the door.

When Quila topped Gussy's four aces with a royal flush, Bowie held his breath.

Quickly, too quickly, Quila shuffled lightly and dealt again. "Ante," she urged impatiently. "Come on, come on. Me auld bones be fallin' ta sleep!"

But Gussy rose quickly like a trapped animal.

"Ye've still Robbie's shirt and Doll's jeans, m'posy. Two more tricks 'till yer in a bind. Ye wouldn't renege on pals? What's the matter, have ye purple hide or somethin'?" Quickly Quila reached up and easily tore the threadbare shirt off of Gussy.

Slim as a stem Gussy had been, sponging herself as she hummed in the suddenly filtered moonlight of the transom. Slim as the faceless wraith in Bowie's mind, she was. And Gussy's belly was just the same. Like a swollen gall on a young twig. And barefooted Lolli had traded that fact to Quila.

Casually, Robbie glanced over at where Gussy bellied out from under a growing chain of safety pins that held her jeans together. Slowly, Robbie lit a cigarette. "Well, what do you know! Our prissy posy's been deflowered!"

Robbie was really drunk and hurting, thought Bowie, or she'd never be so crude.

"Ye made overlabor of concealment, m'dearie. But ye were a fishie in a glass trailer, tryin' ta prove she could fly. Can't scrub scars from a soul, me pet, nor birth from a body. 'What I wouldn't give fer a kosher pickle, Holly.' Tsk, tsk, a fool could see you're spouseless. Not even a shadow on your ring finger!" Quila gathered the cards.

"So that explains the wee cherub I've been ignorin' near handles o' your teacups!"

Gussy looked long and hard, not at Quila, but at Robbie, while a big tear meandered down her cheek. She looked at her now bare feet, unlocked the door and stepped outside, gripping shreds of the shirt against her heart.

"Get out of here Quila! I'm either going to vomit or drown myself!" Robbie sobbed.

That night Gussy forgot all about the Pigpen or raking. Bowie heard her talking to the dark when she settled into bed—evidently there was no doubt about the day's lesson.

"Thank you Life, for proving it: my hero can be no one else outside of me!"

The Chips began to trust Gussy that next afternoon when she gathered up a handful of potato peels from a garbage can and slapped a poultice on the blackened eye of one Chip. From then on, she was a shepherdess and they behaved like lambs for her. She paid attention to their feats, admired and guided them. She seemed to think they were not really bad, just bored and starved for affection like Gussy was. Though she felt two-faced for using their innocent friendship, Gussy knew that she really needed it.

When the Chips threw mud balls at each other, Gussy soon had them chinking spaces and knotholes in her back fence with red dirt "plaster" and scraping it flush with boards until there were no places for snuffing butts, thought Bowie. When the Chips threw rotten fruit at a bull's-eye they had slyly made on her trailer, Gussy seized her opportunity. "Wait, would you like real paint to work with?"

And so her trailer was painted, using old sponges, cylinders from toilet paper, cloth, palms and fingers on paint sediments that she had collected from the Pigpen. She had tried thinning paint dregs with a variety of liquids—vinegar, alcohol, water and wine. But this only created "new" colors with bubbles, blobs and smears that only a child could appreciate. Now, the little trailer became a hodgepodge of colors, textures and shapes like some wildman's canvas. Bowie shook his head. Quila was worried about this tenant? The Chips had never had any freedom, direction and materials with which to be creative, and Bowie had never seen them really happy before.

That night Gussy added the same wild colors to the collage of her little trailer.

The Chips looked at Gussy adoringly; only she could stop their stick-sword defacing, without de-knighting them. When they began gouging grooves in old Lambeth's trailer with wire clothes hangers, Gussy distracted them. "Have you ever made a throwing hoop?" she asked while she fashioned a circle with one of the hangers. Soon, all the kids in the park were ringing wooden stakes that Gussy had pounded into the Pigpen. Yes, Gussy had a way with the little bulls. Around her they seemed to be completely dehorned, reflected Bowie.

It was only because Gussy was so good to them that they resisted her beautiful porch step. They watched her as she painted the outside boards of the stepping box with more of the blobby paint she had created. New flowers brushed on the sides of the step were not flat like the bizarre paint itself they had dimensions all their own. They watched her nail a bit of old rug on top that matched red dirt of the park. What a wonderful toy box that would make! Someday, they might even have some toys to put in it. The enchanting doorstep was always there, something to keep in reserve for a particularly irresistible or revengeful occasion, Bowie figured. When they played near her trailer the twins often stared at Gussy's little work of art, as it sat there, seeming to openly taunt them.

Gussy was mending a clothes pin with flour paste and string when she looked out the window one day to see Juju drifting across the driveway like a bedraggled butterfly. Doll was gone, Gussy remembered. The child had soiled her orange blotched diaper and walked woodenly, "Like a clothes pin doll twist-walking in a child's hand," Gussy sighed out loud as Juju held up the seat of her nightgown so she could walk without tripping. Bowie watched from a curtain gap as Gussy fashioned a face on the mended clothespin. Before she went after the child, she covered one bench of the breakfast nook with layers and layers of newspapers; then she created a newspaper path from there clear out to the porch step.

After placing the child sideways, so she wouldn't have to look at the ugly cheek, Gussy poured weak fruit-peel punch for the two of them. On the table she opened cereal boxes full of rolled material scraps, ice-cream sticks wound with thread, little balls of colored yarn, assorted buttons and a bar of soap stuck with pins and needles. Soon the wooden doll had a bonnet and dresses, a skirt and blouses, tiny shoes and a drawstring wardrobe bag.

Though Gussy talked and answered herself, the child had never showed emotion. By now Juju's squirming and foul odor were unendurable. Gussy gingerly sat the child outside. "Come again tomorrow?" said Gussy, exaggerating her lip movements as though the child were deaf. But I'll never invite you inside again, she vowed. Quickly Bowie ducked beneath the trailer as Gussy wound the windows wider and carried soggy newspapers to the Pigpen.

Though Gussy never asked the child inside again, she found things to do outside with her. Gussy sat on the porch step herself, while Juju sat in the dirt. From cardboard boxes Gussy made a house for the clothespin doll, and she made it a mate.

Juju never even came close to a smile. Yet she began to wait for Gussy with her rag and an empty bottle to suck on, cat-napping beneath the newly painted trailer.

But Gussy was not as bright in Bowie's eyes as she once had been. Though Gussy enjoyed Juju's companionship, she avoided contact with the grubby little hands and the matted black curly head. She seldom looked Juju straight in the face; she was too filled with repulsive pity at the heart-breaking birthmark. There was no way to pretty up the scarred face and no way to camouflage the odor of her diapers, concluded Bowie, without touching the child. Gussy was good at prettying the surface of things but there was absolutely no way to do this with Juju. Often on the hottest days, Juju looked sick and her widely-set eyes seemed to crawl around on her filthy face like huge blue flies. Gussy's heart ached to wash the feverish body, but her hands would not obey. Though bees buzzed around food mashed into the child's hair, Gussy refused to dirty the old brush she had found and sterilized.

Gussy tried to teach Juju to read with uncooked spaghetti pieces, but the child snatched letters unexpectedly, and chewed them up. One day Gussy abandoned the effort and Juju as well. Gussy had spelled "Mama" with pieces of broken shell scattered around the park. Gussy said "Mama," pointing to the filthy rag the child carried. Furiously Juju stomped the beautiful shell letters into the dirt, then limped away on bleeding feet, to hide under Quila's wagon beside Mange Bowie noticed, who wouldn't mind her smelly diaper and soundless sobbing. Mange just licked away the blood and tears and snuggled close to her.

As unexpectedly as she had left, Doll reappeared that day, holding out her arms to the neglected child who waited for her at the mailbox beside Spade. "How's my little whirligig?" she called. Juju twirled as she always did when she first saw Doll. "She really does understand. She's really not dumb!" whispered Doll as she patted Spade and hugged Juju. Doll ruffled the matted curls, kissed the quivering mouth and picked up the limping Juju.

Spade lay curled and purring on a bench now, watching while Doll gently lathered the festered little body and painful wounded feet. Doll washed, played with and unsnarled the dirty hair. She blew bubbles into the soapsuds and played little water games to keep Juju soaking longer. She dried the child with a new white towel, diapered her in some of Pug's clean flannel rags, then hummed the child into a disbelieving sleep.

But Doll had been gone too long, it seemed, for Juju had forgotten how to smile.

Gussy gathered the toys Juju had left in a heap, mended, cleaned and put them in a drawer. "The child doesn't need a pal or a teacher," she reasoned, "she needs a mother!"

But Gussy missed her. Feeling guilty, like a trapper of tiny animals, she tacked some butter wrappers on the trailer ledge. But Juju ignored them. Envy and deep disappointment in herself pestered Gussy. Juju had proved it: though Gussy worked twice as hard to gain the toddler's affection, Juju's love was only for Doll.

Loneliness and a hunger that fed on odors alone crept upon Gussy again. There was a new family in the park now and the Chips spent all of their time with them. It was hard to smell the aroma of pancakes, fried chicken and cobbler that came from Pug's place. Somehow, Quila found out about Gussy's trick of borrowing from Pug in order to have excuses for simply visiting and snacking. Gussy had already paid Quila's bottle for her silence, and couldn't risk the ruse anymore. It was even more agonizing to smell Robbie's spicy coffee or warming Poppycock on Sunday evenings.

Purposely, Gussy neglected to rake one evening. At midnight when the candle was out, she peeked behind a paper curtain and saw what she expected: a small red glow that waxed and waned from breath behind it, as Bowie waited for Gussy to talk to the night. Instead of being outraged, Gussy almost wished she had the courage to invite this homeless, friendless man inside. He was the only one in all of the park who had shown any real and lasting, unconditional interest in her being, who seemed contented just to be close to her, to share her thoughts and feelings once in awhile.

She sat on the bed, unexpectedly, and whispered out loud, "Surely, somewhere in all of this loneliness there must be a lesson hiding, waiting just for me."

The next night Bowie stood again beside Gussy's newspaper curtain. She began to hum while unwinding a length of yarn from her cigar box of colorful balls. Bowie edged closer. She was also creating crochet hooks of different sizes from twigs of the tree.

Late that night Quila painfully kneeled beside her trunk. She swiveled her head like a preying mantis, searching for peekers, listening for eavesdroppers. She pulled the little rug more closely over the sweeping crack. Today's letter to Ginny rested with others in the locked trunk, unripe for Quila's use. She had steamed them open and studied them with her magnifying glass. Now, if she had the nerve, she would slowly put them all back in the mailbox for lonely little Gussy to discover.

Quila was glad she had hidden the first letters. This Tad of Gussy's past seemed such a loose fish then, with irregular habits and superficial nature, a person so unlike what Gussy was becoming. Now that Quila could barely see to do much but analyze the handwriting, she could tell that Tad was growing. His writing now was threaded with tolerance that he was still trying to mask with sophistication. Between the lines his heart bled for Ginny to join him in something which his heart was still afraid to reveal to his head.

Bowie watched and listened outside an enlarged wormhole as she carefully opened the new letter above her steaming teakettle. By candlelight, in her black dress, she was like a bodiless head, a carved mask on a thin stick erected to scare evil spirits away. Without warning he became so sad and drained that he took several swallows from his bottle. Looking at the letter closely, Quila nodded her head, smiled and wiped away a tear. Tad's words proved his progress, and their endings now swept up joyously with newly unfolding love and generosity for all of humanity.

Bowie didn't knock. He entered noiselessly and reached across the table. "I'll take the rest of this bottle, Quila, and another one every night–as well as regular suppers–or I'll tell your biggest secret! I'm sure the post office would be interested in your 'arrangement' with the letter carrier!" he threatened.

"How, Quila, could you keep on hiding Gussy's only hope?"

40. Chloe

The next afternoon Bowie pushed out from under Quila's wagon to watch laughing repairmen working up on a telephone pole. They were also watching Lolli as she curled below them on her towel posing as though for the sun, itself, to admire her.

"Man, look at them sweet sugar loaves!" one deeply sun-tanned curly-headed worker smacked his lips in exaggeration.

Furious, Lolli jumped up, doubled her fist and shouted up at him in a voice unlike herself. "Black nigger!" Why, Lolli was terribly nearsighted, Bowie instantly realized. "Stuff your eyes back in or my man'll shove 'em clean out of your frizzy head!" At just that moment Louie rounded a corner of the adjacent trailer, home from work early and already staggery drunk. Bowie hurried over to Lolli's trailer and rolled beneath it.

Louie grabbed a handful of Lolli's hair and shook her. "They were both staring!" he snarled. "Why would you pick on the darker one?" He straggled into the trailer, tossed dirty dishes into the sink and slammed several drawers trying to locate the beer opener.

"Why do you dress like that? Men–black, white or purple–can't help staring!" The sound of ripping cloth. "Why are you complaining? When the calling card is embossed, you're supposed to feel of it! Even from the street, it's simple to fill in details. Do you dress yourself with a paintbrush?" Above him Bowie could imagine Lolli sidling up to Louie.

"Today?" she suggested, trying to change the subject. Louie roughly pushed her away from him and she hit a wall of the trailer. His voice was draggy but pensive. "Our todays, our tomorrows have no reason." She was probably winding her long brown hair around his neck as she often did, tying it in half-knots behind Louie's head.

"Leave-me-alone," he seethed. Lolli gasped. Louie must have taken both of her hands and held them behind her while he drizzled beer over her head as he had done before. "Wake up! When are you going to quit dressing and acting this way?" He shoved her away in disgust, "God, how I need a wife in my house and not a dummy in a store window!"

Lolli staggered out the door holding torn straps of her sunsuit and headed for the shower with towels and shampoo in her hand. Her usually straight hair was kinking into a froth of dripping 'serpents'. Louie was outside too now, shaking her again.

Bowie watched as women scurried for vantage spots. They loathed Lolli. Whatever she wore was merely thin skin. Even on weekends, if Louie went somewhere, she spread her towel where husbands or boyfriends could admire her before they arrived home, dissatisfied. If Louie intended to rough her up, the women intended to silently cheer him on.

Louie held her hands behind her again, kissed her savagely and forced beer down her mouth. He shook her hard, "Come on! Drink with me! Afraid of letting go, aren't you?"

"What's the matter with everybody?" It was Gussy, rushing up in bare feet with colored ribbons wrapping her toes and ankles like laced sandals. "How can you let a drunkard beat up his wife?" Getting no answers, Gussy herself tore into Louie who was shaking Lolli again.

"You little spitfire!" Even while Louie picked her up tenderly and her flailing feet kept losing their ribbons, Gussy kept beating him with her fists. He carried her into the storeroom and hooked the door. Inside, Gussy pounded until she was exhausted, then she just listened.

Lolli was furious. "You respect a knocked-up pansy more than your own wife!"

"Pansy, my big toe!" Louie bellowed and pointed wildly to the storeroom, "That girl has more guts, more courage in her prissy pinkie than Lolli has in her whole beautiful body! Anybody with her kind of class would have to almost worship a man to chance going through all of that alone, and in a dump like this!" Bowie looked around the barren park. Everyone must be breathlessly watching and listening from hidden viewing places.

Louie took hold of Lolli's wet hair again and shoved her chin up to his. "Listen to me and listen good! I'd rather be shacked with the blackest bitch in town, one that really loved me, that was proudly bearing what's mine, than–"

"You know!" Lolli breathed. "You've always known," she whispered.

"It added up too good!" Louie belched loudly. "I met Lolli's father, but her mother was never around, somehow." He swayed, teetered and finally caught himself.

"Lolli is always furious with every crazy kink in her hair, with every ounce she imagines she gains. Yet–" he pretended to sniff the air, "it's things like chitlins cooked all day, making the house smell funky. It's clabber, cool and sugared." He loudly smacked his lips. "It's corn pone, sow belly, salt-pork and greens–that's the stuff that Lolli's soul craves! Not rabbit food! And not this stupid sunning of herself to PRETEND that's she's TAN!" He smoothed Lolli's dripping curls from her face.

"It hurts me the way you love, yet also hate that funny little panda that your mother gave you. And Whiffet, that phony excuse for a real baby! Your mammy and me," Lolli was sobbing uncontrollably now, "we've waited such a long time. I know and love her well, Lolli. Often, when you think I'm at The Joint, I've really driven to shanty town. She cooks for me in her homey little kitchen all of the things you used to love." He held her chin in his hand.

Lolli's big brown eyes were incredulous. "All along, what you wanted was just to keep up this pretense for my sake?" Her laugh was hysterical.

"There seemed no way to tell you gently, little Chloe."

Chloe! Chloe! The old name echoed through Lolli like a rush of springtime in a tomb. Weeping loudly, she grabbed Louie, kissed every inch of his face, caressed his hair and held him tight against her wet body.

But she closed her eyes for her heart was somewhere else.

Where was little Chloe? Could she still be found in Pansy-Bear's shabby spots where she'd pounded him in despair? Or on his worn little mouth where she'd kissed him and sobbed that she was so sorry? Or in his shabby fur that still smelled like luscious fattening things that Mammy made with big, gentle hands so much like Pug's? Where was that laughing little barefoot native, unaware of black and white, romping through those happy days, spending long evenings safe in the comforting lap of Mammy's vivid, giant skirts?

Mammy had given her the panda to remember her by, when little Chloe went to live with her white father. Big tears fell from her black cheeks as Mammy smoothed curly, creamed-coffee hair from Chloe's tan-colored temples. "Now don't you ever forget, sweet baby, parts of this panda are white, but its soul is a velvety blackness, as comforting as Mammy's lap, as understanding as Mammy's big heart."

Even after her marriage, Lolli had beaten the little panda. "I hate you, I hate you, so why do I also love you? Oh, Mammy, why am I so miserable?"

Somewhere in the deep darkness of her body, could there be a little seed with that same loving soul of Chloe, waiting for new life?

"Oh, Louie! You don't know how deeply I've longed to have your baby!" She was weeping unashamedly and Bowie could feel the whole hidden park weeping with her and for her. "I was afraid that any baby of mine would be too fat, too black, too curly-haired!"

Louie picked her up like a bride. "I wouldn't care if it was a striped, chubby, kinky-haired little zebra!" She had handed him the sun tan bottle and he emptied it dramatically on the ground. Lolli, herself, tossed Whiffet out the door where she skidded on her little nose. Then, as though it were shutting out her whole phony life, Lolli closed the door.

Coughing and sniffling, watchers went back to supper-making. Robbie released Gussy from her prison and Bowie crept back under Quila's wagon.

Settling beside the warmness of Mange, Bowie realized the message that had always been flagged by Lolli's clothes, the message that tenants had been too jealous to decipher and Lolli had been too blind to recognize: "See me exactly as I am, and like me, please?" How long would it take before SHE saw herself exactly as she was? How long would it take for her to realize that the only time she was really contented was when she was cooking, serving others just like Pug, and just like her own wonderful black Mammy?

Bowie took a long swig, remembering Robbie, one long-ago summer day. Robbie was watching Chloe saunter past the washhouse in bare feet. Her big hat was hanging by ribbons, unused on her back. Her sunsuit was merely a sheen on her fabulous figure. Robbie had been leaning against the washhouse wall, sharing suckers with one of Pug's little girls. "Chocolate's the best part, isn't it?" Robbie smiled. "Once you lick off the white coating!" Almost in a whisper, Robbie added "Chloe, I think we'll call you 'Lollipop'. Something that must be licked before unfolding its real gift."

Above him, Quila stomped up her little steps and flung the door open. Angrily she thumped a mug on the table. "Dammit!" she complained.

Bowie had told her of Lolli's peculiar routine whenever Louie was gone at night. Lolli stuck a metal comb into the flame of a candle. Wiping a bit of Vaseline into a lock of hair, she then ran the hot comb through it.

Gradually her hair hung straighter. Finally she crawled into bed with her straight shiny hair on a towel and snuggled up to Whiffet.

"Dammit!" Quila grumbled again. "I waited too long! There was so much more to Lolli that I already 'paid' for and never got to use!"

Bowie smiled tearfully; the last of the suntan water had dribbled away. Whiffet still stood with her feet on the doorstep, sadly whining, her tail between her legs. And inside the trailer, Louie was discovering for the very first time the eager sweetness of little Chloe.

41. Pigpen Fiasco

Except for drunken laughter from the den, the park seemed deserted that next afternoon. Nothing could deaden the heat through Gussy's newspaper curtains. Breezes from the open transom were even hot and sultry, so she carried the big dictionary, pencil and used envelopes to an empty stall and settled down on a cool toilet. So engrossed had she become in reading the dictionary that Gussy didn't realize a crowd was gathering in the Pigpen, until the clamor increased, until she heard Quila's odd words and Robbie's drunken pitch.

Quiet rustling came from the toolroom next to Gussy's stall where Bowie had slipped into darkness and was pulling paper from a peephole. Doll wasn't in the Den, but Bowie had been watching anyway. The girls had been drinking too much wine when they started to play charades. One of the girls went to the Pigpen for a prop and soon they were all there. Gussy felt trapped. There was nothing she could do but listen and watch from the door crack.

"Hey, look here under Gussy's awning. Here's two of my old perfume bottles tinkling in the breeze along with sticks, bones and cans!" protested Mala.

"The little scavenger!" cried Lolli, as Whiffet pushed through Gussy's screen and brought out something familiar. "That's why nobody gets an invite here! Look what she's done with my old bra: whiter than a virgin's reputation, with new straps and lace, the little rag-picker!" Bowie cringed: only he and Gussy knew for whom the "new" bra was intended.

Lolli's words struck like angry fists against Gussy's empty stomach as she pulled toilet paper from an outside peephole. By this time in the afternoon most clothes were off the lines and Gussy could see a cluster of women gathered around and inside her trailer.

Bowie leaned back against the partition as a knot of apprehension gathered in his throat, a knot composed of Gussy's little personal doings which he had traded to Quila.

"Here's your old flowered skirt, Fay–being taken apart!"

"Yuck! This was Juju's diaper, once!" Someone else rushed into and out of the trailer and soon it was filled with laughing drunken looters.

Robbie peeked around the door screen. Perched crazily on her head was a bonnet of Orry's. Robbie fingered the crocheted ruffle that Gussy had added to the frayed edges. "I always whip up a hat when I'm down in the dumps," she tittered in Gussy's genteel voice.

"I wondered where ye got such a unique wardrobe," chortled Quila, and laughter spread through the rest of the girls who couldn't squeeze inside the tiny trailer.

Robbie reappeared with the patched jeans Doll had thrown away and an old shirt of Robbie's, bleached, sleeveless and with flowers appliquéd over burn spots that trademarked the right front sides of Robbie's shirts. With cut-off sleeves Gussy had made fanlike ruffles above the shoulders and embroidered the buttonholes to look like flowers. Both garments seemed like dismembered body parts, stuffed with crumpled newspapers.

"So that's how she irons!" the Oriental girls exclaimed.

Robbie "sat" the jeans against the trailer wall and propped the stuffed shirt into the waist. She balanced a can on the neck of the shirt and tied the bonnet around it.

"Too countrified," said Robbie, studying the dummy. "Needs jewels; a teensy dewdrop will do." Robbie mimicked Gussy. Gussy cringed inside her stall as Robbie dipped her knife into a puddle of slop, then daintily shook it onto the snowy bosom of the shirt.

Quila shook her head, "Too citified," and she sprinkled a handful of dirt overall, creating splashy red blobs.

"Still too plain," chided Robbie, "let's add pokey-dots." Laughingly she poked holes all over the frail shirt with her pocketknife.

Gussy flinched with every stab. Robbie's drollery might have been fascinating had not Gussy spent so many hours saving drops of bleach, grains of soap, wisps of thread, washing, bleaching, mending, altering, disguising. But she was a voluntary captive, spellbound to see herself imitated–though it was also heartbreaking. Tears dammed up in her eyes.

Quila whispered in Robbie's ear. Robbie replied, "Right! No safety pins! Let's make 'her' comfy anyway." She arranged newspapers, so the "stomach" pouched out the fly of the jeans.

"We need a throne," said Robbie. "Help me lift this old car seat."

One girl spread long ragged underwear in front of the now enthroned figure. Another found a fancy half-burned garter for a crown. With a shredded fly swatter Robbie tapped the effigy on the head, a movement which in her drunken state, almost knocked her over. "I dub thee, Posy, Pregnant Prig of the Pigpen!" Everyone bowed while Robbie did a curtsy.

"Down with royalty!" Dago swayed and caught herself against another girl.

"Wait, first the feast!" Robbie reeled, leaned against the trailer wall then raised crossed arms above her head. "Let's do this genteelly, please. Now, everybody bring the food to me, 'Innoc,' for I'm the chef." Robbie staggered over to the dummy, just like Enoch might, preening her hair on top. "I'll name each dish and see if it's fitten for a princess."

The girls began to cull through cans and garbage but unused imaginations could not see beyond the refuse. Shag shyly held up a rotten potato. "Potatoes, Lyonnaise!" Robbie declared, sprinkling onion husks over it. She took the lid off a trashcan, transferred the potato to it and dramatically held the lid above her head before depositing it in front of the dummy.

Confident now that Robbie's naming could colorfully transform whatever they found, the drunken girls over swarmed the Pigpen and filed past Robbie with their offerings.

Fay limped up with eggshells and a broken whiskey bottle. Robbie poured stale drops over the shells. "Eggs Benedict!" She elegantly crumbled Fay's contribution onto the lid.

"Entrée!" Robbie spied the fishbone Opal held. Robbie dredged it in a can of grease Amiko held. "Marinated herring," Robbie held her nose as she deposited the fish on the lid.

"A little jerky," she tore a sliver from the roast bone Quila held, then ran her finger inside an empty pickle jar and spread green tidbits over the meat. "She'll relish this!" Laughter shot through the growing audience.

Each girl competed for limelight. A broken dish became in Robbie's hands, "Ah, Dresden." Broken glass was, "Ah, crystal." Carrot peels were garnish. A chicken carcass was sprinkled with an imaginary can of spice.

Lolli held a lid of Whiffet's tidy mound of excrement. "Ah," Robbie looked down the line of offerings, saw an empty carton of cottage cheese, and dumped Lolli's addition into it. "Head-cheese!" she declared and the audience exploded with laughter again.

The game was beginning to pall though and seem disgusting. Robbie chose the last offering, and sprinkled cantaloupe seeds over the conglomeration, while declaring it, "A masterpiece!"

"Wait, hold out your hand," demanded Lolli. She spit her gum into Robbie's hand. Robbie was quiet. Others were getting restless. But triumph in Lolli's eyes was short-lived.

"You can't discard this! It's only firsthand. Do like Gussy and chink a drafty hole. Like this." Robbie shoved the gum back into Lolli's sneering mouth and loudly knocked her jaw shut. Lolli left the laughers, her eyelids lowered to hide any revenge her eyes might betray. Regardless of her truce with Louie, thought Bowie, old patterns were still a part of her.

Waiting, Lolli was always waiting. The thought tormented Bowie. Eventually just the right moment would arrive for knocking the backbone out of this place and Lolli would slyly smile as she watched the park collapse. Without the keystone, without Robbie's protection, Bowie knew that he would have no place to wait for the unfolding, no method of ever knowing who he was or what was inside that leather, waiting in the groove of Quila's bosom.

Primed now for a grand finale, Robbie wasn't about to disappoint her audience. She twisted a newspaper and lit the end.

"Goodbye, cruel world! I'm tired of cold feet, cold shoulders, and this artless place!" Applause rippled through the audience of girls, and suddenly Gussy was dizzy. She turned and threw up in the toilet. She had to lie down. She opened the door, almost knocking over Quila who seemed upset as she took her airing quilt from the line and hurried from the scene.

Robbie transferred the flame to several places on the paper-stuffed figure just as Pug returned from the store, sized up the scene, and walked toward her. Robbie tore off a piece of the flaming paper and playfully handed it to Pug. "Crepe suzettes?"

Then everybody noticed barefoot Gussy walking from the washhouse with ribbons woven around her toes and ankles. Tears spilled down her cheeks as she walked toward her trailer, tightly hugging the big dictionary as if it were the only friend she had left in the whole world. Bowie, still watching from the tool room could have kicked himself.

Instead, the huge knot of guilt exploded soundlessly from his throat and dribbled down his cheeks.

"I'm ashamed of knowing all of you!" shouted Pug, surveying the burning dummy and the lid full of garbage before it. She rushed to put her arms around Gussy and lead her toward the ransacked trailer. As she smoothed Gussy's hair away from her hot, tearful face, Pug turned and shouted to the guilty-looking girls.

"Gussy's life itself is art. She creates beauty out of our discarded ugliness!" She made a sweeping gesture that took in the whole Pigpen. "Not a one of you would have the imagination or guts to use anything here!" she sobbed. "Not a one of you could find a whole rainbow here to paint with. Not a one of you could find perfume in a geranium leaf, music in hanging debris. Not a one of you could find entertainment here, or a clean bite to eat! You're all too ignorant and insensitive to recognize and respect someone who must and can!" Pug lowered her voice. "Especially, I am disappointed in you, Robbie."

"Don't be a spoil-sport, Pug. There's still more of everything in the old Pigpen. And all for nothing, all for nothing!" gestured Robbie, swaying gallantly.

Pug seemed to be looking way past Robbie to where Gus was heading up the driveway. "One often pays dearest for the thing he gets for nothing, Robbie." Everyone showed astonishment, for Pug seldom spoke at all, much less with any depth.

The fiasco was finished and a painful silence was dropping like a final curtain. The girls separated to make a path for Pug and Gussy, and Robbie bowed as they passed by her. "Humble pie?" she asked, holding out an open hand that Pug ignored.

Robbie had gone too far. Bowie could see it in the faces of the girls. Their adulation ceased as fast as it had begun. All seemed hurt by their own cruelty and sheepishly drifted away. The playlet was over; the third act had come to an inglorious conclusion, and the playwright staggered back to her own trailer to turn on the endless record.

Somehow, thought Bowie, Quila seemed more upset than anybody. When Robbie had lit the firebrand Quila rushed off to her wagon seeming to want no part in the turn of things.

Inside, Gussy's trailer was in shambles. She sat on the bed looking at balls of yarn unrolled all over the room. Broken sticks wound with knotted string were scattered. Gaping cupboards were depleted of what little they had contained. Food collections in the icebox were squandered on the floor. Carefully sharpened pieces of charcoal were heeled into the linoleum and broken pencil stubs were now too small for using. Jars of watered food coloring and "manufactured paint" were drizzled over the table. All those hours of experimenting–boiling holey socks, shriveled beets, dried cabbage leaves, old ties and faded hair ribbons–were wasted now. The only things they hadn't bothered were sketches. In silence, Pug picked up broken glass, wiped the table, rolled the yarn and threw away broken pencils. Gussy swept the bed, stovetop and floor with the whiskbroom.

As Pug left, she picked up the "dummy's plate" and overturned it on a trashcan.

Gussy sat on her doorstep drinking Bowie's wine, staring like she was frozen.

From under the wagon, Bowie watched the dummy dissolve into ashes. He bit his lips, but blood didn't stop their quivering. Poor Gussy, she had no car and no outside friends. She couldn't just leave, like other tenants who had also felt humiliated in the past. At least, they would have hidden away in their own trailer for a while. They wouldn't just sit there in front of the whole park hurting and crying, yet not hating any of their persecutors.

Gussy sat staring at the Pigpen, getting drunker and drunker as time passed.

Rivulets of slop steamed in hot sun. Flies were greedily exploring. Maggots worked in pockets of dampness. Cockroaches and rats waited for darkness.

Her mother was right: life wasn't a happy experience. It was ugly, sordid, horrifying. In her half-starved condition everything seemed unreal. As she drank all of the warm wine on her empty stomach, the wavery Pigpen grew even more revolting, and the smoking incinerator kept spreading a suffocating shadow, engulfing Gussy in nauseating fumes.

From the washhouse Gussy could hear an angry foot descending again and again, but the wash machine wouldn't start. She could hear a woman cursing and knew the child beneath the vengeful hand would never once cry out.

And the very last tenderness that Gussy had felt in her heart for Robbie was now but a putrid clot in her throat, which she could not even swallow.

From the edge of the Pigpen, a vision of Quila's crooked smile leered up from rotten wormholes in an apple. Moldy corks arranged themselves into Bowie's dissipated grin. Pug's face smiled from muddy stones. Robbie seemed to frown from a burned branch hanging out of the incinerator.

Suddenly it came to her, why lovely paintings Flo had hung for Gussy had never sold: the world didn't want beauty to strive toward, but sordidness in which to wallow.

Now Gussy realized that she had used many things in the Pigpen for her art, but not filth and garbage. "Is there even some kind of answer, there?" she whispered.

Gussy went inside, took out her charcoal sketches and began to plan.

As days passed, Gussy began to partially turn sketches into collages, adding every seemingly related bit of dry discard from the Pigpen: smelly slices of cork, dried garbage, sandy driftwood, broken seashells. Yet Bowie saw that basic sketches remained the major part of each picture. Did she plan it that way? Couldn't she find enough right rubbish? Or did the sketches represent the visual part of a person or place, and debris revealed the hidden core? Bowie listened as Gussy actually talked to various materials until they seemed to murmur back, telling her the right picture and the right place where they belonged.

Kindly, Flo hung the hideous new collages in place of Gussy's other lovely paintings.

Miraculously, the new curator of the Plaza Art Gallery saw and wanted all of Gussy's collages hanging on Flo's walls. Gussy almost fainted with both joy and hunger, when Flo shouted the good news over the back fence. That night Bowie listened as Gussy talked to the night. "Thank you, Life. Just by being myself, doing my very best with whatever little I could find, I have been forced to try my own rigid wings. Maybe someday, I will eventually touch my own sky."

Gussy struck a bargain with Flo for whatever she needed from her shop. When the showing at the gallery closed, which would include a whole wall of Gussy's works, they both would get paid.

Gussy had no time to even wash and mend secondhand baby clothes that Flo saved for her. They stayed in a sack beneath her bed. To Bowie, she seemed obsessed with completing all the pictures in her mind. To save time she never curled her hair again. She merely wet it in the shower and tied it in bouncy tails at the sides of her head.

She went to bed at dusk now and slept until midnight, when everyone else would be asleep. After exploring the Pigpen and putting scavenged treasures into order, she worked on choosing, drying and gluing all through the cool night. Three or four pictures a week were all Flo asked, though she promised to take all Gussy could produce. Whenever a picture was finished, Gussy trudged to Flo's to deliver it, trying to get there at lunchtime, even though the sidewalks seemed hottest then, and she was getting blisters on her bare feet. (Flo usually had a few shoes for sale, but they were always too big or high-heeled.)

Living was harder now that Gussy's icebox, closet and cupboards were denuded, yet she seldom took time to scavenge food. There was a burned spot now on the front of Gussy's trailer, a brown blistered shadow of the bonneted dummy. But Gussy didn't have the heart, the time, or the inclination to repair the spot. It just waited, thought Bowie, a daily reminder to the women of that unforgettable day of the Pigpen fiasco.

Strangely though, very usable things began to appear at the tops of garbage cans: new pencils, spools of thread, and longer pieces of already sharpened charcoal. Robbie began to wash out the trash cans every week, straighten the lids with a hammer and kept pounding them down to lock out Spade, cockroaches, flies, ants and rats. Lolli seemed to leave more meat on old ham bones, labeled her throwaway sacks and secured them with rubber bands or string. Quila left more candy in her boxes. Pug often left a whole piece of unpeeled fruit, an onion or potato in with her peelings. One night a set of oil paints was suddenly there on top of clean newspapers.

Several beautiful pictures, painted as Gussy would like Last Resort to look, were ready to take to Flo's, but she needed strength to get there. Shaky and desperate from not eating that day, Gussy uncapped an empty bottle of steak sauce, added a little water, shook it and poured the remnants down her throat. She tucked the pictures into a mended pillowcase.

Stepping off the apple box porch, Gussy paused and looked back at the fence, for the hundredth time it seemed to Bowie. Someday, she was going to get brave, borrow a saw and cut a gate through to Flo's, so she wouldn't have to brave hot sand and sidewalks. Knotted rope would do for hinges. Someday, she would at least paint a picture of the gate that already existed in her mind. She drew a sketch of her dream gate in the diary.

Maybe this time Flo could repay her with some kind of old blanket. Nights were getting chilly and fall was in the air.

"That's not what my client wants," complained Flo. "They're too pretty! There's no dimension!" Yet, even after Flo refused the lovely pictures, she invited Gussy to lunch. Gussy sadly stored the potential loveliness of the park behind a cushion of her little breakfast nook couch.

42. Gypsy Days

Gussy began in earnest now the painstaking acquirement of materials for creating collages. She didn't bother making odd "paints" anymore. Tattered cloth, old magazines and other discarded items could be used for color. Bowie watched her at night sorting things into used cereal boxes. Flo was exceptionally glad to see Gussy's finished pictures and invite her to an elaborate lunch.

Gussy had gotten smart. At first she gave Flo several pictures at once. Now she took only two or three, though she had a lot more ready. She could exist on one good meal a day. She had to walk to Flo's to get it, but what time it saved to only search for art supplies.

She sat on her doorstep a lot, drawing, studying the park and tenants, making notes as they did their work. She continued to look at girls from the Den with numb, disenchanted eyes. With Robbie, it was as though a living cord that somehow linked them together had violently ripped away and only Gussy's side of it kept on bleeding.

Raking? She had no time anymore. What did it matter, anyway, if Bowie peeked into her trailer or watched from restroom rafters? There was nothing he didn't know.

It seemed to Bowie that she was also hurrying in her efforts to wash, cut, mend and crochet when she tired of long hours on her collages. Now Bowie watched as something new began to happen in Gussy's life. From having too little, now Gussy had too much. From having a bareness to her trailer, she now had hardly any room in which to work. She had to take more pictures to Flo, to keep up with frenzied productivity and make more space for new pictures that kept gushing from her mind.

One hot afternoon when Doll was washing Juju, Bowie realized that Gussy must have some artsy need for Juju's rag. There were a lot of women in the washhouse; clothes were sorted in piles all over the floor and Gussy waited on a bench for her turn at the busy shower. From a storeroom peephole, Bowie saw Juju's rag beside Gussy. During the time when Mala left the shower and Gussy entered, Bowie noticed that Juju's rag was missing. The rag must have disappeared before, for the next day Juju was carrying another pair of Fay's panties.

One midnight, when Gussy was quietly at work, Bowie awoke with a jerk beside the hollyhock. "Goodness, I am already rich!" Gussy shouted up to the transom. "I have a treasure that nobody can ever steal. My wealth is just my special way of seeing everything!" Open cereal boxes with their raw materials, a jar of flour paste and odd little "brushes" were scattered on the table, stove, seats and bed. Gussy had a brush in her hand as she twirled and drew in the air. Sketches and collages were leaning in rows and rows against every vertical spot in the over-crowded trailer.

Life could have been fairly comfortable if Gussy could shut from her ears the daytime laughter bubbling from the Den and the nighttime throb of Robbie's bass viol at The Joint down the street. And though she feasted once a day at Flo's, eating just wasn't fun anymore.

Only Gussy and Bowie had noted Quila's reaction to the fiery climax of the Pigpen fiasco. Trembling, Quila had hurriedly grabbed her quilt from the clothesline, returned to her wagon, and took from her sleeve the familiar carved clothespin that she had just stolen from Gussy's table. Quila had finally discarded those same faded, broken pieces, but now, since Gussy had glued them together and repainted them, the pin looked new, as if Lazlo had just created it. Quila opened her door-window to capture breezes, then lying down on her recessed bed, she pressed the sun-warmed quilt and the mended clothespin to her heart. Memories started to gather. Like pieces of the ragged quilt and the restored clothespin they joined together the few happy fragments of her life.

New and uncharred were the quilt colors, and she—not Quila, but Marya—would soon be beneath them with Lazlo in the bed niche that he had carved and painted with babies.

Lazlo had been hidden for weeks in the woods behind his family's camping ground, where he was building, and living in, a honeymoon wagon like the one his father had made for his Italian bride. Marya was permitted only the task of filling the bedroll with feathers and making a flowered curtain, after Lazlo stood before her, gesturing. "Only wan leetle curtain. Theese big! With skylight, who needs more weendows?" He shrugged.

To quiet her curiosity, Marya began a quilt of her favorite cloths. Most prominent were squares of the swirling blue skirt. It was old and worn but it first attracted Lazlo to the dancing figure named Marya, and she wanted that midnight-blue always above their sleeping bodies. Bands of red were made from the vivid scarf that Lazlo loved so much. It was tucked into the throbbing vee of his shirt, only to fly away as they first danced together in a frenzy wild as that wonderful wind whipping that same bit of scarlet away into the forest with the laughing, breathless twosome dashing after it.

When Lazlo finally captured the scarf, he put it around her neck, pulled its ends toward his face and kissed her. Calico squares were from the tablecloth on which they spread their first picnic. Lace of the tiny center square was snipped from the hem of Lazlo's baptismal dress that his mother had given Marya to use again someday.

On the day of the wedding Marya soaked in special herbs, sudsing her long curly hair, rinsing it in rainwater and braiding it.

The wedding party arrived on horseback. Rupa, Nanosh, Liza and Lazlo came first. Lazlo in white ruffled sleeves, bright beads and embroidered vest, rode proudly on his beloved white mare. Her mane and bridle, swishing tail and prancing hooves were entwined with wildflowers. The rest of his family drove wagons behind them. The two families, wild in greeting, grew even wilder with elderberry wine, feasting and fiddling, heady music and dancing, clapping and chanting. Everyone complimented Marya's sourdough loaves, arranged in a circle around a crock of her homemade butter.

From stoneware jugs the laughing men guzzled moonshine liquor, slinging it over the right shoulder, right arm curved around it, head and mouth twisting toward it. They gulped and joked, trying to catch their breath while the liquid ran down their chins and throats, staining their shirts which were unbuttoned to the waist.

Her family kissed Marya and wept together as they symbolically unbraided her hair for the ceremonies. The bridal twosome jumped the broomstick and mingled the blood of their wrists. Everyone danced, ate and drank far into the night. At last, Lazlo whisked Marya up and carried her through darkness to the tiny house on wheels hidden in the forest.

Moonlight shimmered on the brightly painted wagon as Lazlo carried her over the threshold. Under the arched roof a soft many-colored glow sifted down through the stained glass skylight of birds and flowers, softly lighting the room. Almost every inch of space had been pressed into some use. A tiny table for two unfolded from one wall, and above it were hanging varied utensils contributed by members of the families—"To give a push to the new wagon!" A narrow rack above the table held only two of everything: tin plates, metal bowls, ceramic mugs, jars instead of glasses. There was a portable rack for Lazlo's fine-edged carving tools that he had used inside and out of the wagon, the same tools with which he carved quaint clothespin people with which he made his living.

Laying her on the new quilt, he gently undressed her, admired her soft curves and spread her fragrant hair out on the pillow. (Quila sobbed at the remembered joy of it.) Marya smiled up at Lazlo and smoothed his black curls. "The wedding pots smashed into many pieces. We will have many years together."

Lazlo looked up and touched the cherubs carved above the bower. "Soon will have to make beeger wagon. This one too small for leettle Romanos!"

At sundown Bowie stepped up to the wagon door. Looking past the gently blowing curtain, he saw Quila smiling in her sleep. She neither heard his steps nor stirred, but slept the night through, permitting for the first time the complete return of haunting memories.

Hitching the tiny wagon to Lazlo's eager mare, next morning the honeymooners took off in a flurry of shouting and congratulations. Pots and pans, broom and tubs were banging all over the colorful outside walls. Lazlo played his guitar while Marya held the reins as they sang and laughed along the winding dusty back roads.

Their yearlong tour of Gypsy camps throughout the states was exciting and rewarding, especially when they camped by a river or stream, for Gypsy life revolved around water. There Marya washed clothes and hung them to dry on bushes. She cut and stripped willow stems to weave baskets. Lazlo spent long, lazy days carving and painting clothespins, singing love songs to Marya or helping her gather wild mushrooms, potherbs and teaplants.

High among the scroll work of the porch, Lazlo built little shelves and perching branchlets for birds that followed Marya as they traveled, wanting to nest and roost as close to her as possible, thriving on daily crumbs and individual attention.

Following patron–Gypsy clues–from camp to camp was half the fun. Finding shreds of material hanging from branches at the height of Lazlo standing on driving boards was so rewarding. Lazlo delighted in "reading" spots where no trees bordered the road: dark spots left by fire, with nearby stones, bones and broken crockery, objects that didn't seem out of place.

For months life was simple, idyllic. Lazlo was unlike most other Gypsy men who seemed to do as little of their trade as possible, preferring to let their womenfolk sell weaving, embroidery or fortunes. The men teased Lazlo, for he even helped to bury vegetable peels and bones of meat that was "borrowed" from farmers along the way.

Once a week the two of them drove to town for bartering. In gay festoons the baskets, clothespins, Lazlo's guitar and Marya's tambourine were strung about the white mare's neck. They stopped to pluck greenery and wildflowers, for baskets sold much better when stuffed with beauty and sprinkled with stream water. They danced together or Lazlo played his guitar while Marya danced with her tambourine. Often there were fortunes for Marya to tell.

Bartering over, the twosome turned toward camp, taking their time, enjoying the first smells, sights and sounds of Gypsy camps. First the aroma of borrowed chickens or a young lamb from a farmer's yard, mingled with simmering produce from the same field. Sounds of laughing, chanting, clapping, concertina, guitars and fiddles. Rounding the last corner they could see dark silhouettes against bonfires. Their horse whinnied as she passed silent watchdogs, keeping their jaws free for thieves or curiosity-seekers.

Dismounting, Lazlo fed their horse while Marya went inside the wagon to tuck a fresh bread loaf into her shawl. Then dancing together, they whirled toward the music and smiling faces. There was always someone to offer the honeymooners a bite of supper in happy payment for their dancing and a taste of Marya's sourdough.

Meals by the fires were leisurely, followed by boasting and laughing about good sales, the latest pregnancies, news of other camps, skirmishes with the law, or how to get the price of a horse or a bride. Then fires were banked, everyone got comfortable under the starry sky, and old respected Roms resang their youthful songs and told their epic tales again. Finally, the twosome retired to their own wagon. They had eaten well and "paid" for it. Their warm young bodies were entwined; the sun would shine tomorrow.

Feeling cold, Quila pulled the ragged quilt up high around her neck.

43. Lazlo

One time Marya rode to town alone, first patting Lazlo's dog, Blanca and new puppies. "A wife likes to take her time choosing a new material," she whispered to Blanca. Marya wanted to buy some infant flannel and then surprise Lazlo with her wonderful news.

Riding back to camp on Lazlo's mare, it was a heavenly evening. Four yards of blanketing were strapped to the horse. Candles rested safely near her swelling bosom. She had bargained well and next week they might make enough money to choose a small layette. No second-hand clothes for their baby, clothes that maybe a dead child had worn. Willows dangled, caressing her curly, waist long hair. A heavy moon hung low for bats to string patterns across it. She jumped down beside the stream to pluck an evening primrose for her hair, to smell the fragrance of a moonflower before swinging back up on the mare.

Marya rounded the last curve with uneasiness. No odor of simmering food rushed to greet her. No tiny fires flickered beneath trees, no chanting, fiddling or soft clapping, no thud of ax, no neighing or snorting of horses. She strained her eyes in the darkness but there were no familiar silhouettes. Iron cranes with their heavy pots had been yanked up and whisked away. Gone were men in tight trousers and elaborate jackets, women in long busy skirts, children laughing and playing. Even the silent dogs were gone.

There was only Blanca at the edge of the clearing with smoke at the tips of her ears and tail. She had a fierce death hold on the neck of a non-Gypsy, a writhing gorgio. Smoke was drifting from the only wagon left behind–the little honeymoon wagon.

Marya jumped off the horse and dashed into the doorway, past the table strewn with empty wine bottles. Hysterically, she beat the flames from Lazlo's clothes and his still, dear body. With the smoldering quilt she dragged him outside. It was easy to figure that the gorgio had offered Lazlo friendship and laughter, got him drunk with poisoned wine, and had then thrown the firebrand into the sleeping nook. Happily, Lazlo had already passed out and soon had faded forever away, beside Blanca's helpless litter at the foot of the bed.

Gypsies in Lazlo's clan burned all of a dead man's possessions but Marya knew she was strangely different. She could never part with even one scorched scroll or wooden curve of a baby, not one blackened carving tool, or one scrap of charred cloth. In a nightmare of pain and unreality, she cut a dark curl from an unburned part of Lazlo's head, wrapped her shawl around his body, then quickly buried him in a hole from which an uprooted forest tree had fallen. Along with Lazlo she buried all but one pitiful, half-alive male puppy. Blanca would not come when she was finally called. Crazed with revenge and the pain of his trying to beat her off with a jagged stick, she had chosen to die interlocked with the evil gorgio's throat. Marya put the whimpering puppy into the warmth of her smudged blouse, hitched up the horse and, in dazed pain, drove the wagon toward the summer camp of her own family.

Not until her screaming mother dragged her from the smoldering wagon, and forced her to sit for hours in the cold water of a nearby pool did she finally realize how dearly she had paid for her leisurely trip to town. With the lives of beloved Lazlo and her precious, stillborn baby, with all of her lovely hair, and the skin of her young brown hands whose scorched fingers would never function normally again. Forever more, even the gathering of wild food and flowers would be a painful and difficult task. Never again could she create another basket, or support herself in ways that she was used to.

Quila tossed beneath the ragged quilt, "Oh, Lazlo, why did you wait for me?"

44. Jofranka

It was getting cold when Marya prepared to return to her husband's people; her mother's people wanted her gone. Since that first night when she clattered into camp with wild eyes, flame-frizzled hair and smoking wagon, gorgios had begun to throw stones whenever any of the tribe drove through a town. Farmers accused Gypsies of putting hexes on their milk cows, of stealing children and wheedling away their best stallions.

Marya with her painful, scarred, useless hands could do nothing worthwhile to help out in her mother's camp. The ultimate disgrace for a Gypsy woman was to have short hair and now Marya felt like an unfaithful wife, whose husband had cut off her burnt hair. She wore a babushka whenever she left her wagon. She tired of children calling her "raghead," of others' insistence that she burn the wagon and begin a new life, of waking suddenly when someone pricked her to see if, witchlike, she had dead spots on her now curveless, scrawny body.

But things were no different with Lazlo's people. All of them shuddered or crossed themselves when she arrived in a mysterious cloud of birds that never left the vicinity of her wagon. Everyone was cold and silent except the ever-moving loner, old Jofranka, whose husband had also died mysteriously. Jofranka was crouched by her fire, smoking a short-stemmed brass pipe and holding her Turkish coffee maker over restless flames. She invited Marya to her fireside, and Marya learned about Lazlo's last night.

Jofranka had been visiting the same camp as Marya and Lazlo when she "felt" death in the air. Among other dread omens, she had seen an owl perching on top of Lazlo and Marya's wagon in broad daylight. She had been able to persuade everyone but Lazlo to quickly break camp and leave. But Lazlo would not accept the loan of a horse to tow away his wagon when Jofranka offered it. No, he would wait there for Marya, alone.

"Please, Lazlo! Come with us! Marya is very good at following patrin!" But Lazlo had found a paint can in an old shack near the clearing, and was determined to wash and freshen an underpart of the colorful wagon before they moved on.

"No!" scolded Jofranka. "Leave the paint alone!" She grabbed the can from him and threw it into the bushes. "It will be black inside the lid, I feel it! We only stop here long enough for collecting mushrooms and cress, or to make a quick repair on a needy wagon. That clearing yonder belongs to a vengeful gorgio! His daughter ran off with a Gypsy after they were caught together in that same shack! May I die before daylight if it's not true!"

Despite old Jo's warning, Lazlo pried off the lid, then laughed in surprise. "Black not only mean death, Jofranka. It mean night, rest, pleasure! Have you forgotten?"

Jofranka took Marya's withered hand in her own. "I hear that Gypsies never go there anymore. They call it 'Dead Lazlo's Lane.'"

She untied Marya's babushka, swept back her stubby hair wisps, looked past her scarred face and deep into still-grieving eyes.

"God, you are ugly now, child. But let's not waste it anymore!" Jofranka took from her own warm shoulders the lovely blue shawl she had made on huge pins that held her beautiful silver hair. She taught Marya how to drape the shawl around herself, instead of hiding in it like some little cave. With patient exercise, she brought back some use of Marya's hands. Gently, she dabbed her own wild ointments on Marya's scars and wrapped her hands in rags to sleep in. She taught her to use charcoal and chalk to deepen "attributes." "And the way you're inclined to talk, we can mold and use that too!" Jo declared.

Lazlo had loved Marya's funny way of talking, spiced with bits and scraps from all of the books that her father loved reading to her. But both Lazlo's people and her own had always ridiculed her. "She's no Gypsy: she's a mongrel! Like that book-reading, Scotch-Irish gorgio that fathered her!"

Jofranka studied Marya's speech and taught her to savor the very words and phrases that made her different from the rest. "But there's something else that makes you different: a bad habit! Whenever you get tense and don't want to show it, it gives away your nervousness and impatience. You must stop clicking your fingernails together!"

Jo taught her to read and analyze handwriting. She was amazed at how quickly Marya caught on to cards, teacup-reading and palmistry. She taught her when to raise her voice or let it fall, how to pause for a dramatic effect, when to speak fast and when to draw things out.

"It is their eyes, though, that you must really read, their walk, their facial expressions, their gestures, their clothes and mannerisms," advised Jo. "Actually, it's only commonsense, my dear. And, above all else: don't you ever forget, girl," Jofranka clapped her hands loudly to remind her, whenever Marya would sink, silent and depressed into her shawl: "Gypsies are wildflowers of this world, created to spark up and beautify dull stretches of life."

Marya became proficient at her new trade, but things in camp worsened. They were suspicious of a woman who attracted wild birds, picked up a smoldering ember with bare leathery fingers to light Jo's pipe, who told fortunes that too often hit the mark.

Suspicion seemed to precede them in every town they entered. The tribe had to keep on the move with only overnight stops. Their cows dried up. Their horses grew thin and skittish. The men grew irritable, the women quarrelsome and the children impudent and wild.

Times got harder, they broke into units of four wagons to protect themselves against gorgio brutality. Children, women and even some men had to resort to begging.

Their own four wagons stopped at a camping site beside a woodsy pool, and at last they were undisturbed. It was good to remain in one spot, to gather strength, rest the horses, and allow women to launder. Harnesses needed repair, wheels and axles needed greasing.

At last they seemed to appreciate something about Marya as she caught fish with her bare hands instead of a hook and line. But that night before supper, a mass of fish floated dead in the same pool. They had to throw out food that was already cooked, spill coffee, overturn every pail of water, squelch the fire and prepare to leave the next morning on empty stomachs. It was in all of their eyes: Marya was "marhime"–unclean.

The next dawn, Marya strained her eyes in lingering darkness, only to see emptiness. Two wagons had vanished, leaving tracks in trampled grass and dark spots where campfires had burned. Only Jofranka remained. They knew, without searching, there would be no patrin. They hitched up their wagons and decided to follow the carnival circuit.

Fortune-telling proved good. Jofranka taught her to interpret dreams; what to tell, and what to keep untold. Jo taught her to stack cards for "emergencies" that involved a single sloppy shuffle. For a genuine fortune, she taught her to shuffle seven times.

Jo helped her to gather special herbs as the carnival ambled along the back roads. Together, they hung plants from both of their wagon ceilings; at night they prepared teas and ointments that kept the twosome popular. Marya stocked up on groceries and material for a black fortune-teller's dress with special sleeves that Jofranka designed and made for her.

The carnival boss made use of the fact that Marya breathed into nostrils of restless animals, soothing them. He made a big show about the way she called wild birds to her hand, and often told under what zodiacal sign a person was born. He asked her to "weave a web" to restrain his wandering mate, and it worked! The years passed in bland contentment.

But old Jofranka died suddenly as Marya had seen in her teacup. As Jo was dying, she put her herbal notebook and her horse's bridle into Marya's hands. She held up her scarab beetle ring, her mother's symbol of resurrection, for Marya to remove.

But Jofranka's beautiful horse was only a coveted hindrance. And with Jo's death there began a series of evil events that Marya had made the mistake of predicting.

One night someone drugged Marya's coffee and the carnival boss nailed her door shut. He drove Marya's wagon to a dingy trailer park, then untied Jofranka's horse, sawed off the hitching boards and rode away on the beautiful stallion.

Quila awoke and looked around at the dismal wagon. Her curly black hair was long gone and a colorless sort of dodder seemed to swirl in its place. Her skin was scruffy from flame, time and infrequent washing. She listened, then sighed. There was no bubbling stream outside to bathe in, to wash her everyday garments, to drink of, to fall asleep listening to.

But it was dawn; nights were hardest. No stories around a campfire. No one to coax into a singing mood, no reason to keep coffeepots simmering through long magic nights. No one to keep her warm beneath the threadbare, charred quilt of precious memories.

45. Quila Dresses

Bowie awakened as Quila started her day above him. He could hear the teakettle being filled from her metal pitcher of "special" water captured from rain, fog and dew in a little bucket hanging beneath the point of a scroll on her roof. A mug, a loaf of bread and a jar of bacon grease thudded across the table. Quila lit the stove and sat beside it in long white bloomers and camisole, palming her eyes as she waited for the kettle to boil.

Finally, she poured simmering water into a metal teapot that held the often thrice-used herbs she collected on neighborhood walks. She placed the pot on the coolest part of the stove to steep. Bowie could feel the dragging of a stool. She would be sitting beside the door-window now, pulling the ragged curtain aside.

Quila was starting her mornings as usual by collecting sights of the park and filing them in her memory to brighten the dark "night" she knew was inevitable. Quila-like, Bowie squinted his eyes until he could barely see latticework around him through wetness of his eyelids. With a heavy heart, he wondered: is this what life looks like through Quila's eyes?

What an idiot they would think she was, if they knew of simple joy Quila blotted up from daily designs on the clotheslines. She savored every hue, shape, movement. Though taught by her Gypsy mother that it was unsanitary to wash male and female clothes together, Quila delighted in patterns which resulted. Spotless diapers, that one of Robbie's odd girls was always hanging for Pug, were strung like Gypsy teeth smiling in space. Many-colored socks were Gypsy feet, twirling, dancing to guitars and concertinas that nobody else heard. Little dresses curtsied in the breeze. Gus' flannel shirts caressed Pug's giant garments.

Only lines which Mala hung were dull and uninteresting. Her clothes never profited from washing and she let children's clothes hang out at night for evil spirits to enter them.

It was taking longer each day now for humans to materialize from distorted phantom-material that was the park at morning sight. It was harder and harder for Quila to console herself that it was because of outlines, carriage, voices, colors they chose, habits, and mostly what they did and didn't say, that made it possible to match distant personalities to the right bodies! But let humans wait, clotheslines were always first to greet her eager eyes.

Inanimate objects delighted Quila. Afterwards, people could always be heard, but not the visual chorus of clotheslines, gathering clouds or changing moodiness of the tree.

Quila alone had no desire for the tree spot. She loved comforting sunshine on her clammy body. Even now, warmness filtered through the smoke-smudged skylight, enclosing her body in nebulous hues. Anywhere but under this colorful warmth or huddled beside her cozy stove, Quila's bones were heat-proof. She also loved the tree for contrast, changing ground patterns, sylvan sounds. The tree's cousins, willows, were old friends that used to bend and weave as she bid them to. She could tell when it was fall by the tree's yellowing, when it was spring by sparkles of scalloped triangles. Summer was here when seedy "snow" drifted around the park. In winter the tree was leafless, considerably letting sunshine through to whatever trailer was beneath. The tree was much sweeter than an evergreen. It would not burn as fast, would not be chosen as a firebrand.

She poured tea then turned back to the window, watching while she warmed her hands around a pottery mug. Below the wagon Bowie was enjoying the strangely familiar, herby odor that always made him long for things unnamed.

There was Fay Rose limping after Juju with a stick. Fay's nighttime self was an eye-catching mix of color and texture that the world was not ready for. Even in the late mornings with tousled hair in curlers and face speckled with medicine, Fay was not worth spending precious eyesight on.

Robbie, a formless blue blob, jangled to a sink for water. Quila's heart surged toward wrists that bore the pot and turned the faucet, wrists scabbed over and thick-skinned from self-inflicted wounds. Often the blob greeted workers in a smooth tone: Doll was home, all was well. Too often, nowadays, ominous silence meant Doll was gone, beware.

Today the blob was silent and created silence in workers, for Robbie's ears would be tuned for water dripping, unjiggled toilet knobs, the hum of more than one fan, or use of the hose. The jangle of keys faded, and the tiresome record began. Mournful music permeated every space for thinking. It also announced that the door to the Den was probably locked.

Lolli was in the washhouse. How annoyed she'd be to realize that her tawny hair, eyes, skin and clothes merely blended in with dirt of the court, unless she stood her brown self against the light walls of the washhouse or one of the brighter trailers.

There went Gussy, a white "umbrella" on a split blue handle. Each day she went through that ritual of getting to the mailbox first, walking like she was hurrying to some delightful Eden. From flower-fresh skin to the extra place at her table, Gussy was always ready to receive some expected guest. But Gussy's arms and legs were getting thinner, she was so busy that she relied now only on her single meal at Flo's.

Gussy tried hard to seem like the rest of the women. But she could never be accepted as one of the others. Quila shuddered; she was afraid of the girl. If given even half a chance, she would spread herself like springtime throughout the park, upholstering every unbeautiful situation with imagination, hope and simple solutions. Destroying Quila's livelihood.

Quila sipped strong tea as morning grew into its usual routine. From the uncovered floor slit where she swept the wagon's weekly dirt, she heard a garment rustle, and smiled.

Silent as drifting snow was Bowie, moving in staccato spurts or slow imperceptible oozes. Zig, zag, dart, blend. She seldom saw him arriving. She heard his knock, sensed his footfall, or suddenly he was just there. Like Mange, he was invisibly tethered to the park.

Though slowly crumbling beneath the daily onslaught of mostly wine and cigarettes, Quila could still sense a rugged handsomeness in spite of Bowie's thinness. Oh well, if she kept him in wine, cigarettes and occasional meals, no woman would ever notice the potential waiting to be recognized, appreciated, encouraged. Not even the girl with brown skin like Bowie's, and graceful black braids, who'd been secretly watching the park lately.

Maybe Quila should harp on the bad eye. Then Bowie would keep his hat pulled farther down over what little pride was left in that other beautiful brown window, that peeked into his inner soul and secret hell. Stripped of his few reminders of the misty past, he would remain as she needed him to, only a shell, her watchdog and ever-present eye.

Bowie never got closer to his miserable past than when he stood in front of Flo's pawncase, vaguely studying the slowly growing circle of silver dollars with a tassel of rawhide, beads and feathers hanging from the back of each coin.

He was so patient. Like other Navajos she and Lazlo passed on their honeymoon, huddled in blankets, waiting for a snowstorm to blow over or a swollen stream to subside. She pulled off a hunk of sourdough, drizzled bacon grease over it, and munched it to the crust, which she no longer tried to chew. When dried at the back of her table, she crumbled the crusts to feed Mange and a few little birds that still lived among her porch eaves.

Bowie's tales were a gold mine now that Quila's eyesight was quickly fading. Drab things that he described were, with Quila's deft handling, highly colorable, significant little jewels. She patted the metal cigarette box at the back of her table. Only when Bowie was in her wagon could she afford to smoke the mesmerizing herbal cigarettes Jofranka had made for coaxing information. Now, (except for the times that Bowie was being punished) little rent payments to Robbie, food and a few luxuries flowed to her through Bowie's eyes. She settled back on her stool, munching and stretching.

Some days she felt like a fading queen in exile, almost enjoying herself for the first time in precarious widowhood. But enjoyment had always been a warning to Quila. It usually meant a rising crisis.

Hmm, she pondered, beating a tattoo on the tabletop, Bowie didn't seem to really want the leather role she kept in her bodice. He could have grabbed it easily, a hundred times! He seemed afraid of what it might, or might not, reveal. Quila laughed out loud and shook her head as she remembered peeking into the little bundle.

Food, drink and oblivion were all that Bowie desired anymore. Even without her help, he could subsist, at least, on his instinctive knowledge of survival. But Bowie was suspended in some forgotten time-slot, and for the time being was satisfied with being so.

From the very beginning of his amnesia, unknowingly, Bowie had been dependent on Quila for his wine. She had hidden it near particular trailers, those she knew or hoped he would be peeking into. Each bottle was slightly sticking up out of its red hump, waiting for his discovery. When she figured he had found or fashioned peepholes in every trailer, she teased and led him into watching certain trailers even more, for that was where the full, instead of almost empty bottles could be found. Poor Bowie, with this ever-changing, senseless-seeming situation, he must often think that both his mind and memory had flown.

Quila was strangely glad for his presence in yet another way. Bowie was the same age that her own son should have been, the little

Lazlo that was born dead as she waited, numb in the cold water of the stream, while her mother sobbed. Sometimes at night, when she missed the sweet life that never was, she uncovered the sweeping hole just to be closer to Bowie.

The record stopped! Quila shuffled to the door and pulled the curtain aside again. Yes! She was back! Like a blade of blue grass, Doll was hanging up Juju's gaudy diaper. As willowy as a marsh reed, she moved back to the washhouse where Juju was soaking. Calm, graceful, sweet, Doll moved like her heart was hearing cradlesongs. That black "worm" twisting at her legs was Spade. "Your fortune is in the country," Quila's lips longed to tell Doll every time the trees appeared in her teacup. But Robbie's adoring eyes were always across the table: sea and sand were the only "country" for Doll and Robbie together.

Kneeling, she felt beneath the bed nook for an old candy box, put a mirror at the back of the table and lit a candle to imitate lighting in the Den. Across tired valleys and sagging hills of her face, Quila smeared cold cream, removed "makeup" with a rag and looked at herself as she really was—an always aching, tired, hungry, worried, little-old-lady-too-soon.

She was always a pretender now, never herself—Marya Mikhail—anymore. Gorgios and Gypsies alike had always thought she was a witch. "So why not play it up, benefit by it!" Jofranka always said. Quila had much to start with. When she was only a baby, her mother discovered the first essential—the Mongolian spot—that bluish patch near the base of the spine that was also found on some Navahos, Mayas, or Asiatics: "The witch mark!"

Stripped to her underwear, she was the boniest shred of a human that she had ever squinted at. Since the day she arrived at Last Resort, she had never taken a bath in the tub that hung outside her wagon. Aye, that would plump out her skin and pink up her cheeks, but it was too hard to fill and empty. Sponge baths had to do. Her body was ugly anyway, shapeless as a melting candle, and she had no desire to see and feel it totally nude.

In true, old Gypsy style she had no change of clothing. Her only everyday dress, the one Jofranka had made, she tied around herself, kimono-like, only when she heard Bowie's footfalls or when she left the wagon. Otherwise, she hung the shapeless thing wrong side-out, preserving it, precluding the need to wash its weary, smoke-filled threads. Her only recognitions of winter were the wearing of a heavy petticoat, throwing Jofranka's shawl around her shoulders more often, going to bed earlier and getting up later.

She rubbed her aching knees as much as her painful mangled hands would permit. Her skinny arms extended into gnarly fingers that always created a shudder as they traced the lines of a palm. Yes, much as she respected the witch mark, Quila respected her hands even more. They lent authenticism to every fortune. Aye, and if ever she really, really needed to she could apply buttercup juices from the seep in the canyon, and ulcers would appear to further create pity or revulsion. Each day the hands infamized anew her reputation. Children avoided her shadow, and mothers often grabbed clothes off the lines when Quila passed.

She put her arms into the black dress, and chuckled. Neighborhood wives would be even more nervous if they knew that her "emergency" talents included picking locks and whisking away family silverware! She tied the waist sashes.

Moving the candle closer she looked in the mirror. Since the fire her skin was mottled sycamore. To even the color she rubbed chalk and dabbed charcoal on places that were scarred the most. She shunned a comb as her hair fell out by handfuls, matting her shoulders with gray debris, swirling her head like a parasite. She dared but pick it clean of debris, scrunch it with her fingers and smooth it with roughness of her hands.

Gypsy style, she rubbed her few teeth with salt on a moistened finger, took a sip of water, swished it around her painful mouth, held it there to tingle on sore gums, then swallowed. She spoke to her reflection with scarred, ill-fitting lips which met obliquely. The words were stolen, molded into her own style from every Gypsy ever encountered or read about. She hoped more and more that everyone was hearing her fascinating words and not the strange wheeze that seemed to be getting louder with every breath.

As Jo had taught her, Quila darkened the downiness that arched above her upper lip, her brows she thickened and pushed up into peaks. The hairpoint on her forehead she lengthened, and deepened the scowl lurking down the corners of her eyes and mouth. Though the box held but shades and sizes of chalk and charcoal, when she finished, the frightened little old lady had disappeared. In her place was a beetle-browed, hawk-nosed and evil-looking new creature ready for the day's work!

She looked deeply into the mirror. So far, she kidded herself, no one suspected she was going blind. By accident, she had found that she could look between bony spaces of closed fingers and thereby focus her dwindling eyesight. She could sometimes read this way, and better decipher features of nearby people. But she wanted no pity! Sympathy, pity, affection were forbidden to her kind of witch. No, she could afford allegiance to no one save Robbie, the foundation of the park, and her Den, the marketplace.

There, Quila could "buy" her daily ration and maintain a delicate balance between teasing blackmail and the real thing. No, she didn't want wealth, the tree space or Robbie's "throne." She just wanted things to stay as they were, for a little while longer, at least.

The steaminess that covered Quila's wakening eyes had melted into tears which she dabbed away with her sleeve. She knelt and unlocked the chest where she kept secret things, her most beloved possessions, and beautiful gems that her mother had given her for creating moods. Every day she took pride in dressing up the black dress with something different, jewelry which was not just beautiful, but meant something and had "a use."

She gently touched the scattered gems in the top compartment. What should she choose to help her through the day? Without even looking close, she could tell by the feel, the cut and the setting what gem was on what chain. No, not the round faceted diamond today, not the square-cut emerald for love and success—it was too late. No, not the oval amethyst that often helped her headaches and eye pain. Not the smooth egg-shaped lapis lazuli to feel cheerful and fortunate, nor the rectangular aquamarine for courage. She hung the humble mustard seed around her neck to inspire hope. The transformation was completed.

She lifted her nose and sniffed. Coffee was starting to perk. She tidied her morning things, then grabbed a bread crust from the back of the table. With numb leathery fingers she pinched out the flame of the candle and stepped out the door.

46.   Quila Falls

Quila stood on her little porch, sniffing the morning air. Coffee wasn't strong enough yet, but the record wasn't playing! "Saturn's day," she whispered gloomily. She crumbled half the crust and scattered it while birds flew down from fancy roosts. Sitting on the top step, she held a few crumbs in her open hand and talked to the tiny bird who always perched on her finger while he ate. She fondled Mange's ears as he sprawled uneasily on the porch and whimpered a thank-you for his meager share. Did his old eyes seem larger, more watery than usual? He wasn't even vaguely interested in licking at the aroma of bacon grease lingering on her fingertips.

Again, Quila felt a sense of rising change to be suffered through; she hated change as she oldened. Reaching into the pouch-like part of an inner sleeve she felt the assuring presence of corn kernels, which she, as most old Gypsies, often carried to ward off evil. Gorgios would never understand the confidence they gave to a Rom.

She smelled again, yet waited, looking out over the drab trailer park, so unlike a Gypsy encampment where wagons were painted different colors and scrolled in gold or silver. She sighed: there were no arched roofs here, flowered curtains blowing through screenless windows, gaily painted spokes, horses neighing, silent dogs on guard, no foreign gorgeous familiar people.

A strange gloomy pall was pressing down around her. She crossed herself twice.

This crummy trailer park reminded her of a Gypsy tribe that nobody liked to camp near. Their wagons were battered and unrepaired; windows always broken; women silent and sullen; their men repulsive, shifty-eyed toads and children that were wild, dirty and sassy.

But here at Last Resort, at least police didn't pop up every twenty-four hours and urge her to move, "Keep your pockets clean and stay away from back doors, gardens and barnyards!" Here, there were no vigilantes with shotguns, no crazed Gorgios whose daughters had been "stolen" by Gypsies and wanted "to cremate every livin' Gypsy bastard!"

She still dreaded being tricked away again as in the past when her fortunes were too close to bitter truth. But time was shortening: she'd have to be careful, act on concrete things and less on intuition—which always got her into trouble. She smoothed the little bird's head feathers and tossed him into the air.

She stood, nodded, one-stepped painfully down the creaky steps and hobbled toward Robbie's Den. Guy was painting the wheel rims of his trailer as she passed. Quila crossed herself and hurried faster. If Guy were a Rom, she'd swear that someone in his family would die before the new moon: the color on his brush was black! With her right hand she positioned her left one into a protective Gypsy handsign as she walked.

When she entered the Den was empty but it soon became filled with girls, smoke and uncomfortable silence. Doll had come home and left again. When a pack of cigarettes and a pot of coffee were finished, everyone slipped away from the uneasy stillness, and Robbie was left alone again with only the draggy record.

That afternoon was long, but darkness was endless and Quila couldn't sleep. Usual night sounds came from Mange groaning in his sleep, the leaky faucet dripping and Gussy's erratic crickets. While drinking the last of her tea, Quila watched from her door-window as a couple entered the park, their familiar voices laughing softly, their arms entwined.

Later that night, Bowie awoke as Lolli's bare feet climbed the wagon steps and she softly knocked on the door above him.

Quila had taken out the sourdough starter and now Lolli sat watching on a stool. Quila kneaded the dough clumsily, in ways that avoided hurting certain fingers. Lolli tried to make small talk, until Quila was finished, covered the bowl with a dingy dishtowel, and then settled down on the other stool.

When even the whispering above him lowered and Quila covered the sweeping slot, Bowie felt like moonlight, itself, had been swallowed up by evil.

Early next morning, Bowie watched with dread from the slit beside Robbie's window. Something wicked was simmering on Quila's back burner. Deathlike, she alone sat across from Robbie who was still drunk from the night before. Quila's arms were like folded crossbones below her thin skull of a head. Doll had slipped out before daylight, and

Robbie's eyes were spreading gloom. The coffeepot wasn't even ready; why was Quila here so early?

A picture engulfed Bowie's mind where another wrinkled old one was studying bones in the sand and sadly shaking his head. The memory was fearsome as butterflies whose wings kept brushing away familiar scenes, puzzling as the web that waited for his spirit to float through a feather that was always caught there. He proceeded to empty what was left of the liquid grapes that whispered sweet lies when he drank enough of them.

Numb now, he waited for the inevitable.

Quila dealt cards for solitaire. "My, when yer amethyst, Doll, ain't hangin' 'round yer neck-ta keep ye from drink-yer gay as a pallbearer!"

"You old crepehanger, you'd hang shrouds around the sun, itself, if you could just get close enough!" Quila chuckled as though pleased at recognition of her audacity. "More like an old owl every day," Robbie mumbled, "seeing only things of darkness. No wonder you're always cold; you deny there's sunlight left in the world! Always making dark caverns out of everyone's mole holes."

"Necessity has no holidays, pet! Besides, me needments be tidy!" Bowie could imagine Quila's fingernails nervously clicking together beneath the table.

"It's got to stop, Quila. I'm tired of your petty thievery, your mudslinging, and my own hands filthy from it! Why can't you tell mostly good fortunes?"

"Ah, you're pale, Robbie, your blood jest needs more redment." From the arsenal of her sleeve she drew out and uncorked a small bottle of whiskey, wiped its mouth on her hem before handing it to Robbie, who took several swallows. "Ye know, everbody's a thief in some way, pet. Stealin' money, food, naps on the job, fantasies, stolen looks, strange bedfellows." A chill raced though Bowie's body as Quila pushed up her sleeves.

"What's on your mind, Quila?"

"It's not sayable," Quila lowered her eyes and Robbie seemed to pale.

"Somehow, I always thought that you, at least, would be loyal. But no, I don't think you even know the meaning or the feeling of loyalty." Robbie swigged again from the bottle. "All you've ever had for me is 'cupboard love'!"

Suddenly Quila forgot her odd way of talking, forgot to color and season her words for Robbie. "Why, I've paid you back for every crumb you ever doled out from this dreary cupboard!" Angrily, Quila gathered the cards, "I've made you king of this park! And say, Gorgio, I could turn you into the park's jester with only one measly, black word!" Quila usually talked so low, or whispered for effect, but now her voice kept rising.

"Straining facts, aren't you, Quila? Who else would keep you, lately, for the little you add to dull days?" Robbie drank the last of Quila's whiskey in long deep swallows.

Quila grabbed an apple from the fruit bowl, as though it might be her very last. She was sick of Robbie's moodiness, her silent rhapsodizing over Doll. What did Doll ever do for Robbie's Den? Who could count humming, brushing Juju's hair, stroking that bastard, Spade? Doll seldom even recognized the brilliance that unfolded before her! She never even noticed that even little incivilities of Quila and Robbie were superb, carefully planned as they went along. Refill the cups, sometimes Doll did, smiling and pulling at Robbie's curl. Insert toothpicks here and there, and make or pass around paper trays. But, Quila shook her head, it mattered little to Robbie what Doll did or didn't do. If Doll were just there, it was enough. And when she pulled at Robbie's hair, Robbie would have moved a whole mountain and put it back again had Doll but hinted at it!

A blind one would know when Doll was home! Robbie talked in poetry! Gone was the soulless look. Spangles of light, like leaves of the tree in morning sunshine, fluttered in and out of her sky-blue eyes. And aye, Quila herself finally understood the reason why Robbie kept the Den so dark. It had to seem a habit! For, whenever Doll might enter, Robbie was already in shadows of the spotlight, or the flickering camouflage of a candle. When there were no shadows to relax in, Robbie seldom looked at Doll. And mostly, when Doll was home Robbie needed little to drink: she was intoxicated by Doll's mere presence!

Again, Quila forgot that she was a pretender. "You're bewitched with Doll!" she cried. "You play that same old song of hers like it was the Magnificat! You'd let her lead you around on a pink leash in front of the whole wide world if she but asked you to!"

"What a small sin!" Robbie laughed nervously and lit a cigarette. Tensely Bowie waited without breathing, watching Robbie's jaw muscles tense, nostrils flare, teeth silently grind. The crack of Robbie's knuckles and the clicking of Quila's fingernails seemed to intermingle.

Scorn suddenly slipped from Quila's usually cautious lips. "You're passionless around men, Robbie!" she hissed. "And this 'thing' with Doll is a filthy, foul–" Robbie's hand flew out and silenced the cruel offending mouth. The slap was bitter, noted Bowie, but Quila swallowed it, then sat cowlike, chewing the bitter cud of it. Aye, she had gone too far. Perhaps if she acted casual, things would unsnarl themselves.

She rubbed her mouth, then slipped back into the safety of pretending. "My, yer nettlesome this morn'. Maybe, you're jest feelin' too malty from last night!"

"No. You've just swooped too low this time, Aquila!" (Robbie pronounced the name differently this time! Instead of calling her "A-keel'-a" as she always did, she pronounced it now as "Ak'-wee-la.) Gussy, the Chips, Bowie and anyone else who might be listening, could easily hear Robbie shouting from inside the open door.

"Did you ever wonder, Marya Mikail, what your nickname really means? You, with your trashy English, vacant eyes and feasting on dead 'remains,'" Robbie raised the empty bottle. "To 'a'Quila', queen of carrion: vulture!" Robbie threw the empty bottle across the room and it shattered against more glass as it fell into the wastebasket.

Quila hid the shock but her face went eggshell white as Bowie watched it crack into a weak smile. She'd been enjoying her throne-of-sorts. Now, she was aware of its inglorious disgrace. "Aye, I'm a lickspittlin' old fungus, but ye thrive on m'leechin'. I give salt to yer life blood." She twisted the apple into halves to make it easier for biting into.

"Always gnawing the hand that feeds you!" Robbie's voice kept rising. "Well, I'm tired of helping you stuff your bottomless bottle!" Robbie slapped the apple halves far from Quila's hand, "This was your Last Supper, Judas. Get out!" Robbie sobbed.

All was lost anyway, horribly mishandled. But everything added up now, just as Lolli reminded her last night: Robbie's moods running parallel to Doll's absence or presence; Robbie's sadistic pleasure in Doll's injuries and Robbie's envy of Spade's privileges. Quila stepped over to the screen door and flung it open.

Inside her trailer, Gussy had started a sketch, but stopped her pencil and looked out the open window. Quila slammed Robbie's screen, hurried down the step, and the record began again. Everyone could hear Quila now as it spewed from her mouth like she couldn't stand the taste of it one minute longer. Her tongue clawed into everyone's memory, all of the bottled-up, unsaid things condensed into three brain-searing words.

"You're queer, Robbie!" shouted Quila, the one who always sugared and flavored her words for Robbie. Bowie watched as Robbie froze on her bench.

"You were seen!" Quila screamed to the petrified park, just as Doll appeared from the washhouse, headed for Robbie's trailer, holding the just-washed Juju in her towel. "You both came home last night, arm-in-arm, you, Robbie, who can't even stand to be touched and you both slept in the same bed all night!" Quila hurried past Doll, and up the wagon steps as fast as fragile legs and weak eyes permitted, then locked herself, shaking and sobbing into her wagon.

"I'll kill that redskinned bloodhound," breathed Robbie. Quickly and deeply she jammed her glowing cigarette into Bowie's eyehole, then slammed out the door.

In total shock at Quila's words, Doll slid the dripping Juju down onto the driveway as Quila scuttled past her. Robbie exploded out the door and dashed toward the tarpaper shed. But Doll grabbed her arm and stopped her.

"Please don't play that record anymore, Robbie!" sobbed Doll. She turned and ran back through the washhouse, picked up her suitcase and hurried away from the park. Pug rescued shivering little Juju and took her home for drying and diapering.

Gussy sat there stunned and shaking, looking out her window for several minutes. Staying in the same position, she finished new sketches.

47. Bowie, Chased

Holding his burnt eyelid, Bowie had burst out the tarpaper door expecting to see Robbie standing there. But Doll had grabbed Robbie's arm, delaying her, and Robbie hadn't noticed Bowie's flight. The shock, and the pain in his eye, had disoriented Bowie or he would have merely dropped over the side fence and hid in a neighbor's shrubbery. Instead, he scurried from spying place to hideout as Robbie searched for him and the record kept on playing.

"Are you in there, you stalk-eyed wino?" Robbie shouted into the tarpaper shed from which Bowie had previously staggered, unnoticed.

"A rat doesn't trust to one hole!" Robbie searched in both the storeroom and the tool room, throwing things out in back of her as she mumbled angrily to herself.

"Are you hiding up there, you lynx-eyed lecher?" Robbie shouted up to the toilet room rafters. She hefted herself up on the dividing wall, pushed aside a board, and searched the shadowy attic in vain.

Hipped with two bottles, Robbie swigged and swayed as she searched the park. "Come out, you red-nosed wineskin!" Robbie yelled under Quila's wagon.

Bottle-in-hand, Robbie veered to the middle of the driveway (where Gussy could easily sketch her), and bellowed, "I'll find you, you know, and when I do, you bell-mouthed stool-pigeon, I'll rip out your filthy tongue-clapper!" Robbie knitted her fingers together and pressed until they cracked with nervous anticipation. Then Robbie stumbled back to her own trailer, as Gussy finished another sketch, then sank back into shock again.

First scratching the needle across it, in a way she had never done before, Robbie turned off the record player. Gussy felt like sharpness, itself, had scraped across her soul.

Bowie half rushed, half tarried out of the park, feeling the eyes of women as he passed, seeming to say, "Little things were okay, Bowie, but this?" Never had he really minded that people rarely noticed him, but now he ached for someone to speak, touch his arm, or take his hand and say, "I know you'd never rat on Robbie! I know it wasn't you!" But women in the washhouse, hanging clothes, under the tree, at the mailbox, all acted as if he were merely a shadow, or worse, something embarrassing like a blob of feces come upon accidentally on someone's parlor couch, something to ignore for politeness' sake.

Before turning toward the hills, once again Bowie looked back at the park. But there was no place to hide there; Robbie would keep on checking every niche and corner. Bowie hurried up the narrow path and huddled around the scrub oak in the arroyo, getting drunker, awaiting time and perhaps Robbie's sobering up.

That afternoon Bowie hiddenly twined his way back into the park and was starting to dig behind Gussy's trailer, searching for a bottle that might be hidden there, when Robbie, bleary-eyed and grumbling, finally found him. Roaring drunk, Robbie fiercely dragged him by the ear to the washhouse where all of the women were gathered, still murmuring in shock.

"An ass is known by long, listening ears!" shouted Robbie, as women scattered. Lolli had just lifted Whiffet out of rinse water when Robbie grabbed Bowie's shirt, plunged his head into perfumed warmth and held it there. Robbie pulled him up by the hair. "I want you water-cured and stone-sober, to hear what I say! Look me in the eye, not through a crack, a keyhole or around a paper curtain. If the eye offends thee, says the big, black book, then pluck it out! I want you to feel this!" Bowie struggled wildly, but Robbie was suddenly limbed with arms of steel. "I'm going to gouge it out, you one-eyed cyclops!" Deep into Bowie's burnt peeking eye, Robbie plunged a thumb! The pain was unbearable and Bowie fainted into the sink.

With unbelievable strength, Robbie lifted Bowie's limp body up out of the water, and dunked him again and again until he came to.

Bowie shivered convulsively. The last time he was pulled from the water "she" was standing there, golden-skinned and braids shiny, scolding Robbie! Instantly, Bowie's head was trapped in a wind-tossed bell that clanged deafeningly, "Fawna! Fawna! Fawna!"

"What are you doing? Let him up, you'll drown the poor man!" She fought and struggled with Robbie. Sputtering, Bowie shook water from his hair, squeezed his eyes shut, then opened them wide. Yes! She was here! The girl who was always, yet never quite, with him. That voice of sighing wind, whispering leaves, murmuring water. The girl in his dream world, with braids and golden skin. It was she! He began to pass out again. Weakness, pain and shock competed for the reason.

But Robbie would not have it and began dunking him again. "Wake up, you Janus-eyed monster! Face the facts! One way or another, you-yourself, killed your wife! This girl may look like, but she is not, Fawna!"

Suddenly, Doll appeared and dropped her suitcase on the cement. How could she return so soon, gasped Gussy, who had come to get hot water? Doll's gentle hands closed like handcuffs around Robbie's wrists, "Let him go, Robbie. He's had enough!"

Blindly, Bowie threw off Robbie's hands, shivered violently and ran moaning and weeping, holding his eye, to seek refuge, to throw himself again beneath the friendly oak in the arroyo. There he could drink of liquid forgetfulness buried there; he could conjure up the ghostly web, float through gentle arms of the familiar feather and flow into the blackness of nothing.

Luanna shook spatters of water from her hair, wiped her hands on her skirt and stared after the fleeing man in astonished sympathy. Without the grimy hat, his face was handsome with strength showing through despite his pain and habits of recent years. His wet, stringy hair only made her hands ache to wash it leisurely and trim it in ways that would highlight beautiful gray that was taking over. Longing and agony lay unshared in his black mournful eyes. Though he stooped and cowered under the gaze of white people, though his skin and clothes were worn with soil and neglect, Luanna knew that he could stand tall and admirable where there was beauty and familiarity around him, if only someone cared.

Luanna had followed–clear into the park this time–the barefooted, ribbon-shoed blond who looked like the parson's daughter wearing Luanna's clothes! But now, Luanna ran after the weeping, gasping man, retrieving his soggy hat at the corner of the washhouse.

She followed him over a winding trail dense with chaparral, until he curled up on the dirt beneath a scrub oak like a baby in shock. Despite empty bottles of wine beside him, the pain of his eye was excruciating. She cradled his trembling head in her lap and smoothed his muddy, dripping hair. Sensing only that she was female, he was just grateful and wept some more, until utterly exhausted, he slept. But crazy-eyed butterfly wings closed in upon him. He woke up screaming, holding his ears, slapping at imagined insects, digging at his eyes until his cheeks were bleeding. Luanna was close behind as he staggered out through the dark canyon and hurried back into the park.

Gussy opened her eyes and froze on the bed, as Bowie knocked impatiently. "Open the door, Fawna!" his wine-laden voice whispered hopefully. "Fawna, I'm home. Let me in!" His eerie voice rose higher and higher. "I can't find a doctor, Fawna! I must help you by myself! Let me in!" he cried.

Lights blinked on all over the park except in the Den, where Robbie had finally passed out. People were awakening in houses next door and across the street. Bowie was banging so hard that Gussy's whole trailer shook. Collages leaning against walls to dry, began falling. Things inside the cupboards crashed against the doors, Gussy's cup rattled on its hook, and water sloshed loudly in the tank beneath the breakfast nook seat.

"I'll never leave you again," he screamed, putting his finger into the handle hole and shaking the door. "We'll go back home, Fawna. Wait! Wait!" With a powerful thrust his fist broke through the screen and shattered the window inside. He reached through jagged wire and splintered glass, turned the inside handle, and the door finally opened. Bowie rushed into the darkness and flung himself on the bed.

He felt for dark hair on the pillow and crushed it to his face. But the hair was not long, strong and satiny. Without seeing, he knew that it was fine, flyaway and curled a bit on yellow-tasseled ends. Its owner pulled away from his wet bloody hands, gasping in terror at his winey breath.

He groped beneath the pillow where he vaguely remembered tucking the lucky turquoise amulet, before he went in search of more fiery red water, that somehow, always drowned the proud, shy, uneasy, speechless, discouraged manner that prevented him from getting or keeping a job. But the turquoise stone was gone, and there was only a thick little booklet there. He held it in his hands for a moment, bleeding over it, trying to fit the past into the present. He threw the book aside, stood up, and in darkness desperately felt his way along the trailer walls, feeling for warmth of animal skins, friendliness of dried corn and texture of hand-woven baskets that should be hanging there. The moon peeked out from clouds and easily lit the room through its thin newspaper curtains.

Little plants, no bigger than their saucers, were everywhere. Accusing eyes were watching him, not hovering butterfly spots, but Robbie's blue, blue eyes staring from squares and rectangles everywhere, all around the room.

He spied crickets hushed inside their invisible jail, grabbed the jar and smashed it. "Old One says crickets aren't good in a house! Evil spirits that come up through cracks in the ground!" He was weeping, stomping on broken glass and insects fleeing across the floor.

Across the floor, across the spot where Fawna's sheepskin used to be, that "magic carpet" whose very odor of mutton and pinyon smoke could always transport Fawna in dreams, back to her beloved marshland. He fell sobbing onto the empty spot with arms held out to embrace the memory. He stood on his knees in the broken glass and looked wildly around the room. Everything familiar was gone.

He turned back to the bed and ripped off a paper bouquet pasted to the head of the wall. Oh, God, it was there! That bloody, splintery hole he had gouged himself with Fawna's long black knife, still dripping with life from her warm, beautiful body. "If ever I die in here, help my spirit out of this place." Fawna had sighed one night. "It is bad enough for my body!"

"Fawna's gone." Bowie opened the door and slumped down on the apple box step. "I did it!" he screamed to the sky. "Her father warned me that a child would probably kill her! Just as it had killed her mother," he whispered. His eyes were vacant, his body spent and lifeless, as the girl who had looked so much like Fawna appeared from shadows and took him gently by the hand. But someone else was rushing up!

"Wait, Longbow!" The old name sent shivers of faintly remembered joy throughout his weary body. Quila rushed over. "Remember?" she shook him hard. "Fawna didn't die because of childbirth!" Quila was panting, "I only left her for a few minutes. Ran to Pug's for supplies and help. But the little boy had birthed already, fast as a wilding and easy. When I rushed back with Pug, Fawna was there on that bloody sheepskin, as you ran inside and saw her. With that big, black knife in her heart! You pulled it out yourself, then gouged a hole in the wall. Don't you remember? You didn't kill her, Bowie. Birth didn't kill her either!"

Quila put her mangled hand on Bowie's shoulder. She had dropped her odd way of talking; she wasn't angling or setting a scene, she was telling the truth. "The child never breathed, Bowie. Fawna must have felt that she and her ways were fated to pass with that tiny baby. She was of another time; desperately unhappy and out of place. I tried to explain, Bowie. But your eyes were blind, your ears were deaf, and you ran away into the hills for such a long time."

The moon went into, then out of the clouds again, as Quila reached into her bosom and drew out the buckskin pouch. "Fawna had this in her hand. She told me to give it to you, that only you would know when, and what to do with it."

Bowie held the pouch to his chest, sobbed noiselessly, then stuffed it quickly into his shirt. It occurred to him vaguely that Quila had made a great sacrifice. She now had no hold on him and no way to insure a living in her ever-darkening world.

"Come," the girl who looked like Fawna swung the black braid off her firm breast and took him by his bloody trembling hand. As he trailed behind her, headed for the canyon again, she placed her feet cautiously, crossing her line of progress with each step as Fawna used to do, as if her feet were more accustomed to rocks and woods than to sidewalks and roadways.

Beside the scrub oak, they uncovered Bowie's feeble embers. He spread the few coals with kindling, arranged wood snags that he had saved for winter, and fanned up a little flame.

It was time to remember.

There were so many good things, as well as the horror, and he needed those memories to help him start to heal.

"If it happened at all," his voice quivered, "it happened like this." Luanna laid his mud-caked head in her lap again. Many of the words were of his own, now-remembered language. But Luanna understood, and true to Indian women, she never interrupted.

48. Indian Days

It was late spring and the family had followed their sheep, goats and horses up out of the warming desert and onto the high Arizona grasslands.

One morning eight-year-old Pinieten (as Bowie was then called) wandered away on his new pony and soon was lost in a maze of canyons branching endlessly beyond the summer campsite. After hours of desperation his pony walked a wide ledge, following peculiar circles where wildflowers grew denser as the steep-sided canyon narrowed. Plaintive cries of a strange-sounding bird enticed him farther until finally the horse stopped in a sudden shadow. Pinieten looked straight up and almost backward along a jagged cliff. Dismounting, and tying his horse to a bush, he sensed that the birdcalls came from a rock slit into which he could squirm when he sucked in his stomach.

From inside the cleft another strange bird was calling. He followed the sound, groping upwards into dark dampness. Steep frightening blackness followed, filled with sharp curves, a trickle of water, tiny pools, strange echoes and little winds as bats fluttered close to his body.

Suddenly he fell many feet and tumbled into sunshine. He was up on a narrow shelf, high above a sunken boxed-in canyon! Frantically he grabbed a big root, just as he began to slip down the sheer cliff below. A giant earthquake must have produced this unbelievable scene! Slowly peeking beneath him, he felt suspended above a giant oval bowl of salad greens!

Above him were sheer eroded cliffs, whose peaks stretched like a mammoth fort around the small canyon. He heard both distant falling water and murmuring water nearby. A soft wind parted willows and cottonwoods for him to see tiny lakes prickled with cattail and rushes. Palms waded the water's edges, birds on stilted legs teetered and called in the shallows. Even as he hung there trembling, he felt a calmness that he had never known before.

He pulled himself back up onto the shelf. On hands and knees he inched along crumbling edges, fingering unsteady rocks of an ancient cliff ruin, much of which had fallen down into canyon rises. Suddenly the hair on his arms quivered: he wasn't alone on the cliff. He heard the first bird again and other unfamiliar calls.

Slowly he crept near where the sounds were coming from, and peeked up over a rubbled wall. Wide-eyed as a startled elf owl, sat a girl no older than he, pressing together potsherds with wild pitch. She was making up bird sounds, practicing as she worked. She was astonished, her eyes devouring him as though she had never seen a small boy before.

Eager to make friends, the child helped him across the wall. She offered pinyon gum that tasted of mint. She found a nestling bird in a treetop on the cliff below them; gently she put the ball of feathers in his hand and threaded fragile legs between his fingers.

In dimness of the cave behind her, she selected wood from piles of different-sized fuel, then finished assemblling a fire in the hollow of a wall. She mashed dried chia pods for tinder, and with a wooden drill that hung at her waist she produced a flame. She balanced a pot of leaves and water across blackened rocks, and soon, steam and smoke were disappearing into a natural chimney shaft! In disbelief, Pinieten sat on the crumbling wall, stroked the baby bird, and looked down far below him with fright, awe and appreciation.

The girl motioned for him to sit on a molded couch-like rock while she unrolled the piece of deerskin that hung from a thong around her waist. (Bowie turned his head in Luanna's lap, patted the mound beneath his shirt, and sobbed.) Spread out before Pinieten was a small display of plant parts. The girl acted out problems that each relieved, pointing to her forehead, teeth, stomach, and pretending to bite her arm. Carefully she rolled her medicines up and placed them again at her waist. Then she showed him edible leaves, seeds and bulbs cached in lidded pottery jars, hidden in rocky pockets of the cave.

Gently, she took the bird from his hands and placed it back in its nest.

She poured fragrant brew from a tiny lip of the clay teapot, then handed him a steaming "goblet" cut from a swollen buckwheat stem turned upside-down for using. He sipped the tea as though it were liquid gold served to him by a goddess. He sat the cup beside him, wiggling its three branchy legs into dirt. Instead of sweetening the tea, she served him pieces of wild honeycomb broken from oval slabs stacked in their earthen jar.

As she licked honey from her fingers, she turned to a crack in the rocky wall behind her and pulled out a flat leather bag. She slid from it a piece of beautiful wood with a double row of crude depressions in it. With two kinds of stones inside the bag, they played a new game. Her stones had "eyes" of turquoise peeking from uneven sides. When he moved his own stones, flashes of red delighted his eyes.

As she played she poured more tea, including in her comments straw dolls sitting around them in cozy niches. Why, she was "playing house," and he was smiling stupidly like the rest of the dolls. He pinched himself; had he just awakened into some children's heaven?

At first they only talked together in laughter and awkward signs. Her giggles told of his playing mistakes, or how glad she was to have him here. When he took too long with his turn, she pulled a buzzer toy from around her neck, twirled and pulled it while it hummed.

When the game was done, the tea gone, the fire dead and the cave tidied, she took his hand to lead him down a steep narrow path. As they inched along he shuddered: rash-making plants were waiting at every step and handhold.

A baby deer paused on the trail below. She pointed to the deer, then to herself. "Your name must be Deer." She shook her head and made a sign for baby. "I call a baby deer, a fawn." She wasn't pleased, with any way he tried to say it. "You," he pointed to her and the deer, then stamped his foot in dismay. "'Fawna!'" She shrugged, then smiled her okay.

At the bottom of the trail they crossed a bubbly stream, tiptoeing on flat rocks that led to a pool where the girl stopped, smiling at the two of them reflected in the deepness. They sidestepped behind a waterfall rushing high above. They oozed in and out of fissures, where giant rocks seemed barely balanced above them. At last they stood on the floor of the lush canyon, looking up at towering walls whose sharp teeth were eating of the clear blue sky.

Even when they stood before it he didn't recognize her home, hidden in a cliff, seeming like merely a rockslide. They had to push sideways through the hidden slit that was covered with a tattered animal skin door.

Pinieten expected to enter blackness, but sun shone down from a jagged hole above the fire ring, illuminating a snug room and filling it with warmth. The cavern had shelves and benches fashioned from soft stone with fluffy furs for sitting upon. The chamber was floored with round pebbles of an ancient streambed. It was walled with skins, colored corn, onion braids, mushroom strings, basket-making materials and strange instruments. He sat on one of the built-in couches, looking around with admiration. She opened covered baskets on hand-molded shelves to show dried meat and wild fruit. They sat in a circle of sunshine as the girl listened with eagerness to his every word. She felt of his shirt, his pants, and marveled at his worn tennis shoes. He returned the compliment by fingering her unfamiliar clothing.

Suddenly an old one stepped from the dark doorway where he had been watching and listening. His weathered face frowned down on Pinieten.

How did you get here, his angry eyes inquired?

"I don't know, a cave just swallowed me up!"

How long are you going to stay, the old ones hands seemed to ask?

Pinieten closed his eyes, picturing the fabulous valley as he had hung above it, and the cliffside cave that Fawna used for a playhouse. He opened his eyes to the wondrous room and the girl who awaited his answer. Wistfully he sighed, "Forever, if I could."

The old man paused a long time, measuring happiness that had taken over the girl's wide eyes. Having struggled with momentous decisions, he turned and disappeared.

"But when will you show me the way home?" Pinieten's face was anxious.

"Tonight," her hand seemed to answer as it pointed to sunlight above them and made a downward arc. Later that evening they motioned for him to eat corn and wild onions simmered in jerky gravy, and to drink of a strong bitter tea.

Bowie stretched his bent knees and repositioned his head on Luanna's lap. Without opening his eyes, he sighed, "And 'tonight' just never came."

49. Fawna

Scrawny as a Navajo pony was Fawna. Her tough little body thrived on long treks, heat, cold, danger or hunger. Pinieten and Fawna explored every niche and crest of the beautiful wooded valley, then spent hours tracking bugs and lizards, following ants or chasing winged insects. Flitting about in her skirt of shredded bark, she was more fun than a bevy of boys in jeans. In fact, Fawna had to be as much boy as she was girl–the Old One had only Fawna to insure any place for them in the future.

They seldom saw the Old One: he blended like his work into his surroundings. Always stacking and securing "fences" of smelly cheesebush around his gardens, which thrived in volcanic ash that spread like a spongy carpet throughout the strange area. Always clearing mistletoe from mesquite, wading shadowy coves to check fish traps, or working in hidden caves, stashing wood and dried food there. Often he needed their help.

Life was deliciously dangerous with Fawna. She taught him to see and hear all over again. They often ventured in long ways outside the wondrous canyon, so he could never remember the routes. He found himself doing as she had told him to: gripping her small strong hand as they jumped wide chasms; or clinging to her long thick braid as they sought narrow toeholds leading to cloud-capped peaks. "You'll pay me back," she laughed. "When I'm in real trouble, I'll send you a lock of hair and you must come flying! Promise? But that will never happen, I'm stronger than you." (Bowie began to weep and put his arms over his face.)

Fawna loved to play tag when the wind was just right, taunting him, running away, then intentionally entering a little whirlwind. Though stunned and blinded by dust and sticks, Fawna screamed ecstatically, pulled him inside, and together they ran along with squinted eyes, screeching with delight.

She taught him cleverly by playing games. She would shout a plant name and run for it, and he could only follow by using as stepping stones flat plants of the same kind. She taught him not to cringe at unfamiliar food like insect larvae, the inner bark from certain trees and meat sucked from snail shells. She wouldn't feed him until he found exactly the menu she planned. They climbed palm trees to rob hang birds' nests for eggs to scramble. They climbed rocky hills for fern tea and dug bulbs that waited under certain flowers. She cooked by dropping hot stones into watertight baskets of food, water and seasonings.

She was as slender, small and graceful as dwarf willows growing below the lakes where they swam every evening. Wherever they went outside the valley she taught him not to leave a footprint nor a bit of telltale ash; not a single arrow shaft was left to lay or escape in the flesh of a fleeing animal, without being tracked.

They often played in her special cave. She took him farther back into darkness and told him to stay there until she called. He waited in blackness, but only heard a whisper. "Pinieten, our tea is ready." He came into the brightness with a question on his face. "Have you never heard of a whispering cave?" she laughed, as she poured tea into plant goblets.

Fawna taught him secrets of eating poisonous snakes, and insects with pinchers or jagged legs. "You might need to know," she smiled. "Then you will never be dependent on those who can only feast!" Usually they did feast on fish, waterfowl, and produce from the gardens. Yet every day or so they had a small meal of only what could be found in the dry desert outside the fertile valley. Roasted grasshoppers with pigweeds, old dry fruits lingering on bushes, and tea from almost any plant that wasn't poisonous soon became easy to endure.

"It keeps you lean, hungry, alert. Ready for famines that are always waiting," said the Old One's hands. Soon it was second nature for Pinieten to be derooting a weedy plant, defeathering a scrawny bird or skinning a tiny animal while Fawna made the fire.

"And," said Bowie as he shifted position on Luanna's lap again, "I didn't realize that Fawna was also teaching patience: every time we followed humping span worms; waited for spiders to finish webs; for moonflowers to open; for smoke beneath a hand drill, or heat to move from our concentrated minds and enter millions of pores on our shivering little bodies."

Fawna taught him to make and use various stone weapons. "You never know when a rock might be your only weapon," she explained. She fished with crushed plants that merely stunned fish for awhile. The Old One used harpoons and snares–silent weapons. When they were caught by night away from the cave, they dug a shallow trench, filled it with grass and enveloped themselves in a fur that Fawna carried on her back.

Life seemed one long joyous day. But soon, though daytime skies were gentle and hazy, there was a chill in summer nights. Leaves were yellowing, drifting. The lowering sun got dimmer and the rising moon was soft orange.

"Indian Summer," explained Fawna, "a special gift of the gods."

Pinieten helped as Fawna made root baskets and her father pounded hemp for nets and rope. When wind blustered outside, around the fire the Old One taught Pinieten basics that grandfathers at home saved for older boys: twisting plant fibers and animal sinews into bowstrings, splitting granite, chipping flint and fashioning bones into tools.

And always, last thing at night, when embers barely glowed, stomachs were happy and stars twinkled from the ceiling hole, the Old One said exactly the same thing. "People without their history are like wind on the grass." Then, with forked sticks, Fawna lifted a hot stone from the fire ring, lowered it into water and nighttime herbs. Soon fragrant tea was waiting in pottery bowls, keeping their hands warm, as the Old One wove for them his stories of the past.

Suddenly, Pinieten realized that back home it was past time to gather pinole seeds, help with rabbit drives, or gather fuel beneath juniper and pinyon. Happy days of summer were over. It was almost time to learn indoors things from his grandfather's head. It was time to find a lower, warmer winter camp. He didn't want to be left behind.

Pinieten shared his nighttime tea with one of the dogs that now kept him warm at night. But the dog fell into a sleep from which he could not be awakened! The next night Pinieten only pretended to drink his tea and poured it among pebbles of the floor. When Fawna and the dogs had followed the Old One into sleep, Pinieten left the warm cave and tried to scale the walls that stood like fortress sides around the valley.

With bleeding knees and fingers he reached the upper edge of one windswept cliff before he realized why the Old One spent so much time there, where nothing worth eating could grow. Here the Old One encouraged thorny bushes and cactus, tucked stinging plants among fingerholds. Poisonous ivy stretched giant nets over every possible toehold, and its strands would not hold a small boy.

Fawna found Pinieten in a crumpled heap the next morning. The Old One carried him home and laid him on their softest furs. Fawna made sagebrush tea to treat his rashes, and spent hours getting stickers and thorns from his body. She blew puffball spores into his wounds and mended his leg with saguaro splints shaped to fit his ankle and knee. From a basket of poppies and herbs she made a concoction which lessened his pain enough to sleep.

While Pinieten mended, the Old One moved to a mountain spring for autumn hunting, awaiting thirsty animals and migrating birds. When Pinieten awoke in pain, the Old One was back in the cave again, hanging strips of meat across poles beneath the sunhole. Pinieten's shattered shoes were gone, but Fawna sat weaving yucca sandals like her own. He was wearing a shredded skirt of mesquite bark now, that made the tending of his wounds easier.

He slept a lot beside the daylong fire that Fawna kept alive. Fall faded to winter and Fawna replaced his thin shirt with a hooded rabbit skin top. Winds roared outside the cave bringing nightmares to Pinieten. His sobbing startled Fawna from her sleep and he heard the Old One whisper to her: "Only his spirit knows of shadowy specters waiting in front of Pinieten. His young body would never believe!"

That night Fawna brought to the fireside baskets of boughs and fibers. While the Old One told his stories, Fawna created a fiber web within a willow wreath, decorated it with feathers and beads and hung it above Pinieten.

"Here is your own dream catcher. According to legend, bad dreams are caught in these woven webbings while good ones flow through the feathers to guide and protect the dreamer." Bowie told Luanna how that same dream catcher still hung in his haunted memory.

As he drifted into Fawna's "poppy-petal sleep," he heard the Old One's whispered words and watched his talking hands: "Pinieten's great vision quest will not be a formal seeking. It will take him to dark and deathly places before he will realize personal power and attain spiritual growth that will ready him to the grand purpose for which he was intended."

After evening meals they taught him to play on hollow reeds, bone flutes, gourd rattles, a tortoise shell drum and a castanet of rattling things like seedpods, deer hooves and birds' beaks.

Bowie stopped, sobbed, put his hands over his ears.

For a while they were snowbound, they couldn't open the skin door and had to move the fire ring away from the snowdrift that fell from the ceiling hole, and soon became their water supply. Fawna had time to beautify a basket with hanging beads and bone, and colorful feathers that she found as she had gathered food in other seasons. As she worked, the Old One helped Pinieten to practice chipping bird points, knives and scrapers with pieces of antler and bone.

"Your tool depends on how it flakes," the Old One showed him. For the first time Pinieten realized that his own blood was now mixed with ancient drops all over the rocks around them. The two of them practiced throwing and shooting weapons down a dead-end hallway that led away from the main cave. The Old One lit a torch at the end, where he hung dead bats and animal skins as targets.

At night now, Fawna covered the "sitting fire" embers with stones, twigs and dirt. She spread soft skins above the warm area for the three of them to sleep upon. Beneath the starlight, Fawna fell happily asleep, nestled within her sheepskins. Pinieten drifted off beside her, imaging myths and legends that the Old One's soft voice was still sharing. Early every morning Fawna tenderly unearthed the night's embers and blew them back to life again. Once, she really got upset when "mother's" coals were nearly out.

One morning Fawna helped Pinieten walk outside when the valley was covered with snow again. She looked at animal tracks, then stepped on the crusty whiteness and fell up to her knees. "Strong enough to support game," she laughed, "but not the hunter, herself!"

Bowie shuddered in some kind of related memory.

When spring finally returned, Pinieten often lay beside new bubblings at the head of the little lakes, while Fawna massaged his legs. The waterline was fringed with an array of plants that he had seldom seen in a desert place. Marsh trees were alive with migrating wings. For every leaf, flower or feathered songster Fawna taught him a unique name.

Fawna never went hunting without results. She knew secrets of birds, animals, seasons and nature. "Watch those ducks circling the pond," she whispered as she readied her bow. "They'll land just as the breeze slows down." They spent hours watching ravens play and tumble in special kinds of winds that blew above her favorite cliff.

As Pinieten began to walk again, at first it terrified him to wander with Fawna among wild tobacco plants growing rank on the hillside across from the cave; he knew that such plants had a liking for graveyard soil! But Fawna was like a soul released when there. Wild-eyed she became and she talked with strangeness in her voice.

More and more they were able to converse, each in the other's language. As they sat at the edge of her playhouse cave overlooking the luxuriant valley, she told him tales of a wonderful tribe and a terrible earthquake. She lamented coldness of dead squaw fires, the hard-earned, forgotten skills of bodies lost in the earth across from them. And Fawna took it upon herself to teach him lost skills: to count on a crude abacus of twigs and hide circlets, to tell time with a shadow clock. She taught him unique ways to hunt, fish and trap, to subsist on air, water, snow, sunshine or aroma when there was nothing else.

She let him peek into the leather pouch that hung around her waist: a buzzard feather, eagledown and strong-smelling leaves were there.

Bowie cried silently as he touched the swelling on his shirt where Fawna's pouch was always waiting.

"Even gathering dead squaw wood off the trees was fun with Fawna," said Bowie. "Her games and storytelling while we worked were of a long-forgotten, primitive brand.

"The days were too short," he moaned.

Finally Fawna and the Old One gave in to his homesickness. Fawna dried meat and vegetables to hang in a chain around his neck. Pinieten gazed at her soft brown skin as she worked, her haunting smile, and almost changed his mind.

They fed him a potion and when he awoke outside the canyon walls, all that he could remember was being strapped to a travois. Fawna's beautiful black eyes had juiced up with tears, and her voice had implored him, "Come back boy-child, please come back."

After many days the strings of food were empty, his legs were weary with unaccustomed walking, but he finally found his people's new encampment. His mother almost fainted, and his grandfather gasped at the thin boy limping toward them in a bark skirt, rabbit shirt, and a stone club hanging from his waist. He was so tired he collapsed beside his mother's feet and fell asleep while somebody covered him up.

That night the older ones built up a big sitting fire beside him. They put a fresh pot of coffee in the coals and drew their blankets close around them.

"It is strange how little Pinieten dresses like the Old Ones!" His grandfather shook his head, thinking that Pinieten was still asleep on the sand. "He disappears into nowhere, leaving the pony to find her own way home alone. We had given him up for dead!" Again the grandfather told of great earthquakes that walled in the Old Ones until the race was almost extinct. For four generations in a beautiful storied valley, the frightened remnants of a Nation smothered camp smoke, crawled under brush to leave no trail, wiped out their footsteps, used noiseless slings, and hid at the approach of other human beings.

"Five generations ago they wove sandals like Pinieten's and dressed the same way!" great-grandfather whispered.

After that they watched the nine-year-old carefully. They kept him busy herding lambs, caring for horses and chopping wood. They questioned him repeatedly, without results. At night Pinieten snuggled under the beautiful blanket his hopeful mother had woven for his returning. For some reason, he always thought before he fell asleep, the beautiful canyon, Fawna and the Old One should be kept a perfect secret: he told them he couldn't remember.

But, he kept his horse rope beneath his bedroll, where it was always ready.

50. Longbow

Bowie stretched, turned and settled his head again in Luanna's lap.

But it was yet another spring before Pinieten could put on his favorite clothes and sneak away to that special canyon. Walking in front of his horse, he kept his head bowed to the right, searching for strange patterns of wildflowers that now he knew grew bigger and denser in carbon circles of ancient fire rings. Finally he stood in the shadow of a jagged cliff, and there it was, just the right rock face. But no matter how he tried, he had grown too big to squeeze into any of the small slits.

While he was wandering aimlessly, miraculously, in the voice of a strange owl, Fawna hooted to him, and he tied his horse to a bush. She led him with her calls, by devious routes through a black tunnel and out across another canyon, then into a cave behind the shimmering waterfall, playing and fluttering in the distance and often merely taking him into dizzying black or sunny circles in order to confuse him.

Fawna showed him where special manure that her father used was steaming beneath bats asleep on walls of a certain cave. She showed him a new place to bathe in a hidden hot spring pool when it was too cold to use outdoor waters. Life was wonderful, she smiled. Even at its saddest, there were buried seeds of wisdom and joy, and new things to discover if you were patient, she said. He knew that though her waiting had been long, it had also had its own beauty.

By this time Pinieten had no idea of where he was or how they had arrived there at the door of her father's cave.

After dinner they called music from all of the instruments waiting on the walls. A cricket chirped loudly from the entrance to the cave. "Listen!" Pinieten laughed. "He's trying to join us!" But the Old One rushed over and stomped on the insect with the heel of his moccasin.

"Crickets not good in house. Evil spirits of 'gone ones' coming up through cracks in the earth!" (It was the only time that he had disagreed, even silently, with the Old One. But Pinieten respected his wishes. Whenever he heard another cricket nearby, he quickly caught it and gently took it outside.)

The fire died down to a gentle glow and stars added magic from the ceiling hole. Again, the Old One enchanted them with stories until they fell asleep within soft furs.

That very next morning after breakfast, Fawna returned him through a labyrinth of narrow canyons and steep crevasses they had to jump over. It was as though they wanted him to know, now, that he was not a prisoner and could come and go whenever he wanted to.

Pinieten's people began to believe that lions and bears prowled among gloomy shadows of the towering cliff walls. Their sheep disappeared when allowed to graze near certain areas. Though no such plants were visible, paths were strewn with spiny burs of those plants! Though Fawna never called in her owl voice, unless Pinieten was alone, the men secretly followed the network of countless passages that branched beneath and among the granite cliffs. For days they became lost and starving, until strange bird songs enticed them back into sunshine. Secretly, others tried to climb the rocky walls but jagged pinnacles seemed to reach backward to the sky, and one boy fell to his death. Eerie echoes, clouds of bats and mournful sighs among the endless caves finally drove them away for good.

One day while Pinieten was visiting Fawna, the Old One handed him a bow. It was remarkably long and exquisitely detailed with bright feathers and bone beads hanging at the bottom tip. For weeks the Old One had been soaking, chewing, working deer tendons, flaking points and singeing feather edges to produce arrows. Fawna decorated the bow and finished the arrows by rubbing them smooth with coarse rocks and stems of the horsetail plant.

"My father and his father before him were named Longbow," said the Old One as he stroked the finished bow. "There was something magical about the spirit of whatever bow they fashioned. It could send an arrow farther, more accurately, than could be achieved by mere arm alone. So fast were the arrows, they sped unseen. Game that hung from their shoulders was always enough for widows and wizened old men, as well as young squaws that waited with sharpened edge and ready fire." The Old One paused, put one hand on Pinieten's shoulder and gestured with his other hand. "Always I have wanted a son. I will call you 'Longbow.'" Pinieten wanted to say it was impossible to shoot a big weapon from his pony, but, they would think, would any Indian sacrifice power for comfort?

Back home, his family fingered the doeskin shirt Fawna had made him for chilly nights and began to question deeper. Finally, he merely told them about the strange waterfall that rose and disappeared within the same valley, of lakes full of fish and ducks that never went dry. "He draws the 'longbow' cleverly," laughed his uncle. "Let's call him 'Longbow.'" Pinieten was mystified: the Old One and even his very own people had both chosen the same name.

Bowie opened his eyes and Luanna too, was looking mystified.

His family could not believe the power of the springy, sturdy bow that he told them he had "found." Never had they seen such a unique bow cover as the weird mountain lion tail which Fawna had prepared for it! Fawna had also taught him to imitate a rabbit in distress, quail calls and the honk of wild geese, all of which Pinieten could fell with the throw or release of several weapons. He knew the secrets of splitting sinews, and what parts of animal bodies they came from. Grandfathers frowned, for these secrets were saved for older boys!

Longbow had also become an expert axeman. As the Old One had taught him, he cleared ground an ax-length around, so the ax wouldn't catch on anything. He worked with a firm but not a tense grip, controlled rather than hard strokes. Grandfathers shook their heads in dismay. These skills were unheard of in one so young! The woodpile around his mother's hogan was soon higher than all others and divided into several types of fuel.

Nor could anyone explain why Longbow knew his numbers so well or how he could tell time in sand, and do simple arithmetic.

Now he knew the habits and logic of the hunted. Better than adult hunters and without the grandfathers' school, he knew of bear trails that led to unbelievable fishing! In drought months, when sheep could scarcely find grass, Longbow would be able to lead them to some hidden grassy pool or secret crescent of water concealed in rocks. "Like the Old People used to do," they whispered, he often slept in the water of hidden springs on hot summer nights.

If he and friends were gone overnight, nobody worried. Longbow could always find something worthy of eating, and water for drinking. Around the campfire Longbow told the Old One's stories until his friends fell asleep. Like Fawna, he often drank from a three-pronged buckwheat goblet, that he could toss to the wind when finished. For dessert, remembering Fawna, he nourished himself on a beautiful view.

He made replicas of weird drums, rattles and whistles that he and Fawna had played with. Older relatives whispered and left him alone. But with children he had earned a new respect. He could out sprint and out dare every one of them. For ant bite to lightning strike he seemed to know every antidote as well as, or better than, even the medicine man!

Longbow lived with his mother and grandfather. His mother wove blankets to barter with at the trading post. His father worked in town and had grown completely away from old ways and Longbow's mother. "They are the best, the old ways," his mother told Longbow. She hid him when his father or strangers came around.

"Why do you work off of the Reservation, Lone Bear?" she asked the father at first.

"Don't you want more than this?" he pointed to the neat hogan in disgust.

"What more do I need than shelter and fire, food, a few pots, some clothes, Pinieten—and you?" Shaking his head, Lone Bear rode off in his new truck.

One day after the first fall rain, Lone Bear drove up again. A pretty woman and two little girls sat in the bed of the truck. The woman ran red fingernails through blond curly hair, smoothed her knee-length flowered skirt, and lit a cigarette. For the first time Pinieten realized that his mother's braids smelled of mutton and woodsmoke, that the bottom of her heavy, velvet skirt was always dusty or muddy, that her gentle hands were rough and callused.

Before his mother could hide him, his father had lifted the blanket-door and was sitting on sheepskins. "He is still called Pinieten, 'little no-sense'?" his father questioned.

"He is Longbow now."

"Show me what Longbow has learned this year that any schoolboy can't do better!" His mother's face was stricken. "Come, come! What has he learned?" his father repeated. "How to avoid evil, ride a tame burro, kill a blind wood rat?"

Longbow beckoned his parents to come outside.

51. Indian School

On rain-dampened ground Longbow drew a shadow clock to prove it was noon. Proudly he held up the hoe he was fashioning for grandfather, made by tying a deer's shoulder blade to a wooden handle, as the Old One did. He read latest news of clouds, put his ear to the ground and returned with a pack rat's cache of pine nuts. He drew his bow and killed a frightened quail that flew from a hillside bush. His father walked over and picked up the bird.

"Mere mouthfuls, when whole cows, plump chickens and fat lambs are minutes away in a market! What's he to be, just a pot-hunter?" His father spat on the bird and threw it away. "He knows nothing of books! He's been nowhere! He has no schooling!"

"He already knows more than grandfathers teach," his mother replied softly.

"What good are old teachings in today's world? I want my only son to follow highways, waterways, airways—not just ruts worn by weary ignorant moccasins!"

Early next morning Longbow put on the clothes that Fawna had made. His bow hung from his shoulder, he was taking his rope from beneath the bedroll. But suddenly, his father and the sheriff burst through the blanket door. They dragged Longbow out of the hogan, screaming and fighting. His father jerked the bow from its holder, fitted an arrow and killed his pony in the nearby meadow. Over his powerful knee, he then broke the beautiful bow.

He looked at Longbow's deerskin shirt, bark skirt and yucca sandals with disgust. "He looks like some nightmare out of the past! You've held back the wind long enough!" he shouted to Longbow's mother. "I want my son to have nothing to return to here!" He jerked the quiver full of arrows from the boy's shoulder, then threw arrows, pieces of broken bow and the lion tail cover into the breakfast fire.

As they wrenched him away from her, his mother's eyes were icy and the last of her wifely love trickled down her cheeks as her son disappeared across the horizon.

At school he was shorn of his hair like a sheep. Secretly he cried for his mother. He longed for Fawna's dream catcher, for he couldn't stop the nightmares about his dead horse and ashes of his wondrous bow. White teachers burned the clothes Fawna had carefully fashioned. Like pack rats they stole his yucca sandals and left stiff leather "boxes" in their place. His body wandered like a sleepwalker. His heart was a caged bird that only escaped in daydreams to drift with clouds hovering above the magic valley, above the girl who waited.

White teachers stole his legends and heroes, and replaced them with strange values, titles and traditions. Every hour had to be accounted for. Nothing was natural. Seasons were ignored. There was no time for meditation or the quiet enjoyment of just being alive.

Life was hard. Longbow cared for nothing that had to be learned from books. He refused to speak the language of his captors and they punished him for mumbling in Indian. They never mentioned sweat-earned, earthy, practical things that his mother, the grandfathers, the Old One and Fawna had taught. The only thing good was strange food, but there was never enough time to finish it! At night he and his friends stole to the hills to make a fire. They used water, oil and cornmeal taken from the kitchen, to make cakes on hot rocks, while telling stories of their homes and families. Yet by day, it seemed that teachers scrubbed their minds and hearts of music, art, history, love and respect of all they held dear.

One night Longbow found familiar herbs to put in their hidden fire. He had no time to dry herbs, nor look for eagle feathers to direct the healing, long-remembered fragrance. With only his hands he wafted smoke toward himself and the other boys. Before leaving, they rolled in sand to get rid of the telling odor.

Was wonderful food intended to kill the Indian in him? He quit eating! He ran away from school and tramped the country working at odd jobs. "Why should I have studied?" he asked Luanna. "Stolen ventures only taught me the meaning, first-hand, of intolerance."

Brought back to school again and again, he grew sick and weak, and spent most of his time speechless, looking out the window toward where Fawna lived with embers bequeathed by her mother. Never were the embers so weak as to be beyond a breath, and a handful of squaw wood. He remembered now how Fawna got uncommonly concerned when embers burned too low. He felt that the embers of his own small "fire" were almost beyond recall. His friends bound clumps of sage together, and smudged him late at night. Again, there were no eagle feathers to create a bridge from Longbow to the gods. He fasted for days.

Easter vacation came and his father reluctantly allowed him to leave his bed and visit his mother. But there had been flooding and Longbow could not find Fawna's magic valley. As he wandered hopelessly trying to imitate her strange birdcalls, Fawna finally called to him.

While Fawna tended sheep on the spring-flowered hillsides outside the wonderful canyon, she showed him likely places to find quartz, obsidian or jasper for arrowheads. She taught him how to choose the proper rocks for arrow-straighteners, scrapers, manos and metates for grinding seeds. They picked watercress from new little springs and robbed birds' nests for breakfast again. They ran together, he in a buckskin breechcloth of the Old One's, and she still in her skirt of shredded bark. They watched the hummers' mating arcs. Longbow named the birds, and she was proud of his remembering.

"Look!" she shouted. "This old streambed is weeping purple flower-tears! And here, little mushrooms are holding hands around this hollow log!" Sometimes, when they were caught by night, they piled willow branches into a shelter. While they were sleeping, Fawna often got up silently and covered his feet. "To protect them from moonshine," she told him, "so you will never, never turn gray!"

Bowie touched his graying hair and shook his head.

Together they tumbled on a hillside sprinkled with poppies and purple larkspurs. They were a king and queen on a royal carpet spread out just for them, and he fashioned a flower chain to crown her with. She put a rawhide thong around his neck. It held a drop of turquoise on his chest. "For good luck," she said as she placed one hand over her own heart and the other over Longbow's. "I feel that never again will we be so rich, so free of cares," she said wistfully.

Luanna wiped tears from Bowie's cheeks with the hem of her skirt. "That wonderful summer flew so fast," Bowie sighed.

Too soon the leaves turned yellow, nights became chilly and the moon ripened into its soft orange glow. It was Indian Summer once again. Longbow waited at the farewell spot while Fawna slowly disappeared into the brush, covering her footprints with dead leaves, or wiping them out with her fingers. He watched her feet springing from rock to rock until she was out of sight, leaving no signs behind her.

But the hills were blue with woolly plant stars. Their blooming told him that he had stayed away too long, that it was almost October.

52. Navajo Code Talker

His angry father sent him even farther away to school and finally Longbow shaped up. He graduated at the top of his high school class, joined the Marines, and just as his father had planned it, they sent him to a school for Navajo code talkers.

Overseas he was plunged into a warring world where "home" was tents or trenches. Though his only curse word was "coyote," he earned respect as a crack shot, survival expert, and night patroller who could stay alive with absolutely nothing to eat, while probing the best-guarded of any Japanese position.

Injured in mind and body, he finally returned from WWII. He should have felt proud and bejeweled in uniform; his arms should be filled with presents; his voice should be eager to share his part in winning the war. The grandfathers held cleansing ceremonies for the returning warriors. Some felt healed enough to move on. Some, like Longbow, did not.

In the daytime he was thankful for serene, uncomplicated, unthreatening desert. But every night he unwillingly returned to steamy, rain-soaked, death-filled islands. Again and again, he drowned in rivers of mud, leeches and dead bodies. He awoke still dripping with jungle sweat, exhausted from hacking through vine-choked, rotting vegetation, teeming with snakes, booby traps, snipers, dysentery and death. Every morning he was weary from pulling shattered bodies out of red, slimy ditches, sleeping with dead men, trying to ignore screams of the injured and dying. His ultimate duty was "only the radio and the code."

Unexpectedly, he had come home one evening. Mutton ribs were roasting and bread was frying in sizzling lamb fat. That night there was a welcome dance for him, unlike the dances among whites, held in smoke-filled rooms with loud music and unfamiliar faces. Here they danced in clear fresh air with stars and fires for background.

But after ten years, returning to the Reservation was a shock. Hills were parched, gardens pitiful, horses thin and shoddy. His grandfather was gone. Tribal leaders were sad, ineffectual and worn with discouragement. Old ceremonies were uninspired and endless. Scrawny cattle, dwindling sheep, meager crops, poverty and drabness depressed him. Older boys were moving to town after graduating from the white man's school. They wore tight Levi's and wide belts with their private names burned on the back.

Although they goaded him to get a truck, a gun and a girl, for a while he just bummed around the Reservation, pondering old ways, and drowning those agonizing islands in alcohol.

He watched his mother's weaving, changing loom strings, beating patterns down with a rhythm, humming while unwinding yarn and cutting. Yet now, he could choose a dozen rugs, pots or baskets and pay for them with green paper instead of time and sweat.

Finally he bought a horse and sought out the towering cliffs. Beneath their shadows, he tied the mare's front feet together and scattered hay. Maybe she wouldn't wander too far! He called to Fawna in the voice of a bird that would never sing at this time of year.

At last she answered him.

Somehow, he expected that Fawna had grown into a long-limbed horsy sort of a girl, shaggy-maned and unbroken to niceties of life, when suddenly she appeared in shadows beside him. "Longbow?" Her voice was soft wind in pine boughs.

She wore panels of deerskin laced down the sides and caught on bare shoulders with leather ties. Fringe caressed her thighs and danced around her elbows. Her slim waist was circled with rawhide and tasseled with the medicine bag she had always worn. Curved tips of shiny braids on the ridges of her breasts were as fascinating as ravens that played in the winds above her favorite mountain.

Near forks of dark passages she waited for him to catch up. He could smell in cross breezes that she rubbed scented plants on her skin just for her own pleasure.

He ached to hold and kiss her, but Longbow was used to easy girls. Fawna was probably twenty-one now, yet she wouldn't need another human being. She had for company every animal, insect and plant that she came across. And in her lovely head was everything that the Old One had taught her of homemaking, survival, entertainment and defense.

As they rested beneath a stream-side willow, Longbow unwrapped a velvet skirt, peasant blouse and sandals. But he could see that Fawna preferred her own clothes. He unwrapped a squash blossom necklace of silver bells—symbol of fertility, he reminded her—and tenderly asked her to marry him. Tears in her eyes, she handed the necklace back to him.

Was it because Fawna didn't care to own real jewelry? She would much prefer him to encircle her with wildflowers or a necklace of buckwheat balls, as though all she treasured was the day itself. The only things she needed were the leather pouch, her mother's embers, her father's knowledge and sometimes, the childlike company of Longbow.

She kept the clothes and fancy tin box, but insisted he keep the necklace. That evening her father studied scattered bones as they sat around the campfire. The Old One was not pleased with what the bones foretold. He tied a carved mask onto a stick, and stuck the point into soft dirt at the entrance of the cave.

Then he left to walk all night without any words to them of good sleep.

53. Taking Fawna

For several years there had been little rain, Fawna told him as they sat beneath the starry ceiling, around glowing embers. The Old One had had to work very hard bringing water from lowering ponds to thirsty gardens. Longbow decided to stay several months and repay the Old One for his teachings. Fawna led his horse through a narrow slot that led to a natural corral where there was plenty of grass, a constant pool, room to romp, and shade.

Days later, the Old One made a sand painting outside the cave to summon the help of gods in bringing rain and curing his sudden sickness. But when the Old One bent down to wipe the painting out before dark, he hadn't done any singing! Longbow could see that disease had already engulfed him, and sands of time were sweeping rituals from his mind. Without eating that night, the Old One climbed the highest pinnacle of the valley. As they sat around the fire, Fawna and Longbow could hear his distant chanting, and the usually friendly stars above them seemed distant and foreboding.

Next morning while gathering potherbs they watched vultures circling the valley. Shivering, Fawna ran home to find the Old One napping, which he had never done before.

He napped a lot now. Whenever Fawna caught him deeply sleeping, she filled his medicine pipe with certain herbs and blew the healing smoke all over his thin body.

Longbow worked harder now with Fawna and the Old One, putting into practice all the skills they had taught him: leaching acorns in the fastest part of the stream, gathering medicine plants and cattail pollen, stacking wood caves with fuel, tinder and kindling plants.

He helped pound deer meat into powder, mix it with hot fat and wild berries and cut it into cakes. Still it was flavorless to Longbow.

"No matter what it tastes like," said the Old One's weary hands, "pemmican keeps forever, takes little room, and keeps a hunter full without the need of fire!" What a wonderful grandfather he would have made, what a wealth of knowledge would be lost when he was gone. Again, and without results, Longbow pleaded with Fawna to marry him.

As a storm began to gather, Longbow prepared to leave. Though the Old One was bent like a silvery fiddleneck plant, and always smelled of medicinal smoke, the promising clouds were seeming to revive him. Fawna was smiling too.

Fawna tried to hurry Longbow home through just one narrow passage, instead of the usual roundabout way. But as he walked, Longbow had time to drop dried corn he had secretly brought along. Fawna returned home a different way. As Longbow watched her bare feet springing away from rock to rock, he pushed a row of yellow kernels into the highest bank of the streambed so they would be safe from flooding.

Her footsteps were soft as petals falling, but as she disappeared, the storm descended in angry fury. Longbow whistled as Fawna had told him to and his horse came wriggling out of a tall crevice. He could tell that the horse was happy, and felt without knowing, that someone had been visiting, brushing, and bringing little treats.

Longbow returned in a few weeks and urged his horse back through the narrow slot. The soaking rain and sunshine had had time to do their jobs. There was no sign of yellow kernels but, as he had planned, along the rise of the wash was a scraggly green row of corn leading to one of many narrow slits, well-hidden in mesquite bushes. Holding himself just so, he pushed through the slit. With a flashlight, he followed yellow kernels, twisting, squeezing and scraping through narrow passages until he stepped into the beautiful valley.

Along the shore of the biggest pond he waited.

Fawna arrived beside the hidden niche, as she did every evening at this time of year. She untied and dropped her deerskin dress, then straight as sharpened arrowweed she swam the lake and back, her arms making quiet curves. Springing at last from the water she stood before him like a shapely manzanita bough, quivering in surprise. She was more beautiful and breathtaking than even his wildest dream.

"Fawna, since you've grown up, you're touchy as a sandcrack in my mare's hoof. Don't you love me anymore?" She cupped his chin and kissed him, then shrank back, for his breath was heavy with wine and his arms could not be discouraged. "I've tried to wait, Fawna, but it's useless as hacking ironwood with a blade of grass."

Their "marriage bed" was not as he had planned it: a shallow trench lined with fragrant cedar branches and soft furs to enfold them. He couldn't even smell of Fawna, who was always fragrant like flowers or rain. Instead, their bed was a flattened plant mass that smelled of dead fish. But he had to possess her, now–her and all of those mystic old ways that she stood for. Some strange blend of tribes must mingle within her beautiful hair, eyes and skin, that all melted into flowing shapes of the same warm earthy brown.

She didn't scream, she merely sighed, like the last treasured breath of a wounded animal. As he took her, a heavy sadness settled upon them. Without inviting him to follow her she walked away, dragging her clothes behind her like wings of a shattered butterfly, then putting them on as she walked. Her eyes in the moonlight were left behind to haunt him, like black, paired wingspots they would now flutter around him whenever his mind relaxed.

Bowie could not control his weeping.

A cloud had befallen her soft, lustrous eyes, and forever after he knew that he would dread some unknown, fearsome forecast.

Ashamed and disappointed with himself, he found his way through blackness, coaxed his horse from the hidden corral, and stayed away from the valley for many months.

One night as he walked at the edge of his family's summer camp, in the quiet distance he heard a faint death wail, or was it the night wind playing tricks in erosion caves that pocked the sheer canyon walls? Faintly, the eerie sounds continued for almost a week.

Then one afternoon, Fawna in the velvet skirt, peasant blouse and sandals, appeared at the edge of camp, loaded down with the most important of her earthly possessions. She walked slowly, sweeping out her footprints with a yucca broom as she approached the camp. Her beautiful black hair was singed. Knife wounds for her dead father striped her arms. And she was frightened: her stomach was swollen with child. She crumpled at Longbow's feet.

Longbow had just finished dressing for a celebration at the Trading Post. He was wearing new jeans, moccasins, a blue velvet shirt, and a belt of silver dollars that an army buddy created with a tassel of rawhide strings, beads and feathers hanging from every joining.

Disappointment in his mother's eyes was overwhelming. He ducked into the hogan and bundled up the only thing that he cherished now—the beautiful blanket that she had woven for him while he was gone as a child. He took Fawna's hand, headed for the bus depot and never looked back at his family's shock.

"Let's take the long way," Fawna said wistfully, knowing that he was taking her from everything dear and familiar. As they walked, Fawna told him of how she had placed hot stones on her stomach but waited in vain for the fetus to be expelled. She had tried the violent croton and searched for rye with ergot on its grains. But they had only made her weak and sick.

"It was meant to be, Longbow. I'm sorry that I'm to be your burden. I never asked for children or marriage. It was enough that you came back to me sometimes. That we loved the little child that lived in each other." Longbow hugged her and wept.

Before boarding the bus, she kneeled, took two handfuls of warm earth and held them to her cheeks.

For hours and hours in the strange bus, she was silent, yet seemed warmed by the embers in the now hole-punched metal box that once had held the squash blossom necklace. She carried the box in a rabbit skin sling to keep most of the warmth inside. Finally, after Fawna sniffed the air, they shifted to a taxi.

"Hurry, Longbow, hurry! Let's get out right here," she urged at last. She held the cooling box in its furry covering close to her heart. "The stars and wind have told me. We will find our new home near the sound of waves."

Wearily, they walked from apartments, hotels, motels and trailer parks. Fawna, with her burnt hair and slashed bare arms, her burden of baskets, pots and skins, a hand drill, a big knife and a medicine pouch at her waist, seemed a poor risk to all of the landlords.

"This must be the place, at last," sighed Fawna as she looked up at the tall cottonwood at the side of a dingy, rundown trailer park.

"There's a marsh tree!"

54. Fawna at Last Resort

Robbie noted the earthy assortment hanging in crude nets on Fawna's back. Her eyes were frightened but strong as the obsidian knife hanging at the waist of her long skirt. Robbie noted the bulge on her belly, and it seemed to be some secret sign. Robbie didn't hesitate. She handed Longbow the doorknob to the gray trailer and smiled at his name.

"To 'draw the longbow' among some whites, my friend, means to tell tall tales. If you don't mind, we'll just call you 'Bowie' while you're here," Robbie explained.

Despite her original forecast, when Fawna really looked around the dismal park, she knew that it was bad luck to stay on fertile ground which produced only weeds.

Before entering the trailer, Fawna looked sadly at the monotonous sky pierced only by one small range of hills beyond the park. Though unhappy with the whole trailer, she could tolerate it for the door seemed to open more onto the rising, instead of the setting sun! Besides, it was getting dark; stars and sounds had spoken. They stepped inside the gloomy trailer and Bowie slammed the door once, twice. The third time it caught, but the bookcase fell from the wall, the closet door popped open, and one of the bedroom windows shattered and fell to the ground.

From then on they always left the door ajar, said Bowie.

"It has no place for fire!" Fawna cried, dumping everything she was carrying onto the bare mattress and opening the tin box. "It does not matter." her voice was dead as the cold embers inside the box. Nothing seemed of real importance to her after that.

It was a strange and lonely life for Fawna and Longbow. Everything smelled stagnant and the park seemed a hotbed for hatching flies, flu and diarrhea. At night there was not the spicy burning-together of juniper and pinyon, only the half-burned smell of butane. Fawna missed the sounds of desert nights. For substitute there were only loud radios, renewed bickering, sputtering cars and cussing of the tenants.

Though she quickly found the nearby canyon and explored foothills beyond, nowhere were there pools for fishing, not enough water to even sit in and bathe, much less to swim in. She could find no cattail floss for disposable diapers. So Fawna gathered into a drawer cottonwood floss matted into drifts beside the fence, trailer wheels and stepping boxes. She made a tiny leather diaper holder for the tree cotton with tying strings on one side.

The tenants were suspicious of a dark woman who barely spoke their language, who packed water from some hole in the rocks when there was a bottomless lake inside the faucets. They were frankly bewildered by a female who did most of her labor before breakfast, who worked hard and ate sparingly to have a small child.

They watched in astonishment when Fawna cooked wild birds on a small fire in the Pigpen, collected grubs from trees and ate them with no qualms. She placed salad greens around an anthill to capture their vinegary footsteps for flavoring! She stopped the flow of blood from a child's cut with a rolled mat of tough spider webbing!

Fawna had strange pastimes too. Like running into a lightning storm to plant pinches of tobacco, and swirling in tiny whirlwinds. Evenings, she waited breathlessly for weedy moonflowers growing across the fence to "smack" open in cool night air, just so she could smell them before sleeping! She sang strange chants at night when Bowie hadn't come home.

In daytime there was no one for Fawna to relate to. Who was there to care that she could tell the time of year by stars. What good was the knowledge to replace a broken pot when there was no clay around; to make a basket so tightly woven that it could easily carry water when there were no willow trees for framework, or deergrass for weaving? And Fawna had no desire at all to ever be in the Den.

With less and less to do, Fawna became more and more what she used to be–a little child playing house in a cave. She nailed animal skins over windows, hung baskets and nets on walls and too often swept the trailer with her weird yucca broom. Daylight only came down from the open transom, which Fawna pretended to be the skylight of her father's cave. At night Fawna usually sat alone, swaying and softly singing beneath the little square of starlight, pretending she was home.

To Fawna, (said Bowie sadly), most of the tenants seemed like sick rodents inside of gloomy hovels. But soon Fawna found that she and Quila had much in common. Both collected rain water and both scooped up sand for dish washing. They both searched for wild tea leaves, and mushrooms after it rained. They both gathered lambsquarters, though Quila called them baconweeds and Fawna's word for them meant frostbite. Quila was much in awe of Fawna for she knew even more than Quila did about the mischief and magic of wild plants. Fawna's name for Lolli meant "flowers-sewn-on-skin." And, the only one that Fawna really admired in the park was the quiet, hard-working Pug.

Though the park was a place of no seasons, on chilly nights the walls of the gray trailer often "wept" with heat inside and cold without. Their blanket, the wool one his mother had woven, became so damp and smelly with wall and old horse-sweat, that Fawna finally left the bed for her sheepskins on the floor.

Bowie sighed to Luanna, "I never saw her smile anymore, except when she was dreaming on the floor—of times and places past."

Fall brought nothing familiar, except perhaps the cottonwood tree. There was no flowering of goldenrod or rabbitbrush, no rain smell on creosote, no need for gathering squaw wood, no familiar little food seeds and few familiar tea plants to pick for winter use. The only positive thing in Fawna's life was the infrequent nearness of Longbow.

For Longbow it was even harder. The only jobs open to him were part-time labor at half-time pay. Night and day, he spent much time in beer parlors. Early every morning, he gently smoothed the baby that was swelling like a gall on Fawna's thin little body. He removed his turquoise amulet and kept it tucked beneath her pillow for good luck. And he left his belt of silver dollars, buckskin knots and beads on the table. They made him look too Indian, too different. He merely threaded a small rope between the beltloops of his jeans. Then he began anew the endless, degrading search for work. But no one had even heard of his kind of skills. Nor was Longbow experienced in anything else they mentioned. Who would pay now for the skills of war? For tracking, code-talking, shooting, hiding, running, burying dead body parts, shutting out screams of dying friends? Who would pay for skills of surviving in the wilds?

"Nobody," Bowie sighed as he slowly opened, then wearily shut his eyes again.

Longbow asked for work at the second-hand store behind the trailer park. Flo sized him up with greedy eyes and stocked up on wine, cigarettes and chewing gum. At least the weeding and watering that Longbow did for Flo would pay his monthly rent. But it would barely fill one shelf of the tiny barren icebox. And Longbow didn't dare to spend his muster pay: he was saving that for the baby's arrival.

Fawna created a blanket dress that covered her growing stomach. And one day she did the weirdest thing of all: she spread her big, wide hem out over the biggest anthill in the Pigpen. And then she sat shivering in the midst of it. "Indians do that," Quila whispered to the women, "they know that ants will eat such things as lice and nits, and Fay Rose 'aphids'!"

In total desperation, Longbow began a drunken orgy that lasted over a week.

"Someone found me one evening." Bowie wept uncontrollably and squeezed Luanna's wrist until it hurt. "They handed me a lock of Fawna's beautiful black hair-tied with a buckskin knot. It smelled like cigarettes and stale beer, instead of yucca suds and fresh air. It had been passed around by drunks from one familiar haunt to another. I ran for blocks and blocks. It was too late when I got there."

Bowie had talked all night, the moon was almost down. He slept for a short while and when he awoke, Luanna still had not moved his head from her lap.

"The moon has caught you napping outside!" Luanna teased as she touched the muddy gray in his hair. He gazed into eyes that warmed him like sweet dying coals, as comforting as Fawna's eyes. From his old cache among the rocks, she cooked a small meal on the fire he made.

55. Quila's Decline

Quila had been holed up in her trailer for several days now, sobbing and shaking, napping and pacing. She smoked the last of the herbal cigarettes and drank too much wine throughout the long lonely hours. At last she was empty of tears, exhausted emotionally and over-hungry for the Den. Restocked with shaky courage, enthusiasm and a dry throat, Quila plied her way with painful nonchalance back to the silent Den. But the door was locked and there was no smell of coffee. Quila's face was already a dry cracked streambed, waiting for a drop of moisture to roll down over it.

The record had not played once since Quila's outburst and Doll's request. Its absence was even worse than its constant presence. It felt like the whole park was holding its breath.

Bowie tied his rope-of-a-belt even tighter now as he watched Quila dwindle and shrivel in her clothes as if they were shrouds. Her thin hair seemed ragged as a cobweb ensnaring tree cotton and snarls that she was oblivious to. She couldn't have eaten even if she did have any food. It was a struggle for her to reach the toilets or Robbie's doorstep. For awhile she measured distances by how long it took to hum a Gypsy song; but then, Bowie could have sworn that she was measuring footsteps by the numbers of her bone creaks, or wheezing little breaths. Gussy was often sitting on her doorstep sketching as Quila shuffled by with her arms whirling in slow circles, like there were invisible webs along the way instead of clotheslines, children listlessly playing and women sadly working.

Hoping to somehow feel cheerful, Quila wore her blue lapis lazuli day and night, never bothering to remove her dress for even sleeping.

Every morning she knocked at Robbie's door as though this daily drop of penance might in time wear away at Robbie's stony facade. She had to keep trying. She could not, without youth or hitching boards, according to Gypsy nature, simply move on.

"Robbie? Fergive me crudeness. Old age widens me wicked mouth, but it also bends me sorry knee. Gladly would I let ye stitch up me sickly orbs fer seein' and sayin' what ain't true. Aye, I'd lick the dust ye tread upon, if only ye'd have me back."

"For Christ's sake!" came a hoarse growl.

"Surely yer anger's outburned? Let's coffee together again, like it never happened."

"Quit sucking, leech. The blood is dried."

"But I need ye, Robbie!" Without the leather pouch Quila had no hold on Bowie anymore, and without Robbie's Den, no way of eating, at all.

Quila turned away at the long silence, slumped down on the box step and rocked like a mother with a dead child in her arms. "Ah, the good times that we've had," she moaned. "Let me in, wrathy Robbie, so I can soothe ye!

Robbie's door burst open, scraping Quila's back as she rested her head in her lap. "Leave me alone, you pathetic parasite." Robbie breathed, and Quila shuddered from the look in Robbie's drunken spiritless eyes.

"Why don't ye deny it, Robbie? By yer very silence 'they' outcry ye! I cannot see ye suffer so. I love ye, overmuch. Like I would me own son–I mean daughter!" Realizing what she had said, Quila hurried away, rubbing her back, mumbling and sobbing.

Bowie watched as Quila straggled away with arms outstretched for balance. No longer was she interested in stealing candles and matches from the local church, or crackers, salt, pepper or toothpicks from nearby cafes. Instead, Quila often dogged Robbie's footsteps at a pitiful safe distance, as though by her mere presence she was protecting Robbie from nameless danger. It was miraculous how she and Mange arrived at the pier, the store, or The Joint without assistance, when sometimes she could barely find her way across the driveway.

"Quit following me, you doddering old do-nothing!" Robbie turned one afternoon and Gussy was watching as Robbie quickly ripped Quila's dress off one shoulder.

"Sackcloth' doesn't become you!" Robbie was so drunk, she nearly fell over. "Why don't you strew a bit of beauty, or even blarney for the remembering of how good it feels before I have to string wires for you to find the toilet?"

Quila took to silently sitting on Robbie's porch step. "I know you're there," said Robbie one night. "Even though your forked tongue is silent." Robbie started talking to herself, so low that Quila on one side of the trailer and Bowie on the other could barely hear. "Why can't we both quit mourning for ourselves and live for somebody else?"

"Say out there, old scarab beetle!" Robbie shouted. "Why don't you quit collecting the dung of this dump before it sickens you to death? At least start to share some of your knowledge before it rots in your stagnant mind! Gypsy secrets should be shared, they shouldn't molder away in a walking corpse! Don't you want to remember the sight of even one happiness you've created before the long night?" There was a long sigh.

"Why don't you at least uncollar that pitiful 'crutch' of yours? Poor miserable dog! His bulging, cancerous eyes are ready to pop with pain! Look what love has got him. Holding on to love when it's way past time to let it go. Why is that so, so hard?" Was Robbie weeping?

"Sheath yer tongue, Robbie, it's already torn me heart clear out," Quila's hollow voice replied as she hobbled back to her wagon. She had pretended for too long, that Blonco was still regal and handsome. Robbie's name for him, "Mange," should have proved that he was only a bad advertisement. But, outside of her little birds, Mange was the only one in the whole world who loved Quila! Yet Robbie was right. What had it gotten Mange? He did seem to be clinging to his miserable life merely to make her happy.

Mange was lying on the wagon's porch, his tail thumping a slow, yet quickening beat as Quila climbed the steps. Birds fluttered from the eaves and settled hopefully beside her as she eased herself down beside the faithful old friend. She fondled Mange's ears, pressed around his eyes to increase the circulation and loosened his worn collar. He gratefully licked her hands, as she eased out a long, sobbing sigh.

"Tomorrow," she promised herself, she would begin to search for the right herbs.

Each day as Bowie watched, Quila became more pitiful. In search of customers, like a jumping cholla joint, she desperately attached herself and offered fortunes to the most casual passerby or salesman, for daily she needed something to feed the dog and a bite and a sup to keep herself from drying up and blowing away. There was precious little to share with Bowie. There were seldom crusts for little birds; crusts lightly spread with bacon grease were all that she could spare for even Mange. Bowie stoned sparrows or a snake, but Quila shuddered when he offered to share with her. But Bowie always saved a bit for Mange's dish.

Bowie was nearby when Quila and Mange walked the pier. "Give me yer hand," she'd plead of passersby. "I can tell how many loves ye'll have!" But she looked so seedy and forlorn with her scraggly hair, desperate eyes, torn old dress and sick panting dog, that they were only repulsed and hurried away. A few took pity and left a coin or two in her hand.

One morning after her usual attempt at Robbie's locked door, a soft, quivering young arm curved under Quila's armpit. "May I help you home, Quila?"

"Aye, lass. The road steepens with age," she sighed.

"May I fix your hair?" Gussy asked, noticing a dead fly caught in a tangle.

"Pshaw, who'd care to?" objected Quila, startled for anyone to offer touching the gruesome stuff that swirled about her head. Especially Gussy!

"And then I'll just straighten your bed, mend your dress, and fix us both some tea." She helped Quila up into the wagon. "You do have some tea, don't you?" Gussy was desperately hungry. Flo was out of town and Gussy's dependable lunches had stopped for awhile. She was tired of her usual tea mix and slim gleanings from the Pigpen. But the gratitude in Quila's eyes, the straightened back, the hints of a labored smile were more satisfying than food could possibly be. Gussy noticed a mirror on the table, propped against the wall. In front of it was an open box of chalks and charcoal that Quila hadn't used for days. So that's how she looks so mean and threatening. Gussy smiled at Quila's tired little unmade-up granny face.

Quila eased herself down on a stool and groaned with relief.

Gussy took a sidecomb out of Quila's hair and began to untangle. A bunch of the vile stuff came out in her hand! Hiding astonishment, she took the gray bundle and massed it into a "rat," which she tucked beneath the thinnest part of Quila's hair. Smoothing and arranging with one of her little pencils was all that was possible without further damage. As Gussy worked, she tried to ignore the low, frightening wheeze as Quila breathed. She felt the still-warm teapot, and poured two mugs half full. She took mental notes for future pictures while she straightened the tattered quilt on Quila's bed and gently touched the dusty tambourine and web-covered guitar that hung beside the sleeping niche.

At the table, Quila sat drinking tea in her underwear while Gussy took a threaded needle from a pocket of her blouse and began to mend Quila's dress. "You know, Quila, with an outdoor table, a sign and a new dress, you could entice a bevy of neighbors who'd like their palms read, to say nothing of curious sailors!" Quila merely sighed. Gussy sipped the strong, unsweetened strange-tasting tea without relish, merely to be able to go on.

"Wait," said Quila as Gussy started to leave. She kneeled in front of her chest, unlocked it and felt among the gems in the top tray. Choosing the square-cut emerald, she put it into Gussy's hand. "For love and success, Gussy dear. But you won't need luck for those two things. You'll see!"

As she walked back to her trailer, Gussy fastened the chain around her neck. Quila must be getting senile. Never before did she have even a kind word for Gussy!

That night in the Pigpen, Gussy got a brilliant idea! Except for paintbrushes, hair was something she had found little use for, before today when she had fixed Quila's hair. Why, hair was a brand new treasure! In empty toilet paper rolls she began to separately save and label the tenants' hair to add to her collages. She soon found that everybody's hair had a certain texture that could be used for a special kind of painting stroke. Pug always cut or snipped her family's hair on Saturday nights, as she sat them on a stool outside, where often, she also clipped the hair of Robbie's girls. Lolli was always snipping at Whiffet, and often trimmed her own coarse hair as well. And there were always wads of hair that had been pulled from brushes. Gussy laughed as she pictured her mother's certain disgust.

Next morning when the Chips' spit balls hit her on the cheek as she walked toward the washhouse, Quila veered but really didn't care much anymore, and they soon quit.

"You're-an-old-vulture," the Chips sing-songed that evening as Quila patted Mange and talked to birds on her porch.

"Look," Gussy nudged one Chip as she passed by and pointed to the sky. "My Daddy told me that its brightness makes the constellation Aquila so easy to find!" But the Chips ignored her, they weren't interested in any good aspects of Quila. They were off and running, led by the sound of Fay clattering around in her kitchen.

Without the daily marketplace of the Den, Quila often spent mornings in Lolli's shady yard. Seeing an opportunity to keep Robbie eclipsed, Lolli gave Quila matches, cigarettes and often a goody to go with her coffee. Slyly, Quila always saved some of the treats and put them into her sleeve for Bowie, Mange and her birds. But Lolli's sessions were short. A few of the tenants sat their boxes beneath the tree and a few lonely girls leaned against Lolli's trailer for a fast cup of coffee. But neither Quila nor the rest of the girls had the heart, the inspiration or the ability to create a verbal atmosphere without Robbie. It was hard for Quila to lean very long against Lolli's trailer, without sitting down, especially while she juggled a cup of tea or coffee. It was even harder to endure accusing looks of the women, who were silently blaming Quila for the long closure of the Den.

Quila and Bowie were becoming desperate for real food. Without Robbie's get-togethers there were no more supplies for their already skimpy meals and the milk bottle was always empty. For nights she and Bowie had had only withered potherbs boiled with a dab of bacon grease. There was no money for flour and the bread starter had gone sour. Bowie told her that he often roasted grasshoppers, a skinned rat, or even simmered a poisonous snake when his hunger got unbearable. Their usual breakfast was of black coffee and crumbly skillet cakes of cornmeal. Quila went back to brewing Gypsy herb tea in a can. She stirred the brew throughout the day with a stick whenever she remembered to, and Bowie spent hours searching for the right leaves.

Telling fortunes didn't work anymore. Everybody in the park seemed to be losing any pride they might have had upon which Quila could work. Sometimes, when there was a lull at Lolli's place, Quila would grab a girl's hand and recite one of the "no fail fortunes" Jofranka had taught her: "You will soon meet a person who will have great influence on your future!" Or, she'd try to give hope about a new job, or a boyfriend. But neither Quila nor any of the girls believed her anymore.

"I see shells," Quila lied to Fay one morning as she grabbed her empty teacup, "beckoning on a window!"

"Who cares," Fay sighed, "the game's not worth the price. It matters nothing who knows." Without Robbie's occasional snacks and happy atmosphere to anticipate, Fay was fading fast, observed Bowie. Fay's rape by Enoch and her fight with Doll, seemed to have taken something out of her that was essential to survival. She limped away like a skinny clothestree with a negligee hanging on it. About Fay there seemed nothing else to find out.

Or was there, Quila mused, watching Bowie's wary eyes. Fay drifted past the wagon, while Quila and Bowie sat on the porch steps sipping tea in lingering sunshine. Hmm, mused Quila, Robbie wasn't here to protect Fay any more, so this was the time to "use her!"

But the next day as the group sat on boxes having coffee in Lolli's yard, Quila surprised herself and made up a hand fortune for pathetic little Fay: a sugar daddy with a big car to whisk her away. Fay held a fist against the pain in her chest and pulled her hand away.

Fay could often feel now, when tide was due. Each day she walked closer to the sea, where she could feel steady breathings of waves lapping closer to her feet. She ignored the Chips, except when the sea was in storm. Bowie watched, when her beautiful hair was filled with wind and her eyes were the same as the sea. She would grab the Chips by their hands and run, limping down the street with them, until they reached the sand. She'd kick off her shoes and the three of them waded into and out of the cold, frothy, teasing tongues of water.

Back at the trailer park, Bowie watched in horror as Fay step-dragged, step-dragged to and from the shower late at night, her makeup unrepaired between patrons, looking messy and rumpled, often swinging her douche bag without its cover from her shoulder like a dead cat by its tail. The route seemed longer each weary night. Spiritless and saturated with almond flavoring, Fay drifted, seeming to grow more tired and color blind: servicemen were of every colored hair and skin now, and their uniforms were from every branch of the Service. Gussy was often watching and sketching.

From behind her little door curtain, Quila also watched and ached for Fay, yet she merely swallowed once again that growing lump of fear. She just couldn't give in to this mere sample of the pain that she dreaded was yet to overtake them all.

56. Sugar Daddy

"Bowie!" Quila whispered incredulously as she knelt down close to the gazebo. "He's really here, just like I told her! The sugar daddy I predicted for Fay! <u>Hurry</u>!"

Humping out from Mange's door, Bowie could smell onions and herbs, if nothing else, on Quila's hurriedly-wiped hands, awaiting the revelation of his eyes. Quickly he stationed himself in evening shadows and pulled out the chink rag outside of Fay's bedroom.

Fresh from the shower, Fay had been in her bedroom listlessly brushing her hair dry when the knock came.

"You!" she spat the word, for standing there in suit, gloves and wig, carrying a fancy cane, was Enoch! She gathered her robe tighter as he pushed in past her. "What the hell are you doing here!" she hissed.

Enoch pushed her toward the bed. "Sit and listen! I've come to take you away from this treadmill." With his cane he indicated the depression in the bed, then reached beneath it, brought out her notorious campaign ribbons and dropped the box and all in the wastebasket.

"What I'm trying to say is simple: I want to be a master and you <u>need</u> one! I know it will be painful to wean you from sailor boys, but I intend to do it fast. You've been faithful to just a memory, in your own way, of course, long enough. You've never wanted much, have you? Just love really, but now you'd settle for security." Fay's eyes widened.

"You'll need a trousseau," he announced, opening her closet and riffling clothes with his cane. "These colors hurt the eyes and shout your lack of taste."

He held her chin, looked into wary sea-green eyes, ran his fingers through damp hair and studied her weary, childlike face. "You need pale blues and greens to frame you, not distracting circus colors."

His cane thumbed through nightgowns and negligees. "No teasing. I'll expect satisfaction infrequently, but dutifully. This will be your first marriage, won't it?" He looked at her ringless fingers. Again he held her chin, "To understand all is to forgive all."

"I want you to walk down the aisle in a white lace cocktail dress with snowy accessories." He wrote on a calling card, "Give this to Miss Spence at Shards." Fay felt the highly embossed card. It did not say Enoch anywhere, only A. Cunningham, Plaza Funeral Parlor, Waterfront, California.

"Slacks, bowling shoes, a tennis skirt and bathing suit. We'll honeymoon in Florida. You need rest, sun, good food, fun and exercise."

With the finger of his cane he pawed through dresser drawers and gingerly edged crudely-sewn bosom stuffers into the wastebasket. "A lady needn't underscore any lack of so-called 'assets.' Mammary glands are only for babies." He didn't touch her clean silk panties, just edged them into the wastebasket with the tip of his cane. "Underlinens pure white, plain as sheets. You needn't blow tin whistles to keep me interested!"

He turned to the mirrored cabinet and with the hook of his cane scooped all of the bottles and jars into the wastebasket. "You need nothing, Fay, to enhance yourself."

In five minutes Enoch had told her what nobody else ever bothered to explain. Her eyes grew into green velvet, but then he unfolded her robe. Now here "it" always comes, she sighed with disappointment. But he was eyeing her nakedness like a doctor would!

The concavity of her chest was more frightening than he remembered. Too often he had seen tubercular bodies like this one cold and hard on a slab. He'd be taking a chance, but realized that this was the only girl that had ever interested him. The risk would be worth it.

Circling Fay's hair was her only adornment now, a pink ribbon to hold back her damp tousled hair. Scrubbed of makeup it was an innocent face with cheeks and lips that burned with frightening fire. He tied her robe, then drew her face toward his. "You will flourish," he tried to convince them both, "under my green-backed thumb!"

He took a plush box from his breast pocket. "You've not been properly claimed." He slipped a big diamond onto her ring finger, while Fay gaped at the plain band waiting in the box. "I will come for you and the children three weeks from today. Here is money for food and expenses. You never have to 'earn' anymore!"

He stepped out the door, then popped his head back inside. "What do you say?"

Speechless, Fay removed his wig and soundly kissed his bald head. Twirling, she pushed her small rump around to him. "Pinch me!" she teased.

Bowie ducked beneath the trailer as Fay pushed a curtain aside to watch Enoch pausing in the driveway. He took out a handkerchief, spit on it, then carefully erased every bit of chalky rose from the side of her trailer before heading toward his expensive car.

Fay fell on the couch and stared at the transom. Others were tall like Woody and had to stoop out the door. Enoch is bald and short, his eyes the color of chewed tobacco. There isn't a thing about him like Woody. But he is a bit like Papa, assuring her that he still loves her even when she takes pennies from the sugar bowl to buy ribbons for her hair. Her weary mother always ruined those beautiful moments with Papa. "Soon ripe, soon rotten!" declared her mother, gathering up her buckets and brooms and storming out the door.

Fay shivered at the depressing memories, then ran to get her own filthy mop, which she threw violently out the door. "I'll never mop this place, again!" she cried, alerting most of the tenants to the fact that something new was happening in the midst of their humdrum lives. "He likes me as I am! And Juju, the Chips, gray hair, flat chest, everything!" she shouted out to the mop. She twirled around the dark living room, whose unmade beds always smelled like old piddle and poo-poo. So what if Enoch wasn't a fathom tall? Everything else was going to improve!

Fay has finally lost her mind, the tenants thought. She had propped the bedroom door wide open and was throwing out the fishnet still entangled with cheap prizes from the pier. Upon it she threw out her clothes by great armfuls. Onto the heap she tossed the wastebasket full of makeup, black underwear, campaign ribbons and chocolate cherries. Last of all, she pried off the box of seashells and ceremoniously dropped it on top. She drug the heavy weight to the curb, left it by the trashcans, and wiped her hands dramatically.

57. Spade

After sharing with Quila the happenings at Fay's trailer, and a meager dinner of herbed onions, Bowie sat alone on Quila's steps taking a lengthy survey of the mostly darkened trailers. Even though the leather pouch was his now, waiting in his bosom pocket, even though he was no longer bound to peek and listen, there was nothing to take its place. He seemed even more aimless now, than he had ever been before. Finally he strolled to Gussy's trailer and peeked inside at the mass of artworks hanging, balanced, leaning and stacked there. Almost all of the pictures displayed tonight had Robbie's blue, blue eyes staring out at him, but there was nothing new. He took up a useless vigil beneath Robbie's trailer.

At least, Robbie had settled down. Bowie was tired of following her to the beach, The Joint, the pier or the railroad tracks where trains had to slow down at a certain hilly spot and he and Doll could safely swing up into a freight car. Robbie haunted these places, as though to feel or find Doll there. But things were totally quiet now above Bowie. Quila's wagon might make a better lookout.

Mange's breathing was labored tonight. Bowie held his paw like it were a human hand and smoothed it while looking out through the moonlit checkered shadows. In widening semi-circles he moved troubled eyes around the slumbering park. Something was very wrong. All afternoon the silence that Doll's song should be filling was a growing chasm of dread and depression. The weight of the absence was a giant boulder balanced above the park. Bowie felt like a blind tortoise, creeping toward some black crevasse.

But the only thing amiss was Spade prowling from Robbie's trailer to the mailbox, back and forth, again and again, as though frantically looking for Doll. She seemed intoxicated for she wove as she walked and shook her head as though it didn't belong to her.

Above him Quila sat at her table waiting for bedtime tea to cool. She rubbed her aching fingers. Aside from the proven truth of Fay's good fortune, the week had been filled with bad omens: seagulls flying too low, an owl in daylight on top of the washhouse roof, another flew high into the tree and hooted continually, calling some soul from a human body.

Quila poured strong unsweetened tea down her throat, turned the cup over on the table, then gathered leaf shapes into a figure. There was that griffin, or was it a cat, that kept appearing so often now in teacups? Either griffin or cat, it was a sign of imminent danger. Quila shivered, blew out the candle and crawled beneath the quilt.

Below the wagon, Bowie had nothing to do but think. Yet only one thought seemed of importance. In order to sleep longer and not smell odors of early breakfast-making, Bowie had slept on the other side of the back fence last night in Flo's yard. Still, he was awakened early by Flo's expensive-looking customer as she parked her car at the back of Flo's shop. When she left, she was eagerly carrying out armfuls of Gussy's collages! There was nothing left to do or to think, so, with eyes wide open, he snuggled up to Mange's warmth and waited for daylight.

Usually on Monday morning, Bowie saw the park at its busiest from his shadowy lookout: Pug sorting mountains of clothing, Mala complaining about everything as she emptied trash or rinsed her mop, Lolli washing Whiffet, and other women joking and smoking as they worked. Even flies and dust seemed to be lying low this Monday, waiting. Smolder today was unbearable. Gussy pulled her blouse over her nose and sat on doorsteps to sketch.

Doll was still gone and Robbie had been at the lowest ebb that Bowie ever remembered. Even if she were home, Doll would probably spend little time at the Den. By the time Syd arrived in the morning now, Doll's hair was brushed, her lips were bright and she wore a new dress! Tea would be set for the four of them in Lambeth's trailer. Afterwards, Doll and Juju would make the ice rounds with Syd.

Even though Robbie unlocked the door sometimes, put on the coffeepot and was soon surrounded with nervously laughing females, it was never for more than an hour. And Robbie would have spent that time speechless, looking into a candle, cracking her knuckles, smoking incessantly and adding new cellophane to the coil that was now as long as a whip. Bowie dozed beneath the wagon, alone now. Quila had coaxed Mange up her little steps to sample pot-scrapings before she did dishes, and now Mange was too tired to face the steepness of the steps and rejoin his sleeping buddy.

Spade was extremely jittery. She had forgotten her constant checking of the mailbox, and started to wander aimlessly around the trailers. She began to vomit and have diarrhea. When Gussy stepped into her trailer, Spade jumped down from the roof and cruelly dug her claws into Gussy's scalp. That afternoon Spade rushed up the steps to bite Quila as she sat fondling Mange. Mange tried to punish Spade yet even feeble effort tired him. But Spade was immediately sorry for the bite, shaking her head and wiping her tongue on her fur as if she had bitten an angry toad.

That night Bowie slept beneath Robbie's trailer instead of the Gypsy wagon, for Pug had hired him to watch Robbie, his main duty being to follow if Robbie left the park on foot. For the first time since leaving the Marines, Bowie had a job that he was good at, but wished had never been necessary. Pug gave him lunch and money for wine and cigarettes. Now it was Bowie who sneaked food out to share with Mange, Quila and her birds.

The night was hot and humid, every trailer was dark for a change, and there wasn't a sound in Robbie's trailer above him. Bowie could not stay awake.

Springtime, and Doll arrived the next morning and Bowie just couldn't understand her reasoning. No matter how often, or why she left, when she returned everything seemed to start from the beginning again! Her short blond hair was swept up at the sides and formed a delicate line in the back. Wisps tapered around her face in points, and she wore again the old jeans and white shirt. She seemed genuinely happy to see Robbie, to be in the Den again.

Juju had been waiting at the mailbox, but Spade was nowhere in sight. Doll looked worried as she took off Juju's nightgown and rediapered her with cloth from her suitcase.

"Just cattin' around, no doubt," drawled Robbie as she poured a round of coffee to girls sprawled over rustling pillows. The Den was crowded, word spread fast for everyone missed the old routine, the old crowd. Nobody mentioned the episode with Quila; everybody surmised that what Quila had said was true. It just wasn't any of their business. Bowie stayed out of Robbie's sight, and Quila, like Doll, acted as though nothing had ever happened.

Bowie felt happiness, even from the shed, and enjoyed the old feelings. Extra fans went on. Even from her lonely trailer, Gussy felt the difference and didn't take her morning nap. Instead, she watered and raked the driveway, hosed the washhouse, cleaned and raked the trash yard. When Robbie refilled the coffee pot, Doll followed and ran water to bathe Juju.

As she soaped Juju, "Are you sure you haven't seen Spade?" Doll asked as Robbie emptied coffee grounds into the barrel beside the sink.

Robbie mumbled something with a cigarette in her mouth. Doll tried to forget how Robbie rubbed Spade's fur the wrong way whenever she walked across her lap, hurrying to reach the welcome mat of Doll's body.

Lolli had washed and dried Whiffet and sat on a bench brushing her. "When did you last see Spade?" Doll asked. "Hmm, yesterday I think it was. Boy, she was acting strange!"

Robbie rinsed the pot as Doll rinsed Juju. "Haven't seen Spade, have you?" she inquired as Quila hurried home through the washhouse to check on Mange before fresh coffee was ready. Quila didn't bother to answer, and Doll tried not to remember how Quila trembled and crossed herself whenever Spade scurried in front of her path.

That morning Quila decided Mange must be tethered. Suddenly the lethargic dog was obsessed, trying to dig up Gussy's hollyhock! Now his stake was pulled up!

Bowie left his happy listening post beside Robbie's trailer to keep an uneasy lookout beneath Quila's wagon where he could check on the park as a whole. Curiously, he had watched as Mange pulled and chewed at an unaccustomed stake. Finally loose, Mange had feebly ambled over to Gussy's trailer and began digging around the new hollyhock Bowie had planted there.

Bowie watched Mange dig and rest, dig and rest, until he finally uncovered the furry familiar black thing, grasped its tail and pulled until its buried stake broke loose. Sadly he dragged the muddy, net-covered body to the center of the group of women in the washhouse.

Doll gasped at the sight of the stiff, morbid cat. Her eyes were riveted to the cellophane coil tied around its neck outside of the net! Robbie stood there speechless.

"The thing itself speaks," Doll whispered.

Leaving Juju dripping, Doll ran toward the ice truck lumbering out of the park.

"Doll, you don't understand!" Robbie shouted in a heart-stricken voice, fully aware that no reason could be valid. It was plain in everyone's eyes.

"You hateful, hideous heathen!" cried Fay as she limped away pulling the naked Juju.

Lolli walked by with a confident swagger and a trace of a smile on her face.

Pug moved to console Robbie, thought better of it, and hurried to her own trailer.

Slowly, Robbie poured water out of the coffee pot that she had just filled. Alerted by Robbie's shouting, girls streamed from the Den, then decided to leave the park entirely.

The sound of Robbie's keys struck Bowie's soul like deep bells, tolling an ominous chord as she clinked back to the empty Den with the coffeepot dribbling behind her. Bowie had never felt so lonely as he made his way to The Joint.

When Bowie arrived at the window slit that evening, Robbie was sitting before the bottle-strewn table with only the light of a candle. Robbie must have known he arrived, for Bowie heard fingers on seams of the wall, feeling for any small rush of cool air. A wad of paper was poked into the biggest slit and pushed farther in by Robbie's knife. Bowie tried to burn the wad away with his cigarette, but it took two of them to complete the opening. He watched helplessly through the smoky hole as Robbie's jaw muscles tensed, knuckles cracked, and empty eyes became more desperate. Each bottle–gin, whiskey, wine, vanilla, hair tonic, anything that might help to render insensibility–was drained, then lined up on the table. Why was Robbie acting so strangely? Doll would come back. They had had serious misunderstandings before. Why was Robbie taking it so hard this time? Doll always returned, and she would again. And there would always be another stray cat.

Robbie sat in flickering light with hands pressed against her ears, as if to shut out the passing of time without Doll. Occasionally she wrote something on one of the papers littering her table, then stuffed it into a pocket of her shirt. She picked up the base viol and strummed aimlessly. But she didn't play the record.

Though tight with apprehension, Bowie was emotionally exhausted from events of the past week. He finished the bottle that Pug had bought for him, then put his hand on the bulge that filled the pocket over his heart. Why couldn't he open that little pouch and absorb the lingering, beckoning mystery waiting there? But what if there was only emptiness inside? He couldn't handle such final disappointment. He tried to conjure up the dream catcher. At least he could envision the willow hoop now, and he watched as a spider spun her web within it. By the time the little weaver had worked her way to the center, enclosing the feathers, horsehair and beads, Bowie had fallen fast asleep.

58. Last Teardrop

Bowie's eyes snapped open. Strange ominous silence screamed above him! In splintering clatters the base slid from Robbie's hands. She had started to strum familiar chords, then remembered. Shaking his groggy head, Bowie struggled to a slit. Again, something blocked the view, but it took longer this time to burn off the paper. It was hard to see through smoke.

Scattering Pug's sack of fresh cinnamon buns, Robbie stumbled down the step and headed for the only light still on in the park. Bowie hurriedly followed.

There was frenzied jolting and loud banging at Gussy's door and before she could open it, Robbie's angry fist had smashed through jagged, unrepaired screen and glass that Bowie had already shattered. Robbie reached through and twisted the inside handle with bleeding fingers.

The startled Gussy stood before Robbie, her bareness hurriedly wrapped in a towel. Despite growing pregnancy, Gussy was thinner: eating was a minor necessity, finishing pictures had grown into first priority.

Damp clothing still bounced everywhere from strings criss-crossing the small interior and Robbie was ducking to avoid bulky artworks hanging from the ceiling. Bowie could only recognize the piece of rescued glass on the table and a torn paper heart that kept swaying. Though some were still falling, partial pictures were pinned to curtains, balanced along rods, arranged like cards at the backs of the table, stove and breakfast nook cushions. Robbie plopped her drunken body down on a bunch of sketches, not realizing that almost every piece of art had her own face upon it!

"Why didn't you just embalm the damn cat in rosewater and invite us all to the funeral?" Robbie snarled, wiping blood on the back of her jeans. "My ways aren't pretty, but how would YOU gussy-up a dying, miserable cat who was biting and scratching people, vomiting and having diarrhea all over the park?" Robbie's voice became tender, "I thought it would be easier on Doll to think that Spade was just a-wandering."

"But why dump her in a garbage can? Somebody really loved her! When I found her, I just buried her as Doll would have, near some kind of beauty, my hollyhock–not in the garbage!" Carefully, Gussy spread crumpled newspapers over the broken glass, then sat across from Robbie. "Why strangle the poor thing?"

"Faster, less painful than poison. Just threw a net and pulled a noose!" Robbie snapped her fingers. "Over like that! Spade was too tough for any other way. She would've fought to the last wretched hiss.

"Spade was like tenants, and all the people that stick around this neighborhood. Not made of velvet, like you, Gussy, but comfortable as worn slippers, at least for Doll. Even standing in mud, common folks were still likeable in their own beautiful uniqueness. I loved winding them up a little, oiling them, forcing them to think, rewarding them just for staying alive. For being themselves, in spite of life."

Robbie leaned back and smiled. "I enjoyed them that way. No matter how depraved, each had a certain code, her own unique look, some unrecognized talent." Why is Robbie speaking in the past tense, wondered Gussie.

Robbie lit a cigarette, took a long drag then slowly eased it out. "I enjoyed you too, Gussy, though you were using every one of us, in one harmless way or another." As she smoked and gestured, blood continually dripped from Robbie's hand onto the table.

"Others found no poetry here. Unknowingly, you brought your own along with you. The rest cursed darkness, while you not only lit," she pointed with her cigarette to Gussy's candle-making efforts strewn over the table, "you created your own literal and figurative 'candles.' That was the reason I didn't fight for you to have the tree spot. You were dependent upon this space. You had so little, Gussy, yet you made it seem like so much! You lived in spaces that nobody else even knew existed."

Robbie fingered a paper curtain, sniffed potpourri, touched leaves growing from a turnip stub, then held up a sketch that Gussy had started to collage. "This trailer, cluttered as it is, is a masterpiece of 'make-do.' It's been a pleasure watching you discover pearls in this swill. Don't be offended. Swill is beautiful to someone–a pig, a hollyhock, a posy like you. For a moment, I was beautiful to Doll's lovely eyes, and were I <u>any</u> different, I never could have enjoyed Doll in any way."

Robbie sighed heavily, "But beauty is only to be enjoyed for awhile. Ugliness is what we grow from." Robbie took another puff and aimed the smoke away from Gussy's face.

"There's only one thing I can't forgive you for. Trying to change Doll was touching perfume to a rose, adding streamers to a sunset. She was already so special, not giving a damn if anyone ever discovered beauty hiding in those ragged jeans and baggy shirts."

With her blood-dribbling hand, Robbie reached for the wine bottle at the back of the table and uncorked it. "Here's to Gussy's of this world, who whitewash crumbling 'fences' instead of helping lift people over them!" She drank deeply and stared into space.

"Enoch was a saver, trying to get rich. You were a user of things that others were blind to, trying to become independent, trying to find who you really were, trying to test yourself and things that you only hoped were really true.

"It wasn't by accident that you came here. Quila warned us. It was destiny, she said."

A long pause, "Gussy, did you know there are only three despairs that twist and complicate people? Loneliness, hunger of one kind or another, and nature's mistakes. What most of us don't realize is that most mistakes are things that make us real, prized for our own unique ugliness, like gnarly driftwood."

Gussy was shivering. Robbie had never, never been so wordy!

"Take yourself, Gussy, potbound in a milk-and-water parsonage. You would never have become real if you didn't make a mistake and have to live here! Here you were untethered, could test yourself in your own sweet time. Here you found music in old bottles, and insect legs, here you 'ironed' and created 'pillows' with crumpled newspapers. Here you found bits of food that others didn't recognize, tea waiting in orange peels and perfume in leaves. Here you found art lurking everywhere you looked.

"Now you know, firsthand, what it's like to be deprived of food, money, the opposite sex, your pride. Now you know that orthodox friends are not vitally necessary. Who else in all of this world has crickets, an unwanted doll and a plant for best friends?" Robbie shook her head and laughed hysterically.

"You came here with nothing but imagination. Now you know that that is all you'll ever need! The rest is merely frosting.

"But what was the necessity for your 'sin'? It puzzles me. You look in perfect health. It wasn't loneliness or hunger. Was he in the wrong class?

Was it pity? Or wouldn't he have you?" Gussy fidgeted in her damp towel, but Robbie wasn't waiting for answers.

"I'm surprised that you even permitted an affair. You couldn't tolerate ugliness before you came here. Things are different now. You can almost look 'an ugly' in the eye and have it move aside." Robbie took a long swig, while blood trickled down her shirt now.

"It does move aside, by God, or you gussy it up so you can't see the realness! You still can't appreciate some things as they right now exist! Everything has to be charming, but unreal as hell." Robbie ignored the pretty shell of an ashtray and snuffed her cigarette in the dregs of a coffee cup. She took out a new pack of cigarettes and opened it, not carefully as she always did, but twisting the wrapper and throwing it on the table. With cold chills Gussy realized that Robbie was so drunk, she didn't realize that lifeblood was steadily draining away. Still, Gussy didn't interrupt: this was the first time that anybody had analyzed her. She had never before looked closely at herself.

Robbie continued rambling. "Can't you see the folly of gilding or draining bogs of life? Just as they are, bogs create rare plants. An orchid of a Doll, a posy in the sordid pigpen of life. I guess you just couldn't help it, gilding what you couldn't erase! But you're learning, Gussy. Your artwork proves it. " Robbie swayed, gesturing at all the pictures.

"And what would you want me to do," Gussy almost shouted, as Robbie flipped the twisted cellophane onto her clean floor, "rot, like the rest of you? Wallow in endless hours alone with no radio, no money and especially, no friends? You've helped see to that! Just what would you suggest, great Solomon?" Gussy hissed.

"Oh, Robbie, let's quit this!" A fine sweat covered Robbie's face, and the curl was edging away from confinement. Gussy got bold now and took a risky chance: "Robbie, why don't you quit wasting time with Doll and find yourself a man before it's too late?"

Robbie stood up very slowly, trying to control herself. "You could never understand!" Robbie was sobbing as her eyes fell on manicure scissors beside the odd assortment of candlewicks. "You could never understand, but maybe you could be forced to feel a measure of my pain!" She ripped the towel from Gussy's nakedness. While Gussy struggled to rewrap, Robbie grabbed the scissors, and quickly Gussy's hair, parted and tied like corn tassels, lay scattered on the floor. "Now, how feminine do you feel?" breathed Robbie.

"How dare you look at me like an ugly man would?" Gussy snarled.

Robbie slapped her hard. Blood spattered Gussy's face and sketches around the room.

Yet Robbie was strangely calm. "Don't resist the ugly, Gussy. Unspeakable beauty and opportunity can be hidden there, condensed in a single drop. Only when you've fought for that last drop, Gussy, like tackling a last mound of 'swill,' can you possibly find your own 'pearl'. That last pearly teardrop–the essence of all you've been looking for!"

Robbie had come from a state of frenzy, but now her eyes had a frightening glow in the depths of coldness, as though at last she had found some meaning, some purpose to her miserable life. The usual sag had straightened. There was something pitifully heroic about her. As though in a trance, she smiled, opened the door to leave, yet paused.

"I said I'd know my time, Pug," Robbie murmured to the night. Then she was gone.

"Wait, Robbie, wait!" screamed Gussy as she grabbed damp jeans and shirt off the line above her and struggled to tug them on. But she could hear that Robbie was already starting her car.

59. Stolen Doorstep

"Now?" asked one Chip of the other, after Robbie stepped off Gussy's doorstep.

Underneath Gussy's trailer they had crawled, passing the time until Fay was finished with her late visitor. Meanwhile, they waited until Gussy might go to bed.

The perfect time for stealing her step seemed finally to have arrived. It was prettier and more irresistible every time they looked at it. Fantasy flowers, little pigs and hearts were all over it now. But Robbie had been up there inside and the boys were impatient.

"Now!" whispered the other Chip as Robbie hurried toward her car. They scrambled from under the trailer, grabbed the step and scurried to hide it under Fay's trailer.

Just as Robbie's sputtering car was backing into the driveway, Gussy dashed from her doorway with shirt unbuttoned, pulling up damp jeans and screaming, "Wait, Robbie, wait!" Without the step where she expected it, she fell into blackness, biting her tongue as her head struck the ground.

Frantically, Quila rushed from her listening place and shook the bleeding, unconscious Gussy. Oh God, Quila thought, this was not the right time, but any other might be too late. "Gussy! Gussy! There's a letter. Here!" Quila tucked an envelope into the pocket of Gussy's shirt. "Gussy!" she screamed and shook her again. "Tad's coming to claim you! He's grown, he's changed. He's beautiful now, like you are!" She threw herself on the dirt, and cradled Gussy's head. "Forgive me, child. Forgive me Lord. Forgive us all! She outbloomed us. Just a tiny flower and we let her stick too big in our craws!"

Gussy came to slowly and briefly, unable to focus. With all its lights suddenly on the trailer park was an abstract painting, peopled with bodiless voices. "Someone, please find Robbie, before it's too—" A violent pain seized her and she sank back into blackness.

Pug hurried over, leaned down and anxiously felt of Gussy's stomach. "I've called the ambulance."

"No, too long," sobbed Bowie, stepping into the scene. He smoothed jagged hair like muddy petals on a bloody dandelion. He touched Gussy's skin, no longer petal-pink and plump like it used to be, but toughened by too much sun and not enough to eat. He buttoned the top of her wet shirt, wincing at hollow cheeks and thin wrists, while tears raced down his cheeks. Why hadn't he told her of potherbs that grew in vacant lots, shared with her a skinned rabbit or knowledge of wild tea leaves to be gathered any time of year?

He had been too focused on the fact that she was living in his little gray trailer.

He picked her up gently for where her shirt bulged pain was giving a roll of effort. He hurried from the park with Gussy dangling in his arms.

Quila leaned against Gussy's trailer and its little walls shook with her weeping. She should have told Gussy of all those beautiful signs she had always seen in her teacups, of the star of love at the top. She should have told her of the many dots of wealth, of the spades of steady work that led to fame and honors. At least, it would have given her hope. Now it was too late.

Bowie was already sprinting up the steps of the small hospital near the Plaza when he heard the faraway howl of the ambulance.

60. Cellophane Clock

Pug sat up in bed. She had known that Doll would return, but not that very night, when Gussy was in the hospital and everyone's shocked body was finally back in bed. And Doll was screaming, "Help, everybody! Robbie's trailer's on fire!"

Doll tugged on the locked burning door until it gave way, then rushed into the bedroom which was just beginning to burn. But Robbie wasn't there!

Pug ran barefooted down her steps, heading for the tool room opposite Robbie's trailer to get some hoses. But the door was locked! Of course, Robbie had the keys, probably drunk all night, passed out somewhere. She tugged frantically at the door, then looked closely at it. The door was not padlocked, as usual at night. It was fastened somehow from inside.

Weakly Pug turned her back, leaned against the door and braced herself against it. Robbie's trailer blazed away in spite of neighbors hosing it from across the fence.

Pug rubbed at her heart with both hands, picturing the inside of the Den. All of Robbie's full cubbyholes, the carved table, the big bass, the gurglet, Doll's scratchy record, Pug's old comfortable chair, Gussy's impossible pillows–all were now only flames and smoke. All of the bad times were gone, but all of the good times, too. Everything that was part of the Den would now exist only in Gussy's pictures and everyone's memories.

As far as Pug was concerned, this was not really happening. A train whistled in the distance. Did it only seem to slow down at Robbie and Doll's usual boarding place? She listened for a faint murmur of Robbie's beloved ocean, closed her eyes and took a deep sobbing breathful of the balmy night. The tree rustled and she pictured some high spot upon its trunk where Robbie once climbed to carve two initials. Unconsciously, her bare toes caressed the precious blanket of red dirt beneath her feet. Long-controlled tears, bittersweet, liquefied pieces of shattered heart quivered as they hung from her eyes, then fell from her cheeks.

Thank heavens dinner was long over, the children played with, storied and sound asleep. Nothing would ever be the same, again, except for the precious black curl which hung among blond ones tacked on the wall above her pillow.

Black smoke belched as the tarpaper shed exploded into flames and people rushed toward the tool room for more hoses. Pug braced her trembling heart to open the door on what she always knew she would have to face alone. She pulled and pulled until the door gave way and she rushed inside. Cold, bare feet struck her across the face and Pug collapsed.

Bowie rushed up and stood frozen. There hung the strange body he had seen in Fay's bedroom that stormy night. Now it dangled, naked, twisting in violent firelight reflected from the open door. Pug came to and shuddered convulsively, while the body still reeled, swaying from Pug's impact, creating an eerie swishing as it grated back and forth from the rafters.

Fay in her negligee, with Juju and Chips close behind, hurried up and pushed Bowie aside. "Don't just stand there, dummy, grab the hose!" Then she saw the body too, hanging with its back toward her, and Fay gasped. Tattooed dolls were swinging around in slow motion with the skin of the body itself. And the dolls had familiar uniqueness: they were all alike, yet their hair was of every length and color.

"Dear God," she crossed herself and steadied her body against the wall. A soft, beautiful, yet manly body swung around to face Fay now, triumphantly freed, like a prisoner from irons, without the hampering clothing that was dropped on the floor below. Fay put her arms around her ears and screamed. It was Robbie's body! But from its thighs a normal male organ hung like a tag, affixed with God's afterthought: "Oh, I forgot, this is a man!"

Tenderly, Fay drew Juju toward her for the first time in her life. But the shaking child pulled back from her and ran away.

Doll rushed up screaming when she saw Robbie's face twisting above shocked tenants. "Robbie! You knew I'd come back, I always do!" she screamed hysterically. "If you knew it, then why?" her blistered hands implored. Doll shoved Bowie and Fay aside. "Oh, God, you did know it. That's why! You released me." The body swung full around again. "You're not a woman, Robbie!" She grabbed Robbie's feet and rubbed them into hot tears. "Oh God, Robbie, that's why I loved you so much! That's why I couldn't stay away! Why didn't you share with me? I loved you so much!"

Juju pushed up in front of the tenants' legs. Her nightgown was gathered in front of her and she opened it above the clothes at Robbie's feet. Dozens of cellophane wrappers that Juju had been saving in the pocket over Bowie's bed, fell out. Juju dropped in a tiny heap, massing her black rag, the cellophanes and Robbie's clothing beneath her shaking body.

Fay grabbed her own throat with both hands to somewhat control her sobbing, "Juju was Robbie's–all along! And nobody knew it, but God!" And I tried to kill her, she whispered, as gently she held her hand to the ugly birthmark on Juju's cheek.

Still dazed, Pug reached out from where she had collapsed, pulled the child off Robbie's clothes and into her lap. She pushed aside black ringlets and looked into the same familiar, sad, blue, blue defensive eyes of Robbie.

Smiling incredulously through tears Doll took the child from Pug, kissed her eyes, her curls, her tear-stained cheek, her quivering mouth. She too looked into familiar, sad, blue, blue defensive eyes of Robbie. Doll hugged the child fiercely, then handed her back to Fay.

With the overturned chair that Robbie had kicked aside, Pug pushed her way to the front. She fumbled in Robbie's pockets for the strange knife, then held it briefly to one wet cheek, the last reminder of lost hopes to mend people's bodies. This same knife had created kites, carved initials, slashed wrists, pulled out foxtails, speared cheese, cut flowers for lonely old ladies, and carved away time–without Doll–on a wooden table.

Standing in the doorway, Quila began to shake. Only once had she read for Pug. The tea leaves had been so obvious that Quila never offered again. "There's a deep and hidden part o' yer life, Pug," Quila whispered. "Someday, ye'll face it alone, yet in sight o' all yer friends." Quickly, Quila had stirred the leafy picture into a blur. Now, here again was that same picture, life-sized, come true. Pug was cutting down an extension of her own body with Robbie's knife while all around her were stricken, speechless watchers, waiting to catch this dead flower of Pug's soul.

Gus steadied her on the chair, while Pug sawed the cellophane cord. Hands reached out to gently lower Robbie, while Doll and Fay sobbed uncontrollably. Someone spread a sheet and tenderly Robbie was laid upon it. Pug began to reclothe his body, to pull up the shorts and the jeans, to put on the blood-spattered shirt and button it over the bizarre chest.

"Each doll was a passion unfulfilled," Pug looked up at Doll's stricken face. She decided to leave the shirt unbuttoned, to let the dolls breathe unhidden at last, to let sparse chest hair curl free in open air. She resolved to not let anyone shave the slight beard that bristled lightly over the morbid chin. She neatly rolled the shirt sleeves exposing tattooed dolls, old scars and more of the light curly hair on Robbie's arms.

"My son, my little Roberto," sighed Pug for the first time aloud in many years. "My warm little stone is gone," she wept. "The drops have finally hollowed you."

"No." Lolli backed away from the scene. No strange and wonderful being such as Robbie could spring from such commonness. But it was true! They were the same: gentle voice, big heart, silent love. Lolli realized that she too had always, unknowingly, loved Robbie while at the same time being openly jealous. Lolli put her arms around Robbie's mother, feeling strange, forgotten comfort in warm, wonderful bigness.

Pug still sobbed as she unhooked Robbie's keys. "Here, you've waited a long time for these, Lolli." Though Lolli took the keys, Pug knew that having them now was meaningless.

Quila reached over and took Bowie's hands. "You felt it, didn't you? When I asked you for 'something small about Robbie,' you knew there was nothing small. You'd have eaten your own right hand before trading Robbie in! You even thought of him as 'her', so as to never slip or betray him." Bowie hung his head to hide both truth and his trembling mouth.

Quila dropped to Robbie's side now, reaching for his still-warm bloody hand. Her finger traced again the abrupt lifeline, whose continuation she had once looked for so frantically. She nestled Robbie's head in her lap. "It's all my fault." She rocked back and forth as she had rocked with Gussy, as she had rocked outside of Robbie's door. Why, oh why had she kicked Robbie faster toward this end? She'd seen but never believed recurring vases at bottoms of Robbie's cups, always surrounded by clouds: a sacrifice was coming, it insisted, for the benefit of someone very dear to the drinker.

Bewildered, Quila watched another of her predictions as tearfully, Fay began to wrap Robbie "within the winding sheet." Fay put her lips to Robbie's ear, "Kindness is never lost, –not with love, nor even with lust." Sticking from Robbie's pocket was a slip of paper addressed to her! There were more papers, but Fay just took hers and limped away to her trailer, gently pulling Juju behind her while the Chips followed in dazed silence.

Doll crumbled down beside Robbie, rested her head on his bare chest and closed her eyes. Watching her, Lolli felt like a ton of iron had settled onto her body. Why, I've always lumped those two together– Robbie and Doll–as lewd and ugly, when they were both as innocent as rain for each other! Theirs was no back street relationship as we all believed. Theirs was probably one of the purest loves that we will ever know.

The coroner and police arrived. A white-haired reporter began to interview neighbors standing speechless on the sidelines. Doll, with her head still on Robbie's chest, ran her hand inside of Robbie's shirt, caressing him and the barely-warm replicas of herself, bodies that would surround Robbie in his grave. Doll, herself, enclosing him forever in her arms.

Someone began to lift Doll up, but she pulled away. She kissed Robbie full on the mouth, while pulling slowly at the springy curl for the very last time. Her tears fell on Robbie's bare chest. To those who watched—was Robbie's face at last ecstatic? Like a wild stallion he had once caught, thought Bowie. But once unbridled, wild with freedom, it had galloped away and raced off the nearest cliff.

61. Fay's Letter

Fay locked her door as though to keep away any further agony. She tucked the wide-eyed Chips back into their make-do couch bed, picked up Juju and put her between Fay's sheets. Crawling in beside her, Fay cradled the small shaking body into the curve of her arm.

Oh God, it had been a masked Robbie in her bed that stormy night when Juju was conceived. "Please don't talk," Robbie had whispered as he softly put his fingers over her mouth. Fay slid down deeper between the sheets, remembering from an entirely new dimension: she knew now and deeply appreciated just who her lover was!

Tenderly he had kissed and caressed her eyes, her ears, her mouth, her hairline–like nobody else had ever bothered to do. Unlike the rest, he was infinitely gentle. Fay had felt her body parts becoming beautiful under his sensitive hands, and in her heart she was a virgin again. He combed her hair with caring fingers, smelling and kissing its clean lengths.

Drops kept falling from the rain hat he still wore, pulled low on the mask that hid his face. But drops that touched her lips seemed salty, and Fay was filled with wondering: was that rain, sea spray or constant tears? He cupped her face to his mask and kissed her like one might kiss a child, while the storm outside raged on.

Again and again with joy, and yet with shame, it seemed, he repeated the act that always before left Fay untouched, as unawakened as stone above a match. This time, in spite of her struggles, again and again, she could not keep from ecstasy. And then he wept for a while, as though releasing first tears of his manhood. Spent by such tenderly furious a passion, he had slept a moment.

Fay was not intelligent, but she had intuitions that sometimes made up for that loss. When she was only a little girl, she knew when Papa was leaving for the very last time. She knew when the siren song of the sea had finally become irresistible to Woody. Now, she had known with unerring judgment that this was the first time that this man resting so lightly, so considerately, upon her had ever made love to a woman. What puzzled her was the finality in it. It was also to be the last time! He had carefully planned, and patiently waited for this special kind of orgy, to nourish him for a lifetime. And Fay, despite her reasoning, had felt strangely honored. Though now she knew, it was really Doll that Robbie had been making love to.

"Please forgive me for using you, my little Fay Rose. Would it help at all to know that the beautiful memory has made my life bearable?" —was all that Robbie's note had said.

God, forgive me, Fay wept. All of the misdirected hatred! Woody was the one to be hated, not the gentle, kind, considerate one who fathered Juju. It wasn't the deed, Robbie, that I detested, nor the doer, but the result–the result–Oh, God.

Fay's sobbing had awakened Juju. Fay drew the child closer and held the strange little cheek in her own hot palm. But Juju pulled away from her. Like the daily neglect of forgotten toothpicks in her earring holes, Fay's entrance to the child's heart had slowly and finally closed.

62. Madonna

Gently, Guy had helped Pug back to her own home, past the unheeded, smoky wreckage of Robbie's trailer. Vaguely, eyes staring, Pug felt Guy putting her between the sheets. She dozed. Like pus, finally released from an excruciating wound, memories surged back now with all of their sweet and bitter impact.

Pug was a bride of seventeen.

To Andre' Madonna was a slim, beautiful, sedate bride–she was not quite herself yet. She stifled her commonplace words, appetite, desires. She read stuffy books that Andre' suggested and tried to modify her speech. She tried to dress sedately, instead of seductively. Suddenly, Andre' vowed that he could never grow in Arkansas, and insisted that Madonna leave all that she loved behind.

In California, Andre' ordered his home meals scant, balanced, and, to her way of taste, bland. Though Madonna would rather be dancing or sleeping, their evenings were spent in reading or discussion. Occasionally, they attended concerts or operas where Madonna fell asleep. "You'll never be more than a servant!" Andre' once whispered, as he took her by the arm and led her out of the concert hall. "Your elbows are rough as corncobs," he scolded.

After Roberto's birth (too soon for social scrutiny), Madonna retired more from the new life. As Andre' grew more suave and handsome, Madonna seemed only to coarsen, to add even more to her maternity weight, to become harder and harder to fit. Finally, she had only the servility of her charmless mother and the good humor of her Irish father to call upon. "You're as useful as a cogwheel! And just as uninteresting, too!" Andre' complained. "Your clothes are never silky, soft and feminine anymore. They're practical as gunny sacks!"

Andre' brought new people home for long discussions over wine and cheese, but Madonna was too absorbed in her child to do anything but yawn outrageously and go about emptying ashtrays. Andre' began taking his friends elsewhere.

Roberto was the most beautiful baby in the world: he was too beautiful. He had his father's classic features and his mother's placid good humor. His blue, blue eyes were sweet and trusting, but already had a sadness deep inside. His curls hung down on his forehead and she kissed them constantly. Her milk was rich and abundant, and one evening Andre' came home unexpectedly while Madonna was nursing a black neighbor's sickly baby. Quickly she put the child down and took up Roberto.

"Have you no pride, Madonna? You'd wet nurse any thirsty bastard! Maybe that's what ails Roberto!" He pulled Roberto off her breast, looked at his heavenly eyes, long ringlets, beautiful mouth and extravagant lashes. "You've debased everything! Our comradeship, our home, my friends! Even my child! I wanted a real son! Not this, this." He shoved Roberto back into her arms, snatched up his coat and left.

At first Madonna didn't accept his desertion, even after she received proper papers and the checks began to come. But slowly the years folded into each other.

Pug stirred happily in her sleep. She met Guy at a downtown dance and soon he had moved in, as naturally as day follows night. Whereas to Andre' she was dowdy, dull and countrified, to Guy she was everything he needed, and she had ample to give of mothering, pampering, childbearing, cooking and cleaning. He never pushed her and instead of seeming lax, her housekeeping, which revolved around Guy, was merely comfortable. Her meals were wholesome, abundant, unvaried, untrimmed, and they both grew in proportion.

Years filled up with children and resigned contentment. Madonna tried to seem as happy with her own lot as Guy was with his. In a sad way, Roberto was their only thorn.

By fifteen, with Guy's help, Roberto had mastered life's manly skills. He was as versatile outdoors as he was inside. He had read everything that a librarian could mention, yet he could do anything menial and make of it a masterpiece. He repaired the toaster, revived darkened lamps, made fences, pruned, created toys for children and read to them for hours. He talked to his tools, wood and metal as he would to best friends. Especially did he enjoy mending and tending animals, birds and people.

Her only reminders of Andre' were when Roberto teased, "Use perfume once in awhile, Ma." Or, "Put paprika on the potatoes!"

"When I grow up, Ma, I'm going to buy you a frilly apron and flood your house with flowers!" The tiny frilly apron lay unused in Pug's bottom drawer, scattered over it were petals from every bouquet that he had ever brought to her.

Roberto filled home with "longhair" music, as Guy laughingly called it, with instruments he taught himself to play and with well-read people. He graduated early from high school and by seventeen checks from Andre' were enough to put him through college.

"A doctor, that's what I'll be, Ma!" And for luck he bought an unbending knife that he called a scalpel. Roberto loved after-hour conversations with professors. On weekends home he told Madonna of the house that he'd build, of the life that he'd create for his beloved, whenever he found her, (though, most women were just too dense!) He'd make it up to her for long hours of a doctor's life, interrupted mealtimes. He had great plans.

But college was manned with virility and to coeds Roberto was "either a muscular woman, or an effeminate man!" His grades were unbelievable, but socially, he had no place.

After meticulous care, he looked like a dandy; hammy seemed his naturally beautiful gestures. Men tittered and women whispered. No matter what medicinal or mechanical means he employed, Roberto's beard never passed beyond the downy stage. Worse, his beautiful mouth missed by one degree of being masculine and his eyelashes brushed the bottoms of his brows—when he didn't trim them. Conversations he overheard were agonizing.

Shortly before term's end, Roberto stumbled through Madonna's back door. Looking haggard and unkempt, he staggered into his bed. Next morning he tore down the placards tacked on his walls and ceiling, quotes from great thinkers. He made a fire in the backyard and threw into it for hours all of his books, photographs, awards, records—everything but furnishings and linen. "My questions have no answers, Ma."

That summer he chewed tobacco. He could spit out a lighted match! He spent hours slicking curly hair, talking brusquely in front of a mirror; smoking, and drinking black coffee, hoping to achieve sallow skin, lusterless teeth and rugged nonchalance. Regardless, in off guard moments he was still sensitive, wholesome, magnetic.

That fall he returned to college. Refueled with determination, "I'm going to be a writer instead of a doctor, Ma!" he said. "I've got to be somebody, don't I?"

It didn't take long. He stumbled home one night, "Just your old pigeon, Ma, homing in again. Tired of being gazed at and guessed at. The men come near a faint when I enter a restroom. I put a damper on everyone's jokes, a crimp in everyone's style. It's tiresome correcting the 'she'!" He drained the bottle in his hand and threw it far into darkness.

He took the sobbing Madonna in his arms, "It's not your fault, Ma. It must be hard on you as well, not to have a son that you can brag about.

"Any use in shaking my pagoda tree? I could drink up a river all by myself!" Madonna gave him what money she had that night and the next and the next without end, it seemed. At first, he returned just long enough to reel in and say, "Pagoda tree?" with his hand out like a baby pleading, "Bottle?" But as the days passed by he became so drunk and sick that he could only stumble in, hold his hand out and murmur, "Pug–?"

"You'll kill yourself this way," Madonna pleaded, as he put his arms around her to catch himself. "I don't plan on a long life, my dear pug-o-da tree. I don't any longer want to save people's miserable lives, nor preserve them forever on paper. I only want to spend my own simple life, such as it is. I want to experience the deeps, wear old clothes, enjoy just the moment, talk to people, inspire them, and fight for them a little, maybe. People, all kinds are what existence is about. Like my old friend, Thoreau, I have found that I too, am as unfit for any practical purpose as spider webs for the timber of a ship. It is not death, but dying–totally unfulfilled–that scares me, Ma!" he whispered.

So he began calling Madonna, "Pug"–as if being mother to such a freak would mortify her too much. The pet name was sort of a daily reminder between them, that it was important to remain only friends, so their basic pain need never be shared in public. And he became "Robbie"– take it or leave it, for male or for female, whatever suited the onlooker's fancy. Though his lips became pursed from restraint, and his arms stiff from holding back, he never corrected anyone again.

63. Almost Happy

Weary and broken, Robbie lost himself in a shabby waterfront town, in a trailer park that attracted only the debris of tenants, and fate at last granted him a measure of contentment.

She was simple, kind and beautiful in a tomboyish fashion and she loved Robbie in a strange platonic way. A ballerina couldn't move more gracefully. Her feet, arms and hands seemed always poised for a sudden spring into a beautiful world only existing for her delight. She smoothed her hair, smoked cigarettes and gazed into space. She helped Robbie in the Den and stroked Spade in a flow of beautiful arcs that fascinated Robbie.

Her name was Dolores and she despised men. At last Robbie had a seeming advantage. "Doll," as he called her, needed a buddy just like Robbie: not too masculine, yet not feminine enough to remind her of the maternity her deficient body could never accomplish. And suddenly Robbie, who always urged Pug to occasionally rebel at the monotony of her life, became happy with his own narrow rut.

Suddenly it was enough to enjoy the changing sea and sky, the uneventful day, the small uniquenesses of tenants, neighbors and girls from the beach, the pier and The Joint, who drifted in and out of Robbie's always welcoming trailer. Most of all, Robbie enjoyed potentials that might be waiting, evolving just because the daily coffee klatch existed. It was enough now to cheer people, encourage them to discover and appreciate themselves and each other. It was just not important anymore "to become somebody."

A motley bunch of girls was always being attracted to Robbie's trailer. Broke, weary, dirty, cold, sick, homeless, lonely. They usually had a history of poverty, sexual abuse, physical or emotional neglect. Girls with babies, lesbians and prostitutes drifted in and out. At night, Robbie listened in his trailer, consoling someone. Sometimes it took all night to sober and settle a desperate drunk. His coffeepot was always on, the door was seldom locked.

But once again, sick and drunk, Robbie drifted home to Pug. He had to move. The owner wanted to sell, and though the tenants were the refuse of rentery, the owner didn't want "any queers" around, lousing up the desirability of the crummy joint. "I can't leave, Pug. I'm almost happy for the first time in my life!" Robbie's voice had trembled. From her bottom drawer, Pug took out the rest of the college money and handed it to Robbie. Crying ecstatically, he kissed her palms and hurried away.

As well as being the owner-manager, Robbie soon became keystone of the park and Pug persuaded Guy to move there. Pug could easily see that it was going to be hard keeping the park on a going scale. What type of person was it that must settle for Last Resort? Those who were unrooted, unhireable, unskilled, unwanted. Robbie adopted stray people like some folks did stray animals. In fact, for people with no problems, there seemed no vacancy!

Bowie and Fawna were welcomed like Mary and Joseph. Mala had no husband and a trailer bursting with children. Fay Rose had only her body with which to make a living. Gussy hadn't a scrap of baggage. Quila was dumped in front of the park, screaming curses inside her little nailed-shut wagon!

Pug remembered that as a child Robbie showed the same deep longings to help the lost and lonely: when he brought home for meals the old man who lived in a box; when he hid an orphan under his bed and fed her until authorities tracked her down. His room was always harboring sick birds, a dog who'd lost a fight, or exotic pets that people no longer wanted. Pug was not surprised that Robbie's crowded trailer became a haven.

At Robbie's urging, there was always some oddly-nicknamed girl like Frosty, Chi or Shadow willing to help Pug hang endless clothes, sweep or mop her trailer, wash dishes, or baby-sit. Robbie was always there to do the paying. The girls needed work and wages. Plus, it freed Pug to lend her motherly presence to the Den.

And what a difference little Gussy made! At last Robbie needn't try so hard, all alone, to stimulate and entertain girls that just naturally gravitated to the Den.

Nor did it matter how little they were fed, as long as it was something, regularly!

When Robbie had only an apple at the end of one month, creative little Gussy borrowed a tub from Pug and everybody bobbed for the single little treat. Robbie finally brought it up with his teeth, laughing, his hair curling into his eyes. He cut the apple in little squares and the girls took an hour to eat it with their toothpicks.

Once Doll was gone too long and when Robbie's ears tired of the record and longed for laughter, he wheedled Pug into making pretzel dough. The record was silent, so soon the Den filled up with girls. Robbie flattened, cut and rolled the dough. Girls looped and tied, sprinkled with seasonings, and soon delicious-smelling hot circles were ready to eat.

"Wait!" said Gussy. "Let ME pass around." Stacking sketches behind her, she took the tray from Dago. "In olden times, people didn't pray as we do. They crossed their arms in the form of a cross, like this!" She held one pretzel high. "Monks were first to make these rewards for children who learned their prayers. A pretzel looks like a child saying prayers!"

Pug sobbed and smiled, allowing herself to enjoy and relive those magic hours that could never come again.

Some months a tenant could pay nothing for rent. Soon the tarpaper shed began to fill up with boxes of household goods that tenants had used instead of money for overdue rent. "Clothes payments" hung in the storeroom, above the space where Bowie slept.

Though tenants rebelled at leaky faucets, plugged toilets, the crumbling incinerator, the cranky wash machine and lidless trashcans, Pug understood. Repairmen, high utility bills and new equipment meant empty bellies at the Den, no wages for a penniless girl, no little presents to soothe Pug's frequent depression, no gas for St. Vitus, and no money for Blackie, the tattoo artist out on the pier. People were just more important to Robbie, than processes.

Yet Robbie was a tough manager and often seemed miserly; he tried not to go to the store more than twice a month and saved in every possible way. Once there was no coffee, one dry wiener in the icebox, and fourteen hungry girls sitting around in the Den. Robbie added ice, water and lemon juice to empty coffee cups. He divided the wiener into little pieces, fried them, then sprinkled with grated cheese and herbs. Doll speared the feast with toothpicks, while everybody got a peek into the history and makeup of wieners.

At the end of one month, Robbie simply added bread cubes to sizzling bacon grease, passed the golden squares around and talked of bread, bacon and toothpicks! Pug's nostrils flared in her sleep; she could almost smell those special "make-do days."

Crisping leftovers in a skillet, once Robbie dropped thin biscuit dough overall and covered the mixture. After scoring, turning and waiting to cool, the girls were happily munching tiny doll-sized portions of "biscuit bottoms." Pug sighed heavily. Why had so many golden days been gray for her? Except that she was seldom home in the daytime, to keep up with her work and better watch the children, times at the Den were mostly happy! If only she could have forgotten Robbie's stifled potential.

In her big green trailer in California, Pug had tried half-heartedly to create Andre's house in Arkansas. Now it was crystal clear: that was the problem! Part of her was still reluctant to forget Madonna. But Robbie was the only one who remembered how good she looked in the size twelve dresses that hung at the back of her closet.

As though in a dream, she could feel Guy holding and patting her hand. Bless Guy's heart, he still thought her perfect in all phases of mother craft. Her stout, squat dumpiness, and her graying hair were as lovable to him as her big heart. He was always calling her "little cobblestone" when she was allowing someone else to walk over her.

Pug delivered her seven babies at home with Guy's help. They weren't named more than "baby"–sometimes until several years old, for it satisfied Robbie to find exactly the right name for Pug's little daughters. Remembering Robbie's voice, Pug began to weep again.

"You're so little and dainty, even elves can whisper in your ear, my little Elfin."

"You don't like Robbie! Like a cold, dry wind, a mistral. Let's call you Missy!"

"Always running and skipping. Let's name you Peg, Pegasus, a little winged horse!"

"We're going to call you Patrin, our little Gypsy!

For reasons known to only Robbie, one girl was Pal, named for Pallus, Goddess of Wisdom. Cassy was named for Cassandra, who prophesied bad luck but never was believed.

Orra was the only one who had a name change. After rocking her all night through one of her sick spells, Robbie announced: "Pug, when this baby goes to school, don't saddle her with the name Orra, that means leftover, last. Spell it 'Aura!' Though unwanted at first, she has cast a spell, an aura of innocent, magic babyhood over you and me and Guy!"

"I'll never wife or sire," Robbie murmured holding each new baby in his arms. "Men crave sons in their image. But I long for a daughter," he said wistfully. Pretending the happiness was his own, Robbie found some feature that he and his new half-sister shared. "He who feels the joy, should share the burden also!" he would exclaim, as he rocked, changed diapers, hung clothes, or peeled the endless potatoes–anything but do dishes!

Pug almost died having Orra, the last baby. Weakly she whispered, "How I miss the red sod of home." Where Robbie got trucks, help, shovels, and dirt, Pug never found out. But when she left her birth-bed, the park was deeply blanketed with red, surrounded with a fence, and fronted with a low stone wall, all hastily erected by Robbie's friends to keep the dirt inside. Under threat of eviction, Robbie forbade anyone from planting in, or even scratching the surface of "Pug's dirt." Hmm, Gussy was the only one that got away with consistently defying that threat!

Children were forever cutting themselves on broken glass or jagged cans in the trash yard that Robbie called the Pigpen. So Robbie was always removing glass, thorns and splinters from tough little feet and making major productions of antiseptic and bandaging.

Often a child from the neighborhood knocked on the door, offered his "payment" and sat on the bench to wait for treatment. By having a child "pay" Robbie knew that he would not hesitate asking for Robbie's exaggerated "operation," the privilege of sitting on Robbie's lap and sharing the day's treat. Pug shook her head, bit her lip, and Guy wiped her tears.

Only Pug sometimes suspected that when the threesome–Robbie, Doll and Juju–were alone, Robbie must have pretended that Juju belonged to him and Doll. Oddly, it never occurred that Juju could have really belonged to him, to such a freak as he seemed to himself.

Robbie's greatest pleasure was secretly to do a good deed and have it found out by accident, if at all. A dime on her doorstep, so Gussy could wash; five-dollar bills slipped under Fay's bedroom door, when she couldn't pay rent; mysterious boxes of candy beside Quila's bottle, a single stolen flower on Pug's pillow when she seemed depressed. A door in the gazebo for Mange that was big enough for Bowie.

Quila brought Robbie her porch birds whose wings needed splinting, or toes were eaten by fungus. Old Blonco was often there for treatment of itchy, bleeding skin and patchy hair. Afterwards, the relieved dog hunkered down with his head on Robbie's foot. One day Robbie sprinkled cider on the dog's head. "'Mange,' is what I christen thee!" Robbie laughed.

Much as Robbie hated cats, he cut an opening in his own trailer door, so that Spade could wander in and out, be petted by, or lie beside Doll, purring contentedly.

Pug turned in her half-sleep and Guy gently took big pins from her heavy bun.

Robbie was friended among poor blacks in ramshackle houses, forgotten ones rocking on porches, homeless wanderers on the pier, drunks in bars all over town. Where did he find time to play ball in the streets with shabby kids, to leave bouquets on doorknobs or to listen for hours to old men reminisce?

64. Worn-Out Record

When Doll was home Robbie tried hard to keep her mind entertained, hoping there would be less need for her to soothe to sleep, then rob happily mesmerized drunks. Robbie didn't realize how much it took to support Doll's father, old Lambeth, his medicines and doctors.

When Doll was gone Robbie often walked the beach or strolled the pier seeking freakish people, lonely sailors, quiet fishermen, sad-faced children or bored shopkeepers to encourage. Though he smoked, drank and cussed too much, whenever he remembered to, his obvious aims at demeaning himself only seemed to raise him higher in everyone's esteem.

Once, the esteem of the girls was barren as his own supplies. Bread cubes were soon bubbling in butter, spiced with cinnamon and sugar and waiting in a paper tray. He put an inch of wine in one cup, stood, and banged his big metal spoon on the table.

"The word 'toast', a proposal of health, originated in Rome where an actual bit of spiced and toasted bread was dropped into wine to improve flavor and absorb sediment." Robbie dropped a toothpicked cube in the cup and held it high.

"When I say, 'Here's to you!', why do I drink the wine myself?" He had the girls' attention. "Here's to Gussy, who finds beauty wherever it isn't!" He handed the cup to Gussy, who grinned, drank the wine and ate the cube. Robbie refilled the same cup with its tiny dole of wine and dropped another toothpicked cube inside.

"Here's to Pug," toasted Gussy, "the most perfect mother I've ever known!"

Everyone dug into their imagination for some little quality in one another, and made the day seem suddenly shiny. The girls finally left, all wearing contented smiles.

It was easy for Robbie to appear of a neuter gender: he cleaned and serviced restrooms so nobody noticed which facility he used. "I'm coffee-logged." "My kidneys are drowning!" "Don't you ever visit the john, Robbie?" Doll laughed, "There's camel humps where kidneys ought to be!" and she'd pull a curl way down to Robbie's nose and giggle.

Pug sobbed weakly while Guy smoothed her hair and kissed her forehead.

Robbie never washed clothes. When shirts, pants or shorts (that Pug had saved from Guy's leaner days) were really dirty, Pug stole them to wash or else Robbie would rip them up to burn. And Robbie hated washing dishes. For bowls he used jar lids and small cans that Pug saved for him, plus paper sacks for trays and popsicle sticks for spreaders and stirrers. And then there were toothpicks, fingers and even tongues! Pug laughed and cried at once.

It was a relief for Guy to be done with hospitals. Often, before Doll, he was called to get the bandaged Robbie, mouthing drunken curses at doctors for doing their jobs so well.

Life for Robbie was endurable at Last Resort, even when Doll was gone, tingly when she was expected and short of ecstatic when she came back.

Pug stirred happily, remembering how Robbie's step and voice awakened at Doll's unexpected nearness. Like a schoolboy, he climbed the tree one night and carved two initials. To Robbie, Doll was heaven-born, created and winged down just for him. It gave Pug tender joy simply to watch Robbie and Doll in the Den, especially when the company included Quila, Gussy and Juju on Doll's lap. Sometimes a girl would bring her guitar or harmonica. Then Robbie would light a fat candle and settle back listening, his warm, longing eyes embracing Doll from the shadows.

When Doll was gone too long and the neighborhood, The Joint, the pier and long hours at the library had lost their attraction, Robbie began to play Doll's favorite, scratchy old record, plunking along with it on his bass viol. Pug was the only one for whom Robbie would unlock the door. "Hearing Doll's Song makes me feel a part, Pug," he onetime said, "of something that Doll loves, of something intangible that makes her hard exterior instantly soft, makes her eyes get tender and misty. How I love to pretend that that 'something' is me."

"But you've got to eat, Robbie!"

"Don't you know, Pug, that tobacco, wine, music and love are also food?"

"But that scratchy worn-out record is driving everyone crazy, Robbie!"

Robbie had put his arms behind his head, leaned back against the trailer wall and closed his eyes while the record scratched on and on. "Did you know that Wagner wrote his best music while dressed in historical costumes? Haydn wore a special ring? Gluck sat in a field? Whoever wrote Doll's Song was holding someone just like her in his arms."

Robbie and Doll often hung out nights in dark little bars all over town, Robbie keeping time on her bass, while someone else played guitar or accordion. Doll sang for tips, almost whispering sad ballads as she looked into space and pleaded in a windy voice for some unknown prince to discover her. Every night she sang Doll's Song.

Robbie was the kindest of people. Except when overdrunk, when Doll had been hurt, or was merely gone too long. Robbie often lit a candle, just pretending Doll was home again.

When Robbie's cupboard and icebox were totally bare, Robbie took mugs and coffeepot outside to serve in the washhouse. Sitting in an old chair that leaned against the wall, with females all around him, he joked, drank, encouraged, wove endless cellophanes, and laughed in that magic way of his. Pug shook with crying, as she pictured that same old chair when Robbie had kicked it out from under his world-weary body.

65. Tattoos

Doll had confided in Pug that she had tried many kinds of work, but bosses were always more interested in her after-dark potential than the fact that her typing, shorthand and bookkeeping were first rate. Since she couldn't keep a job without compromise, Doll had bitterly decided to pay all men back for their lack of interest in her professional skills. From now on, they'd have to pay for her casual company and new skills of taunting, faking and hedging. She had many tight squeezes, narrow escapes, and scars to prove them. Yet every inch of hurt that Doll brought home endeared her even more to Robbie. It seemed proof that Doll had retained virginity. For Doll it was a necessary, profitable game that kept her and Lambeth afloat. Her "clients" were paying for fun, tenderness, companionship and no more.

At first when Doll was gone, before finding how much he delighted in casual company of "lost" people, Robbie dabbled in every sort of hobby, trying to lose himself. Finally he sank to the task of absently weaving the cellophane that enclosed cigarette wrappers into long chains. This hobby cost nothing and he could do this and still watch Doll if she were in the Den. "Someday Pug, I'll make her the most beautiful purses and belts just from cellophane wrappers. I have chains of them in the closet." It pained Pug to see Robbie's mind sink to such mindless simplicity. Weaving wrappers was no choice of a pastime, for someone with Robbie's intelligence and discrimination. Nor, Pug was sure, would the purseless, beltless Doll be even interested in such gifts. It was merely part of the fantasy that kept Robbie going.

Robbie realized that he had found a symbolic use for his unbending knife, a use that compensated for his lifelong ambition to doctor people. "I am already doctoring people, Ma. Just by using food and facts, I am cutting away at psychological problems, restoring sick hearts, making people appreciate their own minds and bodies, helping them forget their sordid pasts! Most of all, Ma, I'm giving them a taste of what unconditional 'home' should have been for all of them; what it always was for me. You, just being here, Pug, give them that sense of warm motherhood. And, although they don't realize it, I give them fatherly support."

Every time that Robbie used his knife in the Den, Pug had shed a silent tear or two, and yet, she was also smiling!

When Gussy joined the group it was the final spark Robbie needed. Gussy loved words, ideas and the concept of "what else?" She was also openly fascinated with everything that Robbie did! More and more, since Gussy came, Robbie filled the Den days with things that inspired girls to enjoy their everyday life, now, just as it was, before moving on.

Robbie thought there was even room for a person such as Fay. "She's a cool hand on brows of despair," he said when Pug had wanted Fay to leave.

Robbie loved the history and background of things that others took for granted, especially food and famous people. He spent hours at the library, and hours studying each girl as she did or didn't talk. Slyly he fed their bodies, while he fascinated their minds with the tales and tastes of a variety of often unknown, unappreciated foods.

The librarian sat in the same church pew with Pug and her family. "That Robbie in your park has certainly inspired a lot of strange girls to use the library! They ask questions I've never been asked before. 'How did spices prove the world was round?' 'Where is a book on nutmeg?' 'How do I make pretzels?' 'Can a high school drop-out become a chef?'"

Pug trembled and Guy helped her turn over.

Robbie was fascinated with popcorn! It was fast and easy. He could change its look and taste with herbs, brown sugar, cheese, a tidbit of meat or a melted candy bar. It was cheap, and a mere handful turned into twenty handfuls, enough to feed a whole Den of famished girls. On the first pass around, Robbie might have them choose "mushrooms"–the largest, roundest, best-flavored popcorn morsels. Next, Robbie had them choose "butterflies"–irregular, branched tidbits of flavor. Sometimes they had to toss away "bee wings"–tiny flecks attached to the tip of a kernel. Once, there was a prize for who guessed how many "old maids" of unpopped kernels would be at the bottom of the batch.

Pug could almost see Robbie's skillet covered with old screening as he began to shake it, while everyone waited for the first kernel to explode. She could almost smell fragrance as the popping slowed. Robbie turned off the heat and waited for settling before removing the screen. Yet, one or two puffy balls always waited to explode from the skillet. If anyone happened to catch one, they earned a big handful, before others were served.

Once, Robbie filled the skillet with embers from the incinerator, lit a candle and banged his spoon. "In the dark past, people thought a little devil lived inside each kernel. Heating his house made the little devil so mad, that he burst the hull to escape! Scientists now know that each kernel is full of moisture. Heating turns it to steam and it explodes!"

Robbie whispered louder as he walked around handing each girl five kernels. "Some Indians tossed kernels into fire to predict fortunes, by how many kernels popped and in what direction they flew."

Pug remembered how much Quila enjoyed that day. Weighing personalities, potential, and where the popcorn flew, she fabricated forecasts that delighted everybody.

Entertainment, unconditional welcome, and a regular bit of food kept Robbie's Den always full of girls, except when Doll was gone overlong. Then Robbie could insult or evict a coffee klatcher in a blinking of his eyelid. Girls stayed away when Doll's Song was playing.

When Doll was home, Robbie slyly condensed, updated, commented and joked about news, trying to make it a part of girls' limited life. He introduced words; polished lackluster personalities, blew complementary air into deflated egos. He thrived on varied personalities and nationalities. He loved to discover gems that could be encouraged to light the world.

Robbie was comfortable with what the majority would think of as nonconformers, people who insisted on doing their own thing even if it were nothing for the time being.

"We're the lucky ones," Robbie toasted the girls one day, "discovering that it's okay not to join the rest of society yet; okay to bloom slowly, to play with wonders about this enchanting world that others will never have lazy time to enjoy! Wonders that are not required for college degrees, won't help in making a living, aren't great for cocktail conversation. That just add sparkle to dullness that common folks accept as everyday life!"

Robbie had poured another round of wine. "We're the fortunate ones. Not trying to be copies of each other: dressing, doing, going, eating alike. 'They' are the ones with money, education, power. But we still have the one thing that they would never recognize or even desire: freedom to drift, unnoticed, until we discover our own unique space. Someday, if you, too, are one of they, remember that these lazy little 'todays' were priceless steps that most of the world skips over in their frantic rush to the top!"

"But," said Pug that night after dinner in her trailer, "you can't mark time and dabble forever, Robbie. Whatever happened to all of your dreams, your plans?"

"To affect the quality of the day," Thoreau said, "is the highest of the arts." He looked sad. "Even my own mother doesn't realize that I'm an unpaid master of this unrecognized art!" His eyes brightened. "I'm already successful, Ma: exactly where I want to be, doing a few things well that I want to do. I only expect to live in the 'now,' Pug."

Brightening the day, arresting emotional pain, being where people could find him–those were his simple ambitions. His biggest need was merely to have Doll nearby.

Happiness was at its peak when Doll and Robbie went "a-Gypsying," but for red-blooded Robbie it became unbearable.

Only one person, other than Pug and Guy, shared Robbie's secret: Blackie, an old tattoo artist, ex-art teacher that Robbie had met in college. He had a tiny shop out on the pier. He always turned out his "closed" sign, took Robbie to a back room, and locked the door.

"Roberto," the old man examined his body. "There's not an inch of right skin left!"

Robbie's voice was always heavy with wine. "Please, just this once again, discover a place! Next time it'll be easier. This time it's unbearable. Just to watch her asleep on the sand, her soft hair blowing against her cheek. Here, there's a bare spot on this ankle.

"In some places, Blackie, it's only a little tickle. In others it's a clawing cat. Sometimes the pain is almost ecstasy and sublimates the agony." Blackie sighed, shaved and sterilized, adjusted the little spotlight, wiped his magnifying glass and traced the patterns that he knew by heart.

"It's my only fetish, Blackie, a warm blanket around this lonely prison that is me. I even hold my own body sometimes, pretending it's Doll, and drift happily to sleep."

Pug could never understand how Robbie could find relief in such a painful ritual. Yet she was grateful to old Blackie for his secrecy and understanding. When Robbie was gone too long, Pug trudged out to the pier with a loaf of homemade bread, in hopes of seeing Robbie or learning from Blackie that he was still alive.

Yet, Robbie's form of branding was more civilized than that of the crude, homemade tattoos of some girls who sat in the Den. Jack knives, switchblades, beer openers, sharp rings and inkpens had been used to decorate their tender skin. Once, when the smell of burning flesh filled the Den, Pug realized that one girl was holding a lighted cigarette to her own arm. Later, the unwanted boyfriend's name merely fell off with the bloody scab.

There was no scab to end Robbie's torment. Sometimes he got disgusted with the painful abuse, but still returned to its release again and again. "Her hair is black as the rising and falling, nighttime sea, Blackie. Tonight it was a pale lily in moonlight."

"Wouldn't it be easier to tell her?" Pug urged frantically.

"Not once to caress or make love to her, I can stand," he whispered. "Not to ever see her again, I could never endure. No, she would think that I had betrayed her. I've seen her so innocently undress, I've shared her darkest secrets. She must never know until it is time. She always, always comes back when she needs me, Ma. I want to be near until she needs me no more. I'll know my time, Pug. Believe me, I'll know my time."

66.   Robbie's Letters

Dawn was bleeding into the blackness of that long night when Pug finally stirred again. Sleepless, Bowie was peeking into the window as she awoke, dreamed out, emotionally exhausted, to find Guy still sitting at her bedside.

"Here's a note from Robbie," Guy patted her head, "when you're ready to read it."

Robbie's familiar handwriting split her heart and tears began anew. "'Don't depend on fragile threads from the past to carry you across life's chasm, when a stout rope of today is at your command,'" quoted Robbie. "Home is wherever you are happiest, Ma. But you have to believe that with all of your heart! Your loving son, Roberto."

"Hand me the picture, Guy." She opened the frame and removed the photograph of herself as Andre's bride. Carefully she tore it up. She reached up over the pillows, took an armload of dusty books from the shelf and dumped them into the wastebasket. She got up from bed, pulled out a drawer beneath the mattress, took out phonograph records, broke each of them in two on her knee then dropped the halves in the basket. She opened the closet, took out little dresses and sadly watched each one slide off its hanger to join other remnants of the past. Tired from long-delayed decisions, Pug sighed with unexpected relief and leaned back.

Guy went to the bathroom and took out his old-fashioned shaving brush, unscrewed the handle where blades were supposed to be stored and shook something out. Back in the bedroom, he kneeled on the floor beside Pug.

"Every night for fifteen years I've watched you look into your own eyes pictured there and tell 'him' goodnight. Then always, as though I were Andre, you let me love you. You are the mother of my children, my mistress, my only heroine." He slid a plain gold band onto her ring finger. "Will you now be, also, my wife?"

Pug's entire body seemed to dissolve in tears. For the very first time, she hugged Guy with her whole body and soul. The sad thin wall that had always stood between them had crumbled into nothingness.

Louie had gone to a Union meeting that horrible night. So Lolli ran home to hug Whiffet while she read Robbie's note to her.

"At last I am going to really be me," Robbie wrote. "How I wish that I could share with you that same ecstasy, Lolli. We all have some twisted blemish, seen or unseen. But, if I had not been exactly as I was, I would not have had Doll. Nor, would you have had Louie. My very affliction, my horrible curse has brought the greatest beauty into my life. You were born, Lolli, with 'spurs' and therefore always fancied yourself as a ruler. But I have studied you, and you are only really happy when you are serving, not ruling.

"Just be your own wonderful self, Chloe–that alone is much more than enough!" Lolli pushed Whiffet away, grabbed Pansy-Bear from under her pillow and covered him with long-overdue tears.

As they carried Robbie away, Bowie leaned against the washhouse wall, staring at the wet smoldering wreckage.

Doll was sitting on Pug's porch with Robbie's note in her hand. The shocking, yet somehow tender sight of Robbie's death seemed forever engraved in her eyes. Sitting beside Doll, Quila was chewing hollyhock leaves–that Bowie gave her–then applying the sticky paste to burns on Doll's hands. It should have been revolting, instead it was soothing, Doll thought. Light from Pug's door fell on the paper, and a tear began at the sight of Robbie's handwriting.

"To those whose daily life is hell, Doll, it comes very seldom to make the supreme sacrifice for a noble cause, not just from cowardice to face another day. Since we are rich only through what we give, please, please tolerate me to say that, 'I give my life for Doll and her happiness' and I can die ecstatic. As long as I am still here, through pity, habit, friendship and a strange, unfulfillable love, you will always fly back to me.

"I told myself that 'I would know my time,' but I have seen sweet adoration in Syd's eyes, ignored it, and lingered too long. Syd will cherish you, Doll. He is a fortune within himself; he is that 'rich' man, that sweet and gentle prince, that you have always waited for!

"Don't grieve or blame yourself. I have died a little each hour of my miserable adult life. Fear has always been a sentinel, a harness on my eager arms, a gag upon my lovesong, a muzzle on my longing lips. Tonight will be the last, easy and done with.

"I have nothing to leave you, but that most important gift of all—total freedom.

"But let there be truth between us, Doll. I could not leave with my love unsung. My favorite poet said, 'I loved you so bare of any hope, or the slightest expression, with such purity and gentle passion.' May God grant that you be loved this deeply, once again. Forever, Roberto."

Quila had walked away when Doll began to read Robbie's note. Though unspeakably sad, Quila hadn't felt so immediately good for years. It was nice to have truly helped someone again, to use simple medical knowledge and have it appreciated. Perhaps it was time to share her knowledge of curing. She knew it would please Robbie, but she had no idea of how to start. Nor any strength to even think about it.

She patted poor miserable Mange who was sprawled across her porch. She had to step over him to enter the door and her dress dragged soothingly over his panting body.

She lit a candle, then took Robbie's letter from her sleeve. "'Kill slowly the thing that you dearly love, to keep it. Or cut it free from suffering and have it forever just as it is.'"

Quila opened the door and coaxed the bewildered Mange inside her wagon. Carefully she lifted his painful whimpering body up onto the bed where he had been born. She held Robbie's words over her heart and Mange put his weary head upon the writing. They both gave a quivering sigh and drifted off to sleep.

In the days before Robbie's funeral a pall settled over the park, invisible thought Bowie, yet eerie as sunlight through a fire cloud. Puffs of dust and flies arose with the slightest breeze and then resettled, as though intending to take possession of Last Resort. Without Robbie to give each day its hopes and tides, to keep the women's time from slipping into oblivion, the park was body void of soul.

The Pigpen reeked and overflowed its bounds. Even Pug did not wash. The phone rang unanswered. The faucet dripped even more defiantly. Tenants had never realized how much Gussy's little rakings, her washhouse sweepings, her hosing of the women's showers and her picking up of blowing trash had helped Last Resort. But Gussy and her premature baby had almost lost their lives. Gussy was slipping into and out of a coma. No one was permitted to see them. No one knew whether or not they'd ever come home. And Bowie wondered again and again: how could Quila's forecast ever come true, now? How could Gussy's mere existence be enough to miraculously change Last Resort, to say nothing of Waterfront, itself?

Around nine in the morning and two in the afternoon, without realizing it, everyone seemed to be waiting for the jangle of Robbie's keys as he sauntered out to get fresh coffee water. In the quiet night tenants listened unconsciously for Robbie and Doll to return together, arm in arm, softly laughing.

At night Doll stayed secluded in her father's trailer. In the daytime she walked dazedly down the street, along the beach, out on the pier, beside the railroad tracks, or down to The Joint. Everywhere people wanted to share with her their private experiences with Robbie. Her eyes were always red and she never bothered to wipe away tears. She was oblivious to the iceman's worried, caring glances, even to the needs or whereabouts of Juju.

Bowie sometimes watched in shadows as Doll visited Robbie in the mortuary, and then as she squeezed her way again and again into the overcrowded, ever-growing art show to visit Gussy's pictures of Robbie. Here, for a while, it seemed that time could be relived.

The tenants all seemed to suffer the same thought. If only they could apologize to Robbie for the things that they had thought of her–of him.

Lolli kept her trailer tidied up and ready for the klatch twice a day. But she didn't have the heart to bake anything. Nobody stayed long or had much to say. The park remained kingless, without even Quila as the jester. The days were gray and depressing, so often the coffee crowd just quietly sat around Lolli's table inside. Lolli even lit a candle now and then as the even more faded and hungry Quila sometimes told her now bland fortunes. "Ask a silent question, shuffle the cards, cut them three times, then I'll give ye an answer" she droned, as Mange lay panting beneath Lolli's table with his chin on Quila's foot.

Fay dragged around like a broken stick after Robbie died; something new and awful was taking over her fragile body. If Bowie had the right herbs he would fan the healing, soothing smoke over her frailness, like Fawna used to do. But Fay didn't care to be healed. Without thought of her children she'd disappear, come home again, disappear, and then come home again. Thanks to Flo, Juju and the Chips had a place to sleep and eat. They were always in clean clothes now, their hair was clean and brushed, and Flo began to break Juju to a toilet seat. She brought the children to Fay's once in awhile, to see if Fay had come home and to straighten her trailer a bit more each time. But Fay, Doll, Gussy and Robbie were all gone at once: the Chips seemed much happier, but Juju's eyes were vacant and hopeless.

"There'll be a sudden guest!" cried Quila excitedly, as she sat at Lolli's table one afternoon. As she studied her own tea leaves the candle in front of her began to gutter. "See there! That proves it, a double sign! A stranger's due, and soon!

"List!" cried Quila that very evening as she lay sleepless and fully dressed on her bed. "I feel a strange walker," she whispered as she started down the steps to find Bowie.

Eyes closed, Bowie was stretched out beneath Quila's wagon, one finger corking the last inch of wine in the bottle. The belly of the trailer above him was a cool sandstone cave. Mentally he was sifting mingled odors of suppertime and placing each dish on a deerskin tablecloth laid out by Fawna. He was awaiting her call by the stream now, one finger adangle in coolness. She dipped into the stream and handed him water in a three-legged plant cup.

"Bowie!" whispered Quila. "Wake up!"

67. Tad

Quila had alerted Bowie, before the stranger even knocked at Lolli's "Office" sign that Louie had printed. Bowie watched now from under the wagon as Lolli stood in the driveway, pointed to Gussy's colorful trailer and handed the doorknob to the stranger.

Quila limped over to the young man and took his hand. "Be ye the Tad that Ginny's always 'spectin'?" He smiled sadly. "At last, at last! She's still in the hospital ye know!" Teary-eyed, Quila wobbled away to the washhouse with her hands held out for balance.

Three times Tad slammed behind him the door of this wildly-dimensioned, patchwork-colored trailer. He must be in the wrong place, he thought, as he dodged clothes and artworks swaying above and around him. Neat little Ginny could never stand this crowdedness! But he was so tired and this was an oddly cheerful room to rest in. It looked, smelled and sounded so interesting, so different. A spicy fragrance sprang into the air when he ran his fingers through a bowl of dried leaves, blossoms and orange peels. Sweet glassy jingles, woody throbbings and metalic chimings continued in the breeze outside the tiny bedroom area. Great, but often ugly sketches were scattered around the room and crumpled on a bench, as though someone had sat on them! Ginny's sketches were never, never true and real like these. There were dozens of collages too, in various stages of completion.

Whoever the occupant was, she couldn't afford electricity, for Tad had tried the switches. Instead she saved old candles, then melted the wax to make new ones. She was experimenting with wicks and fragrances— evidence was scattered on the table where she had hurriedly left them.

Ginny never touched cigarettes or wine, yet the ashtray was overflowing, an empty wine bottle was overturned. There was broken glass on the floor under crumpled newspaper, a pool of dried blood on the table, red spatters across a big open dictionary and some sketches, a towel on the floor and little manicure scissors that seemed to have been dropped there. Bunches of blond hair were scattered–not Ginny's, hers was soft brown!

It was getting dark, so he lit a candle and settled at the breakfast nook to rest and think awhile. He put his head on the big dictionary and closed his eyes.

Not until he had arrived back home–too early, ingloriously–had Tad's folks told him of Ginny's visit and her request not to burden his year of art scholarship in Mexico with her problems. His folks had given Ginny several checks, enough for one person to live well for a year, and pay for the baby's birth. Whoever lived here wasn't accepting much charity! Whoever lived here could stand alone, take things as they were and adapt to them beautifully.

No, she was not meek, this girl, humble, yes, and her convictions were not idly fought for; they were being proven all around her. She was doing her own thing, regardless of the rest of the world around her. He lifted his head.

The scalloped newspaper curtains made his heart ache. Broken dishes held greenery whose leaves tried to hide the poverty here. He pumped water for drying vines, twisted new growth around curtain rods and watered vegetable ends that were sprouting leaves.

The curved ceiling was a work of art in progress! He moved the hanging heart aside and held the candle higher. The middle of the arch was unfinished, but the sides were an intricate mural, its designs dictated by outrageous pictures in the wood! Now this was the kind of female for which Tad had always yearned–not meek, inefficient, scatterbrained, lovable Ginny. But one like this, who wouldn't be shocked at wherever his new life might lead, who could accept the sordid and help to alleviate it. One who could recognize beautiful new patterns, wherever they might lead. One who would understand that pursuing a caring, nameless occupation was just as important as being a famous artist, or a junior partner in his father's law firm.

Tad had met Ginny's folks and noted that Ginny was the worst of both: as spineless, dependent and impractical as Dom; as superficial, unimaginative and fastidious as Eloise often seemed. But whoever owned this trailer could offer her man a real woman; one who had suffered deeply, scrimped unbelievably, could imagine the unseeable, and now stood tall on her own feet. "I'd love to meet the owner of this place! It couldn't be Ginny!"

This girl filed collage materials in whatever container was available! Like cereal boxes and toilet paper rolls! A jar of paint brushes that were made from human hair, mop threads and broom wisps waited at the back of the table. She must be some strange kind of artist! Of course! This was the studio of Gussy, the girl that everyone was reading about! The girl whose pictures were making such an impact at the local gallery! Whose fame was spreading all over the country!

He looked closely at many of the strong, few-lined sketches stuffed into and hanging from niches all around him, many that were becoming collages. In art school Ginny's people were intricately beautiful, nothing like this horrible picture, entitled "Fay Rose, Pharose, Fey Rose." Plainly revealed were the subject's character, attitudes, and occupation. Only part of the picture was charcoal. The rest was made of debris that only an artist could discover on a walk by the sea or a visit to the dump.

At art school students called Ginny's pictures lacking in academic structure, or, even worse, "pretty." But Ginny loved to draw and made up her own stylized rules. She disliked the business, the rigidity of realistic rules. She romanticized landscapes, idealized everything commonplace, and used nothing but delicate pastels. Colors here were earthy and solid, ugly but real.

Tad hurt Ginny worst of all, labeling her best work, "An unreal, idyllic, flossy bit of trivia. What's dramatic about a sappy smile on a perfect face!" he had shouted.

On one jaunt students were sketching run-down houses of the neighborhood. In Ginny's pictures the sags were straightened, brown lawns were green and bright faces smiled from dingy windows. Tad finished early and sketched the crippled teacher. "What is worse," asked Ginny, "to cover ugliness or to capture it forever?" Yet, whoever lived in this little trailer was doing a masterful job of capturing the ugliness of life!

When it was Tad's turn to model for the class everyone but Ginny portrayed Tad as a sophisticate; Ginny gave him a Lincolnesque look with his hand on the colored student's head that he had snubbed when asked for criticism. Tad was annoyed for pictures were hung around the room for parents to admire. And there it was, for everyone to see, the shell that he really was, with inhibited yearnings that he had been taught to hide toward all minorities.

Tad usually joined the upper, arty clique gathered at the courtyard fountain for their daily brand of lunch talk. Once Tad left the group and followed Ginny. She ate beside the lake while she was sketching. "At last your art is realistic," he commented over her shoulder, for the place was already beautiful and needed no improving.

Such perfect days followed. Tad brought his own sketchpad and at first his work, to Ginny, was slick technical display, his models posing in front of a backdrop. But he relaxed around her and soon his figures were integrated with the landscape. They often spent evenings on the lake in a rented boat, talking of art and life, being closer and closer together.

"Tad," she said one day, "my art is merely design so far, but yours is different, somehow. It's as though you're suppressing a message."

For the term project he began a series called Waifs of Westlake, sifting until he got the most derelict of characters to pose for him. Ginny noticed uneasily, that his work was powerful, but that it had begun to agonize him to reproduce pain and hopelessness.

Tad disappeared from school and to Ginny's puzzlement, hustlers and bums who had posed for Tad also disappeared. When finally he returned to school, tattered and unwashed, Tad's parents threatened to stop his tuition and allowance. Things weren't working as they had planned. Grudgingly, they had consented to art school. It seemed a harmless way to work out lingering bits of idealism that could keep Tad from becoming a successful criminal lawyer like his father.

Tad began a mural around the courtyard of the art school, showing the fountain, the teachers and students gathered in conversation. "A real projection of your personality, Tad." "Beautiful strokes," said another. "Frigid," said the black student. "It has no message," said Ginny. "Where is the 'you' in it?" The self that I really love, he read in her eyes.

But beneath the mural's sophistication and in his series of Waifs there was something different that won a scholarship to float around in Mexico and sketch the misery that he was sure to find there.

"So I miffed the opportunity!" he said aloud to the empty trailer. A pillowslip peeked from behind the breakfast nook cushion. He pulled it out and inside were painted cardboards. On top was an idyllic picture of the faded Gypsy wagon he had passed. But in the picture the wagon was brand new, turned into a little shop that featured things a Gypsy would sell. And in the window was not the ugly, wizened woman that had held his hand in the driveway, but a sweet old lady face, smiling from ear to ear.

Tears of recognition ran down Tad's cheeks.

Here was a girl who collected rotting garbage, moldy seaweed, wine corks, dust curls, hair snarls, soap chips and more to depict the nightmares of living. Yet, from the midst of these same materials, she could also produce a clean, dreamy world of her own imagination.

Her drawings were so spare and true, now. How could little tortoise-paced Ginny have evolved into an artist who displayed such remarkable speed in sketching that just a few lines would give the essence of her subjects?

Her collage collection was made of fragments with interesting form, history and potential that nobody else could recognize, much less appreciate. "How could she live nose-close to this stinking trash yard, and not have to spend all her time fighting pests?" Tad cried.

Outside, Bowie put his hand over his mouth while tears ran down his fingers, remembering how Gussy was always tenderly escorting flies, ants and cockroaches outside of her trailer. Always mending windows with tape, sewing patches on screens, and stuffing cracks with wet newspapers and rags. Gussy had painfully grown accustomed to the ugly and the ugly had become a beautiful challenge.

Yes, decided Tad. It was true what his heart had been insisting. This very trailer itself was proof: this was the Gussy that newspapers were talking about. And Gussy was his own Ginny. A thrilling flood of pride surged throughout his body.

He looked around with new excitement, and saw one picture alone on the closet door. This same wildly-painted trailer was drawn within a magazine picture that looked like the only tree in this trailer park. A newspaper face of a man looked out the trailer window with eyes just like his own! Ginny had scrawled at the bottom, "Someday."

He gently eased down on the handmade quilt for some emotional rest. In trying to fluff up the flat, fragrant pillow, his fingers found a childishly-made, blood-stained booklet underneath it. He returned to the candlelit table to read its contents.

Bowie left the back of Gussy's trailer for there was a commotion out on the sidewalk. Strangers were gathered beneath the glowing streetlight. They were holding newspapers, pointing and noting the tenant's movements with a lip-smacking kind of curiosity.

Bowie felt confused and lonely. He crawled under Quila's wagon and snuggled his head into Mange's warm neck, conjured up the dreamcatcher and fell asleep.

68.   Gallery Office

From speckled shade beneath Quila's wagon, Bowie had watched the white-haired reporter for days. He returned every morning to sit on tenants' doorsteps, drinking coffee, wiping his eyes, blowing his nose, reading Gussy's bloody diary and making too many notes. Sadly he poked around in the ashes of Robbie's trailer. Bowie followed, unseen, while he interviewed kids playing ball, people sitting on porches, waitresses at The Joint, customers at Flo's, strollers along the beach, fishermen and shopkeepers along the pier. The reporter hung around the curve where the train slowed, flagged the engineer and rode along with him.

Around noon the reporter returned to Gussy's trailer with groceries and a stack of newspapers. There he lunched with Tad, shared notes and they read newspapers together.

For nothing else to do, every evening lately Bowie also followed the reporter to the back door of the art gallery, watching through a window as the reporter and the curator drank wine or coffee, ate sandwiches, talked and scribbled in the office for hours. Together they copied Gussy's words, sketched pictures of the gallery walls, and wrote on big diagrams until there were streaks of dawn in the eastern sky. The artist always working beside them enlarging some of Gussy's art and handwriting, had usually fallen asleep on top of his work.

After a light breakfast with Tad, today the reporter took a nap in Gussy's trailer and then returned to his office. Bowie watched beside the hollyhock, as Tad just sat alone now in the silent trailer drinking cold coffee in the cluttered space and looking around in dismay.

Suddenly, Tad rushed down Gussy's fancy step (that had just reappeared one night!), then hurried away to the hospital at the edge of town. As usual, not one nurse allowed him to awaken the weirdly-wired, straw-haired, skinny little person they insisted was Gussy. Nor would they allow him to hold the sleeping baby with Gussy's name on its bassinet.

From the hospital Tad hurried to the main part of town and the overcrowded Plaza. There he tried in vain to press into the silent mass of people attempting to enter the funeral parlor even though the doors were guarded by policemen and the funeral director was shouting from an upstairs window, "All of the seats are taken!" Tad could see that a constant trickle of hand-picked weeds and bouquets in jelly jars was being passed up the jam-packed steps from one loving hand to another, then transferred through a slightly opened door.

Because of crushing crowds, shops around and across the street from the funeral parlor and the art gallery could not even open today. Disappointed and frustrated, Tad walked back to Gussy's trailer and just sat there, looking hopelessly at the mass of artworks sitting, hanging, and crushing in all around him. They left so little room for daily living in their midst! How could neat little Ginny stand this? Robbie's face was constantly staring at Tad from every plane and angle in this small, cramped space. Robbie's haunting blue eyes were so sad and lonely. His trailer was only ash. His girls were scattered, lonely, and more lost than they had ever been before. The tenants of Last Resort were shocked into an eerie quietness and total immobility. Robbie's efforts now seemed to have been useless.

Tad opened Gussy's diary. "All that I care to find in the Pigpen now are paper and cardboard which I have to tear or cut so fast that the unimportant edges are jagged. But I must hurry, hurry, hurry to capture the few significant lines that suddenly, unexpectedly take form in my mind, screaming to be recorded somewhere before new ones, form, crowd them out and erase forever their wonderful being. Collaging will have to wait. This exact moment in time will never come again!"

Suddenly, a need to act creatively, himself, at exactly this moment in time, also overtook Tad!

He rushed to Pug's trailer to borrow pillow slips and big baby-blanket safety pins, then grabbed some newspapers from the Pigpen. Back at Gussy's he gathered sketches into piles, carefully wrapped hanging artworks and collages in crumpled newspaper and packed them all into pillow slips. Feeling Gussy-like, he strung the slips together with safety pins, as her diary had described the transportation of impossible pillows! Outside, he unhooked Gussy's wind chimes and laid them at the top of one stuffed pillowcase. "I'll make her some more," he vowed.

He trudged several blocks to the gallery, explained his mission to the policeman standing guard at the back entrance, then sidestepped into the building carrying Gussy's treasures.

What a strange art gallery office this is, he thought. One excited worker was stirring a fragrant pot of tea with a stick, another was hurriedly peeling onions, someone was shaking popcorn in a skillet and another was dumping the entire contents of a spice can into a giant pot of coffee. Cots were all around the room where weary workers were taking catnaps! Tad put his big bundles on the floor, close beside the desk of the astonished female curator.

He lifted and shook the magic sounds of Gussy's wind chimes, which instantly silenced busyness in the room. He cleared his throat and started with no introduction at all. "You might be interested in Gussy's kind of music."

Again he cleared tightness from his throat, and pointed to the pillow slips. "Most of these works of Gussy's aren't even finished. Or are they? Are they collage fading into sketch? Or are they sketch fading into collage? Anyway, they illustrate the way they grew." The onion-cutter threw the onion into the pot and wiped his hands. The tea-stirrer gave a big stir and turned down the burner. The corn-popper shook the corn and turned off the gas.

All eyes and ears were now Tad's.

"At first, Gussy brought bunches of pictures to the second hand store behind Last Resort, where Flo rewarded her with lunch and whatever else her store could offer," he explained. "Toward the end, Gussy decided to bring only a few pictures every day, so she could be sure that one daily meal could be depended upon. But art began to pile up all around her, to take over, and overwhelm her tiny trailer. Suddenly, Gussy realized she wasn't merely creating for the sake of money or food, but mostly just for the sake of creating, and preserving a very special time at Last Resort! That day she decided she would have to take lots of pictures to Flo, in order to make room, not only for more pictures, but for herself to exist and work in! But, that very night she had her accident and didn't return to her trailer.

"Here are the rest of Gussy's pictures." Eagerly, the curator reached for them.

"Wait," said Tad, putting one pillow slip aside. "Most of the pictures I've brought, like others that are now on your walls, are flat on can labels or torn cardboards. They don't really reflect all of the creative resources that the artist had to use.

"But the artworks in this special case," he lifted it up, "are on backgrounds that Gussy worked on just for herself, on nights when she couldn't find paper or cardboard. Each of these unusual 'canvases' was unearthed in the Pigpen and chosen by Gussy to better enhance a particular aspect of Robbie's character that Gussy was trying so hard to understand. These were exercises that kept Gussy in tune. Then, when she found more paper or cardboard, she was already more advanced in techniques and sensitivity, more accurate and selective with lines. These are just Gussy's practice pieces that show how she evolved."

Tad reached into the first bulging pillowslip for an open book which was glued to a board. He handed it to the curator as if it were made of snowflakes. "Here is Robbie's open book-shaped self when teaching girls. How happy his face is!" Tad reached farther into the case and carefully began to unwrap as workers crowded closer.

"Here, Gussy painted Robbie's beautiful, undistorted real self on a piece of glass. Then, Doll left the park for quite some time, the door to the Den was locked, the record was driving tenants crazy. Lonely, hungry little Gussy, sobbing, threw a cup that was full of coffee at this 'Robbie.' But next morning Doll came home and Gussy dried and glued the broken pieces back together. She knew now," Tad wiped his eyes, "exactly how Robbie felt every time that Doll left. She knew now exactly how it felt to be so fractured, detached, splintered! When the pieces were glued together, and Gussy was happily back in the Den, she really understood how, so often, Robbie had to instantly fit his shattered self together and put on a smooth, even front for people who were so important to him, and he was so important to. Gussy liked this picture better than all of her other works, never thinking that anyone else would ever care to see it, ever understand the importance, the significance of its imperfect being. She kept it just for herself." Tad's tears dribbled across the cardboard-backed mosaic, becoming part of tessellated glass as he handed it to the curator and she in turn carefully passed it around to the workers.

He unwrapped a piece of linen and spread its frayed edges. "Another view of Robbie's tortured face, when life felt flat, shapeless, ragged, useless—Doll was gone too long."

Using elbows and hands, Tad tried by himself to open a tightly-wound scroll. "No matter how hard she tried, Gussy could not get this particular paper to stay opened by itself. So Gussy nailed it to her table until it was finished. See the puncture marks? Then, like Robbie himself, the picture's inward turning instantly came back as soon as it was 'unsecured'. So this is how Gussy drew Robbie, when he finally locked the door and turned inalterably inward, away from everybody, smoking, drinking, listening to Doll's scratchy record." The curator wiped her eyes on the sleeve of her smock, handed the scroll to her main assistant and pointed to square boards stacked in a corner. "A back board! Not entirely opened! Robbie's room!" Reluctantly the assistant left the room.

Very carefully Tad unwrapped the next item. "Here is a Robbie that Gussy painted on a big, flesh-colored, paper heart. She tore it into still-connected pieces that dangled like shreds of flesh, still moving in the air, still barely alive as Robbie himself, too often felt.

"Here Gussy painted Robbie's hard but warm blue eyes on a little piece of metal. She scratched those same eyes onto this piece of rusty iron." Tad began to talk faster, to be sure that everything he wanted to relate would have its own time. And the articles disappeared as soon as they were handed to the curator for fast directions to the workers.

"Doll's face is inside this zippered cloth. Viewers would wear it out in their zeal to glimpse the special woman that Robbie kept warm and secure deep down inside of himself."

Tad was laughing hysterically, yet crying at the same time as he took more things from the bags and talked faster and faster. "Robbie is everywhere inside these cases! His ruggedness is part of bark, his hardness is of rock. His softness is on this velvet, but look how the face seems to bristle when rubbed the wrong way! His rippling laughter is caught within this corduroy; his lost sense of time is on the face of this broken clock.

"And where did Gussy find the exquisite time it must have taken to bring beaten-back elegance out of this scrap of satin; to coax Robbie's common touch from this tattered burlap?"

From another pillowslip Tad took a stack of envelope backs and spread them out: "Robbie's hollowness is here in a knothole, a cavern, an abyss, a grave hole." He closed his eyes and reached inside, again and again, flinging pictures over his head and around the room, to the dismay of the curator. "Suddenly, Gussy was seeing Robbie's face whenever and wherever she opened her eyes."

Tad rescued a piece of paper from the floor, sat on the desk, and tenderly blew the drawing into the air. There was a catch in his voice: "Robbie's zigzagging cellophane chain meanders there, in and out among laughing girls, weaving them together with warmth, food, and acceptance. Now, I understand why Robbie always wore that chain around his neck, and was always adding to it. That chain was a ticking clock that he was always adding precious time to. Only the chain, itself, would know when Robbie's time had run out."

Tad slid to the floor, amidst scattered balls of crumpled newspapers, pillowslips and sketches. He rested his face in his palms and allowed hot tears to flow through his fingers. "Gussy had fallen in love with Robbie and never even knew it!" Silence.

Tad lifted, scattered and blew papers. "Robbie's face is on these paper 'leaves', the crescent of a moon, the curl of a soothing wave, a whisper of wind." He picked up a bigger paper. "Look closely, Robbie's caring eyes are designed into every one of these puzzle-like pieces on this protective turtle shell-on-wheels that was Robbie's trailer."

He squeezed his eyes together. "As hard as she tried, as much, and as fast as she drew, Gussy could not get that arresting face out of her eyes, her mind, her heart, her soul. She was never even seeing him, yet without trying or asking, Robbie was taking over Gussy's space and Gussy's time. He was becoming everywhere, on every discard that Gussy rescued from the Pigpen, insignificant little fragments, in the eyes of everyone but Gussy."

Suddenly Tad was quiet, while the room itself seemed to wait. "But now," he said at last, as he stood up beside the desk, gathered armfuls of the sketches and held them close to his body, "every little fragment of Robbie belongs here in this gallery. It doesn't even matter how this art is displayed. You, me," he pointed around the room, "Gussy, Robbie's girls, tenants, pier people, sloppy drunks from dark bars, homeless people, prostitutes, homosexuals, Negroes and ethnics that Robbie loved so much, ragged little kids, newspaper readers. Every single one of us deserves to enjoy every aspect of Robbie, for one last time, before his very nature is divided, sold, scattered apart forever among friends and strangers alike, who admire, relate to or enjoy the wonderful, lovable, unusual person that he was."

Tad felt in the final pillowslip, took something out, closed his eyes, inhaled the fragrance. "Here is the last, where Gussy carved Doll's virginal face on a new bar of soap!"

Workers descended upon the papery chaos, while the curator got on the telephone to enlist more helpers.

69. On and Under the Balcony

A worker held up cupped fingers making a frame to look at the collage in his other hand. "Fantastic!"

"Open that extra workroom!"

"I know just the caption for this!" The curator took a pencil from her hair bun, wet her fingers and thumbed through her marked-up copy of Gussy's diary.

Caught in the excitement, now Tad <u>had</u> to see the pictures–it would help to better know Gussy and that summer at Last Resort! He <u>was</u> going to enter the packed gallery, <u>now</u>! He jerked down a paint-spattered apron, seized a hammer, slung a tape around his neck and dashed out the back door. Tearful, smiling viewers exiting the rear, hurried to the front again. "Three times, and we still can't even get near Robbie's Wall," a woman sobbed!

Extra policemen were directing at entry doors trying to keep spectators somewhat flowing. Now Tad was even more determined to become part of the pain and ecstasy inside this gallery, where Dom insisted, "Legends are being born!"

People, tightly laddered on the steps, waited to funnel in. Tad held the hammer high and shouted, "Make way! I work here!" Magically, a narrow pathway opened.

Above wide open doors was the only "sign"–an enlargement of the mailbox with "last resort" carved into its wooden post by Robbie's scalpel. Tad would have missed the humble sketch, if he–like other viewers looking up–had not been following Dom's reports in the Wake of daily changes and additions to the gallery. More than any other articles in local and national papers, it was Dom's that kept enticing the same people back, again and again.

Inside the open doors, Tad pushed under a giant blowup hanging above him. Quila was sitting up there at her table across from Bowie. Her prophetic words were below: "Aye, with less than a drop o' printer's ink this lifeless trailer park and this whole dreary town will be reborn!" Her vacant eyes stared past a ragged curtain. Smoke from her herbal cigarette and the glistening of her earrings were, for Bowie, turning gloomy candlelight into a spell-like trance. Tad shuddered ahead. Beside him policemen stood guard at a glass jug, "For Gussy!" People were continually stuffing it with money!

With hammer high, Tad loudly explained his way through the slowly surging crowd. Stepping through the initial archway, he noticed a restraining rope at a staircase and a sudden whim grabbed him! He jumped the barrier and raced up steps that led to a narrow balcony encircling all of the adjacent viewing rooms. Here he could overlook the whole show and get a general feeling before he joined the eager crowd below! (Here, said Dom, gallery workers also kept an eye on the viewers, yet what little scraps they managed to steal just seemed to be okay, and were never reported!) Tad stepped into narrow darkness.

Wow! This curator has guts, Tad thought as his hands slid along the railing. What daring imagination! Only a small, unimportant gallery could risk such shock to the world of art! "Only a shrewd art lover would realize the potential in being first to recognize these raw, rule-ignoring creations!" the San Diego Tribune commented. "Planners must have uncanny feeling for throngs of mostly ordinary people, from far and wide, to keep them coming back, again and again, merely to an art show!" the reporter concluded.

Planned illumination was keeping the gallery in perpetual twilight for during this spectacular show, the gallery never closed! A pleasant mix of odors was playing in warm rising air and a faint haunting melody was coming from the farthest room. The crowd must be expecting this for a profound hush was seizing spectators as they filtered into the entrance. Why, that must be Doll's Song!

Tad peered over and through arches into all the rooms below. Huge reproductions of Gussy's most dramatic works, with enormous captions below, stretched across top portions of every room. With this magnificence high in view, unfortunate viewers in the middle of rooms who were being unwillingly swept into and out of the gallery were at least rewarded with immense emotional impact. At least, these visual giants represented the basic drama of this unheard-of happening.

Readers as well as viewers were being served, for each wall had oversized paragraphs from Gussy's diary, reproduced in her own writing. Slowly, sliding along the handrail, Tad encircled the imposing display. But words, sketches and collages were not the main magnetism. Peeking, exactly like Bowie had done, was the incurable attraction.

At the middle of every wall stood, even larger than life, front walls of the main trailers! According to Dom, these were painted, screened, curtained and "shabbied" in authentic ways. At both ends of these mock trailers Gussy's sketches and collages were displayed, behind plastic over-sheets. Workers on ladders kept moving things, filling empty spaces with works and sketches that Tad had just brought, while cameras clicked and flashed.

At "trailer" fronts people were stooping, stretching, angling to peek, like Bowie had spied. What genius! "Upon each trailer at approximate eye-levels," said the Wake, "watch for Bowie's attached poking wires to push aside a curtain, or one of Bowie's viewing spots which is painted so that the eye is easily led to it. Of course," the reporter added, "there are many more spying spots along each trailer, than Bowie actually had." In fact, workers must have used up the full, extended length of every trailer, thought Tad, watching the wedged-together voyeurs, spying with impossible contortions!

On inaccessible backsides of the trailers, Tad could see from this vantage point, dozens of Gussy's sketches boxed like peepshows, positioned at eye levels. (At the back of each trailer, Dom had told him, was a door to the main utility rooms, from where workers rushed back and forth without being viewed or interrupted. There were also cots for helpers, for everyone was working day and night until after the funeral, or possibly until after the show's closing!) From this high lookout, Tad saw that many boxed scenes were illuminated with spotlights, flickering candles, artificial moonlight or fake lightning!

Why, this showing would be recorded in the history of art galleries!

As crowds sifted through big archways connecting each room, workers on ladders tacked up Gussy's countless practice sketches. Perhaps they were later to be covered with plastic? Or maybe, Tad smiled, they were put there "just because," even in their smallness, they <u>deserved</u> to be included! This action seemed to soothe and slow the ardent viewers, to entertain and satisfy them as they half-inched along. Some even had binoculars!

Tad began his second walk. Why, this really was a huge storybook for adults, as the Wake described it! Happenings within trailers had been observed by Bowie, but frozen in time by Gussy. The tale was illustrated and written on mammoth wall-pages being copied in newspapers all over the country. This original edition had been "published" by the imaginative, gutsy curator, yet, it was common, ordinary listeners, peekers and smellers who inspired constant innovations, bigness and reality that the curator sensed they all deserved.

"What a show! Starting with one wall and ending with five rooms!" Dom, (Gussy's father and reporter from the Wake), had watched it evolve.

Incredible, Tad thought: viewers seem more important to the curator than potential buyers! Perhaps she sensed more value from this far-fetched showing than from sales. "As popularity keeps doubling," said one newspaper, "giant ashtrays at the entryway are overflowing, carpets are wearing to the floorboards. No matter what sad shape it's in, almost very piece of art is already sold or spoken for!" Tad could see below him people vying for new pictures and "sold" tags being applied before the works were even hung! Viewers just wanted to own forever a piece of the once-in-a-lifetime warmth within these walls!

Tad watched the quiet mass below and shook his head in disbelief. At most art shows affluent, well-dressed patrons stood off at a distance. Paintings were flat, without dimension. If anything, they smelled of pigment and turpentine, were static and needed a special vocabulary, some knowledge of technique. But this audience below him was made of largely everyday folks who had probably never even been to any art gallery; they wore old house dresses and dirty work clothes. They cared nothing for techniques, they were looking at colorful character, raw emotion rather than finished art. They already knew intimate details about people and places displayed here–Gussy's diary was in all of the newspapers.

"Odor is so important!" said the Wake. And from above, Tad could catch the secrecy going on! "On most of the pictures a little corner of the protective plastic has been slyly pulled aside. Viewers insist on smelling Pug's homey towel-of-an-apron, smeared with peanut butter kisses and finger wipes of frosting. They want to sniff of Fay's odd perfume, Enoch's paper bag drugstore, Robbie's fragrant Den and Quila's simmering Gypsy tea as she stirs it with a special stick. They want to poke at Gussy's miniature Den pillows–will they too get whiffs of nutmeg, orange peel or bay?"

On the narrow walkway beside him news photographers were adjusting equipment and stringing wires. Commentators were already whispering into microphones.

Arising from Pug's trailer was the scent of a simmering soup bone, herbs and garlic. Above Quila's trailer arose the brewing of wild tea. Over Robbie's Den was the aroma of popcorn, and coffee tinged with nutmeg! Pots were suspended above candles, so rising heat could release their essence slowly, constantly!

Tad was amazed at silence below. "Viewers don't want to intrude their own personalities into this special world; they want to keep it 'pure,' exactly as it was." Another paper added "Although hints of Robbie's endless record can be faintly heard throughout the gallery, observers also strain to hear Pug's endless pitting and snapping, the hiss of Robbie's gurglet, the beat of Lolli's palms. Leaning closer: could Quila's wheeze be captured?"

People below him were feeling an intimate part of Last Resort, and it was time for Tad to feel this same personal closeness. Two-at-a-time he raced down stairs, hopped the rope, held his hammer high and pleaded: an instant pathway was lined with compacted bodies.

He was inside the first room, the very soul of that last joyous, yet terrible summer, standing at Bowie's Wall, through whose eyes the public would mostly be spying. Bowie was standing beside him!

There was no mock trailer of course, thought Bowie, for I live nowhere. Instead, the trellised underpart of Quila's wagon was spreading across the upper wall. Bowie was barely visible in speckled shadows. Bigger than life were his lonely, vacant, staring eyes. Smoke curled from a cigarette, the comforting body of Mange was pillowed beneath his head.

Looking below the enlargement, Bowie's body trembled with forced-back tears. Like hastily torn cardboard pieces of his heart, happiness and agony exploded all over the wall for everyone to gasp at. Bowie stepped closer. Under his shapeless hat, Bowie's non-peeking eye was only a puckered slit that dirty hair stringed over. People beside him were leaning, checking to smell if those puzzled pieces were really sliced from wine bottle corks.

Above now, Bowie was listening in restroom rafters, in the hot center of Robbie's shed, poking aside Gussy's paper curtains, pulling out Fay's chink-rag. He peeked through scratched paint at Gussy and Enoch enjoying odd meals; he stood in back of Pug's trailer savoring the midnight smell of simmering soup. Gussy had imprisoned Bowie's patience as he waited for moonflowers to open, as he suffered loneliness while wrapped in his furry bed, as he hunched closer to tiny embers in the windy darkness of the canyon.

The last group of Bowie's pictures was hardest to bear. Anguish was in every pencil stroke as Bowie's fist shredded wire and shattered glass in Gussy's door window. Hopeless guilt had been caught on paper as Bowie slumped on Gussy's doorstep, shouting, "Her father warned me a child would kill her!" He could almost feel the excruciating pain again, as he burst from Robbie's shed, holding his injured eye. The same despair gripped him as Quila in her underwear put a mangled hand on his paper shoulder: "The child never breathed." How could Gussy have had the composure to sketch in the midst of such shock and despair? Bowie was suddenly torn from this peeper's wall, for the crowd was determined to move across the room, pushing Bowie toward Quila's Wall. But Quila had pushed ahead of him.

Closer to her own wall now, Quila guiltily watched herself stamping up the wagon steps, "Dammit, there was so much more to Lolli that I never got to use!"

Gussy had drawn Quila sitting on her narrow porch, "The only place in the world where Quila allows herself to share love," wrote Gussy. One real-feathered finch sat on Quila's upturned hand and Mange was resting his head in Quila's lap. Quila's milk bottle in another picture was stuffed to overflowing. Gussy called it "Milking Human Guilt." Quila felt the shame of it and huddled deeper into her black dress.

At the middle of the wall stood the angled front and side of Quila's faded wagon. Standing on tiptoe, around bobbing heads, Quila got glimpses of her own flickering silhouette on the shabby door curtain as she sipped from her serving spoon.

All along the weathered wagon viewers were stooping, stretching and angling to squint with one eye and spy into the mysterious world of a Gypsy. Through a little knothole Quila watched as she, herself, darkened eyebrows, widow's peak and scowl, "Transforming her sweet old face into a vile creation that could manipulate any happening into becoming her own advantage!" Again, Quila felt excruciating shame. Sidestepping along, she peered between wooden sideboards as Gussy mended the dress Robbie had torn, as Gussy lifted Quila's own wispy hair with a stubby pencil.

Two women jostled in front of a knothole. Quila stooped down, came up between them and glanced through the coveted space at herself kneeling before the old trunk and feeling, without seeing the scattered gems.

There up on the side wall, Quila rocked on Robbie's doorstep: "I love ye overmuch. Like me own son—I mean, daughter!" Quila shook with grief. And there, with ragged hair, torn dress and desperate eyes, her arms held out, Quila tried to reach Robbie's trailer. Suddenly knocked from position, Quila decided to see the rest of her own pictures another time. Her eyes were hurting, her heart was in agony. Suddenly, she saw Fay, whom she hadn't seen in days, moving toward the next archway, looking even more desperate and fragile, almost dragging herself along into the next room.

A lighthouse with sad, searching beacons—Fay's own eyes—towered down on a beach of broken shells. Seaweed hair hung down and dipped into frothy water. Red finger-nailed hooks were beckoning fishes who were wearing sailor hats! Fay just sighed.

Lower, Fay herself, trudged a rut to the restroom with a douche bag slung on one shoulder. "But how can I put Fay's painful, gagging cough, deep despair and hopelessness into merely lines or color?" Gussy's words agonized below. Over there was a bruised and bloody Fay kneeling beside Doll's suitcase throwing out a real curl, a real feather and a real beetle. A portrait of feverish, childlike Fay was tying a ribbon around damp, uncurled hair. There was Quila pointing into Fay's cup. "A rich suitor is on his way. You'll see!" And there, Fay was throwing things into the fishnet, shouting, "He likes me! Exactly like I am!"

Beside Fay, a blond sailor pressed a finger on Fay's wind-tossed hair as she walked in fancy shoes too close to the hungry sea. The sailor shied back in surprise as he smelled his almond-scented finger. Next to him, a woman in dark glasses fluttered carmine fingertips across Fay's sea-green eyes and folded a dab of color into her handkerchief! Everywhere, workers were trying to protect the pictures with plastic before they were touched, or partially whisked away, something that had never happened before at an art show!

Slowly, Fay moved ahead to the replica of her own trailer, looking for the chalky rose, but compassionate fingers had smudged it out. Round windows were cut from the trailer and curtained like Fay's. Looking into widened windowsill slits, as others were doing, Fay watched herself ironing a bizarre costume, serving canned meals, and cuddling the Chips.

At last it was Fay's turn to stand on a box too high for children, pull out a chink rag and look through real candlelight while she entertained a sailor boy. Then it dawned on Fay: shy, naïve little Gussy had also been using Bowie's peekholes to enlarge upon her drawings!

Juju, or evidence of her, was across the room from Fay's, on half the opposite wall. It took a long time for Fay to worm her way over there. Looking down through Quila's latticework were sad blue eyes as Bowie must have seen them from his shadowy lookout. Lips were blowing out a match as Bowie held it through a square; Juju's mournful blue eyes in the giant picture were saucer-size. Fay held both fists to her chest and struggled along.

Juju was the cherub Doll was bathing up there on cardboard, blowing bubbles into bathwater with a straw, passing a real feather between soapy noses. Doll was up there creating soap sculptures in Juju's hair. Juju was the little body tucked into Doll's lap as she sang a lullaby. Why hadn't Fay ever found those kinds of beautiful moments with Juju?

Beneath Quila's wagon Juju nestled her shivering into the warm curve of Mange. Little hands planted Gussy's bottle fence. Juju's rag, Fay's black panties, trailed patterns across the dirt. Juju was the shadowy urchin licking a butter wrapper. She was the culprit in fancy diapered bottoms that was always, always beneath Fay's spanking boards. Fay sobbed.

Gussy had never once showed Juju's blotched face and many viewers were expressing disappointment. But like a hidden signature, Juju's rag betrayed whenever she was an unseen part of any picture. Though spectators understood that Gussy couldn't bear to have Juju stared at, to reproduce her miscreated face, it was plain they felt cheated. Gazing longer at the soiled piece of Fay's ragged panties, viewers at length sensed the despair and stench of the unseen child. They seemed to sadden with resignation as they sidestepped on to the next pictures. Fay had never seen her own daughter doing these things, but now she saw Juju watching Gussy create a clothespin doll; a woozy ragamuffin sucking her Sunday bottle of mixed liquors; a wistful waif watching Robbie throw some other laughing child into the air.

A giant paragraph from Gussy's diary was beneath Juju's pictures: "How horrible I feel, stealing Juju's rag to finish her pictures. Nothing else would do! I couldn't even cut into her precious treasure, until I saw her hugging another pair of panties, stolen from Fay's drawer." Fay's arms were so constricted by people pressing tightly around her, she couldn't wipe away the hot tears. Oh God, she had had too much. No wonder the same people came back day after day after day. One could not handle, emotionally, all of this in one viewing. Fay leaned her fragile, painful body against other bodies pressing against her.

The bottom of the wall belonged to the Chips. In the dominating picture they sat on the floor of the Den, each with one foot in Robbie's lap. "Can't ya bandage our other two feet, too, so's we can play like other kids with real shoes?"

Mindlessly the Chips jumped on the bedspring, dabbed Gussy's trailer in wild colors, and, lying on their stomachs, gazed enviously at Gussy's pretty doorstep.

There was one group of pictures where the Chips were banging on Fay's door:

"Let us in, Mama, it's scary, cold and rainy out here!"

"Mama, help us! Juju's messed 'er britches, and it's leakin' down 'er legs!"

"It's dark, everyone's in bed! We haven't had supper!" "As usual," said Gussy's diary, "Fay just turns the record player higher and becomes more attentive to her current customer." The last of Fay's emotions shriveled into a single teardrop that she sponged away with her tongue as she watched Louie shyly pushing into the next room.

High on the right hand wall was a giant Lolli on her towel, looking down through her beautiful sly brown eyes, rubbing "suntan oil" into shapely limbs, but, Louie smiled, Gussy had turned the oil into white opera gloves, glistening white hosiery and a white face mask!

Curious fingers had rubbed at the chalked-on curves of a smaller "Lolli" below, until the black interior showed through, just as though Gussy had planned it that way (instead of just doing it for herself?) And there, Lolli dangled Robbie's smoldering shorts by a stick, sauntered to the store in hat and bare feet, or sat in the Den, studying girls with gemlike eyes. Moving along, Louie shook with emotion as he stood before the curled fetus of Lolli, sucking her white thumb and drenching Pansy Bear with black tears. Why, everyone in the park except Lolli must have accepted the fact that she was black!

Gussy's diary words explained the next picture: "Sometimes when Louie is gone at night, I look into Bowie's peeking hole to find some reasons for other Lolli pictures." Above these words was a little treasure of a sketch, where Lolli was heating a metal comb on a kitchen burner, then running it down a kinky strand of oiled hair to straighten it.

There were fewer peepholes in the trailers of this smaller room and few pictures of Lolli on the walls. "All she does is sun herself, dust occasionally, toss countless salads, pamper Whiffet and sneer about everyone who passes her 'throne.'" Lolli shared space with the iceman handing out ice chips, lemonade, flowers and fruit to children crowding around his truck, as his hand puppet made them laugh. There were a few collages of fat little Kasha and some of Mala drying dishes with underwear or kicking the wash machine.

And there was Louie, himself, picking up the beer-drenched Lolli and carrying her into the trailer like a bride over a threshold. "I wouldn't care if our baby was striped like a zebra!" he shouted. Louie was sobbing so hard he could barely see across the room, where a life-sized Enoch and Gussy were dining on a scalloped newspaper. But there was no way Louie could get close to Enoch's trailer. He was too tired from pleading and pushing. Staying closer to the wall this time, Louie shoehorned into the next room.

Gussy's wall is just ahead, thought Tad. After escaping to a worker's cot for a two-hour nap, Tad was ready to resume his consuming tour. Since the gallery was open 24 hours a day, it didn't matter how long his personal viewing might take! Tad had had no idea that each character would have been so emotional, so exhausting.

As Tad pushed past, workers up on ladders were positioning fans to keep little wind chimes constantly playing, adding new dimension to Gussy's special space.

Overshadowing scenes below was a massive, expanded view of the idyllic way Gussy saw the trash yard—a mystic, glittering, overflowing horn of plenty! Moonlight was caught by the jagged rim of a broken bottle. Starlight was captured in shattered splinters of a mirror. Tangles of hair, bits of cloth, a needle, peelings and bones sparkled like jewels from hiding places. Glowing embers of the incinerator revealed cockroaches, maggots and a slobbering rat waiting for yellow pupils and the restless tail of Spade to vanish into darkness. And, whoever had enlarged some of Gussy's diary words, had reproduced them with all of their original impact, even including blood spatters! Tad raised the hammer again, "Workman coming through!" A small path widened so he could get closer.

Sketches and collages were positioned at the first side of Gussy's Wall, preserved behind pieces of plastic. Tad pretended to measure an angle with his hammer where Gussy fed crickets, ate candle drips and dabbed the wine bag on her face as she drew. He never saw more sketches, the crowd was bodily insisting that he move along. He moistened a kiss with a tear and blew it up to Gussy sitting against the mailbox, waiting for letters that never came.

Spectators were so involved! They knew exactly how to peek into Gussy's wee workshop that was angled into the aisle like Quila's trailer. When a wire hung beside a screen, viewers were threading it through an obvious hole. This way Tad watched Gussy gaze out her kitchen window: "I've got to try, Holly, though it's the hardest thing I've ever done!"

Tad wiped wetness from his cheek and pushed aside other paper curtains where Gussy hung clothes on knotted strings, worked from cereal boxes of debris, shivered on her bed under only Luanna's skirt. How could Gussy find time and enough light to capture all of those scenes and emotions? She didn't own even one light bulb!

Poking aside the next curtain, Tad saw the vague torso of Gussy washing herself with the bag of soap chips. Seeing his apron and the tape, viewers allowed him to push farther ahead and watch Gussy studying her dictionary. Specters of Robbie's symbolic names for Pug's daughters and tenants of the court lurked in shadows, awaiting discovery: a lighthouse, a flying horse, a vulture, an elf, a goddess, a Gypsy dropping patrin and the face of wind. Tad wanted to linger, but yielded to pressures.

He moved sideways until it was his turn to peek at Gussy thumbing color up into the wooden tapestry of her ceiling. Moving along he watched Gussy tear, snip and paste. Rows deep of sketches and collages were stacked and hanging around her cramped working space.

Sheepishly, like Bowie, Tad watched rag-curlered Gussy look into the mirror. "Shit! Shit! Shit! There now, I've said it!" He peeked in other places to watch Gussy appliqué flowers on Robbie's shirt and create shoes from ribbons. There were too many tears in his eyes to study pictures. He merely read captions, then closed his eyes and imagined the scene.

On the wall beyond Gussy's trailer was a group of barely discernable pictures of Gussy in her bed, talking to darkness itself, hoping to have somehow proved that less WAS more, that slowness WAS beautiful, that work WAS wonderful when you chose to do it yourself, and that art WAS everywhere you stood! A collage of Gussy's wildly-painted trailer was sitting in the midst of patterned dirt, a bottle fence and toilet paper flowers twining up the awning poles. The bonneted silhouette seemed really burned onto the trailer's front!

Higher on the wall, Gussy added a paper spider to her broken, "webbed" window. Over there she coaxed an ant to leave. Closer by she stood on Pug's doorstep: "Can I borrow a cup of...uh...salt?" In the Den Gussy held out her hand as Quila sneered: "Yer nicotine smells like mustard, dearie!" And over there, she was entering the Den, completely hidden by pins holding "Impossible Pillows." He bit his lip: those pillows were only ashes, now.

Tad stood on tiptoe to look at several sketches over, where Gussy stood on a bench stealing thread from a bird's nest. Wow, what a lot of money on photographing and enlarging. Tad now realized that this curator's future was destined for much bigger museums!

Oh, how this girl has grown artistically! Her earlier painstakingly intricate work is gone. Sometimes a picture is portrayed with less than a dozen lines and a blur of shading!

Gussy's self-portrait possessed no characteristic to hint of any change she might make in the tenants' lives, especially not in Robbie's simple but precarious contentment.

One little sketch knocked the air from his lungs and flooded emptied spaces with tears. "There, looking up through broken glass and squirming maggots was a little cloth smile!"

Trying not to sob, Tad held up his hammer and tape. "Please let me through."

Pug now stood beneath a giant-sized picture of herself in her dark corner of the Den. "Mending, peeling, pitting, cutting, knitting, her bent head with its cinnamon hair always hiding eyes content to watch Robbie's happy nearness to Doll." Pug shook her head, "and I thought I was hiding my feelings," she sobbed.

A dowdy woman stroked a study of Pug, then slyly dislodged a pebble to hide in her pocket. People were sniffing a collage of Pug that reeked of garlic and bleach. A picture farther on was labeled "Walking Through Pug's Marvelous Laundry."

A group of sketches showed Pug tending Robbie's Den girls: sewing buttons, trimming hair, covering Stray with her apron, tearing off a handkerchief for Bones, taking down Too-tall's jeans. At the top of this grouping little girls crawled all over Guy in his lumpy chair; Guy was giving horsy rides, and they were all having a massive tickle fight.

Pug loved the sketch, "Peas." One woman pointed out picturesque names as they popped from Pug's pod-shaped trailer, all in dresses alike. The woman whispered to her husband that Gussy's finest brushes were made from these children's heads! The little peas had wings, a cape of wind, elfin shoes, a sad face, a mad face, a rosebud face. One pea was dropping toys behind her. The last pea could barely be seen, but there was a halo above its placid little face! Pug had to leave the gallery, now. She couldn't stand any more.

Tad was trapped in warm bodies trickling into the next room. Above heads, he held longing arms toward Pug's trailer, toward the kind of mother-love that he had always longed for. All he could do now was slide along until there was a lessening of pressure somewhere. However, this tight condition forced time for thinking, listening to comments, considering the overall scene. He closed his eyes and began to feel like an essential little drop of this human flow, absorbing hope, love and courage from these impossible pieces of art.

What a wonderful, sensual show, he thought dreamily. Everyone smelling, listening and feeling almost as one. Before workers had started to cover the pictures with plastic, Fay's sea-green eyes had been touched away every evening, then someone mysteriously reapplied them! Fay's chalky rose reappeared on her trailer every morning. "There are posted guards now, but it's too late to save certain pictures. The curator seems to know that missing pieces belonged to someone that was hurting, and that Robbie and Gussy would agree. Curiosity is wiping away Quila's spider-web hair. Robbie's curl is only a smudge on the reachable sketches. And there is no way at all to replace many of Juju's real curls, bits of black rag, or little nightgown knots. How strange—the manager of this gallery seems to 'know' that this showing, with Gussy and Robbie's permission, already belongs to Everyman, even if he must steal it!"

Tad was overfilled with emotion. He ducked into an unmarked door and sought one of the unused cots to fall upon again. Two hours of dead sleep passed before he had the energy to enter the gallery again.

It was time to face Robbie.

70. Robbie's Room

Tad closed his eyes as he inched along toward Robbie's Room. It was really true, what newspapers were saying. He was hearing it in countless whispers. He was seeing it in glistening eyes, and now he was feeling it in warm bodies tightly pressed around him. Gussy's "trash can pictures" were digging deeper into human psyche than conventional art could ever do! From common discards Gussy was revealing character. People were silently weeping, aching, and loving each other more. Here was a little "mushroom artist" who had popped up overnight into a notoriety that many established artists had never even approached.

"Gussy is hope with magic!" said the Pennsylvania Post. "She finds flowers in folded toilet paper, perfume in common leaves, an iron in crumpled newspapers. Gussy is merely a stand-in for the common Everyman, trying to find survival and beauty in the midst of Impossible Circumstance. In short, Gussy has made an art out of having nothing!"

Despite Bowie's daily replacements, and gallery workers' constant efforts to raise certain pictures higher or frame behind glass or plastic those collages and sketches which were especially vulnerable, Tad could see that viewers could not help but diminish certain works. From trifles they were snitching–some pictures merely had a corner torn off and stolen–Tad felt that Gussy was merely adding symbolism to lives. Lives of those, who like herself and Robbie's girls had no everyday skills to support themselves, or no one to care if they existed, nothing to work with, no place to really belong.

Pictures were sold or spoken for before they were even hung, regardless of what shape they were in. Treatment here in the gallery only seemed to add one more reason for purchase. Anyway, buyers were not paying for the coveted work of a known artist. They were paying for the sweat, despair and make-do of a sensitive creator who showed great promise. For now, though, this future artist was merely "just another one of us!"

Spectators had come to a total stop. Someone was stepping on Tad's foot, holding him back from the expectant hush waiting at the threshold of the last room. Tad decided to endure the restraint, it seemed to make him an even deeper part of this total experience, gave him time to digest this overwhelming feast for the senses and emotions. Maybe, he could find new pleasures in being slowed. "Enjoying whatever the moment holds!" as Gussy would think of it. Being tall, he could stretch higher and look closely at lesser sketches on the curves of archways. Leaning closer, he could see how Gussy had filled in between hair strands and other strokes with Robbie's words and future ideas to insure her welcomes at the Den.

According to her diary, Gussy had instigated a unique technique on standoffish tenants who never invited company into their trailers. Gussy offered to sketch the flattered subject, there in their own home, and presented them one of the best sketches. Otherwise Gussy would have had no other access to Mala, Fay, Lambeth or Quila's trailers.

Oh, God! That must be an elephant on my foot! Tad closed his eyes trying to think of something else. This was certainly different from all other art shows Tad had ever attended! "Why," according to an editorial in the Gallup Gazette, "do viewers keep coming back again and again, looking so sad and depressed when they enter, yet quietly uplifted when they leave?" Why was it so appealing to the masses, wondered Tad?

Well, secret worlds were always appealing. Without her knowing it, Gussy's secrets were now exposed on every wall, being read in newspapers all over the country! Characters in this, and other so similar stories, lived among these viewers, suffering their same poverty, hunger, despair, anger, deception. Plain charcoals were wonderful but it was the secretive peepshow treatment, odors and sounds, and partial collages that were so compelling.

Was it also more appealing because these materials were totally new to art? What other artist had ever used no-handle "brushes" of sponges, mop threads and human hair? What other artist had used weird "paints" whose refusal to blend created such a fleeting beauty all of their own? Gussy's pathetic materials proved perfect "clay" for "sculpturing" her pictures. All around him, with flashlights, hidden matches and magnifiers, people were delighting in sharing discoveries: Dust curls? Blanket fuzz? Froth? Hair snarls? Ashes? Mold? Some swore that blood, sweat and tears added realism. Some materials continued to defy identification. And, considering what they were made from, most pictures were so ephemeral, they had such a limited lifespan, as though they were made of ice. Audiences, workers and even the curator seemed to be holding their breaths until the show was over!

Many of the intended collages were still only charcoal or pencil sketches; you could tell by minute collage plans in the corners. Gussy had had enough time to discover, choose and sort, but not enough time to add all the bits of abandoned scraps that gave her drawings dimension, made them so distinctive, so personal, so devastating. So, these tiny-penciled plans were just another vital part of many drawings!

Still, it was much, much more than the mystery of Gussy's materials that kept luring viewers, kept selling newspapers still inky off the presses, kept police cars in front of the nondescript trailer park and foretold a funeral the likes of which could never have been imagined in such a drab little town as Waterfront.

How did the Portland Oregonian say it? "With absolutely no orthodox equipment, with only small cut-up hands, lonely battered heart, hungry body, and unique imagination, Gussy has skillfully distilled the character of each tenant, each trailer, each lifestyle. With only tidal debris and gleanings from a trash yard, she has found mediums more natural for her subjects than any pallet of choice colors could ever have offered."

Suddenly the weight was off Tad's foot and he entered the hush of Robbie's Room, biggest in the gallery, "the one that always smells of spiced coffee and popcorn," said Dom. The record began to play again.

Dom warned him this room would be hardest of all to bear. Tad tried to settle the sudden quiver, the catch in his breathing, tears that gathered in readiness, for even as he entered, he could sense the overwhelming presence of Robbie.

Looming over the right-hand wall was Gussy's now giant enlargement of rough, ragged, lonely Robbie sitting in the candle's shadow, behind the spiraling steam of his coffee cup, changing into a totally new being as he looked at Doll. Huge words stretched below. "Robbie is satisfied with so little: the opportunity to secretly help someone, sounds of eating and laughter in the Den, the feel of sea spray, warm sand, but most of all, Doll—just nearby."

Tad was closer to the lefthand wall so he decided to push nearer and look at Doll's Wall before Robbie's. There was no trailer here, for Doll, like Bowie, had no home. Just sketches and collages that often smelled of soap, no doubt. Pictures were farther apart than on the other walls and seemed to be fewer. Therefore, each was being studied and appreciated longer. Above everything was a huge sketch of a pensive Doll, waiting while Quila studied tea leaves in her cup. "I wish that I could meet a kind, rich man. Someone I could really love," sighed Doll. Pictured below was the bloody, clothes-torn Doll, as Gussy had first seen her. As in many pictures, even edges of a peephole were part of the sketch. And over there was that same graceful Doll spearing food with toothpicks and making Robbie trays. Above was Lambeth sitting on his porch step: "Maybe Doll might wave, or stop to have some tea."

Grouped pictures showed Doll diapering Juju in her worn towel, in flannel from Guy's shirt, in Robbie's old shirt with burn holes on it and in a flowered remnant from Pug's dress.

All alone with no other picture near it was Doll in only Robbie's shirt with bruises and bloody bandages, her beautiful legs showing for the first and only time.

Doll and Robbie were up there running for a train, and Robbie's bandanna handkerchief-of-a-suitcase was tied to a belt loop. Tad could almost hear the clacking metal wheels and feel excitement as Robbie swung Doll's little suitcase up inside of an open boxcar.

Over there, Doll touched Robbie's arm, "Please don't play that record anymore!" And there was dead, muddy, net-covered Spade, tenderly held by the grief-stricken Doll. The twisting cord around the cat's neck was the same color as red-handed Robbie, standing in front of Doll, defensively, pathetically. Yet, there above, silhouetted as they sat beside the ocean, still watching a sunset, were Doll and Robbie. They always made up.

Now it was really time to face Robbie. Tad turned around, held his hammer up, and pleaded. A small, tight, grudgingly-given path appeared.

On the right-hand side of the wall that framed his trailer were sketches of Robbie and children, where the back of Robbie's table was always lined with pathetic, glass-jarred, drooping bouquets. Robbie was holding children on his knee while fixing toys and pets, removing splinters and glass, bandaging wounds, wiping tears, sharing food and drink. There he was reading to Pug's little girls as they sat on the floor, lying or dozing on velvet pillows.

Grouped together were symbolic pictures with Robbie's unmistakable eyes staring out of a sphinx, a cottonwood stump, a drab oyster. The only color on those charcoal sketches were those blue, blue eyes! And over there was a sorcerer pulling moods out of the air, a jail with eyelash-bars, an old pier stretching toward the sky but too weighed down by smiling female barnacles to make any progress. Again, the only color on those charcoal sketches were those blue, blue eyes.

Robbie's knife was over there, sticking into his carved tabletop, which in the picture was a mosaic of all the uses made of Robbie's scalpel: slashed wrists, "poky" dots on a dummy, fixing toys, mending kites, minutely dividing food, stuffing and removing Bowie's peeking holes with cigarette wrappers, taking foxtails from puppy paws and glass from tough little toes. Why, even with years behind them, Tad had never seen accomplished the staggering amount of work that Gussy had produced in such a short time!

Underneath Gussy's favorite portrait of Robbie were her own words, "You have the wisdom of a prophet, the curiosity of a child, yet you linger in a timeless sunset, Robbie."

A close-up of things in Robbie's odd cupboard was there and another of Spade pushing into the door Robbie made for her. There was the gurglet, its insides shaped like an hourglass, bubbles like sand dropping to the lower globe, waiting until it was time. "Soother of despair, enchanter of celebration," said Gussy's familiar handwriting. There was Pug's sack of food overturned on Robbie's doorstep.

There were only a few outside pictures of Robbie. "A dewdrop will do!" said drunken Robbie shaking muddy water onto the dummy. "Goodbye cruel world," sighed Robbie as he touched a firebrand to the effigy. Robbie was up there again, playing stickball, slyly hanging a bouquet on a doorknob. Sitting in the wash house with her chair leaning against a wall.

In a group of Thanksgiving pictures, Robbie was holding the wishbone–"I already got my wish!" There, raising a mug up high, he was saying, "I'm thankful it's today, instead of yesterday...or tomorrow!" There the happy, drunken Robbie was giving the final toast: "We're never so boor or proke, that we can't shind fomething to sare!" Tad knew that the real sheet of a tablecloth there, would probably smell of turkey, spices and wine.

The last scenes on the left-hand wall were well-planned and made Tad hold his breath. Robbie, sweeping coffee cups to the floor, "And nature can be so blunderous!" he was sobbing. "Signs arc everywhere," sighed Quila. "Look at that long, shroudlike 'winding sheet' on the candle." "You are affected with a strange malaise, Robbie." There was Quila running from Robbie's trailer, "Yer queer, Robbie! Ye both slept in the same bed last night!" At last, Robbie stood there staggering in the middle of the driveway, "When I find you, Bowie, you bell-mouthed stoolpigeon, I'll rip out your filthy tongue-clapper!"

Even though distracting workers on ladders were still hanging dimensional works that Tad had just delivered, the almost-reverence of this room, the arrested time-span suddenly engulfed Tad. Yet, he gathered courage, held up his hammer and demanded to get back to the first peeping hole in Robbie's trailer. There he stooped like the man before him and angled to the same degree Bowie might, before slowly peeking into slots between window and frame.

Once again, Robbie, big spoon poised, was waiting for silence to share his fascination with foods. Once again, he was weaving tales of popcorn, stirring mugs with a feather, balancing the gurglet on one shoulder and holding up a "fairy umbrella." Time stood still as Tad peeked at Robbie squeezing eggs, playing poker with artichoke leaves, splinting a bird's leg, ducking pillows, shoes and cigarettes while holding up his chamber pot. "Remember," Robbie said at last, "prejudice is just an unfamiliar 'vegetable' not lovingly introduced yet!"

In one peepshow, as Robbie poured champagne into strange containers, Gussy merely held up a cupped hand. At another peephole, "Methinks, we'll call her Gussy!"

Quila was often reading palms, tea leaves and cards. She told Robbie's fortune: "Yer goin' ta be famous overnight and take this whole sleepy town along with ye!" There was often a glimpse of serene, slow-moving, graceful Doll as she automatically helped Robbie, as she enjoyed every little motion that brought Juju any pleasure, as she stared sadly into nowhere. And in the same pictures, there was always Robbie, somewhere at the side, his eyes caressing the spirit of Doll's pristine being from within his well-planned shadows. In every picture Robbie was wearing the cellophane spiral. Now everybody, everywhere, knew why Robbie always wore and worked on that "clock." He was adding precious time to it.

Dominating the last, the Girls' Wall, which surrounded the exit doors was a gigantic flame with Robbie's blue eyes warmly burning in the middle. Moth-winged girls hovered, enchanted, around the Robbie-candle. "Always females of every race and color, grateful for even the smallest space in Robbie's Den, the smallest niche in Robbie's heart."

Single portraits were grouped. "My nose is hooked!" "I'm an orphan." "My toenails turn up." "My eyes are crossed." "I have horrible acne!"

On the floor and totally happy again were Robbie's girls sitting on Gussy's Impossible Pillows. Robbie was blowing out a match, telling Gussy about the special place for everyone's uniqueness. Again, Robbie asked "squashes" and "potatoes" to snuggle up to the black "eggplant." Robbie, inspiring "buds" back to school to become beautiful "flowers."

Opal cried again in Pug's lap, "Black jest don't wash off, burn off or wear off!"

There were sketches named Skunk, Peaches, Bones, Too-Tall, Tex, Dago, Butte, Arkie, Nora, Amiko, Trash and all of the other faces named in Gussy's diary, "All with the very same haunting eyes and very same bottomless stomachs."

What massive amounts of time Gussy's gathering, sorting, sketching and pasting must have taken. Yet she had been hurrying! It was this very hurrying, in fact, that made her sketches so bare, so true. Since the Pigpen fiasco, according to her diary, Gussy reasoned that after the baby was born, not only would she not have time or concentration, but, never again would she have the same intense urgency and gut feelings that were then hers. "Never again will it be exactly now," she had written.

Instantly that same intense urgency again flared inside Tad, as though he, himself, had in a single heartbeat become the final needed note in some grand, unknown, unfinished chord!

It was too much! He was suffocating with exquisite pain and yet, strange joy and indecision. Never again would it be exactly now for Tad either. Gussy was in the hospital, connected to feeding tubes, stuffed with drugs, sleeping pills and pain-killers. For at least three weeks nobody could even risk seeing, infecting or exciting her or the fragile baby. Wonderful Robbie was dead. Doll and Fay Rose were wandering aimlessly, with seldom the heart to even return to the trailer park at night. No one knew where all of the girls were, though many drifted back after dark to lean against the washhouse wall and have a cigarette while they wept or stared at Robbie's empty, blackened shambles.

The park was at its lowest. What could Tad possibly do to take advantage of now? What could he accomplish for Robbie and his girls, for Gussy, the tenants, and all of Robbie's and Gussy's admirers? How could he inspire? How could he make a difference at Last Resort? For the first time since Sunday school he closed his eyes and asked for guidance.

Instead of advice, an "impossible" picture of Last Resort began to unfold in his mind!

He had to get out now, but the only way out was to trickle along with the crowd. Then he heard it too. That noise the Wake often hinted at: a faint jangle of keys, reminiscent of Robbie, as though someone unseen walked among them. Tad shut his eyes and allowed himself to flow, or rather, bleed along with the rest of the hurting, puzzled throng. With closed eyes his ears could focus without distraction on the origin of that telltale sound. Tad glanced upward, wondering if anybody else had figured the answer. The park's new manager, Lolli, was just taking her daily stroll around the dark balcony. Lolli had to be part of all this, but she just couldn't stand to be seen guiltily crying.

Another shove and Tad was out, sobbing his way toward the funeral parlor next door. Even if he couldn't get inside, he had to be close, to be a part of the ceremony, a part of the crowd, to mourn with Robbie's plight, to exalt with Robbie's sacrifice.

He had to share with Robbie, somehow, a golden promise that was taking root within himself of Tad's own final freedom and all of the exciting steps leading up to it!

71. "The" Funeral

Enoch couldn't figure out why this peculiar corpse was out of order again! He scratched his balding head and wrinkled his graying brows as he stood beside the coffin that was curtained off from the organ player, prying eyes, muffled whispers, and indiscreet camera flashes. Ah, he was just too hurried, nervous, and awed by the overplayed magnitude of the whole affair, too anxious that the body live up to what the whole world seemed to expect of it!

He could almost feel the crush of humanity pressing against the policed entrance of his mortuary. The smell of weeds and flowers in dozens of jelly glasses, old cans, little vases and baskets pressing close around the casket and lining sides of the room were overpowering. He was constantly wiping his eyes and suppressing sneezes.

Hours before the funeral hundreds of people had trickled past Robbie's casket, flooded into and out of the adjacent art gallery, and the combination had caused such a traffic jam that officers cordoned off and began to police the whole block, just as they had done to the trailer park. Plainclothesmen arrived early to mingle unnoticed among mourners, for with the notables there also came the commoners who might need a watchful eye.

Instead of cowardly, pondered Enoch, Robbie's suicide has been sanctified! "As one," according to a whispering, on-the-spot radio announcer, "everyone here is grieving. Artists and clergymen are mourning, shopkeepers, housewives, pregnant girls alone, scarlet ladies and effeminate males, Indians, Negroes and ethnics of all kinds, people holding dogs and cats, parents with all their children, fishermen, sad-faced kids that played stickball with Robbie. Sailors are everywhere, salting these mourning multitudes with white uniforms."

But not Fay Rose, thought Enoch.

Even The Joint had closed, so that waitresses, bartenders, and customers could attend the funeral. Old men on porches down the street that Enoch had often seen Robbie talking to, sat waiting on chairs they had brought—hours too early. Old women who had received bouquets and compliments from Robbie stood patiently leaning on anything nearby. An engineer from a train was there in his working outfit, but not Fay Rose. Enoch could have spotted her, smelled her, and heard her in a heartbeat.

Strange, Enoch thought, as he peeked out between heavy drapes surrounding the coffin, how this funeral seems to belong to everybody! Each has come to say his own private goodbye, to grieve, to see the curl, or tuck a "token" into the open coffin.

Almost as much as each wanted to see the body, everyone was eager to see the tenants. Not Gussy, she was still in the hospital. But the others would surely be there: Juju, Doll, Bowie, Pug, Lolli, Quila, and possibly Fay Rose—those wretched, glorified tenants of Last Resort, the objects of Gussy's ugly pictures that were "enshrined" in the gallery next door, the objects of daily newscasts all over the country.

Enoch closed the peeking slit in the curtain. Well, they would all just have to wait, all of them. Press photographers and reporters for whom there were not enough reserved seats, even noteworthy persons of the community who sprinkled themselves anonymously among common folks. The young minister was uneasily shuffling notes and the organist was beginning again her limited repertoire. They'd all just have to wait!

Enoch took unusual pride in details of his funerals. His corpses resembled photographs so exactly they almost seemed to breathe when Enoch was through with them and their big moment arrived. But, however individual his bodily reproductions were, Enoch permitted nothing else to deviate from traditional requirements, that is, until he came upon this corpse, about whom everything was unprecedented, eerie and infamous, or was it famous? Enoch couldn't quite make up his mind about Robbie.

Other irregularities had been easy to spot in viewing days before the funeral. Something obvious had given a clue. A less exacting mortician would never notice that one shirt pocket was ever so slightly mounded, or that the satin pillow raising the head of black curls was slightly awry, but Enoch did. He scooped from one of Robbie's pockets pieces of a torn bridal photograph and painstakingly fitted them together before returning the photo of a beautiful young Pug to its final resting place. Gently he lifted the pillow and drew out, of all things, a melted phonograph record, probably the one that Robbie played incessantly!

Each addition was a token from someone who wanted Robbie to know of the profound effect he had had on that individual's life.

Orientals buried money with their dead, and Enoch had seen rabbits' feet and other common fetishes placed on bodies, but never such an odd assortment as in this unparalleled case: single flowers, popped and unpopped corn, assorted vegetables, a spent candle, little toys, a storybook, etc. It was becoming ridiculous, over-dramatic, Enoch objected to himself. And the organ music was beginning to really sound over-strained.

Many things were being added to Robbie's coffin, but things were subtracted as well! So many little scraps had been torn from his bloody shirt, that now, Robbie's sleeves needn't be rolled up anymore. Their ragged, quickly-torn edges, just naturally came to the spot on Robbie's arms where Pug had wanted them to be. And, except for "the" curl (why was that so sacred?) Robbie's hair was shorter now, all over. Little snips of the hurriedly hacked-off strands betrayed from where the treasures had been stolen!

A last time, Enoch dragged his eyes over the body without success. His imagination was overworked. Again he pushed the stubborn forelock back into the curly mass; it made the face fragile, vulnerable, too sensitive. Automatically, Enoch started to refold the hands.

"That's what's wrong," he whispered with relief, "the hands!"

Enoch folded hands so that a wedding ring might show, if there was one. This time, however, Enoch gently refolded the hands as they had been, the wrong way, right over left.

When the tear rolling down his cheek was tidied, he sat on the bench and shook something out of his shoe. He removed Robbie's shoe and dropped into it a coin with a hole in its center.

He motioned his assistant to pull aside the curtains. The organist left the room, and a new record of Doll's Song began to play softly as Pug had requested.

The minister cleared his throat, "Shall the finished clay say to The Master Potter: 'What is this miscreation that must be called Robbie, instead of Roberto?'"

After the stirring eulogy, those inside filed numbly, slowly past the casket, unheeded tears glistening and a strange exultation in their eyes, as though in this special death there lay a personal resurrection for each one who lingered at the coffin, for each one who surrendered a token to this body that headlines called merely, "Robbie."

The room was finally cleared and police threw open the front doors for the ever-growing mob outside to file past the casket. Enoch kept clucking in satisfaction as he watched grievers viewing his handiwork. He had done a good job on the body, especially considering the circumstances of death, and despite the fact that Pug insisted upon no shave, the shirt unbuttoned to the waist (thereby showing many of the strange-haired dolls), and upon burial in exactly the same soiled and bloody clothing that Robbie was already wearing.

Enoch had allowed all of the strange, added objects to remain, to be buried as they were put on the body, unnoticed. Including what was hidden by Robbie's bloodied right hand, knotted around the wedding-ring finger: a torn off and knotted strip of the black silk rag that Juju loved so much.

It was over for Enoch, now. He was relieved, tired of living at the mortuary since his shameful episode with Fay, tired of no one to talk to unless they were dead. If he were careful, he could live the rest of his life on money he had saved, and even share it with Fay Rose and her little family. How had Quila said it? "It's high time ye chucked the pills, got a mite o' dirt in your craw and lived it up a little!" It was okay to live it up a little, to be himself joyously, for now there was proof–that little strip of black rag–that Fay had returned!

At the back of the workshop he changed to a tee shirt and khaki pants, then dropped his formal clothing into a wastebasket. He stood before a mirror, wondering if Bowie were watching. He removed a small toupee, dropped it also into the basket, then ran a comb through red stubs that were sprouting again.

Bowie started to snuff his cigarette into a crack beneath the window sill of the mortuary workshop, but suddenly he felt sick and guilty. Remembering black remains where Robbie's trailer once stood, he heeled the butt into dirt.

72. Quila's Change

Tap, tap, tapping–like the pecking of a bird's beak. The odd little noise on the door-window of Quila's wagon awakened her the morning after Robbie's funeral. As usual lately, she had slept in her clothes. She poured water from a metal pitcher into a metal glass: Gypsies, always on the go, preferred unbreakable things, but what difference did it make anymore? She wiped at a tear. Beautiful, wandering, bumpy Gypsy roadways would never be driven again. She swished her mouth with water, then swallowed it.

As she listlessly opened the door to leave for Lolli's, she thought she heard a robin sing as he flew from her porch. Her heart fluttered at the old familiar sign of good luck, but quickly the happy feeling settled down with a thud as she glanced toward Robbie's heartbreaking space. Why, oh why, could she still get excited over lucky messengers? They were all as phony as smashed wedding pots, she sobbed. Where were all those years with Lazlo, and all those baby Romanos that broken pottery pieces had promised? Why should she follow the patrin of daily life, when it would only lead to false hopes and disappointments?

Night after night she hadn't slept, though exhausted from non-exertion. Day after day she awoke ambitionless, visionless. She had no food for her and Bowie, but neither one of them had any appetite. Quila was existing on black coffee and a few cookies at Lolli's place; Bowie had only broken cookie bits that had survived when she removed them from her sleeve at night as they sat around the last candle drinking strong tea in silence. Occasionally, one of them picked up the almost empty shakers, sprinkled salt or pepper into their palm, and licked it. Quila couldn't tell fortunes like she used to. Her heart wasn't in it. Whenever she had to go to the toilet or the washhouse, and therefore had to catch a glimpse of Robbie's blackened ruins, she sobbed or trembled for the rest of the day.

She opened the door, scattering birds searching in vain for crumbs. She hurried down past Mange's vacant waiting place and slowly sidestepped down her stairs. Bowie was wiggling out from the dog door, slithering over to Lolli's and settling down in back of her porch step.

Quila paced numbered steps to Lolli's. Mala, Tad, Opal, and Stray were sitting in the breakfast nook. Coffee was ready but its fragrance turned Quila's stomach. Lolli's cookies sat untouched. Everyone was sitting in silence as though just grateful for togetherness.

Like myself, thought Quila, they all look like they've slept in their clothes, had nightmares and haven't bothered to look in the mirror. Though there had often been only a handful at Robbie's klatches, a handful seemed achingly lonely now. So many were gone. Overnight it seemed: Robbie, Spade, Enoch, Gussy, Fay, Doll, and Mange. Quila wondered if she missed Robbie or old faithful Mange the most. Lolli poured coffee, while Quila's thoughts wandered back into grief.

Walking home from Robbie's funeral, Quila had heard Mange howling a block away. Was he howling in pain or because everyone had left at once and he was tethered? Whining, whimpering, wagging, he acted as though someone unseen to Quila accompanied her as she walked, someone unseen who was consoling him with gentle hands! Mange barked feebly, his bulging eyes oozing with effort, while some "presence" left his side, beckoned, and Mange strained at his unaccustomed rope.

Crossing herself, Quila had hurried into her wagon and rummaged in the chest until she located and hung around her neck a sparkling gem. (Roms swore by the power of diamonds to prevent madness!) Meanwhile Mange tossed in misery and tugged on his rope.

Quila rolled a cigarette and smoked it as she sat looking out the window, toward, but not at the edge of the black spot that used to be Robbie's trailer. She sighed heavily, ground out the rest of the cigarette and began what she had to do.

She took the can of bacon grease, Mange's favorite taste, from back of the stove. Standing tiptoe, she took down a packet waiting in darkness. Mumbling the right words, she sprinkled special herbs into the last of the grease, stirred, and crumbled the last heel of bread.

Sitting on her porch, she had hugged the old friend as he ate a bit. She unfastened his collar and rubbed the hairless ring beneath it. He licked her tears, inched feebly down the steps, and then took off gently barking toward the hills, as though an invisible hand were encouraging him. Aye, she would miss her faithful companion, dreadfully, but what would Juju and Bowie do without his dependable warmth and comfort?

Lolli poured more coffee, but nobody broke the silence, nobody could smile, or lessen the total absence of Robbie. Quila could feel the presence of Bowie underneath Lolli's trailer as though he wanted to be close, but not with people who were grieving like he was. The park was kingless. Even Lolli had no desire for Robbie's empty crown.

Tad looked around. How could anyone jolt these lost souls, he thought. Where could anyone start? Robbie's spectacular suicide had not budged them. Gussy's plight and success had not moved them. Though every person at the park was changed, somehow, they were suspended in time. Some unusual kind of inspiration was needed before they could take up a single tangled thread of everydayness and even consider weaving it into a new pattern.

Women at their work were aimless floaters drifting with the slightest current that might distract them. At all hours shabby girls drifted to Robbie's space, standing alone or in silent groups. Occasionally, someone got a shadowy, fleeting glimpse of Fay there. In late hours of a long night (Pug had told Tad), whenever she fell asleep and dreamed of the happy twosome returning, softly laughing, hand in hand, she would get out of bed, pull aside a curtain, and Doll was always standing there, smoking as she stood across from Robbie's space, weeping as she leaned against the tool shed with her arms outstretched against the door.

With Robbie alive, aimless days of girls in the Den had held a vague, warm routine, a dependable, welcoming tide. From Robbie had flowed the only, often infrequent, passive adventure. Now, whenever anyone heard Lolli's keys jangle, smelled fresh coffee, or felt the deep vibration of the new bass player at The Joint, as one they all remembered Robbie and seemed to settle deeper and deeper into their own private mourning.

Without Robbie to scrub sinks occasionally, flies settled down on scum from diapers, dishes, mops, and coffee pots like square-shaped, living crusts. Without Robbie's watchful eye, two toilets were plugged and out of use. The washing machine, without Robbie's urging, oiling, and fiddling, had given up and was silent. Trash containers in the Pigpen were overflowing and trash blew about the park unnoticed. Without either Robbie or Gussy, everything seemed to be crumbling away. And nobody cared.

Trying in his own pathetic way to keep life somewhere as it used to be, daily Bowie haunted the gallery, renewing hollyhock petals and patching collages as the cherished bits of debris were merely stolen away again. Though every month was to be the last month of Gussy's showing, the viewing kept being extended! "Sold" tags didn't deter viewers from taking little items from each already purchased treasure. And workers could not frame collages fast enough to prevent petty thievery. Even quickly tacked-up, crude practice sketches of Robbie's eyes, curl and hands had been slyly whisked away. Even minor collages of Robbie had been slyly robbed of significant pieces.

But at Last Resort, there was nothing left of Robbie.

Tad was seized by a sudden panic to jerk the keys off Lolli's belt, gild them and hang them high over the telephone. He longed to stake off the blackened space and embosom it with golden cord. But from what he had read, heard, seen and felt of Robbie at the gallery and in Gussy's diary, Robbie would hate that. If Robbie were to have any memorial, it had to be more than morbid bleeding hearts, more than a static rectangle of glorified, black wood and metal: it had to have ongoing life! Tad knew that he couldn't even start it all alone.

Huddled in the dark safety of her dress, Quila and her wheeze seemed worse today. Often she trembled unexpectedly, like a wintry wind had suddenly engulfed her. Whenever she picked up her coffee cup the ugly beetle ring hanging from a skinny finger shook like a washer on a knotted wire. Gently Tad took one of Quila's small withered hands in his own.

Quila looked as startled by his touch, as the scabby-looking shoeshine boy whose head Tad had patted during his trip to Mexico.

"You touched me!" the boy had gasped. Falling on the ground, the boy had taken a kiss from his deformed mouth and with filthy, grotesque fingers transferred it to the hem of Tad's trousers. The boy stood up on knob-like knees and with mangled fingers pulled the edges of his mouth into a grateful smile. "What us needs, sometimes, is only a little touch, Senor."

An exquisite exhilaration had filled Tad, surpassing by far the satisfaction of preserving on canvas the agony of the leper. Instead of capturing the misery he had found on every painting jaunt in Mexico, Tad had put down his brushes and rolled up his sleeves. A final curtain had come down on his sophisticated, carefree, arty kind of life. He was sent home disgraced but totally happy to have found some realness in himself at last.

Now he felt a small surge of that same exhilaration.

With his other hand, Tad held Quila's tiny chin and looked into her face. The flesh of her facial emotions seemed kept in check now only by a web of despair lines; she seemed ready to weep at any moment. She had lost any interest in today, much less tomorrow. She was too weary, hungry and listless to get to the store, play cards or work up any fortunes.

She had even quit stealing candles from the church in the Plaza, and, according to worried Bowie, she was down to her very last stub. What did she need to see at night, she asked Bowie? She could stare at the ceiling and weep, without any light at all!

Quila was wearing, as she always did now, not a gem but a worn shell Robbie had given her, hanging by a dirty string knotted through a natural hole. It was as though she had no desire anymore to influence today or tomorrow, just to grieve over yesterday.

Quila's mournful frown was inlaid like a bad design, embedded deeper each day on a lid that nobody had ever cared to raise. Her innermost desires and talents were decaying. Tad took her other hand. Slowly, he raised the "lid," let in daylight, and peeked inside.

"I'll bet that you were a beautiful young girl, Quila. You're still so special. When one is truly gifted like you palms, cards and tea leaves serve mainly to draw the conscious mind to a focus, while the subconscious taps the universal source of knowledge. In this way the intellect enjoys an extension of wisdom and hearing into the infinite, which is not within the scope of the average person."

Tad had totally lost Quila's attention; she was merely enthralled by a gentle voice, gallantry and the touch of strong, warm hands.

"What I'm trying to say, Quila, is that your special touch is so badly needed, right now, by everyone in the park and for blocks and miles around!" Tad took a sip of coffee. "Oh, not your old black magic, sweetie, that tricked people into paying blackmail! But hidden, unused knowledge that drives illness from bodies and hearts in pain, helps people sidestep trouble, helps them find success in their own peculiar fashion, helps weave harmony from discord."

He smoothed wispy hair away from pinched-together eyes that widened in disbelief. "The lonely, sick, wayward, confused—all need consolation and advice that for many kinds of people can only be delivered in the guise of fortune-telling and other mystic-seeming means. And, if it is paid for, the words become even more meaningful and important."

He looked deep into astonished eyes. It was so quiet in Lolli's trailer that everyone heard the pathetic little wheeze as Quila breathed. "People like you, Quila, are so essential in this sad, frightening world." He opened her scarred hands, uncurling stiff bent fingers frozen into some secret Gypsy sign of protection from evil, or something.

He traced what was left of jagged palm lines. "See, it says so here, and—" he opened his own hand and lied a bit, "it says so here, too! I'm the one who's going to help!" (He could hardly contain his excitement. This was "it," Step One, and he hadn't even planned it!) "There's going to be a miraculous change in your life! You're going to rediscover old talents and apply them in new ways. You're going to have a business of your own, a really different, very needed, thriving shop right here in this park! Just like Gussy's picture of it!

"You've been dependent on people's badness for way, way too long; now you will discover their wonderful goodness!"

Quila was crying.

73. Step One

"We're going to 'package' you, Quila! Your knowledge, your intuition, your heritage are all going to waste! You and Bowie are gold mines begging to be tapped!" I'll have to hurry, he thought, there's no time to do things "right." Quila's next "destination" is already in her eyes, and I want her to at least taste of happiness, here, before she moves on.

He took a scroll of paper from his shirt pocket. He had been carrying it, not even knowing why, until now! He unrolled the little sketch Gussy had made of the Gypsy wagon, idealized and ready for Quila's business. She gasped with delight. "Come on, we're doing this together!" Tad promised, as he helped her down from Lolli's step.

There were no pipes or wires to disconnect from Quila's space. With Guy and Bowie on each side, Tad maneuvered Quila's light wagon to a new vacancy next to the street, at the first corner of the park. They reattached latticework and stabilized the tiny house. Tad borrowed supplies from Guy and Flo, briefly cleaned, then brushed yellow, blue and red flourishes onto the main designs of Quila's wagon. While he worked, Quila was already telling fortunes to curious neighbors as she sat beneath a big umbrella at a round table spread with a paisley tablecloth, all brought from Flo's place.

From under the new space, Bowie listened above him as Tad took off the top half of Quila's cupboard and moved it down beside the bottom half. Now, Tad tried to talk himself into cutting a long opening, sort of a counter top, or sample window, on the street side of the wagon, as Gussy's picture suggested.

Suddenly Tad ran down Quila's steps, looked through the reattached latticework, and shouted in to Bowie: "Get the hell out from that stick-in-the-mud place before you take root! I need you, Bowie!" With Guy's supervision they cut a long hole, then added a canvas hood which

Pug devised to shade the opening. From the cut-out portion of the wall, they created a narrow shelf on hinges that could be folded up at night to close the wagon, like Gussy's picture indicated. Tad began to realize that Bowie had a natural feeling for wood.

Tad brought dinner and candles from his mother's house. Afterward, he, Bowie and Quila sat eating apple pie and planning for tomorrow. Late that night under Quila's wagon, Bowie's full stomach and tired body felt satisfied for the first time in years and years. He slept like an innocent child until daylight without a drop of wine.

At dawn Bowie awakened to sounds above him as Quila talked to herself while she dusted and took inventory of things she possessed and things that needed throwing out. She smelled cloth pouches hanging beneath her slender dish shelf. Sometimes she shrugged, dumped the contents into her tea canister and stirred with a cinnamon stick.

Tad and Bowie continued to paint and repair the outside of the wagon. Inside, they removed useless, cobwebby plants hanging from ceiling hooks, and put up little shelves.

Everyone in the park continued to ignore Robbie's ruins. No one could look at the space without sobs or shaking. Tad couldn't even enter the suicide shed for tools so he borrowed things from Flo, the neighbors or Guy. Everyone's heart could barely stand a glimpse of the blackness, yet no one could even think of removing the very last of Robbie's presence.

Tad often paused at his work and stole a look at Bowie. He seemed to be standing straighter and Pug had trimmed his hair. Tad had told Bowie of his fears and plans for Quila, and now Bowie was hurriedly preparing soil beside the front wall in preparation for useful plants that he planned to "borrow" in the night from neighbors' yards or vacant lots. Bowie's remembering and healing will be slow, but sure, thought Tad. A warm feeling spread throughout his body, pushing out the last of his inborn aloofness toward minorities such as Bowie. Tad was slowly beginning to realize that helping redirect lives was the single thing that gave him the most joy!

Quila came out of her wagon and beckoned to Bowie as he tamped dirt around a newly potted plant. Soon, the twosome were excitedly pointing to ordinary trees that grew along the street and in hills beyond the court. Who but Quila, from wandering Gypsy days, would have known that even trees from Europe and Asia had leaves filled with usefulness? Tad took them a pad and pencil for listing and Quila rattled off a bunch of spices that would enhance various mixes. She laughed, realizing that spices were already waiting in her cupboard! "A lot of things have just been waiting," she sighed.

Quila hurried back into her wagon and pulled a big crockery jar from under her bed. "The perfect container ta save time and space!" she almost shouted. "The perfect basis fer me new little business. Medicine, tea, bath herbs, potpourris, scent jars, and sleep pillows can all be made from the same essential plants, Jofranka always said, and stored together, just waitin' fer last-minute ingredients to make the mix special!"

She shooed a spider out and dusted the jar with her hem. Tad took the crock to the washhouse for a good soaping and rinsing, and then positioned it on Quila's porch for sunlight to disinfect it.

From early morning until evening, Bowie was mostly gone now, busy with gathering. Soon fragrant new branches hung from every inch of Quila's ceiling. By candlelight the three of them cleaned and sorted materials for drying. Tad hurried the process by using Pug's low oven heat to fast-dry a bit of everything.

With soothing leaves of willow as the major bulk, they added to the crock other dried and crumbled things from the neighborhood: hollyhocks, roses, honeysuckle, mint, and bay. Bowie brought juniper, sumac berries, and Indian tea from nearby hills and canyons. Bowie was the one who loved to stir the medley, smelling the blend with obvious joy and memory.

Most plants they prepared in fairly uniform small pieces. Bigger, more perfect parts would wait at the top of the mix: flowers, leaves, and seedpods to hold back in their beautiful entirety. Quila could choose from these when needed, to make the basic combination specifically medicinal, more personal, (more dramatic?) for every customer.

Each morning Quila placed clean jars and a few spice cans on her outside table. She dipped from the crock and placed a chosen amount for the day into an earthen bowl, choosing as well several bigger items, according to the average customer's likely problems. She covered the fragrant "waiting bowl" with one of Pug's handmade flannel napkins. At last she brought from the wagon a fresh pot of tea, hung it from a metal crane and lit a candle beneath.

As a patron sat down, Quila poured two cups of tea, smiled and leaned back in her chair to really listen. After awhile, Quila lit the long-burning candle Jofranka had given her, then held her hands above it while she closed her eyes and mumbled. With warmed fingers she crumbled into a jar stronger plant pieces especially chosen as the customer talked. Then she added a scoop full of general mixture, sprinkled a spice or two, gently shook the little jar, and smelled of the contents as though they had fallen from heaven. She told the customer to use it as tea, scent or an herbal bath, according to their specific problem.

If Bowie was working outside he tried to identify some herbs by smell. But the experience made him lonesome for home. It was always then that he felt of the leather roll in the pocket of his shirt. Somehow, he just couldn't look inside, yet. He still needed something to look forward to, something to be sharing with Fawna.

Quila was handing a tiny jar of herbs to an unhappy bride. "Tie some of this love scent into your hanky dearie, then pin it to his pillow," she whispered.

Tad would often rest from his labors at Gussy's table. Elbows up, chin in his hands and eyes closed, he tried (like Gussy so often had) to think up ideas to entice the rest of the tenants into becoming involved in this initial step. Jars and material, he thought one day! Quila soon had a steady flow of little washed and sterilized jars, and clean pieces of material kept coming from Pug, Mala, and Lolli. Quila used colorful squares or rounds as lids secured with string or rubber bands, or tied little pouches of medicinal scents to hang above her wagon's shelf.

Almost every day Quila opened Jofranka's book waiting on the outside table and studied it through the helpful slots of her closed fingers. Sometimes she merely took a strong-smelling medicinal "swisher" from the top of the mixture, for stirring the customer's regular tea at home. Sometimes she picked a fresh flower top from her (almost overnight!) garden that Bowie was creating, and dramatically floated the fragrant medicine in a sufferer's tea.

Bowie never went to the tool shed; he couldn't bear the memory. He never slept in the storeroom; he couldn't stand to be cooped up, anymore. He never climbed to the toilet rafters, or peeked into any of the trailers. But he had still not overcome his wanting to be alone beneath Quila's wagon for a small part of every day. He felt a need to still absorb a lingering aura of Mange's gentle spirit. He felt a need to absorb a growing happiness around the wagon space that existed nowhere else in the morbid, stagnant trailer park. There he rested from his work and listened as Quila put on her little medicine shows.

Bowie often listened to Quila's sly tactics. When there were too many customers for one-to-one encounters, Quila had several means of delay. Sometimes she'd give the customer a leaf plucked from her ceiling and directions on where to find the herb. "Ye need to be involved," she'd insist, "to make the magic work!" Or, she'd send an unsuspecting customer to the store for a spice can, and something she needed for dinner that night. Or to the library to read up on some new plant that Bowie had discovered.

And oh, what Quila could do with nightmares! She'd listen intently, then untwist the scenes into advice that a mother would have been scoffed at for, but Quila was paid for it!

At the Den girls had largely been in big groups; Lolli still had small groups in her klatches. But now, when someone needed special attention there was no Robbie to discover or counsel her. Instead, the hurting girl, attracted by laughter, greenery, flowers, and aroma, would drift over to Quila's place. It stood out like a tiny Eden in the midst of a depressing ghetto.

Little black Opal seemed to need Quila the most, to really enjoy and appreciate the atmosphere and to amble over more often than the rest.

When all the customer needed was a willing ear, Quila poured tea and, remembering Robbie, she sprinkled cloves in the teacup of the melancholy girl who drank too much. She tapped ginger into the cup of the unwed girl with morning sickness, and a dash or two of nutmeg for the girl who just couldn't cope with life. Wiping at a tear of memory, Quila settled back to listen, smile, nod, and pat the girl's hand.

One morning even Lolli sidled up to Quila's table. She seemed listless and nervous as she sat with Whiffet in her lap. "What I probably need is a priest." Lolli complained.

"Pshaw, I can give ye the same relief in half the time confession would take!"

Quila poured tea then sprinkled cardamom in their cups. Tears gathered in Lolli's lovely eyes. "Robbie used to say that cardamom turned any day into a holiday."

"Exactly right, me pet. We're celebratin'! I'd bet me mother's memory that this is the first time ye have ever, ever asked anyone fer help! Give me yer hand."

Quila had figured out what was bothering Lolli the most lately, but it would be much easier on the girl if Quila "found the thing" in her hand. She studied the lines for a while.

"Aha! I see three things." In the past, she thought, I would have drawn things out and made them items to somehow be ashamed of. Now I just want to help, as much and as fast as I can. Like Robbie advised, I want to remember sights of happiness before my dark night.

"First, dearie, yer feelin' guilty fer lettin' another take blame fer wrong tattlin' on Robbie and Doll!" Lolli's eyes were incredulous. "It's right here." Quila crossed her fingers under the table. "See that special place in yer palm? Ye jest don't seem ta realize! That misdeed, me pet, was part o' the process that Bowie needed to wake 'im up and make 'im want ta live agin'! And, part o' the process that helped spur Robbie into fulfillin' his own unique destiny!" Lolli began sobbing.

"The second thing," Quila searched for lines that looked like glasses. "There!" Lolli held her palm up close to her eyes, then realized she had given herself away. "If ye'd jest wear those spectacles that Louie bought, not only could ye read and be a crackerjack housekeeper, but ye'd find that enemies were suddenly friends! Think about it, too-lovely-Lolli!"

"The third thing!" Quila smoothed Lolli's tight brown curls out of her beautiful eyes. "A tiny seed's awaitin' and soon you could be a-rockin' it!" Lolli beamed through her tears.

"Quila, you've made me so happy! I know the perfect payment." She jerked off Whiffet's bow and handed her to Quila. "I don't need a dog as much as you do! She'll stay wherever you want her to: the wagon, the porch, your lap, your chair or just at your feet. She hates baths, bows and perfumes!" Sensing a big change in her canine life, Whiffet joyfully licked Quila's chin and wildly wagged her little tail. Without a backward look, Lolli hurried to her trailer, anxious for a change, to find the eyeglasses and begin a sumptuous dinner for Louie.

Two girls with babies waited on Quila's steps. "Spread the skin of eggshells on these pimples, dearie." Quila patted Whiffet. "Dab garlic soakin's on this baby's ringworm, sweety."

Hot tea would do for mornings or medicine. For afternoons, Quila taught Opal to make Jofranka's sun tea. There was always a big jar of this wild tea brewing on Quila's sunshiny steps, now. "The look of it intrigues people!" Jo used to chuckle. "Any mixture will do," she said, "if patrons see long curls of citrus peelings, a bay leaf and lemon slices!" Syd kept Quila supplied with chipped ice for her teas, in exchange for a shady chat, for news about the seldom seen Doll and a fragrant glassful when he made deliveries.

Quila cared little about medicine for men: her heart ached for lonely girls who missed the Den. At night Quila, Bowie and Tad made tiny sleep pillows, stuffing cloth circles with mugwort, rose petals, citrus, cloves and nutmeg, and then tying them with yarn. With her basketful of these freebies, Quila could at least treat sleepless nights and make the girls forget for a while the total emptiness from the loss of Robbie and his Den.

Quila didn't realize how much Gussy was missed until Tad began to rake the neglected park. Although he didn't have experience, Tad started to keep sinks unplugged and scrubbed, toilets and the wash machine working and trash carried out to the curbing.

It was getting harder for Quila's eyes to distinguish plants. She sorted bigger ones from the crock with her fingers and nose. Tiny rose buds, orange blossoms, fragrant mint and curly lemon peels were easy to identify for a new bride's tea. Quila would smile as she collected, knowing that she would later add hollyhock flowers to help a baby's delivery and increase the new mother's milk.

More and more Opal sat listening on one of the nearby benches that Tad was making, and ran back and forth from the wagon, to the store, the library or a vacant lot.

Business was brisk at Quila's interesting wagon, though she had no prices marked and only a few of anything. On her long shelf were such things as baskets of wild honeycomb for hay fever, licorice ropes (in memory of Robbie) and necklaces of green eucalyptus fruits for flea collars. For mild pain Quila mumbled as she massaged necks and shoulders. But, it wasn't merely herbs, it was Quila's caring, confidant knowledge and touching. Her upturned tambourine sat on the table for "Donations". Soon it held rent money, Whiffet's meat bill, and plenty for food to fill her tiny cupboard and icebox.

At first, curiosity made her little shop popular. Diabolic old woman–it was whispered around the neighborhood and even in the art gallery–this old seer with her odd way of talking, felt more than most could ever see! She juggled horoscopes, dreams, palms, tea leaves, even egg whites! But even more than the earning of happy independence, Quila was learning the joy of giving herself, and the marvel of just living in the beautiful helpful moment!

Step one is finally completed, thought Tad, as he pounded in the last nail of secure new railings fastened to Quila's little steps. He tested their strength, and smiled with satisfaction at the happy customers and colorful, inviting Gypsy space.

74. Jofranka's Ring

As soon as Guy chugged in that afternoon, Tad and Bowie borrowed his truck to move Mala's trailer from beside the Pigpen to the space next to Quila's wagon. Then off they drove for supplies. They worked past midnight hauling things from the Pigpen to the dump.

Before sunup, Tad, Guy and Bowie had planed and sanded the back fence beside the Pigpen. For the first time since Robbie's death, Pug cooked, then invited Tad and Bowie to breakfast.

As soon as Mala's old space and the Pigpen area were raked, they began on the fence. When Tad caught Mala watching he rubbed his hands in eagerness then pried the lid from a new can of paint. He plunged a stick inside and stirred, picked out a new brush, and kissed its potential. Slowly, he dipped it into blue paint. Dramatically he stroked the fence as though it were a painter's canvas, defining the upper third–the sky part of the fence.

"Can't I help?" pleaded Mala.

Flo was looking over the fence to check on the new commotion. Seeing her, Tad took out the rolled-up gate picture waiting in his shirt pocket, and handed it up to her.

Flo jumped down. "Give me the brush, and <u>you</u> begin planning this Gussy Gate!"

Opal, Shag, and Dago stood behind him as he sketched a place for the gate. Again, Tad slyly rubbed his hands in eagerness, opened another can of paint, poured in thinner and stirred its contents. He chose a medium brush, kissed it dramatically, then started to create a rolling green hill along the lower two-thirds of the thirsty wood. Tad was well aware that this hasty method of painting, without primer, was far from perfect, but he had to take advantage of the probably short-term interest in the project. Smugly he looked over his shoulder at the three girls extending a painted hillside all around the park. At lunchtime Lolli served sandwiches and lemonade to the painters.

The rolling hill on the fence at the back of the Pigpen space was somewhat dry by now and soon all of the other girls who stopped in at Lolli's place for coffee were happily creating flat, four to five-petaled "Gussy flowers" to bloom along the barely dry wooden hillside.

Next morning Tad enlisted all the children he could find to make chalk figures of animals, houses, suns, moons, and stars, "Along the playground part of the fence!" Then, just like he had highlighted fading hues on Quila's wagon, following behind the little artists with colors dabbed on a cardboard pallet, he swiftly dabbed, flourished, or stippled main lines of the children's drawings with his fingers, for all of the brushes were in use. He praised and rewarded each child with a dime, and they happily raced away for ice cream.

Late that afternoon a truck drove up to the back of the park and dumped a load of gravel. Tad, Bowie, and Guy worked until almost dawn spreading rocks by moonlight over the new playground area–the old Pigpen. Early the next morning, Tad and Bowie left in search of used items to fill the playground, while women continued painting the fence.

Mala was a frequent visitor at Quila's, now that her trailer sat beside the wagon. Very soon Quila came to realize that it was time to change the negative nickname Robbie had given Mala, when it had seemed to fit so perfectly. As everyday Quila talked to, and worked with the girl, like the mother who deserted her should have, Mala began to drop her hostile approach to life, to show appreciation for herself, her house, and children. She began to share her loneliness, tragic childhood, and empty future with Quila.

That morning Quila pulled out a chair for the tired-looking, paint-spattered Mala, who was having hideous cramps again; the pain was in her eyes. Quila picked a sprig of mint, trimmed it to a swisher and stirred Mala's tea. While the fresh brew of mint and herbs steamed up for Mala to breathe, Quila stood behind her and rubbed her neck, the tightness in her shoulders and the tension at her temples.

"I've the best of news fer ye, me pet! The lady that were jest here be frantic fer a housekeeper. Says that all the others have sour faces, dirty houses, and scream at their children." Quila winked. "I told her I knew jest the answer: a girl who sings while she cleans, constantly kisses her wee ones, and whose face was so bright that I called her 'Smila', when she visits me! She'll be here tomorrow morning to call on ye!"

Mala's distress blossomed into an unbelieving smile, and she drank her tea quickly. Pain and tension had left her now eager eyes, and it wasn't long before Quila heard her humming as she hurried back and forth to the washhouse with her mop and buckets, soap, and a new bottle of bleach.

That afternoon as Tad and Bowie unloaded old playground equipment and giant pieces of chipped clay pipe, Lambeth was listlessly filling his coffeepot at the sink beside Quila. He seldom left his trailer now, never sat on his doorstep opposite Robbie's sad space, and had no idea where Doll was staying from day to day. Quila wiped her wet knotty hands and took Lambeth's bony ones in her own. "Your rheumy ain't improvin'. Walk me over ta the wagon. I have answers fer yer problems!"

Quila served him hot tea spiced with ginger and cayenne. The fragrance rose from his cup and he smelled it with obvious delight. She held her thumb against the opening of the olive oil bottle, then began to massage his painful palms and knuckles.

"Lambie," he was surprised at her impromptu nickname, "I've a proposition fer ye!" He looked startled. "I'll trade ye daily arthritis tea and tender touchin,' jest like this, fer a wee bit o' yardwork every day. Bowie's way too busy now in gatherin' and enjoyin', ta keep up what he started. What say ye?"

"Why yes, yes. Of course!" he replied as she poured him another cupful. "Nothin' beats me auld 'ginger-snappy' fer the rheumy," she cackled knowingly.

From that day on Bowie never watered, trimmed, or raked around the Gypsy wagon. Lambie seldom frowned or ever rubbed his knuckles. And Quila's own gnarled fingers seemed to profit, to pinken up and straighten out a bit, as she rubbed not only the aching notches and bones of Lambie, but the overworked hands of Pug, painful bursitis in Guy's shoulder, headaches of the girls' and sinuses of children in the neighborhood.

Listening to happiness around Quila's wagon and digging his sore digits into healing earth soon put spring into Lambeth's step, confidence in his approach, twinkles in his dull dependable eyes. Neighbors discovered and hired him. Now, Quila and Bowie watched a wonderful progression: since Lambeth didn't need doctors anymore, there was no need for Doll to roll drunks—the tables were turned! Lambeth was easily supplying, when she was home, the listless Doll with food, encouragement, and a place to stay.

As Tad leaned on his rake one evening, he noticed that greenery and flowers around Quila's space were even spreading their beauty and fragrance over the side fence and front wall. Quila and Lambie, as always now, were having evening tea together in Quila's flowery yard, enjoying a new-found pleasure in the mutual company of age and contentment.

Tomorrow, Tad decided, he would make more benches for girls who merely came to Quila's space for tea and conversation; and also for groups of strangers from the gallery who were beginning to join the sad-faced girls that came to stare in silence at Robbie's space.

One evening while Tad was at the hospital, Opal sat inside the wagon with Quila and Bowie having tea by candlelight. A moth fluttered around the candle until it was caught and killed by the flame. "Too bad," sighed Quila. "Poor little innocent. She never even realized 'er own beauty." Quila held the dead body up to the light for Opal to see, (just as Bowie had done last night, as he pointed to beauty that Quila's eyes could not confirm).

"Notice the checkered, milky wings, how light reflects a rainbow," said Quila.

"Were ye born in October, child?" Opal nodded in surprise. "That explains it: yer mother named ye fer the special gem of that month, hopin' ye would ignore harsh realities and reflect instead, the beautiful colors in life! Opals are like a hummer's shimmering throat, or beautiful moth wings. Was your gramma real mean to ye, when yer father left and yer mother died?" Opal nodded again in surprise as a tear sparkled in candlelight.

"That explains it! Mother wasn't married and granny couldn't stand the shame!" Quila took Opal's hands. "I've been a'savin' me prized possession fer someone jest like ye."

Suddenly, Bowie's apprehension increased as Quila started to fondle the loose ring on her finger.

"Me best friend ever, old Jofranka, always wore this. She was the greatest 'teller ever born. She always said that jest the nearness of this metal circle helped 'er discover unique lights within everyone she happened ta meet! She whispered ta me once, that this ring was found in an empty cavity, the heart space inside of a mummy! It stands fer everlastin' life. Jofranka took it from 'er finger when she was a'dyin. Said it were mine, until I knew that it belonged to another. Now I know that it belongs to Opal. It be too big, anymore, fer me twiggy finger. It's cryin' out fer plumpness and youth! Touch it often and remember that you were created to enhance life for others. It will change yer life!"

Quila took the ring from her finger, kissed it, then slipped it snugly on Opal's finger. "Remember this little Opal. Me best friend often telled me: 'Gypsies be human wildflowers scattered in this dark world to beautify dull stretches of life.' Don't ever fergit that the bestest part of ye be Gypsy!" Jofranka's approving face flashed into Quila's mind. "Whenever Quila claps, it means: don't fergit that both of us be wildflowers, waitin' ta be discovered, wherever needed in this often colorless world!"

Then with Opal, like all of the other single girls, Quila tried to steer her into waiting for a Laslo kind of mate: one who was even-tempered, had good luck, sweetness, and was a good money-earner instead of one who was merely intriguing or good-looking.

Every morning, thanks to Opal who wanted to learn their names, there was a fresh bouquet of wildness on the table, and Quila often plucked from it a flower top to float in a customer's teacup while she told of the floral magic. And Opal kept renewing the basket of free good luck pieces: old pennies, pebbles, interesting wood, and seashells, that waited on the outside table, where Quila often invited a tearful child to choose a little charm before leaving.

Bath herbs now hung in knotted nylons from hooks above the display shelf. Every night, while Tad was at the hospital (peeking at, but not visiting Gussy and the baby), Quila, Bowie, and Opal stuffed nylons with dried flowers, leaves and spices, then double-knotted an empty space between the bulges. This way, whenever a customer just needed to escape her boredom or relax in a fragrant tub, Quila snipped off an herbal pouch from the bottom.

Bowie was taking an iced tea break, sitting on Quila's porch, watching girls still painting flowers all around the fence as though they never wanted to stop, as though there would be nothing left then to hold them happily together. Quila was pouring tea, listening, and prescribing: a wet soap bar on itches, a squeeze of lemon for bites, ice for children's wounds, and castor oil for age spots.

Inside Quila's open window, Bowie could see Opal busily dusting. Ecstatic to be recognized as unique, to be of use, fed, and often housed, Opal was beginning to keep the wagon clean and cheerful, the hanging pot filled with hot tea, and the sun tea jar always ready on the sunshiny porch. When there was nothing else to do, she read Jofranka's book or wandered around vacant lots reviewing useful weeds and bringing unknown samples back for identification. (Quila seldom had to clap, reminding Opal that she was special.)

Now Opal was up on a stool, humming a Gypsy tune that Quila had taught her, while she scrubbed years of grime away from the skylight. Bowie turned his tea jar upside down, put it in a far corner of the porch and took off for the arroyo to check on what was blooming today.

Smiling, Quila watched Bowie disappear into the hills. Now she knew that the robin needn't tap at her window anymore, a toad hop up her porch steps, or a bee fly into her open window. She needed no outside luck for the morrow. Nor did she need the box of makeup anymore. She could earn an even better living than when she tried so hard to be somebody else that she wasn't. All she needed to do now was just be her own helpful self.

Quila called the Chips over to her table. She propped up her mirror and on their own little faces she showed them how to use shades of chalk and charcoal for changing a face just for fun. She put the mirror into the makeup box and handed it to the astonished boys. She could see it in their eyes–it was their very first real possession.

For a while, there had been no customers or visitors, so Quila sat back listening to Opal hum as she worked inside the wagon. She poured tea and looked at her happy space. Thanks to Tad, Bowie and Lambeth, in less than two weeks, Quila's shop had become a curiosity that neighbors, people from town, the beach, the pier, and even The Joint could not resist! Many out-of-town gallery visitors also often found their way to Quila's table for a reading, medication, or merely a happy visit. Quila's ceiling was a fragrant umbrella of security where herbs were drying and waiting. And, thanks to Bowie and Jofranka, she learned or remembered each day more of the Indian and Gypsy secrets that she could share.

She sipped and nodded. Changing times needn't frighten her anymore with old visions of a smoking wagon, burying a beloved body, a dead baby floating in a bloody stream, midnight police searches, accusing eyes when a pond was covered with dead fish. Everything evil had already happened. Nothing was left to fear. Instead, there were just happy expectations of each tomorrow, and the sweet reunions that welcome death would bring.

She took a labored breath. She hadn't any real worries now. Life and its surroundings were bright, clean, and orderly. Bowie was almost ready. Jofranka's ring was snug on Opal's finger. Opal loved plants, Jofranka's remedies, Gypsy wagons, and helping people. Quila laughed out loud. It didn't even bother her when Opal plinked on Lazlo's guitar as she was doing now, or at night when she counted donation money and put it in a jar, or pretended to hear Gypsy music, and danced with the emptied tambourine, barefooted, in the tiny wagon. In fact, Opal showed a lot of natural Gypsy talent. Quila had even allowed her to wash the precious quilt by hand, for the very first time.

That night as Quila pulled up the fresh-smelling quilt, she realized that the days were not dragging by as they used to do. They were flying too fast; nights were fleeting too! Opal had, as always, done the dishes and straightened up. Then, like every night, while Quila and Bowie told old stories, Opal had spent a few minutes scrubbing a tiny bit more of the smoky blackness off of the wagon walls. Then she oiled and polished the clean, special woods that Lazlo had included in the wagon's designs. Opal did this in such an unobtrusive way, that it never hurt Quila's heart, or stirred up bad memories.

Opal helped Quila undress, blew out the candle, and snuggled down beside her. They had laughed together, joked, and shared the day's events. Like every day now, Quila had eaten well and shared her food; made several people feel better or happier. She patted Whiffet, who nestled beside her, and then Opal, who had already fallen asleep.

She caressed the precious quilted fragments of the past. All that she really missed now (besides Lazlo's strong young body, Jofranka's friendship, Robbie's Den and Mange's eager greetings) were the old respected Roms who sang songs of their youth, sorrow, and bygone tales. She began to softly hum as Romany words rushed back. But her eyes could not stay open for long. Every morning, when dew was almost dry on plants was the very best time for her, Opal, and Bowie hand in hand to start the daily searching.

75. Bell in a Teacup

Step two was completed, thought Tad, as he rested his head on Gussy's dictionary. The Pigpen was perfectly clean, with a new incinerator and trash cans. The fence was hugging the park with sky, hills, and flowers. Second-hand playground equipment was being reassembled, sanded, and primed by Guy and Bowie.

But the subtle, smoky odor of Robbie's space still permeated Last Resort, and kept astir the endless grief in outsiders who drifted to the black debris at all hours, day or night. And only when they absolutely had to did tenants make hurried trips to the washhouse, keeping their eyes turned away from the depressing eyesore.

Regardless of the park's dramatic improvements, tenants had returned to silent grieving. Pug and Lolli had quit cooking, nobody turned on their radio, and the telephone seldom rang. Every night after visiting the hospital, Tad sat at the table as Gussy had done, turning the problem over in his mind. Wasn't there any way to take care of Robbie's heartbreaking site? At least for now, there was no answer.

One morning near the handle of Quila's cup was the sign of Aquarius. A big social event was on its way. In the midst of this sadness and despair, she shrugged? The next morning a racquet was there, a sign again for merrymaking. That night there was a tiny bell in her teacup and Quila could ignore it no more!

Early the next morning before Opal awoke, Quila lit a candle, opened her trunk, and removed the top compartment. She held up her dark blue wedding skirt, the long-sleeved white blouse, and the wide springy belt that hugged her waist without any fastening at all. She could tell that everything would still fit. Then she felt of her thin hair. That long-ago day when Gussy fixed it, she had not combed it at all. She had merely removed things caught in it, lifted it here and there with her stubby pencil, smoothed only the top layer and tucked in little "rats" of hair she had pulled from Quila's brush! Why, Opal could do the same, and here and there she could add a tiny wildflower for the big event! There, she had planned enough. Opal was dressed, Bowie was waiting on the steps; it was time for gathering.

Early this morning Tad had tidied the Pigpen, fixed another toilet, scrubbed, bleached, and oiled the wash machine again, then scrubbed the washhouse sinks. He had sanded away the depressing bonneted figure and blended colors back into Gussy's wildly-painted trailer front. Now he proceeded to practice raking "Gussy patterns" into the red dirt. Aside from Gussy's bizarre trailer, the only thing left to remind tenants of her presence were a few traces left from this unique little rake that he intended to keep on using.

Quila and Bowie had been easy to help, their potential was already developed inside of them, a part of every cell. But the tenants and girls had only possibilities with no Robbie to discover and nurture them, to interest them in the day itself and the world around them. There was no more of Pug's motherly touch and presence, none of Robbie's fatherly understanding. There was no excitement that Gussy had always added to their drab lives. And it was hard for little Quila to keep on trying to fill those devastating, emotional vacancies all by herself.

Last Resort has put its mark on tenants, Tad thought as he raked. The surface of this place has changed but the grieving heart beneath it grows ever sadder. In fact, he looked over at the morning bunch, they look like they were stamped in ink beneath the shade of Lolli's tree. Girls hardly talked or moved. Those who lived away from the park leaned against Lolli's trailer, occasionally casting an eye toward Robbie's space. They barely sipped coffee as they watched Tad rake. They barely smoked cigarettes which were burning to ashes without any help. Tad _had_ to snap them out of it. Somehow, he had to get _them_ involved!

That evening sitting at Gussy's table, the perfect answer for Robbie's trailer finally appeared in Tad's imagination, and soon he was knocking on the door of the big green trailer. Inside, he held Pug and Guy's hands and shared their agony of indecision, their hope of pleasing Robbie and not hurting Robbie's people. Though any decision was going to wound, they finally agreed that Tad's plan was probably the best.

All the next day Tad sat on one of the benches he had made for those who were always leaning against the washhouse across from Robbie's space. As each one sat down, Tad told his plan and asked them to spread the word.

At sunup, Tad passed out sacks, boxes, and gloves. Borrowed shovels and rakes leaned against the washhouse. He asked workers to sift through just a little bit of black rubble at one time, looking carefully for anything significant enough to save for Pug. Each person was also invited to take mementos. Two trucks waited to take bigger pieces to the dump. Women served snacks, and soon the space was cleared of everything but black dirt.

As workers drifted home in silence, Lolli handed Robbie's big metal spoon to Tad. "I don't think Pug could stand this yet." Lolli ebbed away. Had he done the right thing or not? Nobody seemed relieved or inspired to make any further changes. In fact, they seemed to have slipped even deeper into frightening numbness.

That afternoon Tad sat at Gussy's table with eyes closed, holding Robbie's spoon, and once again inspiration struck! Grabbing Gussy's only pan, he rushed out the door.

Beating the pan with Robbie's metal spoon, he walked twice around the park as the spoon gave him courage and volume. "Hear ye, hear ye!! Potluck tonight in the washhouse!! Bring your eating service, something to share, and be ready for a great announcement! Hear ye, hear ye!" In the center of the washhouse Tad created a long table of boards on top of sawhorses and gathered all the new benches around it.

Your world used to be bounded, he thought as he ate that night, by a rickety fence and a filthy trash yard. But not any more! A playground is rising for your children to play on, the trash yard is an inspiration, toilets are flushing and spotless, and the wash machine works like a charm. But nobody enjoys these things. Are Gussy and Robbie's lives here to be in vain? You all feel somehow responsible for both of their different tragedies, yet you make no move whatsoever to change anything! It's as though the two of them never lived! They only died or left! Without realizing it both Gussy and Robbie were trying to learn and to teach the same thing in different ways, as Shakespeare did centuries ago: "What cannot be shunned, must be embraced!" Why, he couldn't say all of that. He'd sound like a windy preacher. They'd all get up and leave!

Instead, after the pitiful potluck, he simply began: "You're all invited to a wedding! In fact, whoever wants to come is invited!" Quila beamed complacently. "The most gala wedding this side of heaven! I know that it's right after Robbie's funeral, but I also know that Robbie would approve. Gussy, the bride," everybody clapped, "and her baby girl, Cherub," they clapped even harder, "should be able to leave the hospital in less than two weeks. So let's hurry! Let's clean and brighten this whole 'wedding chapel' to surprise her! If you're stuck for ideas, here is how Gussy would enchant the whole trailer park!"

Tad dealt out Gussy's pictures that Flo wouldn't buy, beautiful idyllic ones that she painted before her disillusionment: elaborately raked dirt, brightly painted trailers, long green, color-dotted benches in the shade of potted trees, the green washhouse with giant flowers splashed over it. Tad read aloud from Gussy's little diary: "So desolate is this place, so worn and neglected, I feel like giving it bold, 'impossible' new life! But everybody fights <u>any</u> kind of beauty here, like it was some disease to be avoided."

"But what can I do?" whined Lolli.

"Why not fix up the tree space like Gussy would do it? See in this picture how the tree is trimmed? A big green rug for a lawn? Benches with lots of people sitting on them? The tree creates such a special spot in this greenless park. It deserves to be celebrated and shared!"

"We have nothing to work with, no money," complained Mala.

"Start with what you have: cleaning, scrubbing, weeding! Put your household discards outside, then men will carry things to the front of the park for a yard sale. Also, if you want your trailer painted <u>free</u>, it must be washed, inside and out. I'll provide paint, brushes, painters, and encouragement!" Now, he thought, I'll have to think fast! How can I afford more paint and supplies? How can I attract more workers?

"Here, I'll show you that it's possible to make something out of nothing!"

From a pillow slip, Tad dumped humble packages wrapped in newspaper. "Gussy had little to work with and no real friends." Most of them looked down at the table, guiltily. "So Gussy started Christmas early. I know it isn't December and there isn't something for everyone, but the real presents here are ideas! Christmas was made for man, and we need that day, right now! Robbie declared Thanksgiving in summer." Tad banged the table with Robbie's big spoon. "Now, it's Christmas in September!"

For Mala, (hemmed by hand!) there were dishtowels from discarded print dresses. For Lolli, dingy old bras had been mended and bleached. Lolli held the garments to her chest and tearfully paraded like a model.

Fay still hadn't come home and her absence created apprehension whenever her name was mentioned. But Fay's gift wasn't wrapped, just tied together. It was coat hangers, each wrapped with strips of hosiery imprisoning spices and Fay's dried bouquet parts. Tad squeezed the fragrance then passed the hangers around. The Chips tore eagerly into their package of wildly painted jackstraws made of twigs from the tree. You could see in their expressions, and Quila knew for sure now that this was only the second semblance of a toy that they had ever owned! Juju unwrapped her cardboard doll house and clothespin dolls with new wardrobes. Pug's and Mala's girls unwrapped colorful strings with directions for making a cat's cradle and other figures.

A patchwork apron with pockets was for Pug. One pocket was outfitted with a needle in a piece of soap, colored threads on ice cream sticks, and a string of old buttons.

From unraveled sweaters Gussy was crocheting a shawl for Quila with a crude wooden hook! Wrapped in the center of the crocheting was a circle of cardboard on a neckstring. In the middle of the card was a painted eye. Quila held its hole to one of her eyes and squealed with delight for she could suddenly see much better!

Tad picked up a dried orange on a string. It was stuck all over with cloves and rolled in spices. "Gussy made this for Robbie's smoky Den. I guess it's yours now, Lolli."

Tad handed Quila a brightly-painted walking stick that he had made for her.

And there was one more thing. The Chips had slyly returned Gussy's step. So Tad had added a hinged lid to a new box, painted CHIPS on top, and decorated the sides as Gussy would have done. The Chips were happily speechless when they unwrapped the toy box.

That night Tad cleaned Gussy's trailer and found most of the checks that his parents had given to Gussy. Now he could buy the needed supplies! Only one thing marred the progress: Fay Rose's absence. Remembering Gussy's diary he shared his problems with the darkness.

That next morning, word had spread like gossip. People from everywhere showed up with cleaning supplies, food, and hand tools. Bowie ran errands, mixed paint, cleaned brushes, tore up rags. The Chips kept racing to the store and Tad kept borrowing ladders. By nighttime some of the trailers were cleaned and primed, the washhouse and new benches were planed and sanded. Pug and Lolli served coffee and cake to celebrate.

On Sunday most workers sat on the ground to eat lunch. Seeing this, a shopkeeper delivered lumber, saws, sawhorses, and nails for more benches. A few of the trailers had been painted the basic colors that Gussy pictured. Scores of benches were ready at least to sit upon. After dinner men primed the benches and planned to paint them dark green. Seeing Gussy's pictures, a nurseryman from the Plaza disappeared and returned with potted trees and a big green rug to spread beneath the tree.

Late that night Tad ran to the hospital and peeked in as usual on the sleeping mother and baby. Then far into the night he worked on table-making plans.

Tad encouraged a potluck every night where the throngs of people who arrived to help could also celebrate accomplishments, plan the next day's work, and make of their dull, individual fare, a feast! Often, Tad paused to think: "I hope I'm getting worthy of a Gussy!"

Everywhere he hurried, Tad carried cardboards and can labels showing Gussy's glorified ideas. He held pictures up while women painted swirls on the swing set, and Mala supervised decorations on the crawl-through pipe. Opal held colorful cardboards while painters splashed flowers over the washhouse walls.

Exhausted, Bowie climbed the tree to have a beer, to be alone, and to survey the happy bustle below. It wasn't just togetherness that made these days so special. It was the wedding goal, Gussy, Tad, and Robbie. He squeezed the leather pouch inside his pocket and pressed it closer to his heart. He couldn't think of doing anything more about it yet.

Bowie could see below him piles stacking up in front of the park, where Flo was bargaining and buying, while the Chips were carrying things back to her shop, through the new Gussy Gate! Many of the neighborhood women had brought cleaning supplies, and he watched them happily washing curtains, shining windows, and scrubbing.

One night Quila walked up to the potluck table, proudly using her colorful new walking stick, and took Tad's hand. "Why don't ye insist on seein' Gussy and the wee one?"

"Quila, if Gussy could make things so special out of nothings in her life, waiting months before she heard from me, surely I can wait a few days to surprise her with this impossible transformation that she designed and inspired! I just couldn't keep it from her, Quila, if I had to see her face to face!"

Happily wearing thick glasses, Lolli served coffee and freshly-baked goodies to early birds who gathered beneath the tree to hear Tad's plans for the day. Bowie was having coffee there, the morning Tad handed back to Lolli the big dictionary that she had once thrown away. "This belongs to you now, Lolli. I'll buy Gussy her own! And I'm sure you'll enjoy the penciled additions and comments."

"As long as we're returning things, Tad, this space, itself, belongs to Gussy. My old one is vacant. After we don't need the shade for meals, just before Gussy comes home, could you arrange the trade?" Tad looked at her in astonishment and gave her a big hug.

Without realizing it tenants were taking pride in the potluck. Quila added spices to bread loaves. Lolli made roasts. Lambeth made gourmet catsup. Workers from everywhere brought food to share. Bowie picked fall leaves for centerpieces. After the tables were cleared at night, the Chips proudly opened their toy box, supervised jackstraw games and transformed children's faces.

Some of the women were making personal improvements. As Tad tidied the Pigpen he found that Lolli was discarding flesh-colored sunsuits and a wide-brimmed hat. She was wearing sundresses and sandals now. Like a contented housewife she constantly cooked, served coffee and lemonade to hurried workers.

Once, Guy paused to make a flowerbox for Pug, and planted it with flowers that Bowie "borrowed." Sweetly Guy patted her head, "Now there's no need to disturb Robbie's gift, your 'red dirt of home.'" And it suddenly slapped Pug: how patient and understanding Guy had been all of these years, when she was spending the bulk of each day at Robbie's Den. That night with Guy sound asleep, an eager Pug slipped out of bed. When Guy got up, the trailer was spotless and Pug had made Sunday breakfast on an ordinary weekday!

But Quila felt heavy-hearted whenever she thought of the absent Fay Rose.

As Tad cleaned brushes at night, he speckled tops of green benches with multi-colored spots, laughingly remembering the famous artist Seurat and pictures made from dots. On a whim he added sunflowers to the bottom edge of Pug's now sky-blue trailer. Whenever there was leftover white, he added "Van Gogh clouds" to the top part of her trailer.

While painting Lambeth and Enoch's trailers Tad realized that while most of the new look was Gussy's, he was adding his own frivolous touch. Who cared if the whole place looked like a happy hodgepodge? "Anything would be an improvement!" Pug encouraged.

Tad sighed with relief. Let someone else save the fly belt of Africa, the waifs of Mexico. This place is _my_ "canvas" for now, _my_ kind of "art!" Like Robbie, I can't solve everything; I can only just start and then let someone else carry on.

Fay had returned to her now spotless trailer! She ate fruit that Syd had left beside new ice in her clean icebox. She slept on the new spread Flo had put on her bed. But Fay was gone again by sunup, and ecstatically Flo continued to look after the Chips and Juju.

Only a few more days, pledged Tad. I've got to resist visiting until everything is like Gussy imagined. That will be my wedding gift! He couldn't even glimpse of her that night; her entire room and even the hallway was filling up with dozens of congratulatory bouquets from all over the country.

That night by moonlight, Tad sketched on top of the new pinkness of Fay's vacant trailer. Tomorrow he would paint lace, ribbons, and roses for her eventual return.

76. Eloise

Eloise stepped up into the wildly painted trailer and put Ginny's suitcase on the breakfast nook bench. She placed her prim purse and the wedding dress box on the bed, took off her plain hat and dusted it with fingers and breath. She pulled off her sturdy shoes and lined them evenly on the floor. Gingerly, for it was stitched by hand, she settled down to rest from her long walk, on the thin, unlined patchwork quilt that her daughter had made.

"How unacceptable!" she looked around the room. "Yams were made for eating, not vines! Newspapers were made for reading, not curtains!" She picked up a booklet of envelope backs tied with knotted shoestrings. "Ginny's diary," explained Tad, taking it from under the pillow before he went to work outside, with the whole town, it sounded like! Preparing for a wedding that he had told Ginny nothing about!

"Good Lord! It's spattered with blood! How could Ginny keep such grossness under her pillow? She never did look at anything in the accepted way," Eloise complained. "This pitiful diary proves it!"

Beside the hollyhock, Bowie leaned against the trailer, waiting, listening, resting with a cigarette for awhile, before continuing on to do his errand through the new gate to Flo's.

"Envelope backs belong in trash cans, not strung together letting everyone know your secret thoughts!" In spite of her hatred of reading, Eloise thumbed through the familiar, hurried writings. "She writes like Dom," Eloise observed, emotionless. But why did she dwell on sad, hungry, lonely days? How could she risk others knowing about her nightly scavenging, hard lessons, longings for Tad and Dom, and her strange fascination for Robbie?

Bowie watched her try to plump up the flat, bumpy pillow. "Humph! Pillows should smell of fresh air, not stale spices and dried orange peels!"

She looked at the curved ceiling where a mural seemed to be growing. "And ceilings were made for protection, not amusement!" She shouted up to the ceiling. "Ridiculous!"

Eloise looked out a window. "And front yards were made for grass, white pickets, and vines, not patterns raked in dirt, booze bottle fences, and toilet paper flowers. How humiliating!" She looked above the kitchen sink where hollyhock blooms peeked above the windowsill. Bittersweet memories rushed to overwhelm her, as she lay her head on the fragrant flatness, and allowed herself time to remember.

As a little girl Ginny danced down the winding path that led through the parsonage garden with its tidy rows of plants, interrupted here and there by leggy hollyhocks. Eloise grew mostly vegetables and perfect, long-stemmed flowers suitable for cutting. "I cannot understand why you waste valuable space on useless hollyhocks. They're not practical for bouquets or anything else, Dom!" Eloise always lamented in her precise way.

According to the diary, Dom always answered, "Does everything have to be practical, Eloise? Is nothing to be loved for its own nonconforming self?" Seeing Eloise's bewilderment, Dom consoled her. "You're perfectly right, my dear. There's no room for anything that doesn't carry its own weight. Next year I won't plant hollyhocks." Yet he always allowed them to reseed themselves, said the diary, and Ginny loved him even more for the crumbs he permitted himself to enjoy. Eloise thumbed to a new section.

"Somehow I'll have to create my own niche," the grown-up Ginny had thought as she shoved her packed suitcase back underneath her bed. And the only things that Ginny took were hollyhock seeds strewn all over Eloise's antiseptic-smelling house. "The taxi was honking so loud," said the diary, "there was no time to find any container but my hand!"

Eloise and Dom were away and the cook, Luanna, was off, when Ginny had bleached her brown hair, cleaned her purse of all but comb, manicure kit, and five checks sealed in an envelope for possibly returning to Tad's parents. One check she had cashed: Six twenties for six months' trailer rent. She wore a peasant blouse, a flowered skirt, and brown sandals of Luanna's. She took no other clothes.

She lingered, said the diary, in Dom's study, "the only untidy, creative spot in the house!" She sat in Dom's chair, holding the limp teddy bear that sat in the crease. "Maybe I should stay. Daddy-Dom would understand, and in time Eloise could solve my problem, easily. But in the end, I would still be the same inadequate, resentful, inhibited child. I have to leave home to force solutions upon myself. I must find out if it is really true, what Eloise is always drumming on: Is everything natural for me to do, to be, or to think, of no value whatsoever? Must I always use everyone else's answers for my own unique problems?"

Ginny had hugged the teddy bear, as though saying goodbye to childhood. The taxi honked impatiently. A last time she twirled in Dom's chair, took a deep breath and left.

Eloise rubbed tired eyes; she was used to accomplishing, not lying around reading as Dom and Ginny loved to do. She opened the cupboard doors above a two-burner stove. Inside was a terrycloth bag in a saucer smelling of wine! A jar of "Seed Nuts" contained the inner pits of prunes, apricots and peaches! Ginny didn't smoke, but an empty jar was labeled, "Cleaned Butts." The last jar said "Candle Drips," but it was empty too. "Whatever did Ginny do with candle drips?" she asked out loud with disgust.

Ginny's toiletries in the medicine cabinet were pathetic! A washrag bag of soap chips, a percolator brush for teeth, and a jar of soda and salt labeled, "Toothpowder."

Eloise was feeling uncomfortable, guilty, and remorseful remembering certain entries in Ginny's dairy. "I'm so hungry, mother's breadboard would be a feast!" Until her eating arrangement with Flo, every day for Ginny had been palled by endless searching, for something clean enough to eat, something to do, and to do with. Often, Ginny ate only ice for dinner, then lurked in vain among neighborhood flower beds hoping to find gardeners like Eloise, who bordered roses with garlic, or tucked parsley among flowers.

Eloise noticed Ginny's saucer gardens. "It's hard to eat such darling leaves. But their fresh greenness is more than I can resist!" Eloise spit bitter carrot leaves into the sink.

A strange tinkling came through the window and Eloise shook her head. Ginny's "music" was unlike anyone else's: it came from silence, thunder, rain, and birdsong in the garden. Violin and voice lessons had been wasted, for she could find music only where there was none! Open a window and listen to unraked leaves; listen to branches squeaking together on unpruned trees. Yet, Ginny just could not stand orderly music in a church! And now, it seemed, her music had come from hanging debris swinging in the wind, creepy crickets in a jar, vulgar laughter from the Den, Robbie's drunken voice behind a closed door, children giggling at an iceman's puppet, Dom's church bells in the distance.

She riffled through cardboard pictures. Were these hard eyes really hers? One sketched hand held a blue pencil that crossed out natural activities of happy childhood. The other hand held a rigid tuning fork trying to turn a fiddle (named Dom!) into a classy violin.

Angrily, Eloise restacked the pictures. She jerked out a drawer, labeled "Cherub," where Ginny had nestled a little hand sewn mattress, being stuffed with tree cotton that smelled like baby powder! A ruffle of faded print was glued around the edges.

"And a drawer was made to hold clothes, not a dear little newborn baby!" she sobbed.

Hot tears rolled down Eloise's cheeks. If only she had half the imagination and eagerness for experiment that highlighted Dom and Ginny's lives. At home, Eloise never even changed the furniture around and its sameness drove Dom and Ginny wild! "Nothing should be fixed absolutely, no matter how good it seems," Dom commented. But Eloise's life had always been safely bound and hemmed in by precedents and practicality.

Eloise threw herself on the bed. "Worn, flowered dresses should have been used to dust this dingy trailer, not patched together for a quilt!" "Somehow," said the odd diary, "I feel cherished for just my own uniqueness, when at night I slip beneath these precious fragments of perfect motherhood–Pug." Eloise felt hurt, envious, and terribly sad.

She rolled over, sat up, and saw a threesome of discarded dolls sitting at the foot of the bed: a rag doll with a burned cheek, a bunny with one ear, and a dog with no eyes. Eloise turned diary pages and read out loud: "I can't stand to see loved dolls tossed away just because they're over-used, and over-loved. Like my own stuffingless, worn, and beloved little Tessie-bear."

Eloise fingered the yellowed satin in the open box beside her. Always she had wanted her daughter to be married in this beautiful old wedding gown. Eloise herself, as fresh and untouched as her mother before her, had worn it. "Satin was made for brides, not mothers!" she sobbed. Yet Eloise could not imagine Gussy wearing this dress! Ginny would, dutifully, but resentfully, wear it! But Gussy was not Ginny! "I'm afraid, Holly, that this dress is too conforming for Gussy!" Outside, Bowie smiled and went through the Gussy gate.

Suddenly, Eloise ripped off the overskirt and folded it and the dress back into the box before she could make any practical decision! She put on her shoes, plunked on the hat, tucked the diary into her purse, put the dress box under her arm, and rushed from Ginny's trailer.

She returned the next morning and Tad was already working. Last night she had read the entire diary. Today, stretched out on the bed again, Eloise saw things with brand new eyes.

Nothing in the room seemed to ever have been new. Yet every little thing seemed to sing together, in a perfect harmony of wordless gratitude and unbelieving happiness at being rescued from oblivion. Here at last, every single item had been seen, not for its age nor its wornness, but for its perfect fitness for some never-before-recognized use!

Makeshift things depressed Eloise. Yet now, she didn't scorn strange furnishings, weird foods or cereal boxes full of debris for Gussy's special kind of art. "This whole trailer is a marvelous medley of planned necessity and planned growth, deep love and creative invention," she said softly. This oddly beautiful room had been Ginny's lonely prison and mandatory classroom, where her only companionship had been crickets, unwanted dolls and a hollyhock. Her teachers had been the tenants and the trailer park, good and bad events, discarded pencil stubs, unrecognized paper and canvases, pieces of charcoal and a wealth of collage material unrecognized by anyone else in the world!

"And hollyhocks aren't useless!" Eloise told herself. "Hollyhocks can be tied for a playhouse. They can help in a husband's quiet rebellion," she cried. "They can remind someone of home. They can substitute for a friend's ear or a mother's shoulder to cry on."

She took out the wedding dress and draped it over the box. It was totally remade and shortened. She put the precious diary back beneath the fragrant pillow.

She took from her purse the limp Tessie-bear with pieces of heart material sticking out of its armpits. She kissed the raggedy thing and snuggled it among the other precious dolls. To Eloise, the bear represented Ginny's unobtrusive yet rebellious little nature. Eloise stretched out beside the wedding dress, looked at teddy, and remembered those orderly days.

When timid Ginny rebelled, it was only in writing, and in a very special place in Dom's study. Dom wanted nothing touched in his study, so it was never dusted or tidied except by Dom, himself. Ginny loved the room and escaped there when the sterility and rigidity of the rest of the house became overwhelming. "My church is me!" Ginny's finger first had written in the dust on his practice lectern. The little diary told how Dom had reconstructed the story behind Ginny's brief sentence, while having his regular Friday morning coffee break at Lila's, who used to be their housekeeper and cook.

To Eloise's humiliation, Ginny's favorite friend was Tessie, the daughter of black Lila. Whenever Eloise was gone, Ginny and Tessie played among the hollyhocks, tying them together to make a "hidey house." There they told stories and ate donut holes that Lila made for them, while frying donuts for Eloise's more formal entertaining.

On Saturdays, Dom sat the twosome in his leather chair and read his Sunday sermon. Wherever they squirmed, nodded or licked their suckers loudly, he used his big eraser.

When Sunday arrived the girls knew the sermon by heart. Sitting together in a pew they laughed too long, pretended sleep or licked imaginary suckers at remembered changes in the sermon. After the girls were separated, they sometimes played sick on Sunday mornings and happily spent those hours alone, together.

On those days at home, instead of wearing "Sunday-best," Ginny borrowed a favorite, loose dress of Tessie's. Lila had made it of flannel with no buttons, zippers, sleeves or sash. It had little hearts all over it, and just pulled over her head and down. The girls took Lila's fresh cookies to eat in their hollyhock house. They raced all over the parsonage, slid down banisters and twirled in Dom's chair until they were dizzy. When their stomachs started to growl, they knew that church was out, that Lila would soon be serving lunch to someone that Eloise wanted to impress that week. They ran to their own rooms and pretended to be napping.

On those happy Sundays, Ginny not only shared Tessie's old dress, but Tessie's only "doll," a sawdust teddy bear whose arms they often pulled until one of the girls gave in.

One Sunday, when the girls had played in every room in the parsonage, the twosome and teddy fell asleep in Dom's swivel chair, instead of in their own rooms.

While Dom and the visitor had tea in the garden, Eloise stomped all over the parsonage with a dustpan and whiskbroom, gathering cookie crumbs and sawdust trails. She found them asleep in each other's arms with the limp, empty teddy bear between them.

Lila was dismissed. Eloise had been poised, waiting for any small reason to just be done with Tessie, before Ginny's close relationship with a Negro girl became embarrassing. Tessie was forbidden to visit. Eloise jerked off the shapeless flannel dress that Ginny was wearing. She threw the dress and the limp teddy bear into the trashcan.

That night Ginny rescued the teddy bear, stuffed her with Tessie's beloved dress, and left bits of heart material sticking out from its torn armpits, so she could always see it.

All seven of Ginny's own dolls were locked up in a glass case, in her spotless, uninteresting room. On Ginny's birthdays, Eloise took down the exquisite dolls, lined them against Ginny's pillow and read their story tags. Eloise fingered the elegant materials and pointed to perfect stitches: just right for sleeves, for smocking, for hems. Then Ginny opened her present for that year: another untouchable doll. Eloise admired, read about and then put all of the dolls back into confinement for another year. The dolls had to be locked, remembered Eloise, or Ginny would give them to the first little ragamuffin with longing in her eyes. For Ginny, to possess meant having things to share: owning was a burden!

Tessie and Lila had already moved on Ginny's birthday. Eloise left after the annual doll presentation, then Ginny took the teddy bear from under her pillow. Sobbing and hugging it, she ran to Dom's leather chair, deciding that was the safest, most wonderful place for her treasure, "whose name now and forever was 'Tessie-bear'," said the diary.

Even without Tessie, Ginny still loved to help with Dom's sermons. But in church Ginny yawned outrageously, laughed unexpectedly and put fingers in her ears when people sang. Embarrassed, Eloise explained that Ginny was sick, she couldn't stand loud music or sitting still. Now, Sunday mornings belonged to Ginny, by herself. She could read, think, wander in the garden, twirl in Dom's chair, talk to the young new cook and housekeeper, Luanna, or sit in the hollyhock house and cry for Tessie.

77. Discovering Gussy

It was Dom who had called Eloise to first inform her that she was a grandmother. Now Eloise read from a list that Dom had telephoned from the hospital. She opened one of Ginny's drawers called, "Etc." and took out a matchbox labeled, "Shoes."

"I can't walk much anymore on hot pavement," the diary had said. "I've lost my sandals in one of Robbie's poker games." Sadly, Bowie watched through the man-shaped hole in the newspaper curtain as Eloise coiled up two frayed ribbons, put them in a suitcase and cried.

Looking at the list again, Eloise put her fingers on the handle of the baby clothes drawer. She hesitated for just a moment, seized with an impulse to rush out and buy up all the frills in town for her new grandchild. "My baby, my own little Ginny, a mother," she sobbed. She opened the drawer, then crushed to her lips tiny stitches on an infant's gown. No store-bought garment could ever enclose a baby with the same depth of love embedded with each hand stitch which mended this little second or maybe even third-handmade garment that lay in her hands. She tucked the baby gown into Ginny's suitcase.

Next on the list was an infant's shirt. Ginny had rescued a worn one, and embroidered puckered flowers over old mendings. Eloise folded the garment into the suitcase so that the flowers showed. Then she stacked in the diapers. Where else in the whole wide world, sighed Eloise, could one buy such pricelessness as three-ply flannel print diapers made from a heroine's old dresses and hemmed by hand with pink thread that was gathered by a bird?

Folded at the bottom of the drawer was a worn, hemmed, white terrycloth towel. "This little 'receiving blanket' is very special," said the diary. "I was sitting on the bench watching, when Doll first created it for Juju from her own worn towel. As always, Fay nonchalantly tossed away

Juju's soiled diaper and its messy contents. I rescued, washed and bleached this towel several times. I want my own baby to start life surrounded with that special kind of simple, total, all-giving love." Eloise shuddered, wiped her eyes, added the receiving blanket, Ginny's own nightgown and bathrobe from home, then put the suitcase by the door.

She sat at the table and looked around lovingly. Every inch of this room had been touched by Ginny's slow, creative mind. Yet, as always, Ginny had moved like lightning, once she had made up her mind to do something new that excited her!

Otherwise, Ginny made an art out of slowness! Whenever she was punished for dawdling at her chores, Eloise had had her sit on a stool behind a door. That would have been devastating for Eloise, herself! One day busy Eloise forgot about Ginny, sitting there in a corner of her bedroom. But Ginny had been happily studying her own palms for over an hour! "Mommy!" she shouted, as Eloise rushed in. "I was born with everything in my own hands! My own alphabet! My own pictures too!" Ginny marveled at and shared with Eloise the wigwams, railroad tracks, butterflies, pine trees and little squared-off letters! "I should always write my own story!"

And now she was famous, not for that art of slowness, but for lightning speed when something needed to be drawn and "captured" in only seconds, in only a few swift lines! And, what Eloise had branded as laziness, others tagged as a talent for seeing food, beauty, art, entertainment, and supplies where nobody else had ever recognized them before.

At Last Resort, where no mother pushed or expected anything, Ginny was finally in her own element. There was no right time, proper materials, or rigid rules for doing anything correctly. Ginny's childhood should have been filled with experimentation and fantasy. Yet, it was here in this gross place that she had found those things. It was here that she had grown through and out of childhood without losing childhood's best traits: innocence and awe.

And now, after reading the entire diary, Eloise finally understood that Ginny's personal little customs were just as valuable and meaningful as Eloise's own dutiful traditions. What difference if one kneels or stands on their head! What difference if you call it Mystery, Miracle, Life or some other God-name? What difference if you talk, whisper or shout? What difference if it's called socially accepted reverence, or wildly unique awe, adoration, sharing, gratitude, ecstasy? Ginny did not believe in pleading for "somebody-else-out-there" to change things for her; she just accepted life as it was and tried to learn from it.

Through pages of the diary, Eloise had tearfully watched as Ginny proved all of her little sayings, ones that at home she had only hoped were true: that life for her should be simple, slow, quiet, creative, filled with unconditional love, and confidence in her own answers. "The only things that really count in life are a deep reverence for all of it, a little food, minimum shelter, some one or thing to love and share with, and trying to be the unique self that you were born to express," said the little diary. And, just by being herself, Ginny had become Gussy, and Gussy had become a legend.

Eloise went over to the bed to put on her shoes, she slid the purse under her arm and looked slowly around the happy little "Gussy space" before she left. Anybody, "any Eloise," could have made this trailer into just another spotless room to exist in. But only a Gussy could have fashioned it into an enchanting studio where never-before-recognized food and materials for an artist magically appeared, whenever they were needed.

Suddenly, Eloise desperately wanted to be even a tiny atom, a speck, or whispery part of this magical place-in-time. She walked to the table and with her little finger she wrote in the heavy dust at the back, "Yes!"

Tearfully smiling, Eloise picked up the suitcase, patted the baby drawer, blew a kiss to Holly and the dolls, and left. Bowie sniffed, smiled, wiped his eyes on his sleeve, and walked through Gussy's gate to Flo's, where he had been sent for more nails.

78. Into My Own Picture

Eloise had plenty of time to think as she walked home to the parsonage. She hadn't seen Dom for several months, since that day she rushed into his den with Ginny's note.

Art school was the only big decision that had ever arisen from meek little Ginny and Eloise had been angry and hurt when Ginny first left home. Now, according to the note, Ginny had even decided to leave art school and everything else as well! It served her right, wanting to be an artist was as impractical as Dom wanting to be a reporter and novelist, instead of a minister!

"I've already seen the note," Dom drawled as he turned around from his view of the hollyhocks to face Eloise from his swivel chair. The floppy little teddy bear was in his hands and tears were in his eyes. His sleeves were rolled, his parson collar awry. Eloise had taken a long disgusted look at him.

"Yes, I've been tippling. A celebration with me and myself! We're leaving you, Eloise." Tears reached down to his jaw, now.

"Ginny was the jewel that kept me here in this rigid setting. But you've driven her away. She had no mother to confide in. To you the sudden bloom of womanhood was a red flag of dirty disaster, not a sweet promise of fulfillment. Ginny was kind of like me, an experimenter. She didn't want someone else to have the joy of discovery, then tell her how it's done. And, she had something else to be proud of: a gentle tongue."

Eloise had taken her coat from a hanger and was angrily brushing it off. "Dominic! Of what workaday use is a gentle tongue? Ginny can't stand up for herself! She has no practical skills! She'll never make it in this world! She can't even make change! She can read the dictionary for hours, but her mind can't add or subtract! She doesn't care to drive, detests competition, gives everything away, just plays at doing housework! She has absolutely no memory, can't even remember a grocery list!"

"What extraordinary creations could spring from such an uncluttered mind!"

"Rubbish! She won't even make a good housewife! She thinks that dust is merely the perfect surface for finger-writing when she's inspired! Yes, I've seen it on your lectern, all through the years. 'Love is All!' 'Less is More!' 'Slowness is Beauty!' 'My Church is Me!' 'Silence is My Music!' 'We are Stardust!' 'Insist on Yourself!' She makes up her own silly rules, but never proves them!

"And as for pace, she has only one: snail pace! She can gaze at the 'arty' drippings from a lighted candle and never hear me vacuuming the entire house; she can lie on her belly and, enchanted, watch a caterpillar emerge from an egg, when all around her its creepy relatives are chewing up the garden! And you, you're just like her!" Eloise sobbed. "The two of you, hypnotized, can enjoy the very last log burning away, while I am outside sawing! The two of you, fascinated, can watch a dot of a cloud turn into a rainstorm, while I am trying to find your misplaced umbrellas!"

"You enjoy doing that! Me and Ginny would find more pleasure in a walk by the sea, a good book, interesting people. We can't help being us, and you can't help being you!"

"She was also born with your mushy backbone, Dom! It's impossible for either of you to choose sides! You both see everything through rainbow-colored glasses. Life just isn't that way, Dom! Mostly, it's ugly. Ginny's biggest vice is that she just doesn't recognize ugliness. Cover it up! Grab some perfume! Add color! A fancy word!"

"She's never seen life, except from tinted panes of churchdom. You've raised a caged bird. When she's on her own, she'll test her wings and do what just comes naturally!"

"Exactly what I'm afraid of!" Eloise put on her coat. "I'm going to find her!"

"Turn her loose, Eloise. A wildflower is storm-torn and depetaled, but ecstatic to be free: it has really lived! Let her make mistakes, Eloise!"

"I'm going, Dom!"

"Sit <u>down</u>, <u>Eloise</u>!" For the first time in married life, Dom was insisting upon his own way. Astonished, Eloise sat down. Dom stood up, took a deep breath. "I'm delivering to you, alone, Eloise, a sermon that's been stuck in this parson collar a long, long time." He swigged from the almost empty bottle as he stood beside the lectern.

"The last thing Ginny wrote is still there: Touch the Sky! Try your Wings!"

He loosened his collar. "I'm ready to touch my sky, to try my wings. I'm tired of being a hypocrite! How many dinners I've suffered through, exchanging niceties with some stuffed shirt, while a ragged, but 'rich' Negro was fed in the kitchen. Now I can eat with a darky, share his ale and record his tales. I can dig bare toes into clean mud, throw my shirt off and offer sweat and sympathy, not pompous, untried advice!"

"But what about me, Dom? What about us?"

"I'd rather go on a beer bust with a bum, than go to bed with you!"

"That's not exactly what I meant!"

"It's exactly what I meant, my squeamish spinster! It's time I had a real woman, not an old maid. I'm an earthman, Eloise, not the 'skyman' you insisted I be, like my father and his father before him, God bless. I'm different from them! And now, I suddenly know that that is okay! I like the smell, the feel of things that are earthy: sweat, lovemaking, rotting earth!" She squirmed as he caressed the curve of her breast. He fumbled softly in her hair and drew out big hairpins that always held her fat bun, until the curly mass of soft brown hair fell down on her shoulders. "I love a woman's hair, unconfined.

"I hate high necklines!" He ripped her blouse apart and buttons flew. He ripped the skirt and underwear from her body, then forced her to lie on the floor. "Pull down the shade, Dominic; Luanna is watering roses!" Resigned, she squeezed her eyes shut, turned her head from his winey breath and tensed her body as he dropped his pants beside her.

"Remove your collar, Dominic," she said without opening her eyes.

"By God!" he ripped off his collar and threw it to the floor. "I may break you, but I'll never bend you, will I? You're as rigid and thorned as those long-stemmed roses you revere!"

He put on his pants. "Like I said, but just needed to prove it one last time: I'd rather go on a beer bust with a bum, than go to bed with you!" To Eloise's astonishment, after he stomped and stamped and wiped his parson collar with the soles of his shoes, he stuffed it into his pocket! Then he flipped up the window shade. It flapped around and around while he gazed above the hollyhocks and breathed in fragrance as Luanna watered the garden.

"I don't want to preach it anymore, Eloise, just to try and prove it to myself. I am one with God. My body is his temple, my mind is his instrument. But for me, God has to be more simple than a parson must always see him. Orthodox religion is just too damn complex and numbery! I don't want a congregation anymore. I want a gang to go fishing and laughing with! I want to be free as the wind for awhile!" Eloise sat up on the bed and wrapped the bedspread around her nakedness. He smoothed her loosened hair and searched her frightened eyes. "I'm a schoolboy at heart, Eloise. I need a carefree maiden to <u>play</u> with, not Whistler's Mother to take care of me!

"I want a girl like you used to be, or seemed to be." He looked past her eyes. "She'll wear gossamer webs that dissolve at my loving glance!" He opened the closet door and riffled her clothes. "I've lost that girl; these aren't her clothes! These clothes are blah-brown, funeral black, ghastly-gray! 'She'll be wearing blush-pink when first I see her, then grass-green, sky-blue, pansy-purple. Goodbye, Eloise, I'm going to look for my Ellie."

Sobbing, Eloise turned the last corner, ran up the precisely groomed entryway, opened the polished mahogany door and entered the spotless, empty, silent, lonely parsonage.

There was only one night left before Gussy came home. Tad moved Lolli's trailer back to its old space, but he still had Gussy's trailer to put beneath the tree. Workers still had reception tables to make, more doorstep rugs to cut and nail on. People from The Joint came to serve coffee, sandwiches and cookies until almost dawn. Their three-piece band provided spotlights and played soft encouragement to keep workers awake. As the sun came up, they left with weary bodies and big smiles, parking all the cars outside and stretching a rope to keep the whole area pristine, once Tad had finally "mended" the giant web of dirt. After a short nap, Tad helped Guy to move the little trailer, he arranged bottles to form Gussy's fence again, and then repaired her useless doorknob.

Tenants were tired of skirting the intricate patterns that Tad had finally finished, when Gussy's taxi drove up. Tad was waiting by the mailbox.

Gussy pressed the warm, sweet-smelling bundle close to her loudly-beating heart as Tad flung open the door. She hadn't seen or heard from him in months. Before the taxi even stopped, he was inside, shaking, holding her and the baby as he sobbed.

It had been so hard, leaving her alone in the hospital, not holding, or phoning her even once. But life had been wrong for so long. From now on things were going to be as perfect as Tad could possibly make them!

"You didn't tell me about the baby, Ginny. I had no idea! I would never, never, never have gone any place, or left you all alone!"

"I know."

"She's so beautiful, and you're so different, somehow. Your hair, your skin, you're so thin. You look fragile, but you seem strong!"

Tad helped the two of them out of the cab and paid the driver.

"Come! See my last fling as an artist! The grand tour of the Agean Stables, A. G."

"A. G.?"

"After Gussy!" he said proudly. He grabbed her suitcase and lifted her and the baby into his strong arms. In spite of her nightgown and robe, Gussy seemed weightless as a whisper and she was barefooted! She wore only ribbons woven around her big toes and crossed around her ankles like Roman sandals.

Giddiness took over as a giant feast for the eyes unfolded before Gussy, while Tad loosened the rope that cordoned off the driveway. He knew that every trailer there had wet-eyed peekers smiling from sparkling windows, that Flo was watching over the back fence, that strangers and neighbors alike had quietly gathered at edges of the trailers. Boldly, he began the first footprints in the astonishing patterns encrusted in the redness! Every inch of dirt had been watered and raked into crosshatches, waves, plaids and herringbones which stretched like a carpeted valley nestled in wildly-flowered, make-believe hills.

"It's like walking into my own picture!"

"Exactly!" smiled Tad. "But, I've added something. I hope you won't mind. The plain-colored trailers in your pictures made perfect canvases: I decided to use them for my own 'Frivolous Farewell to Art!'

"When I saw how you and the Chips had painted your trailer, Gussy, it totally freed me!" Tad whirled the three of them in a circle. "According to your materials, or lack of them, you just dabbled with techniques we had learned in art school. You followed no rules: you just enjoyed yourself and the beautiful creative moment! I have done the same thing on a bigger scale. I played with artists' concepts, celebrated their lives with paint and rapture! It was delightful! Pug said I could paint any way I wanted to, if I bought the colors! Now I am done with static art. Now I can start on living, breathing 'creations' of people!"

Fay's trailer was sprinkled with roses on a background of lace and ribbons. "Nobody knows where she is. Don't laugh," he explained. "I call this, 'Rhapsody for Fay Rose.'"

"It's so beautiful, who could possibly laugh!"

All the trailers were tidied up, painted in bright colors, entryways garnished with flowers, greenery or potted trees. Every porch step had a dirt-red foot cloth nailed upon it.

"Look! Over there, those brown, tan, black, and white curves and swirls. That's my 'Lyric to Lolli'. And how do you like that dreamlike Dali across from it?"

"Tad, it's a nightmare!"

"Enoch's trailer. Nobody lives there. I couldn't resist!" Tad laughed hysterically.

Lambeth's trailer was covered in sizes and colors of squares, placed at impossible angles. Tad laughed, "Cubistic Cezanne?"

"Interesting!"

The only flaw in the red-carpeted "valley" was Robbie's vacant black space. Passing it, Gussy sobbed uncontrollably. Tad hugged her, sighed, and moved on.

"Pug's trailer," boasted Tad. "My 'Starry Night', sort of. Dark blue with swirly clouds molded with only fingers. Vague stars and around the bottom, a border of sunflowers by Van Gogh!"

Tad turned the corner and Gussy saw that her space was vacant. "You've outgrown your pigpen, Posy," said Tad gently. Passing by, Gussy saw through blurred eyes that a gate to Flo's was painted with four-petaled flowers and little pink pigs. The hinges were made of knotted rope, like in her pictures! Shiny trashcans and a new incinerator were standing in line on a pebbled floor.

Children were making towers of wildly-painted cans, in the playground of Gussy's dreams! There was a colorful cement pipe for crawling through and a brightly painted swing set. Stick figures, tiny houses, trains, moons, and stars scattered themselves along the back fence. Children threw balls at a bull's-eye and ringed colored stakes with hoops.

"Wait, where's Quila's trailer?" Gussy cried as they rounded the washhouse. "Later," said Tad as he noted the dampness of her yellow hair.

Tad hurried past the flower-splashed washhouse and there was Gussy's trailer. Beneath the tree! Just as she had imagined it so often: green rug "lawn", benches all around it for sharing the shade and tall hollyhocks in pots blooming at the icebox drain. Though repainted in several places, the trailer was still patterned and roughly textured in the same way she had had it before. The bottle fence was there again, but the burned silhouette was gone and the paint was like it used to be.

"That's all I can take, Tad," Gussy sighed and he turned the new, now snug handle.

Tad slid her under the turned-down patchwork sheet and tucked the baby in beside her. "Oh Tessie-bear!" Gussy hugged the flat fuzzy bear with heart material peeking from its armpits as it rested with the other dolls. Tad smoothed her uneven hair which still hung as Robbie had hacked it.

Lambeth fastened the rope again, tipped his cap to policemen across the street, tiptoed around the trailer edges, and took the wash house phone off its hook. Everyone in the park was as quiet as Tad had asked them to be and tasks were all suspended. The baby nursed and the threesome slept in each other's arms.

The next afternoon everyone was drinking and celebrating. It was impossible for Dom to restrain. Way before dawn, Lolli's Mammy, Luanna, Lila, and Tessie, who was now a beautiful serene woman, had been helping Pug with the wedding feast.

Enoch was returning with Flo through the new gate that led to her Thrift Shoppe. With Bowie in the middle, they were carrying a monstrous rug to cover Robbie's space. Enoch had never seen Flo's store before. It needed reorganization, but all of those discarded things were fascinating, the way Flo was displaying them.

Tad had told Enoch that Flo brought beautifully decorated casseroles and pies for the work parties. Enoch could tell that she even made her own clothes. His eyes wandered down past her big-jawed face and appreciatively inched along the newly created wedding clothes.

It was the first time anyone had ever looked at her like that and Flo loved it! Following at her heels were the Chips, carrying chairs. Flo was going to miss them when Fay came back, got married to Enoch and moved away. The Chips' secondhand clothes smelled so fresh lately, they were always ironed and seemed to fit, for Flo knew how to hem and tuck and loved to sew for children. In just a few weeks, she had found love hiding beneath their ornery ways. Warmth and clay were also waiting, eager for molding with tenderness, discipline and security. She dabbed her eyes with the freshly ironed handkerchief she always saved for weddings. Oh, well, she had had their wonderful young nearness for a while.

Enoch was surprised by admiration in Flo's eyes: here was a man who hadn't collected belly fat with birthdays! Both had been unblessed with marriage or babies and their eyes twinkled at the bond. But this was the day Enoch was supposed to pick up Fay.

Dom checked his watch. Any moment Eloise would emerge from Ginny's trailer and begin directing; after all, this was the wedding of her only child and nobody had consulted her! She'd be dressed in that severe suit he hated, smelling like nothing, her hair pulled back into its accustomed bun. Poor Eloise, she'd find it hard to bear publicly, to become a grandmother before becoming a mother-in-law. Especially in front of this motley crowd of "peons."

Dom shifted uneasily, smoked another cigarette, reported more notes on his pad, and waited in one of the few empty chairs lined up in rows beside Gussy's trailer.

Finally, standing up there and ready to step down, like a dream holding Cherub, was Gussy in the same ivory, but shortened, dress that "Ellie" wore twenty years ago! Enoch helped her down, for he was the best man, and Dom noticed that only ribbons were shoe-ing Gussy's bare feet!

Standing in back of Gussy was an apparition! Squeezing his eyes shut, then opening them made no difference. It was Ellie, not Eloise, in a blush-pink mist of a dress! Was it created from dye and merely the veil of a wedding dress? The cloud of pink made crisp curves soft again, and the bodice was indecently low-cut! Long brown hair hung loose and curly. A hint of color was on her cheeks and lips. Underneath the dress was a swish of taffeta, and lingering perfume.

Suddenly Dom felt uncomfortable and seedy. He awaited her disapproval of his appearance. As the new reporter at the Wake, he was so caught up in his first assignment, at this very trailer park, that he had typer's slouch. His hair without Eloise's care was white now, and curled untamed around his ears, neck, and temples. His eyebrows without her constant tweezing and snipping were growing together. His pant knees were baggy, he hadn't pulled them up as she had taught him to, "to preserve the razor crease that a pastor should always have!" He needed a haircut, a shave, a homey meal, more sleep, and less cigarettes. He needed a cup of strong coffee to settle his woozy stomach and bloodshot eyes.

Eloise hadn't seen Dom since he left her well-ordered life. It had been easier to stifle ambitions than to live without Dom. She missed fresh eggs, plucked chickens, new honey, and extra fruit that, like an old-time country parson, Dom attracted to his doorstep, instead of money in the basket. She actually missed his embarrassing sermons when he took onions, fish, or rotten eggs to church for examples. She missed his spur-of-the-moment plans and formal ones were no longer interesting without Dom in the middle of them all.

"It's great to see you, Dommie," was all she said. As he helped her down from Gussy's fancy step, her eyes caressed his entire body without a trace of criticism!

79. Wedding Bouquets

Doll and Syd stood at the fringe of the huge audience, waiting for the wedding group to assemble.

"Why don't we slip away," said Syd who had finished his rounds for the last time. "Big weddings are so unnecessary. Ideal marriage is between the bride and groom. Shouldn't we hurry before that precious child sees you leave and you're both hurt too much?"

Doll dropped his hand. "I'll meet you back at the truck." She walked to where Juju and Fay stood waiting beside their rose-covered trailer, while Flo was fussing over them. As if by magic, it seemed to Doll, Fay had returned to the court, all dressed up and just in time for the wedding! Doll watched as Flo was trying, in vain, to hold the dirty black rag for Juju, at least while she was the flower girl.

Doll crouched down, looking beautiful just in the ordinary white dress and sandals that she always kept in her suitcase, thought Bowie as he watched from a new bench beside Fay's trailer. Flo had dressed Juju in frills of pink ruffles and for the first time in her life she looked adorable. Waiting for Juju on Fay's step was a nosegay of rose geranium leaves with toilet paper flowers "blooming" in the center.

Tenderly, Doll pulled Juju into her arms as though she were Love, itself and held her tight as her eyes pleaded with Fay's. In answer, Fay rubbed her knee defiantly. It had never mended right. She just couldn't walk in quite the same way that used to pay the rent and keep their stomachs from growling. The fight with Doll had been truceless and Fay was still unrevenged. "Humph," she'd sneer, when Doll wanted to talk of adoption, "would that bring back the life back to my leg?"

Doll looked into the same blue, blue Robbie-eyes and slowly pulled out the same Robbie-curl, until it sprang back into place. Fiercely she hugged Juju, caressed her curls and kissed her.

Sobbing, Doll ran to the ice truck, swung up into its empty bed and began waving as it pulled away, plopping giant "tears" of melting ice behind it.

Fay looked down at Juju's scrubbed, apple-bright cheeks, at the giant blotch that would always remind her of Pug's knitting needle. Callused to disappointment, Juju just stood there shaking with silent grief, kneading her black rag as she watched the ice truck drive away for the last time. Fay lifted the small chin so she could look again into Robbie's eyes.

Why was she being contrary? She had always, always been praying that someone would steal Juju away, that she'd never have to look even once again at those dirty black curls and that telltale cheek.

Juju's little mouth was a quivering rosebud as Fay kissed it, loving her like she had never loved anything in life before. Fay gave a long sigh, and her eyes seemed to squeeze from their depths the very last of an aching moisture, before she whispered something into the child's ear, then turned her around and pushed her gently toward the street. Ecstatically Juju ran toward the waving Doll and the dripping truck, forming the single word over and over like Fay had urged her to, until it broke loose from her very heart:

"Mama, Mama, Mama!" The dirty rag streamed like a black tail behind a pink fluffy bunny, then suddenly fluttered out of her hand and whipped along in the gutter. Sobbing with happiness, Doll jumped down from the bed of the truck and with arms outstretched she raced to meet Juju.

In the same instant that Fay had kissed Juju goodbye, it was all settled about the boys as well. Fay found an engulfing peace of mind in the decision. She was the mother of their bodies; it was now in her power to be the mother of their happiness. I am like Robbie, she thought hopelessly, a misfit, with only one real gift to give. She pushed a fist against her painful chest.

The Chips were in the trash yard with Louie preparing tin cans to tie on the car Tad had borrowed from his father. In fine clothes that Enoch had bought them, Fay could see that in Flo's care their little undergrown chests were filling out with flesh and pride. Their hair was freshly cut, and Flo had scrubbed their cheeks so hard their little freckles matched the seeds in watermelon cubes waiting on festive, overloaded tables.

Fay bit her lip and nodded her weary head. Flo had always wished for sons. Enoch and Flo could make a great couple, Fay nodded again: they had much in common. Things that would make a good home life for the Chips. Uprooting them from this place would not be too painful. They had little good to remember, but they could use the Gussy gate to have fun in the new playground with trailer friends. And they would always have shoes and underwear. Perhaps, once in awhile they would remember, and even get a longing for her when a wild wind unleashed the sea.

As the wedding march began, from the band assembled in the driveway, Dom took his place beneath the tree. Its giant arms framed Gussy's new yard in a shimmering, newly-pruned green ceiling. Colorful benches in front of the fence and on each side of Gussy's yard, served as pedestals for pots of Flo's rose-geraniums. Gussy's congratulatory bouquets had all been sent from the hospital and were scattered throughout the park, making it look and smell like a nursery everywhere! But dominating the makeshift altar was a curve of tall hollyhocks that Ellie must have brought from home.

Tenants and neighbors sat in rows before Gussy's front door, but people from the pier, the beach, The Joint, the Plaza, the Waterfront Gallery and complete strangers had brought their own chairs or stood in the overcrowded driveway.

Until today, Dom had not had a single drink since the story of Last Resort had hit the stagnant, now hectic little office where he worked. But suddenly Dom was feeling lightheaded from too much of "Robbie's Champagne." He poured the rest of his current drink into one of the hollyhock vases. He could feel himself weaving as Gussy and Tad finally stood before him.

The wedding march stopped. The groom, and the bride holding little Cherub, stood waiting before him. But Dom felt like a giant clapper suspended from its bell by only a fragile thread. The silence was overwhelming. He hated public speaking, public occasions!

But Gussy's new little chimes that Tad had created began to fill the immense silence. They were playing in a soft breeze as they hung where Tad had placed them in a lower branch of the tree. Dom raised his hands. "Let's all be quiet for just a minute," he almost whispered and put his finger at his lips. "And listen to one of Gussy's favorite kinds of music for any occasion!" Finally, the sweet simple sounds released his tension. It just didn't matter that the old wedding words were completely wiped from his memory. Gussy deserved brand new words, created on the spot, spontaneously, just for her.

Slowly, Dom began in a strange way. "'Homage to Hollyhocks' is what I'm calling this ceremony," he said after excruciating silence.

Dom was here to perform a wedding, but all that he could think of the entire day was how he wished Robbie were here. How could this dead man whom he'd never seen or known, affect him and others so profoundly? Here was a man that was so revered, despite being wrongly considered homosexual, despite hating to bathe, to wash dishes or clothes, despite having a once-in-a-lifetime orgy with a prostitute, and despite fathering an illegitimate child that he knew nothing about!

Dom had lingered for days in the art gallery "visiting" Robbie, Gussy and the other tenants. He had written more than could ever be used in the Wake, probably too much for even a book! And he was sure now: both Robbie and Gussy had found that The Big Answer was merely to discover, enjoy and share one's own unique self.

"You can't grow roses from hollyhock seed," Dom continued. "Some flowers can be cramped into bouquets, but not a hollyhock. They're just not made for vases." He turned and pointed to the hollyhocks in buckets that fringed the altar behind him. "A hollyhock must stick its neck out unhampered, in spite of what the world around it thinks." He swayed.

"But humans are never really content to just be themselves pure hollyhock; they're forever reaching elsewhere, for that awesome uniqueness that's merely waiting deep, deep inside us all." The audience began to cough and shift nervously, feeling themselves in the midst of a sermon. "And, like Juju, we are all expecting sand, stones, and mud, instead of pearls, to be hiding in the swill of life. We cannot comprehend that so very often dirt and debris <u>might</u>, in time, develop into pearls."

Now he was almost whispering again as he put his hands in a prayer position and bowed his head. "Most of us let a mere grain of sand turn into a giant stumbling block, but, we could just keep working in our own humble ways and wait." There was a long silence. "Just wait and watch; that little grain of grit may slowly be turning into a pearl, a gem, a gift that will add its own uniqueness, lessons, color and sparkle to this swill of life! And this is what Robbie, Juju, Gussy, and Tad have done unconsciously." Again he paused.

"Gussy, will you take this boy to be your wedded husband, even if he'd rather comfort a lawyer, than be one?" Gussy looked puzzled, but nodded anyway.

"You've walked your own path, Ginny, until you've become 'a Gussy.' However hard, you've stuck to your own inner architect, not aligning yourself to others' 'vases' for you."

How dainty Gussy looked. How tall and tan Tad had become. Dom took their hands and joined them. "May you have many hybrids and no, hic, high-breds! You may kiss the bride!" Many seemed disappointed in the short ceremony, some seemed glad it was over.

While Tad and Gussy kissed, many in the crowd were clapping and cheering. Some drifted toward reception tables. But Tad raised his hand. "Wait! Gussy and I have something to add!

"First off, I want to thank my parents," he held open hands toward them, "for cutting off my allowance when I was in Mexico. In absolutely no other way could I have learned humility and recognized the real reason that life sent me there." Tad squeezed Gussy's hand.

"And I want to thank my mother," added Gussy, holding her hands toward the shocked Eloise. "Unknowingly, she forced me to find my own answers, prove my own ideas, and discover my own teachers. Also, thanks to Enoch," she bowed her head and hugged little Cherub tighter, "for proving to me that it's not what you have that really counts, but how you 'label' it.

"And, I'm so thankful for my little trailer beside the Pigpen. It taught me the joys of simplicity and the fact that art is all around us, just waiting for recognition.

"And thank you, Daddy-Dom, for always believing in me! And Pug, your loving example has showed me what real, real mothering is all about." She kissed Cherub's head.

"And thank you Tad, for waiting until I grew up."

There was a long pause while Gussy wiped at sudden tears. "Mostly, and especially, I want to thank Robbie. He taught us all that there is a worthy uniqueness in every, single human being. Robbie celebrated the little things in life that we take so much for granted: diversity, history, food, togetherness, and especially, The Moment! He made the plainest food enchanting, instructive, magically delicious. And today at this reception, Robbie has planned all of the refreshments.

"Robbie created a magic space in time that is also permeating this entire day. In Robbie's Den, it was okay not to join society, okay to bloom slowly into specialness. We were always accepted exactly as we presently were, as long as we accepted each other! There it was okay to play with the countless simple wonders of this enchanting world that others will never have the lazy time to enjoy. Robbie gave us the privilege of taking priceless little steps that most of the world has to skip beyond in their frantic rush to the top.

"Robbie gave us precious moments where real home – food, warmth, and total acceptance – could be experienced." Trembling and more tears made Gussy pause again.

"Robbie proved to us all that true love could be forever unconsummated and still be so worthy of having. He shared with us all an agony and ecstatic beauty in his sacrifice for love.

"He proved that affecting the quality of the day is the very highest of all the arts." Gussy closed her eyes and her body could not stop its trembling. "And Robbie, you are doing just that, right now: 'affecting the quality of this day.'" Tad hugged Gussy and the baby.

Music started. Guests began congratulating or drifting toward the tables.

"Wait," said Dom, just for Tad's ears. "I'd like to share one other ceremony with you, alone. This wedding was my last official act, Tad, the crown of a long, unhappy career." He pulled his parson collar from around his neck. "This collar has been chaining me to someone else's ground! Its symbolism was made for another!" He took Tad's hand, put the collar into it and embraced him. "It's just an old used rag, Tad, but it still has some magic left in it. I know that you'll never use it as intended, Tad, it's way, way too confining. Just tuck it away somewhere, a reminder that there are always people to help and inspire, wherever you go, whatever you might label yourself."

Then, Dom lost himself in the throng of congratulators.

At last, he really was what he had always longed to be just one of the crowd.

80. Sea Green Eyes

The wedding was over, music just right for dining, and guests were gathering to choose from the banquet tables.

Fay leaned against her trailer, standing in front of Enoch, who was still in his best man's finery. Fay, herself, wore her own new bridal dress. It only came to her knees, yet would have looked reserved had not Fay "smartened" it up with cheap jewelry. Her cheeks were fiery, noted Enoch, uneasily. She hadn't curled her bangs and they hung in little damp points. The back of her hair was a long curved flame on her shoulders. He touched the white frost which had settled upon the redness since she had been gone.

"Are you ready, my little sea-flower?" She looked so hauntingly beautiful.

"Yes," she whispered, "I'm ready." But her vacant eyes looked through and past him. Past him to the restless green sea from which her eyes must have been plucked from the very beginning.

"I want to save you, Fay. Please want me to!" Lightly he held her arms.

"Save? What would you save me for?" She cringed at the clammy feel of his fingers and pushed them off her arms as though they were too-tight bracelets. Wrenching away, she turned her head, listening.

There it was! That same purring beat! She hadn't heard it once since Woody left. Briefly she looked at Enoch's serious brown eyes, and for the first time ever saw him with compassion. He was really a good man and deserved so much more than she would ever have to offer. She could never, never appreciate his brand of conversation. She could never, never tousle his hair and even pretend that it was curly and blond. She would still be making her living the same old way. Like a worn, resoled shoe, she'd still be the same inside. Enoch saw her as she possibly could be, not as she really was.

"You never really kissed me or told me that you loved me."

Quila had nervously kept herself close to Fay Rose, since she had returned today. Now she gasped as Fay took off the engagement ring and put it in Enoch's hand.

Speechless, Enoch watched as Fay weakly tossed her hair and limped toward the street. Probably headed for the Plaza to meet some poor spineless sailor, he sobbed. He had only been kidding himself that his dreams could all come true, that he could travel the world with Fay and her children. His apprentice was buying him out at a sum that would cover his tidy needs for a lifetime. Florida was to be the first stop on their honeymoon around the world. But Fay could never belong to anyone, much less to him. And suddenly he had no desire either to possess or to save her. Fay was a swamp flower and would always smell like one. Yet, he knew that her odor would linger a lifetime to haunt him.

Good Lord! She could have worn something else besides white lace to Gussy's wedding. She should have saved that particular dress for her own celebration. And, she must be wearing every bracelet that she had ever owned!

Though still attractive from afar, closer up Fay's eyes had sunken deeper. Aside from her cheeks, her skin was blue-white and cadaverous. "I hate her, I hate her," he wept as he watched her walking, slow, undulating, seductive, even with the slight limp. He hurried back to the festive tables.

"Suzette?" Fay lifted her head and stopped a minute to rest against the mailbox. Did the name just arise from hoping? Or was it that same unreal, wavelike sound that used to whisper out from a throng of sailors mulling around the Plaza? No, the whisper was from the sea itself! But now it was calling, "Fay Rose, Fay Rose." She tried to hurry a bit.

Quila looked after her uneasily, remembering the broken engagement in Enoch's cup. The ring and the cross, or was it a ring and a skull in a sea of waves? She gasped again, then started after Fay.

But Bowie stood up from his bench and firmly put out his hand. Quila's old eyes couldn't decipher it now, but Bowie knew that Fay suspected something even worse than tuberculosis.

"Let her go, Quila."

Fay rested against every telephone pole along the street. She sat on running boards, leaned against fences, and once she eased herself down on the curb.

Exhausted, she finally reached the seawall, sat down upon it and dropped off her new white shoes. She lifted weary legs across cool bricks and shivered. She could feel the throb of waves as she painfully drifted over warm sand, closer and closer to the one place where there was no struggle, no hunger, no rent, no pain; no unloved, unfamiliar masculine bodies to be pleased. The sea was applause, a thousand palms slapping ecstatically together, urging her on and on. "Fay Rose, Fay Rose." Was that Robbie's voice? She began to limp faster, faster, almost regally.

Robbie was the only human being who had ever treated her gently, tenderly, carefully, like a real lady. What a difference it would have made to have known over the years that Robbie was the father of Juju. What devotion he would have had to offer the child, and Fay as the mother. If making love to him was that thrilling without love, what could it be now? Perhaps, at least, she could just be near for him, until Doll arrived.

Her bare feet left the sand and she seemed to be gliding into a glowing sunset. It tastes like fresh tears, she thought as she began to tread water, deeper and deeper into the restless, restful calm. An unexpected warmth surrounded her with love and peace. Robbie must be waiting, Somewhere, Near.

The sea and she were finally one and her heart began to surge and ebb with the same pulsing throb. She closed her sea green eyes for the very last time and held out her tired, welcoming arms. Her long red hair floated, serene as seaweed.

As he watched the distant waves, in the hushed space within his heart Bowie thought that he heard Fay's bracelets, like the bells of a lost lamb. Bowie and Quila both listened without breathing. The sea. Was it weeping, or sighing with relief?

81. Bowie in the Tree

High above the merrymaking, draped in a crotch of the tree, Bowie felt like drenched confetti. Though blissful with the park's new look and the wedding, he was limp from heartbreak. Robbie, Mange, and now Fay Rose were gone, but they were done with pain.

Physically and emotionally drained from rushing, he was also fulfilled. It was wonderful to feel useful again. Flo had given him jeans, shirt, shoes, and socks for the wedding and it wasn't hard to let go of ragged clothes, except for his familiar hat. Yet he often pushed up the floppy brim for he needn't hide the shape he was in.

Far below, feasting had begun, but he was full from sampling. The band from The Joint played soft music, air was delicious with still-cooking food. That puffy white dot below was Quila, who used to talk to no one outside the Den. Now she happily stumped around the crowded park with her walking stick for steadiness, creating knots of people that she studied with Gussy's eyepiece, animating guests with her presence, hugs, and pattings. Her leaving dissolved these groups. Then her colorful personality generated new knots, uniting the entire wedding fabric into one caring whole. No plan beneath her words, just making others happy!

Bowie smiled down on the colorful scene, nodding agreement. Never could there ever be another day like this! It was not only Gussy's marriage, motherhood and success. It was not only visual proof of Tad's new direction, hard work and sincerity. Without words, everyone knew that today was the celebration of Robbie's very being; he was the silent soul of everything. He was affecting the quality of the day, his most important, ecstatic reason for living! His blue, blue eyes were overlooking, sanctioning everything about this haunting, treasured, unforgettable "today."

A giant zee of loaded tables extended from Pug's doorstep, angled through the washhouse, then elbowed down the driveway to Gussy's trailer. Dozens of color-speckled benches waited everywhere to be used as they were needed. Potted trees spread lacy shade; blossoming flowers added bouncy colors, happy guests ate and chatted everywhere.

Like Thanksgiving in Robbie's Den, tablecloths were sheets. But the last two sheets were doubling Robbie's honor: they had been dyed the color of blue, blue eyes! From Bowie's viewpoint, they seemed to be gazing at heaven! Napkins were cloth squares nailed to tables! Lolli and Opal were still making platters from paper sacks and Lambeth was lining them with clean rags. Tad was in charge of transferring food into Robbie-trays.

"Everything will be served from a can, a jar lid, or Robbie tray. Everything will be served with a toothpick, lid, ice-cream stick, or a smaller can. "If it doesn't remind us of Robbie," he insisted, "it doesn't belong here, today!" Yes, he seemed to be thinking, Robbie is being returned to this space!

Wedding cake, borrowed cups, and new buckets were Tad's concessions to convention.

Tex kept mixing wine and seltzer for Robbie's Champagne. Dago stirred orange juice and chipped ice, taped a feather outside, and labeled it, "Remember Robbie's Cock-tails?"

Bowie had peeked into Pug's kitchen while women made pretzels and donuts. Pug bustled around wearing lipstick, too much perfume and a ridiculously tiny apron safety-pinned to her dress! Even though she was constantly crying, she looked happier than Bowie had ever seen her. Quila and Opal steamed artichokes. Lolli and her Mammy were pouring tapioca. Luanna was blending lemon juice and mayonnaise into sardines, right in the cans; girls from the pier were bringing in Poppycock, Biscuit-Bottoms and Robbie's Pumpkin Pie.

Toothpicks were everywhere: in tiny onion sandwiches, bites of fruit, bits of donuts, pieces of Thanksgiving-in-Summer Turkey. Doll forked her fingers through bowls of popcorn, selected bee's wings and old maids, then spread them on the table. Girls were bringing labeled Fairy Umbrellas, Classy Queens, Albino Freaks, Music Bells and Carrot Coins. Oriental girls brought Squash Scallops; Dago brought Earth Apples and Opal brought eggplant cubes. Sadly, yet joyfully, Bowie remembered Robbie's comparisons.

Coffeepots were spaced along tables and Doll was surrounding each with spice cans.

Only lambing time could be more exciting! The scenes tore at Bowie's heart while at the same time mending it with healing bliss. Others might not notice but Bowie saw tears as the girls dished up, yet he knew they were rejoicing in fantastic memories of Robbie.

Bowie had helped Tad spread a giant carpet over the black spot. Pug had looked at it tearfully, at first opposing dancing on Robbie's space, but memory changed her mind. "All of my life," Robbie once said wistfully, "I have longed to dance until dawn with the woman I love!" "It would be homage," Pug decided out loud, "not sacrilege, to dance on that space. It would enable the space to be used again, to have a last memory that was happy."

"I can't wait to return from the honeymoon," Tad whispered to Bowie as they unrolled the carpet. "Guy and I are planning a big cabin on Robbie's space. Bed bunks, a homey kitchen, cozy fireplace, and huge table. The director of the art gallery is donating that blowup of Robbie's eyes in the candle flame. We'll call the cabin, 'Robbie's Space, A Last Resort for Homeless Girls.' Pug will change babies, mend, give haircuts; Lolli and Mala will make meals, snacks, coffee. When it's filled, Gussy and I will start Last Resorts everywhere!"

As Bowie and Tad arranged benches around the carpet, Doll asked the band to play Doll's Song before more guests arrived. One last time that simple haunting melody filled every space for thinking or feeling. Everyone stopped, listened, controlled their trembling as Doll danced by herself, around and around the carpet, her arms embracing Robbie. Tears fell, unheeded. A smile tried to mask her quivering lips as she danced a last goodbye.

Too much sampling of Robbie's Champagne, emotional stress and joy were overfilling Bowie. He resettled himself in the tree and snoozed.

Quila trudged the steps to her wagon, placed her new cane beside the door, sat down with a heavy sigh and began to shiver. Birds fluttered expectantly and Whiffet whined pleadingly from inside the wagon. With much effort Quila stood, and holding on to walls she went inside. Returning with crumbs and Whiffet, she wearily sat on the porch again, and tossed crumbs all around her.

She looked at the park through blurry eyes. Because of Tad it was even gayer than a Gypsy camp. He had tried to explain each trailer as she touched its different strokes. In the end Tad merely said that each trailer was just his celebration of an artist he admired.

With Whiffet in her arms, Quila went inside now and opened the door-curtain to capture breeze, music, laughter and odors while she took a nap. She was exhausted in body and soul and needed to prime herself for the last aspect she knew would be part of this bittersweet day. Though Fay had left forever, it seemed to be all right now, the only beautiful way to depart. Quila wouldn't even tell anyone until long after Gussy and Tad drove away.

Her heart whispered that this was the day when Bowie would also leave. His once listless eyes were eager for living now, his limbs required the joy of action. She opened her trunk and unwrapped Jofranka's blue shawl. She curled up on the bed with Whiffet, wrapped Jofranka's loving stitches around the two of them, closed her eyes, and smiled.

Bowie didn't tug on the grimy hat any more, wake up slapping wings or squeezing giant eyes from his mind. He seldom dreamed of a burning bow or a bloody horse. He didn't hang in shadows or need to be alone beneath her wagon. Often he paused in Lolli's trailer or under the tree with the rest of the wedding workers! The only wine he drank was with Quila as they sat at her table preparing herbs or planning the wedding. She turned in her sleep.

Days before the funeral, when Quila had no food to share with Bowie and neither had any appetite for even life itself, Quila had begun to miss Bowie around the park. If she rested often and picked up walking sticks along the way, she could look for Bowie in the canyon. She had found him staring into a tiny fire and squatted beside him. He had cracks at the corners of his mouth, his eyes were more haunted than she remembered, his clothes more grimy and tattered. She had realized for the first time that she had a deep affection for Bowie.

Like her own son he had become and the same age as little Lazlo would have been. She had pushed his hat up and smoothed stringy hair from sad black eyes. She snuffed his feeble fire with her foot and covered it with sand. She took his hand, urging him back to the wagon. While Bowie napped, she washed his fragile shirt by hand and hung it to dry. Leaving pails of warm water beside the bed, she left him to wash his hair, bathe his weak body and sleep for a long time, in a real bed for a change. She put her last dollar bill in his pocket and left his almost dry shirt beside him. She made them both a meal from sliced onions, garlic and herbs. As they ate she smiled at his glistening hair and copper face from which he had pulled long neglected hairs. It was such a simple thing that all of humanity needed: just a little boost from someone else, once in awhile. Robbie had recognized this innocent truth and it was up to those who remembered his warmth, not to ever forget it. Quila arranged the shawl closer, pulled the quilt higher. Warm little Whiffet resettled herself in a different body niche beside her, while Quila remembered.

As Tad and Bowie had begun working on her wagon, Bowie started to bring presents to add to their meals: a branchlet of sage leaves, a cutup rabbit in its own furry skin. Now that she could afford to, Quila kept cigarettes, nuts and canned fruit for Bowie. Remembering Robbie's unexpected presents, Quila started leaving things for Bowie in pockets above his sleeping area: toothpaste, candy bars, gum and spare change.

Quila stirred at polka music, but could tell that it was not dusk yet and drifted back to dozing. One day Bowie left for higher hills. "I need to smell pinyon burning." He returned the next morning with pockets full of pine nuts, hands black with pitch, and a broad smile.

Though Quila knew she'd be a victim in the end, she sent Bowie farther and higher for plants. "They say there be a bigger pool hidden in the right-hand canyon. Maybe there's plantain to gather, miner's lettuce and even yerba mansa," she urged.

When he returned with water plants, eagerly Quila grabbed a mansa leaf, chewed it, then tucked the numbing mass between her gums and aching teeth. That night she could feel excitement and longing in Bowie as they prepared the plants. On the next long treks he took Luanna. Quila knew then that she would have to dole with care the scarce new moisture-loving plants: there was only one real cure for homesickness.

Bowie was ready and it was all right. No longer were they dependent on one another; blackmail had no part in life. The milk bottle was gone, it could not begin to hold money and gifts that appeared in the upturned tambourine. Less and less did she need the special herbs Bowie gathered. More and more it was sympathy and simple suggestions that people sought.

Eagerly Bowie had begun to join the world again, to talk to all kinds of people, to help ready the park for the wedding and to contribute wild things to the nightly potluck. Without having to find trading facts, after the day's work Bowie often climbed the tree, like this evening, and sprawled in a big crotch with moccasins dangling, cleaning his nails of paint and sawdust, smoking, daydreaming. He watched the park as a whole now because watching was beautiful and interesting, not because it was necessary.

Quila knew Robbie would agree that it was okay for Bowie to largely do nothing now, just soak up healing sky, listen to rustling leaves, feel caressing breezes, enjoy people working and children laughing. Still suspended in time, but not sorry now, he carried the leather pouch unopened, afraid he'd find no final answer within it. Quila fell into a light sleep.

Half-awake, Bowie climbed to a more comfortable crotch. Alone with daydreams, imagining he was a cloud, he floated to faraway hills. Below him dreamlike petticoats billowed as they peeked from colorful skirts. Concho buttons twinkled on busy moccasins. Half asleep, he drifted farther inland, where the drip, drip from a single willow leaf was laying raindrops, the first gather of a fall rain. Bowie collected misty sheep into the hollow of a dark overhang then sprinted home to Fawna. He found her dusting with cobwebs, covering the cradle with a bird's wing and washing dishes in a giant dewdrop. Musicians were playing a waltz. As usual he was dreaming. Through drowsy eyes he saw Quila sitting on her porch.

She could hardly wait for dusk as now she watched women lighting candles along the wedding tables. She smelled of steaming food still being brought from Pug's kitchen, and suddenly she was eager to taste again exciting food that had originated in Robbie's mind.

Expectancy was in her life again! Tonight adults would be dancing, drinking, celebrating, and children would need her! At dusk they would gather, eagerly waiting for Gypsy tales. She kept simples in her sleeves now, not blackmail: feathers to chase, straws and soapy bubbles, a hanky for drying tears, and pieces of licorice in memory of Robbie.

She smoothed the wedding clothes she was wearing, and decided: every day from now on she would wear them, instead of her dreary black dress! Why not? Every day that she was still alive, doing for others, receiving from others, was reason to celebrate, to dress up for life itself! Each hour of life was so precious, now that she knew from tea leaves and cards: this was the last season she would watch yellow leaves falling from the tree. Wearing her wedding dress she would be ready anytime for Lazlo's beckoning! Her thoughts were interrupted as laughing children gathered close around her on the steps.

Bowie looked sleepily down at the childlike fence, interesting trailers, flickering candles on festive tables, happy people eating everywhere and dancing on Robbie's space, and giggling children on Quila's steps. How could a single death create such miracles? Yet what was Bowie's miracle? Fawna answered with haunting voice and beautiful hands!

"Few are aware that death and disaster are often gifts. A great fire renews with green carpets; a great flood creates new scenes. Death, like fire and flood, gives new viewpoints, new understanding, new birth. Sometimes Death is best for everyone."

Finally, he brought the warm leather pouch from his bosom and held it to his cheek. Softness whispered that it had been soaked, tanned and chewed by the girl who smelled like wildflowers. Sorrow leaked down his cheeks and over the precious pouch. Why was he afraid to open it? And why was he staying here? There was no place for him with Robbie gone, with Lambeth caring for Quila's garden and Opal attending her daily needs. Quila had herbs to last longer than she could use them all. Tad and Guy were planning a new retreat, right over Robbie's old space, to beckon lost girls. But it was lost boys that were beckoning Bowie, boys needed fathers, brothers and wise men.

The "soil" at Last Resort has changed its character, as though with flood, fire, earthquake, or death. Different things should grow now. Fawna was gone. Longing would never make her walk from that little trailer below him. But he had met the "new" Fawna-Luanna, and he knew the rest could follow, with patience.

Instantly he realized that he had been on a long Vision Quest of healing and learning, one that the Old One and nightmares had hinted at. "I, too, am a special eye of God, but what does He want me to do?" he whispered. "How can my skills fit the world of today?"

He only knew that he was weary of drab seasons, hillside excuses for soaring cliffs and white men's food and pleasures. At home it was back-to-back time when winter meets summer. In Indian country willows were yellow paint blobs, fat acorns and ripe pine nuts waited for picking. Mountains were cheeked with seeds and wind was whispering farewell to fall. It was twilight and axes would be pinging; cook fires being stoked; brown palms would be slapping fry bread, and mutton was sizzling at home! He wanted to hold his mother again.

Below, people were gathering to cut wedding cake.

A gust of wind ruffled his hair and shadows of butterflies, bows and fleeing horses fluttered through his mind. He had thought he was done with those memories, forever!

But, in one thrilling heartbeat he realized he had almost missed that lesson!

Those apparitions should be exciting, not frightening, parts of himself! Instead of denying, he invited their shadows into his being, stretched hands high around the memories until they flowed into his soul: Fawna's eyes, the enchanting bow, the faithful horse.

"I welcome you! Whenever you appear, I will treasure the memories of your being!"

As he said these words, Bowie heard a noise below the tree. Luanna, feather-footed as Fawna, was patiently waiting for him, leaning against the trunk.

He must make a decision. He couldn't part with Fawna's pouch, yet he couldn't keep it: it might become an unseen wall. There couldn't be anything irreplaceable there; Fawna kept herbs, feathers and maybe a splinter struck by lightning. Why was he afraid to find out?

With fear, yet anticipation, he untied the thong and shook something into his hand. Just a tiny shriveled tube of skin, knotted with strong black hair, the only link between Fawna and his son! Bowie's own mother had buried Pinieten's body cord beneath the hogan's entryway, so he would finally come back home. He pressed the shred of skin to his throbbing heart. He would keep it forever. But no, Fawna's words were again in his ear: "Give it to Longbow, Quila. Only he will know the right time to do the right thing with it."

Time was suspended: the music, the breeze. Yet the tree seemed to pulse now and he climbed its gentle throbbing. Slowly at first, limb by limb, then faster and faster until he was near the top, nearer sky and clouds. The tip of the tree, full of life, swayed gently. He looked beyond birds, beyond cliffs and clouds.

"It isn't a pine tree Fawna, but it's the only remembrance you really treasured."

Bowie slit the tree top with his knife, inserted the precious shred of mother-baby skin, then tightly bound the living wood with Fawna's pouch and tied it with the leather thong. He smoothed the bulge, like Fawna's stomach, a gall on a tender twig, remembering one last time.

His son had been sired by wind, rain, campfire smoke, and the hearts of two joyful children. Bowie had finally returned the little spirit to Life itself. And the last of Fawna had been spent.

Exhausted, he climbed to a lower crotch.

Fragile V's of migrating ducks were parting the lowering sun. Without breeze, yellowing leaves floated downward, an orange moon was rising. This was Fawna's Indian Summer, a special gift of the gods! Not the lonesome, somber autumn of white poetry, but clear of clouds and wind. Smoke of hogans would be lifting straight up to the blue sky.

His ears seemed filled with grinding songs, chanting, storytelling. Dropping to lower branches, earthy life melted into a civilization that he needed no part of. A world that brought quick profit, disease, wars, that tossed away tribal wisdom and left nothing to take its place.

His body twitched with eagerness. He couldn't wait to go where he was like everyone else! Cottonwoods like this one would fringe a stream, offer shade and pain relief. People celebrated harvests, frost, the arrival of grass and wildflowers. But how could he be of real use and still make a living? In answer, Bowie remembered Robbie's last newscast. "The white man's experiment with Indian schools has ended: children are coming home!"

"Children coming home!" It was not too late for those who had wildness in their veins! He could create a school where essentials were to know, respect and wisely use Mother Earth. Examples would always be a part of him that could grow with every sharing, thanks to Fawna, the Old One, his mother, his grandfather, Quila, Gussy, and Robbie.

And Robbie. The sky itself would always remind him of Robbie's blue, blue eyes, and Robbie's legacy. Although he would never forget the joys to be found in simple things that are taken so much for granted, and although he would never forget the happiness that is always waiting in the present moment: both Robbie and Gussy's big answer was merely to discover, enjoy and share one's own unique self! He too, really did have something wonderful to offer his people, something that he now knew was uniquely all his own!

Today, young Indians were drowning in alcohol and poverty, knowing nothing about ancestors. "People without history are wind on the grass!" the Old One had said.

Bowie closed his eyes, seeing campfire classes in winter; mesa classes in summer with sheep grazing all around. Learning skills of roping on dogs, chickens, siblings and horses! Learning patience by watching span worms, spider weavers, night flower openings! They'd practice living on air, water, sunshine and aroma, pretending there was nothing else! He'd reveal the mysteries of plants, silent weapons, imitating prey, and Fawna's secrets of scents to warn, locate, relax, and heal. His body started twitching with excitement.

But how could he finance such a school?

He climbed to a lower limb, a bigger one that could hold the weight of possibilities overfilling him. He could teach boys how to ride like wind, make primitive tools, musical instruments, travois and dream catchers. They'd be telling time in sand, listening to secrets of clouds, rocks and smoke. He could prove why elders should be looked upon with pride, admiration, and love, instead of shame.

But how could he make a living?

Cheeked with campfires, wind ruffling their hair, drinking plant-goblet-tea, Longbow would enchant them with the Old One's stories!

But what would he do for money?

Suddenly he knew: He would use Fawna's playing stones! Outside the cave's entrance big ants decorated their craters with garnets brought from below. Inside her cave Fawna worked an endless vein of turquoise with just an antler. Why couldn't he remember until now?

He had had to be away, live through crises, and merely exist until timing was right. Now he recognized skills, resources and perfect "schoolhouses" already in existence! He quivered with anticipation, as yellow leaves fell down around him like rain.

Timing was exactly right now! With Luanna, a small Indian Renaissance was just waiting to be created. While he taught boys to be men, she'd teach girls to wife and mother. Many young Indians found success in modern times; some, like Bowie, preferred the old ways! He'd concentrate on potential leaders, those aware that beautiful land was going unrecognized, or becoming merely a stage for white men.

When boys were ready, he'd share the secret valley, teaching special ones in the Old One's cave to flake tools, adding fresh to ancient drops, becoming blood brothers with past warriors. They would practice shooting and throwing in the long hall of that cave.

Grandfathers would be invited to teach rituals. He couldn't bear to see it happen again, as with the Old One, standing confused above an altar of sand, the last medicine man of his tribe, who had suddenly lost old songs before there was anyone to learn them. They'd resurrect the Old One's gardens, traps and music. Storage caves were still filled with wood, hidden pots were brimming with dried food and tea leaves that he had helped gather.

He jumped down from the last branch. "Luanna, it's so exciting! I just can't wait!" He was crying unashamedly, yet laughing with abandon as he twirled her around and around. "Luanna, we too will be sharing our uniqueness, we too will be affecting the very quality of every day!" He lifted his nose.

"Luanna, can you smell that bubble bread browning? Corn roasting in embers? Deer meat sizzling on a spit?" He laughed hysterically and twirled in a circle by himself.

He tipped his hat and shouted. "Luanna! I'll need a new hat with no morbid memories in it. There's no need anymore to hide in nothingness!" He flung his hands up high. "We have no money for bus fare! But we can walk home!" Dramatically, he stretched a foot toward the street. "We'll start with just one step!"

82.   Blue, Blue Sky

Hand-in-hand Bowie and Luanna twined through the crowded driveway toward Quila's wagon. The air was delicious with all kinds of food, laughter and flowers. Children were spilling down the steps, but Opal sat near to the frail little Gypsy body. She pulled Jofranka's shawl more closely around Quila's shoulders as she began the tale of her own Gypsy wedding. Children were eating from Robbie trays in their laps. Little girls sat at Quila's feet, stirring coffee with cinnamon sticks.

"Goodbye Cassy, goodbye Patty," whispered Bowie. Patty shook her head. "No," she whispered back, "my name is really Patrin. I'm not Patty anymore! My sister here is Cassandra. Over there are Pegasus and Mistral. Pallus and Elfin are down there on the bottom step. Here on my lap is Aura. Mama says we have all grown up now and should be proud of our real names. Our only brother, Roberto, named us all!"

Misty-eyed, Bowie smiled now as Quila enchanted her audience. He reached up and touched her hair where wilted wildflowers were still suspended in their wispy gray whirlwind. Quila had been so good to him lately. She even made special night teas to help him sleep. But it was hard to change old habits, to sleep instead of prowling. He craved exciting things to tire him in the daylight so that sleep would be impossible to avoid!

Quila was fading so fast. Tad, Bowie, Opal and Lambeth could see it happening before their eyes. That was the big reason they had been hurrying to beautify her wagon and her life. She always wore her amethyst now to help her growing headaches and eye pain. This evening she had hung her bloodstone on top of the amethyst for courage. But underneath (as always) was the old seashell that Robbie had given her.

From squinting so much her eyes were just little slits. She had told Bowie that lights of the park were Gypsy fires, growing dimmer every night. Bowie touched her leathery cheek. "Shama," Mother, he said in Navajo and held her tiny, trembling, withered hand in his. Her crooked smile seemed not so jagged anymore. Like a wise old Indian, sorrow, hope and resignation were scribed on her kind face. They would miss each other.

Quila paused in her story, while Opal easily continued on. Quila handed Bowie Fawna's metal box that had been waiting beside her. Bowie had forgotten it even existed! Fawna's "magic rag" had been inside, he remembered. Once she had kept alive here the warmth of her mother, the spirit of the glorious past in embers within this very box.

Bowie closed his eyes and felt of the air holes that Fawna had punched in the sides. He opened the lid and there were the silver dollars that used to encircle his waist, that used to lay in Flo's pawn case! The leather tassels, beads and feathers had all been removed, but tiny remnants of solder still clung to the coins. They were ready to spend now.

"Two tickets for home," Quila explained tearfully. "I was the one who took the coins and the metal box from Fawna's table that awful night. I slowly pawned the coins for you and me to eat, Bowie. Then slowly I bought them back again from Flo and cleaned them of their past. Until today, I didn't even know why. But Flo seemed to understand, somehow, and had only used them for display."

Bowie grabbed Luanna. "Yes! Of course!" he shouted to the sky. He put the coins in his pocket, then removed the itchy socks and heavy shoes that Flo had given him. Barefooted, he twirled down the street with Luanna. "Yes! Yes!" His shouting started to fade.

He could not hurry fast enough. His feet were tired of leather boxes, blacktop and cement. They longed for the feel of moccasin paths. They longed for places where there was always something to gather, to grind, to plan, to teach, to sing, to share. Where people never refused the old, the sick, the confused. Where children were never struck. Where the Great Spirit was with him every place, every minute, not just in a stained glass house on Sundays!

The two of them danced circles toward the sea as they headed for the bus depot in the Plaza. Bowie's head was high as he twirled, as though he were already breathing in the blue, blue sky, as though he were already smelling the warm fires of home, as though he were already hearing the happy bells of sheep being herded home for the night.

Quila waved into the nothingness and children who were standing beside her watched the circling figures getting smaller. The tallest figure jerked off its hat, shook its long hair free, and sailed its hat high up into the blue, blue sky.

Dom wiped away the last bittersweet tear, smiled, and pulled the final sheet of paper from his typewriter.

ABOUT THE AUTHOR

For over a decade, Barbara (Babs) Kobaly was the editor and feature writer for the monthly *Smoke Signal*, the local newspaper in her high desert community. Babs' natural history articles and columns have appeared in the *Hi-Desert Star Newspaper, Desert Magazine, The Sun Runner Magazine, The Western Tanager,* and many other publications. She is also author of *The Guide to Morongo Valley Wildflowers.* Babs has lived in the same home in Morongo Valley for the last fifty-two years.

Swill of Pearls is her first novel.